D1283044

Edgar Allan Poe

LANDOR'S COTTAGE

Edgar Allan Poe

Collected Stories and Poems

Illustrated by Aubrey Beardsley, Harry Clarke, Gustave Doré, Edouard Manet and John Tenniel

This edition first published in 2006 by
CRW Publishing Limited, 69 Gloucester Crescent, London, NW1 7EG

ISBN10 1 904919 77 4
ISBN13 978 1 904919 77 3

2 4 6 8 10 9 7 5 3 1

Designed and typeset in Jenson and Fell Type by Bookcraft Limited,
Stroud, Gloucestershire, UK

Printed and bound in China by Imago

Contents

TALES OF MYSTERY AND IMAGINATION

TALES OF THE GROTESQUE AND ARABESQUE

POEMS

Tales of Mystery and Imagination

The Gold Bug

What ho! what ho! this fellow is dancing mad!
He hath been bitten by the Tarantula.

All in the Wrong

Many years ago I contracted an intimacy with a Mr William Legrand. He was of an ancient Huguenot family, and had once been wealthy; but a series of misfortunes had reduced him to want. To avoid the mortification consequent upon his disasters, he left New Orleans, the city of his forefathers, and took up his residence at Sullivan's Island, near Charleston, South Carolina.

This island is a very singular one. It consists of little else than the sea sand, and is about three miles long. Its breadth at no point exceeds a quarter of a mile. It is separated from the main land by a scarcely perceptible creek, oozing its way through a wilderness of reeds and slime, a favourite resort of the marsh-hen. The vegetation, as might be supposed, is scant, or at least dwarfish. No trees of any magnitude are to be seen. Near the western extremity, where Fort Moultrie stands, and where are some miserable frame buildings, tenanted, during summer, by the fugitives from Charleston dust and fever, may be found, indeed, the bristly palmetto; but the whole island, with the exception of this western point, and a line of hard, white beach on the sea coast, is covered with a dense undergrowth of the sweet myrtle, so much prized by the horticulturists of England. The shrub here often attains the height of fifteen or twenty feet, and forms an almost impenetrable coppice, burdening the air with its fragrance.

In the inmost recesses of this coppice, not far from the eastern or more remote end of the island, Legrand had built himself a small hut, which he occupied when I first, by mere accident, made his acquaintance. This soon ripened into friendship – for there was much in the recluse to excite interest and esteem. I found him well educated, with unusual powers of mind, but infected with misanthropy, and subject to perverse moods of alternate enthusiasm and melancholy. He had with him many books, but rarely employed them. His chief amusements were gunning and fishing, or sauntering along the beach and through the myrtles, in quest of shells or entomological specimens; – his collection of the latter might have been envied by a Swammerdamm. In these excursions he was usually accompanied by an old negro, called Jupiter, who had been manumitted before the reverses of the family, but who could be induced, neither by threats nor by promises, to abandon what he considered his right of attendance upon the footsteps of his young 'Massa Will'. It is not improbable that the relatives of Legrand, conceiving him to be somewhat unsettled in intellect, had contrived to instil this obstinacy into Jupiter, with a view to the supervision and guardianship of the wanderer.

The winters in the latitude of Sullivan's Island are seldom very severe, and in the fall of the year it is a rare event indeed when a fire is considered necessary. About the middle of October, 18—, there occurred, however, a day of remarkable chilliness. Just before sunset I scrambled my way through the evergreens to the hut of my friend, whom I had not visited for several weeks – my residence being, at that time, in Charleston, a distance of nine miles from the island, while the facilities of passage and re-passage were very far behind those of the present day. Upon reaching the hut I rapped, as was my custom, and getting no reply, sought for the key where I knew it was secreted, unlocked the door and went in. A fine fire was blazing upon the hearth. It was a novelty, and by no means an ungrateful one. I threw off an overcoat, took an armchair by the crackling logs, and awaited patiently the arrival of my hosts.

Soon after dark they arrived, and gave me a most cordial welcome. Jupiter, grinning from ear to ear, bustled about to prepare some marsh-hens for supper. Legrand was in one of his fits – how else shall I term them? – of enthusiasm. He had found an unknown bivalve, forming a new genus, and, more than this, he had hunted down and secured, with Jupiter's assistance, a *scarabaeus* which he believed to be totally new, but in respect to which he wished to have my opinion on the morrow.

'And why not tonight?' I asked, rubbing my hands over the blaze, and wishing the whole tribe of *scarabaei* at the devil.

'Ah, if I had only known you were here!' said Legrand, 'but it's so long since I saw you; and how could I foresee that you would pay me a visit this very night of all others? As I was coming home I met Lieutenant G—, from the fort, and, very foolishly, I lent him the bug; so it will be impossible for you to see it until the morning. Stay here tonight, and I will send Jup down for it at sunrise. It is the loveliest thing in creation.'

'What? – sunrise?'

'Nonsense! no! – the bug. It is of a brilliant gold colour – about the size of a large hickory nut – with two jet-black spots near one extremity of the back, and another, somewhat longer, at the other. The *antennae* are – '

'Dey aint *no* tin in him, Massa Will, I keep a-tellin on you,' here interrupted Jupiter; 'de bug is a goole bug, solid, ebery bit of him, inside and all, sep him wing – neber feel half so hebby a bug in my life.'

'Well, suppose it is, Jup,' replied Legrand, somewhat more earnestly, it seemed to me, than the case demanded, 'is that any reason for your letting the birds burn? The colour' – here he turned to me – 'is really almost enough to warrant Jupiter's idea. You never saw a more brilliant metallic lustre than the scales emit – but of this you cannot judge till tomorrow. In the meantime I can give you some idea of the shape.' Saying this, he seated himself at a small table, on which were a pen and ink, but no paper. He looked for some in a drawer, but found none.

'Never mind,' said he at length, 'this will answer;' and he drew from his waistcoat pocket a scrap of what I took to be very dirty foolscap, and made upon it a rough drawing with the pen. While he did this, I retained my seat by the fire, for I was still chilly. When the design was complete, he handed it to me without rising. As I received it, a loud growl was heard, succeeded by a scratching at the door. Jupiter opened it, and a large Newfoundland, belonging to Legrand, rushed in, leaped upon my shoulders, and loaded me with caresses; for I had shown him much attention during previous visits. When his gambols were over, I looked at the paper, and, to speak the truth, found myself not a little puzzled at what my friend had depicted.

'Well!' I said, after contemplating it for some minutes, 'this is a strange *scarabaeus*, I must confess: new to me: never saw anything like it before – unless it was a skull, or a death's-head – which it more nearly resembles than anything else that has come under *my* observation.'

'A death's-head!' echoed Legrand. 'Oh – yes – well, it has something of that appearance upon paper, no doubt. The two upper black spots look like eyes, eh? and the longer one at the bottom like a mouth – and then the shape of the whole is oval.'

'Perhaps so,' said I; 'but, Legrand, I fear you are no artist. I must wait until I see the beetle itself, if I am to form any idea of its personal appearance.'

'Well, I don't know,' said he, a little nettled, 'I draw tolerably – *should* do it at least – have had good masters, and flatter myself that I am not quite a blockhead.'

'But, my dear fellow, you are joking then,' said I, 'this is a very passable *skull* – indeed, I may say that it is a very *excellent* skull, according to the vulgar notions about such specimens of physiology – and your *scarabaeus* must be the queerest *scarabaeus* in the world if it resembles it. Why, we may get up a very thrilling bit of superstition upon this hint. I presume you will call the bug *scarabaeus caput hominis*, or something of that kind – there are many similar titles in the Natural Histories. But where are the *antennae* you spoke of?'

'The *antennae*!' said Legrand, who seemed to be getting unaccountably warm upon the subject; 'I am sure you must see the *antennae*. I made them as distinct as they are in the original insect, and I presume that is sufficient.'

'Well, well,' I said, 'perhaps you have – still I don't see them;' and I handed him the paper without additional remark, not wishing to ruffle his temper; but I was much surprised at the turn affairs had taken; his ill humour puzzled me – and, as for the drawing of the beetle, there were positively *no antennae* visible, and the whole *did* bear a very close resemblance to the ordinary cuts of a death's-head.

He received the paper very peevishly, and was about to crumple it, apparently to throw it in the fire, when a casual glance at the design seemed suddenly to rivet his attention. In an instant his face grew violently red – in another as excessively pale. For some minutes he continued to scrutinise the drawing minutely where he sat. At length he arose, took a candle from the table, and proceeded to seat himself upon a sea-chest in the farthest corner of the room. Here again he made an anxious examination of the paper, turning it in all directions. He said nothing, however, and his conduct greatly astonished me; yet I thought it prudent not to exacerbate the growing moodiness of his temper by any comment. Presently he took from his coat pocket a wallet, placed the paper carefully in it, and deposited both in a writing-desk, which he locked. He now grew more composed in his demeanour; but his original air of enthusiasm had quite disappeared. Yet he seemed not so much sulky as abstracted. As the evening wore away he became more and more absorbed in reverie, from which no sallies of mine could arouse him. It had been my intention to pass the night at the hut, as I had frequently done before, but, seeing my host in this mood, I deemed it proper to take leave. He did not press me to remain, but, as I departed, he shook my hand with even more than his usual cordiality.

It was about a month after this (and during the interval I had seen nothing of Legrand) when I received a visit, at Charleston, from his man, Jupiter. I had never seen the good old negro look so dispirited, and I feared that some serious disaster had befallen my friend.

'Well, Jup,' said I, 'what is the matter now? – how is your master?'

'Why, to speak de troof, massa, him not so berry well as mought be.'

'Not well! I am truly sorry to hear it. What does he complain of?'

'Dar! dat's it! – him neber plain of notin – but him bery sick for all dat.'

'*Very* sick, Jupiter! – why didn't you say so at once! Is he confined to bed?'

'No, dat he aint! – he aint find nowhar – dat's just whar de shoe pinch. My mind is got to be berry hebby bout poor Massa Will.'

'Jupiter, I should like to understand what it is you are talking about. You say your master is sick. Hasn't he told you what ails him?'

'Why, massa, taint worf while for to git mad about de matter – Massa Will say noffin at all aint de matter wid him – but den what make him go about looking dis here way, wid he head down and he soldiers up, and as white as a gose? And den he keep a syphon all de time – '

'Keeps a what, Jupiter?'

'Keeps a syphon wid de figgurs on de slate – de queerest figgurs I ebber did see. Ise gittin to be skeered, I tell you. Hab for to keep mighty tight eye pon him noovers. Todder day he gib me slip fore de sun up and was gone de whole ob de blessed day. I had a big stick ready cut for to gib him deuced good beating when he did come – but Ise sich a fool dat I hadn't de heart arter all – he look so berry poorly.'

'Eh? – what? – ah yes! – upon the whole I think you had better not be too severe with the poor fellow – don't flog him, Jupiter – he can't very well stand it – but can you form no idea of what has occasioned this illness, or rather this change of conduct? Has anything unpleasant happened since I saw you?'

'No, massa, dey aint bin noffin onpleasant *since* den – 'twas *fore* den I'm feared – 'twas de berry day you was dare.'

'How? what do you mean?'

'Why, massa, I mean de bug – dare now.'

'The what?'

'De bug – I'm berry sartain dat Massa Will bin bit somewhere bout de head by dat goole-bug.'

'And what cause have you, Jupiter, for such a supposition?'

'Claws enuff, massa, and mouff too. I nebber did see sich a deuced bug – he kick and he bite ebery ting what cum near him. Massa Will cotch him fuss, but had for to let him go gin mighty quick, I tell you – den was de time he must ha got de bite. I didn't like de look ob de bug mouff, myself, no how, so I wouldn't take hold ob him wid my finger, but I cotch him wid a piece ob paper dat I found. I wrap him up in de paper and stuff piece ob it in he mouff – dat was de way.'

'And you think, then, that your master was really bitten by the beetle, and that the bite made him sick?'

'I don't tink noffin about it – I nose it. What make him dream bout de goole so much, if taint cause he bit by de goole-bug? Ise heerd bout dem goole-bugs fore dis.'

'But how do you know he dreams about gold?'

'How I know? why, cause he talk about it in he sleep – dat's how I nose.'

'Well, Jup, perhaps you are right; but to what fortunate circumstance am I to attribute the honour of a visit from you today?'

'What de matter, massa?'

'Did you bring any message from Mr Legrand?'

'No, massa, I bring dis here pissel;' and here Jupiter handed me a note which ran thus:

> MY DEAR —, Why have I not seen you for so long a time? I hope you have not been so foolish as to take offence at any little *brusquerie* of mine; but no, that is improbable.
>
> Since I saw you I have had great cause for anxiety. I have something to tell you, yet scarcely know how to tell it, or whether I should tell it at all.
>
> I have not been quite well for some days past, and poor old Jup annoys me, almost beyond endurance, by his well-meant attentions. Would you believe it? – he had prepared a huge stick, the other day, with which to chastise me for giving him the slip, and spending the day, *solus*, among the hills on the mainland. I verily believe that my ill looks alone saved me a flogging.
>
> I have made no addition to my cabinet since we met.
>
> If you can, in any way, make it convenient, come over with Jupiter. *Do* come. I wish to see you *tonight*, upon business of importance. I assure you that it is of the *highest* importance. – Ever yours,
>
> WILLIAM LEGRAND

There was something in the tone of this note which gave me great uneasiness. Its whole style differed materially from that of Legrand. What could he be dreaming of? What new crotchet possessed his excitable brain? What 'business of the highest importance' could *he* possibly have to transact? Jupiter's account of him boded no good. I dreaded lest the continued pressure of misfortune had, at length, fairly unsettled the reason of my friend. Without a moment's hesitation, therefore, I prepared to accompany the negro.

Upon reaching the wharf, I noticed a scythe and three spades, all apparently new, lying in the bottom of the boat in which we were to embark.

'What is the meaning of all this, Jup?' I enquired.

'Him syfe, massa, and spade.'

'Very true; but what are they doing here?'

'Him de syfe and de spade what Massa Will sis pon my buying for him in de town, and de debbil's own lot of money I had to gib for em.'

'But what, in the name of all that is mysterious, is your "Massa Will" going to do with scythes and spades?'

'Dat's more dan *I* know, and debbil take me if I don't believe 'tis more dan he know, too. But it's all cum ob de bug.'

Finding that no satisfaction was to be obtained of Jupiter, whose whole intellect seemed to be absorbed by 'de bug', I now stepped into the boat and made sail. With a fair and strong breeze we soon ran into the little cove to the northward of Fort Moultrie, and a walk of some two miles brought us to the hut. It was about three in the afternoon when we arrived. Legrand had been awaiting us in eager expectation. He grasped my hand with a nervous *empressement* which alarmed me and strengthened the suspicions already entertained. His countenance was pale even to ghastliness, and his deep-set eyes glared with unnatural lustre. After some enquiries respecting his health, I asked him, not knowing what better to say, if he had yet obtained the *scarabaeus* from Lieutenant G—.

'Oh yes,' he replied, colouring violently, 'I got it from him the next morning. Nothing should tempt me to part with that *scarabaeus*. Do you know that Jupiter is quite right about it?'

'In what way?' I asked, with a sad foreboding at heart.

'In supposing it to be a bug of *real gold*!' He said this with an air of profound seriousness, and I felt inexpressibly shocked.

'This bug is to make my fortune,' he continued, with a triumphant smile, 'to reinstate me in my family possessions. Is it any wonder, then, that I prize it? Since Fortune has thought fit to bestow it upon me, I have only to use it properly and I shall arrive at the gold of which it is the index. Jupiter, bring me that *scarabaeus*!'

'What! de bug, massa? I'd rudder not go fer trubble dat bug – you mus git him for your own self.' Hereupon Legrand arose, with a grave and stately air, and brought me the beetle from a glass case in which it was enclosed. It was a beautiful *scarabaeus*, and, at that time, unknown to naturalists – of course a great prize in a scientific point of view. There were two round black spots near one extremity of the back, and a long one near the other. The scales were exceedingly hard and glossy, with all the appearance of burnished gold. The weight of the insect was very remarkable, and, taking all things into consideration, I could hardly blame Jupiter for his opinion respecting it; but what to make of Legrand's concordance with that opinion, I could not, for the life of me, tell.

'I sent for you,' said he, in a grandiloquent tone, when I had completed my examination of the beetle, 'I sent for you, that I might have your counsel and assistance in furthering the views of Fate and of the bug – '

'My dear Legrand,' I cried, interrupting him, 'you are certainly unwell, and had better use some little precautions. You shall go to bed, and I will remain with you a few days, until you get over this. You are feverish and – '

'Feel my pulse,' said he.

I felt it, and, to say the truth, found not the slightest indication of fever.

'But you may be ill and yet have no fever. Allow me this once to prescribe for you. In the first place, go to bed. In the next – '

'You are mistaken,' he interposed, 'I am as well as I can expect to be under the excitement which I suffer. If you really wish me well, you will relieve this excitement.'

'And how is this to be done?'

'Very easily. Jupiter and myself are going upon an expedition into the hills, upon the mainland, and, in this expedition, we shall need the aid of some person in whom we can confide. You are the only one we can trust. Whether we succeed or fail, the excitement which you now perceive in me will be equally allayed.'

'I am anxious to oblige you in any way,' I replied; 'but do you mean to say that this infernal beetle has any connection with your expedition into the hills?'

'It has.'

'Then, Legrand, I can become a party to no such absurd proceeding.'

'I am sorry – very sorry – for we shall have to try it by ourselves.'

'Try it by yourselves! The man is surely mad! – but stay! – how long do you propose to be absent?'

'Probably all night. We shall start immediately, and be back, at all events, by sunrise.'

'And will you promise me, upon your honour, that when this freak of yours is over, and the bug business (good God!) settled to your satisfaction, you will then return home and follow my advice implicitly, as that of your physician?'

'Yes; I promise; and now let us be off, for we have no time to lose.'

With a heavy heart I accompanied my friend. We started about four o'clock – Legrand, Jupiter, the dog, and myself. Jupiter had with him the scythe and spades – the whole of which he insisted upon carrying – more through fear, it seemed to me, of trusting either of the implements within reach of his master, than from any excess of industry or complaisance. His demeanour was dogged in the extreme, and 'dat deuced bug' were the sole words which escaped his lips during the journey. For my own part, I had charge of a couple of dark lanterns, while Legrand contented himself with the *scarabaeus*, which he carried attached to the end of a bit of whipcord; twirling it to and fro, with the air of a conjuror, as he went. When I observed this last, plain evidence of my friend's aberration of mind, I could scarcely refrain from tears. I thought it best, however, to humour his fancy, at least for the present, or until I could adopt some more energetic measures with a chance of success. In the meantime I endeavoured, but all in vain, to sound him in regard to the object of the expedition. Having succeeded in inducing me to accompany him, he seemed unwilling to hold conversation upon any topic of minor importance, and to all my questions vouchsafed no other reply than 'we shall see!'

We crossed the creek at the head of the island by means of a skiff, and, ascending the high grounds on the shore of the mainland, proceeded in a north-westerly direction, through a tract of country excessively wild and desolate, where no trace of a human footstep was to be seen. Legrand led the way with decision; pausing only for an instant, here and there, to consult what appeared to be certain landmarks of his own contrivance upon a former occasion.

In this manner we journeyed for about two hours, and the sun was just setting when we entered a region infinitely more dreary than any yet seen. It was a species of tableland, near the summit of an almost inaccessible hill, densely wooded from base to pinnacle, and interspersed with huge crags that appeared to lie loosely upon the soil, and in many cases were prevented from precipitating themselves into the valleys below, merely by the support of the trees against which they reclined. Deep ravines, in various directions, gave an air of still sterner solemnity to the scene.

The natural platform to which we had clambered was thickly overgrown with brambles, through which we soon discovered that it would have been impossible to force our way but for the scythe; and Jupiter, by direction of his master, proceeded to clear for us a path to the foot of an enormously tall tulip tree, which stood, with some eight or ten oaks, upon the level, and far surpassed them all, and all other trees which I had then ever seen, in the beauty of its foliage and form, in the wide spread of its branches, and in the general majesty of its appearance. When we reached this tree, Legrand turned to Jupiter, and asked him if he thought he could climb it. The old man seemed a little staggered by the question, and for some moments made no reply. At length he approached the huge trunk, walked slowly around it, and examined it with minute attention.

When he had completed his scrutiny, he merely said – 'Yes, massa, Jup climb any tree he ebber see in he life.'

'Then up with you as soon as possible, for it will soon be too dark to see what we are about.'

'How far mus go up, massa?' enquired Jupiter.

'Get up the main trunk first, and then I will tell you which way to go – and here – stop! take this beetle with you.'

'De bug, Massa Will! – de goole bug!' cried the negro, drawing back in dismay – 'what for mus tote de bug way up de tree? – d—n if I do!'

'If you are afraid, Jup, a great big negro like you, to take hold of a harmless little dead beetle, why you can carry it up by this string – but, if you do not take it up with you in some way, I shall be under the necessity of breaking your head with this shovel.'

'What de matter now, massa?' said Jup, evidently shamed into compliance; 'always want for to raise fuss wid old nigger. Was only funnin any how. *Me* feered de bug! what I keer for de bug?' Here he took cautiously hold of the extreme end of the string, and, maintaining the insect as far from his person as circumstances would permit, prepared to ascend the tree.

In youth, the tulip tree, or *Liriodendron Tulipiferum*, the most magnificent of American foresters, has a trunk peculiarly smooth, and often rises to a great height without lateral branches; but, in its riper age, the bark becomes gnarled and uneven, while many short limbs make their appearance on the stem. Thus the difficulty of ascension, in the present case, lay more in semblance than in reality. Embracing the huge cylinder, as closely as possible, with his arms and knees, seizing with his hands some projections, and resting his naked toes upon others, Jupiter, after one or two narrow escapes from falling, at length wriggled himself into the first great fork, and seemed to consider the whole business as virtually accomplished. The *risk* of the achievement was, in fact, now over, although the climber was some sixty or seventy feet from the ground.

'Which way mus go now, Massa Will?' he asked.

'Keep up the largest branch – the one on this side,' said Legrand. The negro obeyed him promptly, and apparently with but little trouble; ascending higher and higher, until no glimpse of his squat figure could be obtained through the dense foliage which enveloped it.

Presently his voice was heard in a sort of halloo: 'How much fudder is got for go?'

'How high up are you?' asked Legrand.

'Ebber so fur,' replied the negro; 'can see de sky fru de top ob de tree.'

'Never mind the sky, but attend to what I say. Look down the trunk and count the limbs below you on this side. How many limbs have you passed?'

'One, two, tree, four, fibe – I done pass fibe big limb, massa, pon dis side.'

'Then go one limb higher.'

In a few minutes the voice was heard again, announcing that the seventh limb was attained.

'Now, Jup,' cried Legrand, evidently much excited, 'I want you to work your way out upon that limb as far as you can. If you see anything strange, let me know.'

By this time what little doubt I might have entertained of my poor friend's insanity was put finally at rest. I had no alternative but to conclude him stricken with lunacy, and I became seriously anxious about getting him home. While I was pondering upon what was best to be done, Jupiter's voice was again heard.

'Mos feerd for to ventur pon dis limb berry far – tis dead limb putty much all de way.'

'Did you say it was a *dead* limb, Jupiter?' cried Legrand in a quavering voice.

'Yes, massa, him dead as de doornail – done up for sartain – done departed dis here life.'

'What in the name of heaven shall I do?' asked Legrand, seemingly in the greatest distress.

'Do!' said I, glad of an opportunity to interpose a word, 'why, come home and go to bed. Come now! that's a fine fellow. It's getting late, and besides, you remember your promise.'

'Jupiter,' cried he, without heeding me in the least, 'do you hear me?'

'Yes, Massa Will, hear you ebber so plain.'

'Try the wood well, then, with your knife, and see if you think it *very* rotten.'

'Him rotten, massa, sure nuff,' replied the negro in a few moments, 'but not so berry rotten as mought be. Mought ventur out leetle way pon de limb by myself, dat's true.'

'By yourself! – what do you mean?'

'Why, I mean de bug. 'Tis *berry* hebby bug. Spose I drop him down fuss, and den de limb won't break wid just de weight ob one nigger.'

'You infernal scoundrel!' cried Legrand, apparently much relieved, 'what do you mean by telling me such nonsense as that? As sure as you drop that beetle I'll break your neck. Look here, Jupiter, do you hear me?'

'Yes, massa, needn't hollo at poor nigger dat style.'

'Well! now listen! – if you will venture out on the limb as far as you think safe, and not let go the beetle, I'll make you a present of a silver dollar as soon as you get down.'

'I'm gwine, Massa Will – deed I is,' replied the negro very promptly – 'mos out to the eend now.'

'*Out to the end!*' here fairly screamed Legrand, 'do you say you are out to the end of that limb?'

'Soon be to de end, massa – o–o–o–o–oh! Lor-gol-a-marcy! what *is* dis here pon de tree?'

'Well!' cried Legrand, highly delighted, 'what is it?'

'Why, taint nuffin but a skull – somebody bin lef him head up de tree, and de crows done gobble ebery bit ob de meat off.'

'A skull, you say! – very well! – how is it fastened to the limb? – what holds it on?'

'Sure nuff, massa; mus look. Why, dis berry curous sarcumstance, pon my word – dare's a great big nail in de skull, what fastens ob it on to de tree.'

'Well now, Jupiter, do exactly as I tell you – do you hear?'

'Yes, massa.'

'Pay attention, then! – find the left eye of the skull.'

'Hum! hoo! dat's good! why, dare aint no eye lef at all.'

'Curse your stupidity! do you know your right hand from your left?'

'Yes, I nose dat – nose all bout dat – tis my lef hand what I chops de wood wid.'

'To be sure! you are left-handed; and your left eye is on the same side as your left hand. Now, I suppose, you can find the left eye of the skull, or the place where the left eye has been. Have you found it?'

Here was a long pause. At length the negro asked –

'Is de lef eye of de skull pon de same side as de lef hand of de skull, too? – cause de skull aint got not a bit ob a hand at all – nebber mind! I got de lef eye now – here de lef eye! what mus do wid it?'

'Let the beetle drop through it, as far as the string will reach – but be careful and not let go your hold of the string.'

'All dat done, Massa Will; mighty easy ting for to put de bug fru de hole – look out for him dare below!'

During this colloquy no portion of Jupiter's person could be seen; but the beetle, which he had suffered to descend, was now visible at the end of the string, and glistened like a globe of burnished gold, in the last rays of the setting sun, some of which still faintly illumined the eminence upon which we stood. The *scarabaeus* hung quite clear of any branches, and, if allowed to fall, would have fallen at our feet. Legrand immediately took the scythe, and cleared with it a circular space, three or four yards in diameter, just beneath the insect, and, having accomplished this, ordered Jupiter to let go the string and come down from the tree.

Driving a peg, with great nicety, into the ground, at the precise spot where the beetle fell, my friend now produced from his pocket a tape-measure. Fastening one end of this at that point of the trunk of the tree which was nearest the peg, he unrolled it till it reached the peg, and thence farther unrolled it, in the direction already established by the two points of the tree and the peg, for the distance of fifty feet – Jupiter clearing away the brambles with the scythe. At the spot thus attained a second peg was driven, and about this, as a centre, a rude circle, about four feet in diameter, described. Taking now a spade himself, and giving one to Jupiter and one to me, Legrand begged us to set about digging as quickly as possible.

To speak the truth, I had no especial relish for such amusement at any time, and, at that particular moment, would most willingly have declined it; for the night was coming on, and I felt much fatigued with the exercise already taken; but I saw no mode of escape, and was fearful of disturbing my poor friend's equanimity by a refusal. Could I have depended, indeed, upon Jupiter's aid, I would have had no hesitation in attempting to get the lunatic home by force; but I was too well assured of the old negro's disposition, to hope that he would assist me, under any circumstances, in a personal contest with his master. I made no doubt that the latter had been infected with some of the innumerable Southern superstitions about money buried, and that his fantasy had received confirmation by the finding of the *scarabaeus*, or, perhaps, by Jupiter's obstinacy in maintaining it to be 'a bug of real gold'. A mind disposed to lunacy would readily be led away by such suggestions – especially if chiming in with favourite preconceived ideas – and then I called to mind the poor fellow's speech about the beetle's being 'the index of his fortune'. Upon the whole, I was sadly vexed and puzzled, but, at length, I concluded to make a virtue of necessity – to dig with a good will, and thus the sooner to convince the visionary, by ocular demonstration, of the fallacy of the opinions he entertained.

The lanterns having been lit, we all fell to work with a zeal worthy a more rational cause; and, as the glare fell upon our persons and implements, I could not help thinking how picturesque a group we composed, and how strange and suspicious our labours must have appeared to any interloper who, by chance, might have stumbled upon our whereabouts.

We dug very steadily for two hours. Little was said; and our chief embarrassment lay in the yelpings of the dog, who took exceeding interest in our proceedings. He at length became so obstreperous that we grew fearful of his giving the alarm to some stragglers in the vicinity – or, rather, this was the apprehension of Legrand – for myself, I should have rejoiced at any interruption which might have enabled me to get the wanderer home. The noise was, at length, very effectually silenced by Jupiter, who, getting out of the hole with a dogged air of deliberation, tied the brute's mouth up with one of his suspenders, and then returned, with a grave chuckle, to his task.

When the time mentioned had expired, we had reached a depth of five feet, and yet no signs of any treasure became manifest. A general pause ensued, and I began to hope that the farce was at an end. Legrand, however, although evidently much disconcerted, wiped his brow thoughtfully and recommenced. We had excavated the entire circle of four feet diameter, and now we slightly enlarged the limit, and went to the farther depth of two feet. Still nothing appeared. The gold-seeker, whom I sincerely pitied, at length clambered from the pit, with the bitterest disappointment imprinted upon every feature, and proceeded, slowly and reluctantly, to put on his coat, which he had thrown off at the beginning of his labour. In the meantime I made no remark. Jupiter, at a signal from his master, began to gather up his tools. This done, and the dog having been unmuzzled, we turned in profound silence towards home.

We had taken, perhaps, a dozen steps in this direction, when, with a loud oath, Legrand strode up to Jupiter, and seized him by the collar. The astonished negro opened his eyes and mouth to the fullest extent, let fall the spades, and fell upon his knees.

'You scoundrel!' said Legrand, hissing out the syllables from between his clenched teeth – 'you infernal black villain! – speak, I tell you! – answer me this instant, without prevarication! – which – which is your left eye?'

'Oh, my golly, Massa Will! aint dis here my lef eye for sartain?' roared the terrified Jupiter, placing his hand upon his *right* organ of vision, and holding it there with a desperate pertinacity, as if in immediate dread of his master's attempt at a gouge.

'I thought so! – I knew it! hurrah!' vociferated Legrand, letting the negro go, and executing a series of curvets and caracoles, much to the astonishment of his valet, who, arising from his knees, looked mutely from his master to myself, and them from myself to his master.

'Come! we must go back,' said the latter; 'the game's not up yet;' and he again led the way to the tulip tree.

'Jupiter,' said he, when we reached its foot, 'come here! Was the skull nailed to the limb with the face outwards, or with the face to the limb?'

'De face was out, massa, so dat de crows could get at de eyes good, widout any trouble.'

'Well, then, was it this eye or that through which you dropped the beetle?' – here Legrand touched each of Jupiter's eyes.

''Twas dis eye, massa – de lef eye – jis as you tell me,' and here it was his right eye that the negro indicated.

'That will do – we must try it again.'

Here my friend, about whose madness I now saw, or fancied that I saw, certain indications of method, removed the peg which marked the spot where the beetle fell, to a spot about three inches to the westward of its former position. Taking, now, the tape-measure from the nearest point of the trunk to the peg, as before, and continuing the extension in a straight line to the distance of fifty feet, a spot was indicated, removed, by several yards, from the point at which we had been digging.

Around the new position a circle, somewhat larger than in the former instance, was now described, and we again set to work with the spades. I was dreadfully weary, but, scarcely understanding what had occasioned the change in my thoughts, I felt no longer any great aversion from the labour imposed. I had become most unaccountably interested – nay, even excited. Perhaps there was something, amid all the extravagant demeanour of Legrand – some air of forethought, or of deliberation, which impressed me. I dug eagerly, and now and then caught myself actually looking, with something that very much resembled expectation, for the fancied treasure, the vision of which had demented my unfortunate companion. At a period when such vagaries of thought most fully possessed me, and when we had been at work perhaps an hour and a half, we were again interrupted by the violent howlings of the dog. His uneasiness in the first instance, had been, evidently, but the result of playfulness or caprice, but he now assumed a bitter and serious tone. Upon Jupiter's again attempting to muzzle him, he made furious resistance, and, leaping into the hole, tore up the mould frantically with his claws. In a few seconds he had uncovered a mass of human bones, forming two complete skeletons, intermingled with several buttons of metal, and what appeared to be the dust of decayed woollen. One or two strokes of a spade upturned the blade of a large Spanish knife, and, as we dug farther, three or four loose pieces of gold and silver coin came to light.

At sight of these the joy of Jupiter could scarcely be restrained, but the countenance of his master wore an air of extreme disappointment. He urged us, however, to continue our exertions, and the words were hardly uttered when I stumbled and fell forward, having caught the toe of my boot in a large ring of iron that lay half buried in the loose earth.

We now worked in earnest, and never did I pass ten minutes of more intense excitement. During this interval we had fairly unearthed an oblong chest of wood, which, from its perfect preservation and wonderful hardness, had plainly been subjected to some mineralising process – perhaps that of the bichloride of mercury. This box was three feet and a half long, three feet broad, and two and a half feet deep. It was firmly secured by bands of wrought iron, riveted, and forming a kind of open trellis work over the whole. On each side of the chest, near the top, were three rings of iron – six in all – by means of which a firm hold could be obtained by six persons. Our utmost united endeavours served only to disturb the coffer very slightly in its bed. We at once saw the impossibility of removing so great a weight. Luckily, the sole fastenings of the lid consisted of two sliding bolts. These we drew back – trembling and panting with anxiety. In an instant, a treasure of incalculable value lay gleaming before us. As the rays of the lanterns fell within the pit, there flashed upwards a glow and a glare, from a confused heap of gold and of jewels, that absolutely dazzled our eyes.

I shall not pretend to describe the feelings with which I gazed. Amazement was, of course, predominant. Legrand appeared exhausted with excitement, and spoke very few words. Jupiter's countenance wore, for some minutes, as deadly a pallor as it is possible, in the nature of things, for any negro's visage to assume. He seemed stupefied – thunderstruck. Presently he fell upon his knees in the pit, and, burying his naked arms up to the elbows in gold, let them there remain, as if enjoying the luxury of a bath.

At length, with a deep sigh, he exclaimed, as if in a soliloquy – 'And dis all come ob de goole-bug! de putty goole-bug! de poor little goole-bug, what I boosed in dat sabage kind ob style! Aint you shamed ob yourself, nigger? – answer me dat!'

It became necessary, at last, that I should arouse both master and valet to the expediency of removing the treasure. It was growing late, and it behoved us to make exertion, that we might get everything housed before daylight. It was difficult to say what should be done, and much time was spent in deliberation – so confused were the ideas of all. We, finally, lightened the box by removing two-thirds of its contents, when we were enabled, with some trouble, to raise it from the hole. The articles taken out were deposited among the brambles, and the dog left to guard them, with strict orders from Jupiter, neither, upon any pretence, to stir from the spot, nor to open his mouth until our return. We then hurriedly made for home with the chest; reaching the hut in safety, but after excessive toil, at one o'clock in the morning. Worn out as we were, it was not in human nature to do more immediately. We rested until two, and had supper; starting for the hills immediately afterwards, armed with three stout sacks, which, by good luck, were upon the premises. A little before four we arrived at the pit, divided the remainder of the booty, as equally as might be, among us, and, leaving the holes unfilled, again set out for the hut, at which, for the second time, we deposited our golden burdens, just as the first faint streaks of the dawn gleamed from over the tree-tops in the east.

We were now thoroughly broken down; but the intense excitement of the time denied us repose. After an unquiet

THERE FLASHED UPWARD A GLOW AND A GLARE

slumber of some three or four hours' duration, we arose, as if by preconcert, to make examination of our treasure.

The chest had been full to the brim, and we spent the whole day, and the greater part of the next night, in a scrutiny of its contents. There had been nothing like order or arrangement. Everything had been heaped in promiscuously. Having assorted all with care, we found ourselves possessed of even vaster wealth than we had at first supposed. In coin there was rather more than four hundred and fifty thousand dollars – estimating the value of the pieces, as accurately as we could, by the tables of the period. There was not a particle of silver. All was gold of antique date and of great variety – French, Spanish, and German money, with a few English guineas, and some counters, of which we had never seen specimens before. There were several very large and heavy coins, so worn that we could make nothing of their inscriptions. There was no American money. The value of the jewels we found more difficulty in estimating. There were diamonds – some of them exceedingly large and fine – a hundred and ten in all, and not one of them small; eighteen rubies of remarkable brilliancy; three hundred and ten emeralds, all very beautiful; and twenty-one sapphires, with an opal. These stones had all been broken from their settings and thrown loose in the chest. The settings themselves, which we picked out from among the other gold, appeared to have been beaten up with hammers, as if to prevent identification. Besides all this, there was a vast quantity of solid gold ornaments – nearly two hundred massive finger- and ear-rings; rich chains – thirty of these, if I remember; eighty-three very large and heavy crucifixes; five gold censers of great value; a prodigious golden punchbowl, ornamented with richly-chased vine-leaves and Bacchanalian figures; with two sword handles exquisitely embossed, and many other smaller articles which I cannot recollect. The weight of these valuables exceeded three hundred and fifty pounds avoirdupois; and in this estimate I have not included one hundred and ninety-seven superb gold watches; three of the number being worth each five hundred dollars, if one. Many of them were very old, and as timekeepers valueless; the works having suffered, more or less, from corrosion – but all were richly jewelled and in cases of great worth. We estimated the entire contents of the chest, that night, at a million and a half of dollars; and upon the subsequent disposal of the trinkets and jewels (a few being retained for our own use), it was found that we had greatly undervalued the treasure.

When, at length, we had concluded our examination, and the intense excitement of the time had, in some measure, subsided, Legrand, who saw that I was dying with impatience for a solution of this most extraordinary riddle, entered into a full detail of all the circumstances connected with it.

'You remember,' said he, 'the night when I handed you the rough sketch I had made of the *scarabaeus*. You recollect also, that I became quite vexed at you for insisting that my drawing resembled a death's-head. When you first made this assertion I thought you were jesting; but afterwards I called to mind the peculiar spots on the back of the insect, and admitted to myself that your remark had some little foundation in fact. Still, the sneer at my graphic powers irritated me – for I am considered a good artist – and, therefore, when you handed me the scrap of parchment, I was about to crumple it up and throw it angrily into the fire.'

'The scrap of paper, you mean,' said I.

'No; it had much of the appearance of paper, and at first I supposed it to be such, but when I came to draw upon it, I discovered it, at once, to be a piece of very thin parchment. It was quite dirty, you remember. Well, as I was in the very act of crumpling it up, my glance fell upon the sketch at which you had been looking, and you may imagine my astonishment when I perceived in fact, the figure of a death's-head just where, it seemed to me, I had made the drawing of the beetle. For a moment I was too much amazed to think with accuracy. I knew that my design was very different in detail from this – although there was a certain similarity in general outline. Presently I took a candle, and seating myself at the other end of the room, proceeded to scrutinise the parchment more closely. Upon turning it over, I saw my own sketch upon the reverse, just as I had made it. My first idea, now, was mere surprise at the really remarkable similarity of outline – at the singular coincidence involved in the fact, that unknown to me, there should have been a skull upon the other side of the parchment, immediately beneath my figure of the *scarabaeus*, and that this skull, not only in outline, but in size, should so closely resemble my drawing. I say the singularity of this coincidence absolutely stupefied me for a time. This is the usual effect of such coincidences. The mind struggles to establish a connection – a sequence of cause and effect – and, being unable to do so, suffers a species of temporary paralysis. But, when I recovered from this stupor, there dawned upon me gradually a conviction which startled me even far more than the coincidence. I began distinctly, positively, to remember that there had been *no* drawing upon the parchment when I made my sketch of the *scarabaeus*. I became perfectly certain of this; for I recollected turning up first one side and then the other, in search of the cleanest spot. Had the skull been then there, of course I could not have failed to notice it. Here was indeed a mystery which I felt it impossible to explain; but even at that early moment, there seemed to glimmer, faintly, within the most remote and secret chambers of my intellect, a glow-worm-like conception of that truth which last night's adventure brought to so magnificent a demonstration. I arose at once, and putting the parchment securely away, dismissed all further reflection until I should be alone.

'When you had gone, and when Jupiter was fast asleep, I betook myself to a more methodical investigation of the affair. In the first place I considered the manner in which the parchment had come into my possession. The spot where we discovered the *scarabaeus* was on the coast of the mainland, about a mile eastward of the island, and but a short distance above high-water mark. Upon my taking hold of it, it gave me a sharp bite, which caused me to let it drop. Jupiter, with his accustomed caution, before seizing the insect, which had flown towards him, looked about him for a leaf, or something of that nature, by which to take hold of it. It was at this moment that his eyes, and mine also, fell upon the scrap of parchment, which I then supposed to be paper. It was lying half buried in the sand, a corner sticking up. Near the spot where we found it, I observed the remnants of the hull of what appeared to have been a ship's long-boat. The wreck seemed to have been there for a very great while; for the resemblance to boat timbers could scarcely be traced.

'Well, Jupiter picked up the parchment, wrapped the beetle in it, and gave it to me. Soon afterwards we turned to go home, and on the way met Lieutenant G—. I showed him the insect, and he begged me to let him take it to the fort. Upon my consenting, he thrust it forthwith into his waistcoat pocket, without the parchment in which it had been wrapped, and which I had continued to hold in my hand during his inspection. Perhaps he dreaded my changing my mind, and thought it best to make sure of the prize at once – you know how enthusiastic he is on all subjects connected with Natural History. At the same time, without being conscious of it, I must have deposited the parchment in my own pocket.

'You remember that when I went to the table, for the purpose of making a sketch of the beetle, I found no paper where it was usually kept. I looked in the drawer, and found none there. I searched my pockets, hoping to find an old letter, when my hand fell upon the parchment. I thus detail the precise mode in which it came into my possession; for the circumstances impressed me with peculiar force.

'No doubt you will think me fanciful – but I had already established a kind of *connection*. I had put together two links of a great chain. There was a boat lying upon a sea coast, and not far from the boat was a parchment – *not a paper* – with a skull depicted upon it. You will, of course, ask "where is the connection?" I reply, that the skull, or death's-head, is the well known emblem of the pirate. The flag of the death's-head is hoisted in all engagements.

'I have said that the scrap was parchment, and not paper. Parchment is durable – almost imperishable. Matters of little moment are rarely consigned to parchment; since, for the mere ordinary purposes of drawing or writing, it is not nearly so well adapted as paper. This reflection suggested some meaning – some relevancy – in the death's-head. I did not fail to observe, also, the *form* of the parchment. Although one of its corners had been, by some accident, destroyed, it could be seen that the original form was oblong. It was just such a slip, indeed, as might have been chosen for a memorandum – for a record of something to be long remembered and carefully preserved.'

'But,' I interposed, 'you say that the skull was *not* upon the parchment when you made the drawing of the beetle. How then do you trace any connection between the boat and the skull – since this latter, according to your own admission, must have been designed (God only knows how or by whom) at some period subsequent to your sketching the *scarabaeus?*'

'Ah, hereupon turns the whole mystery; although the secret, at this point, I had comparatively little difficulty in solving. My steps were sure, and could afford but a single result. I reasoned, for example, thus: When I drew the *scarabaeus*, there was no skull apparent upon the parchment. When I had completed the drawing I gave it to you, and observed you narrowly until you returned it. *You*, therefore, did not design the skull, and no one else was present to do it. Then it was not done by human agency. And nevertheless it was done.

'At this stage of my reflections I endeavoured to remember, and *did* remember, with entire distinctness, every incident which occurred about the period in question. The weather was chilly (oh, rare and happy accident!), and a fire was blazing upon the hearth. I was heated with exercise and sat near the table. You, however, had drawn a chair close to the chimney. Just as I placed the parchment in your hand, and as you were in the act of inspecting it, Wolf, the Newfoundland, entered, and leaped upon your shoulders. With your left hand you caressed him and kept him off, while your right, holding the parchment, was permitted to fall listlessly between your knees, and in close proximity to the fire. At one moment I thought the blaze had caught it, and was about to caution you, but before I could speak you had withdrawn it, and were engaged in its examination. When I considered all these particulars, I doubted not for a moment that *heat* had been the agent in bringing to light, upon the parchment, the skull which I saw designed upon it. You are well aware that chemical preparations exist, and have existed time out of mind, by means of which it is possible to write upon either paper or vellum, so that the characters shall become visible only when subjected to the action of fire. Zaffre, digested in *aqua regia*, and diluted with four times its weight of water, is sometimes employed; a green tint results. The regulus of cobalt, dissolved in spirit of nitre, gives a red. These colours disappear at longer or shorter intervals after the material written upon cools, but again become apparent upon the reapplication of heat.

'I now scrutinised the death's-head with care. Its outer edges – the edges of the drawing nearest the edge of the vellum – were far more *distinct* than the others. It was clear that the action of the caloric had been imperfect or unequal. I immediately kindled a fire, and subjected every portion of the parchment to a glowing heat. At first, the only effect was the strengthening of the faint lines in the skull; but, upon persevering in the experiment, there became visible, at the corner of the slip, diagonally opposite to the spot in which the death's-head was delineated, the figure of what I at first supposed to be a goat. A closer scrutiny, however, satisfied me that it was intended for a kid.'

'Ha! ha!' said I, 'to be sure I have no right to laugh at you – a million and a half of money is too serious a matter for mirth – but you are not about to establish a third link in your chain – you will not find any special connection between your pirates and a goat – pirates, you know, have nothing to do with goats; they appertain to the farming interest.'

'But I have just said that the figure was *not* that of a goat.'

'Well, a kid, then – pretty much the same thing.'

'Pretty much, but not altogether,' said Legrand. 'You may have heard of one *Captain* Kidd. I at once looked upon the figure of the animal as a kind of punning or hieroglyphical signature. I say signature; because its position upon the vellum suggested this idea. The death's-head at the corner diagonally opposite, had, in the same manner, the air of a stamp, or seal. But I was sorely put out by the absence of all else – of the body to my imagined instrument – of the text for my context.'

'I presume you expected to find a letter between the stamp and the signature.'

'Something of that kind. The fact is, I felt irresistibly impressed with a presentiment of some vast good fortune impending. I can scarcely say why. Perhaps, after all, it was rather a desire than an actual belief; but do you know that Jupiter's silly words, about the bug being of solid gold, had a remarkable effect upon my fancy? And then the series of accidents and coincidences – these were so *very* extraordinary. Do you observe how mere an accident it was that these events should have occurred upon the *sole* day of all the year in which it has been, or may be, sufficiently cool for fire, and that without the fire, or without the intervention of the dog at the precise moment in which he appeared, I should never have become aware of the death's-head, and so never the possessor of the treasure?'

'But proceed – I am all impatience.'

'Well; you have heard, of course, the many stories current – the thousand vague rumours afloat, about money buried, somewhere upon the Atlantic coast, by Kidd and his associates. These rumours must have had some foundation in fact. And that the rumours have existed so long and so continuous, could have resulted, it appeared to me, only from the circumstance of the buried treasure still *remaining* entombed. Had Kidd concealed his plunder for a time, and afterwards reclaimed it, the rumours would scarcely have reached us in their present unvarying form. You will observe that the stories told are all about money-seekers, not about money-finders. Had the pirate recovered his money, there the affair would have dropped. It seemed to me that some accident – say the loss of a memorandum indicating its locality – had deprived him of the means of recovering it, and that this accident had become known to his followers, who otherwise might never have heard that treasure had been concealed at all, and who, busying themselves in vain, because unguided attempts, to regain it, had given first birth, and then universal currency, to the reports which are now so common. Have you ever heard of any important treasure being unearthed along the coast?'

'Never.'

'But that Kidd's accumulations were immense, is well known. I took it for granted, therefore, that the earth still held them; and you will scarcely be surprised when I tell you that I felt a hope, nearly amounting to certainty, that the parchment so strangely found, involved a lost record of the place of deposit.'

'But how did you proceed?'

'I held the vellum again to the fire, after increasing the heat; but nothing appeared. I now thought it possible that the coating of dirt might have something to do with the failure; so I carefully rinsed the parchment by pouring warm water over it, and, having done this, I placed it in a tin pan, with the skull downwards, and put the pan upon a furnace of lighted charcoal. In a few minutes, the pan having become thoroughly heated, I removed the slip, and, to my inexpressible joy, found it spotted, in several places, with what appeared to be figures arranged in lines. Again I placed it in the pan, and suffered it to remain another minute. Upon taking it off, the whole was just as you see it now.'

Here Legrand, having reheated the parchment, submitted it to my inspection. The following characters were rudely traced, in a red tint, between the death's-head and the goat:

53‡‡† 305))6*;4826)4‡.)4‡);806*;48†8¶
60))85;1‡(;:‡*8†83(88)5*†46(;88*96*?;
8)*‡(;485);5*†2:*‡(;495 6*2(5*–4)8¶
8*;4069285);)6†8)4‡‡;1(‡9;48081;8:8‡
1;48†85;4)485†528806*81(‡9;48;(88;
4(‡?34;48)4‡;161;:188;‡?;

'But,' said I, returning him the slip, 'I am as much in the dark as ever. Were all the jewels of Golconda awaiting me upon my solution of this enigma, I am quite sure that I should be unable to earn them.'

'And yet,' said Legrand, 'the solution is by no means so difficult as you might be led to imagine from the first hasty inspection of the characters. These characters, as anyone might readily guess, form a cipher – that is to say, they convey a meaning; but then, from what is known of Kidd, I could not suppose him capable of constructing any of the more abstruse cryptographs. I made up my mind, at once, that this was of a simple species – such, however, as would appear, to the crude intellect of the sailor, absolutely insoluble without the key.'

'And you really solved it?'

'Readily; I have solved others of an abstruseness ten thousand times greater. Circumstances, and a certain bias of mind, have led me to take interest in such riddles, and it may well be doubted whether human ingenuity can construct an enigma of the kind which human ingenuity may not, by proper application, resolve. In fact, having once established connected and legible characters, I scarcely gave a thought to the mere difficulty of developing their import.

'In the present case – indeed in all cases of secret writing – the first question regards the *language* of the cipher; for the principles of solution, so far, especially, as the more simple ciphers are concerned, depend upon, and are varied by, the genius of the particular idiom. In general there is no alternative but experiment (directed by probabilities) of every tongue known to him who attempts the solution, until the true one be attained. But, with the cipher now before us, all difficulty was removed by the signature. The pun upon the word "Kidd" is appreciable in no other language than the English. But for this consideration I should have begun my attempts with the Spanish and French, as the tongues in which a secret of this kind would most naturally have been written by a pirate of the Spanish main. As it was, I assumed the cryptograph to be English.

'You observe there are no divisions between the words. Had there been divisions, the task would have been comparatively easy. In such case I should have commenced with a collation and analysis of the shorter words, and had a word of a single letter occurred, as is most likely (*a* or *I* for example), I should have considered the solution as assured. But, there being no division, my first step was to ascertain the predominant letters, as well as the least frequent. Counting all, I constructed a table, thus:

'Of the character 8 there are 33.

;	"	26.
4	"	19.
‡)	"	16.
*	"	13.
5	"	12.
6	"	11.
†1	"	8.
0	"	6.
92	"	5.
:3	"	4.
?	"	3.
¶	"	2.
–	"	1.

'Now, in English, the letter which most frequently occurs is *e*. Afterwards, the succession runs thus: *a o i d h n r s t u y c f g l m w b k p q x z*. *E* predominates so remarkably that an individual sentence of any length is rarely seen, in which it is not the prevailing character.

'Here, then, we have, in the very beginning, the groundwork for something more than a mere guess. The general use which may be made of the table is obvious – but in this particular cipher we shall only very partially require its aid. As our predominant character is 8, we will commence by assuming it as the *e* of the natural alphabet. To verify the supposition, let us observe if the 8 be seen often in couples – for *e* is doubled with great frequency in English – in such words, for example, as "meet", "fleet", "speed", "seen", "been", "agree", &c. In the present instance we see it doubled no less than five times, although the cryptograph is brief.

'Let us assume 8, then, as *e*. Now, of all *words* in the language "the" is the most usual; let us see, therefore, whether there are not repetitions of any three characters, in the same order of collocation, the last of them being 8. If we discover repetitions of such letters, so arranged, they will most probably represent the word "the". Upon inspection, we find no less than seven such arrangements, the characters being ;48. We may therefore assume that ; represents *t*, 4 represents *h*, and 8 represents *e* – the last being now well confirmed. Thus a great step has been taken.

'But, having established a single word, we are enabled to establish a vastly important point; that is to say, several commencements and terminations of other words. Let us refer, for example, to the last instance but one, in which the combination ;48 occurs – not far from the end of the cipher. We know that the ; immediately ensuing is the commencement of a word, and of the six characters succeeding this "the", we are cognisant of no less than five. Let us set these characters down, thus, by the letters we know them to represent, leaving a space for the unknown –

t eeth.

'Here we are enabled, at once, to discard the "*th*", as forming no portion of the word commencing with the first *t*; since, by experiment of the entire alphabet for a letter adapted to the vacancy, we perceive that no word can be formed of which this *th* can be a part. We are thus narrowed into

t ee,

and, going through the alphabet, if necessary, as before, we arrive at the word "tree", as the sole possible reading. We thus gain another letter, *r*, represented by (, with the words "the tree" in juxtaposition.

'Looking beyond these words, for a short distance, we again see the combination ;48, and employ it by way of *termination* to what immediately precedes. We have thus this arrangement –

the tree ;4(‡?34 the,

or, substituting the natural letters, where known, it reads thus –

the tree thr‡?3h the.

'Now if, in place of the unknown characters, we leave blank spaces, or substitute dots, we read thus –

the tree thr . . . h the,

when the word "*through*" makes itself evident at once. But this discovery gives us three new letters, *o*, *u*, and *g*, represented by ‡ ? and 3.

'Looking now, narrowly, through the cipher for combinations of known characters, we find, not very far from the beginning, this arrangement –

83(88, or *egree*,

which, plainly, is the conclusion of the word "degree", and gives us another letter, *d*, represented by †.

'Four letters beyond the word "degree", we perceive the combination

;(48;88.

'Translating the known characters, and representing the unknown by dots, as before, we read thus –

th rtee,

an arrangement immediately suggestive of the word "thirteen", and again furnishing us with two new characters, *i* and *n*, represented by 6 and *.

'Referring, now, to the beginning of the cryptograph, we find the combination

53‡‡†.

'Translating, as before, we obtain

. good,

which assures us that the first letter is *A*, and that the first two words are "A good."

'It is now time that we arrange our key, as far as discovered, in a tabular form, to avoid confusion. It will stand thus –

5	represents	a	6	"	i
†	"	d	*	"	n
8	"	e	‡	"	o
3	"	g	(	"	r
4	"	h	;	"	t

'We have, therefore, no less than ten of the most important letters represented, and it will be unnecessary to proceed with the details of the solution. I have said enough to convince you that ciphers of this nature are readily soluble, and to give you some insight into the *rationale* of their development. But be assured that the specimen before us appertains to the very simplest species of cryptograph. It now only remains to give you the full translation of the characters upon the parchment, as unriddled. Here it is:

> A good glass in the bishop's hostel in the devil's seat forty-one degrees and thirteen minutes north-east and by north main branch seventh limb east side shoot from the left eye of the death's-head a bee line from the tree through the shot fifty feet out.'

'But,' said I, 'the enigma seems still in as bad a condition as ever. How is it possible to extort a meaning from all this jargon about "devil's seats", "death's-heads", and "bishop's hotels"?'

'I confess,' replied Legrand, 'that the matter still wears a serious aspect, when regarded with a casual glance. My first endeavour was to divide the sentence into the natural division intended by the cryptographist.'

'You mean to punctuate it?'

'Something of that kind.'

'But how was it possible to effect this?'

'I reflected that it had been a *point* with the writer to run his words together without division, so as to increase the difficulty of solution. Now, a not over-acute man, in pursuing such an object, would be nearly certain to overdo the matter. When, in the course of his composition, he arrived at a break in his subject which would naturally require a pause, or a point, he would be exceedingly apt to run his characters, at this place, more than usually close together. If you will observe the MS, in the present instance, you will easily detect five such cases of unusual crowding. Acting upon this hint, I made the division thus:

> A good glass in the Bishop's hostel in the Devil's seat – forty-one degrees and thirteen minutes – north-east and by north – main branch seventh limb east side – shoot from the left eye of the death's-head – a bee-line from the tree through the shot fifty feet out.'

'Even this division,' said I, 'leaves me still in the dark.'

'It left me also in the dark,' replied Legrand, 'for a few days; during which I made diligent enquiry, in the neighbourhood of Sullivan's Island, for any building which went by the name of the "Bishop's Hotel"; for, of course, I dropped the obsolete word "hostel". Gaining no information on the subject, I was on the point of extending my sphere of search, and proceeding in a more systematic manner, when, one morning, it entered into my head, quite suddenly, that this "Bishop's Hostel" might have some reference to an old family, of the name of Bessop, which, time out of mind, had held possession of an ancient manor-house, about four miles to the northward of the island. I accordingly went over to the plantation, and reinstituted my enquiries among the older negroes of the place. At length one of the most aged of the women said that she had heard of such a place as *Bessop's Castle*, and thought that she could guide me to it, but that it was not a castle, nor a tavern, but a high rock.

'I offered to pay her well for her trouble, and after some demur, she consented to accompany me to the spot. We found it without much difficulty, when, dismissing her, I proceeded to examine the place. The "castle" consisted of an irregular assemblage of cliffs and rocks – one of the latter being quite remarkable for its height as well as for its insulated and artificial appearance. I clambered to its apex, and then felt much at a loss as to what should be next done.

'While I was busied in reflection, my eyes fell upon a narrow ledge in the eastern face of the rock, perhaps a yard below the summit upon which I stood. This ledge projected about eighteen inches, and was not more than a foot wide, while a niche in the cliff just above it, gave it a rude resemblance to one of the hollow-backed chairs used by our ancestors. I made no doubt that here was the "devil's-seat" alluded to in the MS, and now I seemed to grasp the full secret of the riddle.

'The "good glass", I knew, could have reference to nothing but a telescope; for the word "glass" is rarely employed in any other sense by seamen. Now here, I at once saw, was a telescope to be used, and a definite point of view, *admitting no variation*, from which to use it. Nor did I hesitate to believe that the phrases, "forty-one degrees and thirteen minutes", and "north-east and by north", were intended as directions for the levelling of the glass. Greatly excited by these discoveries, I hurried home, procured a telescope, and returned to the rock.

'I let myself down to the ledge, and found that it was impossible to retain a seat upon it except in one particular position. This fact confirmed my preconceived idea. I proceeded to use the glass. Of course, the "forty-one degrees and thirteen minutes" could allude to nothing but elevation above the visible horizon, since the horizontal direction was clearly indicated by the words, "north-east and by north". This latter direction I at once established by means of a pocket-compass; then, pointing the glass as nearly at an angle of forty-one degrees of elevation as I could do it by guess, I moved it cautiously up or down until my attention was arrested by a circular rift or opening in the foliage of a large tree that overtopped its fellows in the distance. In the centre of this rift I perceived a white spot, but could not, at first, distinguish what it was. Adjusting the focus of the telescope, I again looked, and now made it out to be a human skull.

'Upon this discovery I was so sanguine as to consider the enigma solved; for the phrase "main branch, seventh limb, east side", could refer only to the position of the skull upon the tree, while "shoot from the left eye of the death's-head" admitted, also, of but one interpretation, in regard to a search for buried treasure. I perceived that the design was to drop a bullet from the left eye of the skull, and that a beeline, or, in other words, a straight line, drawn from the nearest point of the trunk through "the shot" (or the spot where the bullet fell), and thence extended to a distance of fifty feet, would indicate a definite point – and beneath this point I thought it at least *possible* that a deposit of value lay concealed.'

'All this,' I said, 'is exceedingly clear, and, although ingenious, still simple and explicit. When you left the Bishop's Hotel, what then?'

'Why, having carefully taken the bearings of the tree, I turned homewards. The instant that I left "the devil's seat", however, the circular rift vanished; nor could I get a glimpse of it afterwards, turn as I would. What seems to me the chief ingenuity in this whole business, is the fact (for repeated experiment has convinced me it is a fact) that the circular opening in question is visible from no other attainable point of view than that afforded by the narrow ledge upon the face of the rock.

'In this expedition to the "Bishop's Hotel" I had been attended by Jupiter, who had, no doubt, observed, for some weeks past, the abstraction of my demeanour, and took especial care not to leave me alone. But, on the next day, getting up very early, I contrived to give him the slip, and went into the hills in search of the tree. After much toil I found it. When I came home at night my valet proposed to give me a flogging. With the rest of the adventure I believe you are as well acquainted as myself.'

'I suppose,' said I, 'you missed the spot, in the first attempt at digging, through Jupiter's stupidity in letting the bug fall through the right instead of through the left eye of the skull.'

'Precisely. This mistake made a difference of about two inches and a half in the "shot" – that is to say, in the position of the peg nearest the tree; and had the treasure been *beneath* the "shot", the error would have been of little moment; but the "shot", together with the nearest point of the tree, were merely two points for the establishment of a line of direction; of course the error, however trivial in the beginning, increased as we proceeded with the line, and by the time we had gone fifty feet, threw us quite off the scent. But for my deep-seated impressions that treasure was here somewhere actually buried, we might have had all our labour in vain.'

'But your grandiloquence, and your conduct in swinging the beetle – how excessively odd! I was sure you were mad. And why did you insist upon letting fall the bug, instead of a bullet from the shell?'

'Why, to be frank, I felt somewhat annoyed by your evident suspicions touching my sanity, and so resolved to punish you quietly, in my own way, by a little bit of sober mystification. For this reason I swung the beetle, and for this reason I let it fall from the tree. An observation of yours about its great weight suggested the latter idea.'

'Yes, I perceive; and now there is only one point which puzzles me. What are we to make of the skeletons found in the hole?'

'That is a question I am no more able to answer than yourself. There seems, however, only one plausible way of accounting for them – and yet it is dreadful to believe in such atrocity as my suggestion would imply. It is clear that Kidd – if Kidd indeed secreted this treasure, which I doubt not – it is clear that he must have had assistance in the labour. But this labour concluded, he may have thought it expedient to remove all participants in his secret. Perhaps a couple of blows with a mattock were sufficient, while his coadjutors were busy in the pit; perhaps it required a dozen – who shall tell?'

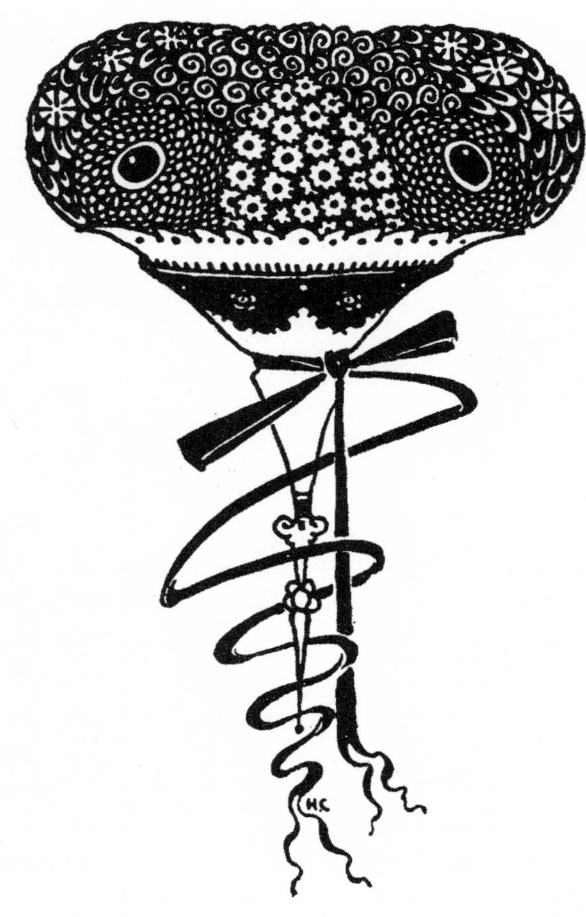

The Facts in the Case of M. Valdemar

Of course I shall not pretend to consider it any matter for wonder that the extraordinary case of M. Valdemar has excited discussion. It would have been a miracle had it not – especially under the circumstances. Through the desire of all parties concerned to keep the affair from the public, at least for the present, or until we had further opportunities for investigation – through our endeavours to effect this – a garbled or exaggerated account made its way into society, and became the source of many unpleasant misrepresentations; and, very naturally, of a great deal of disbelief.

It is now rendered necessary that I give the *facts* – as far as I comprehend them myself. They are, succinctly, these:

My attention, for the last three years, had been repeatedly drawn to the subject of mesmerism; and, about nine months ago, it occurred to me, quite suddenly, that in the series of experiments made hitherto, there had been a very remarkable and most unaccountable omission – no person had as yet been mesmerised *in articulo mortis*. It remained to be seen, first, whether, in such condition, there existed in the patient any susceptibility to the magnetic influence; secondly, whether, if any existed, it was impaired or increased by the condition; thirdly, to what extent, or for how long a period, the encroachments of Death might be arrested by the process. There were other points to be ascertained, but these most excited my curiosity – the last in especial, from the immensely important character of its consequences.

In looking around me for some subject by whose means I might test these particulars, I was brought to think of my friend, M. Ernest Valdemar, the well-known compiler of the *Bibliotheca Forensica*, and author (under the *nom de plume* of Issachar Marx) of the Polish versions of *Wallenstein* and *Gargantua*. M. Valdemar, who has resided principally at Harlem, N.Y., since the year 1839, is (or was) particularly noticeable for the extreme spareness of his person – his lower limbs much resembling those of John Randolph; and, also, for the whiteness of his whiskers, in violent contrast to the blackness of his hair – the latter, in consequence, being very generally mistaken for a wig. His temperament was markedly nervous, and rendered him a good subject for mesmeric experiment. On two or three occasions I had put him to sleep with little difficulty, but was disappointed in other results which his peculiar constitution had naturally led me to anticipate. His will was at no period positively, or thoroughly, under my control; and in regard to *clairvoyance*, I could accomplish with him nothing to be relied upon. I always attributed my failure at these points to the disordered state of his health. For some months previous to my becoming acquainted with him, his physicians had declared him in a confirmed phthisis. It was his custom, indeed, to speak calmly of his approaching dissolution, as of a matter neither to be avoided nor regretted.

When the ideas to which I have alluded first occurred to me, it was of course very natural that I should think of M. Valdemar. I knew the steady philosophy of the man too well to apprehend any scruples from *him*; and he had no relatives in America who would be likely to interfere. I spoke to him frankly upon the subject; and, to my surprise, his interest seemed vividly excited. I say to my surprise; for, although he had always yielded his person freely to my experiments, he had never before given me any tokens of sympathy with what I did. His disease was of that character which would admit of exact calculation in respect to the epoch of its termination in death; and it was finally arranged between us that he would send for me about twenty-four hours before the period announced by his physicians as that of his decease.

It is now rather more than seven months since I received, from M. Valdemar himself, the subjoined note:

> MY DEAR P—, You may as well come *now*. D— and F— are agreed that I cannot hold out beyond tomorrow midnight; and I think they have hit the time very nearly.
>
> VALDEMAR

I received this note within half an hour after it was written, and in fifteen minutes more I was in the dying man's chamber. I had not seen him for ten days, and was appalled by the fearful alteration which the brief interval had wrought in him. His face wore a leaden hue; the eyes were utterly lustreless; and the emaciation was so extreme, that the skin had been broken through by the cheek-bones. His expectoration was excessive. The pulse was barely perceptible. He retained, nevertheless, in a very remarkable manner, both his mental power and a certain degree of physical strength. He spoke with distinctness – took some palliative medicines without aid – and, when I entered the room, was occupied in pencilling memoranda in a pocketbook. He was propped up in the bed by pillows. Drs D— and F— were in attendance. After pressing Valdemar's hand, I took these gentlemen aside, and obtained from them a minute account of the patient's condition. The left lung had been for eighteen months in a semi-osseous or cartilaginous state, and was, of course, entirely useless for all purposes of vitality. The right, in its upper portion, was also partially, if not thoroughly, ossified, while the lower region was merely a mass of purulent tubercles, running one into another. Several extensive perforations existed; and, at one point, permanent adhesion to the ribs had taken place. These appearances in the right lobe were of comparatively recent date. The ossification had proceeded with very unusual rapidity; no sign of it had been discovered a month before, and the adhesion had only been observed during the three previous days. Independently of the phthisis, the patient was suspected of aneurism of the aorta; but on this point the osseous symptoms rendered an exact diagnosis impossible. It was the opinion of both physicians that M. Valdemar would die about midnight on the morrow (Sunday). It was then seven o'clock on Saturday evening.

On quitting the invalid's bedside to hold conversation with myself, Drs D— and F— had bidden him a final farewell. It had not been their intention to return; but, at my request, they agreed to look in upon the patient about ten the next night.

When they had gone, I spoke freely with M. Valdemar on the subject of his approaching dissolution, as well as, more particularly, of the experiment proposed. He still professed himself quite willing and even anxious to have it made, and urged me to commence it at once. A male and a female nurse were in attendance; but I did not feel myself altogether at liberty to engage in a task of this character with no more reliable witnesses than these people, in case of sudden accident, might prove. I therefore postponed operations until about eight the next night, when the arrival of a medical student, with whom I had some acquaintance (Mr Theodore L—l), relieved me from further embarrassment. It had been my design, originally, to wait for the physicians; but I was induced to proceed, first, by the urgent entreaties of M. Valdemar, and secondly, by my conviction that I had not a moment to lose, as he was evidently sinking fast.

Mr L—l was so kind as to accede to my desire that he would take notes of all that occurred; and it is from his memoranda that what I now have to relate is, for the most part, either condensed or copied *verbatim*.

It wanted about five minutes of eight when, taking the patient's hand, I begged him to state, as distinctly as he could, to Mr L—l, whether he (M. Valdemar) was entirely willing that I should make the experiment of mesmerising him in his then condition.

He replied feebly, yet quite audibly, 'Yes, I wish to be mesmerised' – adding immediately afterwards, 'I fear you have deferred it too long.'

While he spoke thus, I commenced the passes which I had already found most effectual in subduing him. He was evidently influenced with the first lateral stroke of my hand across his forehead; but although I exerted all my powers, no further perceptible effect was induced until some minutes after ten o'clock, when Drs D— and F— called, according to appointment. I explained to them, in a few words, what I designed, and as they opposed no objection, saying that the patient was already in the death agony, I proceeded without hesitation – exchanging, however, the lateral passes for downward ones, and directing my gaze entirely into the right eye of the sufferer.

By this time his pulse was imperceptible and his breathing was stertorous, and at intervals of half a minute.

This condition was nearly unaltered for a quarter of an hour. At the expiration of this period, however, a natural, although a very deep sigh, escaped the bosom of the dying man, and the stertorous breathing ceased – that is to say, its stertorousness was no longer apparent; the intervals were undiminished. The patient's extremities were of an icy coldness.

At five minutes before eleven I perceived unequivocal signs of the mesmeric influence. The glassy roll of the eye was changed for that expression of uneasy *inward* examination which is never seen except in cases of sleep-waking, and which it is quite impossible to mistake. With a few rapid lateral passes I made the lids quiver, as in incipient sleep, and with a few more I closed them altogether. I was not satisfied, however, with this, but continued the manipulations vigorously, and with the fullest exertion of the will, until I had completely stiffened the limbs of the slumberer, after placing them in a seemingly easy position. The legs were at full length; the arms were nearly so, and reposed on the bed at a moderate distance from the loins. The head was very slightly elevated.

When I had accomplished this, it was fully midnight, and I requested the gentlemen present to examine M. Valdemar's condition. After a few experiments, they admitted him to be in an unusually perfect state of mesmeric trance. The curiosity of both the physicians was greatly excited. Dr D — resolved at once to remain with the patient all night, while Dr F— took leave with a promise to return at daybreak. Mr L—l and the nurses remained.

We left M. Valdemar entirely undisturbed until about three o'clock in the morning, when I approached him, and found him in precisely the same condition as when Dr F — went away – that is to say, he lay in the same position. The pulse was imperceptible; the breathing was gentle (scarcely noticeable, unless through the application of a mirror to the lips); the eyes were closed naturally; and the limbs were as rigid and as cold as marble. Still, the general appearance was certainly not that of death.

As I approached M. Valdemar I made a kind of half effort to influence his right arm into pursuit of my own, as I passed the latter gently to and fro above his person. In such experiments with this patient I had never perfectly succeeded before, and assuredly I had little thought of succeeding now; but to my astonishment, his arm very readily, although feebly, followed every direction I assigned it with mine. I determined to hazard a few words of conversation.

'M. Valdemar,' I said, 'are you asleep?' He made no answer, but I perceived a tremor about the lips, and was thus induced to repeat the question, again and again. At its third repetition, his whole frame was agitated by a very slight shivering; the eyelids unclosed themselves so far as to display a white line of a ball; the lips moved sluggishly, and from between them, in a barely audible whisper, issued the words –

'Yes; asleep now. Do not wake me! – let me die so!'

I here felt the limbs and found them as rigid as ever. The right arm, as before, obeyed the direction of my hand. I questioned the sleep-waker again – 'Do you still feel pain in the breast, M. Valdemar?'

The answer now was immediate, but even less audible than before – 'No pain – I am dying.'

I did not think it advisable to disturb him further just then, and nothing more was said or done until the arrival of Dr F—, who came a little before sunrise, and expressed unbounded astonishment at finding the patient still alive.

After feeling the pulse and applying a mirror to the lips, he requested me to speak to the sleep-waker again. I did so, saying – 'M. Valdemar, do you still sleep?'

As before, some minutes elapsed ere a reply was made; and during the interval the dying man seemed to be collecting his energies to speak. At my fourth repetition of the question, he said very faintly, almost inaudibly – 'Yes; still asleep – dying.'

It was now the opinion, or rather the wish, of the physicians, that M. Valdemar should be suffered to remain undisturbed in his present apparently tranquil condition, until death should supervene – and this, it was generally agreed, must now take place within a few minutes. I concluded, however, to speak to him once more, and merely repeated my previous question.

While I spoke, there came a marked change over the countenance of the sleep-waker. The eyes rolled themselves slowly open, the pupils disappearing upwardly; the skin generally assumed a cadaverous hue, resembling not so much parchment as white paper; and the circular hectic spots which, hitherto, had been strongly defined in the centre of each cheek, *went out* at once. I use this expression, because the suddenness of their departure put me in mind of nothing so much as the extinguishment of a candle by a puff of the breath. The upper lip, at the same time, writhed itself away from the teeth, which it had previously covered completely; while the lower jaw fell with an audible jerk, leaving the mouth widely extended, and disclosing in full view the swollen and blackened tongue. I presume that no member of the party then present had been unaccustomed to deathbed horrors; but so hideous beyond conception was the appearance of M. Valdemar at this moment, that there was a general shrinking back from the region of the bed.

I now feel that I have reached a point of this narrative at which every reader will be startled into positive disbelief. It is my business, however, simply to proceed.

There was no longer the faintest sign of vitality in M. Valdemar; and concluding him to be dead, we were consigning him to the charge of the nurses, when a strong vibratory motion was observable in the tongue. This continued for perhaps a minute. At the expiration of this period, there issued from the distended and motionless jaws a voice – such as it would be madness in me to attempt describing. There are, indeed, two or three epithets which might be considered as applicable to it in part; I might say, for example, that the sound was harsh, and broken, and hollow; but the hideous whole is indescribable, for the simple reason that no similar sounds have ever jarred upon the ear of humanity. There were two particulars, nevertheless, which I thought then, and still think, might fairly be stated as characteristic of the intonation – as well adapted to convey some idea of its unearthly peculiarity. In the first place, the voice seemed to reach our ears – at least mine – from a vast distance, or from some deep cavern within the earth. In the second place, it impressed me (I fear, indeed, that it will be impossible to make myself comprehended) as gelatinous or glutinous matters impress the sense of touch.

I have spoken both of 'sound' and of 'voice'. I mean to say that the sound was one of distinct – of even wonderfully, thrillingly distinct – syllabification. M. Valdemar *spoke* – obviously in reply to the question I had propounded to him a

UPON THE BED THERE LAY A NEARLY LIQUID MASS OF LOATHSOME –
OF DETESTABLE PUTRIDITY

few minutes before. I had asked him, it will be remembered, if he still slept.

He now said – 'Yes – no – I *have been* sleeping – and now – now – *I am dead*.'

No person present even affected to deny, or attempted to repress, the unutterable, shuddering horror which these few words, thus uttered, were so well calculated to convey. Mr L—l (the student) swooned. The nurses immediately left the chamber, and could not be induced to return. My own impressions I would not pretend to render intelligible to the reader. For nearly an hour, we busied ourselves, silently – without the utterance of a word – in endeavours to revive Mr L—l. When he came to himself, we addressed ourselves again to an investigation of M. Valdemar's condition.

It remained in all respects as I have last described it, with the exception that the mirror no longer afforded evidence of respiration. An attempt to draw blood from the arm failed. I should mention, too, that this limb was no further subject to my will. I endeavoured in vain to make it follow the direction of my hand. The only real indication, indeed, of the mesmeric influence was now found in the vibratory movement of the tongue, whenever I addressed M. Valdemar a question. He seemed to be making an effort to reply, but had no longer sufficient volition. To queries put to him by any other person than myself he seemed utterly insensible – although I endeavoured to place each member of the company in mesmeric *rapport* with him. I believe that I have now related all that is necessary to an understanding of the sleep-waker's state at this epoch. Other nurses were procured; and at ten o'clock I left the house in company with the two physicians and Mr L—l.

In the afternoon we all called again to see the patient. His condition remained precisely the same. We had now some discussion as to the propriety and feasibility of awakening him; but we had little difficulty in agreeing that no good purpose would be served by so doing. It was evident that, so far, death (or what is usually termed death) had been arrested by the mesmeric process. It seemed clear to us all that to awaken M. Valdemar would be merely to insure his instant, or at least his speedy dissolution.

From this period until the close of last week – *an interval of nearly seven months* – we continued to make daily calls at M. Valdemar's house, accompanied, now and then, by medical and other friends. All this time the sleep-waker remained *exactly* as I have last described him. The nurses' attentions were continual.

It was on Friday last that we finally resolved to make the experiment of awakening, or attempting to awaken him; and it is the (perhaps) unfortunate result of this latter experiment which has given rise to so much discussion in private circles – to so much of what I cannot help thinking unwarranted popular feeling.

For the purpose of relieving M. Valdemar from the mesmeric trance, I made use of the customary passes. These for a time were unsuccessful. The first indication of revival was afforded by a partial descent of the iris. It was observed, as especially remarkable, that this lowering of the pupil was accompanied by the profuse outflowing of a yellowish ichor (from beneath the lids) of a pungent and highly offensive odour.

It was now suggested that I should attempt to influence the patient's arm as heretofore. I made the attempt and failed. Dr F— then intimated a desire to have me put a question. I did so, as follows –

'M. Valdemar, can you explain to us what are your feelings or wishes now?'

There was an instant return of the hectic circles on the cheeks; the tongue quivered, or rather rolled violently in the mouth (although the jaws and lips remained rigid as before); and at length the same hideous voice which I have already described, broke forth –

'For God's sake! – quick! – quick – put me to sleep – or quick! – waken me! – quick! – *I say to you that I am dead!*'

I was thoroughly unnerved, and for an instant remained undecided what to do. At first I made an endeavour to recompose the patient; but, failing in this through total abeyance of the will, I retraced my steps, and as earnestly struggled to awaken him. In this attempt I soon saw that I should be successful – or at least I soon fancied that my success would be complete – and I am sure that all in the room were prepared to see the patient awaken.

For what really occurred, however, it is quite impossible that any human being could have been prepared.

As I rapidly made the mesmeric passes, amid ejaculations of 'Dead! dead!' absolutely *bursting* from the tongue and not from the lips of the sufferer, his whole frame at once – within the space of a single minute, or even less, shrunk – crumbled – absolutely *rotted* away beneath my hands. Upon the bed, before that whole company, there lay a nearly liquid mass of loathsome – of detestable putrescence.

MS Found in a Bottle

Qui n'a plus qu'un moment à vivre
N'a plus rien à dissimuler.

QUINAULT, *Atys*

Of my country and of my family I have little to say. Ill usage and length of years have driven me from the one, and estranged me from the other. Hereditary wealth afforded me an education of no common order, and a contemplative turn of mind enabled me to methodise the stories which early study diligently garnered up. Beyond all things, the works of the German moralists gave me a great delight; not from my ill-advised admiration of their eloquent madness, but from the ease with which my habits of rigid thought enabled me to detect their falsities. I have often been reproached with the aridity of my genius; a deficiency of imagination has been imputed to me as a crime; and the Pyrrhonism of my opinions has at all times rendered me notorious. Indeed, a strong relish for physical philosophy has, I fear, tinctured my mind with a very common error of this age – I mean the habit of referring occurrences, even the least susceptible of such reference, to the principles of that science. Upon the whole, no person could be less liable than myself to be led away from the severe precincts of truth by the *ignes fatui* of superstition. I have thought proper to premise thus much, lest the incredible tale I have to tell should be considered rather the raving of a crude imagination, than the positive experience of a mind to which the reveries of fancy have been a dead letter and a nullity.

After many years spent in foreign travel, I sailed in the year 18—, from the port of Batavia, in the rich and populous island of Java, on a voyage to the Archipelago of the Sunda Islands. I went as passenger – having no other inducement than a kind of nervous restlessness which haunted me as a fiend.

Our vessel was a beautiful ship of about four hundred tons, copper-fastened, and built at Bombay of Malabar teak. She was freighted with cotton-wool and oil, from the Lachadive Islands. We had also on board coir, jaggeree, ghee, coconuts, and a few cases of opium. The stowage was clumsily done, and the vessel consequently crank.

We got under way with a mere breath of wind, and for many days stood along the eastern coast of Java, without any other incident to beguile the monotony of our course than the occasional meeting with some of the small grabs of the Archipelago to which we were bound.

One evening, leaning over the taffrail, I observed a very singular isolated cloud, to the north-west. It was remarkable, as well for its colour, as from its being the first we had seen since our departure from Batavia. I watched it attentively until sunset, when it spread all at once to the eastward and westward, girting in the horizon with a narrow strip of vapour, and looking like a long line of low beach. My notice was soon afterwards attracted by the dusky-red appearance of the moon, and the peculiar character of the sea. The latter was undergoing a rapid change, and the water seemed more than usually transparent. Although I could distinctly see the bottom, yet, heaving the lead, I found the ship in fifteen fathoms. The air now became intolerably hot, and was loaded with spiral exhalations similar to those arising from heated iron. As night came on, every breath of wind died away, and a more entire calm it is impossible to conceive. The flame of a candle burned upon the poop without the least perceptible motion, and a long hair, held between the finger and thumb, hung without the possibility of detecting a vibration. However, as the captain said he could perceive no indication of danger, and as we were drifting in bodily to shore, he ordered the sails to be furled, and the anchor let go. No watch was set, and the crew, consisting principally of Malays, stretched themselves deliberately upon deck. I went below – not without a full presentiment of evil. Indeed, every appearance warranted me in apprehending a simoom. I told the captain my fears; but he paid no attention to what I said, and left me without deigning to give a reply. My uneasiness, however, prevented me from sleeping, and about midnight I went upon deck. As I placed my foot upon the upper step of the companion-ladder, I was startled by a loud, humming noise, like that occasioned by the rapid revolution of a mill-wheel, and before I could ascertain its meaning, I found the ship quivering to its centre. In the next instant, a wilderness of foam hurled us upon our beam-ends, and, rushing over us fore and aft, swept the entire decks from stem to stern.

The extreme fury of the blast proved, in a great measure, the salvation of the ship. Although completely waterlogged, yet, as her masts had gone by the board, she rose, after a minute, heavily from the sea, and, staggering awhile beneath the immense pressure of the tempest, finally righted.

By what miracle I escaped destruction, it is impossible to say. Stunned by the shock of the water, I found myself, upon recovery, jammed in between the stern-post and rudder. With great difficulty I gained my feet, and looking dizzily around, was at first struck with the idea of our being among breakers; so terrific, beyond the wildest imagination, was the whirlpool of mountainous and foaming ocean within which we were engulfed. After a while, I heard the voice of an old Swede, who had shipped with us at the moment of leaving port. I hallooed to him with all my strength, and presently he came reeling aft. We soon discovered that we were the sole survivors of the accident. All on deck, with the exception of ourselves, had been swept overboard; the captain and mates must have perished as they slept, for the cabins were deluged with water. Without assistance, we could expect to do little for the security of the ship, and our exertions were at first paralysed by the momentary expectation of going down. Our cable had, of course, parted like pack-thread, at the first breath of the hurricane, or we should have been instantaneously overwhelmed. We scudded with frightful velocity before the sea, and the water made clear breaches over us. The framework of our stern was shattered excessively, and, in almost every respect, we had received considerable injury; but to our extreme joy we found the pumps unchoked, and that we had made no great shifting of our ballast. The main fury of the blast had already blown over, and we apprehended little danger from the violence of the wind; but we looked forward to its total cessation with dismay, well believing, that in our shattered condition, we should inevitably perish in the tremendous swell which would ensue. But this very just apprehension seemed by no means likely to be soon verified. For five entire days and nights – during which our only subsistence was a small quantity of jaggeree, procured with great difficulty from the forecastle – the hulk flew at a rate defying computation, before rapidly succeeding flaws of wind, which without equalling the first violence of the simoom, were still more terrific than any tempest I had before encountered. Our course for the first four days was, with trifling variations, south-east by south; and we must have run down the coast of New Holland. On the fifth day the cold became extreme, although the wind had hauled round a point more to the northward. The sun arose with a sickly yellow lustre, and clambered a very few degrees above the horizon – emitting no decisive light. There were no clouds apparent, yet the wind was upon the increase, and blew with a fitful and unsteady fury. About noon, as nearly as we could guess, our attention was again arrested by the appearance of the sun. It gave out no light, properly so called, but a dull and sullen glow without reflection, as if all its rays were polarised. Just before sinking within the turgid sea, its central fires suddenly went out, as if hurriedly extinguished by some unaccountable power. It was a dim, silver-like rim, alone, as it rushed down the unfathomable ocean.

We waited in vain for the arrival of the sixth day – that day to me has not arrived – to the Swede, never did arrive. Thenceforward we were enshrouded in pitchy darkness, so that we could not have seen an object at twenty paces from the ship. Eternal night continued to envelop us, all unrelieved by the phosphoric sea-brilliancy to which we had been accustomed in the tropics. We observed, too, that, although the tempest continued to rage with unabated violence, there was no longer to be discovered the usual appearance of surf, or foam, which had hitherto attended us. All around were horror, and thick gloom, and a black sweltering desert of ebony. Superstitious terror crept by degrees into the spirit of the old Swede, and my own soul was wrapped up in silent wonder. We neglected all care of the ship, as worse than useless, and securing ourselves, as well as possible, to the stump of the mizzen mast, looked out bitterly into the world of ocean. We had no means of calculating time, nor could we form any guess of our situation. We were, however, well aware of having made farther to the southward than any previous navigators, and felt great amazement at not meeting with the usual impediments of ice. In the meantime every moment threatened to be our last – every mountainous billow hurried to overwhelm us. The swell surpassed anything I had imagined possible, and that we were not instantly buried is a miracle. My companion spoke of the lightness of our cargo, and reminded me of the excellent qualities of our ship; but I could not help feeling the utter hopelessness of hope itself, and prepared myself gloomily for that death which I thought nothing could defer beyond an hour, as with every knot of way the ship made, the swelling of the black stupendous seas became more dismally appalling. At times we gasped for breath at an elevation beyond the albatross – at times became dizzy with the velocity of our descent into some watery hell, where the air grew stagnant, and no sound disturbed the slumbers of the kraken.

We were at the bottom of one of these abysses, when a quick scream from my companion broke fearfully upon the night. 'See! see!' cried he, shrieking in my ears, 'Almighty God! see! see!' As he spoke, I became aware of a dull, sullen glare of red light which streamed down the sides of the vast chasm where we lay, and threw a fitful brilliancy upon our deck. Casting my eyes upwards, I beheld a spectacle which froze the current of my blood. At a terrific height directly above us, and upon the very verge of the precipitous descent, hovered a gigantic ship, of perhaps four thousand tons. Although upreared upon the summit of a wave more than a hundred times her own altitude, her apparent size still exceeded that of any ship of the line or East Indiaman in existence. Her huge hull was of a deep dingy black, unrelieved by any of the customary carvings of a ship. A single row of brass cannon protruded from her open ports, and dashed from their polished surfaces the fires of innumerable battle-lanterns which swung to and fro about her rigging. But what mainly inspired us with horror and astonishment, was that she bore up under a press of sail in the very teeth of that supernatural sea, and of that ungovernable hurricane. When we first discovered her, her bows were alone to be seen, as she rose slowly from the dim and horrible gulf beyond her. For a moment of intense terror she paused upon the giddy pinnacle, as if in contemplation of her own sublimity, then trembled and tottered, and – came down.

At this instant, I know not what sudden self-possession came over my spirit. Staggering as far aft as I could, I awaited fearlessly the ruin that was to overwhelm. Our own vessel was at length ceasing from her struggles, and sinking with her head to the sea. The shock of the descending mass struck her, consequently, in that portion of her frame which was nearly under water, and the inevitable result was to hurl me, with irresistible violence, upon the rigging of the stranger.

As I fell, the ship hove in stays, and went about; and to the confusion ensuing I attributed my escape from the notice of the crew. With little difficulty I made my way, unperceived, to the main hatchway, which was partially open, and soon found an opportunity of secreting myself in the hold. Why I did so I can hardly tell. An indefinite sense of awe, which at first sight of the navigators of the ship had taken hold of my mind, was perhaps the principle of my concealment. I was unwilling to trust myself with a race of people who had offered to the cursory glance I had taken, so many points of vague novelty, doubt, and apprehension. I therefore thought proper to contrive a hiding-place in the hold. This I did by removing a small portion of the shifting-boards, in such a manner as to afford me a convenient retreat between the huge timbers of the ship.

I had scarcely completed my work, when a footstep in the hold forced me to make use of it. A man passed by my place of concealment with a feeble and unsteady gait. I could not see his face, but had an opportunity of observing his general appearance. There was about it an evidence of great age and infirmity. His knees tottered beneath a load of years, and his entire frame quivered under the burthen. He muttered to himself, in a low broken tone, some words of a language which I could not understand, and groped in a corner among a pile of singular-looking instruments, and decayed charts of navigation. His manner was a wild mixture of the peevishness of second childhood and the solemn dignity of a god. He at length went on deck, and I saw him no more.

A feeling, for which I have no name, has taken possession of my soul – a sensation which will admit of no analysis, to which the lessons of bygone time are inadequate, and for which I fear futurity itself will offer me no key. To a mind constituted like my own, the latter consideration is an evil. I shall never – I know that I shall never – be satisfied with regard to the nature of my conceptions. Yet it is not wonderful that these conceptions are indefinite, since they have their origin in sources so utterly novel. A new sense – a new entity is added to my soul.

It is long since I first trod the deck of this terrible ship, and the rays of my destiny are, I think, gathering to a focus. Incomprehensible men! Wrapped up in meditations of a kind which I cannot divine, they pass me by unnoticed. Concealment is utter folly on my part, for the people *will not* see. It was but just now that I passed directly before the eyes of the mate; it was no long while ago that I ventured into the captain's own private cabin, and took thence the materials with which I write, and have written. I shall from time to time continue this journal. It is true that I may not find an opportunity of transmitting it to the world, but I will not fail to make the endeavour. At the last moment I will enclose the MS in a bottle, and cast it within the sea.

An incident has occurred which has given me new room for meditation. Are such things the operation of ungoverned chance? I had ventured upon deck and thrown myself down, without attracting any notice, among a pile of ratlin-stuff and old sails, in the bottom of the yawl. While musing upon the singularity of my fate, I unwittingly daubed with a tar-brush the edges of a neatly-folded studding-sail which lay near me on a barrel. The studding-sail is now bent upon the ship, and the thoughtless touches of the brush are spread out into the word DISCOVERY.

I have made many observations lately upon the structure of the vessel. Although well armed, she is not, I think, a ship of war. Her rigging, build, and general equipment, all negative a supposition of this kind. What she *is not*, I can easily perceive; what she *is*, I fear it is impossible to say. I know not how it is, but in scrutinising her strange model and singular cast of spars, her huge size and overgrown suits of canvas, her severely simple bow and antiquated stern, there will

"INCOMPREHENSIBLE MEN! WRAPPED UP IN MEDITATIONS OF A KIND WHICH I CANNOT DIVINE, THEY PASS ME BY UNNOTICED"

occasionally flash across my mind a sensation of familiar things, and there is always mixed up with such indistinct shadows of recollection, an unaccountable memory of old foreign chronicles and ages long ago.

I have been looking at the timbers of the ship. She is built of a material to which I am a stranger. There is a peculiar character about the wood which strikes me as rendering it unfit for the purpose to which it has been applied. I mean its extreme *porousness*, considered independently of the worm-eaten condition which is a consequence of navigation in these seas, and apart from the rottenness attendant upon age. It will appear, perhaps, an observation somewhat over-curious, but this wood would have every characteristic of Spanish oak, if Spanish oak were distended by any unnatural means.

In reading the above sentence, a curious apothegm of an old weather-beaten Dutch navigator comes full upon my recollection. 'It is as sure,' he was wont to say, when any doubt was entertained of his veracity, 'as sure as there is a sea where the ship itself will grow in bulk like the living body of the seaman.'

About an hour ago I made bold to trust myself among a group of the crew. They paid me no manner of attention, and, although I stood in the very midst of them all, seemed utterly unconscious of my presence. Like the one I had at first seen in the hold, they all bore about them the marks of a hoary old age. Their knees trembled with infirmity; their shoulders were bent double with decrepitude; their shrivelled skins rattled in the wind; their voices were low, tremulous, and broken; their eyes glistened with the rheum of years; and their grey hairs streamed terribly in the tempest. Around them, on every part of the deck, lay scattered mathematical instruments of the most quaint and obsolete construction.

I mentioned, some time ago, the bending of a studding-sail. From that period, the ship, being thrown dead off the wind, has continued her terrific course due south, with every rag of canvas packed upon her, from her truck to her lower studding-sail booms, and rolling every moment her top-gallant yard-arms into the most appalling hell of water which it can enter into the mind of man to imagine. I have just left the deck, where I find it impossible to maintain a footing, although the crew seem to experience little inconvenience. It appears to me a miracle of miracles that our enormous bulk is not swallowed up at once and for ever. We are surely doomed to hover continually upon the brink of eternity, without taking a final plunge into the abyss. From billows a thousand times more stupendous than any I have ever seen, we glide away with the facility of the arrowy seagull; and the colossal waters rear their heads above us like demons of the deep, but like demons confined to simple threats, and forbidden to destroy. I am led to attribute these frequent escapes to the only natural cause which can account for such effect. I must suppose the ship to be within the influence of some strong current, or impetuous undertow.

I have seen the captain face to face, and in his own cabin – but, as I expected, he paid me no attention. Although in his appearance there is, to a casual observer, nothing which might bespeak him more or less than man, still a feeling of irrepressible reverence and awe mingled with the sensation of wonder with which I regarded him. In stature, he is nearly my own height; that is, about five feet eight inches. He is of a well-knit and compact frame of body, neither robust nor remarkable otherwise. But it is the singularity of the expression which reigns upon the face – it is the intense, the wonderful, the thrilling evidence of old age so utter, so extreme, which excites within my spirit a sense – a sentiment ineffable. His forehead, although little wrinkled, seems to bear upon it the stamp of a myriad of years. His grey hairs are records of the past, and his greyer eyes are sibyls of the future. The cabin floor was thickly strewn with strange, iron-clasped folios, and mouldering instruments of science, and obsolete long-forgotten charts. His head was bowed down upon his hands, and he pored, with a fiery, unquiet eye, over a paper which I took to be a commission, and which, at all events, bore the signature of a monarch. He muttered to himself – as did the first seaman whom I saw in the hold – some low peevish syllables of a foreign tongue; and although the speaker was close at my elbow, his voice seemed to reach my ears from the distance of a mile.

The ship and all in it are imbued with the spirit of Eld. The crew glide to and fro like the ghosts of buried centuries; their eyes have an eager and uneasy meaning; and when their fingers fall athwart my path in the wild glare of the battle-lanterns, I feel as I have never felt before, although I have been all my life a dealer in antiquities, and have imbibed the shadows of fallen columns at Balbec, and Tadmor, and Persepolis, until my very soul has become a ruin.

When I look around me, I feel ashamed of my former apprehensions. If I trembled at the blast which has hitherto attended us, shall I not stand aghast at a warring of wind and ocean, to convey any idea of which, the words tornado and simoom are trivial and ineffective? All in the immediate vicinity of the ship is the blackness of eternal night, and a chaos of foamless water; but, about a league on either side of us, may be seen, indistinctly, and at intervals, stupendous ramparts of ice, towering away into the desolate sky, and looking like the walls of the universe.

As I imagined, the ship proves to be in a current – if that appellation can properly be given to a tide which, howling and shrieking by the white ice, thunders on to the southward with a velocity like the headlong dashing of a cataract.

To conceive the horror of my sensations is, I presume, utterly impossible; yet a curiosity to penetrate the mysteries of these awful regions predominates even over my despair, and will reconcile me to the most hideous aspect of death. It is evident that we are hurrying onwards to some exciting knowledge – some never-to-be-imparted secret, whose attainment is destruction. Perhaps this current leads us to the southern pole itself. It must be confessed that a supposition apparently so wild has every probability in its favour.

The crew pace the deck with unquiet and tremulous step; but there is upon their countenance an expression more of the eagerness of hope than of the apathy of despair.

In the meantime the wind is still in our poop, and, as we carry a crowd of canvas, the ship is at times lifted bodily from out the sea! Oh, horror upon horror! – the ice opens suddenly to the right, and to the left, and we are whirling dizzily, in immense concentric circles, round and round the borders of a gigantic amphitheatre, the summit of whose walls is lost in the darkness and the distance. But little time will be left me to ponder upon my destiny! The circles rapidly grow small – we are plunging madly within the grasp of the whirlpool – and amid a roaring, and bellowing, and thundering of ocean and tempest, the ship is quivering – O God! and – going down!

Note. – The 'MS Found in a Bottle' was originally published in 1831; and it was not until many years afterwards that I became acquainted with the maps of Mercator, in which the ocean is represented as rushing, by four mouths, into the (northern) Polar Gulf, to be absorbed into the bowels of the earth; the Pole itself being represented by a black rock, towering to a prodigious height.

A Descent into the Maelström

> The ways of God in Nature, as in Providence, are not as *our* ways; nor are the models that we frame any way commensurate to the vastness, profundity, and unsearchableness of His works, *which have a depth in them greater than the well of Democritus.*
>
> JOSEPH GLANVILL

We had now reached the summit of the loftiest crag. For some minutes the old man seemed too much exhausted to speak.

'Not long ago,' said he at length, 'and I could have guided you on this route as well as the youngest of my sons; but, about three years past, there happened to me an event such as never happened before to mortal man – or at least such as no man ever survived to tell of – and the six hours of deadly terror which I then endured have broken me up body and soul. You suppose me a *very* old man – but I am not. It took less than a single day to change these hairs from a jetty black to white, to weaken my limbs, and to unstring my nerves, so that I tremble at the least exertion, and am frightened at a shadow. Do you know I can scarcely look over this little cliff without getting giddy?'

The 'little cliff', upon whose edge he had so carelessly thrown himself down to rest, that the weightier portion of his body hung over it, while he was only kept from falling by the tenure of his elbow on its extreme and slippery edge – this 'little cliff' arose, a sheer unobstructed precipice of black shining rock, some fifteen or sixteen hundred feet from the world of crags beneath us. Nothing would have tempted me to within half a dozen yards of its brink. In truth, so deeply was I excited by the perilous position of my companion, that I fell at full length upon the ground, clung to the shrubs around me, and dared not even glance upward at the sky – while I struggled in vain to divest myself of the idea that the very foundations of the mountain were in danger from the fury of the winds. It was long before I could reason myself into sufficient courage to sit up and look out into the distance.

'You must get over these fancies,' said the guide, 'for I have brought you here that you might have the best possible view of the scene of that event I mentioned – and to tell you the whole story with the spot just under your eye.'

'We are now,' he continued, in that particularising manner which distinguished him – 'we are now close upon the Norwegian coast – in the sixty-eighth degree of latitude – in the great province of Nordland – and in the dreary district of Lofoden. The mountain upon whose top we sit is Helseggen, the Cloudy. Now raise yourself up a little higher – hold on to the grass if you feel giddy – so – and look out, beyond the belt of vapour beneath us, into the sea.'

I looked dizzily, and beheld a wide expanse of ocean, whose waters wore so inky a hue as to bring at once to my mind the Nubian geographer's account of the *Mare Tenebrarum*. A panorama more deplorably desolate no human imagination can conceive. To the right and left, as far as the eye could reach, there lay outstretched, like ramparts of the world, lines of horribly black and beetling cliff, whose character of gloom was but the more forcibly illustrated by the surf which reared high up against it its white and ghastly crest, howling and shrieking for ever. Just opposite the promontory upon whose apex we were placed, and at a distance of some five or six miles out at sea, there was visible a small, bleak-looking island; or, more properly, its position was discernible through the wilderness of surge in which it was enveloped. About two miles nearer the land, arose another of smaller size, hideously craggy and barren, and encompassed at various intervals by a cluster of dark rocks.

The appearance of the ocean, in the space between the more distant island and the shore, had something very unusual about it. Although, at the time, so strong a gale was blowing landward that a brig in the remote offing lay to under a double-reefed trysail, and constantly plunged her whole hull out of sight, still there was here nothing like a regular swell, but only a short, quick, angry cross dashing of water in every direction – as well in the teeth of the wind as otherwise. Of foam there was little except in the immediate vicinity of the rocks.

'The island in the distance,' resumed the old man, 'is called by the Norwegians Vurrgh. The one midway is Moskoe. That a mile to the northward is Ambaaren. Yonder are Islesen, Hotholm, Keildhelm, Suarven, and Buckholm. Farther off – between Moskoe and Vurrgh – are

Otterholm, Flimen, Sandflesen, and Stockholm. These are the true names of the places – but why it has been thought necessary to name them at all, is more than either you or I can understand. Do you hear anything? Do you see any change in the water?'

We had now been about ten minutes upon the top of Helseggen, to which we had ascended from the interior of Lofoden, so that we had caught no glimpse of the sea until it had burst upon us from the summit. As the old man spoke, I became aware of a loud and gradually increasing sound, like the moaning of a vast herd of buffaloes upon an American prairie; and at the same moment I perceived what seamen term the *chopping* character of the ocean beneath us, was rapidly changing into a current which set to the eastward. Even while I gazed, this current acquired a monstrous velocity. Each moment added to its speed – to its headlong impetuosity. In five minutes the whole sea, as far as Vurrgh, was lashed into ungovernable fury; but it was between Moskoe and the coast that the main uproar held its sway. Here the vast bed of the waters, seamed and scarred into a thousand conflicting channels, burst suddenly into frenzied convulsion – heaving, boiling, hissing – gyrating in gigantic and innumerable vortices, and all whirling and plunging on to the eastward with a rapidity which water never elsewhere assumes, except in precipitous descents.

In a few minutes more, there came over the scene another radical alteration. The general surface grew somewhat more smooth, and the whirlpools, one by one, disappeared, while prodigious streaks of foam became apparent where none had been seen before. These streaks, at length, spreading out to a great distance, and entering into combination, took unto themselves the gyratory motion of the subsided vortices, and seemed to form the germ of another more vast. Suddenly – very suddenly – this assumed a distinct and definite existence, in a circle of more than a mile in diameter. The edge of the whirl was represented by a broad belt of gleaming spray; but no particle of this slipped into the mouth of the terrific funnel, whose interior, as far as the eye could fathom it, was a smooth, shining, and jet-black wall of water, inclined to the horizon at an angle of some forty-five degrees, speeding dizzily round and round with a swaying and sweltering motion, and sending forth to the winds an appalling voice, half-shriek, half-roar, such as not even the mighty cataract of Niagara ever lifts up in its agony to Heaven.

The mountain trembled to its very base, and the rock rocked. I threw myself upon my face, and clung to the scant herbage in an excess of nervous agitation.

'This,' said I at length, to the old man – 'this *can* be nothing else than the great whirlpool of the Maelström.'

'So it is sometimes termed,' said he. 'We Norwegians call it the Moskoe-ström, from the island of Moskoe in the midway.'

The ordinary accounts of this vortex had by no means prepared me for what I saw. That of Jonas Ramus, which is perhaps the most circumstantial of any, cannot impart the faintest conception either of the magnificence, or of the horror of the scene – or of the wild bewildering sense of *the novel* which confounds the beholder. I am not sure from what point of view the writer in question surveyed it, nor at what time; but it could neither have been from the summit of Helseggen, nor during a storm. There are some passages of his description, nevertheless, which may be quoted for their details, although their effect is exceedingly feeble in conveying an impression of the spectacle.

'Between Lofoden and Moskoe,' he says, 'the depth of the water is between thirty-six and forty fathoms; but on the other side, toward Ver (Vurrgh), this depth decreases so as not to afford a convenient passage for a vessel, without the risk of splitting on the rocks, which happens even in the calmest weather. When it is flood, the stream runs up the country between Lofoden and Moskoe with a boisterous rapidity; but the roar of its impetuous ebb to the sea is scarce equalled by the loudest and most dreadful cataracts, the noise being heard several leagues off; and the vortices or pits are of such an extent and depth, that if a ship comes within its attraction, it is inevitably absorbed and carried down to the bottom, and there beat to pieces against the rocks; and when the water relaxes, the fragments thereof are thrown up again. But these intervals of tranquillity are only at the turn of the ebb and flood, and in calm weather, and last but a quarter of an hour, its violence gradually returning. When the stream is most boisterous, and its fury heightened by a storm, it is dangerous to come within a Norway mile of it. Boats, yachts, and ships have been carried away by not guarding against it before they were within its reach. It likewise happens frequently, that whales come too near the stream, and are overpowered by its violence; and then it is impossible to describe their howlings and bellowings in their fruitless struggles to disengage themselves. A bear once, attempting to swim from Lofoden to Moskoe, was caught by the stream and borne down, while he roared terribly, so as to be heard on shore. Large stocks of firs and pine trees, after being absorbed by the current, rise again broken and torn to such a degree as if bristles grew upon them. This plainly shows the bottom to consist of craggy rocks, among which they are whirled to and fro. This stream is regulated by the flux and reflux of the sea – it being constantly high and low water every six hours. In the year 1645, early in the morning of Sexagesima Sunday, it raged with such noise and impetuosity that the very stones of the houses on the coast fell to the ground.'

In regard to the depth of the water, I could not see how this could have been ascertained at all in the immediate vicinity of the vortex. The 'forty fathoms' must have reference only to portions of the channel close upon the shore either of Moskoe or Lofoden. The depth in the centre of the Moskoe-ström must be immeasurably greater; and no better proof of this fact is necessary than can be obtained from even the sidelong glance into the abyss of the whirl which may be had from the highest crag of Helseggen. Looking down from this pinnacle upon the howling Phlegethon below, I could not help smiling at the simplicity with which the honest Jonas Ramus records, as a matter difficult of belief, the anecdotes of the whales and the bears; for it appeared to me, in fact, a self-evident thing, that the largest ship of the line in existence, coming within the influence of that deadly attraction, could resist it as little as a feather the hurricane, and must disappear bodily and at once.

The attempts to account for the phenomenon – some of which, I remember, seemed to me sufficiently plausible in perusal – now wore a very different and unsatisfactory aspect. The idea generally received is that this, as well as three smaller vortices among the Faroe Islands, 'have no other cause than the collision of waves rising and falling, at flux and reflux, against a ridge of rocks and shelves, which confines the water so that it precipitates itself like a cataract; and thus the higher the flood rises, the deeper must the fall be, and the natural result of all is a whirlpool or vortex, the prodigious suction of which is sufficiently known by lesser experiments.' – These are the words of the *Encyclopaedia Britannica*. Kircher and others imagine that in the centre of the channel of the Maelström is an abyss penetrating the globe, and issuing in some very remote part – the Gulf of Bothnia being somewhat decidedly named in one instance. This opinion, idle in itself, was the one to which, as I gazed, my imagination most readily assented; and, mentioning it to the guide, I was rather surprised to hear him say that, although it was the view almost universally entertained of the subject by the Norwegians, it nevertheless was not his own. As to the former notion, he confessed his inability to comprehend it; and here I agreed with him – for, however conclusive on paper, it becomes altogether unintelligible, and even absurd, amid the thunder of the abyss.

'You have had a good look at the whirl now,' said the old man, 'and if you will creep round this crag, so as to get in its lee, and deaden the roar of the water, I will tell you a story that will convince you I ought to know something of the Moskoe-ström.'

I placed myself as desired, and he proceeded.

'Myself and my two brothers once owned a schooner-rigged smack of about seventy tons burden, with which we were in the habit of fishing among the islands beyond Moskoe, nearly to Vurrgh. In all violent eddies at sea there is good fishing, at proper opportunities, if one has only the courage to attempt it; but among the whole of the Lofoden coastmen, we three were the only ones who made a regular business of going out to the islands, as I tell you. The usual grounds are a great way lower down to the southward. There fish can be got at all hours, without much risk, and therefore these places are preferred. The choice spots over here among the rocks, however, not only yield the finest variety, but in far greater abundance; so that we often got in a single day, what the more timid of the craft could not scrape together in a week. In fact, we made it a matter of desperate speculation – the risk of life standing instead of labour, and courage answering for capital.

'We kept the smack in a cove about five miles higher up the coast than this; and it was our practice, in fine weather, to take advantage of the fifteen minutes' slack to push across the main channel of the Moskoe-ström, far above the pool, and then drop down upon anchorage somewhere near Otterholm, or Sandflesen, where the eddies are not so violent as elsewhere. Here we used to remain until nearly time for slack-water again, when we weighed and made for home. We never set out upon this expedition without a steady side wind for going and coming – one that we felt sure would not fail us before our return – and we seldom made a miscalculation upon this point. Twice, during six years, we were forced to stay all night at anchor on account of a dead calm, which is a rare thing indeed just about here; and once we had to remain on the grounds nearly a week, starving to death, owing to a gale which blew up shortly after our arrival, and made the channel too boisterous to be thought of. Upon this occasion we should have been driven out to sea in spite of everything (for the whirlpools threw us round and round so violently, that, at length, we fouled our anchor and dragged it), if it had not been that we drifted into one of the innumerable cross currents – here today and gone tomorrow – which drove us under the lee of Flimen, where, by good luck, we brought up.

'I could not tell you the twentieth part of the difficulties we encountered "on the grounds" – it is a bad spot to be in, even in good weather – but we made shift always to run the gauntlet of the Moskoe-ström itself without accident; although at times my heart has been in my mouth when we happened to be a minute or so behind or before the slack. The wind sometimes was not as strong as we thought it at starting, and then we made rather less way than we could wish, while the current rendered the smack unmanageable. My eldest brother had a son eighteen years old, and I had two stout boys of my own. These would have been of great assistance at such times, in using the sweeps, as well as afterwards in fishing – but, somehow, although we ran the risk ourselves, we had not the heart to let the young ones get into danger – for, after all said and done, it *was* a horrible danger, and that is the truth.

'It is now within a few days of three years since what I am going to tell you occurred. It was on the 10th of July 18—, a day which the people of this part of the world will never forget – for it was one in which blew the most terrible hurricane that ever came out of the heavens. And yet all the morning, and indeed until late in the afternoon, there was a gentle and steady breeze from the south-west, while the sun shone brightly, so that the oldest seamen among us could not have foreseen what was to follow.

'The three of us – my two brothers and myself – had crossed over to the islands about two o'clock that afternoon, and soon nearly loaded the smack with fine fish, which, we all remarked, were more plenty that day than we had ever known them. It was just seven, *by my watch*, when we weighed and started for home, so as to make the worst of the Ström at slack water, which we knew would be at eight.

'We set out with a fresh wind on our starboard quarter, and for some time spanked along at a great rate, never dreaming of danger, for indeed we saw not the slightest reason to apprehend it. All at once we were taken aback by a breeze from over Helseggen. This was most unusual – something that had never happened to us before – and I began to feel a little uneasy, without exactly knowing why. We put the boat on the wind, but could make no headway at all for the eddies, and I was upon the point of proposing to return to the anchorage, when, looking astern, we saw the whole horizon covered with a singular copper-coloured cloud that rose with the most amazing velocity.

'In the meantime the breeze that had headed us off fell away, and we were dead becalmed, drifting about in every direction. This state of things, however, did not last long enough to give us time to think about it. In less than a minute the storm was upon us – in less than two the sky was entirely overcast – and what with this and the driving spray, it became suddenly so dark that we could not see each other in the smack.

'Such a hurricane as then blew it is folly to attempt describing. The oldest seamen in Norway never experienced anything like it. We had let our sails go by the run before it cleverly took us; but, at the first puff, both our masts went by the board as if they had been sawed off – the mainmast taking with it my youngest brother, who had lashed himself to it for safety.

'Our boat was the lightest feather of a thing that ever sat upon water. It had a complete flush deck, with only a small hatch near the bow, and this hatch it had always been our custom to batten down when about to cross the Ström, by way of precaution against the chopping seas. But for this circumstance we should have foundered at once – for we lay entirely buried for some moments. How my elder brother escaped destruction I cannot say, for I never had an opportunity of ascertaining. For my part, as soon as I had let the foresail run, I threw myself flat on deck, with my feet against the narrow gunwale of the bow, and with my hands grasping a ring-bolt near the foot of the foremast. It was mere instinct that prompted me to do this – which was undoubtedly the very best thing I could have done – for I was too much flurried to think.

'For some moments we were completely deluged, as I say, and all this time I held my breath, and clung to the bolt. When I could stand it no longer, I raised myself upon my knees, still keeping hold with my hands, and thus got my head clear. Presently our little boat gave herself a shake, just as a dog does in coming out of the water, and thus rid herself, in some measure, of the seas. I was now trying to get the better of the stupor that had come over me, and to collect my senses, so as to see what was to be done, when I felt somebody grasp my arm. It was my elder brother, and my heart leaped for joy, for I had made sure that he was overboard; but the next moment all this joy was turned into horror, for he put his mouth close to my ear, and screamed out the word "*Moskoe-ström!*"

'No one ever will know what my feelings were at that moment. I shook from head to foot as if I had the most violent fit of the ague. I knew what he meant by that one word well enough – I knew what he wished to make me understand. With the wind that now drove us on, we were bound for the whirl of the Ström, and nothing could save us!

'You perceive that in crossing the Ström *channel*, we always went a long way up above the whirl, even in the calmest weather, and then had to wait and watch carefully for the slack – but now we were driving right upon the pool itself, and in such a hurricane as this! "To be sure," I thought, "we shall get there just about the slack – there is some little hope in that" – but in the next moment I cursed myself for being so great a fool as to dream of hope at all. I knew very well that we were doomed, had we been ten times a ninety-gun ship.

'By this time the first fury of the tempest had spent itself, or perhaps we did not feel it so much, as we scudded before it, but at all events the seas, which at first had been kept down by the wind, and lay flat and frothing, now got up into absolute mountains. A singular change, too, had come over the heavens. Around in every direction it was still as black as pitch, but nearly overhead there burst out, all at once, a circular rift of clear sky – as clear as I ever saw – and of a deep bright blue – and through it there blazed forth the full moon with a lustre that I never before knew her to wear. She lit up everything about us with the greatest distinctness – but, O God, what a scene it was to light up!

'I now made one or two attempts to speak to my brother – but in some manner which I could not understand, the din had so increased that I could not make him hear a single word, although I screamed at the top of my voice in his ear. Presently he shook his head, looking as pale as death, and held up one of his fingers, as if to say *"listen!"*

'At first I could not make out what he meant – but soon a hideous thought flashed upon me. I dragged my watch from its fob. It was not going. I glanced at its face by the moonlight, and then burst into tears as I flung it far away into the ocean. *It had run down at seven o'clock! We were behind the time of the slack, and the whirl of the Ström was in full fury!*

'When a boat is well built, properly trimmed, and not deep laden, the waves in a strong gale, when she is going large, seem always to slip from beneath her – which appears very strange to a landsman – and this is what is called *riding*, in sea phrase.

'Well, so far we had ridden the swells very cleverly; but presently a gigantic sea happened to take us right under the counter, and bore us with it as it rose – up – up – as if into the sky. I would not have believed that any wave could rise so high. And then down we came with a sweep, a slide, and a plunge, that made me feel sick and dizzy, as if I was falling from some lofty mountain-top in a dream. But while we were up I had thrown a quick glance around – and that one glance was all sufficient. I saw our exact position in an instant. The Moskoe-Ström whirlpool was about a quarter of a mile dead ahead – but no more like the everyday Moskoe-Ström, than the whirl as you now see it, is like a mill-race. If I had not known where we were, and what we had to expect, I should not have recognised the place at all. As it was, I involuntarily closed my eyes in horror. The lids clenched themselves together as if in a spasm.

'It could not have been more than two minutes afterwards until we suddenly felt the waves subside, and were enveloped in foam. The boat made a sharp half turn to larboard, and then shot off in its new direction like a thunderbolt. At the same moment the roaring noise of the water was completely drowned in a kind of shrill shriek – such a sound as you might imagine given out by the waste-pipes of many thousand steam-vessels, letting off their steam all together. We were now in the belt of surf that always surrounds the whirl; and I thought, of course, that another moment would plunge us into the abyss – down which we could only see indistinctly on account of the amazing velocity with which we were borne along. The boat did not seem to sink into the water at all, but to skim like an air-bubble upon the surface of the surge. Her starboard side was next the whirl, and on the larboard arose the world of ocean we had left. It stood like a huge writhing wall between us and the horizon.

'It may appear strange, but now, when we were in the very jaws of the gulf, I felt more composed than when we were only approaching it. Having made up my mind to hope no more, I got rid of a great deal of that terror which unmanned me at first. I suppose it was despair that strung my nerves.

'It may look like boasting – but what I tell you is truth – I began to reflect how magnificent a thing it was to die in such a manner, and how foolish it was in me to think of so paltry a consideration as my own individual life, in view of so wonderful a manifestation of God's power. I do believe that I blushed with shame when this idea crossed my mind. After a little while I became possessed with the keenest curiosity about the whirl itself. I positively felt a *wish* to explore its depths, even at the sacrifice I was going to make; and my principal grief was that I should never be able to tell my old companions on shore about the mysteries I should see. These, no doubt, were singular fancies to occupy a man's mind in such extremity – and I have often thought since, that the revolutions of the boat around the pool might have rendered me a little light-headed.

'There was another circumstance which tended to restore my self-possession; and this was the cessation of the wind, which could not reach us in our present situation – for, as you saw yourself, the belt of surf is considerably lower than the general bed of the ocean, and this latter now towered above us, a high, black, mountainous ridge. If you have never been at sea in a heavy gale, you can form no idea of the confusion of mind occasioned by the wind and spray together. They blind, deafen, and strangle you, and take away all power of action or reflection. But we were now, in a great measure, rid of these annoyances – just as death-condemned felons in prison are allowed petty indulgences, forbidden them while their doom is yet uncertain.

'How often we made the circuit of the belt it is impossible to say. We careered round and round for perhaps an hour, flying rather than floating, getting gradually more and more into the middle of the surge, and then nearer and nearer to its horrible inner edge. All this time I had never let go of the ring-bolt. My brother was at the stern, holding on to a small empty water-cask, which had been securely lashed under the coop of the counter, and was the only thing on deck that had not been swept overboard when the gale first took us. As we approached the brink of the pit he let go his hold upon this,

THE BOAT APPEARED TO BE HANGING, AS IF BY MAGIC ...
UPON THE INTERIOR SURFACE OF A FUNNEL

and made for the ring, from which, in the agony of his terror, he endeavoured to force my hands, as it was not large enough to afford us both a secure grasp. I never felt deeper grief than when I saw him attempt this act – although I knew he was a madman when he did it – a raving maniac through sheer fright. I did not care, however, to contest the point with him. I knew it could make no difference whether either of us held on at all; so I let him have the bolt, and went astern to the cask. This there was no great difficulty in doing; for the smack flew round steadily enough, and upon an even keel – only swaying to and fro, with the immense sweeps and swelters of the whirl. Scarcely had I secured myself in my new position, when we gave a wild lurch to starboard, and rushed headlong into the abyss. I muttered a hurried prayer to God, and thought all was over.

'As I felt the sickening sweep of the descent, I had instinctively tightened my hold upon the barrel, and closed my eyes. For some seconds I dared not open them – while I expected instant destruction, and wondered that I was not already in my death-struggles with the water. But moment after moment elapsed. I still lived. The sense of falling had ceased; and the motion of the vessel seemed much as it had been before, while in the belt of foam, with the exception that she now lay more along. I took courage and looked once again upon the scene.

'Never shall I forget the sensations of awe, horror, and admiration with which I gazed about me. The boat appeared to be hanging, as if by magic, midway down, upon the interior surface of a funnel, vast in circumference, prodigious in depth, and whose perfectly smooth sides might have been mistaken for ebony, but for the bewildering rapidity with which they spun around, and for the gleaming and ghastly radiance they shot forth, as the rays of the full moon, from that circular rift amid the clouds which I have already described, streamed in a flood of golden glory along the black walls, and far away down into the inmost recesses of the abyss.

'At first I was too much confused to observe anything accurately. The general burst of terrific grandeur was all that I beheld. When I recovered myself a little, however, my gaze fell instinctively downward. In this direction I was able to obtain an unobstructed view, from the manner in which the smack hung on the inclined surface of the pool. She was quite upon an even keel – that is to say, her deck lay in a plane parallel with that of the water – but this latter sloped at an angle of more than forty-five degrees, so that we seemed to be lying upon our beam-ends. I could not help observing, nevertheless, that I had scarcely more difficulty in maintaining my hold and footing in this situation, than if we had been upon a dead level; and this, I suppose, was owing to the speed at which we revolved.

'The rays of the moon seemed to search the very bottom of the profound gulf; but still I could make out nothing distinctly, on account of a thick mist in which everything there was enveloped, and over which there hung a magnificent rainbow, like that narrow and tottering bridge which Mussulmans say is the only pathway between Time and Eternity. This mist, or spray, was no doubt occasioned by the clashing of the great walls of the funnel, as they all met together at the bottom – but the yell that went up to the heavens from out of that mist, I dare not attempt to describe.

'Our first slide into the abyss itself, from the belt of foam above, had carried us to a great distance down the slope; but our farther descent was by no means proportionate. Round and round we swept – not with any uniform movement – but in dizzying swings and jerks, that sent us sometimes only a few hundred yards – sometimes nearly the complete circuit of the whirl. Our progress downward, at each revolution, was slow, but very perceptible.

'Looking about me upon the wide waste of liquid ebony on which we were thus borne, I perceived that our boat was not the only object in the embrace of the whirl. Both above and below us were visible fragments of vessels, large masses of building timber and trunks of trees, with many smaller articles, such as pieces of house furniture, broken boxes, barrels and staves. I have already described the unnatural curiosity which had taken the place of my original terrors. It appeared to grow upon me as I drew nearer and nearer to my dreadful doom. I now began to watch, with a strange interest, the numerous things that floated in our company. I *must* have been delirious – for I even sought *amusement* in speculating upon the relative velocities of their several descents toward the foam below. "This fir tree," I found myself at one time saying, "will certainly be the next thing that takes the awful plunge and disappears," and then I was disappointed to find that the wreck of a Dutch merchant ship overtook it and went down before. At length, after making several guesses of this nature, and being deceived in all – this fact – the fact of my invariable miscalculation, set me upon a train of reflection that made my limbs again tremble, and my heart beat heavily once more.

'It was not a new terror that thus affected me, but the dawn of a more exciting *hope*. This hope arose partly from memory and partly from present observation. I called to mind the great variety of buoyant matter that strewed the coast of Lofoden, having been absorbed and then thrown forth by the Moskoe-ström. By far the greater number of the articles were shattered in the most extraordinary way – so chafed and roughened as to have the appearance of being stuck full of splinters – but then I distinctly recollected that there were *some* of them which were not disfigured at all.

Now I could not account for this difference except by supposing that the roughened fragments were the only ones which had been *completely absorbed* – that the others had entered the whirl at so late a period of the tide, or, from some reason, had descended so slowly after entering, that they did not reach the bottom before the turn of the flood came, or of the ebb as the case might be. I conceived it possible, in either instance, that they might thus be whirled up again to the level of the ocean, without undergoing the fate of those which had been drawn in more early or absorbed more rapidly. I made, also, three important observations. The first was, that as a general rule, the larger the bodies were, the more rapid their descent – the second, that, between two masses of equal extent, the one spherical, and the other *of any other shape*, the superiority in speed of descent was with the sphere – the third, that, between two masses of equal size, the one cylindrical, and the other of any other shape, the cylinder was absorbed the more slowly. Since my escape, I have had several conversations on this subject with an old schoolmaster of the district; and it was from him that I learned the use of the words "cylinder" and "sphere". He explained to me – although I have forgotten the explanation – how what I observed was, in fact, the natural consequence of the forms of the floating fragments – and showed me how it happened that a cylinder, swimming in a vortex, offered more resistance to its suction, and was drawn in with greater difficulty than an equally bulky body of any form whatever.

'There was one startling circumstance which went a great way in enforcing these observations, and rendering me anxious to turn them to account, and this was that, at every revolution, we passed something like a barrel, or else the yard or the mast of a vessel, while many of these things, which had been on our level when I first opened my eyes upon the wonders of the whirlpool, were now high up above us, and seemed to have moved but little from their original station.

'I no longer hesitated what to do. I resolved to lash myself securely to the water cask upon which I now held, to cut it loose from the counter, and to throw myself with it into the water. I attracted my brother's attention by signs, pointed to the floating barrels that came near us, and did everything in my power to make him understand what I was about to do. I thought at length that he comprehended my design – but whether this was the case or not, he shook his head despairingly, and refused to move from his station by the ring-bolt. It was impossible to reach him; the emergency admitted of no delay; and so, with a bitter struggle, I resigned him to his fate, fastened myself to the cask by means of the lashings which secured it to the counter, and precipitated myself with it into the sea, without another moment's hesitation.

'The result was precisely what I had hoped it might be. As it is myself who now tell you this tale – as you see that I *did* escape – and as you are already in possession of the mode in which this escape was effected, and must therefore anticipate all that I have further to say – I will bring my story quickly to conclusion. It might have been an hour, or thereabout, after my quitting the smack, when, having descended to a vast distance beneath me, it made three or four wild gyrations in rapid succession, and, bearing my loved brother with it, plunged headlong, at once and for ever, into the chaos of foam below. The barrel to which I was attached sunk very little farther than half the distance between the bottom of the gulf and the spot at which I leaped overboard, before a great change took place in the character of the whirlpool. The slope of the sides of the vast funnel became momentarily less and less steep, the gyrations of the whirl grew gradually less and less violent. By degrees, the froth and the rainbow disappeared, and the bottom of the gulf seemed slowly to uprise. The sky was clear, the winds had gone down, and the full moon was setting radiantly in the west, when I found myself on the surface of the ocean, in full view of the shores of Lofoden, and above the spot where the pool of the Moskoe-ström *had been*. It was the hour of the slack – but the sea still heaved in mountainous waves from the effects of the hurricane. I was borne violently into the channel of the Ström, and in a few minutes, was hurried down the coast into the "grounds" of the fishermen. A boat picked me up – exhausted from fatigue – and (now that the danger was removed) – speechless from the memory of its horror. Those who drew me on board were my old mates and daily companions – but they knew me no more than they would have known a traveller from the spirit-land. My hair, which had been raven-black the day before, was as white as you see it now. They say, too, that the whole expression of my countenance had changed. I told them my story – they did not believe it. I now tell it to *you* – and I can scarcely expect you to put more faith in it than did the merry fishermen of Lofoden.'

The Murders in the Rue Morgue

What song the Syrens sang, or what name Achilles assumed when he hid himself among women, although puzzling questions, are not beyond *all* conjecture.

SIR THOMAS BROWNE

The mental features discoursed of as the analytical, are, in themselves, but little susceptible of analysis. We appreciate them only in their effects. We know of them, among other things, that they are always to their possessor, when inordinately possessed, a source of the liveliest enjoyment. As the strong man exults in his physical ability, delighting in such exercises as call his muscles into action, so glories the analyst in that moral activity which *disentangles*. He derives pleasure from even the most trivial occupations bringing his talent into play. He is fond of enigmas, of conundrums, of hieroglyphics; exhibiting in his solutions of each a degree of acumen which appears to the ordinary apprehension preternatural. His results, brought about by the very soul and essence of method, have, in truth, the whole air of intuition.

The faculty of resolution is possibly much invigorated by mathematical study, and especially by that highest branch of it which, unjustly, and merely on account of its retrograde operations, has been called, as if *par excellence*, analysis. Yet to calculate is not in itself to analyse. A chess-player, for example, does the one, without effort at the other. It follows that the game of chess, in its effects upon mental character, is greatly misunderstood. I am not now writing a treatise, but simply prefacing a somewhat peculiar narrative by observations very much at random; I will, therefore, take occasion to assert that the higher powers of the reflective intellect are more decidedly and more usefully tasked by the unostentatious game of draughts than by all the elaborate frivolity of chess. In this latter, where the pieces have different and bizarre motions, with various and variable values, what is only complex, is mistaken (a not unusual error) for what is profound. The *attention* is here called powerfully into play. If it flag for an instant, an oversight is committed, resulting in injury or defeat. The possible moves being not only manifold, but involute, the chances of such oversights are multiplied; and in nine cases out of ten, it is the more concentrative rather than the more acute player who conquers. In draughts, on the contrary, where the moves are *unique* and have but little variation, the probabilities of inadvertence are diminished, and the mere attention being left comparatively unemployed, what advantages are obtained by either party are obtained by superior acumen. To be less abstract – Let us suppose a game of draughts where the pieces are reduced to four kings, and where, of course, no oversight is to be expected. It is obvious that here the victory can be decided (the players being at all equal) only by some *recherché* movement, the result of some strong exertion of the intellect. Deprived of ordinary resources, the analyst throws himself into the spirit of his opponent, identifies himself therewith, and not unfrequently sees thus, at a glance, the sole methods (sometimes indeed absurdly simple ones) by which he may seduce into error or hurry into miscalculation.

Whist has long been noted for its influence upon what is termed the calculating power; and men of the highest order of intellect have been known to take an apparently unaccountable delight in it, while eschewing chess as frivolous. Beyond doubt there is nothing of a similar nature so greatly tasking the faculty of analysis. The best chess-player in Christendom *may* be little more than the best player of chess; but proficiency in whist implies capacity for success in all these more important undertakings where mind struggles with mind. When I say proficiency, I mean that perfection in the game which includes a comprehension of *all* the sources whence legitimate advantage may be derived. These are not only manifold, but multiform, and lie frequently among recesses of thought altogether inaccessible to the ordinary understanding. To observe attentively is to remember distinctly; and, so far, the concentrative chess-player will do very well at whist; while the rules of Hoyle (themselves based upon the mere mechanism of the game) are sufficiently and generally comprehensible. Thus to have a retentive memory, and to proceed by 'the book,' are points commonly regarded as the sum total of good playing. But it is in matters beyond the limits of mere rule that the skill of the analyst is evinced. He makes, in silence, a host of observations and inferences. So, perhaps, do his companions; and the difference in the extent of the information obtained, lies not so much in the validity of the inference as in the quality of the observation.

The necessary knowledge is that of *what* to observe. Our player confines himself not at all; nor, because the game is the object, does he reject deductions from things external to the game. He examines the countenance of his partner, comparing it carefully with that of each of his opponents. He considers the mode of assorting the cards in each hand; often counting trump by trump, and honour by honour, through the glances bestowed by their holders upon each. He notes every variation of face as the play progresses, gathering a fund of thought from the differences in the expression of certainty, of surprise, of triumph, or chagrin. From the manner of gathering up a trick he judges whether the person taking it can make another in the suit. He recognises what is played through feint, by the air with which it is thrown upon the table. A casual or inadvertent word; the accidental dropping or turning of a card, with the accompanying anxiety or carelessness in regard to its concealment; the counting of the tricks, with the order of their arrangement; embarrassment, hesitation, eagerness or trepidation – all afford, to his apparently intuitive perception, indications of the true state of affairs. The first two or three rounds having been played, he is in full possession of the contents of each hand, and thenceforward puts down his cards with as absolute a precision of purpose as if the rest of the party had turned outward the faces of their own.

The analytical power should not be confounded with simple ingenuity; for while the analyst is necessarily ingenious, the ingenious man is often remarkably incapable of analysis. The constructive or combining power, by which ingenuity is usually manifested, and to which the phrenologists (I believe erroneously) have assigned a separate organ, supposing it a primitive faculty, has been so frequently seen in those whose intellect bordered otherwise upon idiocy, as to have attracted general observation among writers on morals. Between ingenuity and the analytic ability there exists a difference far greater, indeed, than that between the fancy and the imagination, but of a character very strictly analogous. It will be found, in fact, that the ingenious are always fanciful, and the *truly* imaginative never otherwise than analytic.

The narrative which follows will appear to the reader somewhat in the light of a commentary upon the propositions just advanced.

Residing in Paris during the spring and part of the summer of 18—, I there became acquainted with a Monsieur C. Auguste Dupin. This young gentleman was of an excellent – indeed of an illustrious family, but, by a variety of untoward events, had been reduced to such poverty that the energy of his character succumbed beneath it, and he ceased to bestir himself in the world, or to care for the retrieval of his fortunes. By courtesy of his creditors there still remained in his possession a small remnant of his patrimony; and, upon the income arising from this, he managed, by means of a rigorous economy, to procure the necessaries of life, without troubling himself about its superfluities. Books, indeed, were his sole luxuries, and in Paris these are easily obtained.

Our first meeting was at an obscure library in the Rue Montmartre, where the accident of our both being in search of the same very rare and very remarkable volume, brought us into closer communion. We saw each other again and again. I was deeply interested in the little family history which he detailed to me with all that candour which a Frenchman indulges whenever mere self is the theme. I was astonished, too, at the vast extent of his reading; and, above all, I felt my soul enkindled within me by the wild fervour, and the vivid freshness of his imagination. Seeking in Paris the objects I then sought, I felt that the society of such a man would be to me a treasure beyond price; and this feeling I frankly confided to him. It was at length arranged that we should live together during my stay in the city; and as my worldly circumstances were somewhat less embarrassed than his own, I was permitted to be at the expense of renting, and furnishing in a style which suited the rather fantastic gloom of our common temper, a time-eaten and grotesque mansion, long deserted through superstitions into which we did not enquire, and tottering to its fall in a retired and desolate portion of the Faubourg St Germain.

Had the routine of our life at this place been known to the world, we should have been regarded as madmen – although, perhaps, as madmen of a harmless nature. Our seclusion was perfect. We admitted no visitors. Indeed the locality of our retirement had been carefully kept a secret from my own former associates; and it had been many years since Dupin had ceased to know or be known in Paris. We existed within ourselves alone.

It was a freak of fancy in my friend (for what else shall I call it?) to be enamoured of the night for her own sake; and into this *bizarrerie*, as into all his others, I quietly fell, giving myself up to his wild whims with a perfect abandon. The sable divinity would not herself dwell with us always; but we could counterfeit her presence. At the first dawn of the morning we closed all the massy shutters of our old building; lighted a couple of tapers which, strongly perfumed, threw out only the ghastliest and feeblest of rays. By the aid of these we then busied our souls in dreams – reading, writing, or conversing, until warned by the clock of the advent of the true Darkness. Then we sallied forth into the streets, arm in arm, continuing the topics of the day, or roaming far and wide until a late hour, seeking, amid the wild lights and shadows of the populous city, that infinity of mental excitement which quiet observation can afford.

At such times I could not help remarking and admiring (although from his rich ideality I had been prepared to expect it) a peculiar analytic ability in Dupin. He seemed, too, to take an eager delight in its exercise – if not exactly in its display – and did not hesitate to confess the pleasure thus derived. He boasted to me, with a low chuckling laugh, that most men, in respect to himself, wore windows in their bosoms, and was wont to follow up such assertions by direct and very startling proofs of his intimate knowledge of my own. His manner at these moments was frigid and abstract; his eyes were vacant in expression; while his voice, usually a rich tenor, rose into a treble which would have sounded petulantly but for the deliberateness and entire distinctness of the enunciation. Observing him in these moods, I often dwelt meditatively upon the old philosophy of the Bi-Part Soul, and amused myself with the fancy of a double Dupin – the creative and the resolvent.

Let it not be supposed, from what I have just said, that I am detailing any mystery, or penning any romance. What I have described in the Frenchman, was merely the result of an excited, or perhaps of a diseased intelligence. But of the character of his remarks at the periods in question an example will best convey the idea.

We were strolling one night down a long dirty street, in the vicinity of the Palais Royal. Being both, apparently, occupied with thought, neither of us had spoken a syllable for fifteen minutes at least. All at once Dupin broke forth with these words –

'He is a very little fellow, that's true, and would do better for the *Théâtre des Variétés*.'

'There can be no doubt of that,' I replied unwittingly, and not at first observing (so much had I been absorbed in reflection) the extraordinary manner in which the speaker had chimed in with my meditations. In an instant afterward I recollected myself, and my astonishment was profound.

'Dupin,' said I, gravely, 'this is beyond my comprehension. I do not hesitate to say that I am amazed, and can scarcely credit my senses. How was it possible you should know I was thinking of —?' Here I paused, to ascertain beyond a doubt whether he really knew of whom I thought.

'Of Chantilly,' said he; 'why do you pause? You were remarking to yourself that his diminutive figure unfitted him for tragedy.'

This was precisely what had formed the subject of my reflections. Chantilly was a quondam cobbler of the Rue St Denis, who, becoming stage-mad, had attempted the role of Xerxes, in Crébillon's tragedy so called, and been notoriously pasquinaded for his pains.

'Tell me, for Heaven's sake,' I exclaimed, 'the method – if method there is – by which you have been enabled to fathom my soul in this matter.' In fact I was even more startled than I would have been willing to express.

'It was the fruiterer,' replied my friend, 'who brought you to the conclusion that the mender of soles was not of sufficient height for Xerxes *et id genus omne*.'

'The fruiterer! – you astonish me – I know no fruiterer whomsoever.'

'The man who ran up against you as we entered the street – it may have been fifteen minutes ago.'

I now remembered that, in fact, a fruiterer, carrying upon his head a large basket of apples, had nearly thrown me down, by accident, as we passed from the Rue C— into the thoroughfare where we stood; but what this had to do with Chantilly I could not possibly understand.

There was not a particle of *charlatanerie* about Dupin.

'I will explain,' he said, 'and that you may comprehend all clearly, we will first retrace the course of your meditations, from the moment in which I spoke to you until that of the rencontre with the fruiterer in question. The larger links of the chain run thus – Chantilly, Orion, Dr Nichols, Epicurus, Stereotomy, the street stones, the fruiterer.'

There are few persons who have not, at some period of their lives, amused themselves in retracing the steps by which particular conclusions of their own minds have been attained. The occupation is often full of interest; and he who attempts it for the first time is astonished by the apparently illimitable distance and incoherence between the starting-point and the goal. What, then, must have been my amazement when I heard the Frenchman speak what he had just spoken, and when I could not help acknowledging that he had spoken the truth! He continued –

'We had been talking of horses, if I remember aright, just before leaving the Rue C—. This was the last subject we discussed. As we crossed into the street, a fruiterer, with a large basket upon his head, brushing quickly past us, thrust you upon a pile of paving-stones collected at a spot where the causeway is undergoing repair. You stepped upon one of the loose fragments, slipped, slightly strained your ankle, appeared vexed or sulky, muttered a few words, turned to look at the pile, and then proceeded in silence. I was not particularly attentive to what you did; but observation has become with me, of late, a species of necessity.

'You kept your eyes upon the ground – glancing, with a petulant expression, at the holes and ruts in the pavement (so that I saw you were still thinking of the stones), until we reached the little alley called Lamartine, which has been paved, by way of experiment, with the overlapping and riveted blocks. Here your countenance brightened up, and, perceiving your lips move, I could not doubt that you murmured the word "stereotomy", a term very affectedly applied to this species of pavement. I knew that you could not say to yourself "stereotomy" without being brought to think of atomics, and thus of the theories of Epicurus; and since, when we discussed this subject not very long ago, I mentioned to you how singularly, yet with how little notice, the vague guesses of that noble Greek had met with confirmation in the late nebular cosmogony, I felt that you could not avoid casting your eyes upward to the great nebula in Orion, and I certainly expected that you would do so. You did look up; and I was now assured that I had correctly followed your steps. But in that bitter tirade upon Chantilly, which appeared in yesterday's *Musée*, the satirist, making some disgraceful allusions to the cobbler's change of name upon assuming the buskin, quoted a Latin line about which we have often conversed. I mean the line

Perdidit antiquum litera prima sonum.

I had told you that this was in reference to Orion, formerly written Urion; and, from certain pungencies connected with this explanation, I was aware that you could not have forgotten it. It was clear, therefore, that you would not fail to combine the two ideas of Orion and Chantilly. That you did combine them I saw by the character of the smile which passed over your lips. You thought of the poor cobbler's immolation. So far, you had been stooping in your gait; but now I saw you draw yourself up to your full height. I was then sure that you reflected upon the diminutive figure of Chantilly. At this point I interrupted your meditations to remark that as, in fact, he *was* a very little fellow, that Chantilly, he would do better at the *Théâtre des Variétés*.'

Not long after this, we were looking over an evening edition of the *Gazette des Tribunaux* when the following paragraphs arrested our attention:

'Extraordinary Murders – This morning, about three o'clock, the inhabitants of the Quartier St Roch were aroused from sleep by a succession of terrific shrieks, issuing, apparently, from the fourth storey of a house in the Rue Morgue, known to be in the sole occupancy of one Mme L'Espanaye, and her daughter, Mlle Camille L'Espanaye. After some delay, occasioned by a fruitless attempt to procure admission in the usual manner, the gateway was broken in with a crowbar, and eight or ten of the neighbours entered, accompanied by two gendarmes. By this time the cries had ceased; but, as the party rushed up the first flight of stairs, two or more rough voices, in angry contention, were distinguished, and seemed to proceed from the upper part of the house. As the second landing was reached, these sounds, also, had ceased, and everything remained perfectly quiet. The party spread themselves, and hurried from room to room. Upon arriving at a large back chamber in the fourth storey (the door of which, being found locked, with the key inside, was forced open), a spectacle presented itself which struck everyone present not less with horror than with astonishment.

'The apartment was in the wildest disorder – the furniture broken and thrown about in all directions. There was only one bedstead; and from this the bed had been removed, and thrown into the middle of the floor. On a chair lay a razor, besmeared with blood. On the hearth were two or three long and thick tresses of grey human hair, also dabbled in blood, and seeming to have been pulled out by the roots. Upon the floor were found four napoleons, an earring of topaz, three large silver spoons, three smaller of *métal d'Alger*, and two bags, containing nearly four thousand francs in gold. The drawers of a bureau, which stood in one corner, were open, and had been, apparently, rifled, although many articles still remained in them. A small iron safe was discovered under the *bed* (not under the bedstead). It was open, with a key still in the door. It had no contents beyond a few old letters, and other papers of little consequence.

'Of Mme L'Espanaye no traces were here seen; but an unusual quantity of soot being observed in the fireplace, a search was made in the chimney, and (horrible to relate!) the corpse of the daughter, head downward, was dragged therefrom; it having been thus forced up the narrow aperture for a cons iderable distance. The body was quite warm. Upon examining it, many excoriations were perceived, no doubt occasioned by the violence with which it had been thrust up and disengaged. Upon the face were many severe scratches, and, upon the throat, dark bruises, and deep indentations of finger nails, as if the deceased had been throttled to death.

'After a thorough investigation of every portion of the house, without further discovery, the party made its way into a small paved yard in the rear of the building, where lay the corpse of the old lady, with her throat so entirely cut that, upon an attempt to raise her, the head fell off. The body, as well as the head, was fearfully mutilated – the former so much so as scarcely to retain any semblance of humanity.

'To this horrible mystery there is not as yet, we believe, the slightest clue.

The next day's paper had these additional particulars:

'THE TRAGEDY IN THE RUE MORGUE – Many individuals have been examined in relation to this most extraordinary and frightful affair' [the word '*affaire*' has not yet in France that levity of import which it conveys with us], 'but nothing whatever has transpired to throw light upon it. We give below all the material testimony elicited.

'*Pauline Dubourg*, laundress, deposes that she has known both the deceased for three years, having washed for them during that period. The old lady and her daughter seemed on good terms – very affectionate towards each other. They were excellent pay. Could not speak in regard to their mode or means of living. Believed that Mme L. told fortunes for a living. Was reputed to have money put by. Never met any persons in the house when she called for the clothes or took them home. Was sure that they had no servant in employ. There appeared to be no furniture in any part of the building, except in the fourth storey.

'*Pierre Moreau*, tobacconist, deposes that he has been in the habit of selling small quantities of tobacco and snuff to Mme L'Espanaye for nearly four years. Was born in the neighbourhood, and has always resided there. The deceased and her daughter had occupied the house in which the corpses were found for more than six years. It was formerly occupied by a jeweller, who under-let the upper rooms to various persons. The house was the property of Mme L. She became dissatisfied with the abuse of the premises by her tenant, and moved into them herself, refusing to let any portion. The old lady was childish. Witness had seen the daughter some five or six times during the six years. The two lived an exceedingly retired life – were reputed to have money. Had heard it said among the neighbours that Mme L. told fortunes – did not believe it. Had never seen any person enter the door except the old lady and her daughter, a porter once or twice, and a physician some eight or ten times.

Many other persons, neighbours, gave evidence to the same effect. No one was spoken of as frequenting the house. It was not known whether there were any living connections of Mme L. and her daughter. The shutters of the front windows were seldom opened. Those in the rear were always closed, with the exception of the large back room, fourth storey. The house was a good house – not very old.

'*Isidore Mustè*, gendarme, deposes that he was called to the house about three o'clock in the morning, and found some twenty or thirty persons at the gateway, endeavouring to gain admittance. Forced it open, at length, with a bayonet – not with a crowbar. Had but little difficulty in getting it open, on account of its being a double or folding gate, and bolted neither at bottom nor top. The shrieks were continued until the gate was forced – and then suddenly ceased. They seemed to be screams of some person (or persons) in great agony – were loud and drawn out, not short and quick. Witness led the way upstairs. Upon reaching the first landing, heard two voices in loud and angry contention – the one a gruff voice, the other much shriller – a very strange voice. Could distinguish some words of the former, which was that of a Frenchman. Was positive that it was not a woman's voice. Could distinguish the words '*sacré*' and '*diable*'. The shrill voice was that of a foreigner. Could not be sure whether it was the voice of a man or of a woman. Could not make out what was said, but believed the language to be Spanish. The state of the room and of the bodies was described by this witness as we described them yesterday.

'*Henri Duval*, a neighbour, and by trade a silversmith, deposes that he was one of the party who first entered the house. Corroborates the testimony of Mustè in general. As soon as they forced an entrance, they reclosed the door, to keep out the crowd, which collected very fast, notwithstanding the lateness of the hour. The shrill voice, this witness thinks, was that of an Italian. Was certain it was not French. Could not be sure that it was a man's voice. It might have been a woman's. Was not acquainted with the Italian language. Could not distinguish the words, but was convinced by the intonation that the speaker was an Italian. Knew Mme L. and her daughter. Had conversed with both frequently. Was sure that the shrill voice was not that of either of the deceased.

'— *Odenheimer*, restaurateur. This witness volunteered his testimony. Not speaking French, was examined through an interpreter. Is a native of Amsterdam. Was passing the house at the time of the shrieks. They lasted for several minutes – probably ten. They were long and loud – very awful and distressing. Was one of those who entered the building. Corroborated the previous evidence in every respect but one. Was sure that the shrill voice was that of a man – of a Frenchman. Could not distinguish the words uttered. They were loud and quick – unequal – spoken apparently in fear as well as in anger. The voice was harsh – not so much shrill as harsh. Could not call it a shrill voice. The gruff voice said repeatedly '*sacré*', '*diable*', and once '*mon Dieu*'.

'*Jules Mignaud*, banker, of the firm of Mignaud et Fils, Rue Deloraine. Is the elder Mignaud. Mme L'Espanaye had some property. Had opened an account with his banking house in the spring of the year — (eight years previously). Made frequent deposits in small sums. Had checked for nothing until the third day before her death, when she took out in person the sum of 4000 francs. This sum was paid in gold, and a clerk sent home with the money.

'*Adolphe Le Bon*, clerk to Mignaud et Fils, deposes that on the day in question, about noon, he accompanied Mme

L'Espanaye to her residence with the 4000 francs put up in two bags. Upon the door being opened, Mlle L. appeared and took from his hands one of the bags, while the old lady relieved him of the other. He then bowed and departed. Did not see any person in the street at the time. It is a by-street – very lonely.

'*William Bird*, tailor, deposes that he was one of the party who entered the house. Is an Englishman. Has lived in Paris two years. Was one of the first to ascend the stairs. Heard the voices in contention. The gruff voice was that of a Frenchman. Could make out several words, but cannot now remember all. Heard distinctly '*sacré*' and '*mon Dieu*'. There was a sound at the moment as if of several persons struggling – a scraping and scuffling sound. The shrill voice was very loud – louder than the gruff one. Is sure that it was not the voice of an Englishman. Appeared to be that of a German. Might have been a woman's voice. Does not understand German.

'Four of the above-named witnesses, being recalled, deposed that the door of the chamber in which was found the body of Mlle L. was locked on the inside when the party reached it. Everything was perfectly silent – no groans or noises of any kind. Upon forcing the door no person was seen. The windows, both of the back and front room, were down and firmly fastened from within. A door between the two rooms was closed, but not locked. The door leading from the front room into the passage was locked, with the key on the inside. A small room in the front of the house, on the fourth storey, at the head of the passage, was open, the door being ajar. This room was crowded with old beds, boxes, and so forth. These were carefully removed and searched. There was not an inch of any portion of the house which was not carefully searched. Sweeps were sent up and down the chimneys. The house was a four-storey one, with garrets (*mansardes*). A trap-door on the roof was nailed down very securely – did not appear to have been opened for years. The time elapsing between the hearing of the voices in contention and the breaking open of the room door, was variously stated by the witnesses. Some made it as short as three minutes – some as long as five. The door was opened with difficulty.

'*Alfonzo Garcio*, undertaker, deposes that he resides in the Rue Morgue. Is a native of Spain. Was one of the party who entered the house. Did not proceed upstairs. Is nervous, and was apprehensive of the consequences of agitation. Heard the voices in contention. The gruff voice was that of a Frenchman. Could not distinguish what was said. The shrill voice was that of an Englishman – is sure of this. Does not understand the English language, but judges by the intonation.

'*Alberto Montani*, confectioner, deposes that he was among the first to ascend the stairs. Heard the voices in question. The gruff voice was that of a Frenchman. Distinguished several words. The speaker appeared to be expostulating. Could not make out the words of the shrill voice. Spoke quick and unevenly. Thinks it the voice of a Russian. Corroborates the general testimony. Is an Italian. Never conversed with a native of Russia.

'Several witnesses, recalled, here testified that the chimneys of all the rooms on the fourth storey were too narrow to admit the passage of a human being. By 'sweeps' were meant cylindrical sweeping-brushes, such as are employed by those who clean chimneys. These brushes were passed up and down every flue in the house. There is no back passage by which anyone could have descended while the party proceeded upstairs. The body of Mlle L'Espanaye was so firmly wedged in the chimney that it could not be got down until four or five of the party united their strength.

'*Paul Dumas*, physician, deposes that he was called to view the bodies about daybreak. They were both then lying on the sacking of the bedstead in the chamber where Mlle L. was found. The corpse of the young lady was much bruised and excoriated. The fact that it had been thrust up the chimney would sufficiently account for these appearances. The throat was greatly chafed. There were several deep scratches just below the chin, together with a series of livid spots which were evidently the impression of fingers. The face was fearfully discoloured, and the eyeballs protruded. The tongue had been partially bitten through. A large bruise was discovered upon the pit of the stomach, produced apparently, by the pressure of a knee. In the opinion of M. Dumas, Mlle L'Espanaye had been throttled to death by some person or persons unknown. The corpse of the mother was horribly mutilated. All the bones of the right leg and arm were more or less shattered. The left tibia much splintered, as well as all the ribs of the left side. Whole body dreadfully bruised and discoloured. It was not possible to say how the injuries had been inflicted. A heavy club of wood, or a broad bar of iron – a chair – any large, heavy, and obtuse weapon would have produced such results, if wielded by the hands of a very powerful man. No woman could have inflicted the blows with any weapon. The head of the deceased, when seen by witness, was entirely separated from the body, and was also greatly shattered. The throat had evidently been cut with some very sharp instrument – probably with a razor.

'*Alexandre Etienne*, surgeon, was called with M. Dumas, to view the bodies. Corroborated the testimony, and the opinions of M. Dumas.

'Nothing further of importance was elicited, although several other persons were examined. A murder so mysterious, and so perplexing in all its particulars, was never before committed in Paris – if indeed a murder has been committed at all. The police are entirely at fault – an unusual occurrence in affairs of this nature. There is not, however, the shadow of a clue apparent.'

The evening edition of the paper stated that the greatest excitement still continued in the Quartier St Roch – that the premises in question had been carefully re-searched, and fresh examinations of witnesses instituted, but all to no purpose. A postscript, however, mentioned that Adolphe Le Bon had been arrested and imprisoned – although nothing appeared to criminate him, beyond the facts already detailed.

Dupin seemed singularly interested in the progress of this affair – at least so I judged from his manner, for he made no comments. It was only after the announcement that Le Bon had been imprisoned, that he asked me my opinion respecting the murders.

I could merely agree with all Paris in considering them an insoluble mystery. I saw no means by which it would be possible to trace the murderer.

'We must not judge of the means,' said Dupin, 'by this shell of an examination. The Parisian police, so much extolled for acumen, are cunning, but no more. There is no method in their proceedings, beyond the method of the moment. They make a vast parade of measures; but, not unfrequently, these are so ill adapted to the objects proposed, as to put us in mind of M. Jourdain's calling for his *robe-de-chambre – pour mieux entendre la musique*. The results attained by them are not unfrequently surprising, but, for the most part, are brought about by simple diligence and activity. When these qualities are unavailing, their schemes fail. Vidocq, for example, was a good guesser, and a persevering man. But, without educated thought, he erred continually by the very intensity of his investigations. He impaired his vision by holding the object too close. He might see, perhaps, one or two points with unusual clearness, but in so doing, he, necessarily, lost sight of the matter as a whole. Thus there is such a thing as being too profound. Truth is not always in a well. In fact, as regards the more important knowledge, I do believe that she is invariably superficial. The depth lies in the valleys where we seek her, and not upon the mountain-top where she is found. The modes and sources of this kind of error are well typified in the contemplation of the heavenly bodies. To look at a star by glances – to view it in a sidelong way, by turning toward it the exterior portions of the retina (more susceptible of feeble impressions of light than the interior), is to behold the star distinctly – is to have the best appreciation of its lustre – a lustre which grows dim just in proportion as we turn our vision *fully* upon it. A greater number of rays actually fall upon the eye in the latter case, but, in the former, there is the more refined capacity for comprehension. By undue profundity we perplex and enfeeble thought; and it is possible to make even Venus herself vanish from the firmament by a scrutiny too sustained, too concentrated, or too direct.

'As for these murders, let us enter into some examinations for ourselves, before we make up an opinion respecting them. An enquiry will afford us amusement' [I thought this an odd term, so applied, but said nothing], 'and, besides, Le Bon once rendered me a service for which I am not ungrateful. We will go and see the premises with our own eyes. I know G—, the Prefect of Police, and shall have no difficulty in obtaining the necessary permission.'

The permission was obtained, and we proceeded at once to the Rue Morgue. This is one of those miserable thoroughfares which intervene between the Rue Richelieu and the Rue St Roch. It was late in the afternoon when we reached it; as this quarter is at a great distance from that in which we resided. The house was readily found; for there were still many persons gazing up at the closed shutters, with an objectless curiosity, from the opposite side of the way. It was an ordinary Parisian house, with a gateway, on one side of which was a glazed watch-box, with a sliding panel in the window, indicating a *loge de concierge*. Before going in we walked up the street, turned down an alley, and then, again turning, passed in the rear of the building – Dupin, meanwhile, examining the whole neighbourhood, as well as the house, with a minuteness of attention for which I could see no possible object.

Retracing our steps, we came again to the front of the dwelling, rang, and having shown our credentials, were admitted by the agents in charge. We went upstairs – into the chamber where the body of Mlle L'Espanaye had been found, and where both the deceased still lay. The disorders of the room had, as usual, been suffered to exist. I saw nothing beyond what had been stated in the *Gazette des Tribunaux*. Dupin scrutinised everything – not excepting the bodies of the victims. We then went into the other rooms, and into the yard; a gendarme accompanying us throughout. The examination occupied us until dark, when we took our departure. On our way home my companion stepped in for a moment at the office of one of the daily papers.

I have said that the whims of my friend were manifold, and that *Je les ménageais* – for this phrase there is no English equivalent. It was his humour, now, to decline all conversation on the subject of the murders, until about noon the next day. He then asked me, suddenly, if I had observed anything *peculiar* at the scene of the atrocity.

There was something in his manner of emphasising the word 'peculiar,' which caused me to shudder, without knowing why.

'No, nothing *peculiar*,' I said; 'nothing more, at least, than we both saw stated in the paper.'

The *Gazette*,' he replied, 'has not entered, I fear into the unusual horror of the thing. But dismiss the idle opinions of this print. It appears to me that this mystery is considered insoluble, for the very reason which should cause it to be regarded as easy of solution – I mean for the *outré* character of its features. The police are confounded by the seeming absence of motive – not for the murder itself – but for the atrocity of the murder. They are puzzled, too, by the seeming impossibility of reconciling the voices heard in contention, with the facts that no one was discovered upstairs but the assassinated Mlle L'Espanaye, and that there were no means of egress without the notice of the party ascending. The wild disorder of the room; the corpse thrust, with the head downward, up the chimney; the frightful mutilation of the body of the old lady; these considerations, with those just mentioned, and others which I need not mention, have sufficed to paralyse the powers, by putting completely at fault the boasted acumen of the government agents. They have fallen into the gross but common error of confounding the unusual with the abstruse. But it is by these deviations from the plane of the ordinary, that reason feels its way, if at all, in its search for the true. In investigations such as we are now pursuing, it should not be so much asked "what has occurred?" as "what has occurred that has never occurred before?" In fact, the facility with which I shall arrive, or have arrived, at the solution of this mystery, is in the direct ratio of its apparent insolubility in the eyes of the police.'

I stared at the speaker in mute astonishment.

'I am now awaiting,' continued he, looking toward the door of our apartment – 'I am now awaiting a person who, although perhaps not the perpetrator of these butcheries, must have been in some measure implicated in their perpetration. Of the worst portion of the crimes committed, it is probable that he is innocent. I hope that I am right in this supposition; for upon it I build my expectation of reading the entire riddle. I look for the man here – in this room – every moment. It is true that he may not arrive; but the probability is that he will. Should he come, it will be necessary to detain him. Here are pistols; and we both know how to use them when occasion demands their use.'

I took the pistols, scarcely knowing what I did, or believing what I heard, while Dupin went on, very much as if in a soliloquy. I have already spoken of his abstract manner at such times. His discourse was addressed to myself; but his voice, although by no means loud, had that intonation which is commonly employed in speaking to someone at a great distance. His eyes, vacant in expression, regarded only the wall.

'That the voices heard in contention,' he said, 'by the party upon the stairs, were not the voices of the women themselves, was fully proved by the evidence. This relieves us of all doubt upon the question whether the old lady could have first destroyed the daughter, and afterward have committed suicide. I speak of this point chiefly for the sake of method; for the strength of Mme L'Espanaye would have been utterly unequal to the task of thrusting her daughter's corpse up the chimney as it was found; and the nature of the wounds upon her own person entirely precludes the idea of self-destruction. Murder, then, has been committed by some third party; and the voices of this third party were those heard in contention. Let me now advert – not to the whole testimony respecting these voices – but to what was peculiar in that testimony. Did you observe anything peculiar about it?'

I remarked that, while all the witnesses agreed in supposing the gruff voice to be that of a Frenchman, there was much disagreement in regard to the shrill, or, as one individual termed it, the harsh voice.

'That was the evidence itself,' said Dupin, 'but it was not the peculiarity of the evidence. You have observed nothing distinctive. Yet there *was* something to be observed. The witnesses, as you remark, agreed about the gruff voice; they were here unanimous. But in regard to the shrill voice, the peculiarity is – not that they disagreed – but that, while an Italian, an Englishman, a Spaniard, a Hollander, and a Frenchman attempted to describe it, each one spoke of it as that *of a foreigner*. Each is sure that it was not the voice of one of his own countrymen. Each likens it – not to the voice of an individual of any nation with whose language he is conversant – but the converse. The Frenchman supposes it the voice of a Spaniard, and "might have distinguished some words *had he been acquainted with the Spanish*." The Dutchman maintains it to have been that of a Frenchman; but we find it stated that, "*not understanding French, this witness was examined through an interpreter.*" The Englishman thinks it the voice of a German, and "*does not understand German.*" The Spaniard "is sure" that it was that of an Englishman, but "judges by the intonation" altogether, "*as he has no knowledge of the English.*" The Italian believes it the voice of a Russian, but "*has never conversed with a native of Russia.*" A second Frenchman differs, moreover, with the first, and is positive that the voice was that of an Italian; but, *not being cognisant of that tongue*, is, like the Spaniard, "convinced by the intonation". Now, how strangely unusual must that voice have really been, about which such testimony as this *could* have been elicited! – in whose *tones*, even, denizens of the five great divisions of Europe could recognise nothing familiar! You will say that it might have been the voice of an Asiatic – of an African. Neither Asiatics nor Africans abound in Paris; but, without denying the inference, I will now merely call your attention to three points. The voice is termed by one witness "harsh rather than shrill". It is represented by two others to have been "quick and *unequal*". No words – no sounds resembling words – were by any witness mentioned as distinguishable.

'I know not,' continued Dupin, 'what impression I may have made, so far, upon your own understanding; but I do not hesitate to say that legitimate deductions even from this portion of the testimony – the portion respecting the gruff and shrill voices – are in themselves sufficient to engender a suspicion which should give direction to all further progress in the investigation of the mystery. I said "legitimate deductions"; but my meaning is not thus fully expressed. I designed to imply that the deductions are the *sole* proper ones, and that the suspicion arises *inevitably* from them as the single result. What the suspicion is, however, I will not say just yet. I merely wish you to bear in mind that, with myself, it was sufficiently forcible to give a definite form – a certain tendency – to my enquiries in the chamber.

'Let us now transport ourselves, in fancy, to this chamber. What shall we first seek here? The means of egress employed by the murderers. It is not too much to say that neither of us believe in preternatural events. Mme and Mlle L'Espanaye were not destroyed by spirits. The doers of the deed were material, and escaped materially. Then how? Fortunately, there is but one mode of reasoning upon the point, and that mode *must* lead us to a definite decision. Let us examine, each by each, the possible means of egress. It is clear that the assassins were in the room where Mlle L'Espanaye was found, or at least in the room adjoining, when the party ascended the stairs. It is, then, only from these two apartments that we have to seek issues. The police have laid bare the floors, the ceilings, and the masonry of the walls, in every direction. No *secret* issues could have escaped their vigilance. But, not trusting to *their* eyes, I examined with my own. There were, then, *no* secret issues. Both doors leading from the rooms into the passage were securely locked, with the keys inside. Let us turn to the chimneys. These, although of ordinary width for some eight or ten feet above the hearths, will not admit, throughout their extent, the body of a large cat. The impossibility of egress, by means already stated, being thus absolute, we are reduced to the windows. Through those of the front room no one could have escaped without notice from the crowd in the street. The murderers *must* have passed, then, through those of the back room. Now, brought to this conclusion in so unequivocal a manner as we are, it is not our part, as reasoners, to reject it on account of apparent impossibilities. It is only left for us to prove that these apparent "impossibilities" are, in reality, not such.

'There are two windows in the chamber. One of them is unobstructed by furniture, and is wholly visible. The lower portion of the other is hidden from view by the head of the unwieldy bedstead which is thrust close up against it. The former was found securely fastened from within. It resisted the utmost force of those who endeavoured to raise it. A large gimlet hole had been pierced in its frame to the left, and a very stout nail was found fitted therein, nearly to the head. Upon examining the other window, a similar nail was seen similarly fitted in it; and a vigorous attempt to raise this sash, failed also. The police were now entirely satisfied that egress had not been in these directions. And, *therefore*, it was thought a matter of supererogation to withdraw the nails and open the windows.

'My own examination was somewhat more particular, and was so for the reason I have just given – because here it was, I knew, that all apparent impossibilities *must* be proved to be not such in reality.

'I proceeded to think thus – *a posteriori*. The murderers *did* escape from one of these windows. This being so, they could not have re-fastened the sashes from the inside, as they were found fastened – the consideration which put a stop, through its obviousness, to the scrutiny of the police in this quarter. Yet the sashes *were* fastened. They *must*, then, have the power of fastening themselves. There was no escape from this conclusion. I stepped to the unobstructed casement, withdrew the nail with some difficulty, and attempted to raise the sash. It resisted all my efforts, as I had anticipated. A concealed spring must, I now knew, exist; and this corroboration of my idea convinced me that my premises, at least, were correct, however mysterious still appeared the circumstances attending the nails. A careful search soon brought to light the hidden spring. I pressed it, and, satisfied with the discovery, forbore to upraise the sash.

'I now replaced the nail and regarded it attentively. A person passing out through this window might have reclosed it, and the spring would have caught – but the nail could not have been replaced. The conclusion was plain, and again narrowed in the field of my investigations. The assassins *must* have escaped through the other window. Supposing, then, the springs upon each sash to be the same, as was probable, there *must* be found a difference between the nails, or at least between the modes of their fixture. Getting upon the sacking of the bedstead, I looked over the headboard minutely at the second casement. Passing my hand down behind the board, I readily discovered and pressed the spring, which was, as I had supposed, identical in character with its neighbour. I now looked at the nail. It was as stout as the other, and apparently fitted in the same manner – driven in nearly up to the head.

'You will say that I was puzzled; but, if you think so, you must have misunderstood the nature of the inductions. To use a sporting phrase, I had not been once "at fault". The scent had never for an instant been lost. There was no flaw in any link of the chain. I had traced the secret to its ultimate result – and that result was *the nail*. It had, I say, in every respect, the appearance of its fellow in the other window; but this fact was an absolute nullity (conclusive as it might seem to be) when compared with the consideration that here, at this point, terminated the clue. "There *must* be something wrong," I said, "about the nail." I touched it; and the head, with about a quarter of an inch of the shank, came off in my fingers. The rest of the shank was in the gimlet hole, where it had been broken off. The fracture was an old one (for its edges were incrusted with rust), and had apparently been accomplished by the blow of a hammer, which had partially embedded, in the top of the bottom sash, the head portion of the nail. I now carefully replaced this head portion in the indentation whence I had taken it, and the resemblance to a perfect nail was complete – the fissure was invisible. Pressing the spring, I gently raised the sash for a few inches; the head went up with it, remaining firm in its bed. I closed the window, and the semblance of the whole nail was again perfect.

'The riddle, so far, was now unriddled. The assassin had escaped through the window which looked upon the bed. Dropping of its own accord upon his exit (or perhaps purposely closed), it had become fastened by the spring; and it was the retention of this spring which had been mistaken by the police for that of the nail – further enquiry being thus considered unnecessary.

'The next question is that of the mode of descent. Upon this point I had been satisfied in my walk with you around the building. About five feet and a half from the casement in question there runs a lightning-rod. From this rod it would have been impossible for anyone to reach the window itself, to say nothing of entering it. I observed, however, that the shutters of the fourth storey were of the peculiar kind called by Parisian carpenters *ferrades* – a kind rarely employed at the present day, but frequently seen upon very old mansions at Lyons and Bordeaux. They are in the form of an ordinary door (a single, not a folding door), except that the lower half is latticed or worked in open trellis – thus affording an excellent hold for the hands. In the present instance these shutters are fully three feet and a half broad. When we saw them from the rear of the house, they were both about half open – that is to say, they stood off at right angles from the wall. It is probable that the police, as well as myself, examined the back of the tenement; but, if so, in looking at these *ferrades* in the line of their breadth (as they must have done), they did not perceive this great breadth itself, or, at all events, failed to take it into due consideration. In fact, having once satisfied themselves that no egress could have been made in this quarter, they would naturally bestow here a very cursory examination. It was clear to me, however, that the shutter belonging to the window at the head of the bed, would, if swung fully back to the wall, reach to within two feet of the lightning-rod. It was also evident that, by exertion of a very unusual degree of activity and courage, an entrance into the window, from the rod, might have been thus effected. By reaching to the distance of two feet and a half (we now suppose the shutter open to its whole extent) a robber might have taken a firm grasp upon the trellis-work. Letting go, then, his hold upon the rod, placing his feet securely against the wall, and springing boldly from it, he might have swung the shutter so as to close it, and, if we imagine the window open at the time, might even have swung himself into the room.

'I wish you to bear especially in mind that I have spoken of a *very* unusual degree of activity as requisite to success in so hazardous and so difficult a feat. It is my design to show you, first, that the thing might possibly have been accomplished; but, secondly and *chiefly*, I wish to impress upon your understanding the *very extraordinary* – the almost preternatural character of that agility which could have accomplished it.

'You will say, no doubt, using the language of the law, that "to make out my case", I should rather undervalue, than insist upon a full estimation of the activity required in this matter. This may be the practice in law, but it is not the usage of reason. My ultimate object is only the truth. My immediate purpose is to lead you to place in juxtaposition, that *very unusual* activity of which I have just spoken, with that *very peculiar* shrill (or harsh) and *unequal* voice, about whose nationality no two persons could be found to agree, and in whose utterance no syllabification could be detected.'

At these words a vague and half-formed conception of the meaning of Dupin flitted over my mind. I seemed to be upon the verge of comprehension, without power to comprehend – as men, at times, find themselves upon the brink of remembrance, without being able in the end, to remember. My friend went on with his discourse.

'You will see,' he said, 'that I have shifted the question from the mode of egress to that of ingress. It was my design to convey the idea that both were effected in the same manner, at the same point. Let us now revert to the interior of the room. Let us survey the appearances here. The drawers of the bureau, it is said, had been rifled, although many articles of apparel still remained within them. The conclusion here is absurd. It is a mere guess – a very silly one – and no more. How are we to know that the articles found in the drawers were not all these drawers had originally contained? Mme L'Espanaye and her daughter lived an exceedingly retired life – saw no company – seldom went out – had little use for numerous changes of habiliment. Those found were at least of as good quality as any likely to be possessed by these ladies. If a thief had taken any, why did he not take the best – why did he not take all? In a word, why did he abandon four thousand francs in gold to encumber himself with a bundle of linen? The gold *was* abandoned. Nearly the whole sum mentioned by M. Mignaud, the banker, was discovered, in bags, upon the floor. I wish you, therefore, to discard from your thoughts the blundering idea of *motive*, engendered in the brains of the police by that portion of the evidence which speaks of money delivered at the door of the house. Coincidences ten times as remarkable as this (the delivery of the money, and murder committed within three days upon the party receiving it), happen to all of us every hour of our lives, without attracting even momentary notice. Coincidences, in general, are great stumbling-blocks in the way of that class of thinkers who have been educated to know nothing of the theory of probabilities – that theory to which the most glorious objects of human research are indebted for the most glorious of illustration. In the present instance, had the gold been gone, the fact of its delivery three days before would have formed something more than a coincidence. It would have been corroborative of this idea of motive. But, under the real circumstances of the case, if we are to suppose gold the motive of this outrage, we must also imagine the perpetrator so vacillating an idiot as to have abandoned his gold and his motive together.

'Keeping now steadily in mind the points to which I have drawn your attention – that peculiar voice, that unusual agility, and that startling absence of motive in a murder so singularly atrocious as this – let us glance at the butchery itself. Here is a woman strangled to death by manual strength, and thrust up a chimney, head downward. Ordinary assassins employ no such modes of murder as this. Least of all, do they thus dispose of the murdered. In the manner of thrusting the corpse up the chimney, you will admit that there was something *excessively outré* – something altogether irreconcilable with our common notions of human action, even when we suppose the actors the most depraved of men. Think, too, how great must have been that strength which could have thrust the body *up* such an aperture so forcibly that the united vigour of several persons was found barely sufficient to drag it *down!*

'Turn, now, to other indications of the employment of a vigour most marvellous. On the hearth were thick tresses – very thick tresses – of grey human hair. These had been torn out by the roots. You are aware of the great force necessary in tearing thus from the head even twenty or thirty hairs together. You saw the locks in question as well as myself. Their roots (a hideous sight!) were clotted with fragments of the flesh of the scalp – sure token of the prodigious power which had been exerted in uprooting perhaps half a million of hairs at a time. The throat of the old lady was not merely cut, but the head absolutely severed from the body: the instrument was a mere razor. I wish you also to look at the *brutal* ferocity of these deeds. Of the bruises upon the body of Mme L'Espanaye I do not speak. M. Dumas, and his worthy coadjutor M. Etienne, have pronounced that they were inflicted by some obtuse instrument; and so far these gentlemen are very correct. The obtuse instrument was clearly the stone pavement in the yard, upon which the victim had fallen from the window which looked in upon the bed. This idea, however simple it may now seem, escaped the police for the same reason that the breadth of the shutters escaped them – because, by the affair of the nails, their perceptions had been hermetically sealed against the possibility of the windows having ever been opened at all.

'If now, in addition to all these things, you have properly reflected upon the odd disorder of the chamber, we have gone so far as to combine the ideas of an agility astounding, a strength superhuman, a ferocity brutal, a butchery without motive, a *grotesquerie* in horror absolutely alien from humanity, and a voice foreign in tone to the ears of men of many nations, and devoid of all distinct or intelligible syllabification. What result, then, has ensued? What impression have I made upon your fancy?'

I felt a creeping of the flesh as Dupin asked me the question. 'A madman,' I said, 'has done this deed – some raving maniac escaped from a neighbouring *Maison de Santé*.'

'In some respects,' he replied, 'your idea is not irrelevant. But the voices of madmen, even in their wildest paroxysms, are never found to tally with that peculiar voice heard upon the stairs. Madmen are of some nation, and their language, however incoherent in its words, has always the coherence of syllabification. Besides, the hair of a madman is not such as I now hold in my hand. I disentangled this little tuft from the rigidly clutched fingers of Mme L'Espanaye. Tell me what you can make of it.'

'Dupin,' I said, completely unnerved; 'this hair is most unusual – this is no *human* hair.'

'I have not asserted that it is,' said he; 'but, before we decide this point, I wish you to glance at the little sketch I have here traced upon this paper. It is a *facsimile* drawing of what has been described in one portion of the testimony as "dark bruises, and deep indentations of finger nails", upon the throat of Mlle L'Espanaye, and in another (by Messrs Dumas and Etienne), as a "series of livid spots, evidently the impression of fingers".

'You will perceive,' continued my friend, spreading out the paper upon the table before us, 'that this drawing gives the idea of a firm and fixed hold. There is no *slipping* apparent. Each finger has retained – possibly until the death of the victim – the fearful grasp by which it originally embedded itself. Attempt, now, to place all your fingers, at the same time, in the respective impressions as you see them.'

I made the attempt in vain.

'We are possibly not giving this matter a fair trial,' he said. 'The paper is spread out upon a plane surface; but the human throat is cylindrical. Here is a billet of wood, the circumference of which is about that of the throat. Wrap the drawing round it, and try the experiment again.'

I did so; but the difficulty was even more obvious than before. 'This,' I said, 'is the mark of no human hand.'

'Read now,' replied Dupin, 'this passage from Cuvier.'

It was a minute anatomical and generally descriptive account of the large fulvous orang-utan of the East Indian Islands. The gigantic stature, the prodigious strength and activity, the wild ferocity, and the imitative propensities of these mammalia are sufficiently well known to all. I understood the full horrors of the murder at once.

'The description of the digits,' said I, as I made an end of reading, 'is in exact accordance with this drawing. I see that no animal but an orang-utan, of the species here mentioned, could have impressed the indentations, as you have traced them. This tuft of tawny hair, too, is identical in character with that of the beast of Cuvier. But I cannot possibly comprehend the particulars of this frightful mystery. Besides, there were *two* voices heard in contention, and one of them was unquestionably the voice of a Frenchman.'

'True; and you will remember an expression attributed almost unanimously, by the evidence, to this voice – the expression "*Mon Dieu!*" This, under the circumstances, has been justly characterised by one of the witnesses (Montani, the confectioner) as an expression of remonstrance or expostulation. Upon these two words, therefore, I have mainly built my hopes of a full solution of the riddle. A Frenchman was cognisant of the murder. It is possible – indeed it is far more than probable – that he was innocent of all participation in the bloody transactions which took place. The orang-utan may have escaped from him. He may have traced it to the chamber; but, under the agitating circumstances which ensued, he could never have re-captured it. It is still at large. I will not pursue these guesses – for I have no right to call them more – since the shades of reflection upon which they are based are scarcely of sufficient depth to be appreciable to my own intellect, and since I could not pretend to make them intelligible to the understanding of another. We will call them guesses, then, and speak of them as such. If the Frenchman in question is indeed, as I suppose, innocent of this atrocity, this advertisement, which I left last night, upon our return home, at the office of *Le Monde* (a paper devoted to the shipping interest, and much sought by sailors), will bring him to our residence.'

He handed me a paper, and I read thus:

> 'CAUGHT – In the Bois de Boulogne, early in the morning of the — inst. [the morning of the murder], a very large, tawny orang-utan of the Bornese species. The owner (who is ascertained to be a sailor, belonging to a Maltese vessel), may have the animal again, upon identifying it satisfactorily, and paying a few charges arising from its capture and keeping. Call at No. —, Rue —, Faubourg St Germain – au troisième.

'How was it possible,' I asked, 'that you should know the man to be a sailor, and belonging to a Maltese vessel?'

'I do *not* know it,' said Dupin. 'I am not *sure* of it. Here, however, is a small piece of ribbon, which from its form, and from its greasy appearance, has evidently been used in tying the hair in one of those long *queues* of which sailors are so fond. Moreover, this knot is one which few besides sailors can tie, and is peculiar to the Maltese. I picked the ribbon up at the foot of the lightning-rod. It could not have belonged to either of the deceased. Now if, after all, I am wrong in my induction from this ribbon, that the Frenchman was a sailor belonging to a Maltese vessel, still I can have done no harm in saying what I did in the advertisement. If I am in error, he will merely suppose that I have been misled by some circumstance into which he will not take the trouble to enquire. But if I am right, a great point is gained. Cognisant although innocent of the murder, the Frenchman will naturally hesitate about replying to the advertisement – about demanding the orang-utan. He will reason thus: "I am innocent; I am poor; my orang-utan is of great value – to one in my circumstances a fortune of itself – why should I lose it through idle apprehensions of danger? Here it is within my grasp. It was found in the Bois de Boulogne – at a vast distance from the scene of that butchery. How can it ever be suspected that a brute beast should have done the deed? The police are at fault – they have failed to procure the slightest clue. Should they even trace the animal, it would be impossible to prove me cognisant of the murder, or to implicate me in guilt on account of that cognisance. Above all, *I am known*. The advertiser designates me as the possessor of the beast. I am not sure to what limit his knowledge may extend. Should I avoid claiming a property of so great value, which it is known that I possess, I will render the animal at least liable to suspicion. It is not my policy to attract attention either to myself or to the beast. I will answer the advertisement, get the orang-utan, and keep it close until this matter has blown over."'

At this moment we heard a step upon the stairs.

'Be ready,' said Dupin, 'with your pistols, but neither use them nor show them until at a signal from myself.'

The front door of the house had been left open, and the visitor had entered, without ringing, and advanced several steps upon the staircase. Now, however, he seemed to hesitate. Presently we heard him descending. Dupin was moving quickly to the door, when we again heard him coming up. He did not turn back a second time, but stepped up with decision, and rapped at the door of our chamber.

'Come in,' said Dupin, in a cheerful and hearty tone.

A man entered. He was a sailor, evidently – a tall, stout, and muscular-looking person, with a certain daredevil expression of countenance, not altogether unprepossessing. His face, greatly sunburnt, was more than half hidden by whisker and mustachio. He had with him a huge oaken cudgel, but appeared to be otherwise unarmed. He bowed awkwardly, and bade us 'good-evening', in French accents, which, although somewhat Neufchatelish, were still sufficiently indicative of a Parisian origin.

'Sit down, my friend,' said Dupin. 'I suppose you have called about the orang-utan. Upon my word, I almost envy you the possession of him; a remarkably fine, and no doubt a very valuable animal. How old do you suppose him to be?'

The sailor drew a long breath, with the air of a man relieved of some intolerable burden, and then replied, in an assured tone –

'I have no way of telling – but he can't be more than four or five years old. Have you got him here?'

'Oh no; we had no conveniences for keeping him here. He is at a livery stable in the Rue Dubourg, just by. You can get him in the morning. Of course you are prepared to identify the property?'

'To be sure I am, sir.'

'I shall be sorry to part with him,' said Dupin.

'I don't mean that you should be at all this trouble for nothing, sir,' said the man. 'Couldn't expect it. Am very willing to pay a reward for the finding of the animal – that is to say, anything in reason.'

'Well,' replied my friend, 'that is all very fair, to be sure. Let me think! – what should I have? Oh! I will tell you. My reward shall be this. You shall give me all the information in your power about these murders in the Rue Morgue.'

Dupin said the last words in a very low tone, and very quietly. Just as quietly, too, he walked toward the door, locked it, and put the key in his pocket. He then drew a pistol from his bosom, and placed it, without the least flurry, upon the table.

The sailor's face flushed up as if he were struggling with suffocation. He started to his feet and grasped his cudgel; but the next moment he fell back into his seat, trembling violently, and with the countenance of death itself. He spoke not a word. I pitied him from the bottom of my heart.

'My friend,' said Dupin, in a kind tone, 'you are alarming yourself unnecessarily – you are indeed. We mean you no harm whatever. I pledge you the honour of a gentleman, and of a Frenchman, that we intend you no injury. I perfectly well know that you are innocent of the atrocities in the Rue Morgue. It will not do, however, to deny that you are in some measure implicated in them. From what I have already said, you must know that I have had means of information about this matter – means of which you could never have dreamed. Now the thing stands thus. You have done nothing which you could have avoided – nothing, certainly, which renders you culpable. You were not even guilty of robbery, when you might have robbed with impunity. You have nothing to conceal. You have no reason for concealment. On the other hand, you are bound by every principle of honour to confess all you know. An innocent man is now imprisoned, charged with that crime of which you can point out the perpetrator.'

The sailor had recovered his presence of mind, in a great measure, while Dupin uttered these words; but his original boldness of bearing was all gone.

'So help me God,' said he, after a brief pause, 'I *will* tell you all I know about this affair; but I do not expect you to believe one half I say – I would be a fool indeed if I did. Still, I *am* innocent, and I will make a clean breast if I die for it.'

What he stated was, in substance, this. He had lately made a voyage to the Indian Archipelago. A party, of which he formed one, landed at Borneo, and passed into the interior on an excursion of pleasure. Himself and a companion had captured the orang-utan. This companion dying, the animal fell into his own exclusive possession. After great

GNASHING ITS TEETH, AND FLASHING FIRE FROM ITS EYES,
IT FLEW UPON THE BODY OF THE GIRL

trouble, occasioned by the intractable ferocity of his captive during the home voyage, he at length succeeded in lodging it safely at his own residence in Paris, where, not to attract toward himself the unpleasant curiosity of his neighbours, he kept it carefully secluded, until such time as it should recover from a wound in the foot, received from a splinter on board ship. His ultimate design was to sell it.

Returning home from some sailors' frolic on the night, or rather in the morning of the murder, he found the beast occupying his own bedroom, into which it had broken from a closet adjoining, where it had been, as was thought, securely confined. Razor in hand, and fully lathered, it was sitting before a looking-glass, attempting the operation of shaving, in which it had no doubt previously watched its master through the keyhole of the closet. Terrified at the sight of so dangerous a weapon in the possession of an animal so ferocious, and so well able to use it, the man, for some moments, was at a loss what to do. He had been accustomed, however, to quiet the creature, even in its fiercest moods, by the use of a whip, and to this he now resorted. Upon sight of it, the orang-utan sprang at once through the door of the chamber, down the stairs, and thence, through a window, unfortunately open, into the street.

The Frenchman followed in despair; the ape, razor still in hand, occasionally stopping to look back and gesticulate at its pursuer, until the latter had nearly come up with it. It then again made off. In this manner the chase continued for a long time. The streets were profoundly quiet, as it was nearly three o'clock in the morning. In passing down an alley in the rear of the Rue Morgue, the fugitive's attention was arrested by a light gleaming from the open window of Mme L'Espanaye's chamber, in the fourth storey of her house. Rushing to the building, it perceived the lightning-rod, clambered up with inconceivable agility, grasped the shutter, which was thrown fully back against the wall, and, by its means, swung itself directly upon the headboard of the bed. The whole feat did not occupy a minute. The shutter was kicked open again by the orang-utan as it entered the room.

The sailor, in the meantime, was both rejoiced and perplexed. He had strong hopes of now recapturing the brute, as it could scarcely escape from the trap into which it had ventured, except by the rod, where it might be intercepted as it came down. On the other hand, there was much cause for anxiety as to what it might do in the house. This latter reflection urged the man still to follow the fugitive. A lightning-rod is ascended without difficulty, especially by a sailor; but, when he had arrived as high as the window, which lay far to his left, his career was stopped; the most that he could accomplish was to reach over so as to obtain a glimpse of the interior of the room. At this glimpse he nearly fell from his hold through excess of horror. Now it was that those hideous shrieks arose upon the night, which had startled from slumber the inmates of the Rue Morgue. Mme L'Espanaye and her daughter, habited in their night clothes, had apparently been occupied in arranging some papers in the iron chest already mentioned, which had been wheeled into the middle of the room. It was open, and its contents lay beside it on the floor. The victims must have been sitting with their backs toward the window; and, from the time elapsing between the ingress of the beast and the screams, it seems probable that it was not immediately perceived. The flapping-to of the shutter would naturally have been attributed to the wind.

As the sailor looked in, the gigantic animal had seized Mme L'Espanaye by the hair (which was loose, as she had been combing it), and was flourishing the razor about her face, in imitation of the motions of a barber. The daughter lay prostrate and motionless; she had swooned. The screams and struggles of the old lady (during which the hair was torn from her head) had the effect of changing the probably pacific purposes of the orang-utan into those of wrath. With one determined sweep of its muscular arm it nearly severed her head from her body. The sight of blood inflamed its anger into frenzy. Gnashing its teeth, and flashing fire from its eyes, it flew upon the body of the girl, and embedded its fearful talons in her throat, retaining its grasp until she expired. Its wandering and wild glances fell at this moment upon the head of the bed, over which the face of its master, rigid with horror, was just discernible. The fury of the beast, who no doubt bore still in mind the dreaded whip, was instantly converted into fear. Conscious of having deserved punishment, it seemed desirous of concealing its bloody deeds, and skipped about the chamber in an agony of nervous agitation; throwing down and breaking the furniture as it moved, and dragging the bed from the bedstead. In conclusion, it seized first the corpse of the daughter, and thrust it up the chimney, as it was found; then that of the old lady, which it immediately hurled through the window headlong.

As the ape approached the casement with its mutilated burden, the sailor shrank aghast to the rod, and rather gliding than clambering down it, hurried at once home – dreading the consequences of the butchery, and gladly abandoning, in his terror, all solicitude about the fate of the orang-utan. The words heard by the party upon the staircase were the Frenchman's exclamations of horror and affright, commingled with the fiendish jabberings of the brute.

I have scarcely anything to add. The orang-utan must have escaped from the chamber, by the rod, just before the breaking of the door. It must have closed the window as it passed through it. It was subsequently caught by the owner himself, who obtained for it a very large sum at the *Jardin des Plantes*. Le Bon was instantly released upon our narration of the circumstances (with some comments from Dupin) at the bureau of the Prefect of Police. This functionary, however well disposed to my friend, could not altogether conceal his chagrin at the turn which affairs had taken, and was fain to indulge in a sarcasm or two, about the propriety of every person minding his own business.

'Let him talk,' said Dupin, who had not thought it necessary to reply. 'Let him discourse; it will ease his conscience. I am satisfied with having defeated him in his own castle. Nevertheless, that he failed in the solution of this mystery is by no means that matter for wonder which he supposes it; for, in truth, our friend the prefect is somewhat too cunning to be profound. In his wisdom is no *stamen*. It is all head and no body, like the pictures of the goddess Laverna – or, at best, all head and shoulders, like a codfish. But he is a good creature after all. I like him especially for one masterstroke of cant, by which he has attained his reputation for ingenuity. I mean the way he has *"de nier ce qui est, et d'expliquer ce qui n'est pas."*'

The Mystery of Marie Rogêt

A sequel to 'The Murders in the Rue Morgue'

Es giebt eine Reihe idealischer Begebenheiten, die der Wirklichkeit parallel lauft. Selten fallen sie zusammen. Menschen und Zufälle modificiren gewöhnlich die idealische Begebenheit, so dass sie unvollkommen erscheint, und ihre Folgen gleichfalls unvollkommen sind. So bei der Reformation; statt des Protestantismus kam das Lutherthum hervor.

There are ideal series of events which run parallel with the real ones. They rarely coincide. Men and circumstances generally modify the ideal train of events, so that it seems imperfect, and its consequences are equally imperfect. Thus with the Reformation; instead of Protestantism came Lutheranism.

NOVALIS (the *nom de plume* of von Hardenberg)
Moral Ansichten

There are few persons, even amongst the calmest thinkers, who have not occasionally been startled into a vague yet thrilling half-credence in the supernatural, by *coincidences* of so seemingly marvellous a character that, as *mere* coincidences, the intellect has been unable to receive them. Such sentiments – for the half credences of which I speak have never the full force of *thought* – such sentiments are seldom thoroughly stifled unless by reference to the doctrine of chance, or, as it is technically termed, the calculus of probabilities. Now this calculus is, in its essence, purely mathematical; and thus we have the anomaly of the most rigidly exact in science applied to the shadow and spirituality of the most intangible in speculation.

The extraordinary details which I am now called upon to make public, will be found to form, as regards sequence of time, the primary branch of a series of scarcely intelligible *coincidences*, whose secondary or concluding branch will be recognised by all readers in the late murder of MARY CECILIA ROGERS, at New York.

When, in an article entitled 'The Murders in the Rue Morgue', I endeavoured, about a year ago, to depict some very remarkable features in the mental character of my friend, the Chevalier C. Auguste Dupin, it did not occur to me that I should ever resume the subject. The depicting of character constituted my design; and this design was thoroughly fulfilled in the wild train of circumstances brought to instance Dupin's idiosyncrasy. I might have adduced other examples, but I should have proven no more. Late events, however, in their surprising development, have startled me into some further details, which will carry with them the air of extorted confession. Hearing what I have lately heard, it would be indeed strange should I remain silent in regard to what I both heard and saw so long ago.

Upon the winding up of the tragedy involved in the deaths of Mme L'Espanaye and her daughter, the Chevalier dismissed the affair at once from his attention, and relapsed into his old habits of moody reverie. Prone, at all times, to abstraction, I readily fell in with his humour; and continuing to occupy our chambers in the Faubourg Saint Germain, we gave the future to the winds, and slumbered tranquilly in the present, weaving the dull world around us into dreams.

But these dreams were not altogether uninterrupted. It may readily be supposed that the part played by my friend, in the drama at the Rue Morgue, had not failed of its impression upon the fancies of the Parisian police. With its emissaries, the name of Dupin had grown into a household word. The simple character of those inductions by which he had disentangled the mystery never having been explained even to the Prefect, or to any other individual than myself, of course it is not surprising that the affair was regarded as little less than miraculous, or that the Chevalier's analytical abilities acquired for him the credit of intuition. His frankness would have led him to disabuse every enquirer of such prejudice; but his indolent humour forbade all further agitation of a topic whose interest to himself had long ceased. It thus happened that he found himself the cynosure of the policial eyes; and the cases were not few in which attempt was made to engage his services at the prefecture. One of the most remarkable instances was that of the murder of a young girl named Marie Rogêt.

This event occurred about two years after the atrocity in the Rue Morgue. Marie, whose Christian and family name will at once arrest attention from their resemblance to those of the unfortunate 'cigar-girl', was the only daughter of the widow Estelle Rogêt. The father had died during the child's infancy, and from the period of his death, until within eighteen months before the assassination which forms the subject of our narrative, the mother and daughter had dwelt together in the Rue Pavée St Andrée; Madame there keeping a *pension*, assisted by Marie. Affairs went on thus until the latter had attained her twenty-second year, when her great beauty attracted the notice of a perfumer, who occupied one of the shops in the basement of the Palais Royal, and whose custom lay chiefly among the desperate adventurers infesting that neighbourhood. M. Le Blanc was not unaware of the advantages to be derived from the attendance of the fair Marie in his perfumery; and his liberal proposals were accepted eagerly by the girl, although with somewhat more of hesitation by Madame.

The anticipations of the shopkeeper were realised, and his rooms soon became notorious through the charms of the sprightly *grisette*. She had been in his employ about a year, when her admirers were thrown into confusion by her sudden disappearance from the shop. M. Le Blanc was unable to account for her absence, and Mme Rogêt was distracted with anxiety and terror. The public papers immediately took up the theme, and the police were upon the point of making serious investigations, when, one fine morning, after the lapse of a week, Marie, in good health, but with a somewhat saddened air, made her reappearance at her usual counter in the perfumery. All enquiry, except that of a private character, was of course immediately hushed. M. Le Blanc professed total ignorance, as before. Marie, with Madame, replied to all questions, that the last week had been spent at the house of a relation in the country. Thus the affair died away, and was generally forgotten; for the girl, ostensibly to relieve herself from the impertinence of curiosity, soon bade a final adieu to the perfumer, and sought the shelter of her mother's residence in the Rue Pavée St Andrée.

It was about five months after this return home, that her friends were alarmed by her sudden disappearance for the second time. Three days elapsed, and nothing was heard of her. On the fourth her corpse was found floating in the Seine, near the shore which is opposite the Quartier of the Rue Saint Andrée, and at a point not very far distant from the secluded neighbourhood of the Barrière du Roule.

The atrocity of this murder (for it was at once evident that murder had been committed), the youth and beauty of the victim, and, above all, her previous notoriety, conspired to produce intense excitement in the minds of the sensitive Parisians. I can call to mind no similar occurrence producing so general and so intense an effect. For several weeks, in the discussion of this one absorbing theme, even the momentous political topics of the day were forgotten. The Prefect made unusual exertions; and the powers of the whole Parisian police were, of course, tasked to the utmost extent.

Upon the first discovery of the corpse, it was not supposed that the murderer would be able to elude, for more than a very brief period, the inquisition which was immediately set on foot. It was not until the expiration of a week that it was deemed necessary to offer a reward; and even then this reward was limited to a thousand francs. In the meantime the investigation proceeded with vigour, if not always with judgement, and numerous individuals were examined to no purpose; while, owing to the continual absence of all clue to the mystery, the popular excitement greatly increased. At the end of the tenth day it was thought advisable to double the sum originally proposed; and, at length, the second week having elapsed without leading to any discoveries, and the prejudice which always exists in Paris against the police having given vent to itself in several serious *émeutes*, the Prefect took it upon himself to offer the sum of twenty thousand francs 'for the conviction of the assassin', or, if more than one should prove to have been implicated, 'for the conviction of any one of the assassins'. In the proclamation setting forth this reward, a full pardon was promised to any accomplice who should come forward in evidence against his fellow; and to the whole was appended, wherever it appeared, the private placard of a committee of citizens, offering ten thousand francs, in addition to the amount proposed by the prefecture. The entire reward thus stood at no less than thirty thousand francs, which will be regarded as an extraordinary sum when we consider the humble condition of the girl, and the great frequency, in large cities, of such atrocities as the one described.

No one doubted now that the mystery of this murder would be immediately brought to light. But although, in one or two instances, arrests were made which promised elucidation, yet nothing was elicited which could implicate the parties suspected; and they were discharged forthwith. Strange as it may appear, the third week from the discovery of the body had passed, and passed without any light being thrown upon the subject, before even a rumour of the events which had so agitated the public mind reached the ears of Dupin and myself. Engaged in researches which had absorbed our whole attention, it had been nearly a month since either of us had gone abroad, or received a visitor, or more than glanced at the leading political articles in one of the daily papers. The first intelligence of the murder was brought us by G—, in person. He called upon us early in the afternoon of the 13th of July 18—, and remained with us until late in the night. He had been piqued by the failure of all his endeavours to ferret out the assassins. His reputation – so he said, with a peculiarly Parisian air – was at stake. Even his honour was concerned. The eyes of the public were upon him; and there was really no sacrifice which he would not be willing to make for the development of the mystery. He concluded a somewhat droll speech with a compliment upon what he was pleased to term the *tact* of Dupin, and made him a direct, and certainly a liberal proposition, the precise nature of which I do not feel myself at liberty to disclose, but which has no bearing upon the proper subject of my narrative.

The compliment my friend rebutted as best he could, but the proposition he accepted at once, although its advantages were altogether provisional. This point being settled, the Prefect broke forth at once into explanations of his own views, interspersing them with long comments upon the evidence; of which latter we were not yet in possession. He discoursed much, and beyond doubt learnedly; while I hazarded an occasional suggestion as the night wore drowsily away. Dupin, sitting steadily in his accustomed armchair, was the embodiment of respectful attention. He wore spectacles during the whole interview; and an occasional glance beneath their green glasses sufficed to convince me that he slept not the less soundly, because silently, throughout the seven or eight leaden-footed hours which immediately preceded the departure of the Prefect.

In the morning I procured, at the prefecture, a full report of all the evidence elicited, and, at the various newspaper offices, a copy of every paper in which, from first to last, had been published any decisive information in regard to this sad affair. Freed from all that was positively disproved, this mass of information stood thus:

Marie Rogêt left the residence of her mother, in the Rue Pavée St Andrée, about nine o'clock in the morning of Sunday, June the 22nd, 18 —. In going out she gave notice to a M. Jacques St Eustache, and to him only, of her intention to spend the day with an aunt who resided in the Rue des Drômes. The Rue des Drômes is a short and narrow but populous thoroughfare, not far from the banks of the river, and at a distance of some two miles, in the most direct course possible from the *pension* of Mme Rogêt. St Eustache was the accepted suitor of Marie, and lodged, as well as took his meals, at the *pension*. He was to have gone for his betrothed at dusk, and to have escorted her home. In the afternoon, however, it came on to rain heavily; and, supposing that she would remain all night at her aunt's (as she had done under similar circumstances before), he did not think it necessary to keep his promise. As night drew on, Mme Rogêt (who was an infirm old lady, seventy years of age) was heard to express a fear 'that she should never see Marie again'; but this observation attracted little attention at the time.

On Monday, it was ascertained that the girl had not been to the Rue des Drômes; and when the day elapsed without tidings of her, a tardy search was instituted at several points in the city and its environs. It was not, however, until the fourth day from the period of her disappearance that anything satisfactory was ascertained respecting her. On this day (Wednesday, the 25th of June), a M. Beauvais, who, with a friend, had been making enquiries for Marie near the Barrière du Roule, on the shore of the Seine which is opposite the Rue Pavée St Andrée, was informed that a corpse had just been towed ashore by some fishermen, who had found it floating in the river. Upon seeing the body, Beauvais, after some hesitation, identified it as that of the perfumery girl. His friend recognised it more promptly.

The face was suffused with dark blood, some of which issued from the mouth. No foam was seen, as in the case of the merely drowned. There was no discoloration in the cellular tissue. About the throat were bruises and impressions of fingers. The arms were bent over on the chest, and were rigid. The right hand was clenched; the left partially open. On the left wrist were two circular excoriations, apparently the effect of ropes, or of a rope in more than one volution. A part of the right wrist, also, was much chafed, as well as the back throughout its extent, but more especially at the shoulder-blades. In bringing the body to the shore the fishermen had attached to it a rope, but none of the excoriations had been effected by this. The flesh of the neck was much swollen. There were no cuts apparent, or bruises which appeared the effect of blows. A piece of lace was found tied so tightly around the neck as to be hidden from sight; it was completely buried in the flesh, and was fastened by a knot which lay just under the left ear. This alone would have sufficed to produce death. The medical testimony spoke confidently of the virtuous character of the deceased. She had been subjected, it said, to brutal violence. The corpse was in such condition when found that there could have been no difficulty in its recognition by friends.

The dress was much torn and otherwise disordered. In the outer garment, a slip, about a foot wide, had been torn upward from the bottom hem to the waist, but not torn off. It was wound three times around the waist, and secured by a sort of hitch in the back. The dress immediately beneath the frock was of fine muslin; and from this a slip eighteen inches wide had been torn entirely out – torn very evenly and with great care. It was found around her neck, fitting loosely, and secured with a hard knot. Over this muslin slip and the slip of lace, the strings of a bonnet were attached, the bonnet being appended. The knot by which the strings of the bonnet were fastened, was not a lady's, but a slip or sailor's knot.

After the recognition of the corpse, it was not, as usual, taken to the Morgue (this formality being superfluous), but hastily interred not far from the spot at which it was brought ashore. Through the exertions of Beauvais the matter was industriously hushed up, as far as possible; and several days had elapsed before any public emotion resulted. A weekly paper, however, at length took up the theme; the corpse was disinterred, and a re-examination instituted; but nothing was elicited beyond what has been already noted. The clothes, however, were now submitted to the mother and friends of the deceased, and fully identified as those worn by the girl upon leaving home.

Meantime, the excitement increased hourly. Several individuals were arrested and discharged. St Eustache fell especially under suspicion; and he failed, at first, to give an intelligible account of his whereabouts during the Sunday on which Marie left home. Subsequently, however, he submitted to M. G— affidavits, accounting satisfactorily for every hour of the day in question. As time passed and no discovery ensued, a thousand contradictory rumours were circulated, and journalists busied themselves in *suggestions*. Among these, the one which attracted the most notice, was the idea that Marie Rogêt still lived – that the corpse found in the Seine was that of some other unfortunate. It will be proper that I submit to the reader some passages which embody the suggestion alluded to. These passages are *literal* translations from *L'Etoile*, a paper conducted, in general, with much ability:

'Mlle Rogêt left her mother's house on Sunday morning, June the 22nd, 18—, with the ostensible purpose of going to see her aunt, or some other connection, in the Rue des Drômes. From that hour nobody is proved to have seen her. There is no trace or tidings of her at all ... There has no person, whatever, come forward, so far, who saw her at all, on that day, after she left her mother's door ... Now, though we have no evidence that Marie Rogêt was in the land of the living after nine o'clock on Sunday, June the 22nd, we have proof that, up to that hour, she was alive. On Wednesday noon, at twelve, a female body was discovered afloat on the shore of the Barrière du Roule. This was, even if we presume that Marie Rogêt was thrown into the river within three hours after she left her mother's house, only three days from the time she left her home – three days to an hour. But it is folly to suppose that the murder, if murder was committed on her body, could have been consummated soon enough to have enabled her murderers to throw the body into the river before midnight. Those who are guilty of such horrid crimes, choose darkness rather than light ... Thus we see that if the body found in the river *was* that of Marie Rogêt, it could only have been in the water two and a half days, or three at the outside. All experience has shown that drowned bodies, or bodies thrown into the water immediately after death by violence, require from six to ten days for sufficient decomposition to take place to bring them to the top of the water. Even where a cannon is fired over a corpse, and it rises before at least five or six day's immersion, it sinks again, if let alone. Now, we ask, what was there in this case to cause a departure from the ordinary course of nature? ... If the body had been kept in its mangled state on shore until Tuesday night, some trace would be found on shore of the murderers. It is a doubtful point, also, whether the body would be so soon afloat, even were it thrown in after having been dead two days. And, furthermore, it is exceedingly improbable that any villains who had committed such a murder as is here supposed, would have thrown the body in without weight to sink it, when such a precaution could have so easily been taken.'

The editor here proceeds to argue that the body must have been in the water 'not three days merely, but, at least, five times three days', because it was so far decomposed that Beauvais had great difficulty in recognising it. This latter point, however, was fully disproved. I continue the translation:

'What, then, are the facts on which M. Beauvais says that he has no doubt the body was that of Marie Rogêt? He ripped up the gown sleeve, and says he found marks which satisfied him of the identity. The public generally supposed those marks to have consisted of some description of scars. He rubbed the arm and found *hair* upon it – something as indefinite, we think, as can readily be imagined – as little conclusive as finding an arm in the sleeve. M. Beauvais did not return that night, but sent word to Mme Rogêt, at seven o'clock on Wednesday evening, that an investigation was still in progress respecting her daughter. If we allow that Mme Rogêt, from her age and grief, could not go over (which is allowing a great deal), there certainly must have been someone who would have thought it worth while to go over and attend the investigation, if they thought the body was that of Marie. Nobody went over. There was nothing said or heard about the matter in the Rue Pavée St Andrée, that reached even the occupants of the same building. M. St Eustache, the lover and intended husband of Marie, who boarded in her mother's house, deposes that he did not hear of the discovery of the body of his intended until the next morning, when M. Beauvais came into his chamber and told him of it. For an item of news like this, it strikes us it was very coolly received.'

In this way the journal endeavoured to create the impression of an apathy on the part of the relatives of Marie, inconsistent with the supposition that these relatives believed the corpse to be hers. Its insinuations amount to this – that Marie, with the connivance of her friends, had absented herself from the city for reasons involving a charge against her chastity; and that these friends, upon the discovery of a corpse in the Seine, somewhat resembling that of the girl, had availed themselves of the opportunity to impress the public with the belief of her death. But *L'Etoile* was again over-hasty. It was distinctly proved that no apathy, such as was imagined, existed; that the old lady was exceedingly feeble, and so agitated as to be unable to attend to any duty; that St Eustache, so far from receiving the news coolly, was distracted with grief, and bore himself so frantically, that M. Beauvais prevailed upon a friend and relative to take charge of him, and prevent his attending the examination at the disinterment. Moreover, although it was stated by *L'Etoile* that the corpse was reinterred at the public expense – that an advantageous offer of private sepulture was absolutely declined by the family – and that no member of the family attended the ceremonial – although, I say, all this was asserted by *L'Etoile* in furtherance of the impression it designed to convey – yet *all* this was satisfactorily disproved. In a subsequent number of the paper an attempt was made to throw suspicion upon Beauvais himself. The editor says:

'Now, then, a change comes over the matter. We are told that, on one occasion, while a Mme B— was at Mme Rogêt's house, M. Beauvais, who was going out, told her that a gendarme was expected there, and that she, Mme B., must not say anything to the gendarme until he returned, but let the matter be for him ... In the present posture of affairs, M. Beauvais appears to have the whole matter locked up in his head. A single step cannot be taken without M. Beauvais; for, go which way you will, you run against him ... For some reason, he determined that nobody shall have anything to do with the proceedings but himself, and he has elbowed the male relatives out of the way, according to their representations, in a very singular manner. He seems to have been very much averse to permitting the relatives to see the body.'

By the following fact, some colour was given to the suspicion thus thrown upon Beauvais. A visitor at his office, a few days prior to the girl's disappearance, and during the absence of its occupant, had observed *a rose* in the keyhole of the door, and the name *'Marie'* inscribed upon a slate which hung near at hand.

The general impression, so far as we were enabled to glean it from the newspapers, seemed to be, that Marie had been the victim of *a gang* of desperadoes – that by these she had been borne across the river, maltreated and murdered. *Le Commerciel*, however, a print of extensive influence, was earnest in combating this popular idea. I quote a passage or two from its columns:

'We are persuaded that pursuit has hitherto been on a false scent, so far as it has been directed to the Barrière du Roule. It is impossible that a person so well known to thousands as this young woman was, should have passed three blocks without someone having seen her; and anyone who saw her would have remembered it, for she interested all who knew her. It was when the streets were full of people, when she went out ... It is impossible that she could have gone to the Barrière du Roule, or to the Rue des Drômes, without being recognised by a dozen persons; yet no one has come forward who saw her outside of her mother's door, and there is no evidence, except the testimony concerning her expressed intentions, that she did go out at all. Her gown was torn, bound round her, and tied; and by that the body was carried as a bundle. If the murder had been committed at the Barrière du Roule, there would have been no necessity for any such arrangement. The fact that the body was found floating near the Barrière, is no proof as to where it was thrown into the water ... A piece of one of the unfortunate girl's petticoats, two feet long and one foot wide, was torn out and tied under her chin around the back of her head, probably to prevent screams. This was done by fellows who had no pocket-handkerchief.'

A day or two before the prefect called upon us, however, some important information reached the police, which seemed to overthrow, at least, the chief portion of *Le Commerciel's* argument. Two small boys, sons of a Mme Deluc, while roaming among the woods near the Barrière du Roule, chanced to penetrate a close thicket, within which were three or four large stones, forming a kind of seat, with a back and footstool. On the upper stone lay a white petticoat; on the second a silk scarf. A parasol, gloves, and a pocket-handkerchief were also here found. The handkerchief bore the name 'Marie Rogêt'. Fragments of dress were discovered on the brambles around. The earth was trampled, the bushes were broken, and there was every evidence of a struggle. Between the thicket and the river, the fences were found taken down, and the ground bore evidence of some heavy burden having been dragged along it.

A weekly paper, *Le Soleil*, had the following comments upon this discovery – comments which merely echoed the sentiment of the whole Parisian press:

'The things had all evidently been there at least three or four weeks; they were all mildewed down hard with the action of the rain, and stuck together from mildew. The grass had grown around and over some of them. The silk on the parasol was strong, but the threads of it were run together within. The upper part, where it had been doubled and folded, was all mildewed and rotten, and tore on its being opened ... The pieces of her frock torn out by the bushes were about three inches wide and six inches long. One part was the hem of the frock, and it had been mended; the other piece was part of the skirt, not the hem. They looked like strips torn off, and were on the thorn bush, about a foot from the ground ... There can be no doubt, therefore, that the spot of this appalling outrage has been discovered.'

Consequent upon this discovery, new evidence appeared. Mme Deluc testified that she keeps a roadside inn not far from the bank of the river, opposite the Barrière du Roule. The neighbourhood is secluded – particularly so. It is the usual Sunday resort of blackguards from the city, who cross the river in boats. About three o'clock, in the afternoon of the Sunday in question, a young girl arrived at the inn, accompanied by a young man of dark complexion. The two remained here for some time. On their departure, they took the road to some thick woods in the vicinity. Mme Deluc's attention was called to the dress worn by the girl on account of its resemblance to one worn by a deceased relative. A scarf was particularly noticed. Soon after the departure of the couple, a gang of miscreants made their appearance, behaved boisterously, ate and drank without making payment, followed in the route of the young man and girl, returned to the inn about dusk, and recrossed the river as if in great haste.

It was soon after dark, upon this same evening, that Mme Deluc, as well as her eldest son, heard the screams of a female in the vicinity of the inn. The screams were violent but brief. Mme D. recognised not only the scarf which was found in the thicket, but the dress which was discovered upon the corpse. An omnibus-driver, Valence, now also testified that he saw Marie Rogêt cross a ferry on the Seine, on the Sunday in question, in company with a young man of dark complexion. He, Valence, knew Marie, and could not be mistaken in her identity. The articles found in the thicket were fully identified by the relatives of Marie.

The items of evidence and information thus collected by myself, from the newspapers, at the suggestion of Dupin, embraced only one more point – but this was a point of seemingly vast consequence. It appears that, immediately after the discovery of the clothes as above described, the lifeless, or nearly lifeless body of St Eustache, Marie's betrothed, was found in the vicinity of what all now supposed the scene of the outrage. A phial labelled 'laudanum', and emptied, was found near him. His breath gave evidence of the poison. He died without speaking. Upon his person was found a letter, briefly stating his love for Marie, with his design of self-destruction.

'I need scarcely tell you,' said Dupin, as he finished the perusal of my notes, 'that this is a far more intricate case than that of the Rue Morgue; from which it differs in one important respect. This is an *ordinary*, although an atrocious instance of crime. There is nothing peculiarly *outré* about it. You will observe that, for this reason, the mystery has been considered easy, when, for this reason, it should have been considered difficult of solution. Thus, at first, it was thought unnecessary to offer a reward. The myrmidons of G— were able at once to comprehend how and why such an atrocity *might have been* committed. They could picture to their imaginations a mode – many modes – and a motive – many motives; and because it was not impossible that either of these numerous modes and motives *could* have been the actual one, they have taken it for granted that one of them *must*. But the ease with which these variable fancies were entertained, and the very plausibility which each assumed, should have been understood as indicative rather of the difficulties than of the facilities which must attend elucidation. I have before observed that it is by prominences above the plane of the ordinary, that reason feels her way, if at all, in her search for the true, and that the proper question in cases such as this, is not so much "what has occurred?" as "what has occurred that has never occurred before?" In the investigations at the house of Mme L'Espanaye, the agents of G— were discouraged and confounded by that very *unusualness* which, to a properly regulated intellect, would have afforded the surest omen of success; while this same intellect might have been plunged in despair at the ordinary character of all that met the eye in the case of the perfumery girl, and yet told of nothing but easy triumph to the functionaries of the prefecture.

'In the case of Mme L'Espanaye and her daughter, there was, even at the beginning of our investigation, no doubt that murder had been committed. The idea of suicide was excluded at once. Here, too, we are freed, at the commencement, from all supposition of self-murder. The body found at the Barrière du Roule, was found under such circumstances as to leave us no room for embarrassment upon this important point. But it has been suggested that the corpse discovered is not that of the Marie Rogêt for the conviction of whose assassin, or assassins, the reward is offered, and respecting whom, solely, our agreement has been arranged with the Prefect. We both know this gentleman well. It will not do to trust him too far. If, dating our enquiries from the body found, and thence tracing a murderer, we yet discover this body to be that of some other individual than Marie; or if, starting from the living Marie, we find her, yet find her unassassinated – in either case we lose our labour; since it is M. G— with whom we have to deal. For our own purpose, therefore, if not for the purpose of justice, it is indispensable that our first step should be the determination of the identity of the corpse with the Marie Rogêt who is missing.

'With the public the arguments of *L'Etoile* have had weight; and that the journal itself is convinced of their importance would appear from the manner in which it commences one of its essays upon the subject: "Several of the morning papers of the day," it says, "speak of the *conclusive* article in Monday's *Etoile*." To me, this article appears conclusive of little beyond the zeal of its inditer. We should bear in mind that, in general, it is the object of our newspapers rather to create a sensation – to make a point – than to further the cause of truth. The latter end is only pursued when it seems coincident with the former. The print which merely falls in with ordinary opinion (however well-founded this opinion may be) earns for itself no credit with the mob. The mass of the people regard as profound only him who suggests *pungent contradictions* of the general idea. In ratiocination, not less than in literature, it is the *epigram* which is the most immediately and the most universally appreciated. In both, it is of the lowest order of merit.

'What I mean to say is, that it is the mingled epigram and melodrama of the idea that Marie Rogêt still lives, rather than any true plausibility in this idea, which have suggested it to *L'Etoile*, and secured it a favourable reception with the public. Let us examine the heads of this journal's argument; endeavouring to avoid the incoherence with which it is originally set forth.

'The first aim of the writer is to show, from the brevity of the interval between Marie's disappearance and the finding of the floating corpse, that this corpse cannot be that of Marie. The reduction of this interval to its smallest possible dimension, becomes thus, at once, an object with the reasoner. In the rash pursuit of this object, he rushes into mere assumption at the outset. "It is folly to suppose," he says, "that the murder, if murder was committed on her body, could have been consummated soon enough to have enabled her murderers to throw the body into the river before midnight." We demand at once, and very naturally, *why?* Why is it folly to suppose that the murder was committed *within five minutes* after the girl's quitting her mother's house? Why is it folly to suppose that the murder was committed at any given period of the day? There have been assassinations at all hours. But, had the murder taken place at any moment between nine o'clock in the morning of Sunday, and a quarter before midnight, there would still have been time enough "to throw the body into the river before midnight". This assumption, then, amounts precisely to this – that the murder was not committed on Sunday at all – and, if we allow *L'Etoile* to assume this, we may permit it any liberties whatever. The paragraph beginning "It is folly to suppose that the murder," &c., however it appears as printed in *L'Etoile*, may be imagined to have existed actually *thus* in the brain of its inditer: "It is folly to suppose that the murder, if murder was committed on the body, could have been committed soon enough to have enabled her murderers to throw the body into the river before midnight; it is folly, we say, to suppose all this, and to suppose at the same time (as we are resolved to suppose), that the body was *not* thrown in until *after* midnight" – a sentence sufficiently inconsequential in itself, but not so utterly preposterous as the one printed.

'Were it my purpose,' continued Dupin, 'merely to *make out a case* against this passage of *L'Etoile*'s argument, I might safely leave it where it is. It is not, however, with *L'Etoile* that we have to do, but with the truth. The sentence in question has but one meaning, as it stands; and this meaning I have fairly stated: but it is material that we go behind the mere words for an idea which these words have obviously intended, and failed to convey. It was the design of the journalist to say that, at whatever period of the day or night of Sunday this murder was committed, it was improbable that the assassins would have ventured to bear the corpse to the river before midnight. And herein lies, really, the assumption of which I complain. It is assumed that the murder was committed at such a position, and under such circumstances that *the bearing it* to the river became necessary. Now, the assassination might have taken place upon the river's brink, or on the river itself; and, thus, the throwing the corpse in the water might have been resorted to, at any period of the day or night, as the most obvious and most immediate mode of disposal. You will understand that I suggest nothing here as probable, or as coincident with my own opinion. My design, so far, has no reference to the facts of the case. I wish merely to caution you against the whole tone of *L'Etoile*'s *suggestion*, by calling your attention to its *ex parte* character at the outset.

'Having prescribed thus a limit to suit its own preconceived notions; having assumed that, if this were the body of Marie, it could have been in the water but a very brief time; the journal goes on to say:

' "All experience has shown that drowned bodies, or bodies thrown into the water immediately after death by violence, require from six to ten days for sufficient decomposition to take place to bring them to the top of the water. Even when a cannon is fired over a corpse, and it rises before at least five or six days' immersion, it sinks again if let alone."

'These assertions have been tacitly received by every paper in Paris, with the exception of *Le Moniteur*. This latter print endeavours to combat that portion of the paragraph which has reference to "drowned bodies" only, by citing some five or six instances in which the bodies of individuals known to be drowned were found floating after the lapse of less time than is insisted upon by *L'Etoile*. But there is something excessively unphilosophical in the attempt on the part of *Le Moniteur*, to rebut the general assertion of *L'Etoile*, by a citation of particular instances militating against that assertion. Had it been possible to adduce fifty instead of five examples of bodies found floating at the end of two or three days, these fifty examples could still have been properly regarded only as exceptions to *L'Etoile*'s rule, until such time as the rule itself should be confuted. Admitting the rule (and this *Le Moniteur* does not deny, insisting merely upon its exceptions), the argument of *L'Etoile* is suffered to remain in full force; for this argument does not pretend to involve more than a question of the probability of the body having risen to the surface in less than three days; and this probability will be in favour of *L'Etoile*'s position until the instances so childishly adduced shall be sufficient in number to establish an antagonistical rule.

'You will see at once that all argument upon this head should be urged, if at all, against the rule itself, and for this end we must examine the *rationale* of the rule. Now the human body, in general, is neither much lighter nor much heavier than the water of the Seine; that is to say, the specific gravity of the human body, in its natural condition, is about equal to the bulk of fresh water which it displaces. The bodies of fat and fleshy persons, with small bones, and of women generally, are lighter than those of the lean and large-boned, and of men; and the specific gravity of the water of a river is somewhat influenced by the presence of the tide from sea. But, leaving this tide out of the question, it may be said that *very* few human bodies will sink at all, even in fresh water, *of their own accord*. Almost anyone, falling into a river, will be enabled to float, if he suffer the specific gravity of the water fairly to be adduced in comparison with his own – that is to say, if he suffer his whole person to be immersed with as little exception as possible. The proper position for one who cannot swim, is the upright position of the walker on land, with the head thrown fully back, and immersed; the mouth and nostrils alone remaining above the surface. Thus circumstanced, we shall find that we float without difficulty and without exertion. It is evident, however, that the gravities of the body, and of the bulk of water displaced, are very nicely balanced, and that a trifle will cause either to preponderate. An arm, for instance, uplifted from the water, and thus deprived of its support, is an additional weight sufficient to immerse the whole head, while the accidental aid of the smallest piece of timber will enable us to elevate the head so as to look about. Now, in the struggles of one unused to swimming, the arms are invariably thrown upwards, while an attempt is made to keep the head in its usual perpendicular position. The result is the immersion of the mouth and nostrils, and the inception, during efforts to breathe while beneath the surface, of water into the lungs. Much is also received into the stomach, and the whole body becomes heavier by the difference between the weight of the air originally distending these cavities, and that of the fluid which now fills them. This difference is sufficient to cause the body to sink, as a general rule; but it is insufficient in the cases of individuals with small bones and an abnormal quantity of flaccid or fatty matter. Such individuals float even after drowning.

'The corpse, being supposed at the bottom of the river, will there remain until, by some means, its specific gravity again becomes less than that of the bulk of water which it displaces. This effect is brought about by decomposition, or otherwise. The result of decomposition is the generation of gas, distending the cellular tissues and all the cavities, and giving the *puffed* appearance which is so horrible. When this distension has so far progressed that the bulk of the corpse is materially increased without a corresponding increase of *mass* or weight, its specific gravity becomes less than that of the water displaced, and it forthwith makes its appearance at the surface. But decomposition is modified by innumerable circumstances – is hastened or retarded by innumerable agencies; for example, by the heat or cold of the season, by the mineral impregnation or purity of the water, by its depth or shallowness, by its currency or stagnation, by the temperament of the body, by its infection or freedom from disease before death. Thus it is evident that we can assign no period, with anything like accuracy, at which the corpse shall rise through decomposition. Under certain conditions this result would be brought about within an hour; under others, it might not take place at all. There are chemical infusions by which the animal frame can be preserved *for ever* from corruption; the bi-chloride of mercury is one. But, apart from decomposition, there may be, and very usually is, generation of gas within the stomach, from the acetous fermentation of vegetable matter (or within other cavities from other causes) sufficient to induce a distension which will bring the body to the surface. The effect produced by the firing of a cannon is that of simple vibration. This may either loosen the corpse from the soft mud or ooze in which it is embedded, thus permitting it to rise when other agencies have already prepared it for so doing; or it may overcome the tenacity of some putrescent portions of the cellular tissue, allowing the cavities to distend under the influence of the gas.

'Having thus before us the whole philosophy of this subject, we can easily test by it the assertions of *L'Etoile*. "All experience shows," says this paper, "that drowned bodies, or bodies thrown into the water immediately after death by violence, require from six to ten days for sufficient decomposition to take place to bring them to the top of the water. Even when a cannon is fired over a corpse, and it rises before at least five or six days' immersion, it sinks again if let alone."

'The whole of this paragraph must now appear a tissue of inconsequence and incoherence. All experience does *not* show that "drowned bodies" *require* from six to ten days for sufficient decomposition to take place to bring them to the surface. Both science and experience show that the period of their rising is, and necessarily must be, indeterminate. If, moreover, a body has risen to the surface through firing of cannon, it will *not* "sink again if let alone", until decomposition has so far progressed as to permit the escape of the generated gas. But I wish to call your attention to the distinction which is made between "drowned bodies", and "bodies thrown into the water immediately after death by violence." Although the writer admits the distinction, he yet includes them all in the same category. I have shown how it is that the body of a drowning man becomes specifically heavier than its bulk of water, and that he would not sink at all, except for the struggles by which he elevates his arms above the surface, and his gasps for breath while beneath the surface – gasps which supply by water the place of the original air in the lungs. But these struggles and these gasps would not occur in the body "thrown into the water immediately after death by violence". Thus, in the latter instance, *the body, as a general rule, would not sink at all* – a fact of which *L'Etoile* is evidently ignorant. When decomposition had proceeded to a very great extent – when the flesh had in a great measure left the bones – then, indeed, but not *till* then, should we lose sight of the corpse.

'And now what are we to make of the argument, that the body found could not be that of Marie Rogêt, because three days only having elapsed, the body was found floating? If drowned, being a woman, she might never have sunk; or having sunk, might have reappeared in twenty-four hours, or less. But no one supposes her to have been drowned; and, dying before being thrown into the river, she might have been found floating at any period afterwards whatever.

' "But," says *L'Etoile*, "if the body had been kept in its mangled state on shore until Tuesday night, some trace would be found on shore of the murderers." Here it is at first difficult to perceive the intention of the reasoner. He means to anticipate what he imagines would be an objection to his theory – viz., that the body was kept on shore two days, suffering rapid decomposition – *more* rapid than if immersed in water. He supposes that, had this been the case, it *might* have appeared at the surface on the Wednesday, and thinks that *only* under such circumstances it could so have appeared. He is accordingly in haste to show that it *was not* kept on shore; for, if so, "some trace would be found on shore of the murderers." I presume you smile at the *sequitur*. You cannot be made to see how the mere *duration* of the corpse on the shore could operate to *multiply traces* of the assassins. Nor can I.

' "And furthermore, it is exceedingly improbable," continues our journal, "that any villains who had committed such a murder as is here supposed, would have thrown the body in without weight to sink it, when such a precaution could have so easily been taken." Observe, here, the laughable confusion of thought! No one – not even *L'Etoile* – disputes the murder committed *on the body found*. The marks of violence are too obvious. It is our reasoner's object merely to show that this body is not Marie's. He wishes to prove that *Marie* is not assassinated – not that the corpse was not. Yet his observation proves only the latter point. Here is a corpse without weight attached. Murderers, casting it in, would not have failed to attach a weight. Therefore it was not thrown in by murderers. This is all which is proved, if anything is. The question of identity is not even approached, and *L'Etoile* has been at great pains merely to gainsay now what it has admitted only a moment before. "We are perfectly convinced," it says, "that the body found was that of the murdered female."

'Nor is this the sole instance, even in this division of his subject, where our reasoner unwittingly reasons against himself. His evident object, I have already said, is to reduce, as much as possible, the interval between Marie's disappearance and the finding of the corpse. Yet we find him *urging* the point that no person saw the girl from the moment of her leaving her mother's house. "We have no evidence," he says, "that Marie Rogêt was in the land of the living after nine o'clock on Sunday, June the 22nd." As his argument is obviously an *ex parte* one, he should, at least, have left this matter out of sight; for had anyone been known to see Marie, say on Monday, or on Tuesday, the interval in question would have been much reduced, and, by his own ratiocination, the probability much diminished of the corpse being that of the *grisette*. It is, nevertheless, amusing to observe that *L'Etoile* insists upon its point in the full belief of its furthering its general argument.

'Re-peruse now that portion of this argument which has reference to the identification of the corpse by Beauvais. In regard to the *hair* upon the arm, *L'Etoile* has been obviously disingenuous. M. Beauvais, not being an idiot, could never have urged, in identification of the corpse, simply *hair upon its arm*. No arm is *without* hair. The *generality* of the expression of *L'Etoile* is a mere perversion of the witness's phraseology. He must have spoken of some *peculiarity* in this hair. It must have been a peculiarity of colour, of quantity, of length, or of situation.

' "Her foot," says the journal, "was small – so are thousands of feet. Her garter is no proof whatever – nor is her shoe – for shoes and garters are sold in packages. The same may be said of the flowers in her hat. One thing upon which M. Beauvais strongly insists is, that the clasp on the garter found had been set back to take it in. This amounts to nothing; for most women find it proper to take a pair of garters home and fit them to the size of the limbs they are to encircle, rather than to try them in the store where they purchase." Here it is difficult to suppose the reasoner in earnest. Had M. Beauvais, in his search for the body of Marie, discovered a corpse corresponding in general size and appearance to the missing girl, he would have been warranted (without reference to the question of habiliment at all) in forming an opinion that his search had been successful. If, in addition to the point of general size and contour, he had found upon the arm a peculiar hairy appearance which he had observed upon the living Marie, his opinion might have been justly strengthened; and the increase of positiveness might well have been in the ratio of the peculiarity, or unusualness, of the hairy mark. If, the feet of Marie being small, those of the corpse were also small, the increase of probability that the body was that of Marie would not be an increase in a ratio merely arithmetical, but in one highly geometrical, or accumulative. Add to all this, shoes such as she had been known to wear upon the day of her disappearance, and, although these shoes may be "sold in packages", you so far augment the probability as to verge upon the certain. What, of itself, would be no evidence of identity, becomes through its corroborative position, proof most sure. Give us, then, flowers in the hat corresponding to those worn by the missing girl, and we seek for nothing further. If only *one* flower, we seek for nothing further – what then if two or three, or more? Each successive one is multiple evidence – proof not *added* to proof, but *multiplied* by hundreds or thousands. Let us now discover, upon the deceased, garters such as the living used, and it is almost folly to proceed. But these garters are found to be tightened, by the setting back of a clasp, in just such a manner as her own had been tightened by Marie shortly previous to her leaving home. It is now madness or hypocrisy to doubt. What *L'Etoile* says in respect to this abbreviation of the garters being an usual occurrence, shows nothing beyond its own pertinacity in error. The elastic nature of the clasp-garter is self-demonstration of the *unusualness* of the abbreviation. What is made to adjust itself, must of necessity require foreign adjustment but rarely. It must have been by an accident, in its strictest sense, that these garters of Marie needed the tightening described. They alone would have amply established her identity. But it is not that the corpse was found to have the garters of the missing girl, or found to have her shoes, or her bonnet, or the flowers of her bonnet, or her feet, or a peculiar mark upon the arm, or her general size and appearance – it is that the corpse had each and *all collectively*. Could it be proved that the editor of *L'Etoile really* entertained a doubt, under the circumstances, there would be no need, in his case, of a commission *de lunatico inquirendo*. He has thought it sagacious to echo the small-talk of the lawyers, who, for the most part, content themselves with echoing the rectangular precepts of the courts. I would here observe that very much of what is rejected as evidence by a court, is the best of evidence to the intellect. For the court, guiding itself by the general principles of evidence – the recognised and *booked* principles – is averse from swerving at particular instances. And this steadfast adherence to principle, with rigorous disregard of the conflicting exception, is a sure mode of attaining the *maximum* of attainable truth, in any long sequence of time. The practice, *en masse*, is therefore philosophical; but it is not the less certain that it engenders vast individual error.

'In respect to the insinuations levelled at Beauvais, you will be willing to dismiss them in a breath. You have already fathomed the true character of this good gentleman. He is a *busybody*, with much of romance and little of wit. Anyone so constituted will readily so conduct himself, upon occasion of *real* excitement, as to render himself liable to suspicion on the part of the over-acute, or the ill-disposed. M. Beauvais (as it appears from your notes) had some personal interviews with the editor of *L'Etoile*, and offended him by venturing an opinion that the corpse, notwithstanding the theory of the editor, was, in sober fact, that of Marie. "He persists," says the paper, "in asserting the corpse to be that of Marie, but cannot give a circumstance, in addition to those which we have commented upon, to make others believe." Now, without re-adverting to the fact that stronger evidence "to make others believe", could *never* have been adduced, it may be remarked that a man may very well be understood to believe, in a case of this kind, without the ability to advance a single reason for the belief of a second party. Nothing is more vague than impressions of individual identity. Each man recognises his neighbour, yet there are few instances in which anyone is prepared *to give a reason* for his recognition. The editor of *L'Etoile* had no right to be offended at M. Beauvais' unreasoning belief.

'The suspicious circumstances which invest him will be found to tally much better with my hypothesis of *romantic busybodyism*, than with the reasoner's suggestion of guilt. Once adopting the more charitable interpretation, we shall find no difficulty in comprehending the rose in the keyhole; the "Marie" upon the slate; the "elbowing the male relatives out of the way"; the "aversion to permitting them to see the body"; the caution given to Mme B—, that she must hold no conversation with the gendarme until his return (Beauvais'); and, lastly, his apparent determination "that nobody should have anything to do with the proceedings except himself". It seems to me unquestionable that Beauvais was a suitor of Marie's; that she coquetted with him; and that he was ambitious of being thought to enjoy her fullest intimacy and confidence. I shall say nothing more upon this point; and, as the evidence fully rebuts the assertion of *L'Etoile*, touching the matter of *apathy* on the part of the mother and other relatives – an apathy inconsistent with the supposition of their believing the corpse to be that of the perfumery girl – we shall now proceed as if the question of *identity* were settled to our perfect satisfaction.'

'And what,' I here demanded, 'do you think of the opinions of *Le Commerciel?*'

'That, in spirit, they are far more worthy of attention than any which have been promulgated upon the subject. The deductions from the premises are philosophical and acute; but the premises, in two instances at least, are founded in imperfect observation. *Le Commerciel* wishes to intimate that Marie was seized by some gang of low ruffians not far from her mother's door. "It is impossible," it urges, "that a person so well known to thousands as this young woman was, should have passed three blocks without someone having seen her." This is the idea of a man long resident in Paris – a public man – and one whose walks to and fro in the city have been mostly limited to the vicinity of the public offices. He is aware that *he* seldom passes so far as a dozen blocks from his own bureau, without being recognised and accosted. And, knowing the extent of his personal acquaintance with others, and of others with him, he compares his notoriety with that of the perfumery girl, finds no great difference between them, and reaches at once the conclusion that she, in her walks, would be equally liable to recognition with himself in his. This could only be the case were her walks of the same unvarying, methodical character, and within the same *species* of limited region as are his own. He passes to and fro, at regular intervals, within a confined periphery, abounding in individuals who are led to observation of his person through interest in the kindred nature of his occupation with their own. But the walks of Marie may, in general, be supposed discursive. In this particular instance, it will be understood as most probable, that she proceeded upon a route of more than average diversity from her accustomed ones. The parallel which we imagine to have existed in the mind of *Le Commerciel* would only be sustained in the event of the two individuals traversing the whole city. In this case, granting the personal acquaintances to be equal, the chances would be also equal that an equal number of personal rencounters would be made. For my own part, I should hold it not only as possible, but as very far more than probable, that Marie might have proceeded, at any given period, by any one of the many routes between her own residence and that of her aunt, without meeting a single individual whom she knew, or by whom she was known. In viewing this question in its full and proper light, we must hold steadily in mind the great disproportion between the personal acquaintances of even the most noted individual in Paris, and the entire population of Paris itself.

'But whatever force there may still appear to be in the suggestion of *Le Commerciel*, will be much diminished when we take into consideration *the hour* at which the girl went abroad. "It was when the streets were full of people," says *Le Commerciel*, "that she went out." But not so. It was at nine o'clock in the morning. Now at nine o'clock of every morning in the week, *with the exception of Sunday*, the streets of the city are, it is true, thronged with people. At nine on Sunday, the populace are chiefly within doors *preparing for church*. No observing person can have failed to notice the peculiarly deserted air of the town, from about eight until ten on the morning of every Sabbath. Between ten and eleven the streets are thronged, but not at so early a period as that designated.

'There is another point at which there seems a deficiency of *observation* on the part of *Le Commerciel*. "A piece," it says, "of one of the unfortunate girl's petticoats, two feet long, and one foot wide, was torn out and tied under her chin, and around the back of her head, probably to prevent screams.

This was done by fellows who had no pocket-handkerchiefs." Whether this idea is, or is not well founded, we will endeavour to see hereafter; but by "fellows who have no pocket-handkerchiefs", the editor intends the lowest class of ruffians. These, however, are the very description of people who will always be found to have handkerchiefs even when destitute of shirts. You must have had occasion to observe how absolutely indispensable, of late years, to the thorough blackguard, has become the pocket-handkerchief.'

'And what are we to think,' I asked, 'of the article in *Le Soleil?*'

'That it is a vast pity its inditer was not born a parrot – in which case he would have been the most illustrious parrot of his race. He has merely repeated the individual items of the already published opinion; collecting them, with a laudable industry, from this paper and from that. "The things had all *evidently* been there," he says, "at least three or four weeks, and there can be *no doubt* that the spot of this appalling outrage has been discovered." The facts here restated by *Le Soleil*, are very far indeed from removing my own doubts upon this subject, and we will examine them more particularly hereafter in connection with another division of the theme.

'At present we must occupy ourselves with other investigations. You cannot fail to have remarked the extreme laxity of the examination of the corpse. To be sure the question of identity was readily determined, or should have been; but there were other points to be ascertained. Had the body been in any respect *despoiled?* Had the deceased any articles of jewellery about her person upon leaving home? If so, had she any when found? These are important questions utterly untouched by the evidence; and there are others of equal moment, which have met with no attention. We must endeavour to satisfy ourselves by personal enquiry. The case of St Eustache must be re-examined. I have no suspicion of this person; but let us proceed methodically. We will ascertain beyond a doubt the validity of the affidavits in regard to his whereabouts on the Sunday. Affidavits of this character are readily made matter of mystification. Should there be nothing wrong here, however, we will dismiss St Eustache from our investigations. His suicide, however corroborative of suspicion, were there found to be deceit in the affidavits, is, without such deceit, in no respect an unaccountable circumstance, or one which need cause us to deflect from the line of ordinary analysis.

'In that which I now propose, we will discard the interior points of this tragedy, and concentrate our attention upon its outskirts. Not the least usual error, in investigations such as this, is the limiting of enquiry to the immediate, with total disregard of the collateral or circumstantial events. It is the malpractice of the courts to confine evidence and discussion to the bounds of apparent relevancy. Yet experience has shown, and a true philosophy will always show, that a vast, perhaps the larger portion of truth, arises from the seemingly irrelevant. It is through the spirit of this principle, if not precisely through its letter, that modern science resolved to *calculate upon the unforeseen*. But perhaps you do not comprehend me. The history of human knowledge has so uninterruptedly shown that to collateral, or incidental, or accidental events we are indebted for the most numerous and most valuable discoveries, that it has at length become necessary, in any prospective view of improvement, to make not only large, but the largest allowances for inventions that shall arise by chance, and quite out of the range of ordinary expectation. It is no longer philosophical to base, upon what has been, a vision of what is to be. *Accident* is admitted as a portion of the substructure. We make chance a matter of absolute calculation. We subject the unlooked-for and unimagined, to the mathematical formulae of the schools.

'I repeat that it is no more than fact, that the *larger* portion of all truth has sprung from the collateral; and it is but in accordance with the spirit of the principle involved in this fact, that I would divert enquiry, in the present case, from the trodden and hitherto unfruitful ground of the event itself, to the contemporary circumstances which surround it. While you ascertain the validity of the affidavits, I will examine the newspapers more generally than you have as yet done. So far, we have only reconnoitred the field of investigation; but it will be strange indeed if a comprehensive survey, such as I propose, of the public prints, will not afford us some minute points which shall establish a *direction* for enquiry.'

In pursuance of Dupin's suggestions, I made scrupulous examination of the affair of the affidavits. The result was a firm conviction of their validity, and of the consequent innocence of St Eustache. In the meantime my friend occupied himself, with what seemed to me a minuteness altogether objectless, in a scrutiny of the various newspaper files. At the end of a week he placed before me the following extracts:

'About three years and a half ago, a disturbance very similar to the present was caused by the disappearance of this same Marie Rogêt, from the *parfumerie* of M. Le Blanc in the Palais Royal. At the end of a week, however, she reappeared at her customary *comptoir*, as well as ever, with the exception of a slight paleness not altogether usual. It was given out by M. Le Blanc and her mother, that she had merely been on a visit to some friend in the country; and the affair was speedily hushed up. We presume that the present absence is a freak of the same nature, and that, at the expiration of a week, or perhaps of a month, we shall have her among us again.' – *Evening Paper*, Monday, June 23.

'An evening journal of yesterday, refers to a former mysterious disappearance of Mlle Rogêt. It is well known that, during the week of her absence from Le Blanc's *parfumerie*, she was in the company of a young naval officer, much noted for his debaucheries. A quarrel, it is supposed, providentially led to her return home. We have the name of the Lothario in question, who is, at present, stationed in Paris, but, for obvious reasons, forbear to make it public.' – *Le Mercurie*, Tuesday morning, June 24.

'An outrage of the most atrocious character was perpetrated near this city the day before yesterday. A gentleman, with his wife and daughter, engaged about dusk the services of six young men, who were idly rowing a boat to and fro near the banks of the Seine, to convey him across the river. Upon reaching the opposite shore, the three passengers stepped out, and had proceeded so far as to be beyond the view of the boat, when the daughter discovered that she had left in it her parasol. She returned for it, was seized by the gang, carried out into the stream, gagged, brutally treated, and finally taken to the shore at a point not far from that at which she had originally entered the boat with her parents. The villains have escaped for the time, but the police are upon their trail, and some of them will soon be taken.' – *Morning Paper*, June 25.

'We have received one or two communications, the object of which is to fasten the crime of the late atrocity upon Mennais; but as this gentleman has been fully exonerated by a legal enquiry, and as the arguments of our several correspondents appear to be more zealous than profound, we do not think it advisable to make them public.' – *Morning Paper*, June 28.

'We have received several forcibly written communications, apparently from various sources, and which go far to render it a matter of certainty that the unfortunate Marie Rogêt has become a victim of one of the numerous bands of blackguards which infest the vicinity of the city upon Sunday. Our own opinion is decidedly in favour of this supposition. We shall endeavour to make room for some of these arguments hereafter.' – *Evening Paper*, June 30.

'On Monday, one of the bargemen connected with the revenue service, saw an empty boat floating down the Seine. Sails were lying in the bottom of the boat. The bargemen towed it under the barge office. The next morning it was taken from thence, without the knowledge of any of the officers. The rudder is now at the barge office.' – *Le Diligence*, Thursday, June 26.

Upon reading these various extracts, they not only seemed to me irrelevant, but I could perceive no mode in which any one of them could be brought to bear upon the matter in hand. I waited for some explanation from Dupin.

'It is not my present design,' he said, 'to *dwell* upon the first and second of these extracts. I have copied them chiefly to show you the extreme remissness of the police, who, as far as I can understand from the Prefect, have not troubled themselves, in any respect, with an examination of the naval officer alluded to. Yet it is mere folly to say that between the first and second disappearance of Marie, there is no *supposable* connection. Let us admit the first elopement to have resulted in a quarrel between the lovers, and the return home of the betrayed. We are now prepared to view a second *elopement* (if we *know* that an elopement has again taken place) as indicating a renewal of the betrayer's advances, rather than as the result of new proposals by a second individual – we are prepared to regard it as a "making up" of the old amour, rather than as the commencement of a new one. The chances are ten to one, that he who had once eloped with Marie, would again propose an elopement, rather than that she to whom proposals of elopement had been made by one individual, should have them made to her by another. And here let me call your attention to the fact, that the time elapsing between the first ascertained, and the second supposed elopement, is a few months more than the general period of the cruises of our men-of-war. Had the lover been interrupted in his first villainy by the necessity of departure to sea, and had he seized the first moment of his return to renew the base designs not yet altogether accomplished – or not yet altogether accomplished *by him?* Of all these things we know nothing.

'You will say, however, that, in the second instance, there was *no* elopement as imagined. Certainly not – but are we prepared to say that there was not the frustrated design? Beyond St Eustache, and perhaps Beauvais, we find no recognised, no open, no honourable suitors of Marie. Of none other is there anything said. Who, then, is the secret lover, of whom the relatives (*at least most of them*) know nothing, but whom Marie meets upon the morning of Sunday, and who is so deeply in her confidence, that she hesitates not to remain with him until the shades of the evening descend, amid the solitary groves of the Barrière du Roule? Who is that secret lover, I ask, of whom, at least, *most* of the relatives know nothing? And what means the singular prophecy of Mme Rogêt on the morning of Marie's departure – "I fear that I shall never see Marie again"?

'But if we cannot imagine Mme Rogêt privy to the design of elopement, may we not at least suppose this design entertained by the girl? Upon quitting home, she gave it to be understood that she was about to visit her aunt in the Rue des Drômes, and St Eustache was requested to call for her at dark. Now, at first glance, this fact strongly militates against my suggestion; but let us reflect. That she *did* meet some companion, and proceed with him across the river, reaching the Barrière du Roule at so late an hour as three o'clock in the afternoon, is known. But in consenting so to accompany this individual (*for whatever purpose – to her mother known or unknown*), she must have thought of her expressed intention when leaving home, and of the surprise and suspicion aroused in the bosom of her affianced suitor, St Eustache, when, calling for her at the hour appointed, in the Rue des Drômes, he should find that she had not been there, and when, moreover, upon returning to the *pension* with this alarming intelligence, he should become aware of her continued absence from home. She must have thought of these things, I say. She must have foreseen the chagrin of St Eustache, the suspicion of all. She could not have thought of returning to brave this suspicion; but the suspicion becomes a point of trivial importance to her, if we suppose her *not* intending to return.

'We may imagine her thinking thus – "I am to meet a certain person for the purpose of elopement, or for certain other purposes known only to myself. It is necessary that there be no chance of interruption – there must be sufficient time given us to elude pursuit – I will give it to be understood that I shall visit and spend the day with my aunt at the Rue des Drômes – I will tell St Eustache not to call for me until dark – in this way, my absence from home for the longest possible period, without causing suspicion or anxiety, will be accounted for, and I shall gain more time than in any other manner. If I bid St Eustache call for me at dark, he will be sure not to call before; but, if I wholly neglect to bid him call, my time for escape will be diminished, since it will be expected that I return the earlier, and my absence will the sooner excite anxiety. Now, if it were my design to return *at all* – if I had in contemplation merely a stroll with the individual in question – it would not be my policy to bid St Eustache call; for, calling he will be *sure* to ascertain that I have played him false – a fact of which I might keep him for ever in ignorance, by leaving home without notifying him of my intention, by returning before dark, and by then stating that I had been to visit my aunt in the Rue des Drômes. But, as it is my design *never* to return – or not for some weeks – or not until certain concealments are effected – the gaining of time is the only point about which I need give myself any concern."

'You have observed, in your notes, that the most general opinion in relation to this sad affair is, and was from the first, that the girl had been the victim of *a gang* of blackguards. Now, the popular opinion, under certain conditions, is not to be disregarded. When arising of itself – when manifesting itself in a strictly spontaneous manner – we should look upon it as analogous with that *intuition* which is the idiosyncrasy of the individual man of genius. In ninety-nine cases from the hundred I would abide by its decision. But it is important that we find no palpable traces of *suggestion*. The opinion must be rigorously *the public's own*; and the distinction is often exceedingly difficult to perceive and to maintain. In the present instance, it appears to me that this "public opinion", in respect to a *gang*, has been superinduced by the collateral event which is detailed in the third of my extracts. All Paris is excited by the discovered corpse of Marie, a girl young, beautiful, and notorious. This corpse is found, bearing marks of violence, and floating in the river. But it is now made known that, at the very period, or about the very period, in which it is supposed that the girl was assassinated, an outrage similar in nature to that endured by the deceased, although less in extent, was perpetrated, by a gang of young ruffians, upon the person of a second young female. Is it wonderful that the one known atrocity should influence the popular judgement in regard to the other unknown? This judgement awaited direction, and the known outrage seemed so opportunely to afford it? Marie, too, was found in the river; and upon this very river was this known outrage committed. The connection of the two events had about it so much of the palpable, that the true wonder would have been a *failure* of the populace to appreciate and to seize it. But, in fact, the one atrocity, known to be so committed, is, if anything, evidence that the other, committed at a time nearly coincident, was *not* so committed. It would have been a miracle indeed, if, while a gang of ruffians were perpetrating, at a given locality, a most unheard-of wrong, there should have been another similar gang, in a similar locality, in the same city, under the same circumstances, with the same means and appliances, engaged in a wrong of precisely the same aspect, at precisely the same period of time! Yet in what, if not in this marvellous train of coincidence, does the accidentally *suggested* opinion of the populace call upon us to believe?

'Before proceeding farther, let us consider the supposed scene of the assassination, in the thicket at the Barrière du Roule. This thicket, although dense, was in the close vicinity of a public road. Within were three or four large stones, forming a kind of seat, with a back and footstool. On the upper stone was discovered a white petticoat; on the second, a silk scarf. A parasol, gloves, and a pocket-handkerchief, were also here found. The handkerchief bore the name, "Marie Rogêt". Fragments of dress were seen on the branches around. The earth was trampled, the bushes were broken, and there was every evidence of a violent struggle.

'Notwithstanding the acclamation with which the discovery of this thicket was received by the press, and the unanimity with which it was supposed to indicate the precise scene of the outrage, it must be admitted that there was some very good reason for doubt. That it *was* the scene, I may or I may not believe – but there was excellent reason for doubt. Had the *true* scene been, as *Le Commerciel* suggested, in the neighbourhood of the Rue Pavée St Andrée, the perpetrators of the crime, supposing them still resident in Paris, would naturally have been stricken with terror at the public attention thus acutely directed into the proper channel; and, in certain classes of minds, there would have arisen, at once, a sense of the necessity of some exertion to re-divert this attention. And thus, the thicket of the Barrière du Roule having been already suspected, the idea of placing the articles where they were found, might have been naturally entertained. There is no real evidence, although *Le Soleil* so supposes, that the articles discovered had been more than a very few days in the thicket; while there is much circumstantial proof that they could not have remained there, without attracting attention, during the twenty days elapsing between the fatal Sunday and the afternoon upon which they were found by the boys. "They were all *mildewed* down hard," says *Le Soleil*, adopting the opinions of its predecessors, "with the action of the rain, and stuck together from *mildew*. The grass had grown around and over some of them. The silk of the parasol was strong, but the threads of it were run together within. The upper part, where it had been doubled and folded, was all *mildewed* and rotten, and tore on being opened." In respect to the grass having "grown around and over some of them", it is obvious that the fact could only have been ascertained from the words, and thus from the recollections, of two small boys; for these boys removed the articles and took them home before they had been seen by a third party. But grass will grow, especially in warm and damp weather (such as was that of the period of the murder), as much as two or three inches in a single day. A parasol lying upon a newly turfed ground, might, in a single week, be entirely concealed from sight by the upspringing grass. And touching that *mildew* upon which the editor of *Le Soleil* so pertinaciously insists that he employs the word no less than three times in the brief paragraph just quoted, is he really unaware of the nature of this *mildew*? Is he to be told that it is one of the many classes of fungus, of which the most ordinary feature is its upspringing and decadence within twenty-four hours?

'Thus we see, at a glance, that what has been most triumphantly adduced in support of the idea that the articles had been "for at least three or four weeks" in the thicket, is most absurdly null as regards any evidence of that fact. On the other hand, it is exceedingly difficult to believe that these articles could have remained in the thicket specified, for a longer period than a single week – for a longer period than from one Sunday to the next. Those who know anything of the vicinity of Paris, know the extreme difficulty of finding *seclusion* unless at a great distance from its suburbs. Such a thing as an unexplored, or even an unfrequently visited recess, amid its woods or groves, is not for a moment to be imagined. Let anyone who, being at heart a lover of nature, is yet chained by duty to the dust and heat of this great metropolis – let any such one attempt, even during the weekdays, to slake his thirst for solitude amid the scenes of natural loveliness which immediately surround us. At every second step, he will find the growing charm dispelled by the voice and personal intrusion of some ruffian or party of carousing blackguards. He will seek privacy amid the densest foliage, all in vain. Here are the very nooks where the unwashed most abound – here are the temples most desecrate. With sickness of the heart the wanderer will flee back to the polluted Paris as to a less odious because less incongruous sink of pollution. But if the vicinity of the city is so beset during the working days of the week, how much more so on the Sabbath! It is now especially that, released from the claims of labour, or deprived of the customary opportunities of crime, the town blackguard seeks the precincts of the town, not through love of the rural, which in his heart he despises, but by way of escape from the restraints and conventionalities of society. He desires less the fresh air and the green trees, than the utter *license* of the country. Here, at the roadside inn, or beneath the foliage of the woods, he indulges, unchecked by any eye except those of his boon companions, in all the mad excess of a counterfeit hilarity – the joint offspring of liberty and of rum. I say nothing more than what must be obvious to every dispassionate observer, when I repeat that the circumstance of the articles in question having remained undiscovered, for a longer period than from one Sunday to another, in *any* thicket in the immediate neighbourhood of Paris, is to be looked upon as little less than miraculous.

'But there are not wanting other grounds for the suspicion that the articles were placed in the thicket with the view of diverting attention from the real scene of the outrage. And, first, let me direct your notice to the *date* of the discovery of the articles. Collate this with the date of the fifth extract made by myself from the newspapers. You will find that the discovery followed, almost immediately, the urgent communications sent to the evening paper. These communications, although various, and apparently from various sources, tended all to the same point – viz., the directing of attention to a *gang* as the perpetrators of the outrage, and to the neighbourhood of the Barrière du Roule as its scene. Now here, of course, the suspicion is not that, in consequence of these communications, or of the public attention by them directed, the articles were found by the boys; but the suspicion might and may well have been, that the articles were not *before* found by the boys, for the reason that the articles had not before been in the thicket; having been deposited there only at so late a period as at the date, or shortly prior to the date of the communications, by the guilty authors of these communications themselves.

'This thicket was a singular – an exceedingly singular one. It was unusually dense. Within its naturally walled enclosure were three extraordinary stones, *forming a seat with a back and footstool.* And this thicket, so full of a natural art, was in the immediate vicinity, *within a few rods,* of the dwelling of Mme Deluc, whose boys were in the habit of closely examining the shrubberies about them in search of the bark of the sassafras. Would it be a rash wager – a wager of one thousand to one – that *a day* never passed over the heads of these boys without finding at least one of them ensconced in the umbrageous hall, and enthroned upon its natural throne? Those who would hesitate at such a wager, have either never been boys themselves, or have forgotten the boyish nature. I repeat – it is exceedingly hard to comprehend how the articles could have remained in this thicket, undiscovered, for a longer period than one or two days; and that thus there is good ground for suspicion, in spite of the dogmatic ignorance of *Le Soleil,* that they were, at a comparatively late date, deposited where found.

'But there are still other and stronger reasons for believing them so deposited, than any which I have as yet urged. And now, let me beg your notice to the highly artificial arrangement of the articles. On the *upper* stone lay a white petticoat; on the *second* a silk scarf; scattered around, were a parasol, gloves, and a pocket-handkerchief bearing the name, "Marie Rogêt". Here is just such an arrangement as would *naturally* be made by a not over acute person wishing to dispose the articles *naturally.* But it is by no means a *really* natural arrangement. I should rather have looked to see the things *all* lying on the ground and trampled under foot. In the narrow limits of that bower, it would have been scarcely possible that the petticoat and scarf should have retained a position upon the stones, when subjected to the brushing to and fro of many struggling persons. "There was evidence," it is said, "of a struggle; and the earth was trampled, the bushes were broken" – but the petticoat and scarf are found deposited as if upon shelves. "The pieces of the frock torn out by the bushes were about three inches wide and six inches long. One part was the hem of the frock, and it had been mended. They *looked like strips torn off.*" Here, inadvertently, *Le Soleil* has employed an exceedingly suspicious phrase. The pieces, as described, do indeed "look like strips torn off"; but purposely and by hand. It is one of the rarest of accidents that a piece is "torn off", from any garment such as is now in question, by the agency *of a thorn.* From the very nature of such fabrics, a thorn or nail becoming entangled in them, tears them rectangularly – divides them into two longitudinal rents, at right angles with each other, and meeting at an apex where the thorn enters – but it is scarcely possible to conceive the piece "torn off". I never so knew it, nor did you. To tear a piece *off* from such fabric, two distinct forces, in different directions, will be, in almost every case, required. If there be two edges to the fabric – if, for example, it be a pocket-handkerchief, and it is desired to tear from it a slip, then, and then only will the one force serve the purpose. But in the present case the question is of a dress, presenting but one edge. To tear a piece from the interior, where no edge is presented, could only be effected by a miracle through the agency of thorns, and no *one* thorn could accomplish it. But, even where an edge is presented, two thorns will be necessary, operating, the one in two distinct directions, and the other in one. And this in the supposition that the edge is unhemmed. If hemmed, the matter is nearly out of the question. We thus see the numerous and great obstacles in the way of pieces being "torn off" through the simple agency of "thorns"; yet we are required to believe not only that one piece but that many have been so torn. "And one part," too, "*was the hem of the frock*"! Another piece was "*part of the skirt, not the hem*" – that is to say, was torn completely out through the agency of thorns, from the unedged interior of the dress! These, I say, are things which one may well be pardoned for disbelieving; yet, taken collectedly, they form, perhaps, less of reasonable ground for suspicion, than the one startling circumstance of the articles having been left in this thicket at all, by any *murderers* who had enough precaution to think of removing the corpse. You will not have apprehended me rightly, however, if you suppose it my design to *deny* this thicket as the scene of the outrage. There might have been a wrong *here,* or, more possibly, an accident at Mme Deluc's. But, in fact, this is a part of minor importance. We are not engaged in an attempt to discover the scene, but to produce the perpetrators of the murder. What I have adduced, notwithstanding the minuteness with which I have adduced it, has been with the view, first, to show the folly of the positive and headlong assertions of *Le Soleil,* but secondly and chiefly, to bring you, by the most natural route, to a further contemplation of the doubt whether this assassination has, or has not, been the work of *a gang.*

'We will resume this question by mere allusion to the revolting details of the surgeon examined at the inquest. It is only necessary to say that his published *inferences,* in regard to the number of the ruffians, have been properly ridiculed as unjust and totally baseless, by all the reputable anatomists of Paris. Not that the matter *might not* have been as inferred, but that there was no ground for the inference – was there not much for another?

'Let us reflect now upon "the traces of a struggle"; and let me ask what these traces have been supposed to demonstrate. A gang. But do they not rather demonstrate the absence of a gang? What *struggle* could have taken place – what struggle so violent and so enduring as to have left its "traces" in all directions – between a weak and defenceless girl and the *gang* of ruffians imagined? The silent grasp of a few rough arms and all would have been over, the victim must have been absolutely passive at their will. You will here bear in mind that the arguments urged against the thicket as the scene, are applicable, in chief part, only against it as the scene of an outrage committed by *more than a single individual*. If we imagine but one violator, we can conceive, and thus only conceive, the struggle of so violent and so obstinate a nature as to have left the "traces" apparent.

'And again. I have already mentioned the suspicion to be excited by the fact that the articles in question were suffered to remain *at all* in the thicket where discovered. It seems almost impossible that these evidences of guilt should have been accidentally left where found. There was sufficient presence of mind (it is supposed) to remove the corpse; and yet a more positive evidence than the corpse itself (whose features might have been quickly obliterated by decay), is allowed to lie conspicuously in the scene of the outrage – I allude to the handkerchief with the *name* of the deceased. If this was accident, it was not the accident *of a gang*. We can imagine it only the accident of an individual. Let us see. An individual has committed the murder. He is alone with the ghost of the departed. He is appalled by what lies motionless before him. The fury of his passion is over, and there is abundant room in his heart for the natural awe of the deed. His is none of that confidence which the presence of numbers inevitably inspires. He is *alone* with the dead. He trembles and is bewildered. Yet there is a necessity for disposing of the corpse. He bears it to the river, but leaves behind him the other evidences of guilt; for it is difficult, if not impossible to carry all the burden at once, and it will be easy to return for what is left. But in his toilsome journey to the water his fears redouble within him. The sounds of life encompass his path. A dozen times he hears or fancies the step of an observer. Even the very lights from the city bewilder him. Yet, in time, and by long and frequent pauses of deep agony, he reaches the river's brink, and disposes of his ghastly charge – perhaps through the medium of a boat. But *now* what treasure does the world hold – what threat of vengeance could it hold out – which would have power to urge the return of that lonely murderer over that toilsome and perilous path, to the thicket and its blood-chilling recollections? He returns *not*, let the consequences be what they may. He *could* not return if he would. His sole thought is immediate escape. He turns his back *for ever* upon those dreadful shrubberies, and flees as from the wrath to come.

'But how with a gang? Their number would have inspired them with confidence; if, indeed, confidence is ever wanting in the breast of the arrant blackguard; and of arrant blackguards alone are the supposed *gangs* ever constituted. Their number, I say, would have prevented the bewildering and unreasoning terror which I have imagined to paralyse the single man. Could we suppose an oversight in one, or two, or three, this oversight would have been remedied by a fourth. They would have left nothing behind them; for their number would have enabled them to carry *all* at once. There would have been no need of *return*.

'Consider now the circumstance that, in the outer garment of the corpse when found, "a slip, about a foot wide, had been torn upward from the bottom hem to the waist, wound three times round the waist, and secured by a sort of hitch in the back". This was done with the obvious design of affording *a handle* by which to carry the body. But would any *number* of men have dreamed of resorting to such an expedient? To three or four, the limbs of the corpse would have afforded not only a sufficient, but the best possible hold. The device is that of a single individual; and this brings us to the fact that "between the thicket and the river, the rails of the fences were found taken down, and the ground bore evident traces of some heavy burden having been dragged along it"! But would a *number* of men have put themselves to the superfluous trouble of taking down a fence, for the purpose of dragging through it a corpse which they might have *lifted over* any fence in an instant? Would a *number* of men have so *dragged* a corpse at all as to have left evident *traces* of the dragging?

'And here we must refer to an observation of *Le Commerciel*; an observation upon which I have already, in some measure, commented. "A piece," says this journal, "of one of the unfortunate girl's petticoats was torn out and tied under her chin, and around the back of her head, probably to prevent screams. This was done by fellows who had no pocket-handkerchiefs."

'I have before suggested that a genuine blackguard is never *without* a pocket-handkerchief. But it is not to this fact that I now especially advert. That it was not through want of a handkerchief for the purpose imagined by *Le Commerciel*, that this bandage was employed, is rendered apparent by the handkerchief left in the thicket; and that the object was not "to prevent screams" appears, also, from the bandage having

IN HIS TOILSOME JOURNEY TO THE WATER
HIS FEARS REDOUBLE

been employed in preference to what would so much better have answered the purpose. But the language of the evidence speaks of the strip in question as "found around the neck, fitting loosely, and secured with a hard knot." These words are sufficiently vague, but differ materially from those of *Le Commerciel*. The slip was eighteen inches wide, and therefore, although of muslin, would form a strong band when folded or rumpled longitudinally. And thus rumpled it was discovered. My inference is this. The solitary murderer, having borne the corpse, for some distance (whether from the thicket or elsewhere), by means of the bandage *hitched* around its middle, found the weight, in this mode of procedure, too much for his strength. He resolved to drag the burthen – the evidence goes to show that it was dragged. With this object in view, it became necessary to attach something like a rope to one of the extremities. It could be best attached about the neck, where the head would prevent it slipping off. And now the murderer bethought him, unquestionably, of the bandage about the loins. He would have used this, but for its volution about the corpse, the *hitch* which embarrassed it, and the reflection that it had not been "torn off" from the garment. It was easier to tear a new slip from the petticoat. He tore it, made it fast about the neck, and so *dragged* his victim to the brink of the river. That this "bandage," only attainable with trouble and delay, and but imperfectly answering its purpose – that this bandage was employed *at all*, demonstrates that the necessity for its employment sprang from circumstances arising at a period when the handkerchief was no longer attainable – that is to say, arising, as we have imagined, after quitting the thicket (if the thicket it was), and on the road between the thicket and the river.

'But the evidence, you will say, of Mme Deluc (!) points especially to the presence of *a gang*, in the vicinity of the thicket, at or about the epoch of the murder. This I grant. I doubt if there were not a *dozen* gangs, such as described by Mme Deluc, in and about the vicinity of the Barrière du Roule at *or about* the period of this tragedy. But the gang which has drawn upon itself the pointed animadversion, although the somewhat tardy and very suspicious evidence of Mme Deluc, is the *only* gang which is represented by that honest and scrupulous old lady as having eaten her cakes and swallowed her brandy, without putting themselves to the trouble of making her payment. *Et hinc illae irae?*

'But what *is* the precise evidence of Mme Deluc? "A gang of miscreants made their appearance, behaved boisterously, ate and drank without making payment, followed in the route of the young man and girl, returned to the inn *about dusk*, and recrossed the river as if in great haste."

'Now this "great haste" very possibly seemed *greater* haste in the eyes of Mme Deluc, since she dwelt lingeringly and lamentingly upon her violated cakes and ale – cakes and ale for which she might still have entertained a faint hope of compensation. Why, otherwise, since it was *about dusk*, should she make a point of the *haste?* It is no cause for wonder, surely, that even a gang of blackguards should make *haste* to get home, when a wide river is to be crossed in small boats, when storm impends, and when night *approaches*.

'I say *approaches*; for the night had *not yet arrived*. It was only *about dusk* that the indecent haste of these "miscreants" offended the sober eyes of Mme Deluc. But we are told that it was upon this very evening that Mme Deluc, as well as her eldest son, "heard the screams of a female in the vicinity of the inn". And in what words does Mme Deluc designate the period of the evening at which these screams were heard? It was "*soon after dark*", she says. But "soon *after* dark", is at least *dark*; and "*about dusk*" is as certainly daylight. Thus it is abundantly clear that the gang quitted the Barrière du Roule *prior* to the screams overheard (?) by Mme Deluc. And although, in all the many reports of the evidence, the relative expressions in question are distinctly and invariably employed just as I have employed them in this conversation with yourself, no notice whatever of the gross discrepancy has, as yet, been taken by any of the public journals, or by any of the myrmidons of police.

'I shall add but one to the arguments against *a gang*; but this *one* has, to my own understanding at least, a weight altogether irresistible. Under the circumstances of large reward offered, and full pardon to any king's evidence, it is not to be imagined, for a moment, that some member of *a gang* of low ruffians, or of any body of men, would not long ago have betrayed his accomplices. Each one of a gang so placed is not so much greedy of reward, or anxious for escape, as *fearful of betrayal*. He betrays eagerly and early that *he may not himself be betrayed*. That the secret has not been divulged, is the very best of proof that it is, in fact, a secret. The horrors of this dark deed are known only to *one*, or two, living human beings, and to God.

'Let us sum up now the meagre yet certain fruits of our long analysis. We have attained the idea either of a fatal accident under the roof of Mme Deluc, or of a murder perpetrated, in the thicket at the Barrière du Roule, by a lover, or at least by an intimate and secret associate of the deceased. This associate is of swarthy complexion. This complexion, the "hitch" in the bandage, and the "sailor's knot" with which the bonnet-ribbon is tied, point to a seaman. His companionship with the deceased, a gay, but not an abject young girl, designates him as above the grade of the common sailor. Here the well-written and urgent communications to the journals are much in the way of corroboration. The circumstance of the first elopement, as mentioned by *Le Mercurie*, tends to blend the idea of this seaman with that of the "naval officer" who is first known to have led the unfortunate into crime.

'And here, most fittingly, comes the consideration of the continued absence of him of the dark complexion. Let me pause to observe that the complexion of this man is dark and swarthy; it was no common swarthiness which constituted the *sole* point of remem brance, both as regards Valence and Mme Deluc. But why is this man absent? Was he murdered by the gang? If so, why are there only *traces* of the assassinated *girl*? The scene of the two outrages will naturally be supposed identical. And where is his corpse? The assassins would most probably have disposed of both in the same way. But it may be said that this man lives, and is deterred from making himself known, through dread of being charged with the murder. This consideration might be supposed to operate upon him now – at this late period – since it has been given in evidence that he was seen with Marie – but it would have had no force at the period of the deed. The first impulse of an innocent man would have been to announce the outrage, and to aid in identifying the ruffians. This, *policy* would have suggested. He had been seen with the girl. He had crossed the river with her in an open ferryboat. The denouncing of the assassins would have appeared, even to an idiot, the surest and sole means of relieving himself from suspicion. We cannot suppose him, on the night of the fatal Sunday, both innocent himself and incognisant of an outrage committed. Yet only under such circumstances is it possible to imagine that he would have failed, if alive, in the denouncement of the assassins.

'And what means are ours of attaining the truth? We shall find these means multiplying and gathering distinctness as we proceed. Let us sift to the bottom this affair of the first elopement. Let us know the full history of "the officer", with his present circumstances, and his whereabouts at the precise period of the murder. Let us carefully compare with each other the various communications sent to the evening paper, in which the object was to inculpate a *gang*. This done, let us compare these communications, both as regards style and MS, with those sent to the morning paper, at a previous period, and insisting so vehemently upon the guilt of Mennais. And, all this done, let us again compare these various communications with the known MSS of the officer. Let us endeavour to ascertain, by repeated questionings of Mme Deluc and her boys, as well as of the omnibus-driver, Valence, something more of the personal appearance and bearing of the "man of dark complexion". Queries, skilfully directed, will not fail to elicit, from some of these parties, information on this particular point (or upon others) – information which the parties themselves may not even be aware of possessing. And let us now trace *the boat* picked up by the bargeman on the morning of Monday the 23rd of June, and which was removed from the barge-office, without the cognisance of the officer in attendance, and *without the rudder*, at some period prior to the discovery of the corpse. With a proper caution and perseverance we shall infallibly trace this boat; for not only can the bargeman who picked it up identify it, but the *rudder is at hand*. The rudder *of a sail-boat* would not have been abandoned, without enquiry, by one altogether at ease in heart. And here let me pause to insinuate a question. There was no *advertisement* of the picking up of this boat. It was silently taken to the barge-office, and as silently removed. But its owner or employer – how *happened* he, at so early a period as Tuesday morning, to be informed, without the agency of advertisement, of the locality of the boat taken up on Monday, unless we imagine some connection with the *navy* – some personal permanent connection leading to cognisance of its minute interests – its petty local news?

'In speaking of the lonely assassin dragging his burden to the shore, I have already suggested the probability of his availing himself *of a boat*. Now we are to understand that Marie Rogêt *was* precipitated from a boat. This would naturally have been the case. The corpse could not have been trusted to the shallow waters of the shore. The peculiar marks on the back and shoulders of the victim tell of the bottom ribs of a boat. That the body was found without weight is also corroborative of the idea. If thrown from the shore a weight would have been attached. We can only account for its absence by supposing the murderer to have neglected the precaution of supplying himself with it before pushing off. In the act of consigning the corpse to the water, he would unquestionably have noticed his oversight; but then no remedy would have been at hand. Any risk would have been preferred to a return to that accursed shore. Having rid himself of his ghastly charge, the murderer would have hastened to the city. There, at some obscure wharf, he would have leaped on land. But the boat – would he have secured it? He would have been in too great haste for such things as securing a boat. Moreover, in fastening it to the wharf, he would have felt as if securing evidence against himself. His natural thought would have been to cast from him, as far as possible, all that had held connection with his crime. He would not only have fled from the wharf, but he would not have permitted *the boat* to remain. Assuredly he would have cast it adrift. Let us pursue our fancies. In the morning, the wretch is stricken with unutterable horror at finding that the boat has been picked up and detained at a locality which he is in the daily habit of frequenting – at a locality, perhaps, which his duty compels him to frequent.

The next night, *without daring to ask for the rudder*, he removes it. Now *where* is that rudderless boat? Let it be one of our first purposes to discover. With the first glimpse we obtain of it, the dawn of our success shall begin. This boat shall guide us, with a rapidity which will surprise even ourselves, to him who employed it in the midnight of the fatal Sabbath. Corroboration will rise upon corroboration, and the murderer will be traced.'

[For reasons which we shall not specify, but which to many readers will appear obvious, we have taken the liberty of here omitting, from the MSS placed in our hands, such portion as details the *following up* of the apparently slight clue obtained by Dupin. We feel it advisable only to state, in brief, that the result desired was brought to pass; and that the Prefect fulfilled punctually, although with reluctance, the terms of his compact with the Chevalier. Mr Poe's article concludes with the following words. – *Eds.*]

It will be understood that I speak of coincidence *and no more*. What I have said above upon this topic must suffice. In my own heart there dwells no faith in preternature. That Nature and its God are two, no man who thinks will deny. That the latter, creating the former, can, at will, control or modify it, is all unquestionable. I say 'at will'; for the question is of will, and not, as the insanity of logic has assumed, of power. It is not that the Deity *cannot* modify His laws, but that we insult Him in imagining a possible necessity for modification. In their origin these laws were fashioned to embrace *all* contingencies which *could* lie in the Future. With God all is *Now*.

I repeat, then, that I speak of these things only as of coincidences. And further: in what I relate it will be seen that between the fate of the unhappy Marie Cecilia Rogers, so far as that fate is known, and the fate of one Marie Rogêt up to a certain epoch in her history, there has existed a parallel in the contemplation of whose wonderful exactitude the reason becomes embarrassed. I say all this will be seen. But let it not for a moment be supposed that, in proceeding with the sad narrative of Marie from the epoch just mentioned, and in tracing to its *dénouement* the mystery which enshrouded her, it is my covert design to hint at an extension of the parallel, or even to suggest that the measures adopted in Paris for the discovery of the assassin of a *grisette*, or measures founded in any similar ratiocination, would produce any similar result.

For, in respect to the latter branch of the supposition, it should be considered that the most trifling variation in the facts of the two cases might give rise to the most important miscalculations, by diverting thoroughly the two courses of events; very much as, in arithmetic, an error which, in its own individuality, may be inappreciable, produces, at length, by dint of multiplication at all points of the process, a result enormously at variance with truth. And, in regard to the former branch, we must not fail to hold in view that the very Calculus of Probabilities to which I have referred, forbids all idea of the extension of the parallel – forbids it with a positiveness strong and decided just in proportion as this parallel has already been long-drawn and exact. This is one of those anomalous propositions which, seemingly appealing to thought altogether apart from the mathematical, is yet one which only the mathematician can fully entertain. Nothing, for example, is more difficult than to convince the merely general reader that the fact of sixes having been thrown twice in succession by a player at dice, is sufficient cause for betting the largest odds that sixes will not be thrown in the third attempt. A suggestion to this effect is usually rejected by the intellect at once. It does not appear that the two throws which have been completed, and which lie now absolutely in the past, can have influence upon the throw which exists only in the future. The chance for throwing sixes seems to be precisely as it was at any ordinary time – that is to say, subject only to the influence of the various other throws which may be made by the dice. And this is a reflection which appears so exceedingly obvious that attempts to controvert it are received more frequently with a derisive smile than with anything like respectful attention. The error here involved – a gross error redolent of mischief – I cannot pretend to expose within the limits assigned me at present; and with the philosophical it needs no exposure. It may be sufficient here to say that it forms one of an infinite series of mistakes which arise in the path of Reason through her propensity for seeking truth *in detail*.

The Purloined Letter

Nil sapientiae odiosius acumine nimio.

SENECA

At Paris, just after dark one gusty evening in the autumn of 18—, I was enjoying the twofold luxury of meditation and a meerschaum, in company with my friend, C. Auguste Dupin, in his little back library or book-closet, *au troisième*, No. 33 Rue Dunôt, Faubourg St Germain. For one hour at least we had maintained a profound silence; while each, to any casual observer, might have seemed intently and exclusively occupied with the curling eddies of smoke that oppressed the atmosphere of the chamber. For myself, however, I was mentally discussing certain topics which had formed matter for conversation between us at an earlier period of the evening; I mean the affair of the Rue Morgue, and the mystery attending the murder of Marie Rogêt. I looked upon it, therefore, as something of a coincidence, when the door of our apartment was thrown open and admitted our old acquaintance, M. G—, the Prefect of the Parisian police.

We gave him a hearty welcome; for there was nearly half as much of the entertaining as of the contemptible about the man, and we had not seen him for several years. We had been sitting in the dark, and Dupin now arose for the purpose of lighting a lamp, but sat down again, without doing so, upon G's saying that he had called to consult us, or rather to ask the opinion of my friend, about some official business which had occasioned a great deal of trouble.

'If it is any point requiring reflection,' observed Dupin, as he forbore to enkindle the wick, 'we shall examine it to better purpose in the dark.'

'That is another of your odd notions,' said the Prefect, who had a fashion of calling everything 'odd' that was beyond his comprehension, and thus lived amid an absolute legion of 'oddities'.

'Very true,' said Dupin, as he supplied his visitor with a pipe, and rolled towards him a comfortable chair.

'And what is the difficulty now?' I asked. 'Nothing more in the assassination way, I hope?'

'Oh, no; nothing of that nature. The fact is, the business is *very* simple indeed, and I make no doubt that we can manage it sufficiently well ourselves; but then I thought Dupin would like to hear the details of it, because it is so excessively *odd*.'

'Simple and odd,' said Dupin.

'Why, yes; and not exactly that, either. The fact is, we have all been a good deal puzzled because the affair *is* so simple, and yet baffles us altogether.'

'Perhaps it is the very simplicity of the thing which puts you at fault,' said my friend.

'What nonsense you *do* talk!' replied the Prefect, laughing heartily.

'Perhaps the mystery is a little *too* plain,' said Dupin.

'Oh, good heavens! who ever heard of such an idea?'

'A little *too* self-evident.'

'Ha! ha! ha! – ha! ha! ha! – ho! ho! ho!' roared our visitor, profoundly amused; 'O Dupin, you will be the death of me yet!'

'And what, after all, *is* the matter on hand?' I asked.

'Why, I will tell you,' replied the Prefect, as he gave a long, steady, and contemplative puff, and settled himself in his chair. 'I will tell you in a few words; but, before I begin, let me caution you that this is an affair demanding the greatest secrecy, and that I should most probably lose the position I now hold, were it known that I confided it to anyone.'

'Proceed,' said I.

'Or not,' said Dupin.

'Well, then; I have received personal information, from a very high quarter, that a certain document of the last importance has been purloined from the royal apartments. The individual who purloined it is known; this beyond a doubt; he was seen to take it. It is known, also, that it still remains in his possession.

'How is this known?' asked Dupin.

'It is clearly inferred,' replied the Prefect, 'from the nature of the document, and from the non-appearance of certain results which would at once arise from its passing *out* of the robber's possession – that is to say, from his employing it as he must design in the end to employ it.'

'Be a little more explicit,' I said.

'Well, I may venture so far as to say that the paper gives its holder a certain power in a certain quarter where such power is immensely valuable.' The Prefect was fond of the cant of diplomacy.

'Still I do not quite understand,' said Dupin.

'No? Well; the disclosure of the document to a third person, who shall be nameless, would bring in question the honour of a personage of most exalted station; and this fact gives the holder of the document an ascendency over the illustrious personage whose honour and peace are so jeopardised.'

'But this ascendency,' I interposed, 'would depend upon the robber's knowledge of the loser's knowledge of the robber. Who would dare – '

'The thief,' said G, 'is the Minister D—, who dares all things, those unbecoming as well as those becoming a man. The method of the theft was not less ingenious than bold. The document in question – a letter, to be frank – had been received by the personage robbed while alone in the royal *boudoir*. During its perusal she was suddenly interrupted by the entrance of the other exalted personage from whom especially it was her wish to conceal it. After a hurried and vain endeavour to thrust it in a drawer, she was forced to place it, open as it was, upon a table. The address, however, was uppermost, and, the contents thus unexposed, the letter escaped notice. At this juncture enters the Minister D—. His lynx eye immediately perceives the paper, recognises the handwriting of the address, observes the confusion of the personage addressed, and fathoms her secret. After some business transactions, hurried through in his ordinary manner, he produces a letter somewhat similar to the one in question, opens it, pretends to read it, and then places it in close juxtaposition to the other. Again he converses, for some fifteen minutes, upon the public affairs. At length, in taking leave, he takes also from the table the letter to which he had no claim. Its rightful owner saw, but, of course, dared not call attention to the act, in the presence of the third personage who stood at her elbow. The minister decamped, leaving his own letter – one of no importance – upon the table.'

'Here, then,' said Dupin to me, 'you have precisely what you demand to make the ascendency complete – the robber's knowledge of the loser's knowledge of the robber.'

'Yes,' replied the Prefect; 'and the power thus attained has, for some months past, been wielded, for political purposes, to a very dangerous extent. The personage robbed is more thoroughly convinced, every day, of the necessity of reclaiming her letter. But this, of course, cannot be done openly. In fine, driven to despair, she has committed the matter to me.'

'Than whom,' said Dupin, amid a perfect whirlwind of smoke, 'no more sagacious agent could, I suppose, be desired, or even imagined.'

'You flatter me,' replied the Prefect; 'but it is possible that some such opinion may have been entertained.'

'It is clear,' said I, 'as you observe, that the letter is still in the possession of the minister; since it is this possession, and not any employment of the letter, which bestows the power. With the employment the power departs.'

'True,' said G—; 'and upon this conviction I proceeded. My first care was to make thorough search of the minister's hotel; and here my chief embarrassment lay in the necessity of searching without his knowledge. Beyond all things, I have been warned of the danger which would result from giving him reason to suspect our design.'

'But,' said I, 'you are quite *au fait* in these investigations. The Parisian police have done this thing often before.'

'Oh yes; and for this reason I did not despair. The habits of the minister gave me, too, a great advantage. He is frequently absent from home all night. His servants are by no means numerous. They sleep at a distance from their master's apartment, and, being chiefly Neapolitans, are readily made drunk. I have keys, as you know, with which I can open any chamber or cabinet in Paris. For three months a night has not passed, during the greater part of which I have not been engaged, personally, in ransacking the D— Hôtel. My honour is interested, and, to mention a great secret, the reward is enormous. So I did not abandon the search until I had become fully satisfied that the thief is a more astute man than myself. I fancy that I have investigated every nook and corner of the premises in which it is possible that the paper can be concealed.'

'But is it not possible,' I suggested, 'that although the letter may be in possession of the minister, as it unquestionably is, he may have concealed it elsewhere than upon his own premises?'

'This is barely possible,' said Dupin. 'The present peculiar condition of affairs at court, and especially of those intrigues in which D— is known to be involved, would render the instant availability of the document – its susceptibility of being produced at a moment's notice – a point of nearly equal importance with its possession.'

'Its susceptibility of being produced?' said I.

'That is to say, of being *destroyed*,' said Dupin.

'True,' I observed; 'the paper is clearly then upon the premises. As for its being upon the person of the minister, we may consider that as out of the question.'

'Entirely,' said the Prefect. 'He has been twice waylaid, as if by footpads, and his person rigorously searched under my own inspection.'

'You might have spared yourself this trouble,' said Dupin. 'D—, I presume, is not altogether a fool, and, if not, must have anticipated these waylayings, as a matter of course.'

'Not *altogether* a fool,' said G—; 'but then he's a poet, which I take to be only one remove from a fool.'

'True,' said Dupin, after a long and thoughtful whiff from his meerschaum, 'although I have been guilty of certain doggerel myself.'

'Suppose you detail,' said I, 'the particulars of your search.'

'Why, the fact is we took our time, and we searched *everywhere*. I have had long experience in these affairs. I took the entire building, room by room; devoting the nights of a whole week to each. We examined, first, the furniture of each department. We opened every possible drawer; and I presume you know that, to a properly trained police agent, such a thing as a *secret* drawer is impossible. Any man is a dolt who permits a "secret" drawer to escape him in a search of this kind. The thing is *so* plain. There is a certain amount of bulk – of space – to be accounted for in every cabinet. Then we have accurate rules. The fiftieth part of a line could not escape us. After the cabinets we took the chairs. The cushions we probed with the fine long needles you have seen me employ. From the tables we removed the tops.'

'Why so?'

'Sometimes the top of a table, or other similarly arranged piece of furniture, is removed by the person wishing to conceal an article; then the leg is excavated, the article deposited within the cavity, and the top replaced. The bottoms and tops of bedposts are employed in the same way.'

'But could not the cavity be detected by sounding?' I asked.

'By no means, if, when the article is deposited, a sufficient wadding of cotton be placed around it. Besides, in our case, we were obliged to proceed without noise.'

'But you could not have removed – you could not have taken to pieces *all* articles of furniture in which it would have been possible to make a deposit in the manner you mention. A letter may be compressed into a thin spiral roll, not differing much in shape or bulk from a large knitting-needle, and in this form it might be inserted into the rung of a chair, for example. You did not take to pieces all the chairs?'

'Certainly not; but we did better – we examined the rungs of every chair in the hotel, and, indeed, the jointings of every description of furniture, by the aid of a most powerful microscope. Had there been any traces of recent disturbance we should not have failed to detect it instantly. A single grain of gimlet-dust, for example, would have been as obvious as an apple. Any disorder in the gluing – any unusual gaping in the joints – would have sufficed to ensure detection.'

'I presume you looked to the mirrors, between the boards and the plates, and you probed the beds and the bedclothes, as well as the curtains and carpets.'

'That of course; and when we had absolutely completed every article of the furniture in this way, then we examined the house itself. We divided its entire surface into compartments, which we numbered, so that none might be missed; then we scrutinised each individual square inch throughout the premises, including the two houses immediately adjoining, with the microscope, as before.'

'The two houses adjoining!' I exclaimed; 'you must have had a great deal of trouble.'

'We had; but the reward offered is prodigious.'

'You include the *grounds* about the houses?'

'All the grounds are paved with brick. They gave us comparatively little trouble. We examined the moss between the bricks, and found it undisturbed.'

'You looked among D—'s papers, of course, and into the books of the library?'

'Certainly; we opened every package and parcel; we not only opened every book, but we turned over every leaf in each volume, not contenting ourselves with a mere shake, according to the fashion of some of our police officers. We also measured the thickness of every book-*cover*, with the most accurate admeasurement, and applied to each the most jealous scrutiny of the microscope. Had any of the bindings been recently meddled with, it would have been utterly impossible that the fact should have escaped observation. Some five or six volumes, just from the hands of the binder, we carefully probed longitudinally, with the needles.'

'You explored the floors beneath the carpets?'

'Beyond doubt. We removed every carpet, and examined the boards with the microscope.'

'And the paper on the walls?'

'Yes.'

'You looked into the cellars?'

'We did.'

'Then,' I said, 'you have been making a miscalculation, and the letter is *not* upon the premises, as you suppose.'

'I fear you are right there,' said the Prefect. 'And now, Dupin, what would you advise me to do?'

'To make a thorough research of the premises.'

'That is absolutely needless,' replied G —. 'I am not more sure than I breathe than I am that the letter is not at the hotel.'

'I have no better advice to give you,' said Dupin. 'You have, of course, an accurate description of the letter?'

'Oh yes!' And here the Prefect, producing a memorandum-book, proceeded to read aloud a minute account of the internal, and especially of the external appearance of the missing document. Soon after finishing the perusal of this description, he took his departure more entirely depressed in spirits than I had ever known the good gentleman before.

In about a month afterwards he paid us another visit, and found us occupied very nearly as before. He took a pipe and a chair and entered into some ordinary conversation.

At length I said – 'Well, but G—, what of the purloined letter? I presume you have at last made up your mind that there is no such thing as overreaching the minister?'

'Confound him, say I – yes; I made the re-examination, however, as Dupin suggested – but it was all labour lost, as I knew it would be.'

'How much was the reward offered, did you say?' asked Dupin.

'Why, a very great deal – a *very* liberal reward – I don't like to say how much, precisely; but I *will* say, that I wouldn't mind giving my individual cheque for fifty thousand francs to anyone who could obtain me that letter. The fact is, it is becoming of more and more importance every day; and the reward has been lately doubled. If it were trebled, however, I could do no more than I have done.'

'Why, yes,' said Dupin drawlingly, between the whiffs of his meerschaum, 'I really – think, G—, you have not exerted yourself – to the utmost – in this matter. You might – do a little more, I think, eh?'

'How? – In what way?'

'Why – puff, puff – you might – puff, puff – employ counsel in the matter, eh? – puff, puff, puff. Do you remember the story they tell of Abernethy?'

'No; hang Abernethy!'

'To be sure! hang him and welcome. But once upon a time, a certain rich miser conceived the design of sponging upon this Abernethy for a medical opinion. Getting up, for this purpose, an ordinary conversation in a private company, he insinuated his case to the physician, as that of an imaginary individual.

' "We will suppose," said the miser, "that his symptoms are such and such; now, doctor, what would *you* have directed him to take?"

' "Take!" said Abernethy, "why, take *advice*, to be sure." '

'But,' said the Prefect, a little discomposed, 'I am *perfectly* willing to take advice, and to pay for it. I would *really* give fifty thousand francs to anyone who would aid me in the matter.'

'In that case,' replied Dupin, opening a drawer, and producing a chequebook, 'you may as well fill me up a cheque for the amount mentioned. When you have signed it, I will hand you the letter.'

I was astounded. The Prefect appeared absolutely thunderstruck. For some minutes he remained speechless and motionless, looking incredulously at my friend with open mouth, and eyes that seemed starting from their sockets; then, apparently recovering himself in some measure, he seized a pen, and after several pauses and vacant stares, finally filled up and signed a cheque for fifty thousand francs, and handed it across the table to Dupin. The latter examined it carefully and deposited it in his pocketbook; then, unlocking an *escritoire*, took thence a letter and gave it to the Prefect. This functionary grasped it in a perfect agony of joy, opened it with a trembling hand, cast a rapid glance at its contents, and then, scrambling and struggling to the door, rushed at length unceremoniously from the room and from the house, without having uttered a syllable since Dupin had requested him to fill up the cheque.

When he had gone, my friend entered into some explanations.

'The Parisian police,' he said, 'are exceedingly able in their way. They are persevering, ingenious, cunning, and thoroughly versed in the knowledge which their duties seem chiefly to demand. Thus, when G— detailed to us his mode of searching the premises at the Hôtel D—, I felt entire confidence in his having made a satisfactory investigation – so far as his labours extended.'

'So far as his labours extended?' said I.

'Yes,' said Dupin. 'The measures adopted were not only the best of their kind, but carried out to absolute perfection. Had the letter been deposited within the range of their search, these fellows would, beyond a question, have found it.'

I merely laughed – but he seemed quite serious in all that he said.

'The measures, then,' he continued, 'were good in their kind, and well executed; their defect lay in their being inapplicable to the case, and to the man. A certain set of highly ingenious resources are, with the Prefect, a sort of Procrustean bed, to which he forcibly adapts his designs. But he perpetually errs by being too deep or too shallow for the matter in hand; and many a schoolboy is a better reasoner than he. I knew one about eight years of age, whose success at guessing in the game of "even and odd" attracted universal admiration. This game is simple, and is played with marbles. One player holds in his hand a number of these toys, and demands of another whether that number is even or odd. If the guess is right, the guesser wins one; if wrong, he loses one. The boy to whom I allude won all the marbles of the school. Of course he had some principle of guessing; and this lay in mere observation and admeasurement of the astuteness of his opponents. For example, an arrant simpleton is his opponent, and, holding up his closed hand, asks, "Are they even or odd?" Our schoolboy replies "Odd", and loses; but upon the second trial he wins, for he then says to himself, "The simpleton had them even upon the first trial, and his amount of cunning is just sufficient to make him have them odd upon the second; I will therefore guess odd" – he guesses odd, and wins. Now, with a simpleton a degree above the first, he would have reasoned thus: "This fellow finds that in the first instance I guessed odd, and, in the second, he will propose to himself, upon the first impulse, a simple variation from even to odd, as did the first simpleton; but then a second thought will suggest that this is too simple a variation, and finally he will decide upon putting it even as before. I will therefore guess even" – he guesses even, and wins. Now this mode of reasoning in the schoolboy, whom his fellows termed "lucky" – what, in its last analysis, is it?'

'It is merely,' I said, 'an identification of the reasoner's intellect with that of his opponent.'

'It is,' said Dupin; 'and upon enquiring of the boy by what means be effected the *thorough* identification in which his success consisted, I received answer as follows: "When I wish to find out how wise, or how stupid, or how good, or how wicked is anyone, or what are his thoughts at the moment, I fashion the expression of my face, as accurately as possible, in accordance with the expression of his, and then wait to see what thoughts or sentiments arise in my mind or heart, as if to match or correspond with the expression." This response of the schoolboy lies at the bottom of all the spurious profundity which has been attributed to Rochefoucauld, to La Bougive, to Machiavelli, and to Campanella.'

'And the identification,' I said, 'of the reasoner's intellect with that of his opponent, depends, if I understand you aright, upon the accuracy with which the opponent's intellect is admeasured.'

'For its practical value it depends upon this,' replied Dupin; 'and the Prefect and his cohort fail so frequently, first, by default of his identification, and, secondly, by ill-admeasurement, or rather through non-admeasurement, of the intellect with which they are engaged. They consider only their *own* ideas of ingenuity; and, in searching for anything hidden, advert only to the modes in which *they* would have hidden it. They are right in this much – that their own ingenuity is a faithful representative of that of *the mass;* but when the cunning of the individual felon is diverse in character from their own, the felon foils them, of course. This always happens when it is above their own, and very usually when it is below. They have no variation of principle in their investigations; at best, when urged by some unusual emergency – by some extraordinary reward – they extend or exaggerate their old modes of *practice*, without touching their principles. What, for example, in this case of D—, has been done to vary the principle of action? What is all this boring, and probing, and sounding, and scrutinising with the microscope, and dividing the surface of the building into registered square inches – what is it all but an exaggeration *of the application* of the one principle or set of principles of search, which are based upon the one set of notions regarding human ingenuity, to which the Prefect, in the long routine of his duty, has been accustomed? Do you not see he has taken it for granted that *all* men proceed to conceal a letter – not exactly in a gimlet-hole bored in a chair-leg – but, at least, in *some* out-of-the-way hole or corner suggested by the same tenor of thought which would urge a man to secrete a letter in a gimlet-hole bored in a chair-leg? And do you not see also, that such *recherchés* nooks for concealment are adapted only for ordinary occasions, and would be adopted only by ordinary intellects; for, in all cases of concealment, a disposal of the article concealed – a disposal of it in this *recherché* manner – is, in the very first instance, presumable and presumed; and thus its discovery depends, not at all upon the acumen, but altogether upon the mere care, patience, and determination of the seekers; and where the case is of importance – or, what amounts to the same thing in the policial eyes, when the reward is of magnitude – the qualities in question have *never* been known to fail. You will now understand what I meant in suggesting that, had the purloined letter been hidden anywhere within the limits of the Prefect's examination – in other words, had the principle of its concealment been comprehended within the principles of the Prefect – its discovery would have been a matter altogether beyond question. This functionary, however, has been thoroughly mystified; and the remote source of his defeat lies in the supposition that the minister is a fool, because he has acquired renown as a poet. All fools are poets – this the Prefect *feels;* and he is merely guilty of a *non distributio medii* in thence inferring that all poets are fools.'

'But is this really the poet?' I asked. 'There are two brothers, I know; and both have attained reputation in letters. The minister, I believe, has written learnedly on the differential calculus. He is a mathematician, and no poet.'

'You are mistaken; I know him well; he is both. As poet *and* mathematician, he would reason well; as mere mathematician, he could not have reasoned at all, and thus would have been at the mercy of the Prefect.'

'You surprise me,' I said, 'by these opinions, which have been contradicted by the voice of the world. You do not mean to set at naught the well-digested idea of centuries. The mathematical reason has long been regarded as *the* reason *par excellence*.'

'"*Il y a à parièr,*"' replied Dupin, quoting from Chamfort, '"*que toute idée publique, toute convention reçue, est une sottise, car elle a convenue au plus grand nombre.*" The mathematicians, I grant you, have done their best to promulgate the popular error to which you allude, and which is none the less an error for its promulgation as truth. With an art worthy a better cause, for example, they have insinuated the term "analysis" into application to algebra. The French are the originators of this particular deception; but if a term is of any importance – if words derive any value from applicability – then "analysis" conveys "algebra" about as much as, in Latin, "*ambitus*" implies "ambition", "*religio*" "religion", or "*homines honesti*" a set of *honourable* men.'

'You have a quarrel on hand, I see,' said I, 'with some of the algebraists of Paris; but proceed.'

'I dispute the availability, and thus the value, of that reason which is cultivated in any especial form other than the abstractly logical. I dispute, in particular, the reason educed by mathematical study. The mathematics are the science of form and quantity; mathematical reasoning is merely logic applied to observation upon form and quantity. The great error lies in supposing that even the truths of what is called *pure* algebra, are abstract or general truths. And this error is so egregious that I am confounded at the universality with which it has been received. Mathematical axioms are *not* axioms of general truth. What is true of *relation* – of form and quantity – is often grossly false in regard to morals, for example. In this latter science it is very usually *untrue* that the aggregated parts are equal to the whole. In chemistry also the axiom fails. In the consideration of motive it fails; for two motives, each of a given value, have not, necessarily, a value when united, equal to the sum of their values apart. There are numerous other mathematical truths which are only truths within the limits of *relation*. But the mathematician argues, from his *finite truths*, through habit, as if they were of an absolutely general applicability – as the world indeed imagines them to be. Bryant, in his very learned "Mythology", mentions an analogous source of error, when he says that "although the Pagan fables are not believed, yet we forget ourselves continually, and make inferences from them as existing realities." With the algebraists, however, who are Pagans themselves, the "Pagan fables" *are* believed, and the inferences are made, not so much through lapse of memory, as through an unaccountable addling of the brains. In short, I never yet encountered the mere mathematician who could be trusted out of equal roots, or one who did not clandestinely hold it as a point of his faith that $x^2 + px$ was absolutely and unconditionally equal to q. Say to one of these gentlemen, by way of experiment, if you please, that you believe occasions may occur where $x^2 + px$ is not altogether equal to q, and, having made him understand what you mean, get out of his reach as speedily as convenient, for, beyond doubt, he will endeavour to knock you down.

'I mean to say,' continued Dupin, while I merely laughed at his last observations, 'that if the minister had been no more than a mathematician, the Prefect would have been under no necessity of giving me this cheque. I knew him, however, as both mathematician and poet, and my measures were adapted to his capacity, with reference to the circumstances by which he was surrounded. I knew him as a courtier, too, and as a bold *intriguant*. Such a man, I considered, could not fail to be aware of the ordinary policial modes of action. He could not have failed to anticipate – and events have proved that he did not fail to anticipate – the waylayings to which he was subjected. He must have foreseen, I reflected, the secret investigations of his premises. His frequent absences from home at night, which were hailed by the Prefect as certain aids to his success, I regarded only as ruses, to afford opportunity for thorough search to the police, and thus the sooner to impress them with the conviction to which G—, in fact, did finally arrive – the conviction that the letter was not upon the premises. I felt, also, that the whole train of thought, which I was at some pains in detailing to you just now, concerning the invariable principle of policial action in searches for articles concealed – I felt that this whole train of thought would necessarily pass through the mind of the minister. It would imperatively lead him to despise all the ordinary *nooks* of concealment. *He* could not, I reflected, be so weak as not to see that the most intricate and remote recess of his hotel would be as open as his commonest closets to the eyes, to the probes, to the gimlets, and to the microscopes of the prefect. I saw, in fine, that he would be driven, as a matter of course, to *simplicity*, if not deliberately induced to it as a matter of choice. You will remember, perhaps, how desperately the Prefect laughed when I suggested, upon our first interview, that it was just possible this mystery troubled him so much on account of its being so *very* self-evident.'

'Yes,' said I, 'I remember his merriment well. I really thought he would have fallen into convulsions.'

'The material world,' continued Dupin, 'abounds with very strict analogies to the immaterial; and thus some colour of truth has been given to the rhetorical dogma, that metaphor, or simile, may be made to strengthen an argument, as well as to embellish a description. The principle of the *vis inertiae*, for example, seems to be identical in physics and metaphysics. It is not more true in the former, that a large body is with more difficulty set in motion than a smaller one, and that its subsequent momentum is commensurate with this difficulty, than it is, in the latter, that intellects of the vaster capacity, while more forcible, more constant, and more eventful in their movements than those of inferior grade, are yet the less readily moved, and more embarrassed and full of hesitation in the first few steps of their progress. Again, have you ever noticed which of the street signs over the shop-doors are the most attractive of attention?'

'I have never given the matter a thought,' I said.

'There is a game of puzzles,' he resumed, 'which is played upon a map. One party playing requires another to find a given word – the name of town, river, state or empire – any word, in short, upon the motley and perplexed surface of the chart. A novice in the game generally seeks to embarrass his opponents by giving them the most minutely lettered names; but the adept selects such words as stretch, in large characters, from one end of the chart to the other. These, like the over-largely lettered signs and placards of the street, escape observation by dint of being excessively obvious; and here the physical oversight is precisely analogous with the moral inapprehension by which the intellect suffers to pass unnoticed those considerations which are too obtrusively and too palpably self-evident. But this is a point, it appears, somewhat above or beneath the understanding of the Prefect. He never once thought it probable, or possible, that the minister had deposited the letter immediately beneath the nose of the whole world, by way of best preventing any portion of that world from perceiving it.

'But the more I reflected upon the daring, dashing, and discriminating ingenuity of D—; upon the fact that the document must always have been *at hand*, if he intended to use it to good purpose; and upon the decisive evidence, obtained by the Prefect, that it was not hidden within the limits of that dignitary's ordinary search – the more satisfied I became that, to conceal this letter, the minister had resorted to the comprehensive and sagacious expedient of not attempting to conceal it at all.

'Full of these ideas, I prepared myself with a pair of green spectacles, and called one fine morning, quite by accident, at the ministerial hotel. I found D— at home, yawning, lounging, and dawdling, as usual, and pretending to be in the last extremity of *ennui*. He is, perhaps, the most really energetic human being now alive – but that is only when nobody sees him.

'To be even with him, I complained of my weak eyes, and lamented the necessity of the spectacles, under cover of which I cautiously and thoroughly surveyed the whole apartment, while seemingly intent only upon the conversation of my host.

'I paid especial attention to a large writing-table near which he sat, and upon which lay confusedly some miscellaneous letters and other papers, with one or two musical instruments and a few books. Here, however, after a long and very deliberate scrutiny, I saw nothing to excite particular suspicion.

'At length my eyes, in going the circuit of the room, fell upon a trumpery filigree card-rack of pasteboard, that hung dangling by a dirty blue ribbon, from a little brass knob just beneath the middle of the mantelpiece. In this rack, which had three or four compartments, were five or six visiting cards and a solitary letter. This last was much soiled and crumpled. It was torn nearly in two, across the middle – as if a design, in the first instance, to tear it entirely up as worthless, had been altered, or stayed, in the second. It had a large black seal, bearing the D— cipher *very* conspicuously, and was addressed, in a diminutive female hand, to D—, the minister, himself. It was thrust carelessly, and even, as it seemed, contemptuously, into one of the uppermost divisions of the rack.

'No sooner had I glanced at this letter, than I concluded it to be that of which I was in search. To be sure, it was, to all appearance, radically different from the one of which the Prefect had read us so minute a description. Here the seal was large and black, with the D— cipher; there it was small and red, with the ducal arms of the S— family. Here, the address, to the minister, was diminutive and feminine; there the superscription, to a certain royal personage, was markedly bold and decided; the size alone formed a point of correspondence. But then the *radicalness* of these differences, which was excessive; the dirt; the soiled and torn condition of the paper, so inconsistent with the *true* methodical habits of D—, and so suggestive of a design to delude the beholder into an idea of the worthlessness of the document; these things, together with the hyper-obtrusive situation of this document, full in the view of every visitor, and thus exactly in accordance with the conclusions to which I had previously arrived; these things, I say, were strongly corroborative of suspicion, in one who came with the intention to suspect.

'I protracted my visit as long as possible, and, while I maintained a most animated discussion with the minister, upon a topic which I knew well had never failed to interest and excite him, I kept my attention really riveted upon the letter. In this examination, I committed to memory its external appearance and arrangement in the rack; and also fell, at length, upon a discovery, which set at rest whatever trivial doubt I might have entertained. In scrutinising the edges of the paper, I observed them to be more *chafed* than seemed necessary. They presented the *broken* appearance which is manifested when a stiff paper, having been once folded and pressed with a folder, is refolded in a reversed direction, in the same creases or edges which had formed the original fold. This discovery was sufficient. It was clear to me that the letter had been turned, as a glove, inside out, redirected and resealed. I bade the minister good-morning, and took my departure at once, leaving a gold snuffbox upon the table.

'The next morning I called for the snuffbox, when we resumed, quite eagerly, the conversation of the preceding day. While thus engaged, however, a loud report, as if of a pistol, was heard immediately beneath the windows of the hotel, and was succeeded by a series of fearful screams, and the shoutings of a terrified mob. D— rushed to a casement, threw it open, and looked out. In the meantime, I stepped to the card-rack, took the letter, put it in my pocket, and replaced it by a facsimiles (so far as regards externals) which I had carefully prepared at my lodgings – imitating the D— cipher, very readily, by means of a seal formed of bread.

'The disturbance in the street had been occasioned by the frantic behaviour of a man with a musket. He had fired it among a crowd of women and children. It proved, however, to have been without ball, and the fellow was suffered to go his way as a lunatic or a drunkard. When he had gone, D— came from the window, whither I had followed him immediately upon securing the object in view. Soon afterwards I bade him farewell. The pretended lunatic was a man in my own pay.'

'But what purpose had you,' I asked, 'in replacing the letter by a facsimile? Would it not have been better, at the first visit, to have seized it openly, and departed?'

'D—,' replied Dupin, 'is a desperate man, and a man of nerve. His hotel, too, is not without attendants devoted to his interests. Had I made the wild attempt you suggest, I might never have left the ministerial presence alive. The good people of Paris might have heard of me no more. But I had an object apart from these considerations. You know my political prepossessions. In this matter, I act as a partisan of the lady concerned. For eighteen months the minister has had her in his power. She has now him in hers – since, being unaware that the letter is not in his possession, he will proceed with his exactions as if it was. Thus will he inevitably commit himself, at once, to his political destruction. His downfall, too, will not be more precipitate than awkward. It is all very well to talk about the *facilis descensus Averni*; but in all kinds of climbing, as Catalani said of singing, it is far more easy to get up than to come down. In the present instance I have no sympathy – at least no pity – for him who descends. He is that *monstrum horrendum*, an unprincipled man of genius. I confess, however, that I should like very well to know the precise character of his thoughts, when, being defied by her whom the Prefect terms "a certain personage", he is reduced to opening the letter which I left for him in the card-rack.'

'How? did you put anything particular in it?'

'Why – it did not seem altogether right to leave the interior blank – that would have been insulting. D—, at Vienna once, did me an evil turn, which I told him, quite good-humouredly, that I should remember. So, as I knew he would feel some curiosity in regard to the identity of the person who had outwitted him, I thought it a pity not to give him a clue. He is well acquainted with my MS, and I just copied into the middle of the blank sheet the words:

" – Un dessein si funeste,
S'il n'est digne d'Atrée, est digne de Thyeste."

'They are to be found in Crébillon's *Atrée*.'

The Fall of the House of Usher

Son coeur est un luth suspendu;
Sitôt qu'on le touche il résonne.

De Béranger

During the whole of a dull, dark, and soundless day in the autumn of the year, when the clouds hung oppressively low in the heavens, I had been passing alone, on horseback, through a singularly dreary tract of country; and at length found myself, as the shades of evening drew on, within view of the melancholy House of Usher. I know not how it was – but, with the first glimpse of the building, a sense of insufferable gloom pervaded my spirit. I say insufferable; for the feeling was unrelieved by any of that half-pleasurable, because poetic, sentiment, with which the mind usually receives even the sternest natural images of the desolate or terrible. I looked upon the scene before me – upon the mere house, and the simple landscape features of the domain – upon the bleak walls – upon the vacant eye-like windows – upon a few rank sedges – and upon a few white trunks of decayed trees – with an utter depression of soul which I can compare to no earthly sensation more properly than to the after-dream of the reveller upon opium – the bitter lapse into everyday life – the hideous dropping off of the veil. There was an iciness, a sinking, a sickening of the heart – an unredeemed dreariness of thought which no goading of the imagination could torture into aught of the sublime. What was it – I paused to think – what was it that so unnerved me in the contemplation of the House of Usher? It was a mystery all insoluble; nor could I grapple with the shadowy fancies that crowded upon me as I pondered. I was forced to fall back upon the unsatisfactory conclusion, that while, beyond doubt, there *are* combinations of very simple natural objects which have the power of thus affecting us, still the analysis of this power lies among considerations beyond our depth. It was possible, I reflected, that a mere different arrangement of the particulars of the scene, of the details of the picture, would be sufficient to modify, or perhaps to annihilate its capacity for sorrowful impression; and, acting upon this idea, I reined my horse to the precipitous brink of a black and lurid tarn that lay in unruffled lustre by the dwelling, and gazed down – but with a shudder even more thrilling than before – upon the remodelled and inverted images of the grey sedge, and the ghastly tree-stems, and the vacant and eye-like windows.

Nevertheless, in this mansion of gloom I now proposed to myself a sojourn of some weeks. Its proprietor, Roderick Usher, had been one of my boon companions in boyhood; but many years had elapsed since our last meeting. A letter, however, had lately reached me in a distant part of the country – a letter from him – which, in its wildly importunate nature, had admitted of no other than the personal reply. The MS gave evidence of nervous agitation. The writer spoke of acute bodily illness – of a mental disorder which oppressed him – and of an earnest desire to see me, as his best, and indeed his only personal friend, with a view of attempting, by the cheerfulness of my society, some alleviation of his malady. It was the manner in which all this, and much more, was said – it was the apparent *heart* that went with his request – which allowed me no room for hesitation; and I accordingly obeyed forthwith what I still considered a very singular summons.

Although, as boys, we had been even intimate associates, yet I really knew little of my friend. His reserve had been always excessive and habitual. I was aware, however, that his very ancient family had been noted, time out of mind, for a peculiar sensibility of temperament, displaying itself, through long ages, in many works of exalted art, and manifested, of late, in repeated deeds of munificent yet unobtrusive charity, as well as in a passionate devotion to the intricacies, perhaps even more than to the orthodox and easily recognisable beauties of musical science. I had learned, too, the very remarkable fact, that the stem of the Usher race, all time-honoured as it was, had put forth, at no period, any enduring branch; in other words, that the entire family lay in the direct line of descent, and had always, with very trifling and very temporary variation, so lain. It was this deficiency, I considered, while running over in thought the perfect keeping of the character of the premises with the accredited character of the people, and while speculating upon the possible influence which the one, in the long lapse of centuries, might have exercised upon the other – it was this deficiency, perhaps, of collateral issue, and the consequent undeviating transmission, from sire to son, of the patrimony with the name, which had, at length, so identified the two as to merge the original title of the estate in the quaint and equivocal appellation of the 'House of Usher' – an appellation which seemed to include, in the minds of the peasantry who used it, both the family and the family mansion.

I have said that the sole effect of my somewhat childish experiment – that of looking down within the tarn – had been to deepen the first singular impression. There can be no doubt that the consciousness of the rapid increase of my superstition – for why should I not so term it? – served mainly to accelerate the increase itself. Such, I have long known, is the paradoxical law of all sentiments having terror as a basis. And it might have been for this reason only, that, when I again uplifted my eyes to the house itself, from its image in the pool, there grew in my mind a strange fancy – a fancy so ridiculous, indeed, that I but mention it to show the vivid force of the sensations which oppressed me. I had so worked upon my imagination as really to believe that about the whole mansion and domain there hung an atmosphere peculiar to themselves and their immediate vicinity – an atmosphere which had no affinity with the air of heaven, but which had reeked up from the decayed trees, and the grey wall, and the silent tarn – a pestilent and mystic vapour, dull, sluggish, faintly discernible, and leaden-hued.

Shaking off from my spirit what *must* have been a dream, I scanned more narrowly the real aspect of the building. Its principal feature seemed to be that of an excessive antiquity. The discoloration of ages had been great. Minute fungi overspread the whole exterior, hanging in a fine tangled webwork from the eaves. Yet all this was apart from any extraordinary dilapidation. No portion of the masonry had fallen: and there appeared to be a wild inconsistency between its still perfect adaptation of parts, and the crumbling condition of the individual stones. In this there was much that reminded me of the specious totality of old woodwork which has rotted for long years in some neglected vault, with no disturbance from the breath of the external air. Beyond this indication of extensive decay, however, the fabric gave little token of instability. Perhaps the eye of a scrutinising observer might have discovered a barely perceptible fissure, which, extending from the roof of the building in front, made its way down the wall in a zigzag direction, until it became lost in the sullen waters of the tarn.

Noticing these things, I rode over a short causeway to the house. A servant in waiting took my horse, and I entered the Gothic archway of the hall. A valet, of stealthy step, thence conducted me, in silence, through many dark and intricate passages in my progress to the studio of his master. Much that I encountered on the way contributed, I know not how, to heighten the vague sentiments of which I have already spoken. While the objects around me – while the carvings of the ceilings, the sombre tapestries of the walls, the ebon blackness of the floors, and the phantasmagoric armorial trophies which rattled as I strode, were but matters to which, or to such as which, I had been accustomed from my infancy – while I hesitated not to acknowledge how familiar was all this – I still wondered to find how unfamiliar were the fancies which ordinary images were stirring up. On one of the staircases I met the physician of the family. His countenance, I thought, wore a mingled expression of low cunning and perplexity. He accosted me with trepidation and passed on. The valet now threw open a door and ushered me into the presence of his master. The room in which I found myself was very large and lofty. The windows were long, narrow, and pointed, and at so vast a distance from the black oaken floor as to be altogether inaccessible from within. Feeble gleams of encrimsoned light made their way through the trellised panes, and served to render sufficiently distinct the more prominent objects around; the eye, however, struggled in vain to reach the remoter angles of the chamber, or the recesses of the vaulted and fretted ceiling. Dark draperies hung upon the walls. The general furniture was profuse, comfortless, antique, and tattered. Many books and musical instruments lay scattered about, but failed to give any vitality to the scene. I felt that I breathed an atmosphere of sorrow. An air of stern, deep, and irredeemable gloom hung over and pervaded all.

Upon my entrance, Usher arose from a sofa on which he had been lying at full length, and greeted me with a vivacious warmth which had much in it, I at first thought, of an overdone cordiality – of the constrained effort of the *ennuyé* man of the world. A glance, however, at his countenance, convinced me of his perfect sincerity. We sat down; and for some moments, while he spoke not, I gazed upon him with a feeling half of pity, half of awe. Surely, man had never before so terribly altered, in so brief a period, as had Roderick Usher! It was with difficulty that I could bring myself to admit the identity of the wan being before me with the companion of my early boyhood. Yet the character of his face had been at all times remarkable. A cadaverousness of complexion; an eye large, liquid, and luminous beyond comparison; lips somewhat thin and very pallid, but of a surpassingly beautiful curve; a nose of a delicate Hebrew model, but with a breadth of nostril unusual in similar formations; a finely moulded chin, speaking, in its want of prominence, of a want of moral energy; hair of a more than weblike softness and tenuity; these features, with an inordinate expansion above the regions of the temple, made up altogether a countenance not easily to be forgotten. And now in the mere exaggeration of the prevailing character of these features, and of the expression they were wont to convey, lay so much of change that I doubted to whom I spoke. The now ghastly pallor of the skin, and the now miraculous lustre of the eye, above all things startled and even awed me. The silken hair, too, had been suffered to grow all unheeded, and as, in its wild gossamer texture, it floated rather than fell about the face, I could not, even with effort, connect its Arabesque expression with any idea of simple humanity.

In the manner of my friend I was at once struck with an incoherence – an inconsistency; and I soon found this to arise from a series of feeble and futile struggles to overcome an habitual trepidancy – an excessive nervous agitation. For something of this nature I had indeed been prepared, no less by his letter, than by reminiscences of certain boyish traits, and by conclusions deduced from his peculiar physical conformation and temperament. His action was alternately vivacious and sullen. His voice varied rapidly from a tremulous indecision (when the animal spirits seemed utterly in abeyance) to that species of energetic concision – that abrupt, weighty, unhurried, and hollow-sounding enunciation – that leaden, self-balanced, and perfectly modulated guttural utterance, which may be observed in the lost drunkard, or the irreclaimable eater of opium, during the periods of his most intense excitement.

It was thus that he spoke of the object of my visit, of his earnest desire to see me, and of the solace he expected me to afford him. He entered, at some length, into what he conceived to be the nature of his malady. It was, he said, a constitutional and a family evil, and one for which he despaired to find a remedy – a mere nervous affection, he immediately added, which would undoubtedly soon pass off. It displayed itself in a host of unnatural sensations. Some of these, as he detailed them, interested and bewildered me; although, perhaps, the terms, and the general manner of the narration had their weight. He suffered much from a morbid acuteness of the senses; the most insipid food was alone endurable; he could wear only garments of certain texture; the odours of all flowers were oppressive; his eyes were tortured by even a faint light; and there were but peculiar sounds, and these from stringed instruments, which did not inspire him with horror.

To an anomalous species of terror I found him a bounden slave. 'I shall perish,' said he, 'I *must* perish in this deplorable folly. Thus, thus, and not otherwise, shall I be lost. I dread the events of the future, not in themselves, but in their results. I shudder at the thought of any, even the most trivial, incident, which may operate upon this intolerable agitation of soul. I have, indeed, no abhorrence of danger, except in its absolute effect – in terror. In this unnerved – in this pitiable condition – I feel that the period will sooner or later arrive when I must abandon life and reason together, in some struggle with the grim phantasm, FEAR.'

I learned, moreover, at intervals, and through broken and equivocal hints, another singular feature of his mental condition. He was enchained by certain superstitious impressions in regard to the dwelling which he tenanted, and whence, for many years, he had never ventured forth – in regard to an influence whose supposititious force was conveyed in terms too shadowy here to be restated – an influence which some peculiarities in the mere form and substance of his family mansion, had, by dint of long sufferance, he said, obtained over his spirit – an effect which the *physique* of the grey walls and turrets, and of the dim tarn into which they all looked down, had at length brought about upon the *morale* of his existence.

He admitted, however, although with hesitation, that much of the peculiar gloom which thus afflicted him could be traced to a more natural and far more palpable origin – to the severe and long-continued illness – indeed to the evidently approaching dissolution – of a tenderly beloved sister – his sole companion for long years – his last and only relative on earth. 'Her decease,' he said, with a bitterness which I can never forget, 'would leave him (him the hopeless and the frail) the last of the ancient race of the Ushers.' While he spoke, the Lady Madeline (for so was she called) passed slowly through a remote portion of the apartment, and, without having noticed my presence, disappeared. I regarded her with an utter astonishment not unmingled with dread – and yet I found it impossible to account for such feelings. A sensation of stupor oppressed me, as my eyes followed her retreating steps. When a door at length closed upon her, my glance sought instinctively and eagerly the countenance of the brother – but he had buried his face in his hands, and I could only perceive that a far more than ordinary wanness had overspread the emaciated fingers through which trickled many passionate tears.

The disease of the Lady Madeline had long baffled the skill of her physicians. A settled apathy, a gradual wasting away of the person, and frequent although transient affections of a partially cataleptical character, were the unusual diagnosis. Hitherto she had steadily borne up against the pressure of her malady, and had not betaken herself finally to bed; but, on the closing in of the evening of my arrival at the house, she succumbed (as her brother told me at night with inexpressible agitation) to the prostrating power of the destroyer; and I learned that the glimpse I had obtained of her person would thus probably be the last I should obtain – that the lady, at least while living, would be seen by me no more.

For several days ensuing, her name was unmentioned by either Usher or myself; and during this period I was busied in earnest endeavours to alleviate the melancholy of my friend. We painted and read together; or I listened, as if in a dream, to the wild improvisations of his speaking guitar. And thus, as a closer and still closer intimacy admitted me more unreservedly into the recesses of his spirit, the more bitterly did I perceive the futility of all attempt at cheering a mind from which darkness, as if an inherent positive quality, poured forth upon all objects of the moral and physical universe, in one unceasing radiation of gloom.

I shall ever bear about me a memory of the many solemn hours I thus spent alone with the master of the House of Usher. Yet I should fail in any attempt to convey an idea of the exact character of the studies, or of the occupations, in which he involved me, or led me the way. An excited and highly distempered ideality threw a sulphurous lustre over all. His long improvised dirges will ring for ever in my ears. Among other things, I hold painfully in mind a certain singular perversion and amplification of the wild air of the last waltz of Von Weber. From the paintings over which his elaborate fancy brooded, and which grew, touch by touch, into vaguenesses at which I shuddered the more thrillingly, because I shuddered knowing not why – from these paintings (vivid as their images now are before me) I would in vain endeavour to educe more than a small portion which should lie within the compass of merely written words. By the utter simplicity, by the nakedness of his designs, he arrested and overawed attention. If ever mortal painted an idea, that mortal was Roderick Usher. For me at least – in the circumstances then surrounding me – there arose out of the pure abstractions which the hypochondriac contrived to throw upon his canvas, an intensity of intolerable awe, no shadow of which felt I ever yet in the contemplation of the certainly glowing yet too concrete reveries of Fuseli.

One of the phantasmagoric conceptions of my friend, partaking not so rigidly of the spirit of abstraction, may be shadowed forth, although feebly, in words. A small picture presented the interior of an immensely long and rectangular vault or tunnel, with low walls, smooth, white, and without interruption or device. Certain accessory points of the design served well to convey the idea that this excavation lay at an exceeding depth below the surface of the earth. No outlet was observed in any portion of its vast extent, and no torch, or other artificial source of light, was discernible; yet a flood of intense rays rolled throughout, and bathed the whole in a ghastly and inappropriate splendour.

I have just spoken of that morbid condition of the auditory nerve which rendered all music intolerable to the sufferer, with the exception of certain effects of stringed instruments. It was, perhaps, the narrow limits to which he thus confined himself upon the guitar, which gave birth, in great measure, to the fantastic character of his performances. But the fervid facility of his impromptus could not be so accounted for. They must have been, and were, in the notes, as well as in the words, of his wild fantasias (for he not unfrequently accompanied himself with rhymed verbal improvisations), the result of that intense mental collectedness and concentration to which I have previously alluded as observable only in particular moments of the highest artificial excitement. The words of one of these rhapsodies I have easily remembered. I was, perhaps, the more forcibly impressed with it, as he gave it, because, in the under or mystic current of its meaning, I fancied that I perceived, and for the first time, a full consciousness on the part of Usher, of the tottering of his lofty reason upon her throne. The verses, which were entitled 'The Haunted Palace', ran very nearly, if not accurately, thus:

I

In the greenest of our valleys,
  By good angels tenanted,
Once a fair and stately palace –
  Radiant palace – reared its head.
In the monarch Thought's dominion –
  It stood there!
Never seraph spread a pinion
  Over fabric half so fair.

II

Banners yellow, glorious, golden,
  On its roof did float and flow
(This – all this – was in the olden
  Time long ago);
  And every gentle air that dallied,
In that sweet day,
  Along the ramparts plumed and pallid,
A wingèd odour went away.

III

Wanderers in that happy valley
  Through two luminous windows saw
Spirits moving musically
  To a lute's well-tunèd law,
Round about a throne, where sitting
  (Porphyrogene!)
In state his glory well befitting,
  The ruler of the realm was seen.

IV

And all with pearl and ruby glowing
  Was the fair palace door,
Through which came flowing, flowing, flowing
  And sparkling evermore,
A troop of Echoes, whose sweet duty
  Was but to sing,
In voices of surpassing beauty,
  The wit and wisdom of their king.

V

But evil things, in robes of sorrow,
  Assailed the monarch's high estate.
(Ah, let us mourn, for never morrow
  Shall dawn upon him, desolate!)
And, round about his home, the glory
  That blushed and bloomed
Is but a dim-remembered story
  Of the old time entombed.

VI

And travellers now within that valley,
  Through the red-litten windows, see
Vast forms that move fantastically
  To a discordant melody;
While, like a rapid ghastly river,
  Through the pale door,
A hideous throng rush out for ever,
  And laugh – but smile no more.

I well remember that suggestions arising from this ballad led us into a train of thought wherein there became manifest an opinion of Usher's, which I mention not so much on account of its novelty (for other men have thought thus), as on account of the pertinacity with which he maintained it. This opinion, in its general form, was that of the sentience of all vegetable things. But, in his disordered fancy, the idea had assumed a more daring character, and trespassed, under certain conditions, upon the kingdom of inorganisation. I lack words to express the full extent, or the earnest *abandon* of his persuasion. The belief, however, was connected (as I have previously hinted) with the grey stones of the home of his forefathers. The conditions of the sentience had been here, he imagined, fulfilled in the method of collocation of these stones – in the order of their arrangement, as well as in that of the many fungi which overspread them, and of the decayed trees which stood around – above all, in the long undisturbed endurance of this arrangement, and in its reduplication in the still waters of the tarn. Its evidence – the evidence of the sentience – was to be seen, he said (and I here started as he spoke), in the gradual yet certain condensation of an atmosphere of their own about the waters and the walls. The result was discoverable, he added, in that silent, yet importunate and terrible influence which for centuries had moulded the destinies of his family, and which made *him* what I now saw him – what he was. Such opinions need no comment, and I will make none.

Our books – the books which, for years, had formed no small portion of the mental existence of the invalid – were, as might be supposed, in strict keeping with this character of phantasm. We pored together over such works as the Ververt et Chartreuse of Gresset; the Belphegor of Machiavelli; the Heaven and Hell of Swedenborg; the Subterranean Voyage of Nicholas Klimn, by Holberg; the Chiromancy of Robert Flud, of Jean D'Indaginé, and of De la Chambre; the Journey into the Blue Distance of Tieck; and the City of the Sun of Campanella. One favourite volume was a small octavo edition of the *Directorium Inquisitorium*, by the Dominican Eymeric de Gironne; and there were passages in Pomponius Mela, about the old African Satyrs and Oegipans, over which Usher would sit dreaming for hours. His chief delight, however, was found in the perusal of an exceedingly rare and curious book in quarto Gothic – the manual of a forgotten church – the *Vigiliae Mortuorum secundum Chorum Ecclesiae Maguntinae*.

I could not help thinking of the wild ritual of this work, and of its probable influence upon the hypochondriac, when, one evening, having informed me abruptly that the Lady Madeline was no more, he stated his intention of preserving her corpse for a fortnight (previously to its final interment), in one of the numerous vaults within the main walls of the building. The worldly reason, however, assigned for this singular proceeding, was one which I did not feel at liberty to dispute. The brother had been led to his resolution (so he told me) by consideration of the unusual character of the malady of the deceased, of certain obtrusive and eager enquiries on the part of her medical men, and of the remote and exposed situation of the burial-ground of the family. I will not deny that when I called to mind the sinister countenance of the person whom I met upon the staircase, on the day of my arrival at the house, I had no desire to oppose what I regarded as at best but a harmless, and by no means an unnatural, precaution.

At the request of Usher, I personally aided him in the arrangements for the temporary entombment. The body having been encoffined, we two alone bore it to its rest. The vault in which we placed it (and which had been so long unopened that our torches, half smothered in its oppressive atmosphere, gave us little opportunity for investigation) was small, damp, and entirely without means of admission for light; lying, at great depth, immediately beneath that portion of the building in which was my own sleeping apartment. It had been used, apparently, in remote feudal times, for the worst purposes of a donjon-keep, and, in latter days, as a place of deposit for powder, or some other highly combustible substance, as a portion of its floor, and the whole interior of a long archway through which we reached it, were carefully sheathed with copper. The door, of massive iron, had been, also, similarly protected. Its immense weight caused an unusually sharp grating sound, as it moved upon its hinges.

Having deposited our mournful burden upon trestles within this region of horror, we partially turned aside the yet unscrewed lid of the coffin, and looked upon the face of the tenant. A striking similitude between the brother and sister now first arrested my attention; and Usher, divining, perhaps, my thoughts, murmured out some few words from which I learned that the deceased and himself had been twins, and that sympathies of a scarcely intelligible nature had always existed between them. Our glances, however, rested not long upon the dead – for we could not regard her unawed. The disease which had thus entombed the lady in the maturity of youth, had left, as usual in all maladies of a strictly cataleptical character, the mockery of a faint blush upon the bosom and the face, and that suspiciously lingering smile upon the lip which is so terrible in death. We replaced and screwed down the lid, and, having secured the door of iron, made our way, with toil, into the scarcely less gloomy apartments of the upper portion of the house.

And now, some days of bitter grief having elapsed, an observable change came over the features of the mental disorder of my friend. His ordinary manner had vanished. His ordinary occupations were neglected or forgotten. He roamed from chamber to chamber with hurried, unequal, and objectless step. The pallor of his countenance had assumed, if possible, a more ghastly hue – but the luminousness of his eye had utterly gone out. The more occasional huskiness of his tone was heard no more; and a tremulous quaver, as if of extreme terror, habitually characterised his utterance. There were times, indeed, when I thought his unceasingly agitated mind was labouring with some oppressive secret, to divulge which he struggled for the necessary courage. At times, again, I was obliged to resolve all into the mere inexplicable vagaries of madness, for I beheld him gazing upon vacancy for long hours, in an attitude of the profoundest attention, as if listening to some imaginary sound. It was no wonder that his condition terrified – that it infected me. I felt creeping upon me, by slow yet certain degrees, the wild influences of his own fantastic yet impressive superstitions.

It was, especially, upon retiring to bed late in the night of the seventh or eighth day after the placing of the Lady Madeline within the donjon, that I experienced the full power of such feelings. Sleep came not near my couch – while the hours waned and waned away. I struggled to reason off the nervousness which had dominion over me. I endeavoured to believe that much, if not all of what I felt, was due to the bewildering influence of the gloomy furniture of the room – of the dark and tattered draperies, which, tortured into motion by the breath of a rising tempest, swayed fitfully to and fro upon the walls, and rustled uneasily about the decorations of the bed. But my efforts were fruitless. An irrepressible tremor gradually pervaded my frame; and, at length, there sat upon my very heart an incubus of utterly causeless alarm. Shaking this off with a gasp and a struggle, I uplifted myself upon the pillows, and, peering earnestly within the intense darkness of the chamber, hearkened – I know not why, except that an instinctive spirit prompted me – to certain low and indefinite sounds which came, through the pauses of the storm, at long intervals, I knew not whence. Overpowered by an intense sentiment of horror, unaccountable yet unendurable, I threw on my clothes with haste (for I felt that I should sleep no more during the night), and endeavoured to arouse myself from the pitiable condition into which I had fallen, by pacing rapidly to and fro through the apartment.

I had taken but few turns in this manner, when a light step on an adjoining staircase arrested my attention. I presently recognised it as that of Usher. In an instant afterward he rapped with a gentle touch, at my door, and entered, bearing a lamp. His countenance was, as usual, cadaverously wan – but, moreover, there was a species of mad hilarity in his eyes – an evidently restrained hysteria in his whole demeanour. His air appalled me – but anything was preferable to the solitude which I had so long endured, and I even welcomed his presence as a relief.

'And you have not seen it?' he said abruptly, after having stared about him for some moments in silence – 'you have not then seen it? – but, stay! you shall.' Thus speaking, and having carefully shaded his lamp, he hurried to one of the casements, and threw it freely open to the storm.

The impetuous fury of the entering gust nearly lifted us from our feet. It was, indeed, a tempestuous yet sternly beautiful night, and one wildly singular in its terror and its beauty. A whirlwind had apparently collected its force in our vicinity; for there were frequent and violent alterations in the direction of the wind; and the exceeding density of the clouds (which hung so low as to press upon the turrets of the house) did not prevent our perceiving the lifelike velocity with which they flew careering from all points against each other, without passing away into the distance. I say that even their exceeding density did not prevent our perceiving this – yet we had no glimpse of the moon or stars – nor was there any flashing forth of the lightning. But the under surfaces of the huge masses of agitated vapour, as well as all terrestrial objects immediately around us, were glowing in the unnatural light of a faintly luminous and distinctly visible gaseous exhalation which hung about and enshrouded the mansion.

'You must not – you shall not behold this!' said I, shudderingly, to Usher, as I led him, with a gentle violence, from the window to a seat. 'These appearances, which bewilder you, are merely electrical phenomena not uncommon – or it may be that they have their ghastly origin in the rank miasma of the tarn. Let us close this casement – the air is chilling and dangerous to your frame. Here is one of your favourite romances. I will read, and you shall listen – and so we will pass away this terrible night together.'

The antique volume which I had taken up was the 'Mad Trist' of Sir Launcelot Canning; but I had called it a favourite of Usher's more in sad jest than in earnest; for, in truth, there is little in its uncouth and unimaginative prolixity which could have had interest for the lofty and spiritual ideality of my friend. It was, however, the only book immediately at hand; and I indulged a vague hope that the excitement which now agitated the hypochondriac, might find relief (for the history of mental disorder is full of similar anomalies) even in the extremeness of the folly which I should read. Could I have judged, indeed, by the wild overstrained air of vivacity with which he hearkened, or apparently hearkened, to the words of the tale, I might well have congratulated myself upon the success of my design.

I had arrived at that well-known portion of the story where Ethelred, the hero of the Trist, having sought in vain for peaceable admission into the dwelling of the hermit, proceeds to make good an entrance by force. Here, it will be remembered, the words of the narrative run thus: –

'And Ethelred, who was by nature of a doughty heart, and who was now mighty withal, on account of the powerfulness of the wine which he had drunken, waited no longer to hold parley with the hermit, who, in sooth, was of an obstinate and maliceful turn, but, feeling the rain upon his shoulders, and fearing the rising of the tempest, uplifted his mace outright, and, with blows, made quickly room in the plankings of the door for his gauntleted hand; and now pulling therewith sturdily, he so cracked, and ripped, and tore all asunder, that the noise of the dry and hollow-sounding wood alarummed and reverberated throughout the forest.'

At the termination of this sentence I started, and for a moment paused; for it appeared to me (although I at once concluded that my excited fancy had deceived me) – it appeared to me that, from some very remote portion of the mansion, there came, indistinctly, to my ears, what might have been, in its exact similarity of character, the echo (but a stifled and dull one certainly) of the very cracking and ripping sound which Sir Launcelot had so particularly described. It was, beyond doubt, the coincidence alone which had arrested my attention; for, amid the rattling of the sashes of the casements, and the ordinary commingled noises of the still increasing storm, the sound, in itself, had nothing, surely, which should have interested or disturbed me. I continued the story:

'But the good champion Ethelred, now entering within the door, was sore enraged and amazed to perceive no signal of the maliceful hermit; but, in the stead thereof, a dragon of a scaly and prodigious demeanour, and of a fiery tongue, which sate in guard before a palace of gold, with a floor of silver; and upon the wall there hung a shield of shining brass with this legend enwritten:

> Who entereth herein, a conqueror hath bin;
> Who slayeth the dragon, the shield he shall win.

And Ethelred uplifted his mace, and struck upon the head of the dragon, which fell before him, and gave up his pesty breath, with a shriek so horrid and harsh, and withal so piercing, that Ethelred had fain to close his ears with his hands against the dreadful noise of it, the like whereof was never before heard.'

Here again I paused abruptly, and now with a feeling of wild amazement – for there could be no doubt whatever that, in this instance, I did actually hear (although from what direction it proceeded I found it impossible to say) a low and apparently distant, but harsh, protracted, and most unusual screaming or grating sound – the exact counterpart of what my fancy had already conjured up for the dragon's unnatural shriek as described by the romancer.

Oppressed as I certainly was, upon the occurrence of this second and most extraordinary coincidence, by a thousand conflicting sensations, in which wonder and extreme terror were predominant, I still retained sufficient presence of mind to avoid exciting, by any observation, the sensitive nervousness of my companion. I was by no means certain that he had noticed the sound in question; although, assuredly, a strange alteration had, during the last few minutes, taken place in his demeanour. From a position fronting my own, he had gradually brought round his chair, so as to sit with his face to the door of the chamber; and thus I could but partially perceive his features, although I saw that his lips trembled as if he were murmuring inaudibly. His head had

BUT THEN WITHOUT THOSE DOORS THERE DID STAND THE LOFTY AND ENSHROUDED FIGURE OF THE LADY MADELINE OF USHER dropped upon his breast – yet I knew that he was not asleep, from the wide and rigid opening of the eye as I caught a glance of it in profile. The motion of his body, too, was at variance with this idea – for he rocked from side to side with a gentle yet constant and uniform sway. Having rapidly taken notice of all this, I resumed the narrative of Sir Launcelot, which thus proceeded:

'And now, the champion, having escaped from the terrible fury of the dragon, bethinking himself of the brazen shield, and of the breaking up of the enchantment which was upon it, removed the carcass from out of the way before him, and approached valorously over the silver pavement of the castle to where the shield was upon the wall; which in sooth tarried not for his full coming, but fell down at his feet upon the silver floor, with a mighty great and terrible ringing sound.'

No sooner had these syllables passed my lips, than – as if a shield of brass had indeed, at the moment, fallen heavily upon a floor of silver – I became aware of a distinct, hollow, metallic, and clangorous, yet apparently muffled reverberation. Completely unnerved, I leaped to my feet; but the measured rocking movement of Usher was undisturbed. I rushed to the chair in which he sat. His eyes were bent fixedly before him, and throughout his whole countenance there reigned a stony rigidity. But, as I placed my hand upon his shoulder, there came a strong shudder over his whole person; a sickly smile quivered on his lips; and I saw that he spoke in a low, hurried, and gibbering murmur, as if unconscious of my presence. Bending closely over him, I at length drank in the hideous import of his words.

'Not hear it? – yes, I hear it, and *have* heard it. Long – long – long – many minutes, many hours, many days, have I heard it – yet I dared not – oh, pity me, miserable wretch that I am! – I dared not – I *dared* not speak! *We have put her living in the tomb!* Said I not that my senses were acute? I *now* tell you that I heard her first feeble movements in the hollow coffin. I heard them – many, many days ago – yet I dared not – *I dared not speak!* And now – tonight – Ethelred – ha! ha! – the breaking of the hermit's door, and the death-cry of the dragon, and the clangour of the shield! – say, rather, the rending of her coffin, and the grating of the iron hinges of her prison, and her struggles within the coppered archway of the vault! Oh, whither shall I fly? Will she not be here anon? Is she not hurrying to upbraid me for my haste? Have I not heard her footstep on the stair? Do I not distinguish that heavy and horrible beating of her heart? Madman!' – here he sprang furiously to his feet, and shrieked out his syllables, as if in the effort he were giving up his soul – *'Madman! I tell you that she now stands without the door!'*

As if in the superhuman energy of his utterance there had been found the potency of a spell – the huge antique panels to which the speaker pointed threw slowly back, upon the instant, their ponderous and ebony jaws. It was the work of the rushing gust – but then without those doors there *did* stand the lofty and enshrouded figure of the Lady Madeline of Usher. There was blood upon her white robes, and the evidence of some bitter struggle upon every portion of her emaciated frame. For a moment she remained trembling and reeling to and fro upon the threshold – then, with a low moaning cry, fell heavily inward upon the person of her brother, and in her violent and now final death-agonies, bore him to the floor a corpse, and a victim to the terrors he had anticipated.

From that chamber, and from that mansion, I fled aghast. The storm was still abroad in all its wrath as I found myself crossing the old causeway. Suddenly there shot along the path a wild light, and I turned to see whence a gleam so unusual could have issued; for the vast house and its shadows were alone behind me. The radiance was that of the full, setting, and blood-red moon, which now shone vividly through that once barely-discernible fissure, of which I have before spoken as extending from the roof of the building, in a zigzag direction, to the base. While I gazed, this fissure rapidly widened – there came a fierce breath of the whirlwind – the entire orb of the satellite burst at once upon my sight – my brain reeled as I saw the mighty walls rushing asunder – there was a long tumultuous shouting sound like a voice of a thousand waters – and the deep and dank tarn at my feet closed sullenly and silently over the fragments of the 'House of Usher'.

The Pit and the Pendulum

'Impia tortorum longas hic turba furores
Sanguinis innocui, non satiata, aluit.
Sospite nunc patria, fracto nunc funeris antro,
Mors ubi dira fuït vita salusque patent.'

Quatrain composed for the gates of a market to be erected upon the site of the Jacobin Club House at Paris.

I was sick – sick unto death with that long agony; and when they at length unbound me, and I was permitted to sit, I felt that my senses were leaving me. The sentence – the dread sentence of death – was the last of distinct accentuation which reached my ears. After that, the sound of the inquisitorial voices seemed merged in one dreamy indeterminate hum. It conveyed to my soul the idea of *revolution* – perhaps from its association in fancy with the burr of a mill-wheel. This only for a brief period; for presently I heard no more. Yet, for a while, I saw; but with how terrible an exaggeration! I saw the lips of the black-robed judges. They appeared to me white – whiter than the sheet upon which I trace these words – and thin even to grotesqueness; thin with the intensity of their expression of firmness – of immovable resolution – of stern contempt of human torture. I saw that the decrees of what to me was Fate, were still issuing from those lips. I saw them writhe with a deadly locution. I saw them fashion the syllables of my name; and I shuddered because no sound succeeded. I saw, too, for a few moments of delirious horror, the soft and nearly imperceptible waving of the sable draperies which enwrapped the walls of the apartment. And then my vision fell upon the seven tall candles upon the table. At first they wore the aspect of charity, and seemed white slender angels who would save me; but then, all at once, there came a most deadly nausea over my spirit, and I felt every fibre in my frame thrill as if I had touched the wire of a galvanic battery, while the angel forms became meaningless spectres, with heads of flame, and I saw that from them there would be no help. And then there stole into my fancy, like a rich musical note, the thought of what sweet rest there must be in the grave. The thought came gently and stealthily, and it seemed long before it attained full appreciation; but just as my spirit came at length properly to feel and entertain it, the figures of the judges vanished, as if magically, from before me; the tall candles sank into nothingness; their flames went out utterly; the blackness of darkness supervened; all sensations appeared swallowed up in a mad rushing descent as of the soul into Hades. Then silence, and stillness, and night were the universe.

I had swooned; but still will not say that all of consciousness was lost. What of it there remained I will not attempt to define, or even to describe; yet all was not lost. In the deepest slumber – no! In delirium – no! In a swoon – no! In death – no! even in the grave all *is not* lost. Else there is no immortality for man. Arousing from the most profound of slumbers, we break the gossamer web of *some* dream. Yet in a second afterward (so frail may that web have been) we remember not that we have dreamed. In the return to life from the swoon there are two stages: first, that of the sense of mental or spiritual; secondly, that of the sense of physical existence. It seems probable that if, upon reaching the second stage, we could recall the impressions of the first, we should find these impressions eloquent in memories of the gulf beyond. And that gulf is – what? How at least shall we distinguish its shadows from those of the tomb? But if the impressions of what I have termed the first stage are not, at will, recalled, yet, after long interval, do they not come unbidden, while we marvel whence they come? He who has never swooned, is not he who finds strange palaces and wildly familiar faces in coals that glow; is not he who beholds floating in mid-air the sad visions that the many may not view; is not he who ponders over the perfume of some novel flower – is not he whose brain grows bewildered with the meaning of some musical cadence which has never before arrested his attention.

Amid frequent and thoughtful endeavours to remember; amid earnest struggles to regather some token of the state of seeming nothingness into which my soul had lapsed, there have been moments when I have dreamed of success; there have been brief, very brief periods when I have conjured up remembrances which the lucid reason of a later epoch assures me could have had reference only to that condition of seeming unconsciousness. These shadows of memory tell, indistinctly, of tall figures that lifted and bore me in silence down – down – still down – till a hideous dizziness oppressed me at the mere idea of the interminableness of the descent. They tell also of a vague horror at my heart, on account of that heart's unnatural stillness. Then comes a sense of sudden motionlessness throughout all things; as if those who bore me (a ghastly train!) had outrun, in their descent, the limits of the limitless, and paused from the wearisomeness of their toil. After this I call to mind flatness and dampness; and then all is *madness* – the madness of a memory which busies itself among forbidden things.

Very suddenly there came back to my soul motion and sound – the tumultuous motion of the heart, and, in my ears, the sound of its beating. Then a pause, in which all is blank. Then again sound, and motion, and touch – a tingling sensation pervading my frame. Then the mere consciousness of existence, without thought – a condition which lasted long. Then, very suddenly, *thought*, and shuddering terror, and earnest endeavour to comprehend my true state. Then a strong desire to lapse into insensibility. Then a rushing revival of soul and a successful effort to move. And now a full memory of the trial, of the judges, of the sable draperies, of the sentence, of the sickness, of the swoon. Then entire forgetfulness of all that followed; of all that a later day and much earnestness of endeavour have enabled me vaguely to recall.

So far, I had not opened my eyes. I felt that I lay upon my back, unbound. I reached out my hand, and it fell heavily upon something damp and hard. There I suffered it to remain for many minutes, while I strove to imagine where and *what* I could be. I longed, yet dared not to employ my vision. I dreaded the first glance at objects around me. It was not that I feared to look upon things horrible, but that I grew aghast lest there should be *nothing* to see. At length, with a wild desperation at heart, I quickly unclosed my eyes. My worst thoughts, then, were confirmed. The blackness of eternal night encompassed me. I struggled for breath. The intensity of the darkness seemed to oppress and stifle me. The atmosphere was intolerably close. I still lay quietly, and made effort to exercise my reason. I brought to mind the inquisitorial proceedings, and attempted from that point to deduce my real condition. The sentence had passed; and it appeared to me that a very long interval of time had since elapsed. Yet not for a moment did I suppose myself actually dead. Such a supposition, notwithstanding what we read in fiction, is altogether inconsistent with real existence – but where and in what state was I? The condemned to death, I knew, perished usually at the *autos da fé*, and one of these had been held on the very night of the day of my trial. Had I been remanded to my dungeon, to await the next sacrifice, which would not take place for many months? This I at once saw could not be. Victims had been in immediate demand. Moreover, my dungeon, as well as all the condemned cells at Toledo, had stone floors, and light was not altogether excluded.

A fearful idea now suddenly drove the blood in torrents upon my heart, and for a brief period I once more relapsed into insensibility. Upon recovering, I at once started to my feet, trembling convulsively in every fibre. I thrust my arms wildly above and around me in all directions. I felt nothing; yet dreaded to move a step, lest I should be impeded by the walls of a *tomb*. Perspiration burst from every pore, and stood in cold beads upon my forehead. The agony of suspense grew at length intolerable, and I cautiously moved forward, with my arms extended, and my eyes straining from their sockets, in the hope of catching some faint ray of light. I proceeded for many paces; but still all was blackness and vacancy. I breathed more freely. It seemed evident that mine was not, at least, the most hideous of fates.

And now, as I still continued to step cautiously onward, there came thronging upon my recollection a thousand vague rumours of the horrors of Toledo. Of the dungeons there had been strange things narrated – fables I had always deemed them – but yet strange, and too ghastly to repeat, save in a whisper. Was I left to perish of starvation in this subterranean world of darkness; or what fate, perhaps even more fearful, awaited me? That the result would be death, and a death of more than customary bitterness, I knew too well the character of my judges to doubt. The mode and the hour were all that occupied or distracted me.

My outstretched hands at length encountered some solid obstruction. It was a wall, seemingly of stone masonry – very smooth, slimy, and cold. I followed it up, stepping with all the careful distrust with which certain antique narratives had inspired me. This process, however, afforded me no means of ascertaining the dimensions of my dungeon, as I might make its circuit, and return to the point whence I set out, without being aware of the fact, so perfectly uniform seemed the wall. I therefore sought the knife which had been in my pocket, when led into the inquisitorial chamber, but it was gone; my clothes had been exchanged for a wrapper of coarse serge. I had thought of forcing the blade in some minute crevice of the masonry, so as to identify my point of departure. The difficulty, nevertheless, was but trivial; although, in the disorder of my fancy, it seemed at first insuperable. I tore a part of the hem from the robe and placed the fragment at full length, and at right angles to the wall. In groping my way around the prison, I could not fail to encounter this rag upon completing the circuit. So, at least, I thought; but I had not counted upon the extent of the dungeon, or upon my own weakness. The ground was moist and slippery. I staggered onward for some time, when I stumbled and fell. My excessive fatigue induced me to remain prostrate; and sleep soon overtook me as I lay.

Upon awaking, and stretching forth an arm, I found beside me a loaf and a pitcher with water. I was too much exhausted to reflect upon this circumstance, but ate and drank with avidity. Shortly afterward I resumed my tour around the prison, and, with much toil, came at last upon the fragment of the serge. Up to the period when I fell, I had counted fifty-two paces, and, upon resuming my walk, I had counted forty-eight more – when I arrived at the rag. There were in all, then, a hundred paces; and, admitting two paces to the yard, I presumed the dungeon to be fifty yards in circuit. I had met, however, with many angles in the wall, and thus I could form no guess at the shape of the vault; for vault I could not help supposing it to be.

I had little object – certainly no hope – in these researches; but a vague curiosity prompted me to continue them. Quitting the wall, I resolved to cross the area of the enclosure. At first, I proceeded with extreme caution, for the floor, although seemingly of solid material, was treacherous with slime. At length, however, I took courage, and did not hesitate to step firmly – endeavouring to cross in as direct a line as possible. I had advanced some ten or twelve paces in this manner, when the remnant of the torn hem of my robe became entangled between my legs. I stepped on it, and fell violently on my face.

In the confusion attending my fall, I did not immediately apprehend a somewhat startling circumstance, which yet, in a few seconds afterward, and while I still lay prostrate, arrested my attention. It was this: my chin rested upon the floor of the prison, but my lips, and the upper portion of my head, although seemingly at a less elevation than the chin, touched nothing. At the same time, my forehead seemed bathed in a clammy vapour, and the peculiar smell of decayed fungus arose to my nostrils. I put forward my arm, and shuddered to find that I had fallen at the very brink of a circular pit, whose extent, of course, I had no means of ascertaining at the moment. Groping about the masonry just below the margin, I succeeded in dislodging a small fragment, and let it fall into the abyss. For many seconds I hearkened to its reverberations as it dashed against the sides of the chasm in its descent. At length, there was a sullen plunge into water, succeeded by loud echoes. At the same moment, there came a sound resembling the quick opening, and as rapid closing of a door overhead, while a faint gleam of light flashed suddenly through the gloom, and as suddenly faded away.

I saw clearly the doom which had been prepared for me, and congratulated myself upon the timely accident by which I had escaped. Another step before my fall, and the world had seen me no more. And the death just avoided was of that very character which I had regarded as fabulous and frivolous in the tales respecting the Inquisition. To the victims of its tyranny, there was the choice of death with its direst physical agonies, or death with its most hideous moral horrors. I had been reserved for the latter. By long suffering my nerves had been unstrung, until I trembled at the sound of my own voice, and had become in every respect a fitting subject for the species of torture which awaited me.

Shaking in every limb, I groped my way back to the wall – resolving there to perish rather than risk the terrors of the wells, of which my imagination now pictured many in various positions about the dungeon. In other conditions of mind, I might have had courage to end my misery at once, by a plunge into one of these abysses; but now I was the veriest of cowards. Neither could I forget what I had read of these pits – that the *sudden* extinction of life formed no part of their most horrible plan.

Agitation of spirit kept me awake for many long hours; but at length I again slumbered. Upon arousing, I found by my side, as before, a loaf and a pitcher of water. A burning thirst consumed me, and I emptied the vessel at a draught. It must have been drugged – for scarcely had I drunk, before I became irresistibly drowsy. A deep sleep fell upon me – a sleep like that of death. How long it lasted, of course, I know not; but when, once again, I unclosed my eyes, the objects around me were visible. By a wild, sulphurous lustre, the origin of which I could not at first determine, I was enabled to see the extent and aspect of the prison.

In its size I had been greatly mistaken. The whole circuit of its walls did not exceed twenty-five yards. For some minutes this fact occasioned me a world of vain trouble; vain indeed – for what could be of less importance, under the terrible circumstances which environed me, than the mere dimensions of my dungeon? But my soul took a wild interest in trifles, and I busied myself in endeavours to account for the error I had committed in my measurement. The truth at length flashed upon me. In my first attempt at exploration I had counted fifty-two paces, up to the period when I fell; I must then have been within a pace or two of the fragment of serge; in fact, I had nearly performed the circuit of the vault. I then slept – and, upon awaking, I must have returned upon my steps – thus supposing the circuit nearly double what it actually was. My confusion of mind prevented me from observing that I began my tour with the wall to the left, and ended it with the wall to the right.

I had been deceived, too, in respect to the shape of the enclosure. In feeling my way, I had found many angles, and thus deduced an idea of great irregularity; so potent is the effect of total darkness upon one arousing from lethargy or sleep! The angles were simply those of a few slight depressions, or niches, at odd intervals. The general shape of the prison was square. What I had taken for masonry seemed now to be iron, or some other metal, in huge plates, whose sutures or joints occasioned the depression. The entire surface of this metallic enclosure was rudely daubed in all the hideous and repulsive devices to which the charnel superstition of the monks has given rise. The figures of fiends in aspects of menace, with skeleton forms, and other more really fearful images, overspread and disfigured the walls. I observed that the outlines of these monstrosities were sufficiently distinct, but that the colours seemed faded and blurred, as if from the effects of a damp atmosphere. I now noticed the floor, too, which was of stone. In the centre yawned the circular pit from whose jaws I had escaped; but it was the only one in the dungeon.

All this I saw indistinctly and by much effort – for my personal condition had been greatly changed during slumber. I now lay upon my back, and at full length, on a species of low framework of wood. To this I was securely bound by a long strap resembling a surcingle. It passed in many convolutions about my limbs and body, leaving at liberty only my head and my left arm to such extent, that I could, by dint of much exertion, supply myself with food from an earthen dish which lay by my side on the floor. I saw, to my horror, that the pitcher had been removed. I say, to my horror – for I was consumed with intolerable thirst. This thirst it appeared to be the design of my persecutors to stimulate – for the food in the dish was meat pungently seasoned.

Looking upward, I surveyed the ceiling of my prison. It was some thirty or forty feet overhead, and constructed much as the side walls. In one of its panels a very singular figure riveted my whole attention. It was the painted figure of Time as he is commonly represented, save that, in lieu of a scythe, he held what, at a casual glance, I supposed to be the pictured image of a huge pendulum, such as we see on antique clocks. There was something, however, in the appearance of this machine which caused me to regard it more attentively. While I gazed directly upward at it (for its position was immediately over my own), I fancied that I saw it in motion. In an instant afterward the fancy was confirmed. Its sweep was brief, and, of course, slow. I watched it for some minutes, somewhat in fear, but more in wonder. Wearied at length with observing its dull movement, I turned my eyes upon the other objects in the cell.

A slight noise attracted my notice, and looking to the floor, I saw several enormous rats traversing it. They had issued from the well, which lay just within view to my right. Even then, while I gazed, they came up in troops, hurriedly, with ravenous eyes, allured by the scent of the meat. From this it required much effort and attention to scare them away.

It might have been half an hour, perhaps even an hour (for I could take but imperfect note of time) before I again cast my eyes upward. What I then saw, confounded and amazed me. The sweep of the pendulum had increased in extent by nearly a yard. As a natural consequence, its velocity was also much greater. But what mainly disturbed me, was the idea that it had perceptibly *descended*. I now observed – with what horror it is needless to say – that its nether extremity was formed of a crescent of glittering steel, about a foot in length from horn to horn; the horns upward, and the under edge evidently as keen as that of a razor. Like a razor also, it seemed massy and heavy, tapering from the edge into a solid and broad structure above. It was appended to a weighty rod of brass, and the whole *hissed* as it swung through the air.

I could no longer doubt the doom prepared for me by monkish ingenuity in torture. My cognisance of the pit had become known to the inquisitorial agents – *the pit*, whose horrors had been destined for so bold a recusant as myself – *the pit*, typical of hell, and regarded by rumour as the Ultima Thule of all their punishments. The plunge into this pit I had avoided by the merest of accidents, and I knew that surprise, or entrapment into torment, formed an important portion of all the grotesquerie of these dungeon deaths. Having failed to fall, it was no part of the demon plan to hurl me into the abyss; and thus (there being no alternative) a different and a milder destruction awaited me. Milder! I half smiled in my agony as I thought of such application of such a term.

What boots it to tell of the long, long hours of horror more than mortal, during which I counted the rushing oscillations of the steel! Inch by inch – line by line – with a descent only appreciable at intervals that seemed ages – down and still down it came! Days passed – it might have been that many days passed – ere it swept so closely over me as to fan me with its acrid breath. The odour of the sharp steel forced itself into my nostrils. I prayed – I wearied heaven with my prayer for its more speedy descent. I grew frantically mad, and struggled to force myself upward against the sweep of the fearful scimitar. And then I fell suddenly calm, and lay smiling at the glittering death, as a child at some rare bauble.

There was another interval of utter insensibility; it was brief; for, upon again lapsing into life, there had been no perceptible descent in the pendulum. But it might have been long – for I knew there were demons who took note of my swoon, and who could have arrested the vibration at pleasure. Upon my recovery, too, I felt very – oh, inexpressibly – sick and weak, as if through long inanition. Even amid the agonies of that period the human nature craved food. With painful effort I outstretched my left arm as far as my bonds permitted, and took possession of the small remnant which had been spared me by the rats. As I put a portion of it within my lips, there rushed to my mind a half-formed thought of joy – of hope. Yet what business had *I* with hope? It was, as I say, a half-formed thought – man has many such, which are never completed. I felt that it was of joy – of hope; but I felt also that it had perished in its formation. In vain I struggled to perfect – to regain it. Long suffering had nearly annihilated all my ordinary powers of mind. I was an imbecile – an idiot.

The vibration of the pendulum was at right angles to my length. I saw that the crescent was designed to cross the region of the heart. It would fray the serge of my robe – it would return and repeat its operations – again – and again. Notwithstanding its terrifically wide sweep (some thirty feet or more), and the hissing vigour of its descent, sufficient to sunder these very walls of iron, still the fraying of my robe would be all that, for several minutes, it would accomplish. And at this thought I paused. I dared not go farther than this reflection. I dwelt upon it with a pertinacity of attention – as if, in so dwelling, I could arrest *here* the descent of the steel. I forced myself to ponder upon the sound of the crescent as it should pass across the garment – upon the peculiar thrilling sensation which the friction of cloth produces on the nerves. I pondered upon all this frivolity until my teeth were on edge.

Down – steadily down it crept. I took a frenzied pleasure in contrasting its downward with its lateral velocity. To the right – to the left – far and wide – with the shriek of a damned spirit! to my heart, with the stealthy pace of the tiger! I alternately laughed and howled, as the one or the other idea grew predominant.

Down – certainly, relentlessly down! It vibrated within three inches of my bosom! I struggled violently – furiously – to free my left arm. This was free only from the elbow to the hand. I could reach the latter, from the platter beside me, to my mouth, with great effort, but no farther. Could I have broken the fastenings above the elbow, I would have seized and attempted to arrest the pendulum. I might as well have attempted to arrest an avalanche!

Down – still unceasingly – still inevitably down! I gasped and struggled at each vibration. I shrunk convulsively at its every sweep. My eyes followed its outward or upward whirls with the eagerness of the most unmeaning despair; they closed themselves spasmodically at the descent, although death would have been a relief, oh, how unspeakable! Still I quivered in every nerve to think how slight a sinking of the machinery would precipitate that keen, glistening axe upon my bosom. It was *hope* that prompted the nerve to quiver – the frame to shrink. It was *hope* – the hope that triumphs on the rack – that whispers to the death-condemned even in the dungeons of the Inquisition.

I saw that some ten or twelve vibrations would bring the steel in actual contact with my robe – and with this observation there suddenly came over my spirit all the keen, collected calmness of despair. For the first time during many hours – or perhaps days – I *thought*. It now occurred to me, that the bandage, or surcingle, which enveloped me, was *unique*. I was tied by no separate cord. The first stroke of the razor-like crescent athwart any portion of the band, would so detach it that it might be unwound from my person by means of my left hand. But how fearful, in that case, the proximity of the steel! The result of the slightest struggle, how deadly! Was it likely, moreover, that the minions of the torturer had not foreseen and provided for this possibility? Was it probable that the bandage crossed my bosom in the track of the pendulum? Dreading to find my faint, and, as it seemed, my last hope frustrated, I so far elevated my head as to obtain a distinct view of my breast. The surcingle enveloped my limbs and body close in all directions – *save in the path of the destroying crescent.*

Scarcely had I dropped my head back into its original position, when there flashed upon my mind what I cannot better describe than as the unformed half of that idea of deliverance to which I have previously alluded, and of which a moiety only floated indeterminately through my brain when I raised food to my burning lips. The whole thought was now present – feeble, scarcely sane, scarcely definite – but still entire. I proceeded at once, with the nervous energy of despair, to attempt its execution.

For many hours the immediate vicinity of the low framework upon which I lay, had been literally swarming with rats. They were wild, bold, ravenous – their red eyes glaring upon me as if they waited but for motionlessness on my part to make me their prey. 'To what food,' I thought, 'have they been accustomed in the well?'

They had devoured, in spite of all my efforts to prevent them, all but a small remnant of the contents of the dish. I had fallen into an habitual see-saw, or wave of the hand, about the platter; and at length the unconscious uniformity of the movement deprived it of effect. In their voracity, the vermin frequently fastened their sharp fangs in my fingers. With the particles of the oily and spicy viand which now remained, I thoroughly rubbed the bandage wherever I could reach it; then, raising my hand from the floor, I lay breathlessly still.

"THEY SWARMED UPON ME IN EVER ACCUMULATING HEAPS"

At first, the ravenous animals were startled and terrified at the change – at the cessation of movement. They shrank alarmedly back; many sought the well. But this was only for a moment. I had not counted in vain upon their voracity. Observing that I remained without motion, one or two of the boldest leaped upon the framework, and smelt at the surcingle. This seemed the signal for a general rush. Forth from the well they hurried in fresh troops. They clung to the wood – they overran it, and leaped in hundreds upon my person. The measured movement of the pendulum disturbed them not at all. Avoiding its strokes, they busied themselves with the anointed bandage. They pressed – they swarmed upon me in ever accumulating heaps. They writhed upon my throat; their cold lips sought my own; I was half stifled by their thronging pressure; disgust, for which the world has no name, swelled my bosom, and chilled, with a heavy clamminess, my heart. Yet one minute, and I felt that the struggle would be over. Plainly I perceived the loosening of the bandage. I knew that in more than one place it must be already severed. With a more than human resolution I lay still.

Nor had I erred in my calculations – nor had I endured in vain. I at length felt that I was *free*. The surcingle hung in ribands from my body. But the stroke of the pendulum already pressed upon my bosom. It had divided the serge of the robe. It had cut through the linen beneath. Twice again it swung, and a sharp sense of pain shot through every nerve. But the moment of escape had arrived. At a wave of my hand my deliverers hurried tumultuously away. With a steady movement – cautious, sidelong, shrinking, and slow – I slid from the embrace of the bandage and beyond the reach of the scimitar. For the moment, at least, *I was free*.

Free! – and in the grasp of the Inquisition! I had scarcely stepped from my wooden bed of horror upon the stone floor of the prison, when the motion of the hellish machine ceased, and I beheld it drawn up, by some invisible force, through the ceiling. This was a lesson which I took desperately to heart. My every motion was undoubtedly watched. Free! – I had but escaped death in one form of agony, to be delivered unto worse than death in some other. With that thought I rolled my eyes nervously around on the barriers of iron that hemmed me in. Something unusual – some change which, at first, I could not appreciate distinctly – it was obvious, had taken place in the apartment. For many minutes of a dreamy and trembling abstraction, I busied myself in vain, unconnected conjecture. During this period, I became aware, for the first time, of the origin of the sulphurous light which illumined the cell. It proceeded from a fissure, about half an inch in width, extending entirely around the prison at the base of the walls, which thus appeared, and were completely separated from the floor. I endeavoured, but of course in vain, to look through the aperture.

As I arose from the attempt, the mystery of the alteration in the chamber broke at once upon my understanding. I have observed that, although the outlines of the figures upon the walls were sufficiently distinct, yet the colours seemed blurred and indefinite. These colours had now assumed, and were momentarily assuming, a startling and most intense brilliancy, that gave to the spectral and fiendish portraitures an aspect that might have thrilled even firmer nerves than my own. Demon eyes, of a wild and ghastly vivacity, glared upon me in a thousand directions, where none had been visible before, and gleamed with the lurid lustre of a fire that I could not force my imagination to regard as unreal.

Unreal! Even while I breathed there came to my nostrils the breath of the vapour of heated iron! A suffocating odour pervaded the prison! A deeper glow settled each moment in the eyes that glared at my agonies! A richer tint of crimson diffused itself over the pictured horrors of blood. I panted! I gasped for breath! There could be no doubt of the design of my tormentors – oh! most unrelenting! oh! most demoniac of men! I shrank from the glowing metal to the centre of the cell. Amid the thought of the fiery destruction that impended, the idea of the coolness of the well came over my soul like balm. I rushed to its deadly brink. I threw my straining vision below. The glare from the enkindled roof illumined its inmost recesses. Yet, for a wild moment, did my spirit refuse to comprehend the meaning of what I saw. At length it forced – it wrestled its way into my soul – it burned itself in upon my shuddering reason. Oh! for a voice to speak! – oh! horror! – oh! any horror but this! With a shriek, I rushed from the margin, and buried my face in my hands – weeping bitterly.

The heat rapidly increased, and once again I looked up, shuddering as with a fit of the ague. There had been a second change in the cell – and now the change was obviously in the *form*. As before, it was in vain that I at first endeavoured to appreciate or understand what was taking place. But not long was I left in doubt. The inquisitorial vengeance had been hurried by my twofold escape, and there was to be no more dallying with the King of Terrors. The room had been square. I saw that two of its iron angles were now acute – two, consequently, obtuse. The fearful difference quickly increased with a low rumbling or moaning sound. In an instant the apartment had shifted its form into that of a lozenge. But the alteration stopped not here – I neither hoped nor desired it to stop. I could have clasped the red walls to my bosom as a garment of eternal peace. 'Death,' I said, 'any death but that of the pit!' Fool! Might I not have known that *into the pit* it was the object of the burning iron to urge me? Could I resist its glow? or if even that, could I withstand its pressure? And now, flatter and flatter grew the lozenge, with a rapidity that left me no time for contemplation. Its centre, and of course, its greatest width, came just over the yawning gulf. I shrank back – but the closing walls pressed me resistlessly onward. At length for my seared and writhing body there was no longer an inch of foothold on the firm floor of the prison. I struggled no more, but the agony of my soul found vent in one loud, long, and final scream of despair. I felt that I tottered upon the brink – I averted my eyes –

There was a discordant hum of human voices! There was a loud blast as of many trumpets! There was a harsh grating as of a thousand thunders! The fiery walls rushed back! An outstretched arm caught my own as I fell, fainting, into the abyss. It was that of General Lasalle. The French army had entered Toledo. The Inquisition was in the hands of its enemies.

The Premature Burial

There are certain themes of which the interest is all-absorbing, but which are too entirely horrible for the purposes of legitimate fiction. These the mere romanticist must eschew, if he do not wish to offend, or to disgust. They are with propriety handled only when the severity and majesty of truth sanctify and sustain them. We thrill, for example, with the most intense of 'pleasurable pains', over the accounts of the Passage of the Beresina, of the Earthquake at Lisbon, of the Plague at London, of the Massacre of St Bartholomew, or of the stifling of the hundred and twenty-three prisoners in the Black Hole at Calcutta. But, in these accounts, it is the fact – it is the reality – it is the history which excites. As inventions, we should regard them with simple abhorrence.

I have mentioned some few of the more prominent and august calamities on record; but in these it is the extent, not less than the character of the calamity, which so vividly impresses the fancy. I need not remind the reader that, from the long and weird catalogue of human miseries, I might have selected many individual instances more replete with essential suffering than any of these vast generalities of disaster. The true wretchedness, indeed – the ultimate woe – is particular, not diffuse. That the ghastly extremes of agony are endured by man the unit, and never by man the mass – for this let us thank a merciful God!

To be buried while alive is, beyond question, the most terrific of these extremes which has ever fallen to the lot of mere mortality. That it has frequently, very frequently, so fallen, will scarcely be denied by those who think. The boundaries which divide Life from Death are at best shadowy and vague. Who shall say where the one ends, and where the other begins? We know that there are diseases in which occur total cessations of all the apparent functions of vitality, and yet in which these cessations are merely suspensions, properly so called. They are only temporary pauses in the incomprehensible mechanism. A certain period elapses, and some unseen mysterious principle again sets in motion the magic pinions and the wizard wheels. The silver cord was not for ever loosed, nor the golden bowl irreparably broken. But where, meantime, was the soul?

Apart, however, from the inevitable conclusion, *a priori*, that such causes must produce such effects – that the well-known occurrence of such cases of suspended animation must naturally give rise, now and then, to premature interments – apart from this consideration, we have the direct testimony of medical and ordinary experience, to prove that a vast number of such interments have actually taken place. I might refer at once, if necessary, to a hundred well-authenticated instances. One of very remarkable character, and of which the circumstances may be fresh in the memory of some of my readers, occurred, not very long ago, in the neighbouring city of Baltimore, where it occasioned a painful, intense, and widely extended excitement. The wife of one of the most respectable citizens – a lawyer of eminence and a member of Congress – was seized with a sudden and unaccountable illness, which completely baffled the skill of her physicians. After much suffering, she died, or was supposed to die. No one suspected, indeed, or had reason to suspect, that she was not actually dead. She presented all the ordinary appearances of death. The face assumed the usual pinched and sunken outline. The lips were of the usual marble pallor. The eyes were lustreless. There was no warmth. Pulsation had ceased. For three days the body was preserved unburied, during which it had acquired a stony rigidity. The funeral, in short, was hastened, on account of the rapid advance of what was supposed to be decomposition.

The lady was deposited in her family vault, which, for three subsequent years, was undisturbed. At the expiration of this term, it was opened for the reception of a sarcophagus – but, alas! how fearful a shock awaited the husband, who, personally, threw open the door. As its portals swung outwardly back, some white-apparelled object fell rattling within his arms. It was the skeleton of his wife in her yet unmouldered shroud.

A careful investigation rendered it evident that she had revived within two days after her entombment – that her struggles within the coffin had caused it to fall from a ledge, or shelf, to the floor, where it was so broken as to permit her escape. A lamp which had been accidentally left, full of oil, within the tomb, was found empty; it might have been exhausted, however, by evaporation. On the uppermost of the steps which led down into the dread chamber, was a large fragment of the coffin, with which it seemed that she had endeavoured to arrest attention, by striking the iron door. While thus occupied, she probably swooned, or possibly died, through sheer terror; and, in falling, her shroud became entangled in some ironwork which projected interiorly. Thus she remained, and thus she rotted, erect.

In the year 1810, a case of living inhumation happened in France, attended with circumstances which go far to warrant the assertion that truth is, indeed, stranger than fiction. The heroine of the story was a Mlle Victorine Lafourcade, a young girl of illustrious family, of wealth, and of great personal beauty. Among her numerous suitors was Julien Bossuet, a poor *litterateur*, or journalist, of Paris. His talents and general amiability had recommended him to the notice of the heiress, by whom he seems to have been truly beloved; but her pride of birth decided her, finally, to reject him, and to wed a M. Renelle, a banker, and a diplomatist of some eminence. After marriage, however, this gentleman neglected, and, perhaps, even more positively ill-treated her. Having passed with him some wretched years, she died – at least her condition so closely resembled death as to deceive everyone who saw her. She was buried – not in a vault – but in an ordinary grave in the village of her nativity. Filled with despair, and still inflamed by the memory of a profound attachment, the lover journeys from the capital to the remote province in which the village lies, with the romantic purpose of disinterring the corpse, and possessing himself of its luxuriant tresses. He reaches the grave. At midnight he unearths the coffin, opens it, and is in the act of detaching the hair, when he is arrested by the unclosing of the beloved eyes. In fact, the lady had been buried alive. Vitality had not altogether departed; and she was aroused, by the caresses of her lover, from the lethargy which had been mistaken for death. He bore her frantically to his lodgings in the village. He employed certain powerful restoratives suggested by no little medical learning. In fine, she revived. She recognised her preserver. She remained with him until, by slow degrees, she fully recovered her original health. Her woman's heart was not adamant, and this last lesson of love sufficed to soften it. She bestowed it upon Bossuet. She returned no more to her husband, but concealing from him her resurrection, fled with her lover to America. Twenty years afterwards, the two returned to France, in the persuasion that time had so greatly altered the lady's appearance, that her friends would be unable to recognise her. They were mistaken, however; for, at the first meeting, M. Renelle did actually recognise and make claim to his wife. This claim she resisted; and a judicial tribunal sustained her in her resistance; deciding that the peculiar circumstances, with the long lapse of years, had extinguished, not only equitably, but legally, the authority of the husband.

The *Chirurgical Journal* of Leipzig – a periodical of high authority and merit, which some American bookseller would do well to translate and republish – records, in a late number, a very distressing event of the character in question.

An officer of artillery, a man of gigantic stature and of robust health, being thrown from an unmanageable horse, received a very severe contusion upon the head, which rendered him insensible at once; the skull was slightly fractured; but no immediate danger was apprehended. Trepanning was accomplished successfully. He was bled, and many other of the ordinary means of relief were adopted. Gradually, however, he fell into a more and more hopeless state of stupor; and, finally, it was thought that he died.

The weather was warm; and he was buried, with indecent haste, in one of the public cemeteries. His funeral took place on Thursday. On the Sunday following, the grounds of the cemetery were, as usual, much thronged with visitors; and about noon, an intense excitement was created by the declaration of a peasant, that, while sitting upon the grave of the officer, he had distinctly felt a commotion of the earth, as if occasioned by someone struggling beneath. At first, little attention was paid to the man's asseveration; but his evident terror, and the dogged obstinacy with which he persisted in his story, had at length their natural effect upon the crowd. Spades were hurriedly procured, and the grave, which was shamefully shallow, was, in a few minutes, so far thrown open that the head of its occupant appeared. He was then, seemingly, dead; but he sat nearly erect within his coffin, the lid of which, in his furious struggles, he had partially uplifted.

He was forthwith conveyed to the nearest hospital, and there pronounced to be still living, although in an asphytic condition. After some hours he revived, recognised individuals of his acquaintance, and in broken sentences, spoke of his agonies in the grave.

From what he related, it was clear that he must have been conscious of life for more than an hour, while inhumed, before lapsing into insensibility. The grave was carelessly and loosely filled with an exceedingly porous soil; and thus some air was necessarily admitted. He heard the footsteps of the crowd overhead, and endeavoured to make himself heard in turn. It was the tumult within the grounds of the cemetery, he said, which appeared to awaken him from a deep sleep – but no sooner was he awake than he became fully aware of the awful horrors of his position.

This patient, it is recorded, was doing well, and seemed to be in a fair way of ultimate recovery, but fell a victim to the quackeries of medical experiment. The galvanic battery was applied, and he suddenly expired in one of those ecstatic paroxysms which, occasionally, it superinduces.

The mention of the galvanic battery, nevertheless, recalls to my memory a well-known and very extraordinary case in point, where its action proved the means of restoring to animation a young attorney of London, who had been interred for two days. This occurred in 1831, and created, at the time, a very profound sensation wherever it was made the subject of converse.

The patient, Mr Edward Stapleton, had died, apparently, of typhus fever, accompanied with some anomalous symptoms which had excited the curiosity of his medical attendants. Upon his seeming decease, his friends were requested to sanction a post-mortem examination, but declined to permit it. As often happens, when such refusals are made, the practitioners resolved to disinter the body and dissect it at leisure, in private. Arrangements were easily effected with some of the numerous corps of body-snatchers with which London abounds; and, upon the third night after the funeral, the supposed corpse was unearthed from a grave eight feet deep, and deposited in the operating chamber of one of the private hospitals.

An incision of some extent had been actually made in the abdomen, when the fresh and undecayed appearance of the subject suggested an application of the battery. One experiment succeeded another, and the customary effects supervened, with nothing to characterise them in any respect, except, upon one or two occasions, a more than ordinary degree of lifelikeness in the convulsive action.

It grew late. The day was about to dawn; and it was thought expedient, at length, to proceed at once to the dissection. A student, however, was especially desirous of testing a theory of his own, and insisted upon applying the battery to one of the pectoral muscles. A rough gash was made, and a wire hastily brought in contact; when the patient, with a hurried, but quite unconvulsive movement, arose from the table, stepped into the middle of the floor, gazed about him uneasily for a few seconds, and then – spoke. What he said was unintelligible; but the words were uttered; the syllabification was distinct. Having spoken, he fell heavily to the floor.

For some moments all were paralysed with awe – but the urgency of the case soon restored them their presence of mind. It was seen that Mr Stapleton was alive, although in a swoon. Upon exhibition of ether he revived and was rapidly restored to health, and to the society of his friends – from whom, however, all knowledge of his resuscitation was withheld, until a relapse was no longer to be apprehended. Their wonder – their rapturous astonishment – may be conceived.

The most thrilling peculiarity of this incident, nevertheless, is involved in what Mr S. himself asserts. He declares that at no period was he altogether insensible – that, dully and confusedly, he was aware of everything which happened to him, from the moment in which he was pronounced *dead* by his physicians, to that in which he fell swooning to the floor of the hospital. 'I am alive,' were the uncomprehended words which, upon recognising the locality of the dissecting-room, he had endeavoured, in his extremity, to utter.

It were an easy matter to multiply such histories as these – but I forbear – for, indeed, we have no need of such to establish the fact that premature interments occur. When we reflect how very rarely, from the nature of the case, we have it in our power to detect them, we must admit that they may *frequently* occur without our cognisance. Scarcely, in truth, is a graveyard ever encroached upon, for any purpose, to any great extent, that skeletons are not found in postures which suggest the most fearful of suspicions.

Fearful indeed the suspicion – but more fearful the doom! It may be asserted, without hesitation, that *no* event is so terribly well adapted to inspire the supremeness of bodily and of mental distress, as is burial before death. The unendurable oppression of the lungs – the stifling fumes of the damp earth – the clinging to the death garments – the rigid embrace of the narrow house – the blackness of the absolute Night – the silence like a sea that overwhelms – the unseen but palpable presence of the Conqueror Worm – these things, with thoughts of the air and grass above, with memory of dear friends who would fly to save us if but informed of our fate, and with consciousness that of this fate they can *never* be informed – that our hopeless portion is that of the really dead – these considerations, I say, carry into the heart, which still palpitates, a degree of appalling and intolerable horror from which the most daring imagination must recoil. We know of nothing so agonising upon Earth – we can dream of nothing half so hideous in the realms of the nethermost Hell. And thus all narratives upon this topic have an interest profound; an interest, nevertheless, which, through the sacred awe of the topic itself, very properly and very peculiarly depends upon our conviction of the *truth* of the matter narrated. What I have now to tell, is of my own actual knowledge – of my own positive and personal experience.

For several years I had been subject to attacks of the singular disorder which physicians have agreed to term catalepsy, in default of a more definite title. Although both the immediate and the predisposing causes, and even the actual diagnosis of this disease, are still mysteries, its obvious and apparent character is sufficiently well understood. Its variations seem to be chiefly of degree. Sometimes the patient lies, for a day only, or even for a shorter period, in a species of exaggerated lethargy. He is senseless and externally motionless; but the pulsation of the heart is still faintly perceptible; some traces of warmth remain; a slight colour lingers within the centre of the cheek; and, upon application of a mirror to the lips, we can detect a torpid, unequal, and vacillating action of the lungs. Then, again, the duration of the trance is for weeks – even for months; while the closest scrutiny, and the most rigorous medical tests, fail to establish any material distinction between the state of the sufferer and what we conceive of absolute death. Very usually, he is saved from premature interment solely by the knowledge of his friends that he has been previously subject to catalepsy, by the consequent suspicion excited, and, above all, by the non-appearance of decay. The advances of the malady are, luckily, gradual. The first manifestations, although marked, are unequivocal. The fits grow successively more and more distinctive, and endure each for a longer term than the preceding. In this lies the principal security from inhumation. The unfortunate whose *first* attack should be of the extreme character which is occasionally seen, would almost inevitably be consigned alive to the tomb.

My own case differed in no important particular from those mentioned in medical books. Sometimes, without any apparent cause, I sank, little by little, into a condition of semi-syncope, or half swoon; and, in this condition, without pain, without ability to stir, or strictly speaking, to think, but with a dull lethargic consciousness of life and of the presence of those who surrounded my bed, I remained, until the crisis of the disease restored me, suddenly, to perfect sensation. At other times I was quickly and impetuously smitten. I grew sick, and numb, and chilly, and dizzy, and so fell prostrate at once. Then, for weeks, all was void, and black, and silent, and Nothing became the universe. Total annihilation could be no more. From these latter attacks I awoke, however, with a gradation slow in proportion to the suddenness of the seizure. Just as the day dawns to the friendless and houseless beggar who roams the streets throughout the long desolate winter night – just so tardily – just so wearily – just so cheerily came back the light of the Soul to me.

Apart from the tendency to trance, however, my general health appeared to be good; nor could I perceive that it was at all affected by the one prevalent malady – unless, indeed, an idiosyncrasy in an ordinary *sleep* may be looked upon as superinduced. Upon awaking from slumber, I could never gain, at once, thorough possession of my senses, and always remained, for many minutes, in much bewilderment and perplexity – the mental faculties in general, but the memory in especial, being in a condition of absolute abeyance.

In all that I endured there was no physical suffering, but of moral distress an infinitude. My fancy grew charnel. I talked 'of worms, of tombs and epitaphs'. I was lost in reveries of death, and the idea of premature burial held continual possession of my brain. The ghastly danger to which I was subjected haunted me day and night. In the former, the torture of meditation was excessive – in the latter, supreme. When the grim darkness overspread the earth, then, with very horror of thought, I shook – shook as the quivering plumes upon the hearse. When nature could endure wakefulness no longer, it was with a struggle that I consented to sleep – for I shuddered to reflect that, upon awaking, I might find myself the tenant of a grave. And when, finally, I sank into slumber, it was only to rush at once into a world of phantasms, above which, with vast, sable, overshadowing wings, hovered, predominant, the one sepulchral idea.

From the innumerable images of gloom which thus oppressed me in dreams, I select for record but a solitary vision. Methought I was immersed in a cataleptic trance of more than usual duration and profundity. Suddenly there came an icy hand upon my forehead, and an impatient, gibbering voice whispered the word 'Arise!' within my ear.

I sat erect. The darkness was total. I could not see the figure of him who had aroused me. I could call to mind neither the period at which I had fallen into the trance, nor the locality in which I then lay. While I remained motionless, and busied in endeavours to collect my thoughts, the cold hand grasped me fiercely by the wrist, shaking it petulantly, while the gibbering voice said again – 'Arise! did I not bid thee arise?'

'And who,' I demanded, 'art thou?'

'I have no name in the regions which I inhabit,' replied the voice mournfully; 'I was mortal, but am fiend. I was merciless, but am pitiful. Thou dost feel that I shudder. My teeth chatter as I speak, yet it is not with the chilliness of the night – of the night without end. But this hideousness is insufferable. How canst *thou* tranquilly sleep? I cannot rest for the cry of these great agonies. These sights are more than I can bear. Get thee up! Come with me into the outer night, and let me unfold to thee the graves. Is not this a spectacle of woe? Behold!'

I looked; and the unseen figure, which still grasped me by the wrist, had caused to be thrown open the graves of all mankind; and from each issued the faint phosphoric radiance of decay, so that I could see into the innermost recesses, and there view the shrouded bodies in their sad and solemn slumbers with the worm. But, alas! the real sleepers were fewer, by many millions, than those who slumbered not at all; and there was a feeble struggling; and there was a general sad unrest; and from out the depths of the countless pits there came a melancholy rustling from the garments of the buried. And, of those who seemed tranquilly to repose, I saw that a vast number had changed, in a greater or less degree, the rigid and uneasy position in which they had originally been entombed.

And the voice again said to me, as I gazed – 'Is it not – oh, is it *not* a pitiful sight?' But, before I could find words to reply, the figure had ceased to grasp my wrist, the phosphoric lights expired, and the graves were closed with a sudden violence, while from out them arose a tumult of despairing cries, saying again, 'Is it not – O God! is it *not* a very pitiful sight?'

Phantasies such as these, presenting themselves at night, extended their terrific influence far into my waking hours. My nerves became thoroughly unstrung, and I fell a prey to perpetual horror. I hesitated to ride, or to walk, or to indulge in any exercise that would carry me from home. In fact, I no longer dared trust myself out of the immediate presence of those who were aware of my proneness to catalepsy, lest, falling into one of my usual fits, I should be buried before my real condition could be ascertained. I doubted the care, the fidelity of my dearest friends. I dreaded that, in some trance of more than customary duration, they might be prevailed upon to regard me as irrecoverable. I even went so far as to fear that, as I occasioned much trouble, they might be glad to consider any very protracted attack as sufficient excuse for getting rid of me altogether. It was in vain they endeavoured to reassure me by the most solemn promises. I exacted the most sacred oaths, that under no circumstances they would bury me until decomposition had so materially advanced as to render further preservation impossible. And, even then, my mortal terrors would listen to no reason – would accept no consolation. I entered into a series of elaborate precautions. Among other things, I had the family vault so remodelled as to admit of being readily opened from within. The slightest pressure upon a long lever that extended far into the tomb would cause the iron portals to fly back. There were arrangements also for the free admission of air and light, and convenient receptacles for food and water, within immediate reach of the coffin intended for my reception. This coffin was warmly and softly padded, and was provided with a lid, fashioned upon the principle of the vault-door, with the addition of springs so contrived that the feeblest movement of the body would be sufficient to set it at liberty. Besides all this, there was suspended from the roof of the tomb a large bell, the rope of which, it was designed, should extend through a hole in the coffin, and so be fastened to one of the hands of the corpse. But, alas! what avails the vigilance against the destiny of man? Not even these well-contrived securities sufficed to save from the uttermost agonies of living inhumation a wretch to these agonies foredoomed!

There arrived an epoch – as often before there had arrived – in which I found myself emerging from total unconsciousness into the first feeble and indefinite sense of existence. Slowly – with a tortoise gradation – approached the faint grey dawn of the physical day. A torpid uneasiness. An apathetic endurance of dull pain. No care – no hope – no effort. Then, after long interval, a ringing in the ears; then, after a lapse still longer, a prickling or tingling sensation in the extremities;

DEEP, DEEP, AND FOR EVER, INTO SOME ORDINARY AND NAMELESS GRAVE then a seemingly eternal period of pleasurable quiescence, during which the awakening feelings are struggling into thought; then a brief re-sinking into nonentity; then a sudden recovery. At length the slight quivering of an eyelid, and immediately thereupon an electric shock of a terror, deadly and indefinite, which sends the blood in torrents from the temples to the heart. And now the first positive effort to think. And now the first endeavour to remember. And now a partial and evanescent success. And now the memory has so far regained its dominion, that, in some measure, I am cognisant of my state. I feel that I am not awaking from ordinary sleep. I recollect that I have been subject to catalepsy. And now, at last, as if by the rush of an ocean, my shuddering spirit is overwhelmed by the one grim danger – by the one spectral and ever-prevalent idea.

For some minutes after this fancy possessed me, I remained without motion. And why? I could not summon courage to move. I dared not make the effort which was to satisfy me of my fate – and yet there was something at my heart which whispered me *it was sure*. Despair – such as no other species of wretchedness ever calls into being – despair alone urged me, after long irresolution, to uplift the heavy lids of my eyes. I uplifted them. It was dark – all dark. I knew that the fit was over. I knew that the crisis of my disorder had long passed. I knew that I had now fully recovered the use of my visual faculties – and yet it was dark – all dark – the intense and utter raylessness of the night that endureth for evermore.

I endeavoured to shriek; and my lips and my parched tongue moved convulsively together in the attempt – but no voice issued from the cavernous lungs, which, oppressed as if by the weight of some incumbent mountain, gasped and palpitated, with the heart, at every elaborate and struggling inspiration.

The movement of the jaws, in this effort to cry aloud, showed me that they were bound up, as is usual with the dead. I felt, too, that I lay upon some hard substance; and by something similar my sides were, also, closely compressed. So far, I had not ventured to stir any of my limbs – but now I violently threw up my arms, which had been lying at length, with the wrists crossed. They struck a solid wooden substance, which extended above my person at an elevation of not more than six inches from my face. I could no longer doubt that I reposed within a coffin at last.

And now, amid all my infinite miseries, came sweetly the cherub Hope – for I thought of my precautions. I writhed, and made spasmodic exertions to force open the lid; it would not move. I felt my wrists for the bell-rope; it was not to be found. And now the comforter fled for ever, and a still sterner Despair reigned triumphant; for I could not help perceiving the absence of the paddings which I had so carefully prepared – and then, too, there came suddenly to my nostrils the strong peculiar odour of moist earth. The conclusion was irresistible. I was *not* within the vault. I had fallen into a trance while absent from home – while among strangers – when, or how, I could not remember – and it was they who had buried me as a dog – nailed up in some common coffin – and thrust, deep, deep, and for ever, into some ordinary and nameless *grave*.

As this awful conviction forced itself, thus, into the innermost chambers of my soul, I once again struggled to cry aloud. And in this second endeavour I succeeded. A long, wild, and continuous shriek, or yell, of agony, resounded through the realms of the subterrene night.

'Hillo! hillo, there!' said a gruff voice, in reply.

'What the devil's the matter now?' said a second.

'Get out o' that!' said a third.

'What do you mean by yowling in that ere kind of style, like a cattymount?' said a fourth; and hereupon I was seized and shaken without ceremony, for several minutes, by a junto of very rough-looking individuals. They did not arouse me from my slumber – for I was wide awake when I screamed – but they restored me to full possession of my memory.

This adventure occurred near Richmond, in Virginia. Accompanied by a friend, I had proceeded, upon a gunning expedition, some miles down the banks of James River. Night approached, and we were overtaken by a storm. The cabin of a small sloop lying at anchor in the stream, and laden with garden mould, afforded us the only available shelter. We made the best of it, and passed the night on board. I slept in one of the only two berths in the vessel – and the berths of a sloop of sixty or seventy tons need scarcely be described. That which I occupied had no bedding of any kind. Its extreme width was eighteen inches. The distance of its bottom from the deck overhead was precisely the same. I found it a matter of exceeding difficulty to squeeze myself in. Nevertheless, I slept soundly; and the whole of my vision – for it was no dream, and no nightmare – arose naturally from the circumstances of my position – from my ordinary bias of thought – and from the difficulty, to which I have alluded, of collecting my senses, and especially of regaining my memory, for a long time after awaking from slumber. The men who shook me were the crew of the sloop, and some labourers engaged to unload it. From the load itself came the earthy smell. The bandage about the jaws was a silk handkerchief in which I bound up my head, in default of my customary nightcap.

The tortures endured, however, were indubitably quite equal, for the time, to those of actual sepulture. They were ey were inconceivably hideous; but out of evil ood; for their very excess wrought in my spirit an evulsion. My soul acquired tone – acquired vent abroad. I took vigorous exercise. I breathed the free air of heaven. I thought upon other subjects than death. I discarded my medical books. 'Buchan' I burned. I read no 'Night Thoughts' – no fustian about churchyards – no bugaboo tales – *such as this*. In short I became a new man, and lived a man's life. From that memorable night I dismissed for ever my charnel apprehensions, and with them vanished the cataleptic disorder, of which, perhaps, they had been less the consequence than the cause.

There are moments when, even to the sober eye of Reason, the world of our sad Humanity may assume the semblance of a Hell – but the imagination of man is no Carathis, to explore with impunity its every cavern. Alas! the grim legion of sepulchral terrors cannot be regarded as altogether fanciful – but, like the demons in whose company Afrasiab made his voyage down the Oxus, they must sleep, or they will devour us – they must be suffered to slumber, or we perish.

The Black Cat

For the most wild, yet most homely narrative which I am about to pen, I neither expect nor solicit belief. Mad indeed would I be to expect it, in a case where my very senses reject their own evidence. Yet, mad am I not – and very surely do I not dream. But tomorrow I die, and today I would unburden my soul. My immediate purpose is to place before the world, plainly, succinctly, and without comment, a series of mere household events. In their consequences, these events have terrified – have tortured – have destroyed me. Yet I will not attempt to expound them. To me, they have presented little but horror – to many they will seem less terrible than *baroques*. Hereafter, perhaps, some intellect may be found which will reduce my phantasm to the commonplace – some intellect more calm, more logical, and far less excitable than my own, which will perceive, in the circumstances I detail with awe, nothing more than an ordinary succession of very natural causes and effects.

From my infancy I was noted for the docility and humanity of my disposition. My tenderness of heart was even so conspicuous as to make me the jest of my companions. I was especially fond of animals, and was indulged by my parents with a great variety of pets. With these I spent most of my time, and never was so happy as when feeding and caressing them. This peculiarity of character grew with my growth, and, in my manhood, I derived from it one of my principal sources of pleasure. To those who have cherished an affection for a faithful and sagacious dog, I need hardly be at the trouble of explaining the nature or the intensity of the gratification thus derivable. There is something in the unselfish and self-sacrificing love of a brute, which goes directly to the heart of him who has had frequent occasion to test the paltry friendship and gossamer fidelity of mere *Man*.

I married early, and was happy to find in my wife a disposition not uncongenial with my own. Observing my partiality for domestic pets, she lost no opportunity of procuring those of the most agreeable kind. We had birds, goldfish, a fine dog, rabbits, a small monkey, and *a cat*.

This latter was a remarkably large and beautiful animal, entirely black, and sagacious to an astonishing degree. In speaking of his intelligence, my wife, who at heart was not a little tinctured with superstition, made frequent allusion to the ancient popular notion, which regarded all black cats as witches in disguise. Not that she was ever *serious* upon this point – and I mention the matter at all for no better reason than that it happens, just now, to be remembered.

Pluto – this was the cat's name – was my favourite pet and playmate. I alone fed him, and he attended me wherever I went about the house. It was even with difficulty that I could prevent him from following me through the streets.

Our friendship lasted, in this manner, for several years, during which my general temperament and character – through the instrumentality of the fiend intemperance – had (I blush to confess it) experienced a radical alteration for the worse. I grew, day by day, more moody, more irritable, more regardless of the feelings of others. I suffered myself to use intemperate language to my wife. At length, I even offered her personal violence. My pets, of course, were made to feel the change in my disposition. I not only neglected, but ill-used them. For Pluto, however, I still retained sufficient regard to restrain me from maltreating him, as I made no scruple of maltreating the rabbits, the monkey, or even the dog, when by accident, or through affection, they came in my way. But my disease grew upon me – for what disease is like alcohol? – and at length even Pluto, who was now becoming old, and consequently somewhat peevish – even Pluto began to experience the effects of my ill temper.

One night, returning home, much intoxicated, from one of my haunts about town, I fancied that the cat avoided my presence. I seized him; when, in his fright at my violence, he inflicted a slight wound upon my hand with his teeth. The fury of a demon instantly possessed me. I knew myself no longer. My original soul seemed, at once, to take its flight from my body; and a more than fiendish malevolence, gin-nurtured, thrilled every fibre of my frame. I took from my waistcoat pocket a penknife, opened it, grasped the poor beast by the throat, and deliberately cut one of its eyes from the socket! I blush, I burn, I shudder, while I pen the damnable atrocity.

When reason returned with the morning – when I had slept off the fumes of the night's debauch – I experienced a sentiment half of horror, half of remorse, for the crime of which I had been guilty; but it was, at best, a feeble and equivocal feeling, and the soul remained untouched. I again plunged into excess, and soon drowned in wine all memory of the deed.

In the meantime the cat slowly recovered. The socket of the lost eye presented, it is true, a frightful appearance, but he no longer appeared to suffer any pain. He went about the house as usual, but, as might be expected, fled in extreme terror at my approach. I had so much of my old heart left, as to be at first grieved by this evident dislike on the part of a creature which had once so loved me. But this feeling soon gave place to irritation. And then came, as if to my final and irrevocable overthrow, the spirit of PERVERSENESS. Of this spirit philosophy takes no account. Yet I am not more sure that my soul lives, than I am that perverseness is one of the primitive impulses of the human heart – one of the indivisible primary faculties, or sentiments, which give direction to the character of man. Who has not, a hundred times, found himself committing a vile or a silly action, for no other reason than because he knows he should *not*? Have we not a perpetual inclination, in the teeth of our best judgement, to violate that which is *Law*, merely because we understand it to be such? This spirit of perverseness, I say, came to my final overthrow. It was this unfathomable longing of the soul *to vex itself* – to offer violence to its own nature – to do wrong for the wrong's sake only – that urged me to continue and finally to consummate the injury I had inflicted upon the unoffending brute. One morning, in cool blood, I slipped a noose about its neck and hung it to the limb of a tree – hung it with the tears streaming from my eyes, and with the bitterest remorse at my heart – hung it *because* I knew that it had loved me, and *because* I felt it had given me no reason of offence – hung it *because* I knew that in so doing I was committing a sin – a deadly sin that would so jeopardise my immortal soul as to place it – if such a thing were possible – even beyond the reach of the infinite mercy of the most merciful and most terrible God.

On the night of the day on which this cruel deed was done, I was aroused from sleep by the cry of 'Fire!' The curtains of my bed were in flames. The whole house was blazing. It was with great difficulty that my wife, a servant, and myself, made our escape from the conflagration. The destruction was complete. My entire worldly wealth was swallowed up, and I resigned myself thenceforward to despair.

I am above the weakness of seeking to establish a sequence of cause and effect between the disaster and the atrocity. But I am detailing a chain of facts, and wish not to leave even a possible link imperfect. On the day succeeding the fire, I visited the ruins. The walls, with one exception, had fallen in. This exception was found in a compartment wall, not very thick, which stood about the middle of the house, and against which had rested the head of my bed. The plastering had here, in great measure, resisted the action of the fire – a fact which I attributed to its having been recently spread. About this wall a dense crowd were collected, and many persons seemed to be examining a particular portion of it with very minute and eager attention. The words 'strange!' 'singular!' and other similar expressions, excited my curiosity. I approached and saw, as if graven in bas-relief upon the white surface, the figure of a gigantic *cat*. The impression was given with an accuracy truly marvellous. There was a rope about the animal's neck.

When I first beheld this apparition – for I could scarcely regard it as less – my wonder and my terror were extreme. But at length reflection came to my aid. The cat, I remembered, had been hung in a garden adjacent to the house. Upon the alarm of fire, this garden had been immediately filled by the crowd – by someone of whom the animal must have been cut from the tree and thrown, through an open window, into my chamber. This had probably been done with the view of arousing me from sleep. The falling of other walls had compressed the victim of my cruelty into the substance of the freshly-spread plaster; the lime of which, with the flames and the *ammonia* from the carcass, had then accomplished the portraiture as I saw it.

Although I thus readily accounted to my reason, if not altogether to my conscience, for the startling fact just detailed, it did not the less fail to make a deep impression upon my fancy. For months I could not rid myself of the phantasm of the cat; and, during this period, there came back into my spirit a half-sentiment that seemed, but was not, remorse. I went so far as to regret the loss of the animal, and to look about me, among the vile haunts which I now habitually frequented, for another pet of the same species, and of somewhat similar appearance, with which to supply its place.

One night as I sat, half stupefied, in a den of more than infamy, my attention was suddenly drawn to some black object, reposing upon the head of one of the immense hogsheads of gin, or of rum, which constituted the chief furniture of the apartment. I had been looking steadily at the top of this hogshead for some minutes, and what now caused me surprise was the fact that I had not sooner perceived the object thereupon. I approached it, and touched it with my hand. It was a black cat – a very large one – fully as large as Pluto, and closely resembling him in every respect but one. Pluto had not a white hair upon any portion of his body; but this cat had a large, although indefinite, splotch of white, covering nearly the whole region of the breast.

Upon my touching him, he immediately arose, purred loudly, rubbed against my hand, and appeared delighted with my notice. This, then, was the very creature of which I was in search. I at once offered to purchase it of the landlord; but this person made no claim to it – knew nothing of it – had never seen it before.

I continued my caresses, and when I prepared to go home, the animal evinced a disposition to accompany me. I permitted it to do so; occasionally stooping and patting it as I proceeded. When it reached the house it domesticated itself at once, and became immediately a great favourite with my wife.

For my own part, I soon found a dislike to it arising within me. This was just the reverse of what I had anticipated; but – I know not how or why it was – its evident fondness for myself rather disgusted and annoyed me. By slow degrees, these feelings of disgust and annoyance rose into the bitterness of hatred. I avoided the creature; a certain sense of shame, and the remembrance of my former deed of cruelty, preventing me from physically abusing it. I did not, for some weeks, strike, or otherwise violently ill-use it; but gradually – very gradually – I came to look upon it with unutterable loathing, and to flee silently from its odious presence, as from the breath of a pestilence.

What added, no doubt, to my hatred of the beast, was the discovery, on the morning after I brought it home, that, like Pluto, it also had been deprived of one of its eyes. This circumstance, however, only endeared it to my wife, who, as I have already said, possessed, in a high degree, that humanity of feeling which had once been my distinguishing trait, and the source of many of my simplest and purest pleasures.

With my aversion to this cat, however, its partiality for myself seemed to increase. It followed my footsteps with a pertinacity which it would be difficult to make the reader comprehend. Whenever I sat, it would crouch beneath my chair, or spring upon my knees, covering me with its loathsome caresses. If I arose to walk, it would get between my feet, and thus nearly throw me down, or, fastening its long and sharp claws in my dress, clamber, in this manner, to my breast. At such times, although I longed to destroy it with a blow, I was yet withheld from so doing, partly by a memory of my former crime, but chiefly – let me confess it at once – by absolute *dread* of the beast.

This dread was not exactly a dread of physical evil – and yet I should be at a loss how otherwise to define it. I am almost ashamed to own – yes, even in this felon's cell, I am almost ashamed to own – that the terror and horror with which the animal inspired me, had been heightened by one of the merest chimeras it would be possible to conceive. My wife had called my attention, more than once, to the character of the mark of white hair, of which I have spoken, and which constituted the sole visible difference between the strange beast and the one I had destroyed. The reader will remember that this mark, although large, had been originally very indefinite; but, by slow degrees – degrees nearly

"I HAD WALLED THE MONSTER UP WITHIN THE TOMB!"

imperceptible, and which for a long time my reason struggled to reject as fanciful – it had, at length, assumed a rigorous distinctness of outline. It was now the representation of an object that I shudder to name – and for this, above all, I loathed, and dreaded, and would have rid myself of the monster *had I dared* – it was now, I say, the image of a hideous – of a ghastly thing – of the GALLOWS! – oh, mournful and terrible engine of horror and of crime – of agony and of death!

And now was I indeed wretched beyond the wretchedness of mere humanity. And *a brute beast* – whose fellow I had contemptuously destroyed – *a brute beast* to work out for *me* – for me, a man, fashioned in the image of the high God – so much of insufferable woe! Alas! neither by day nor by night knew I the blessing of rest any more! During the former the creature left me no moment alone; and, in the latter, I started, hourly, from dreams of unutterable fear, to find the hot breath of *the thing* upon my face, and its vast weight – an incarnate nightmare that I had no power to shake off – incumbent eternally upon my *heart!*

Beneath the pressure of torments such as these, the feeble remnant of the good within me succumbed. Evil thoughts became my sole intimates – the darkest and most evil of thoughts. The moodiness of my usual temper increased to hatred of all things and of all mankind; while, from the sudden, frequent, and ungovernable outbursts of a fury to which I now blindly abandoned myself, my uncomplaining wife, alas! was the most usual and the most patient of sufferers.

One day she accompanied me, upon some household errand, into the cellar of the old building which our poverty compelled us to inhabit. The cat followed me down the steep stairs, and, nearly throwing me headlong, exasperated me to madness. Uplifting an axe, and forgetting, in my wrath, the childish dread which had hitherto stayed my hand, I aimed a blow at the animal which, of course, would have proved instantly fatal had it descended as I wished. But this blow was arrested by the hand of my wife. Goaded, by the interference, into a rage more than demoniacal, I withdrew my arm from her grasp, and buried the axe in her brain. She fell dead upon the spot, without a groan.

This hideous murder accomplished, I set myself forthwith, and with entire deliberation, to the task of concealing the body. I knew that I could not remove it from the house, either by day or by night, without the risk of being observed by the neighbours. Many projects entered my mind. At one period I thought of cutting the corpse into minute fragments, and destroying them by fire. At another, I resolved to dig a grave for it in the floor of the cellar. Again, I deliberated about casting it into the well in the yard – about packing it in a box, as if merchandise, with the usual arrangements, and so getting a porter to take it from the house. Finally I hit upon what I considered a far better expedient than either of these. I determined to wall it up in the cellar – as the monks of the Middle Ages are recorded to have walled up their victims.

For a purpose such as this the cellar was well adapted. Its walls were loosely constructed, and had lately been plastered throughout with a rough plaster, which the dampness of the atmosphere had prevented from hardening. Moreover, in one of the walls was a projection, caused by a false chimney, or fireplace, that had been filled up, and made to resemble the rest of the cellar. I made no doubt that I could readily displace the bricks at this point, insert the corpse, and wall the whole up as before, so that no eye could detect anything suspicious.

And in this calculation I was not deceived. By means of a crowbar I easily dislodged the bricks, and, having carefully deposited the body against the inner wall, I propped it in that position, while, with little trouble, I relaid the whole structure as it originally stood. Having procured mortar, sand, and hair, with every possible precaution, I prepared a plaster which could not be distinguished from the old, and with this I very carefully went over the new brickwork. When I had finished, I felt satisfied that all was right. The wall did not present the slightest appearance of having been disturbed. The rubbish on the floor was picked up with the minutest care. I looked around triumphantly, and said to myself, 'Here at least, then, my labour has not been in vain.'

My next step was to look for the beast which had been the cause of so much wretchedness; for I had, at length, firmly resolved to put it to death. Had I been able to meet with it, at the moment, there could have been no doubt of its fate; but it appeared that the crafty animal had been alarmed at the violence of my previous anger, and forebore to present itself in my present mood. It is impossible to describe, or to imagine, the deep, the blissful sense of relief which the absence of the detested creature occasioned in my bosom. It did not make its appearance during the night – and thus for one night at least, since its introduction into the house, I soundly and tranquilly slept; aye, *slept* even with the burden of murder upon my soul!

The second and the third day passed, and still my tormentor came not. Once again I breathed as a free man. The monster, in terror, had fled the premises for ever! I should behold it no more! My happiness was supreme! The guilt of my dark deed disturbed me but little. Some few enquiries had been made, but these had been readily answered. Even a search had been instituted – but of course nothing was to be discovered. I looked upon my future felicity as secured.

Upon the fourth day of the assassination, a party of the police came, very unexpectedly, into the house, and proceeded again to make rigorous investigation of the premises. Secure, however, in the inscrutability of my place of concealment, I felt no embarrassment whatever. The officers bade me accompany them in their search. They left no nook or corner unexplored. At length, for the third or fourth time, they descended into the cellar. I quivered not in a muscle. My heart beat calmly as that of one who slumbers in innocence. I walked the cellar from end to end. I folded my arms upon my bosom, and roamed easily to and fro. The police were thoroughly satisfied, and prepared to depart. The glee at my heart was too strong to be restrained. I burned to say if but one word, by way of triumph, and to render doubly sure their assurance of my guiltlessness.

'Gentlemen,' I said at last, as the party ascended the steps, 'I delight to have allayed your suspicions. I wish you all health, and a little more courtesy. By the by, gentlemen, this – this is a very well-constructed house.' (In the rabid desire to say something easily, I scarcely knew what I uttered at all.) 'I may say an *excellently* well-constructed house. These walls – are you going, gentlemen? – these walls are solidly put together;' and here, through the mere frenzy of bravado, I rapped heavily, with a cane which I held in my hand, upon that very portion of the brickwork behind which stood the corpse of the wife of my bosom.

But may God shield and deliver me from the fangs of the Arch-Fiend! No sooner had the reverberation of my blows sunk into silence, than I was answered by a voice from within the tomb! – by a cry, at first muffled and broken, like the sobbing of a child, and then quickly swelling into one long, loud, and continuous scream, utterly anomalous and inhuman – a howl – a wailing shriek, half of horror and half of triumph, such as might have arisen only out of hell, conjointly from the throats of the damned in their agony and of the demons that exult in the damnation.

Of my own thoughts it is folly to speak. Swooning, I staggered to the opposite wall. For one instant the party upon the stairs remained motionless, through extremity of terror and of awe. In the next, a dozen stout arms were toiling at the wall. It fell bodily. The corpse, already greatly decayed and clotted with gore, stood erect before the eyes of the spectators. Upon its head, with red extended mouth and solitary eye of fire, sat the hideous beast whose craft had seduced me into murder, and whose informing voice had consigned me to the hangman. I had walled the monster up within the tomb!

The Masque of the Red Death

The 'Red Death' had long devastated the country. No pestilence had ever been so fatal, or so hideous. Blood was its Avatar and its seal – the redness and the horror of blood. There were sharp pains, and sudden dizziness, and then profuse bleeding at the pores, with dissolution. The scarlet stains upon the body and especially upon the face of the victim, were the pest ban which shut him out from the aid and from the sympathy of his fellow-men. And the whole seizure, progress, and termination of the disease, were the incidents of half an hour.

But the Prince Prospero was happy and dauntless and sagacious. When his dominions were half depopulated, he summoned to his presence a thousand hale and light-hearted friends from among the knights and dames of his court, and with these retired to the deep seclusion of one of his castellated abbeys. This was an extensive and magnificent structure, the creation of the prince's own eccentric yet august taste. A strong and lofty wall girdled it in. This wall had gates of iron. The courtiers, having entered, brought furnaces and massy hammers and welded the bolts. They resolved to leave means neither of ingress or egress to the sudden impulses of despair or of frenzy from within. The abbey was amply provisioned. With such precautions the courtiers might bid defiance to contagion. The external world could take care of itself. In the meantime it was folly to grieve, or to think. The prince had provided all the appliances of pleasure. There were buffoons, there were improvisatori, there were ballet-dancers, there were musicians, there was beauty, there was wine. All these and security were within. Without was the 'Red Death'.

It was toward the close of the fifth or sixth month of his seclusion, and while the pestilence raged most furiously abroad, that the Prince Prospero entertained his thousand friends at a masked ball of the most unusual magnificence.

It was a voluptuous scene, that masquerade. But first let me tell of the rooms in which it was held. There were seven – an imperial suite. In many palaces, however, such suites form a long and straight vista, while the folding doors slide back nearly to the walls on either hand, so that the view of the whole extent is scarcely impeded. Here the case was very different, as might have been expected from the duke's love of the bizarre. The apartments were so irregularly disposed that the vision embraced but little more than one at a time. There was a sharp turn at every twenty or thirty yards, and at each turn a novel effect. To the right and left, in the middle of each wall, a tall and narrow Gothic window looked out upon a closed corridor which pursued the windings of the suite. These windows were of stained glass, whose colour varied in accordance with the prevailing hue of the decorations of the chamber into which it opened. That at the eastern extremity was hung, for example, in blue – and vividly blue were its windows. The second chamber was purple in its ornaments and tapestries, and here the panes were purple. The third was green throughout, and so were the casements. The fourth was furnished and lighted with orange – the fifth with white – the sixth with violet. The seventh apartment was closely shrouded in black velvet tapestries that hung all over the ceiling and down the walls, falling in heavy folds upon a carpet of the same material and hue. But in this chamber only the colour of the windows failed to correspond with the decorations. The panes here were scarlet – a deep blood colour. Now in no one of the seven apartments was there any lamp or candelabrum, amid the profusion of golden ornaments that lay scattered to and fro, or depended from the roof. There was no light of any kind emanating from lamp or candle within the suite of chambers. But in the corridors that followed the suite, there stood, opposite to each window, a heavy tripod, bearing a brazier of fire, that projected its rays through the tinted glass, and so glaringly illumined the room. And thus were produced a multitude of gaudy and fantastic appearances. But in the western or black chamber the effect of the firelight that streamed upon the dark hangings through the blood-tinted panes, was ghastly in the extreme, and produced so wild a look upon the countenances of those who entered, that there were few of the company bold enough to set foot within its precincts at all.

It was in this apartment, also, that there stood against the western wall a gigantic clock of ebony. Its pendulum swung to and fro with a dull, heavy, monotonous clang; and when the minute-hand made the circuit of the face, and the hour was to be stricken, there came from the brazen lungs of the clock a sound which was clear and loud and deep and exceedingly musical; but of so peculiar a note and emphasis that, at each lapse of an hour, the musicians of the orchestra were constrained to pause, momentarily, in their performance, to hearken to the sound; and thus the waltzers perforce ceased their evolutions; and there was a brief disconcert of the whole gay company; and, while the chimes of the clock yet rang, it was observed that the giddiest grew pale, and the more aged and sedate passed their hands over their brows as if in confused reverie or meditation. But when the echoes had fully ceased, a light laughter at once pervaded the assembly; the musicians looked at each other and smiled as if at their own nervousness and folly, and made whispering vows, each to the other, that the next chiming of the clock should produce in them no similar emotion; and then, after the lapse of sixty minutes (which embrace three thousand and six hundred seconds of the Time that flies), there came yet another chiming of the clock, and then were the same disconcert and tremulousness and meditation as before.

But, in spite of these things, it was a gay and magnificent revel. The tastes of the duke were peculiar. He had a fine eye for colours and effects. He disregarded the *decora* of mere fashion. His plans were bold and fiery, and his conceptions glowed with barbaric lustre. There are some who would have thought him mad. His followers felt that he was not. It was necessary to hear and see and touch him to be *sure* that he was not.

He had directed, in great part, the movable embellishments of the seven chambers, upon occasion of this great fête; and it was his own guiding taste which had given character to the masqueraders. Be sure they were grotesque. There were much glare and glitter and piquancy and phantasm – much of what has been since seen in *Hernani*. There were arabesque figures with unsuited limbs and appointments. There were delirious fancies as the madman fashions. There were much of the beautiful, much of the wanton, much of the bizarre, something of the terrible, and not a little of that which might have excited disgust. To and fro in the seven chambers there stalked, in fact, a multitude of dreams. And these – the dreams – writhed in and about, taking hue from the rooms, and causing the wild music of the orchestra to seem as the echo of their steps. And, anon, there strikes the ebony clock which stands in the hall of the velvet. And then, for a moment, all is still, and all is silent save the voice of the clock. The dreams are stiff-frozen as they stand. But the echoes of the chime die away – they have endured but an instant – and a light, half-subdued laughter floats after them as they depart. And now again the music swells, and the dreams live, and writhe to and fro more merrily than ever, taking hue from the many tinted windows through which stream the rays from the tripods. But to the chamber which lies most westwardly of the seven, there are

THE DAGGER DROPPED GLEAMING UPON THE SABLE CARPET

now none of the maskers who venture; for the night is waning away; and there flows a ruddier light through the blood-coloured panes; and the blackness of the sable drapery appals; and to him whose foot falls upon the sable carpet, there comes from the near clock of ebony a muffled peal more solemnly emphatic than any which reaches *their* ears who indulge in the more remote gaieties of the other apartments.

But these other apartments were densely crowded, and in them beat feverishly the heart of life. And the revel went whirlingly on, until at length there commenced the sounding of midnight upon the clock. And then the music ceased, as I have told; and the evolutions of the waltzers were quieted; and there was an uneasy cessation of all things as before. But now there were twelve strokes to be sounded by the bell of the clock; and thus it happened, perhaps, that more of thought crept, with more of time, into the meditations of the thoughtful among those who revelled. And thus, too, it happened, perhaps, that before the last echoes of the last chime had utterly sunk into silence, there were many individuals in the crowd who had found leisure to become aware of the presence of a masked figure which had arrested the attention of no single individual before. And the rumour of this new presence having spread itself whisperingly around, there arose at length from the whole company a buzz, or murmur, expressive of disapprobation and surprise – then, finally, of terror, of horror, and of disgust.

In an assembly of phantasms, such as I have painted, it may well be supposed that no ordinary appearance could have excited such sensation. In truth the masquerade license of the night was nearly unlimited; but the figure in question had out-Heroded Herod, and gone beyond the bounds of even the prince's indefinite decorum. There are chords in the hearts of the most reckless which cannot be touched without emotion. Even with the utterly lost, to whom life and death are equally jests, there are matters of which no jests can be made. The whole company, indeed, seemed now deeply to feel that in the costume and bearing of the stranger neither wit nor propriety existed. The figure was tall and gaunt, and shrouded from head to foot in the habiliments of the grave. The mask which concealed the visage was made so nearly to resemble the countenance of a stiffened corpse that the closest scrutiny must have had difficulty in detecting the cheat. And yet all this might have been endured, if not approved, by the mad revellers around. But the mummer had gone so far as to assume the type of the Red Death. His vesture was dabbled in *blood* – and his broad brow, with all the features of the face, was besprinkled with the scarlet horror.

When the eyes of Prince Prospero fell upon this spectral image (which with a slow and solemn movement, as if more fully to sustain its *rôle*, stalked to and fro among the waltzers), he was seen to be convulsed, in the first moment, with a strong shudder either of terror or distaste; but, in the next, his brow reddened with rage.

'Who dares?' he demanded hoarsely of the courtiers who stood near him – 'who dares insult us with this blasphemous mockery? Seize him and unmask him – that we may know whom we have to hang at sunrise from the battlements!'

It was in the eastern or blue chamber in which stood the Prince Prospero as he uttered these words. They rang throughout the seven rooms loudly and clearly – for the prince was a bold and robust man, and the music had become hushed at the waving of his hand.

It was in the blue room where stood the prince with a group of pale courtiers by his side. At first, as he spoke, there was a slight rushing movement of this group in the direction of the intruder, who, at the moment, was also near at hand, and now, with deliberate and stately step, made closer approach to the speaker. But from a certain nameless awe with which the mad assumptions of the mummer had inspired the whole party, there were found none who put forth hand to seize him; so that, unimpeded, he passed within a yard of the prince's person; and, while the vast assembly, as if with one impulse, shrank from the centres of the rooms to the walls, he made his way uninterruptedly, but with the same solemn and measured step which had distinguished him from the first, through the blue chamber to the purple – through the purple to the green – through the green to the orange – through this again to the white – and even thence to the violet, ere a decided movement had been made to arrest him. It was then, however, that the Prince Prospero, maddened with rage and the shame of his own momentary cowardice, rushed hurriedly through the six chambers, while none followed him on account of a deadly terror that had seized upon all. He bore aloft a drawn dagger, and had approached, in rapid impetuosity, to within three or four feet of the retreating figure, when the latter, having attained the extremity of the velvet apartment, turned suddenly and confronted his pursuer. There was a sharp cry – and the dagger dropped gleaming upon the sable carpet, upon which, instantly afterwards, fell prostrate in death the Prince Prospero. Then, summoning the wild courage of despair, a throng of the revellers at once threw themselves into the black apartment, and, seizing the mummer, whose tall figure stood erect and motionless within the shadow of the ebony clock, gasped in unutterable horror at finding the grave cerements and corpse-like mask which they handled with so violent a rudeness, untenanted by any tangible form.

And now was acknowledged the presence of the Red Death. He had come like a thief in the night. And one by one dropped the revellers in the blood-bedewed halls of their revel, and died each in the despairing posture of his fall. And the life of the ebony clock went out with that of the last of the gay. And the flames of the tripods expired. And Darkness and Decay and the Red Death held illimitable dominion over all.

The Cask of Amontillado

The thousand injuries of Fortunato I had borne as I best could; but when he ventured upon insult, I vowed revenge. You, who so well know the nature of my soul, will not suppose, however, that I gave utterance to a threat. *At length* I would be avenged; this was a point definitely settled – but the very definitiveness with which it was resolved, precluded the idea of risk. I must not only punish, but punish with impunity. A wrong is unredressed when retribution overtakes its redresser. It is equally unredressed when the avenger fails to make himself felt as such to him who has done the wrong.

It must be understood, that neither by word nor deed had I given Fortunato cause to doubt my goodwill. I continued, as was my wont, to smile in his face, and he did not perceive that my smile *now* was at the thought of his immolation.

He had a weak point – this Fortunato – although in other regards he was a man to be respected and even feared. He prided himself on his connoisseurship in wine. Few Italians have the true virtuoso spirit. For the most part their enthusiasm is adapted to suit the time and opportunity – to practise imposture upon the British and Austrian millionaires. In painting and gemmary Fortunato, like his countrymen, was a quack – but in the matter of old wines he was sincere. In this respect I did not differ from him materially: I was skilful in the Italian vintages myself, and bought largely whenever I could.

It was about dusk, one evening during the supreme madness of the Carnival season, that I encountered my friend. He accosted me with excessive warmth, for he had been drinking much. The man wore motley. He had on a tight-fitting parti-striped dress, and his head was surmounted by the conical cap and bells. I was so pleased to see him, that I thought I should never have done wringing his hand.

I said to him, 'My dear Fortunato, you are luckily met. How remarkably well you are looking today! But I have received a pipe of what passes for Amontillado, and I have my doubts.'

'How?' said he; 'Amontillado? A pipe? Impossible! And in the middle of the Carnival!'

'I have my doubts,' I replied; 'and I was silly enough to pay the full Amontillado price without consulting you in the matter. You were not to be found, and I was fearful of losing a bargain.'

'Amontillado!'

'I have my doubts.'

'Amontillado!'

'And I must satisfy them.'

'Amontillado!'

'As you are engaged, I am on my way to Luchesi. If any one has a critical turn, it is he. He will tell me – '

'Luchesi cannot tell Amontillado from Sherry.'

'And yet some fools will have it that his taste is match for your own.'

'Come, let us go.'

'Whither?'

'To your vaults.'

'My friend, no; I will not impose upon your good nature. I perceive you have an engagement. Luchesi – '

'I have no engagement; come.'

'My friend, no. It is not the engagement, but the severe cold with which I perceive you are afflicted. The vaults are insufferably damp. They are encrusted with nitre.'

'Let us go nevertheless. The cold is merely nothing. Amontillado! You have been imposed upon. And as for Luchesi – he cannot distinguish Sherry from Amontillado.'

Thus speaking, Fortunato possessed himself of my arm. Putting on a mask of black silk, and drawing a *roquelaire* closely about my person, I suffered him to hurry me to my palazzo.

There were no attendants at home; they had absconded to make merry in honour of the time. I had told them that I should not return until the morning, and had given them explicit orders not to stir from the house. These orders were sufficient, I well knew, to ensure their immediate disappearance, one and all, as soon as my back was turned.

I took from their sconces two flambeaux, and giving one to Fortunato, bowed him through several suites of rooms to the archway that led into the vaults. I passed down a long and winding staircase, requesting him to be cautious as he followed. We came at length to the foot of the descent, and stood together on the damp ground of the catacombs of the Montresors.

The gait of my friend was unsteady, and the bells upon his cap jingled as he strode.

'The pipe,' said he.

'It is farther on,' said I; 'but observe the white webwork which gleams from these cavern walls.'

He turned towards me, and looked into my eyes with two filmy orbs that distilled the rheum of intoxication.

'Nitre?' he asked, at length.

'Nitre,' I replied. 'How long have you had that cough?'

'Ugh! ugh! ugh! – ugh! ugh! ugh! – ugh! ugh! ugh! – ugh! ugh! ugh! – ugh! ugh! ugh!'

My poor friend found it impossible to reply for many minutes.

'It is nothing,' he said, at last.

'Come,' I said, with decision, 'we will go back; your health is precious. You are rich, respected, admired, beloved; you are happy, as once I was. You are a man to be missed. For me it is no matter. We will go back; you will be ill, and I cannot be responsible. Besides, there is Luchesi – '

'Enough,' he said, 'the cough is a mere nothing; it will not kill me. I shall not die of a cough.'

'True – true,' I replied; 'and, indeed, I had no intention of alarming you unnecessarily – but you should use all proper caution. A draught of this Medoc will defend us from the damps.'

Here I knocked off the neck of a bottle which I drew from a long row of its fellows that lay upon the mould.

'Drink,' I said, presenting him the wine.

He raised it to his lips with a leer. He paused and nodded to me familiarly, while his bells jingled.

'I drink,' he said, 'to the buried that repose around us.'

'And I to your long life.'

He again took my arm, and we proceeded.

'These vaults,' he said, 'are extensive.'

'The Montresors,' I replied, 'were a great and numerous family.'

'I forget your arms.'

'A huge human foot d'or, in a field azure; the foot crushes a serpent rampant whose fangs are embedded in the heel.'

'And the motto?'

'*Nemo me impune lacessit.*'

'Good!' he said.

The wine sparkled in his eyes and the bells jingled. My own fancy grew warm with the Medoc. We had passed through walls of piled bones, with casks and puncheons intermingling, into the inmost recesses of the catacombs. I paused again, and this time I made bold to seize Fortunato by an arm above the elbow.

'The nitre!' I said; 'see, it increases. It hangs like moss upon the vaults. We are below the river's bed. The drops of moisture trickle among the bones. Come, we will go back ere it is too late. Your cough – '

'It is nothing,' he said; 'let us go on. But first, another draught of the Medoc.'

I broke and reached him a flagon of De Grâve. He emptied it at a breath. His eyes flashed with a fierce light. He laughed and threw the bottle upwards with a gesticulation I did not understand.

I looked at him in surprise. He repeated the movement – a grotesque one.

'You do not comprehend?' he said.

"FOR THE LOVE OF GOD! MONTRESOR!"
"YES," I SAID, "FOR THE LOVE OF GOD!"

'Not I,' I replied.

'Then you are not of the brotherhood.'

'How?'

'You are not of the masons.'

'Yes, yes,' I said; 'yes, yes.'

'You? Impossible! A mason?'

'A mason,' I replied.

'A sign,' he said.

'It is this,' I answered, producing a trowel from beneath the folds of my *roquelaire*.

'You jest,' he exclaimed, recoiling a few paces. 'But let us proceed to the Amontillado.'

'Be it so,' I said, replacing the tool beneath the cloak, and again offering him my arm. He leaned upon it heavily. We continued our route in search of the Amontillado. We passed through a range of low arches, descended, passed on, and descending again, arrived at a deep crypt, in which the foulness of the air caused our flambeaux rather to glow than flame.

At the most remote end of the crypt there appeared another less spacious. Its walls had been lined with human remains, piled to the vault overhead, in the fashion of the great catacombs of Paris. Three sides of this interior crypt were still ornamented in this manner. From the fourth the bones had been thrown down, and lay promiscuously upon the earth, forming at one point a mound of some size. Within the wall thus exposed by the displacing of the bones, we perceived a still interior recess, in depth about four feet, in width three, in height six or seven. It seemed to have been constructed for no especial use within itself, but formed merely the interval between two of the colossal supports of the roof of the catacombs, and was backed by one of their circumscribing walls of solid granite.

It was in vain that Fortunato, uplifting his dull torch, endeavoured to pry into the depth of the recess. Its termination the feeble light did not enable us to see.

'Proceed,' I said; 'herein is the Amontillado. As for Luchesi – '

'He is an ignoramus,' interrupted my friend, as he stepped unsteadily forward, while I followed immediately at his heels. In an instant he had reached the extremity of the niche, and finding his progress arrested by the rock, stood stupidly bewildered. A moment more and I had fettered him to the granite. In its surface were two iron staples, distant from each other about two feet, horizontally. From one of these depended a short chain, from the other a padlock. Throwing the links about his waist, it was but the work of a few seconds to secure it. He was too much astounded to resist. Withdrawing the key, I stepped back from the recess.

'Pass your hand,' I said, 'over the wall; you cannot help feeling the nitre. Indeed it is *very* damp. Once more let me *implore* you to return. No? Then I must positively leave you. But I must first render you all the little attentions in my power.'

'The Amontillado!' ejaculated my friend, not yet recovered from his astonishment.

'True,' I replied, 'the Amontillado.'

As I said these words I busied myself among the pile of bones of which I have before spoken. Throwing them aside, I soon uncovered a quantity of building stone and mortar. With these materials, and with the aid of my trowel, I began vigorously to wall up the entrance of the niche.

I had scarcely laid the first tier of the masonry when I discovered that the intoxication of Fortunato had in a great measure worn off. The earliest indication I had of this was a low moaning cry from the depth of the recess. It was *not* the cry of a drunken man. There was then a long and obstinate silence. I laid the second tier, and the third, and the fourth; and then I heard the furious vibrations of the chain. The noise lasted for several minutes, during which, that I might hearken to it with the more satisfaction, I ceased my labours and sat down upon the bones. When at last the clanking subsided, I resumed the trowel, and finished without interruption the fifth, the sixth, and the seventh tier. The wall was now nearly upon a level with my breast. I again paused, and holding the flambeaux over the masonwork, threw a few feeble rays upon the figure within.

A succession of loud and shrill screams, bursting suddenly from the throat of the chained form, seemed to thrust me violently back. For a brief moment I hesitated – I trembled. Unsheathing my rapier, I began to grope with it about the recess; but the thought of an instant reassured me. I placed my hand upon the solid fabric of the catacombs, and felt satisfied. I re-approached the wall. I replied to the yells of him who clamoured. I re-echoed – I aided – I surpassed them in volume and in strength. I did this, and the clamourer grew still.

It was now midnight, and my task was drawing to a close. I had completed the eighth, the ninth, and the tenth tier. I had finished a portion of the last and the eleventh; there remained but a single stone to be fitted and plastered in. I struggled with its weight; I placed it partially in its destined position. But now there came from out the niche a low laugh that erected the hairs upon my head. It was succeeded by a sad voice, which I had difficulty in recognising as that of the noble Fortunato.

The voice said – 'Ha! ha! ha! – he! he! – a very good joke indeed – an excellent jest. We will have many a rich laugh about it at the palazzo – he! he! he! – over our wine – he! he! he!'

'The Amontillado!' I said.

'He! he! he! – he! he! he! – yes, the Amontillado. But is it not getting late? Will not they be awaiting us at the palazzo, the Lady Fortunato and the rest? Let us be gone.'

'Yes,' I said, 'let us be gone.'

'For the love of God, Montresor!'

'Yes,' I said, 'for the love of God!'

But to these words I hearkened in vain for a reply. I grew impatient. I called aloud – 'Fortunato!'

No answer. I called again – 'Fortunato!'

No answer still. I thrust a torch through the remaining aperture and let it fall within. There came forth in return only a jingling of the bells. My heart grew sick – on account of the dampness of the catacombs. I hastened to make an end of my labour. I forced the last stone into its position; I plastered it up. Against the new masonry I re-erected the old rampart of bones. For the half of a century no mortal has disturbed them. *In pace requiescat!*

The Oval Portrait

The château into which my valet had ventured to make forcible entrance, rather than permit me, in my desperately wounded condition, to pass a night in the open air, was one of those piles of commingled gloom and grandeur which have so long frowned among the Appenines, not less in fact than in the fancy of Mrs Radcliffe. To all appearance it had been temporarily and very lately abandoned. We established ourselves in one of the smallest and least sumptuously furnished apartments. It lay in a remote turret of the building. Its decorations were rich, yet tattered and antique. Its walls were hung with tapestry and bedecked with manifold and multiform armorial trophies, together with an unusually great number of very spirited modern paintings in frames of rich golden arabesque. In these paintings, which depended from the walls not only in their main surfaces, but in very many nooks which the bizarre architecture of the château rendered necessary – in these paintings my incipient delirium, perhaps, had caused me to take deep interest; so that I bade Pedro to close the heavy shutters of the room – since it was already night – to light the tongues of a tall candelabrum which stood by the head of my bed – and to throw open far and wide the fringed curtains of black velvet which enveloped the bed itself. I wished all this done that I might resign myself, if not to sleep, at least alternately to the contemplation of these pictures, and the perusal of a small volume which had been found upon the pillow, and which purported to criticise and describe them.

Long, long I read – and devoutly, devotedly I gazed. Rapidly and gloriously the hours flew by, and the deep midnight came. The position of the candelabrum displeased me, and outreaching my hand with difficulty, rather than disturb my slumbering valet, I placed it so as to throw its rays more fully upon the book.

But the action produced an effect altogether unanticipated. The rays of the numerous candles (for there were many) now fell within a niche of the room which had hitherto been thrown into deep shade by one of the bedposts. I thus saw in vivid light a picture all unnoticed before. It was the portrait of a young girl just ripening into womanhood. I glanced at the painting hurriedly, and then closed my eyes. Why I did this was not at first apparent even to my own perception. But while my lids remained thus shut, I ran over in mind my reason for so shutting them. It was an impulsive movement to gain time for thought – to make sure that my vision had not deceived me – to calm and subdue my fancy for a more sober and more certain gaze. In a very few moments I again looked fixedly at the painting.

That I now saw aright I could not and would not doubt; for the first flashing of the candles upon that canvas had seemed to dissipate the dreamy stupor which was stealing over my senses, and to startle me at once into waking life.

The portrait, I have already said, was that of a young girl. It was a mere head and shoulders, done in what is technically termed a *vignette* manner – much in the style of the favourite heads of Sully. The arms, the bosom, and even the ends of the radiant hair, melted imperceptibly into the vague yet deep shadow which formed the background of the whole. The frame was oval, richly gilded and filigreed in Moresque. As a thing of art nothing could be more admirable than the painting itself. But it could have been neither the execution of the work, nor the immortal beauty of the countenance, which had so suddenly and so vehemently moved me. Least of all could it have been that my fancy, shaken from its half slumber, had mistaken the head for that of a living person. I saw at once that the peculiarities of the design, of the vignetting, and of the frame, must have instantly dispelled such idea – must have prevented even its momentary entertainment. Thinking earnestly upon these points, I remained for an hour, perhaps, half sitting, half reclining, with my vision riveted upon the portrait. At length, satisfied with the true secret of its effect, I fell back within the bed. I had found the spell of the picture in an absolute *lifelikeness* of expression, which, at first startling, finally confounded, subdued, and appalled me. With deep and reverent awe I replaced the candelabrum in its former position. The cause of my deep agitation being thus shut from view, I sought eagerly the volume which discussed the paintings and their histories. Turning to the number which designated the oval portrait, I there read the vague and quaint words which follow:

'She was a maiden of rarest beauty, and not more lovely than full of glee. And evil was the hour when she saw, and loved, and wedded the painter. He, passionate, studious, austere, and having already a bride in his Art. She, a maiden of rarest beauty, and not more lovely than full of glee – all light and smiles, and frolicsome as the young fawn; loving and cherishing all things; hating only the Art which was her rival; dreading only the palette and brushes and other untoward instruments which deprived her of the countenance of her lover. It was thus a terrible thing for this lady to hear the painter speak of his desire to portray even his young bride. But she was humble and obedient, and sat meekly for many weeks in the dark high turret-chamber where the light dripped upon the pale canvas only from overhead. But he, the painter, took glory in his work, which went on from hour to hour, and from day to day. And he was a passionate, and wild, and moody man, who became lost in reveries; so that he *would* not see that the light which fell so ghastlily in that lone turret withered the health and the spirits of his bride, who pined visibly to all but him. Yet she smiled on and still on, uncomplainingly, because she saw that the painter (who had high renown), took a fervid and burning pleasure in his task, and wrought day and night to depict her who so loved him, yet who grew daily more dispirited and weak. And in sooth some who beheld the portrait spoke of its resemblance in low words, as of a mighty marvel, and a proof not less of the power of the painter than of his deep love for her whom he depicted so surpassingly well. But at length, as the labour drew nearer to its conclusion, there were admitted none into the turret; for the painter had grown wild with the ardour of his work, and turned his eyes from the canvas rarely, even to regard the countenance of his wife. And he *would* not see that the tints which he spread upon the canvas were drawn from the cheeks of her who sat beside him. And when many weeks had passed, and but little remained to do, save one brush upon the mouth and one tint upon the eye, the spirit of the lady again flickered up as the flame within the socket of the lamp. And then the brush was given, and then the tint was placed; and, for one moment, the painter stood entranced before the work which he had wrought; but in the next, while he yet gazed, he grew tremulous and very pallid, and aghast, and crying with a loud voice, "This is indeed *Life* itself!" turned suddenly to regard his beloved – *she was dead!*'

The Oblong Box

Some years ago, I engaged passage from Charleston, SC, to the city of New York, in the fine packet-ship *Independence*, Captain Hardy. We were to sail on the fifteenth of the month (June), weather permitting; and on the fourteenth, I went on board to arrange some matters in my stateroom.

I found that we were to have a great many passengers, including a more than usual number of ladies. On the list were several of my acquaintances; and among other names, I was rejoiced to see that of Mr Cornelius Wyatt, a young artist, for whom I entertained feelings of warm friendship. He had been with me a fellow-student at C— University, where we were very much together. He had the ordinary temperament of genius, and was a compound of misanthropy, sensibility, and enthusiasm. To these qualities he united the warmest and truest heart which ever beat in a human bosom.

I observed that his name was carded upon *three* staterooms; and, upon again referring to the list of passengers, I found that he had engaged passage for himself, wife, and two sisters – his own. The staterooms were sufficiently roomy, and each had two berths, one above the other. These berths, to be sure, were so exceedingly narrow as to be insufficient for more than one person; still, I could not comprehend why there were three staterooms for these four persons. I was, just at that epoch, in one of those moody frames of mind which make a man abnormally inquisitive about trifles; and I confess, with shame, that I busied myself in a variety of ill-bred and preposterous conjectures about this matter of the supernumerary stateroom. It was no business of mine, to be sure; but with none the less pertinacity did I occupy myself in attempts to resolve the enigma. At last I reached a conclusion which wrought in me great wonder why I had not arrived at it before. 'It is a servant, of course,' I said; 'what a fool I am not sooner to have thought of so obvious a solution!' And then I again repaired to the list – but here I saw distinctly that *no* servant was to come with the party; although, in fact, it had been the original design to bring one – for the words 'and servant' had been first written and then over-scored. 'Oh, extra baggage, to be sure,' I now said to myself – 'something he wishes not to be put in the hold – something to be kept under his own eye – ah, I have it – a painting or so – and this is what he has been bargaining about with Nicolino, the Italian Jew.' This idea satisfied me, and I dismissed my curiosity for the nonce.

Wyatt's two sisters I knew very well, and most amiable and clever girls they were. His wife he had newly married, and I had never yet seen her. He had often talked about her in my presence, however, and in his usual style of enthusiasm. He described her as of surpassing beauty, wit, and accomplishment. I was, therefore, quite anxious to make her acquaintance.

On the day in which I visited the ship (the fourteenth), Wyatt and party were also to visit it – so the captain informed me – and I waited on board an hour longer than I had designed, in hope of being presented to the bride; but then an apology came. 'Mrs W. was a little indisposed, and would decline coming on board until tomorrow, at the hour of sailing.'

The morrow having arrived, I was going from my hotel to the wharf, when Captain Hardy met me and said that, 'owing to circumstances' (a stupid but convenient phrase), 'he rather thought the *Independence* would not sail for a day or two, and that when all was ready, he would send up and let me know.' This I thought strange, for there was a stiff southerly breeze; but as 'the circumstances' were not forthcoming, although I pumped for them with much perseverance, I had nothing to do but to return home and digest my impatience at leisure.

I did not receive the expected message from the captain for nearly a week. It came at length, however, and I immediately went on board. The ship was crowded with passengers, and everything was in the bustle attendant upon making sail. Wyatt's party arrived in about ten minutes after myself. There were the two sisters, the bride, and the artist – the latter in one of his customary fits of moody misanthropy. I was too well used to these, however, to pay them any special attention. He did not even introduce me to his wife; this courtesy devolving, perforce, upon his sister Marian – a very sweet and intelligent girl, who, in a few hurried words, made us acquainted.

Mrs Wyatt had been closely veiled; and when she raised her veil, in acknowledging my bow, I confess that I was very profoundly astonished. I should have been much more so, however, had not long experience advised me not to trust, with too implicit a reliance, the enthusiastic description of my friend, the artist, when indulging in comments upon the loveliness of woman. When beauty was the theme, I well knew with what facility he soared into the regions of the purely ideal.

The truth is, I could not help regarding Mrs Wyatt as a decidedly plain-looking woman. If not positively ugly, she was not, I think, very far from it. She was dressed, however, in exquisite taste – and then I had no doubt that she had captivated my friend's heart by the more enduring graces of the intellect and soul. She said very few words, and passed at once into her stateroom with Mr W.

My old inquisitiveness now returned. There was *no* servant – *that* was a settled point. I looked, therefore, for the extra baggage. After some delay, a cart arrived at the wharf with an oblong pine box, which was everything that seemed to be expected. Immediately upon its arrival we made sail, and in a short time were safely over the bar and standing out at sea.

The box in question was, as I say, oblong. It was about six feet in length by two and a half in breadth; I observed it attentively, and like to be precise. Now this shape was *peculiar*; and no sooner had I seen it, than I took credit to myself for the accuracy of my guessing. I had reached the conclusion, it will be remembered, that the extra baggage of my friend, the artist, would prove to be pictures, or at least a picture – for I knew he had been for several weeks in conference with Nicolino; and now here was a box which, from its shape, *could* possibly contain nothing in the world but a copy of Leonardo's *Last Supper*; and a copy of this very *Last Supper*, done by Rubini the younger, at Florence, I had known, for some time, to be in the possession of Nicolino. This point, therefore, I considered as sufficiently settled. I chuckled excessively when I thought of my acumen. It was the first time I had ever known Wyatt to keep from me any of his artistical secrets; but here he evidently intended to steal a march upon me, and smuggle a fine picture to New York, under my very nose; expecting me to know nothing of the matter. I resolved to quiz him well, now and hereafter.

One thing, however, annoyed me not a little. The box did *not* go into the extra stateroom. It was deposited in Wyatt's own; and there, too, it remained, occupying very nearly the whole of the floor – no doubt to the exceeding discomfort of the artist and his wife; this the more especially as the tar or paint with which it was lettered in sprawling capitals emitted a strong, disagreeable, and, to *my* fancy, a peculiarly disgusting odour. On the lid were painted the words – '*Mrs Adelaide Curtis, Albany, New York. Charge of Cornelius Wyatt, Esq. This side up. To be handled with care.*'

Now, I was aware that Mrs Adelaide Curtis, of Albany, was the artist's wife's mother; but then I looked upon the whole address as a mystification, intended especially for myself. I made up my mind, of course, that the box and contents would never get farther north than the studio of my misanthropic friend in Chambers Street, New York.

For the first three or four days we had fine weather, although the wind was dead ahead; having chopped round to the northward, immediately upon our losing sight of the coast. The passengers were, consequently, in high spirits, and disposed to be social. I must except, however, Wyatt and his sisters, who behaved stiffly, and I could not help thinking, uncourteously to the rest of the party. *Wyatt's* conduct, I did not so much regard. He was gloomy, even beyond his usual habit – in fact he was *morose* – but in him I was prepared for eccentricity. For the sisters, however, I could make no excuse. They secluded themselves in their staterooms during the greater part of the passage, and absolutely refused, although I repeatedly urged them, to hold communication with any person on board.

Mrs Wyatt herself was far more agreeable. That is to say, she was *chatty*; and to be chatty is no slight recommendation at sea. She became *excessively* intimate with most of the ladies; and, to my profound astonishment, evinced no equivocal disposition to coquet with the men. She amused us all very much. I say '*amused*' – and scarcely know how to explain myself. The truth is, I soon found that Mrs W. was far oftener laughed *at* than *with*. The gentlemen said little about her; but the ladies, in a little while, pronounced her 'a good-hearted thing, rather indifferent-looking, totally uneducated, and decidedly vulgar.' The great wonder was how Wyatt had been entrapped into such a match. Wealth was the general solution – but this I knew to be no solution at all; for Wyatt had told me she neither brought him a dollar nor had any expectations from any source whatever. 'He had married,' he said, 'for love, and for love only; and his bride was far more than worthy of his love.' When I thought of these expressions, on the part of my friend, I confess that I felt indescribably puzzled. Could it be possible that he was taking leave of his senses? What else could I think? *He*, so refined, so intellectual, so fastidious, with so exquisite a perception of the faulty, and so keen an appreciation of the beautiful! To be sure, the lady seemed especially fond of *him* – particularly so in his absence – when she made herself ridiculous by frequent quotations of what had been said by her 'beloved husband, Mr Wyatt'. The word 'husband' seemed for ever – to use one of her own delicate expressions – for ever 'on the tip of her tongue'. In the meantime, it was observed by all on board, that he avoided *her* in the most pointed manner, and, for the most part, shut himself up alone in his stateroom, where, in fact, he might have been said to live altogether, leaving his wife at full liberty to amuse herself as she thought best, in the public society of the main cabin.

My conclusion, from what I saw and heard, was, that the artist, by some unaccountable freak of fate, or perhaps in some fit of enthusiastic and fanciful passion, had been induced to unite himself with a person altogether beneath him, and that the natural result, entire and speedy disgust, had ensued. I pitied him from the bottom of my heart – but could not, for that reason, quite forgive his incommunicativeness in the matter of the *Last Supper*. For this I resolved to have my revenge.

One day he came upon deck, and, taking his arm as had been my wont, I sauntered with him backwards and forwards. His gloom, however (which I considered quite natural under the circumstances), seemed entirely unabated. He said little, and that moodily, and with evident effort. I ventured a jest or two, and he made a sickening attempt at a smile. Poor fellow! – as I thought of *his wife*, I wondered that he could have heart to put on even the semblance of mirth. At last I ventured a home thrust. I determined to commence a series of covert insinuations, or innuendoes, about the oblong box – just to let him perceive, gradually, that I was *not* altogether the butt, or victim, of his little bit of pleasant mystification. My first observation was by way of opening a masked battery. I said something about the 'peculiar shape of *that* box'; and, as I spoke the words, I smiled knowingly, winked, and touched him gently with my forefinger in the ribs.

The manner in which Wyatt received this harmless pleasantry convinced me at once that he was mad. At first he stared at me as if he found it impossible to comprehend the witticism of my remark; but as its point seemed slowly to make its way into his brain, his eyes in the same proportion seemed protruding from their sockets. Then he grew very red – then hideously pale – then, as if highly amused with what I had insinuated, he began a loud and boisterous laugh, which, to my astonishment, he kept up with gradually increasing vigour, for ten minutes or more. In conclusion, he fell flat and heavily upon the deck. When I ran to uplift him, to all appearance he was *dead*.

I called assistance, and, with much difficulty, we brought him to himself. Upon reviving, he spoke incoherently for some time. At length we bled him and put him to bed. The next morning he was quite recovered, so far as regarded his mere bodily health. Of his mind I say nothing, of course. I avoided him during the rest of the passage, by advice of the captain, who seemed to coincide with me altogether in my views of his insanity, but cautioned me to say nothing on this head to any person on board.

Several circumstances occurred immediately after this fit of Wyatt's, which contributed to heighten the curiosity with which I was already possessed. Among other things, this: I had been nervous – drank too much strong green tea, and slept ill at night – in fact, for two nights I could not be properly said to sleep at all. Now, my stateroom opened into the main cabin, or dining-room, as did those of all the single men on board. Wyatt's three rooms were in the after-cabin, which was separated from the main one by a slight sliding door, never locked even at night. As we were almost constantly on a wind, and the breeze was not a little stiff, the ship heeled to leeward very considerably; and whenever her starboard side was to leeward, the sliding door between the cabins slid open, and so remained, nobody taking the trouble to get up and shut it. But my berth was in such a position, that when my own stateroom door was open, as well as the sliding door in question (and my own door was *always* open on account of the heat), I could see into the after-cabin quite distinctly, and just at that portion of it, too, where were situated the staterooms of Mr Wyatt. Well, during two nights (*not* consecutive) while I lay awake, I clearly saw Mrs W., about eleven o'clock upon each night, steal cautiously from the stateroom of Mr W., and enter the extra room, where she remained until daybreak, when she was called by her husband and went back. That they were virtually separated was clear. They had separate apartments – no doubt in contemplation of a more permanent divorce; and here after all, I thought, was the mystery of the extra stateroom.

There was another circumstance, too, which interested me much. During the two wakeful nights in question, and immediately after the disappearance of Mrs Wyatt into the extra stateroom, I was attracted by certain singular, cautious, subdued noises in that of her husband. After listening to them for some time, with thoughtful attention, I at length succeeded perfectly in translating their import. They were sounds occasioned by the artist in prising open the oblong box by means of a chisel and mallet – the latter being apparently muffled or deadened by some soft woollen or cotton substance in which its head was enveloped.

In this manner I fancied I could distinguish the precise moment when he fairly disengaged the lid – also, that I could determine when he removed it altogether, and when he deposited it upon the lower berth in his room; this latter point I knew, for example, by certain slight taps which the lid made in striking against the wooden edges of the berth, as he endeavoured to lay it down very gently – there being no room for it on the floor. After this there was a dead stillness, and I heard nothing more, upon either occasion, until nearly daybreak; unless, perhaps, I may mention a low sobbing or murmuring sound, so very much suppressed as to be nearly inaudible – if, indeed, the whole of this latter noise were not rather produced by my own imagination. I say it seemed to *resemble* sobbing or sighing – but, of course, it could not have been either. I rather think it was a ringing in my own ears. Mr Wyatt, no doubt, according to custom, was merely giving the rein to one of his hobbies – indulging in one of his fits of artistic enthusiasm. He had opened his oblong box in order to feast his eyes on the pictorial treasure within. There was nothing in this, however, to make him *sob*. I repeat, therefore, that it must have been simply a freak of my own fancy, distempered by good Captain Hardy's green tea. Just before dawn, on each of the two nights of which I speak, I distinctly heard Mr Wyatt replace the lid upon the oblong box, and force the nails into their old places, by means of the muffled mallet. Having done this, he issued from his stateroom, fully dressed, and proceeded to call Mrs W. from hers.

We had been at sea seven days, and were now off Cape Hatteras, when there came a tremendously heavy blow from the south-west. We were, in a measure, prepared for it, however, as the weather had been holding out threats for some time. Everything was made snug, alow and aloft; and as the wind steadily freshened, we lay to, at length, under spanker and foretopsail, both double-reefed.

In this trim we rode safely enough for forty-eight hours – the ship proving herself an excellent sea-boat, in many respects, and shipping no water of any consequence. At the end of this period, however, the gale had freshened into a hurricane, and our after-sail split into ribbons, bringing us so much in the trough of the water that we shipped several prodigious seas, one immediately after the other. By this accident we lost three men overboard with the caboose, and nearly the whole of the larboard bulwarks. Scarcely had we recovered our senses before the foretopsail went into shreds, when we got up a storm staysail, and with this did pretty well for some hours, the ship heading the sea much more steadily than before.

The gale still held on, however, and we saw no signs of its abating. The rigging was found to be ill-fitted and greatly strained; and on the third day of the blow, about five in the afternoon, our mizzen mast, in a heavy lurch to windward, went by the board. For an hour or more we tried in vain to get rid of it on account of the prodigious rolling of the ship; and, before we had succeeded, the carpenter came aft and announced four feet of water in the hold. To add to our dilemma, we found the pumps choked and nearly useless.

All was now confusion and despair – but an effort was made to lighten the ship by throwing overboard as much of her cargo as could be reached, and by cutting away the two masts that remained. This we at last accomplished – but we were still unable to do anything at the pumps; and, in the meantime, the leak gained on us fast.

At sundown, the gale had sensibly diminished in violence, and, as the sea went down with it, we still entertained faint hopes of saving ourselves in the boats. At eight o'clock the clouds broke away to windward, and we had the advantage of a full moon – a piece of good fortune which served wonderfully to cheer our drooping spirits.

After incredible labour we succeeded, at length, in getting the long-boat over the side without material accident, and into this we crowded the whole of the crew and most of the passengers. This party made off immediately, and, after undergoing much suffering, finally arrived, in safety, at Ocracoke Inlet, on the third day after the wreck.

Fourteen passengers, with the captain, remained on board, resolving to trust their fortunes to the jolly-boat at the stern. We lowered it without difficulty, although it was only by a miracle that we prevented it from swamping as it touched the water. It contained, when afloat, the captain and his wife, Mr Wyatt and party, a Mexican officer, wife, four children, and myself, with a negro valet.

We had no room, of course, for anything except a few positively necessary instruments, some provisions, and the clothes upon our backs. No one had thought of even attempting to save anything more. What must have been the astonishment of all then, when, having proceeded a few fathoms from the ship, Mr Wyatt stood up in the stern-sheets, and coolly demanded of Captain Hardy that the boat should be put back for the purpose of taking in his oblong box!

'Sit down, Mr Wyatt,' replied the captain, somewhat sternly, 'you will capsize us if you do not sit quite still. Our gunwale is almost in the water now.'

'The box!' vociferated Mr Wyatt, still standing – 'the box, I say! Captain Hardy, you cannot, you *will* not refuse me. Its weight will be but a trifle – it is nothing – mere nothing. By the mother who bore you – for the love of Heaven – by your hope of salvation, I *implore* you to put back for the box!'

The captain, for a moment, seemed touched by the earnest appeal of the artist; but he regained his stern composure, and merely said –

'Mr Wyatt, you are mad. I cannot listen to you. Sit down, I say, or you will swamp the boat. Stay – hold him – seize him! – he is about to spring overboard! There – I knew it – he is over!'

As the captain said this, Mr Wyatt, in fact, sprang from the boat, and, as we were yet in the lee of the wreck, succeeded, by almost superhuman exertion, in getting hold of a rope which hung from the fore-chains. In another moment he was on board, and rushing frantically down into the cabin.

In the meantime, we had been swept astern of the ship, and being quite out of her lee, were at the mercy of the tremendous sea which was still running. We made a determined effort to put back, but our little boat was like a feather in the breath of the tempest. We saw at a glance that the doom of the unfortunate artist was sealed.

As our distance from the wreck rapidly increased, the madman (for as such only could we regard him) was seen to emerge from the companionway, up which, by dint of a strength that appeared gigantic, he dragged, bodily, the oblong box. While we gazed in the extremity of astonishment, he passed, rapidly, several turns of a three-inch rope, first around the box and then around his body. In another instant both body and box were in the sea – disappearing suddenly, at once and for ever.

We lingered awhile sadly upon our oars, with our eyes riveted upon the spot. At length we pulled away. The silence remained unbroken for an hour. Finally, I hazarded a remark.

'Did you observe, captain, how suddenly they sank? Was not that an exceedingly singular thing? I confess that I entertained some feeble hope of his final deliverance, when I saw him lash himself to the box, and commit himself to the sea.'

'They sank as a matter of course,' replied the captain, 'and that like a shot. They will soon rise again, however – *but not till the salt melts.*'

'The salt!' I ejaculated.

'Hush!' said the captain, pointing to the wife and sisters of the deceased. 'We must talk of these things at some more appropriate time.'

We suffered much, and made a narrow escape; but fortune befriended us, as well as our mates in the longboat. We landed, in fine, more dead than alive, after four days of intense distress, upon the beach opposite Roanoke Island. We remained here a week, were not ill-treated by the wreckers, and at length obtained a passage to New York.

About a month after the loss of the *Independence*, I happened to meet Captain Hardy in Broadway. Our conversation turned, naturally, upon the disaster, and especially upon the sad fate of poor Wyatt. I thus learned the following particulars.

The artist had engaged passage for himself, wife, two sisters, and a servant. His wife was, indeed, as she had been represented, a most lovely and most accomplished woman. On the morning of the fourteenth of June (the day in which I first visited the ship), the lady suddenly sickened and died. The young husband was frantic with grief – but circumstances imperatively forbade the deferring his voyage to New York. It was necessary to take to her mother the corpse of his adored wife, and on the other hand, the universal prejudice which would prevent his doing so openly was well known. Nine-tenths of the passengers would have abandoned the ship rather than take passage with a dead body.

In this dilemma, Captain Hardy arranged that the corpse, being first partially embalmed, and packed, with a large quantity of salt, in a box of suitable dimensions, should be conveyed on board as merchandise. Nothing was to be said of the lady's decease; and, as it was well understood that Mr Wyatt had engaged passage for his wife, it became necessary that some person should personate her during the voyage. This the deceased's lady's-maid was easily prevailed on to do. The extra stateroom, originally engaged for this girl, during her mistress' life, was now merely retained. In this stateroom the pseudo wife slept, of course, every night. In the daytime she performed, to the best of her ability, the part of her mistress – whose person, it had been carefully ascertained, was unknown to any of the passengers on board.

My own mistakes arose, naturally enough, through too careless, too inquisitive, and too impulsive a temperament. But of late, it is a rare thing that I sleep soundly at night. There is a countenance which haunts me, turn as I will. There is an hysterical laugh which will for ever ring within my ears.

The Tell-Tale Heart

True! – nervous – very, very dreadfully nervous I had been and am; but why *will* you say that I am mad? The disease had sharpened my senses – not destroyed – not dulled them. Above all was the sense of hearing acute. I heard all things in the heaven and in the earth. I heard many things in hell. How, then, am I mad? Hearken! and observe how healthily – how calmly I can tell you the whole story.

It is impossible to say how first the idea entered my brain; but once conceived, it haunted me day and night. Object there was none. Passion there was none. I loved the old man. He had never wronged me. He had never given me insult. For his gold I had no desire. I think it was his eye! yes, it was this! One of his eyes resembled that of a vulture – a pale blue eye, with a film over it. Whenever it fell upon me, my blood ran cold; and so by degrees – very gradually – I made up my mind to take the life of the old man, and thus rid myself of the eye for ever.

Now this is the point. You fancy me mad. Madmen know nothing. But you should have seen *me*. You should have seen how wisely I proceeded – with what caution – with what foresight – with what dissimulation I went to work! I was never kinder to the old man than during the whole week before I killed him. And every night, about midnight, I turned the latch of his door and opened it – oh, so gently! And then, when I had made an opening sufficient for my head, I put in a dark lantern, all closed, closed, so that no light shone out, and then I thrust in my head. Oh, you would have laughed to see how cunningly I thrust it in! I moved it slowly – very, very slowly, so that I might not disturb the old man's sleep. It took me an hour to place my whole head within the opening so far that I could see him as he lay upon his bed. Ha! – would a madman have been so wise as this? And then, when my head was well in the room, I undid the lantern, cautiously – oh, so cautiously – cautiously (for the hinges creaked) I undid it just so much that a single thin ray fell upon the vulture eye. And this I did for seven long nights – every night just at midnight – but I found the eye always closed; and so it was impossible to do the work; for it was not the old man who vexed me, but his Evil Eye. And every morning, when the day broke, I went boldly into the chamber, and spoke courageously to him, calling him by name in a hearty tone, and enquiring how he had passed the night. So you see he would have been a very profound old man, indeed, to suspect that every night, just at twelve, I looked in upon him while he slept.

Upon the eighth night I was more than usually cautious in opening the door. A watch's minute hand moves more quickly than did mine. Never before that night had I *felt* the extent of my own powers – of my sagacity. I could scarcely contain my feelings of triumph. To think that there I was, opening the door, little by little, and he not even to dream of my secret deeds or thoughts. I fairly chuckled at the idea; and perhaps he heard me – for he moved on the bed suddenly, as if startled. Now you may think that I drew back – but no. His room was as black as pitch with the thick darkness (for the shutters were close-fastened, through fear of robbers), and so I knew that he could not see the opening of the door, and I kept pushing it on steadily, steadily.

I had my head in, and was about to open the lantern, when my thumb slipped upon the tin fastening, and the old man sprang up in the bed, crying out, 'Who's there?'

I kept quite still and said nothing. For a whole hour I did not move a muscle, and in the meantime I did not hear him lie down. He was still sitting up in the bed, listening – just as I have done, night after night, hearkening to the death-watches in the wall.

Presently I heard a groan, and I knew it was the groan of mortal terror. It was not a groan of pain or of grief – oh, no! – it was the low stifled sound that arises from the bottom of the soul when overcharged with awe. I knew the sound well. Many a night, just at midnight, when all the world slept, it has welled up from my own bosom, deepening, with its dreadful echo, the terrors that distracted me. I say I knew it well. I knew what the old man felt, and pitied him, although I chuckled at heart. I knew that he had been lying awake ever since the first slight noise, when he had turned in the bed. His fears had been ever since growing upon him. He had been trying to fancy them causeless, but could not. He had been saying to himself, 'It is nothing but the wind in the chimney – it is only a mouse crossing the floor,' or, 'It is merely a cricket which has made a single chirp.' Yes, he had been trying to comfort himself with these suppositions; but he had found all in vain. *All in vain*; because Death, in approaching him, had stalked with his black shadow before him, and enveloped the victim. And it was the mournful influence of the unperceived shadow that caused him to feel

BUT, FOR MANY MINUTES, THE HEART BEAT ON WITH A MUFFLED SOUND

– although he neither saw nor heard – to *feel* the presence of my head within the room.

When I had waited a long time, very patiently, without hearing him lie down, I resolved to open a little – a very, very little crevice in the lantern. So I opened it – you cannot imagine how stealthily, stealthily – until, at length, a single dim ray, like the thread of the spider, shot from out the crevice and fell upon the vulture eye.

It was open – wide, wide open – and I grew furious as I gazed upon it. I saw it with perfect distinctness – all a dull blue, with a hideous veil over it that chilled the very marrow in my bones; but I could see nothing else of the old man's face or person, for I had directed the ray, as if by instinct, precisely upon the damned spot.

And now have I not told you that what you mistake for madness is but over-acuteness of the senses? – now, I say, there came to my ears a low, dull, quick sound, such as a watch makes when enveloped in cotton. I knew *that* sound well, too. It was the beating of the old man's heart. It increased my fury, as the beating of a drum stimulates the soldier into courage.

But even yet I refrained and kept still. I scarcely breathed. I held the lantern motionless. I tried how steadily I could maintain the ray upon the eye. Meantime the hellish tattoo of the heart increased. It grew quicker and quicker, and louder and louder every instant. The old man's terror *must* have been extreme! It grew louder, I say, louder every moment! – do you mark me well? I have told you that I am nervous: so I am. And now, at the dead hour of the night, amid the dreadful silence of that old house, so strange a noise as this excited me to uncontrollable terror. Yet, for some minutes longer, I refrained and stood still. But the beating grew louder, louder! I thought the heart must burst. And now a new anxiety seized me – the sound would be heard by a neighbour! The old man's hour had come! With a loud yell I threw open the lantern and leaped into the room. He shrieked once – once only. In an instant I dragged him to the floor, and pulled the heavy bed over him. I then smiled gaily, to find the deed so far done. But, for many minutes, the heart beat on with a muffled sound. This, however, did not vex me; it would not be heard through the wall. At length it ceased. The old man was dead. I removed the bed and examined the corpse. Yes, he was stone, stone dead. I placed my hand upon the heart and held it there many minutes. There was no pulsation. He was stone dead. His eye would trouble me no more.

If still you think me mad, you will think so no longer when I describe the wise precautions I took for the concealment of the body. The night waned, and I worked hastily, but in silence. First of all I dismembered the corpse. I cut off the head and the arms and the legs.

I then took up three planks from the flooring of the chamber and deposited all between the scantlings. I then replaced the boards so cleverly, so cunningly, that no human eye – not even *his* – could have detected anything wrong. There was nothing to wash out – no stain of any kind – no blood-spot whatever. I had been too wary for that. A tub had caught all – ha! ha!

When I had made an end of these labours, it was four o'clock – still dark as midnight. As the bell sounded the hour, there came a knocking at the street door. I went down to open it with a light heart – for what had I *now* to fear? There entered three men, who introduced themselves, with perfect suavity, as officers of the police. A shriek had been heard by a neighbour during the night; suspicion of foul play had been aroused; information had been lodged at the police office, and they (the officers) had been deputed to search the premises.

I smiled – for *what* had I to fear? I bade the gentlemen welcome. The shriek, I said, was my own in a dream. The old man, I mentioned, was absent in the country. I took my visitors all over the house. I bade them search – search *well*. I led them, at length, to *his* chamber. I showed them his treasures, secure, undisturbed. In the enthusiasm of my confidence, I brought chairs into the room, and desired them *here* to rest from their fatigues, while I myself, in the wild audacity of my perfect triumph, placed my own seat upon the very spot beneath which reposed the corpse of the victim.

The officers were satisfied. My manner had convinced them. I was singularly at ease. They sat, and while I answered cheerily, they chatted of familiar things. But, ere long, I felt myself getting pale and wished them gone. My head ached, and I fancied a ringing in my ears; but still they sat and still chatted. The ringing became more distinct – it continued and became more distinct. I talked more freely to get rid of the feeling; but it continued and gained definitiveness – until, at length, I found that the noise was *not* within my ears.

No doubt I now grew very pale; but I talked more fluently, and with a heightened voice. Yet the sound increased – and what could I do? It was a *low, dull, quick sound – much such a sound as a watch makes when enveloped in cotton*. I gasped for breath – and yet the officers heard it not. I talked more quickly – more vehemently; but the noise steadily increased. I arose and argued about trifles, in a high key and with violent gesticulations; but the noise steadily increased. Why *would* they not be gone? I paced the floor to and fro with heavy strides, as if excited to fury by the observations of the men – but the noise steadily increased. O God! what *could* I do? I foamed – I raved – I swore! I swung the chair upon which I had been sitting, and grated it upon the boards, but the noise arose over all and continually increased. It grew louder – louder – *louder!* And still the men chatted pleasantly, and smiled. Was it possible they heard not? Almighty God! – no, no! They heard! – they suspected! – they *knew!* – they were making a mockery of my horror! – this I thought, and this I think. But anything was better than this agony! Anything was more tolerable than this derision! I could bear those hypocritical smiles no longer! I felt that I must scream or die! – and now – again! hark! louder! louder! louder! *louder!* –

'Villains!' I shrieked, 'dissemble no more! I admit the deed! – tear up the planks! – here, here! – it is the beating of his hideous heart!'

Ligeia

And the will therein lieth, which dieth not. Who knoweth the mysteries of the will, with its vigour? For God is but a great will pervading all things by nature of its intentness. Man doth not yield himself to the angels, nor unto death utterly, save only through the weakness of his feeble will.

JOSEPH GLANVILL

I cannot, for my soul, remember how, when, or even precisely where, I first became acquainted with the Lady Ligeia. Long years have since elapsed, and my memory is feeble through much suffering. Or, perhaps, I cannot *now* bring these points to mind, because, in truth, the character of my beloved, her rare learning, her singular yet placid cast of beauty, and the thrilling and enthralling eloquence of her low musical language, made their way into my heart by paces so steadily and stealthily progressive, that they have been unnoticed and unknown. Yet I believe that I met her first and most frequently in some large, old, decaying city near the Rhine. Of her family – I have surely heard her speak. That it is of a remotely ancient date cannot be doubted. Ligeia! Ligeia! Buried in studies of a nature more than all else adapted to deaden impressions of the outward world, it is by that sweet word alone – by Ligeia – that I bring before mine eyes in fancy the image of her who is no more. And now, while I write, a recollection flashes upon me that I have *never known* the paternal name of her who was my friend and my betrothed, and who became the partner of my studies, and finally the wife of my bosom. Was it a playful charge on the part of my Ligeia? Or was it a test of my strength of affection, that I should institute no enquiries upon this point? Or was it rather a caprice of my own – a wildly romantic offering on the shrine of the most passionate devotion? I but indistinctly recall the fact itself – what wonder that I have utterly forgotten the circumstances which originated or attended it? And, indeed, if ever that spirit which is entitled *Romance* – if ever she, the wan and the misty-winged *Ashtophet* of idolatrous Egypt, presided, as they tell, over marriages ill-omened, then most surely she presided over mine.

There is one dear topic, however, on which my memory fails me not. It is the *person* of Ligeia. In stature she was tall, somewhat slender, and, in her latter days, even emaciated. I would in vain attempt to portray the majesty, the quiet ease, of her demeanour, or the incomprehensible lightness and elasticity of her footfall. She came and departed as a shadow. I was never made aware of her entrance into my closed study, save by the dear music of her low sweet voice, as she placed her marble hand upon my shoulder. In beauty of face no maiden ever equalled her. It was the radiance of an opium-dream – an airy and spirit-lifting vision more wildly divine than the fantasies which hovered about the slumbering souls of the daughters of Delos. Yet her features were not of that regular mould which we have been falsely taught to worship in the classical labours of the heathen. 'There is no exquisite beauty,' says Bacon, Lord Verulam, speaking truly of all the forms and genera of beauty, 'without some *strangeness* in the proportion.' Yet, although I saw that the features of Ligeia were not of a classic regularity – although I perceived that her loveliness was indeed 'exquisite', and felt that there was much of 'strangeness' pervading it, yet I have tried in vain to detect the irregularity and to trace home my own perception of 'the strange'. I examined the contour of the lofty and pale forehead – it was faultless – how cold indeed that word when applied to a majesty so divine! – the skin rivalling the purest ivory, the commanding extent and repose, the gentle prominence of the regions above the temples; and then the raven-black, the glossy, the luxuriant and naturally-curling tresses, setting forth the full force of the Homeric epithet, 'hyacinthine'! I looked at the delicate outlines of the nose – and nowhere but in the graceful medallions of the Hebrews had I beheld a similar perfection. There were the same luxurious smoothness of surface, the same scarcely perceptible tendency to the aquiline, the same harmoniously curved nostrils speaking the free spirit. I regarded the sweet mouth. Here was indeed the triumph of all things heavenly – the magnificent turn of the short upper lip – the soft, voluptuous slumber of the under – the dimples which sported, and the colour which spoke – the teeth glancing back, with a brilliancy almost startling, every ray of the holy light which fell upon them in her serene and placid, yet most exultingly radiant of all smiles. I scrutinised the formation of the chin – and here, too, I found the gentleness of breadth, the softness and the majesty, the fullness and the spirituality, of the Greek – the contour which the god Apollo revealed but in a dream, to Cleomenes, the son of the Athenian. And then I peered into the large eyes of Ligeia.

For eyes we have no models in the remotely antique. It might have been, too, that in these eyes of my beloved lay the secret to which Lord Verulam alludes. They were, I must believe, far larger than the ordinary eyes of our own race. They were even fuller than the fullest of the gazelle eyes of the tribe of the valley of Nourjahad. Yet it was only at intervals – in moments of intense excitement – that this peculiarity became more than slightly noticeable in Ligeia. And at such moments was her beauty – in my heated fancy thus it appeared, perhaps – the beauty of beings either above or apart from the earth – the beauty of the fabulous Houri of the Turk. The hue of the orbs was the most brilliant of black, and, far over them, hung jetty lashes of great length. The brows, slightly irregular in outline, had the same tint. The 'strangeness', however, which I found in the eyes, was of a nature distinct from the formation, or the colour, or the brilliancy of the features, and must, after all, be referred to the *expression*. Ah, word of no meaning! behind whose vast latitude of mere sound we entrench our ignorance of so much of the spiritual. The expression of the eyes of Ligeia – how for long hours have I pondered upon it! How have I, through the whole of a midsummer night, struggled to fathom it! What was it – that something more profound than the well of Democritus – which lay far within the pupils of my beloved? what *was* it? I was possessed with a passion to discover. Those eyes, those large, those shining, those divine orbs? they became to me twin stars of Leda, and I to them devoutest of astrologers.

There is no point, among the many incomprehensible anomalies of the science of mind, more thrillingly exciting than the fact – never, I believe, noticed in the schools – that in our endeavours to recall to memory something long forgotten, we often find ourselves *upon the very verge* of remembrance, without being able, in the end, to remember. And thus how frequently, in my intense scrutiny of Ligeia's eyes, have I felt approaching the full knowledge of their expression – felt it approaching – yet not quite be mine – and so at length entirely depart! And (strange – oh, strangest mystery of all!) I found in the commonest objects of the universe, a circle of analogies to that expression. I mean to say that, subsequently to the period when Ligeia's beauty passed into my spirit, there dwelling as in a shrine, I derived, from many existences in the material world, a sentiment such as I felt always around, within me, by her large and luminous orbs. Yet not the more could I define that sentiment, or analyse, or even steadily view it. I recognised it, let me repeat, sometimes in the survey of a rapidly growing vine – in the contemplation of a moth, a butterfly, a chrysalis, a stream of running water. I have felt it in the ocean; in the falling of a meteor. I have felt it in the glances of unusually aged people. And there are one or two stars in heaven (one especially, a star of the sixth magnitude, double and changeable, to be found near the large star in Lyra), in a telescopic scrutiny of which I have been made aware of the feeling. I have been filled with it by certain sounds from stringed instruments, and not infrequently by passages from books. Among innumerable other instances, I well remember something in a volume of Joseph Glanvill, which (perhaps merely from its quaintness – who shall say?) never failed to inspire me with the sentiment: 'And the will therein lieth, which dieth not. Who knoweth the mysteries of the will, with its vigour? For God is but a great will pervading all things by nature of its intentness. Man doth not yield him to the angels, nor unto death utterly, save only through the weakness of his feeble will.'

Length of years and subsequent reflection have enabled me to trace, indeed, some remote connection between this passage in the English moralist and a portion of the character of Ligeia. An *intensity* in thought, action, or speech, was possibly, in her, a result, or at least an index, of that gigantic volition which, during our long intercourse, failed to give other and more immediate evidence of its existence. Of all the women whom I have ever known, she, the outwardly calm, the ever-placid Ligeia, was the most violently a prey to the tumultuous vultures of stern passion. And of such passion I could form no estimate, save by the miraculous expansion of those eyes which at once so delighted and appalled me – by the almost magical melody, modulation, distinctness, and placidity of her very low voice – and by the fierce energy (rendered doubly effective by contrast with her manner of utterance) of the wild words which she habitually uttered.

I have spoken of the learning of Ligeia: it was immense – such as I have never known in woman. In the classical tongues was she deeply proficient, and, as far as my own acquaintance extended in regard to the modern dialects of Europe, I have never known her at fault. Indeed upon any theme of the most admired, because simply the most abstruse of the boasted erudition of the academy, have I *ever* found Ligeia at fault? How singularly – how thrillingly, this one point in the nature of my wife has forced itself, at this late period only, upon my attention! I said her knowledge was such as I have never known in woman – but where breathes the man who has traversed, and successfully, *all* the wide areas of moral, physical, and mathematical science? I saw not then what I now clearly perceive, that the acquisitions of Ligeia were gigantic, were astounding; yet I was sufficiently aware of her infinite supremacy to resign myself, with a childlike confidence, to her guidance through the chaotic world of metaphysical investigation at which I was most busily occupied during the earlier years of our marriage. With how vast a triumph – with how vivid a delight – with how much of all that is ethereal in hope – did I *feel*, as she bent over me in studies but little sought – but less known – that delicious vista by slow degrees expanding before me, down whose long, gorgeous, and all untrodden path, I might at length pass onward to the goal of a wisdom too divinely precious not to be forbidden!

How poignant, then, must have been the grief with which, after some years, I beheld my well-grounded expectations take wings to themselves and fly away! Without Ligeia I was but as a child groping benighted. Her presence, her readings alone, rendered vividly luminous the many mysteries of the transcendentalism in which we were immersed. Wanting the radiant lustre of her eyes, letters, lambent and golden, grew duller than Saturnian lead. And now those eyes shone less and less frequently upon the pages over which I pored. Ligeia grew ill. The wild eyes blazed with a too – too glorious effulgence; the pale fingers became of the transparent waxen hue of the grave; and the blue veins upon the lofty forehead swelled and sank impetuously with the tides of the most gentle emotion. I saw that she must die – and I struggled desperately in spirit with the grim Azrael. And the struggles of the passionate wife were, to my astonishment, even more energetic than my own. There had been much in her stern nature to impress me with the belief that, to her, death would have come without its terrors; but not so. Words are impotent to convey any just idea of the fierceness of resistance with which she wrestled with the Shadow. I groaned in anguish at the pitiable spectacle. I would have soothed – I would have reasoned; but, in the intensity of her wild desire for life – for life – *but* for life – solace and reason were alike the uttermost of folly. Yet not until the last instance, amid the most convulsive writhings of her fierce spirit, was shaken the external placidity of her demeanour. Her voice grew more gentle – grew more low – yet I would not wish to dwell upon the wild meaning of the quietly uttered words. My brain reeled as I hearkened, entranced, to a melody more than mortal – to assumptions and aspirations which mortality had never before known.

That she loved me I should not have doubted; and I might have been easily aware that, in a bosom such as hers, love would have reigned no ordinary passion. But in death only was I fully impressed with the strength of her affection. For long hours, detaining my hand, would she pour out before me the overflowing of a heart whose more than passionate devotion amounted to idolatry. How had I deserved to be so blessed by such confessions? – how had I deserved to be so cursed with the removal of my beloved in the hour of her making them? But upon this subject I cannot bear to dilate. Let me say only, that in Ligeia's more than womanly abandonment to a love, alas! all unmerited, all unworthily bestowed, I at length recognised the principle of her longing, with so wildly earnest a desire, for the life which was now fleeing so rapidly away. It is this wild longing – it is this eager vehemence of desire for life – *but* for life – that I have no power to portray – no utterance capable of expressing.

At high noon of the day in which she departed, beckoning me, peremptorily, to her side, she bade me repeat certain verses composed by herself not many days before. I obeyed her. They were these:

Lo! 'tis a gala night
  Within the lonesome latter years!
An angel throng, bewinged, bedight
  In veils, and drowned in tears,
Sit in a theatre, to see
  A play of hopes and fears,
While the orchestra breathes fitfully
  The music of the spheres.

Mimes, in the form of God on high,
  Mutter and mumble low,
And hither and thither fly;
  Mere puppets they, who come and go
At bidding of vast formless things
  That shift the scenery to and fro,
Flapping from out their condor wings
  Invisible Woe!

That motley drama! – oh, be sure
  It shall not be forgot!
With its Phantom chased for evermore,
  By a crowd that seize it not,
Through a circle that ever returneth in
  To the selfsame spot;
And much of Madness, and more of Sin,
  And Horror, the soul of the plot!

But see, amid the mimic rout
  A crawling shape intrude!
A blood-red thing that writhes from out
  The scenic solitude!
It writhes! – it writhes! – with mortal pangs
  The mimes become its food,
And the seraphs sob at vermin fangs
  In human gore imbued.

Out – out are the lights – out all!
  And over each quivering form,
The curtain, a funeral pall,
  Comes down with the rush of a storm –
And the angels, all pallid and wan,
  Uprising, unveiling, affirm
That the play is the tragedy, 'Man',
  And its hero, the Conqueror Worm.

'O God!' half-shrieked Ligeia, leaping to her feet and extending her arms aloft with a spasmodic movement, as I made an end of these lines – 'O God! O Divine Father! – shall these things be undeviatingly so? – shall this conqueror be not once conquered? Are we not part and parcel in Thee? Who – who knoweth the mysteries of the will, with its vigour? Man doth not yield him to the angels, *nor unto death utterly*, save only through the weakness of his feeble will.'

And now, as if exhausted with emotion, she suffered her white arms to fall, and returned solemnly to her bed of death. And as she breathed her last sighs, there came mingled with them a low murmur from her lips. I bent to them my ear, and distinguished again the concluding words of the passage in Glanvill: *'Man doth not yield him to the angels, nor unto death utterly, save only through the weakness of his feeble will.'*

She died; and I, crushed into the very dust with sorrow, could no longer endure the lonely desolation of my dwelling in the dim and decaying city by the Rhine. I had no lack of what the world calls wealth. Ligeia had brought me far more, very far more than ordinarily falls to the lot of mortals. After a few months, therefore, of weary and aimless wandering, I purchased, and put in some repair, an abbey, which I shall not name, in one of the wildest and least frequented portions of fair England. The gloomy and dreary grandeur of the building, the almost savage aspect of the domain, the many melancholy and time-honoured memories connected with both, had much in unison with the feelings of utter abandonment which had driven me into that remote and unsocial region of the country. Yet although the external abbey, with its verdant decay hanging about it, suffered but little alteration, I gave way, with a childlike perversity, and perchance with a faint hope of alleviating my sorrows, to a display of more than regal magnificence within. For such follies, even in childhood, I had imbibed a taste, and now they came back to me as if in the dotage of grief. Alas, I feel how much even of incipient madness might have been discovered in the gorgeous and fantastic draperies, in the solemn carvings of Egypt, in the wild cornices and furniture, in the Bedlam patterns of the carpets of tufted gold? I had become a bounden slave in the trammels of opium, and my labours and my orders had taken a colouring from my dreams. But these absurdities I must not pause to detail. Let me speak only of that one chamber, ever accursed, whither in a moment of mental alienation, I led from the altar as my bride

– as the successor of the unforgotten Ligeia – the fair-haired and blue-eyed Lady Rowena Trevanion, of Tremaine.

There is no individual portion of the architecture and decoration of that bridal chamber which is not now visibly before me. Where were the souls of the haughty family of the bride, when, through thirst of gold, they permitted to pass the threshold of an apartment so bedecked, a maiden and a daughter so beloved? I have said that I minutely remember the details of the chamber – yet I am sadly forgetful on topics of deep moment – and here there was no system, no keeping, in the fantastic display, to take hold upon the memory. The room lay in a high turret of the castellated abbey, was pentagonal in shape, and of capacious size. Occupying the whole southern face of the pentagon was the sole window – an immense sheet of unbroken glass from Venice – a single pane, and tinted of a leaden hue, so that the rays of either the sun or moon passing through it, fell with a ghastly lustre on the objects within. Over the upper portion of this huge window extended the trellis-work of an aged vine, which clambered up the massy walls of the turret. The ceiling, of gloomy-looking oak, was excessively lofty, vaulted, and elaborately fretted with the wildest and most grotesque specimens of a semi-Gothic, semi-Druidical device. From out the most central recess of this melancholy vaulting, depended, by a single chain of gold with long links, a huge censer of the same metal, Saracenic in pattern, and with many perforations so contrived that there writhed in and out of them, as if endued with a serpent vitality, a continual succession of parti-coloured fires.

Some few ottomans and golden candelabra, of Eastern figure, were in various stations about; and there was the couch, too – the bridal couch – of an Indian model, and low, and sculptured of solid ebony, with a pall-like canopy above. In each of the angles of the chamber stood on end a gigantic sarcophagus of black granite, from the tombs of the kings over against Luxor, with their aged lids full of immemorial sculpture. But in the draping of the apartment lay, alas! the chief fantasy of all. The lofty walls, gigantic in height – even unproportionably so – were hung from summit to foot, in vast folds, with a heavy and massive-looking tapestry – tapestry of a material which was found alike as a carpet on the floor, as a covering for the ottomans and the ebony bed, as a canopy for the bed, and as the gorgeous volutes of the curtains which partially shaded the window. The material was the richest cloth of gold. It was spotted all over, at irregular intervals, with arabesque figures, about a foot in diameter, and wrought upon the cloth in patterns of the most jetty black. But these figures partook of the true character of the arabesque only when regarded from a single point of view. By a contrivance now common, and indeed traceable to a very remote period of antiquity, they were made changeable in aspect. To one entering the room, they bore the appearance of simple monstrosities; but upon a farther advance, this appearance gradually departed; and, step by step, as the visitor moved his station in the chamber, he saw himself surrounded by an endless succession of the ghastly forms which belong to the superstition of the Norman, or arise in the guilty slumbers of the monk. The phantasmagoric effect was vastly heightened by the artificial introduction of a strong continual current of wind behind the draperies – giving a hideous and uneasy animation to the whole.

In halls such as these – in a bridal chamber such as this – I passed, with the Lady of Tremaine, the unhallowed hours of the first month of our marriage – passed them with but little disquietude. That my wife dreaded the fierce moodiness of my temper – that she shunned me, and loved me but little – I could not help perceiving; but it gave me rather pleasure than otherwise. I loathed her with a hatred belonging more to demon than to man. My memory flew back (oh, with what intensity of regret!) to Ligeia, the beloved, the august, the beautiful, the entombed. I revelled in recollections of her purity; of her wisdom; of her lofty, her ethereal nature; of her passionate, her idolatrous love. Now, then, did my spirit fully and freely burn with more than all the fires of her own. In the excitement of my opium dreams (for I was habitually fettered in the shackles of the drug) I would call aloud upon her name, during the silence of the night, or among the sheltered recesses of the glens by day, as if, through the wild eagerness, the solemn passion, the consuming ardour of my longing for the departed, I could restore her to the pathway she had abandoned – ah, *could* it be for ever? – upon the earth.

About the commencement of the second month of the marriage, the Lady Rowena was attacked with sudden illness, from which her recovery was slow. The fever which consumed her rendered her nights uneasy; and in her perturbed state of half-slumber, she spoke of sounds, and of motions, in and about the chamber of the turret, which I concluded had no origin save in the distemper of her fancy, or perhaps in the phantasmagoric influences of the chamber itself. She became at length convalescent – finally, well. Yet but a brief period elapsed ere a second more violent disorder again threw her upon a bed of suffering; and from this attack her frame, at all times feeble, never altogether recovered. Her illnesses were, after this epoch, of alarming character, and of more alarming recurrence, defying alike the knowledge and the great exertions of her physicians. With the increase of the chronic disease, which had thus, apparently, taken too sure hold upon her constitution to be eradicated

"I WOULD CALL ALOUD UPON HER NAME"

by human means, I could not fail to observe a similar increase in the nervous irritation of her temperament, and in her excitability by trivial causes of fear. She spoke again, and now more frequently and pertinaciously, of the sounds – of the slight sounds – and of the unusual motions among the tapestries, to which she had formerly alluded.

One night, near the closing in of September, she pressed this distressing subject with more than usual emphasis upon my attention. She had just awakened from an unquiet slumber, and I had been watching, with feelings half of anxiety, half of vague terror, the workings of her emaciated countenance. I sat by the side of her ebony bed, upon one of the ottomans of India. She partly arose, and spoke, in an earnest low whisper, of sounds which she *then* heard, but which I could not hear – of motions which she *then* saw, but which I could not perceive. The wind was rushing hurriedly behind the tapestries, and I wished to show her (what, let me confess it, I could not *all* believe) that those almost inarticulate breathings, and those very gentle variations of the figures upon the wall, were but the natural effects of that customary rushing of the wind. But a deadly pallor, overspreading her face, had proved to me that my exertions to reassure her would be fruitless. She appeared to be fainting, and no attendants were within call. I remembered where was deposited a decanter of light wine which had been ordered by her physicians, and hastened across the chamber to procure it. But, as I stepped beneath the light of the censer, two circumstances of a startling nature attracted my attention. I had felt that some palpable although invisible object had passed lightly by my person; and I saw that there lay upon the golden carpet, in the very middle of the rich lustre thrown from the censer, a shadow – a faint, indefinite shadow of angelic aspect – such as might be fancied for the shadow of a shade. But I was wild with the excitement of an immoderate dose of opium, and heeded these things but little, nor spoke of them to Rowena. Having found the wine, I recrossed the chamber, and poured out a gobletful, which I held to the lips of the fainting lady. She had now partially recovered, however, and took the vessel herself, while I sank upon an ottoman near me, with my eyes fastened upon her person. It was then that I became distinctly aware of a gentle footfall upon the carpet, and near the couch; and in a second thereafter, as Rowena was in the act of raising the wine to her lips, I saw, or may have dreamed that I saw, fall within the goblet, as if from some invisible spring in the atmosphere of the room, three or four large drops of a brilliant and ruby-coloured fluid. If this I saw – not so Rowena. She swallowed the wine unhesitatingly, and I forbore to speak to her of a circumstance which must, after all, I considered, have been but the suggestion of a vivid imagination, rendered morbidly active by the terror of the lady, by the opium, and by the hour.

Yet I cannot conceal it from my own perception that, immediately subsequent to the fall of the ruby drops, a rapid change for the worse took place in the disorder of my wife; so that, on the third subsequent night, the hands of her menials prepared her for the tomb, and on the fourth, I sat alone, with her shrouded body, in that fantastic chamber which had received her as my bride. Wild visions, opium-engendered, flitted, shadow-like, before me. I gazed with unquiet eye upon the sarcophagi in the angles of the room, upon the varying figures of the drapery, and upon the writhing of the parti-coloured fires in the censer overhead. My eyes then fell, as I called to mind the circumstances of a former night, to the spot beneath the glare of the censer where I had seen the faint traces of the shadow. It was there, however, no longer; and breathing with greater freedom, I turned my glances to the pallid and rigid figure upon the bed. Then rushed upon me a thousand memories of Ligeia – and then came back upon my heart, with the turbulent violence of a flood, the whole of that unutterable woe with which I had regarded *her* thus enshrouded. The night waned; and still, with a bosom full of bitter thoughts of the one only and supremely beloved, I remained gazing upon the body of Rowena.

It might have been midnight, or perhaps earlier, or later, for I had taken no note of time, when a sob, low, gentle, but very distinct, startled me from my reverie. I *felt* that it came from the bed of ebony – the bed of death. I listened in an agony of superstitious terror – but there was no repetition of the sound. I strained my vision to detect any motion in the corpse – but there was not the slightest perceptible. Yet I could not have been deceived. I *had* heard the noise, however faint, and my soul was awakened within me. I resolutely and perseveringly kept my attention riveted upon the body. Many minutes elapsed before any circumstance occurred tending to throw light upon the mystery. At length it became evident that a slight, a very feeble, and barely noticeable tinge of colour had flushed up within the cheeks, and along the sunken small veins of the eyelids. Through a species of unutterable horror and awe, for which the language of mortality has no sufficiently energetic expression, I felt my heart cease to beat, my limbs grow rigid where I sat. Yet a sense of duty finally operated to restore my self-possession. I could no longer doubt that we had been precipitate in our preparations – that Rowena still lived. It was necessary that some immediate exertion be made; yet the turret was altogether apart from the portion of the abbey tenanted by the servants – there were none within call – I had no means of summoning them to my aid without leaving the room for many minutes – and this I could not venture to do. I therefore struggled alone in my endeavours to call back the spirit still hovering. In a short period it was certain, however, that a relapse had taken place; the colour disappeared from both eyelid and cheek, leaving a wanness even more than that of marble; the lips became doubly shrivelled and pinched up in the ghastly expression of death; a repulsive clamminess and coldness overspread rapidly the surface of the body; and all the usual rigorous stiffness immediately supervened. I fell back with a shudder upon the couch from which I had been so startlingly aroused, and again gave myself up to passionate waking visions of Ligeia.

An hour thus elapsed, when (could it be possible?) I was a second time aware of some vague sound issuing from the region of the bed. I listened – in extremity of horror. The sound came again – it was a sigh. Rushing to the corpse, I saw – distinctly saw – a tremor upon the lips. In a minute afterwards they relaxed, disclosing a bright line of the pearly teeth. Amazement now struggled in my bosom with the profound awe which had hitherto reigned there alone. I felt that my vision grew dim, that my reason wandered; and it was only by a violent effort that I at length succeeded in nerving myself to the task which duty thus once more had pointed out. There was now a partial glow upon the forehead and upon the cheek and throat; a perceptible warmth pervaded the whole frame; there was even a slight pulsation at the heart. The lady *lived*; and with redoubled ardour I betook myself to the task of restoration. I chafed and bathed the temples and the hands, and used every exertion which experience, and no little medical reading, could suggest. But in vain. Suddenly, the colour fled, the pulsation ceased, the lips resumed the expression of the dead, and, in an instant afterward, the whole body took upon itself the icy chilliness, the livid hue, the intense rigidity, the sunken outline, and all the loathsome peculiarities of that which has been, for many days, a tenant of the tomb.

And again I sunk into visions of Ligeia – and again (what marvel that I shudder while I write?) *again* there reached my ears a low sob from the region of the ebony bed. But why shall I minutely detail the unspeakable horrors of that night? Why shall I pause to relate how, time after time, until near the period of the grey dawn, this hideous drama of revivification was repeated; how each terrific relapse was only into a sterner and apparently more irredeemable death; how each agony wore the aspect of a struggle with some invisible foe; and how each struggle was succeeded by I know not what of wild change in the personal appearance of the corpse? Let me hurry to a conclusion.

The greater part of the fearful night had worn away, and she who had been dead, once again stirred – and now more vigorously than hitherto, although arousing from a dissolution more appalling in its utter hopelessness than any. I had long ceased to struggle or to move, and remained sitting rigidly upon the ottoman, a helpless prey to a whirl of violent emotions, of which extreme awe was perhaps the least terrible, the least consuming. The corpse, I repeat, stirred, and now more vigorously than before. The hues of life flushed up with unwonted energy into the countenance – the limbs relaxed – and, save that the eyelids were yet pressed heavily together and that the bandages and draperies of the grave still imparted their charnel character to the figure, I might have dreamed that Rowena had indeed shaken off, utterly, the fetters of death. But if this idea was not, even then, altogether adopted, I could at least doubt no longer, when arising from the bed, tottering, with feeble steps, with closed eyes, and with the manner of one bewildered in a dream, the thing that was enshrouded advanced boldly and palpably into the middle of the apartment.

I trembled not – I stirred not – for a crowd of unutterable fancies connected with the air, the stature, the demeanour of the figure, rushing hurriedly through my brain, had paralysed – had chilled me into stone. I stirred not – but gazed upon the apparition. There was a mad disorder in my thoughts – a tumult unappeasable. Could it, indeed, be the *living* Rowena who confronted me? Could it indeed be Rowena *at all* – the fair-haired, the blue-eyed Lady Rowena Trevanion of Tremaine? Why, *why* should I doubt it? The bandage lay heavily about the mouth – but then might it not be the mouth of the breathing Lady of Tremaine? And the cheeks – there were the roses as in her noon of life – yes, these might indeed be the fair cheeks of the living Lady of Tremaine. And the chin, with its dimples, as in health, might it not be hers? – but *had she then grown taller since her malady?* What inexpressible madness seized me with that thought? One bound, and I had reached her feet! Shrinking from my touch, she let fall from her head, unloosened, the ghastly cerements which had confined it, and there streamed forth, into the rushing atmosphere of the chamber, huge masses of long and dishevelled hair; *it was blacker than the raven wings of midnight!* And now slowly opened *the eyes* of the figure which stood before me. 'Here then, at least,' I shrieked aloud, 'can I never – can I never be mistaken – these are the full, and the black, and the wild eyes – of my lost love – of the Lady – of the LADY LIGEIA.'

Loss of Breath

A tale neither in nor out of 'Blackwood'

'Oh, breathe not,' &c.

MOORE'S *Melodies*

The most notorious ill-fortune must in the end yield to the untiring courage of philosophy – as the most stubborn city to the ceaseless vigilance of an enemy. Shalmaneser, as we have it in the holy writings, lay three years before Samaria; yet it fell. Sardanapalus – see Diodorus – maintained himself seven in Nineveh; but to no purpose. Troy expired at the close of the second lustrum; and Azoth, as Aristaeus declares upon his honour as a gentleman, opened at last her gates to Psammetichus, after having barred them for the fifth part of a century.

'Thou wretch! – thou vixen – thou shrew!' said I to my wife on the morning after our wedding, 'thou witch! – thou hag! – thou whipper-snapper! – thou sink of iniquity! – thou fiery-faced quintessence of all that is abominable! – thou – thou – ' here standing upon tiptoe, seizing her by the throat, and placing my mouth close to her ear, I was preparing to launch forth a new and more decided epithet of opprobrium, which should not fail, if ejaculated, to convince her of her insignificance, when, to my extreme horror and astonishment, I discovered that *I had lost my breath.*

The phrases 'I am out of breath', 'I have lost my breath', &c., are often enough repeated in common conversation; but it had never occurred to me that the terrible accident of which I speak could *bona fide* and actually happen! Imagine – that is, if you have a fanciful turn – imagine, I say, my wonder – my consternation – my despair!

There is a good genius, however, which has never entirely deserted me. In my most ungovernable moods I still retain a sense of propriety, *et le chemin des passions me conduit* – as Lord Edouard in the 'Julie' says it did him – *à la philosophie veritable.*

Although I could not at first precisely ascertain to what degree the occurrence had affected me, I determined, at all events, to conceal the matter from my wife until further experience should discover to me the extent of this my unheard-of calamity. Altering my countenance, therefore, in a moment, from its bepuffed and distorted appearance, to an expression of arch and coquettish benignity, I gave my lady a pat on the one cheek, and a kiss on the other, and without saying one syllable (Furies! I could not), left her astonished at my drollery, as I pirouetted out of the room in a *Pas de Zephyr.*

Behold me, then, safely ensconced in my private boudoir, a fearful instance of the ill consequences attending upon irascibility – alive, with the qualifications of the dead – dead, with the propensities of the living – an anomaly on the face of the earth – being very calm, yet breathless.

Yes! breathless. I am serious in asserting that my breath was entirely gone. I could not have stirred with it a feather if my life had been at issue, or sullied even the delicacy of a mirror. Hard fate! – yet there was some alleviation to the first overwhelming paroxysm of my sorrow. I found, upon trial, that the powers of utterance which, upon my inability to proceed in the conversation with my wife, I then concluded to be totally destroyed, were in fact only partially impeded, and I discovered that had I at that interesting crisis dropped my voice to a singularly deep guttural, I might still have continued to her the communication of my sentiments; this pitch of voice (the guttural) depending, I find, not upon the current of the breath, but upon a certain spasmodic action of the muscles of the throat.

Throwing myself upon a chair, I remained for some time absorbed in meditation. My reflections, be sure, were of no consolatory kind. A thousand vague and lachrymatory fancies took possession of my soul – and even the idea of suicide flitted across my brain; but it is a trait in the perversity of human nature to reject the obvious and the ready, for the far-distant and equivocal. Thus I shuddered at self-murder as the most decided of atrocities, while the tabby cat purred strenuously upon the rug, and the very water-dog wheezed assiduously under the table; each taking to itself much merit for the strength of its lungs, and all obviously done in derision of my own pulmonary incapacity.

Oppressed with a tumult of vague hopes and fears, I at length heard the footsteps of my wife descending the staircase. Being now assured of her absence, I returned with a palpitating heart to the scene of my disaster.

Carefully locking the door in the inside, I commenced a vigorous search. It was possible, I thought, that concealed in some obscure corner, or lurking in some closet or drawer, might be found the lost object of my enquiry. It might have a vapoury – it might even have a tangible form. Most philosophers, upon many points of philosophy, are still very unphilosophical. William Godwin, however, says in his *Mandeville*, that 'invisible things are the only realities', and this, all will allow, is a case in point. I would have the judicious reader pause before accusing such asseverations of an undue quantum of absurdity. Anaxagoras, it will be remembered, maintained that snow is black, and this I have since found to be the case.

Long and earnestly did I continue the investigation; but the contemptible reward of my industry and perseverance proved to be only a set of false teeth, two pair of hips, an eye, and a bundle of *billets-doux* from Mr Windenough to my wife. I might as well here observe that this confirmation of my lady's partiality for Mr W. occasioned me little uneasiness. That Mrs Lackobreath should admire anything so dissimilar to myself was a natural and necessary evil. I am, it is well known, of a robust and corpulent appearance, and at the same time somewhat diminutive in stature. What wonder, then, that the lath-like tenuity of my acquaintance, and his altitude, which has grown into a proverb, should have met with all due estimation in the eyes of Mrs Lackobreath. But to return.

My exertions, as I have before said, proved fruitless. Closet after closet – drawer after drawer – corner after corner – were scrutinised to no purpose. At one time, however, I thought myself sure of my prize, having, in rummaging a dressing-case, accidentally demolished a bottle of Grandjean's Oil of Archangels – which, as an agreeable perfume, I here take the liberty of recommending.

With a heavy heart I returned to my boudoir – there to ponder upon some method of eluding my wife's penetration, until I could make arrangements prior to my leaving the country, for to this I had already made up my mind. In a foreign climate, being unknown, I might, with some probability of success, endeavour to conceal my unhappy calamity – a calamity calculated, even more than beggary, to estrange the affections of the multitude, and to draw down upon the wretch the well-merited indignation of the virtuous and the happy. I was not long in hesitation. Being naturally quick, I committed to memory the entire tragedy of *Metamora*. I had the good fortune to recollect that in the accentuation of this drama, or at least of such portion of it as is allotted to the hero, the tones of voice in which I found myself deficient were altogether unnecessary, and that the deep guttural was expected to reign monotonously throughout.

I practised for some time by the borders of a well-frequented marsh – herein, however, having no reference to a similar proceeding of Demosthenes, but from a design peculiarly and conscientiously my own. Thus armed at all points, I determined to make my wife believe that I was suddenly smitten with a passion for the stage. In this I succeeded to a miracle; and to every question or suggestion found myself at liberty to reply in my most frog-like and sepulchral tones with some passage from the tragedy – any portion of which, as I soon took great pleasure in observing, would apply equally well to any particular subject. It is not to be supposed, however, that in the delivery of such passages I was found at all deficient in the looking asquint – the showing my teeth – the working my knees – the shuffling my feet – or in any of those unmentionable graces which are now justly considered the characteristics of a popular performer. To be sure they spoke of confining me in a strait-jacket – but, good God! they never suspected me of having lost my breath.

Having at length put my affairs in order, I took my seat very early one morning in the mail stage for —, giving it to be understood, among my acquaintances, that business of the last importance required my immediate personal attendance in that city.

The coach was crammed to repletion; but, in the uncertain twilight, the features of my companions could not be distinguished. Without making any effectual resistance, I suffered myself to be placed between two gentlemen of colossal dimensions; while a third, of a size larger, requesting pardon for the liberty he was about to take, threw himself upon my body at full length, and falling asleep in an instant, drowned all my guttural ejaculations for relief, in a snore which would have put to blush the roarings of the bull of Phalaris. Happily the state of my respiratory faculties rendered suffocation an accident entirely out of the question.

As, however, the day broke more distinctly in our approach to the outskirts of the city, my tormentor arose, and adjusting his shirt-collar, thanked me in a very friendly manner for my civility. Seeing that I remained motionless (all my limbs were dislocated and my head twisted on one side), his apprehensions began to be excited; and arousing the rest of the passengers, he communicated, in a very decided manner, his opinion that a dead man had been palmed upon them during the night for a living and responsible fellow-traveller; here giving me a thump on the right eye, by way of demonstrating the truth of his suggestion.

Hereupon all, one after another (there were nine in company), believed it their duty to pull me by the ear. A young practising physician, too, having applied a pocket-mirror to my mouth, and found me without breath, the assertion of my persecutor was pronounced a true bill; and the whole party expressed a determination to endure tamely no such impositions for the future, and to proceed no farther with any such carcasses for the present.

I was here, accordingly, thrown out at the sign of the 'Crow' (by which tavern the coach happened to be passing), without meeting with any further accident than the breaking of both my arms, under the left hind wheel of the vehicle. I must, besides, do the driver the justice to state that he did not forget to throw after me the largest of my trunks, which, unfortunately falling on my head, fractured my skull in a manner at once interesting and extraordinary.

The landlord of the 'Crow', who is a hospitable man, finding that my trunk contained sufficient to indemnify him for any little trouble he might take in my behalf, sent forthwith for a surgeon of his acquaintance, and delivered me to his care with a bill and receipt for ten dollars.

The purchaser took me to his apartments and commenced operations immediately. Having cut off my ears, however, he discovered signs of animation. He now rang the bell, and sent for a neighbouring apothecary with whom to consult in the emergency. In case of his suspicions with regard to my existence proving ultimately correct, he, in the meantime, made an incision in my stomach, and removed several of my viscera for private dissection.

The apothecary had an idea that I was actually dead. This idea I endeavoured to confute, kicking and plunging with all my might, and making the most furious contortions – for the operations of the surgeon had, in a measure, restored me to the possession of my faculties. All, however, was attributed to the effects of a new galvanic battery, wherewith the apothecary, who was really a man of information, performed several curious experiments, in which, from my personal share in their fulfilment, I could not help feeling deeply interested. It was a source of mortification to me, nevertheless, that, although I made several attempts at conversation, my powers of speech were so entirely in abeyance that I could not even open my mouth; much less then make reply to some ingenious but fanciful theories of which, under other circumstances, my minute acquaintance with the Hippocratian pathology would have afforded me a ready confutation.

Not being able to arrive at a conclusion, the practitioners remanded me for further examination. I was taken up into a garret; and the surgeon's lady having accommodated me with drawers and stockings, the surgeon himself fastened my hands, and tied up my jaws with a pocket handkerchief – then bolted the door on the outside as he hurried to his dinner, leaving me to silence and to meditation.

I now discovered, to my extreme delight, that I could have spoken had not my mouth been tied up by the pocket handkerchief. Consoling myself with this reflection, I was mentally repeating some passages of the 'Omnipresence of the Deity', as is my custom before resigning myself to sleep, when two cats, of a greedy and vituperative turn, entering at a hole in the wall, leaped up with a flourish *à la Catalani*, and alighting opposite one another on my visage, betook themselves to indecorous contention for the paltry consideration of my nose.

But, as the loss of his ears proved the means of elevating to the throne of Cyrus the Magian or Mige-Gush of Persia, and as the cutting off his nose gave Zopyrus possession of Babylon, so the loss of a few ounces of my countenance proved the salvation of my body. Aroused by the pain, and burning with indignation, I burst, at a single effort, the fastenings and the bandage. Stalking across the room I cast a glance of contempt at the belligerents, and throwing open the sash, to their extreme horror and disappointment, precipitated myself very dexterously from the window.

The mail-robber W—, to whom I bore a singular resemblance, was at this moment passing from the city jail to the scaffold erected for his execution in the suburbs. His extreme infirmity, and long-continued ill-health, had obtained him the privilege of remaining unmanacled; and habited in his gallows costume – one very similar to my own

– he lay at full length in the bottom of the hangman's cart (which happened to be under the windows of the surgeon at the moment of my precipitation) without any other guard than the driver, who was asleep, and two recruits of the sixth infantry, who were drunk.

As ill-luck would have it, I alit upon my feet within the vehicle. W—, who was an acute fellow, perceived his opportunity. Leaping up immediately, he bolted out behind, and turning down an alley, was out of sight in the twinkling of an eye. The recruits, aroused by the bustle, could not exactly comprehend the merits of the transaction. Seeing, however, a man, the precise counterpart of the felon, standing upright in the cart before their eyes, they were of opinion that the rascal (meaning W—) was after making his escape (so they expressed themselves), and, having communicated this opinion to one another, they took each a dram, and then knocked me down with the butt-ends of their muskets.

It was not long ere we arrived at the place of destination. Of course nothing could be said in my defence. Hanging was my inevitable fate. I resigned myself thereto with a feeling half stupid, half acrimonious. Being little of a cynic, I had all the sentiments of a dog. The hangman, however, adjusted the noose about my neck. The drop fell.

I forbear to depict my sensations upon the gallows; although here, undoubtedly, I could speak to the point, and it is a topic upon which nothing has been well said. In fact, to write upon such a theme, it is necessary to have been hanged. Every author should confine himself to matters of experience. Thus Mark Antony composed a treatise upon getting drunk.

I may just mention, however, that die I did not. My body *was*, but I had no breath *to be* suspended; and but for the knot under my left ear (which had the feel of a military stock), I dare say that I should have experienced very little inconvenience. As for the jerk given to my neck upon the falling of the drop, it merely proved a corrective to the twist afforded me by the fat gentleman in the coach.

For good reasons, however, I did my best to give the crowd the worth of their trouble. My convulsions were said to have been extraordinary. My spasms it would have been difficult to beat. The populace *encored*. Several gentlemen swooned; and a multitude of ladies were carried home in hysterics. Pinxit availed himself of the opportunity to retouch, from a sketch taken upon the spot, his admirable painting of the 'Marsyas flayed alive'.

When I had afforded sufficient amusement, it was thought proper to remove my body from the gallows; this the more especially as the real culprit had in the meantime been retaken and recognised – a fact which I was so unlucky as not to know.

Much sympathy was, of course, exercised in my behalf, and as no one made claim to my corpse, it was ordered that I should be interred in a public vault.

Here, after due interval, I was deposited. The sexton departed, and I was left alone. A line of Marston's 'Malcontent' –

> Death's a good fellow and keeps open house –

struck me at that moment as a palpable lie.

I knocked off, however, the lid of my coffin, and stepped out. The place was dreadfully dreary and damp, and I became troubled with *ennui*. By way of amusement, I felt my way among the numerous coffins ranged in order around. I lifted them down, one by one, and breaking open their lids, busied myself in speculations about the mortality within.

'This,' I soliloquised, tumbling over a carcass, puffy, bloated, and rotund – 'this has been, no doubt, in every sense of the word, an unhappy – an unfortunate man. It has been his terrible lot not to walk, but to waddle – to pass through life not like a human being, but like an elephant – not like a man, but like a rhinoceros.

'His attempts at getting on have been mere abortions, and his circumgyratory proceedings a palpable failure. Taking a step forward, it has been his misfortune to take two towards the right, and three towards the left. His studies have been confined to the poetry of Crabbe. He can have no idea of a *pirouette*. To him a *pas de papillon* has been an abstract conception. He has never ascended the summit of a hill. He has never viewed from any steeple the glories of a metropolis. Heat has been his mortal enemy. In the dog-days his days have been the days of a dog. Therein, he has dreamed of flames and suffocation – of mountains upon mountains – of Pelion upon Ossa. He was short of breath – to say all in a word, he was short of breath. He thought it extravagant to play upon wind instruments. He was the inventor of self-moving fans, wind-sails, and ventilators. He patronised Du Pont, the bellows-maker, and died miserably in attempting to smoke a cigar. His was a case in which I feel a deep interest – a lot in which I sincerely sympathise.

'But here,' said I – 'here' – and I dragged spitefully from its receptacle a gaunt, tall, and peculiar-looking form, whose remarkable appearance struck me with a sense of unwelcome familiarity – 'here is a wretch entitled to no earthly commiseration.' Thus saying, in order to obtain a more distinct view of my subject, I applied my thumb and forefinger to its nose, and causing it to assume a sitting position on the ground, held it thus, at the length of my arm, while I continued my soliloquy –

'Entitled,' I repeated, 'to no earthly commiseration. Who, indeed, would think of compassionating a shadow? Besides, has he not had his full share of the blessings of mortality? He was the originator of tall monuments – shot-towers – lightning-rods – Lombardy poplars. His treatise upon *Shades and Shadows* has immortalised him. He edited with distinguished ability the last edition of *South on the Bones*. He went early to college and studied pneumatics. He then came home, talked eternally, and played upon the French-horn. He patronised the bagpipes. Captain Barclay, who walked against Time, would not walk against *him*. Windham and Allbreath were his favourite writers – his favourite artist, Phiz. He died gloriously while inhaling gas – *levique flatu corripitur*, like the *fama pudicitiae* in Hieronymus. He was indubitably a – '

'How *can* you? – how – *can* – you?' interrupted the object of my animadversions, gasping for breath, and tearing off, with a desperate exertion, the bandage around its jaws – 'how *can* you, Mr Lackobreath, be so infernally cruel as to pinch me in that manner by the nose? Did you not see how they had fastened up my mouth – and you *must* know – if you know anything – how vast a superfluity of breath I have to dispose of! If you do *not* know, however, sit down and you shall see. In my situation it is really a great relief to be able to open one's mouth – to be able to expatiate – to be able to communicate with a person like yourself, who do not think yourself called upon at every period to interrupt the thread of a gentleman's discourse. Interruptions are annoying, and should undoubtedly be abolished – don't you think so? – no reply, I beg you – one person is enough to be speaking at a time. I shall be done by and by, and then you may begin. How the devil, sir, did you get into this place? – not a word, I beseech you – been here some time myself – terrible accident! – heard of it, I suppose – awful calamity! – walking under your windows – some short while ago – about the time you were stage-struck – horrible occurrence! – heard of "catching one's breath", eh? – hold your tongue, I tell you! – I caught somebody else's! – had always too much of my own – met Blab at the corner of the street – wouldn't give me a chance for a word – couldn't get in a syllable edgeways – attacked, consequently, with epilepsis – Blab made his escape – damn all fools! – they took me up for dead, and put me in this place – pretty doings all of them! – heard all you said about me – every word a lie – horrible! – wonderful! – outrageous! – hideous! – incomprehensible! – et cetera – et cetera – et cetera – et cetera – '

It is impossible to conceive my astonishment at so unexpected a discourse; or the joy with which I became gradually convinced that the breath so fortunately caught by the gentleman (whom I soon recognised as my neighbour Windenough) was, in fact, the identical expiration mislaid by myself in the conversation with my wife. Time, place, and circumstance rendered it a matter beyond question. I did not, however, immediately release my hold upon Mr W—'s proboscis – not at least during the long period in which the inventor of Lombardy poplars continued to favour me with his explanations.

In this respect I was actuated by that habitual prudence which has ever been my predominating trait. I reflected that many difficulties might still lie in the path of my preservation which only extreme exertion on my part would be able to surmount. Many persons, I considered, are prone to estimate commodities in their possession – however valueless to the then proprietor, however troublesome, or distressing – in direct ratio with the advantages to be derived by others from their attainment, or by themselves from their abandonment. Might not this be the case with Mr Windenough? In displaying anxiety for the breath of which he was at present so willing to get rid, might I not lay myself open to the exactions of his avarice? There are scoundrels in this world, I remembered with a sigh, who will not scruple to take unfair opportunities with even a next-door neighbour, and (this remark is from Epictetus) it is precisely at that time when men are most anxious to throw off the burden of their own calamities that they feel the least desirous of relieving them in others.

Upon considerations similar to these, and still retaining my grasp upon the nose of Mr W—, I accordingly thought proper to model my reply.

'Monster!' I began, in a tone of the deepest indignation, 'monster! and double-winded idiot! – dost *thou*, whom for thine iniquities it has pleased heaven to accurse with a twofold respiration – dost *thou*, I say, presume to address me in the familiar language of an old acquaintance? "I lie", forsooth! and "hold my tongue", to be sure! – pretty conversation, indeed, to a gentleman with a single breath! – all this, too, when I have it in my power to relieve the calamity under which thou dost so justly suffer – to curtail the superfluities of thine unhappy respiration.'

Like Brutus, I paused for a reply – with which, like a tornado, Mr Windenough immediately overwhelmed me. Protestation followed upon protestation, and apology upon apology. There were no terms with which he was unwilling to comply, and there were none of which I failed to take the fullest advantage.

Preliminaries being at length arranged, my acquaintance delivered me the respiration; for which (having carefully examined it) I gave him afterwards a receipt.

I am aware that by many I shall be held to blame for speaking, in a manner so cursory, of a transaction so impalpable. It will be thought that I should have entered more minutely into the details of an occurrence by which – and this is very true – much new light might be thrown upon a highly interesting branch of physical philosophy.

To all this I am sorry that I cannot reply. A hint is the only answer which I am permitted to make. There were *circumstances* – but I think it much safer upon consideration to say as little as possible about an affair so delicate – *so delicate*, I repeat, and at the time involving the interests of a third party whose sulphurous resentment I have not the least desire, at this moment, of incurring.

We were not long after this necessary arrangement in effecting an escape from the dungeons of the sepulchre. The united strength of our resuscitated voices was soon sufficiently apparent. Scissors, the Whig editor, republished a treatise upon 'The nature and origin of subterranean noises'. A reply – rejoinder – confutation – and justification – followed in the columns of a Democratic gazette. It was not until the opening of the vault to decide the controversy, that the appearance of Mr Windenough and myself proved both parties to have been decidedly in the wrong.

I cannot conclude these details of some very singular passages in a life at all times sufficiently eventful, without again recalling to the attention of the reader the merits of that indiscriminate philosophy which is a sure and ready shield against those shafts of calamity which can neither be seen, felt, nor fully understood. It was in the spirit of this wisdom that, among the ancient Hebrews, it was believed the gates of heaven would be inevitably opened to that sinner, or saint, who, with good lungs and implicit confidence, should vociferate the word '*Amen!*' It was in the spirit of this wisdom that, when a great plague raged at Athens, and every means had been attempted for its removal, Epimenides, as Laertius relates in his second book of that philosopher, advised the erection of a shrine and temple 'to the proper God'.

Shadow – A Parable

Yea! though I walk through the valley of the *Shadow*.
Psalm of David

Ye who read are still among the living; but I who write shall have long since gone my way into the region of shadows. For indeed strange things shall happen, and secret things be known, and many centuries shall pass away, ere these memorials be seen of men. And, when seen, there will be some to disbelieve, and some to doubt, and yet a few who will find much to ponder upon in the characters here graven with a stylus of iron.

The year had been a year of terror, and of feelings more intense than terror, for which there is no name upon the earth. For many prodigies and signs had taken place, and far and wide, over sea and land, the black wings of the pestilence were spread abroad. To those, nevertheless, cunning in the stars, it was not unknown that the heavens wore an aspect of ill; and to me, the Greek Oinos, among others, it was evident that now had arrived the alternation of that seven hundred and ninety-fourth year when, at the entrance of Aries, the planet Jupiter is conjoined with the red ring of the terrible Saturnus. The peculiar spirit of the skies, if I mistake not greatly, made itself manifest not only in the physical orb of the earth, but in the souls, imaginations, and meditations of mankind.

Over some flasks of the red Chian wine, within the walls of a noble hall, in a dim city called Ptolemais, we sat, at night, a company of seven. And to our chamber there was no entrance save by a lofty door of brass; and the door was fashioned by the artisan Corinnos, and, being of rare workmanship, was fastened from within. Black draperies, likewise, in the gloomy room, shut out from our view the moon, the lurid stars, and the peopleless streets – but the boding and the memory of Evil, they would not be so excluded. There were things around us and about of which I can render no distinct account – things material and spiritual – heaviness in the atmosphere – a sense of suffocation – anxiety – and, above all, that terrible state of existence which the nervous experience when the senses are keenly living and awake, and meanwhile the powers of thought lie dormant. A dead weight hung upon us. It hung upon our limbs – upon the household furniture – upon the goblets from which we drank; and all things were depressed, and borne down thereby – all things save only the flames of the seven iron lamps which illumined our revel. Uprearing themselves in tall slender lines of light, they thus remained burning, all pallid and motionless; and in the mirror which their lustre formed upon the round table of ebony at which we sat, each of us there assembled beheld the pallor of his own countenance, and the unquiet glare in the downcast eyes of his companions. Yet we laughed and were merry in our proper way – which was hysterical; and sang the songs of Anacreon – which are madness; and drank deeply – although the purple wine reminded us of blood. For there was yet another tenant of our chamber in the person of young Zoilus. Dead, and at full length he lay, enshrouded – the genius and the demon of the scene. Alas! he bore no portion in our mirth, save that his countenance, distorted with the plague, and his eyes, in which death had but half extinguished the fire of the pestilence, seemed to take such interest in our merriment as the dead may haply take in the merriment of those who are to die. But, although I, Oinos, felt that the eyes of the departed were upon me, still I forced myself not to perceive the bitterness of their expression, and, gazing down steadily into the depths of the ebony mirror, sang with a loud and sonorous voice the songs of the son of Teios. But gradually my songs they ceased, and their echoes, rolling afar off among the sable draperies of the chamber, became weak, and undistinguishable, and so faded away. And lo! from among those sable draperies, where the sounds of the song departed, there came forth a dark and undefined shadow – a shadow such as the moon, when low in heaven, might fashion from the figure of a man: but it was the shadow neither of man nor of God, nor of any familiar thing. And quivering awhile among the draperies of the room, it at length rested in full view upon the surface of the door of brass. But the shadow was vague, and formless, and indefinite, and was the shadow neither of man nor God – neither God of Greece, nor God of Chaldea, nor any Egyptian God. And the shadow rested upon the brazen doorway, and under the arch of the entablature of the door, and moved not, nor spoke any word, but there became stationary and remained. And the door whereupon the shadow rested was, if I remember aright, over against the feet of the young Zoilus enshrouded. But we, the seven there assembled, having seen the shadow as it came out from among the draperies, dared not steadily behold it, but cast down our eyes, and gazed continually into the depths of the mirror of ebony. And at length I, Oinos, speaking some low words, demanded of the shadow its dwelling and its appellation. And the shadow answered, 'I am Shadow, and my dwelling is near to the catacombs of Ptolemais, and hard by those dim plains of Helusion which border upon the foul Charonian canal.' And then did we, the seven, start from our seats in horror, and stand trembling, and shuddering, and aghast: for the tones in the voice of the shadow were not the tones of any one being, but of a multitude of beings, and, varying in their cadences from syllable to syllable, fell duskily upon our ears in the well-remembered and familiar accents of many thousand departed friends.

BUT THERE WAS NO VOICE THROUGHOUT THE VAST, ILLIMITABLE DESERT

Silence – A Fable

> Ἐυδουσιν δ'ορεων κορυφαι τε και φαραγγες
> Πρωνες τε και χαραδραι.
>
> ALCMAN

> The mountain pinnacles slumber; valleys, crags, and caves *are silent.*

'Listen to *me*,' said the Demon, as he placed his hand upon my head. 'The region of which I speak is a dreary region in Libya, by the borders of the river Zäire. And there is no quiet there, nor silence.

'The waters of the river have a saffron and sickly hue; and they flow not onward to the sea, but palpitate for ever and for ever beneath the red eye of the sun with a tumultuous and convulsive motion. For many miles on either side of the river's oozy bed is a pale desert of gigantic water-lilies. They sigh one unto the other in that solitude, and stretch towards the heaven their long and ghastly necks, and nod to and fro their everlasting heads. And there is an indistinct murmur which cometh out from among them like the rushing of subterrene water. And they sigh one unto the other.

'But there is a boundary to their realm – the boundary of the dark, horrible, lofty forest. There, like the waves about the Hebrides, the low underwood is agitated continually. But there is no wind throughout the heaven. And the tall primeval trees rock eternally hither and thither with a crashing and mighty sound. And from their high summits, one by one, drop everlasting dews. And at the roots strange poisonous flowers lie writhing in perturbed slumber. And overhead, with a rustling and loud noise, the grey clouds rush westwardly for ever, until they roll, a cataract, over the fiery wall of the horizon. But there is no wind throughout the heaven. And by the shores of the river Zäire there is neither quiet nor silence.

'It was night, and the rain fell; and, falling, it was rain, but, having fallen, it was blood. And I stood in the morass among the tall lilies, and the rain fell upon my head – and the lilies sighed one unto the other in the solemnity of their desolation.

'And, all at once, the moon arose through the thin ghastly mist, and was crimson in colour. And mine eyes fell upon a huge grey rock which stood by the shore of the river, and was lighted by the light of the moon. And the rock was grey, and ghastly, and tall – and the rock was grey. Upon its front were characters engraven in the stone; and I walked through the morass of water-lilies, until I came close unto the shore, that I might read the characters upon the stone. But I could not decipher them. And I was going back into the morass, when the moon shone with a fuller red, and I turned and looked again upon the rock, and upon the characters – and the characters were "DESOLATION".

'And I looked upwards, and there stood a man upon the summit of the rock; and I hid myself among the water-lilies that I might discover the actions of the man. And the man was tall and stately in form, and was wrapped up from his shoulders to his feet in the toga of old Rome. And the outlines of his figure were indistinct – but his features were the features of a deity; for the mantle of the night, and of the mist, and of the moon, and of the dew, had left uncovered the features of his face. And his brow was lofty with thought, and his eye wild with care; and in the few furrows upon his cheek I read the fables of sorrow, and weariness, and disgust with mankind, and a longing after solitude.

'And the man sat upon the rock, and leaned his head upon his hand, and looked out upon the desolation. He looked down into the low unquiet shrubbery, and up into the tall primeval trees, and up higher at the rustling heaven, and into the crimson moon. And I lay close within shelter of the lilies, and observed the actions of the man. And the man trembled in the solitude; but the night waned, and he sat upon the rock.

'And the man turned his attention from the heaven, and looked out upon the dreary river Zäire, and upon the yellow ghastly waters, and upon the pale legions of the water-lilies. And the man listened to the sighs of the water-lilies, and to the murmur that came up from among them. And I lay close within my covert, and observed the actions of the man. And the man trembled in the solitude; but the night waned and he sat upon the rock.

'Then I went down into the recesses of the morass, and waded far in among the wilderness of the lilies, and called unto the hippopotami which dwelt among the fens in the recesses of the morass. And the hippopotami heard my call, and came, with the behemoth, unto the foot of the rock, and roared loudly and fearfully beneath the moon. And I lay close within my covert, and observed the actions of the man. And the man trembled in the solitude; but the night waned, and he sat upon the rock.

'Then I cursed the elements with the curse of tumult; and a frightful tempest gathered in the heaven, where, before, there had been no wind. And the heaven became livid with the violence of the tempest – and the rain beat upon the head of the man – and the floods of the river came down – and the river was tormented into foam – and the water-lilies shrieked within their beds – and the forest crumbled before the wind – and the thunder rolled – and the lightning fell – and the rock rocked to its foundation. And I lay close within my covert, and observed the actions of the man. And the man trembled in the solitude; but the night waned, and he sat upon the rock.

'Then I grew angry and cursed, with the curse of *silence*, the river, and the lilies, and the wind, and the forest, and the heaven, and the thunder, and the sighs of the water-lilies. And they became accursed, and *were still*. And the moon ceased to totter up its pathway to heaven – and the thunder died away – and the lightning did not flash – and the clouds hung motionless – and the waters sunk to their level and remained – and the trees ceased to rock – and the water-lilies sighed no more – and the murmur was heard no longer from among them, nor any shadow of sound throughout the vast illimitable desert. And I looked upon the characters of the rock, and they were changed; and the characters were "SILENCE".

'And mine eyes fell upon the countenance of the man, and his countenance was wan with terror. And, hurriedly, he raised his head from his hand, and stood forth upon the rock and listened. But there was no voice throughout the vast illimitable desert, and the characters upon the rock were "SILENCE". And the man shuddered, and turned his face away, and fled afar off, in haste, so that I beheld him no more.'

Now there are fine tales in the volumes of the Magi – in the iron-bound, melancholy volumes of the Magi. Therein, I say, are glorious histories of the heaven, and of the earth, and of the mighty sea – and of the Genii that overruled the sea, and the earth, and the lofty heaven. There was much lore, too, in the sayings which were said by the Sibyls; and holy, holy things were heard of old by the dim leaves that trembled around Dodona – but, as Allah liveth, that fable which the Demon told me as he sat by my side in the shadow of the tomb, I hold to be the most wonderful of all! And as the Demon made an end of his story, he fell back within the cavity of the tomb and laughed. And I could not laugh with the Demon, and he cursed me because I could not laugh. And the lynx which dwelleth for ever in the tomb came out therefrom, and lay down at the feet of the Demon, and looked at him steadily in the face.

The Man of the Crowd

Ce grand malheur, de ne pouvoir être seul.
LA BRUYÈRE

It was well said of a certain German book that '*er lasst sich nicht lesen*' – it does not permit itself to be read. There are some secrets which do not permit themselves to be told. Men die nightly in their beds, wringing the hands of ghostly confessors, and looking them piteously in the eyes – die with despair of heart and convulsion of throat, on account of the hideousness of mysteries which will not *suffer themselves* to be revealed. Now and then, alas, the conscience of man takes up a burden so heavy in horror that it can be thrown down only into the grave. And thus the essence of all crime is undivulged.

Not long ago, about the closing in of an evening in autumn, I sat at the large bow window of the D— Coffee-House in London. For some months I had been ill in health, but was now convalescent, and, with returning strength, found myself in one of those happy moods which are so precisely the converse of *ennui* – moods of the keenest appetency, when the film from the mental vision departs – the ἀχλυς ὀς πριν ἐπηεν – and the intellect, electrified, surpasses as greatly its everyday condition, as does the vivid yet candid reason of Leibnitz, the mad and flimsy rhetoric of Gorgias. Merely to breathe was enjoyment, and I derived positive pleasure even from many of the legitimate sources of pain. I felt a calm but inquisitive interest in everything. With a cigar in my mouth and a newspaper in my lap, I had been amusing myself for the greater part of the afternoon, now in poring over advertisements, now in observing the promiscuous company in the room, and now in peering through the smoky panes into the street.

This latter is one of the principal thoroughfares of the city, and had been very much crowded during the whole day. But, as the darkness came on, the throng momently increased; and, by the time the lamps were well lighted, two dense and continuous tides of population were rushing past the door. At this particular period of the evening I had never before been in a similar situation, and the tumultuous sea of human heads filled me, therefore, with a delicious novelty of emotion. I gave up, at length, all care of things within the hotel, and became absorbed in contemplation of the scene without.

At first my observations took an abstract and generalising turn. I looked at the passengers in masses, and thought of them in their aggregate relations. Soon, however, I descended to details, and regarded with minute interest the innumerable varieties of figure, dress, air, gait, visage, and expression of countenance.

By far the greater number of those who went by had a satisfied businesslike demeanour, and seemed to be thinking only of making their way through the press. Their brows were knit, and their eyes rolled quickly; when pushed against by fellow-wayfarers they evinced no symptom of impatience, but adjusted their clothes and hurried on. Others, still a numerous class, were restless in their movements, had flushed faces, and talked and gesticulated to themselves, as if feeling in solitude on account of the very denseness of the company around. When impeded in their progress, these people suddenly ceased muttering, but redoubled their gesticulations, and awaited, with an absent and overdone smile upon their lips, the course of the persons impeding them. If jostled, they bowed profusely to the jostlers, and appeared overwhelmed with confusion. There was nothing very distinctive about these two large classes beyond what I have noted. Their habiliments belonged to that order which is pointedly termed the decent. They were undoubtedly noblemen, merchants, attorneys, tradesmen, stockjobbers – the Eupatrids and the commonplaces of society – men of leisure and men actively engaged in affairs of their own – conducting business upon their own responsibility. They did not greatly excite my attention.

The tribe of clerks was an obvious one; and here I discerned two remarkable divisions. There were the junior clerks of flash houses – young gentlemen with tight coats, bright boots, well-oiled hair, and supercilious lips. Setting aside a certain dapperness of carriage, which may be termed *deskism* for want of a better word, the manner of these persons seemed to me an exact facsimile of what had been the perfection of *bon ton* about twelve or eighteen months before. They wore the cast-off graces of the gentry – and this, I believe, involves the best definition of the class.

The division of the upper clerks of staunch firms, or of the 'steady old fellows', it was not possible to mistake. These were known by their coats and pantaloons of black or brown, made to sit comfortably, with white cravats and waistcoats, broad, solid-looking shoes, and thick hose or gaiters. They had all slightly bald heads, from which the right ears, long used to penholding, had an odd habit of standing off on end. I observed that they always removed or settled their hats with both hands, and wore watches, with short gold chains of a substantial and ancient pattern. Theirs was the affection of respectability; if indeed there be an affectation so honourable.

There were many individuals of dashing appearance, whom I easily understood as belonging to the race of swell pickpockets, with which all great cities are infested. I watched these gentry with much inquisitiveness, and found it difficult to imagine how they should ever be mistaken for gentlemen by gentlemen themselves. Their voluminousness of wristband, with an air of excessive frankness, should betray them at once.

The gamblers, of whom I descried not a few, were still more easily recognisable. They wore every variety of dress, from that of the desperate thimble-rig bully, with velvet waistcoat, fancy neckerchief, gilt chains, and filigreed buttons, to that of the scrupulously inornate clergyman, than which nothing could be less liable to suspicion. Still all were distinguished by a certain sodden swarthiness of complexion, a filmy dimness of eye, and pallor and compression of lip. There were two other traits, moreover, by which I could always detect them – a guarded lowness of tone in conversation, and a more than ordinary extension of the thumb in a direction at right angles with the fingers. Very often, in company with these sharpers, I observed an order of men somewhat different in habits, but still birds of a kindred feather. They may be defined as the gentlemen who live by their wits. They seem to prey upon the public in two battalions – that of the dandies and that of the military men. Of the first grade the leading features are long locks and smiles; of the second frogged coats and frowns.

Descending in the scale of what is termed gentility, I found darker and deeper themes for speculation. I saw Jew pedlars, with hawk eyes flashing from countenances whose every other feature wore only an expression of abject humility; sturdy professional street beggars scowling upon mendicants of a better stamp, whom despair alone had driven forth into the night for charity; feeble and ghastly invalids, upon whom death had placed a sure hand, and who sidled and tottered through the mob, looking everyone beseechingly in the face, as if in search of some chance consolation, some lost hope; modest young girls returning from long and late labour to a cheerless home, and shrinking more tearfully than indignantly from the glances of ruffians, whose direct contact, even, could not be avoided; women of the town of all kinds and of all ages – the unequivocal beauty in the prime of her womanhood, putting one in mind of the statue in Lucian, with the surface of Parian marble, and the interior filled with filth – the loathsome and utterly lost leper in rags – the wrinkled, bejewelled and paint-begrimed beldame, making a last effort at youth – the mere child of immature form, yet, from long association, an adept in the dreadful coquetries of her trade, and burning with a rabid ambition to be ranked the equal of her elders in vice; drunkards innumerable and indescribable – some in shreds and patches, reeling, inarticulate, with bruised visage and lack-lustre eyes – some in whole although filthy garments, with a slightly unsteady swagger, thick sensual lips, and hearty-looking rubicund faces – others clothed in materials which had once been good, and which even now were scrupulously well brushed – men who walked with a more than naturally firm and springy step, but whose countenances were fearfully pale, whose eyes were hideously wild and red, and who clutched with quivering fingers, as they strode through the crowd, at every object which came within their reach; beside these, pie-men, porters, coal-heavers, sweeps; organ-grinders, monkey-exhibitors, and ballad-mongers, those who vended with those who sang; ragged artisans and exhausted labourers of every description, and all full of a noisy and inordinate vivacity which jarred discordantly upon the ear, and gave an aching sensation to the eye.

As the night deepened, so deepened to me the interest of the scene; for not only did the general character of the crowd materially alter (its gentler features retiring in the gradual withdrawal of the more orderly portion of the people, and its harsher ones coming out into bolder relief, as the late hour brought forth every species of infamy from its den), but the rays of the gas-lamps, feeble at first in their struggle with the dying day, had now at length gained ascendency, and threw over everything a fitful and garish lustre. All was dark yet splendid – as that ebony to which has been likened the style of Tertullian.

The wild effects of the light enchained me to an examination of individual faces; and although the rapidity with which the world of light flitted before the window, prevented me from casting more than a glance upon each visage, still it seemed that, in my then peculiar mental state, I could frequently read, even in that brief interval of a glance, the history of long years.

With my brow to the glass, I was thus occupied in scrutinising the mob, when suddenly there came into view a countenance (that of a decrepit old man, some sixty-five or seventy years of age) – a countenance which at once arrested and absorbed my whole attention, on account of the absolute idiosyncrasy of its expression. Anything even remotely resembling that expression I had never seen before. I well remember that my first thought, upon beholding it, was that Retzch, had he viewed it, would have greatly preferred it to his own pictorial incarnations of the fiend. As I endeavoured, during the brief minute of my original survey, to form some analysis of the meaning conveyed, there arose confusedly and paradoxically within my mind, the ideas of vast mental power, of caution, of penuriousness, of avarice, of coolness, of malice, of bloodthirstiness, of triumph, of merriment, of excessive terror, of intense – of supreme despair. I felt singularly aroused, startled, fascinated. 'How wild a history,' I said to myself, 'is written within that bosom!' Then came a craving desire to keep the man in view – to know more of him. Hurriedly putting on an overcoat, and seizing my hat and cane, I made my way into the street, and pushed through the crowd in the direction which I had seen him take; for he had already disappeared. With some little difficulty I at length came within sight of him, approached, and followed him closely, yet cautiously, so as not to attract his attention.

I had now a good opportunity of examining his person. He was short in stature, very thin, and apparently very feeble. His clothes, generally, were filthy and ragged; but as he came, now and then, within the strong glare of a lamp, I perceived that his linen, although dirty, was of beautiful texture; and my vision deceived me, or, through a rent in a closely-buttoned and evidently second-hand *roquelaire* which enveloped him, I caught a glimpse both of a diamond and of a dagger. These observations heightened my curiosity, and I resolved to follow the stranger whithersoever he should go.

It was now fully nightfall, and a thick humid fog hung over the city, soon ending in a settled and heavy rain. This change of weather had an odd effect upon the crowd, the whole of which was at once put into new commotion, and overshadowed by a world of umbrellas. The waver, the jostle, and the hum increased in a tenfold degree. For my own part I did not much regard the rain – the lurking of an old fever in my system rendering the moisture somewhat too dangerously pleasant. Tying a handkerchief about my mouth, I kept on. For half an hour the old man held his way with difficulty along the great thoroughfare; and I here walked close at his elbow through fear of losing sight of him. Never once turning his head to look back, he did not observe me. By and by he passed into a cross street, which, although densely filled with people, was not quite so much thronged as the main one he had quitted. Here a change in his demeanour became evident. He walked more slowly, and with less object than before – more hesitatingly. He crossed and recrossed the way repeatedly, without apparent aim; and the press was still so thick that, at every such movement, I was obliged to follow him closely. The street was a narrow and long one, and his course lay within it for nearly an hour, during which the passengers had gradually diminished to about that number which is ordinarily seen at noon in Broadway near the park – so vast a difference is there between a London populace and that of the most frequented American city. A second turn brought us into a square, brilliantly lighted, and overflowing with life. The old manner of the stranger reappeared. His chin fell upon his breast, while his eyes rolled wildly from under his knit brows, in every direction, upon those who hemmed him in. He urged his way steadily and perseveringly. I was surprised, however, to find, upon his having made the circuit of the square, that he turned and retraced his steps. Still more was I astonished to see him repeat the same walk several times – once nearly detecting me as he came round with a sudden movement.

In this exercise he spent another hour, at the end of which we met with far less interruption from passengers than at first. The rain fell fast; the air grew cool; and the people were retiring to their homes. With a gesture of impatience, the wanderer passed into a by-street comparatively deserted. Down this, some quarter of a mile long, he rushed with an activity I could not have dreamed of seeing in one so aged, and which put me to much trouble in pursuit. A few minutes brought us to a large and busy bazaar, with the localities of which the stranger appeared well acquainted, and where his original demeanour again became apparent, as he forced his way to and fro, without aim, among the host of buyers and sellers.

During the hour and a half, or thereabouts, which we passed in this place, it required much caution on my part to keep him within reach without attracting his observation. Luckily I wore a pair of caoutchouc over-shoes, and could move about in perfect silence. At no moment did he see that I watched him. He entered shop after shop, priced nothing, spoke no word, and looked at all objects with a wild and vacant stare. I was now utterly amazed at his behaviour, and firmly resolved that we should not part until I had satisfied myself in some measure respecting him.

A loud-toned clock struck eleven, and the company were fast deserting the bazaar. A shopkeeper, in putting up a shutter, jostled the old man, and at the instant I saw a strong shudder come over his frame. He hurried into the street, looked anxiously around him for an instant, and then ran with incredible swiftness through many crooked and peopleless lanes, until we emerged once more upon the great thoroughfare whence we had started – the street of the D— Hôtel. It no longer wore, however, the same aspect. It was still brilliant with gas; but the rain fell fiercely, and there were few persons to be seen. The stranger grew pale. He walked moodily some paces up the once populous avenue, then, with a heavy sigh, turned in the direction of the river, and, plunging through a great variety of devious ways, came out, at length, in view of one of the principal theatres. It was about being closed, and the audience were thronging from the doors. I saw the old man gasp as if for breath while he threw himself amid the crowd; but I thought that the intense agony of his countenance had in some measure abated. His head again fell upon his breast; he appeared as I had seen him at first. I observed that he now took the course in which had gone the greater number of the audience; but, upon the whole, I was at a loss to comprehend the waywardness of his actions.

As he proceeded, the company grew more scattered, and his old uneasiness and vacillation were resumed. For some time he followed closely a party of some ten or twelve roisterers; but from this number one by one dropped off, until three only remained together, in a narrow and gloomy lane little frequented. The stranger paused, and, for a moment, seemed lost in thought; then, with every mark of agitation, pursued rapidly a route which brought us to the verge of the city, amid regions very different from those we had hitherto traversed. It was the most noisome quarter of London, where everything wore the worst impress of the most deplorable poverty, and of the most desperate crime. By the dim light of an accidental lamp, tall, antique, worm-eaten, wooden tenements were seen tottering to their fall, in directions so many and capricious, that scarce the semblance of a passage was discernible between them. The paving-stones lay at random, displaced from their beds by the rankly-growing grass. Horrible filth festered in the dammed-up gutters. The whole atmosphere teemed with desolation. Yet, as we proceeded, the sounds of human life revived by sure degrees, and at length large bands of the most abandoned of a London populace were seen reeling to and fro. The spirits of the old man again flickered up, as a lamp which is near its death-hour. Once more he strode onward with elastic tread. Suddenly a corner was turned, a blaze of light burst upon our sight, and we stood before one of the huge suburban temples of intemperance – one of the palaces of the fiend, Gin.

It was now nearly daybreak; but a number of wretched inebriates still pressed in and out of the flaunting entrance. With a half shriek of joy the old man forced a passage within, resumed at once his original bearing, and stalked backward and forward, without apparent object, among the throng. He had not been thus long occupied, however, before a rush to the doors gave token that the host was closing them for the night. It was something even more intense than despair that I then observed upon the countenance of the singular being whom I had watched so pertinaciously. Yet he did not hesitate in his career, but, with a mad energy, retraced his steps at once, to the heart of the mighty London. Long and swiftly he fled, while I followed him in the wildest amazement, resolute not to abandon a scrutiny in which I now felt an interest all-absorbing. The sun arose while we proceeded, and, when we had once again reached that most thronged mart of the populous town, the street of the D— Hôtel, it presented an appearance of human bustle and activity scarcely inferior to what I had seen on the evening before. And here, long, amid the momently increasing confusion, did I persist in my pursuit of the stranger. But, as usual, he walked to and fro, and during the day did not pass from out the turmoil of that street. And, as the shades of the second evening came on, I grew wearied unto death, and, stopping fully in front of the wanderer, gazed at him steadfastly in the face. He noticed me not, but resumed his solemn walk, while I, ceasing to follow, remained absorbed in contemplation. 'This old man,' I said at length, 'is the type and the genius of deep crime. He refuses to be alone. *He is the man of the crowd*. It will be in vain to follow; for I shall learn no more of him, nor of his deeds. The worst heart of the world is a grosser book than the *Hortulus Animæ*; and perhaps it is but one of the great mercies of God that *er lasst sich nicht lesen*.'

Some Words with a Mummy

The *symposium* of the preceding evening had been a little too much for my nerves. I had a wretched headache, and was desperately drowsy. Instead of going out, therefore, to spend the evening, as I had proposed, it occurred to me that I could not do a wiser thing than just eat a mouthful of supper and go immediately to bed.

A *light* supper, of course. I am exceedingly fond of Welsh rabbit. More than a pound at once, however, may not at all times be advisable. Still, there can be no material objection to two. And really between two and three, there is merely a single unit of difference. I ventured, perhaps, upon four. My wife will have it five; but, clearly, she has confounded two very distinct affairs. The abstract number, five, I am willing to admit; but, concretely, it has reference to bottles of brown stout, without which, in the way of condiment, Welsh rabbit is to be eschewed.

Having thus concluded a frugal meal and donned my nightcap, with the serene hope of enjoying it till noon the next day, I placed my head upon the pillow, and through the aid of a capital conscience, fell into a profound slumber forthwith.

But when were the hopes of humanity fulfilled? I could not have completed my third snore when there came a furious ringing at the street-door bell, and then an impatient thumping at the knocker, which awakened me at once. In a minute afterward, and while I was still rubbing my eyes, my wife thrust in my face a note, from my old friend, Dr Ponnonner. It ran thus:

> Come to me, by all means, my dear good friend, as soon as you receive this. Come and help us to rejoice. At last, by long persevering diplomacy, I have gained the assent of the Directors of the City Museum, to my examination of the mummy – you know the one I mean. I have permission to unswathe it, and open it, if desirable. A few friends only will be present – you, of course. The mummy is now at my house, and we shall begin to unroll it at eleven tonight.
>
> Yours ever,
>
> PONNONNER

By the time I had reached the 'Ponnonner', it struck me that I was as wide awake as a man need be. I leaped out of bed in an ecstasy, overthrowing all in my way; dressed myself with a rapidity truly marvellous; and set off, at the top of my speed, for the doctor's.

There I found a very eager company assembled. They had been awaiting me with much impatience. The mummy was extended upon the dining-table; and the moment I entered, its examination was commenced.

It was one of a pair brought, several years previously, by Captain Arthur Sabretash, a cousin of Ponnonner's, from a tomb near Eleithias, in the Lybian Mountains, a considerable distance above Thebes on the Nile. The grottoes at this point, although less magnificent than the Theban sepulchres, are of higher interest, on account of affording more numerous illustrations of the private life of the Egyptians. The chamber from which our specimen was taken, was said to be very rich in such illustrations – the walls being completely covered with fresco-paintings and bas-reliefs, while statues, vases, and mosaic work of rich patterns, indicated the vast wealth of the deceased.

The treasure had been deposited in the museum precisely in the same condition in which Captain Sabretash had found it – that is to say, the coffin had not been disturbed. For eight years it had thus stood, subject only externally to public inspection. We had now, therefore, the complete mummy at our disposal; and to those who are aware how very rarely the unransacked antique reaches our shores, it will be evident, at once, that we had great reason to congratulate ourselves upon our good fortune.

Approaching the table, I saw on it a large box, or case, nearly seven feet long, and perhaps three feet wide, by two feet and a half deep. It was oblong – not coffin-shaped. The material was at first supposed to be the wood of the sycamore (*platanus*), but upon cutting into it, we found it to be pasteboard, or, more properly, *papier-mâché*, composed of papyrus. It was thickly ornamented with paintings, representing funeral scenes, and other mournful subjects – interspersed among which, in every variety of position, were certain series of hieroglyphical characters, intended, no doubt, for the name of the departed. By good luck, Mr Gliddon formed one of our party; and he had no difficulty in translating the letters, which were simply phonetic, and represented the word, *Allamistakeo*.

We had some difficulty in getting this case open without injury; but, having at length accomplished the task, we came to a second, coffin-shaped, and very considerably less in size than the exterior one, but resembling it precisely in every other respect. The interval between the two was filled with resin, which had, in some degree, defaced the colours of the interior box.

Upon opening this latter (which we did quite easily) we arrived at a third case, also coffin-shaped, and varying from the second one in no particular, except in that of its material, which was cedar, and still emitted the peculiar and highly aromatic odour of that wood. Between the second and the third case there was no interval – the one fitting accurately within the other.

Removing the third case, we discovered and took out the body itself. We had expected to find it, as usual, enveloped in frequent rolls or bandages of linen; but, in place of these, we found a sort of sheath, made of papyrus, and coated with a layer of plaster, thickly gilt and painted. The paintings represented subjects connected with the various supposed duties of the soul, and its presentation to different divinities, with numerous identical human figures, intended, very probably, as portraits of the persons embalmed. Extending from head to foot, was a columnar, or perpendicular inscription, in phonetic hieroglyphics, giving again his name and titles, and the names and titles of his relations.

Around the neck thus ensheathed, was a collar of cylindrical glass beads, diverse in colour, and so arranged as to form images of deities, of the scarabaeus, &c., with the winged globe. Around the small of the waist was a similar collar or belt.

Stripping off the papyrus, we found the flesh in excellent preservation, with no perceptible odour. The colour was reddish. The skin was hard, smooth, and glossy. The teeth and hair were in good condition. The eyes (it seemed) had been removed, and glass ones substituted, which were very beautiful, and wonderfully lifelike, with the exception of somewhat too determined a stare. The fingers and the nails were brilliantly gilded.

Mr Gliddon was of opinion, from the redness of the epidermis, that the embalmment had been effected altogether by asphaltum; but, on scraping the surface with a steel instrument, and throwing into the fire come of the powder thus obtained, the flavour of camphor and other sweet-scented gums became apparent.

We searched the corpse very carefully for the usual openings through which the entrails are extracted, but, to our surprise, we could discover none. No member of the party was at that period aware that entire or unopened mummies are not infrequently met. The brain it was customary to withdraw through the nose; the intestines through an incision in the side; the body was then shaved, washed, and salted; then laid aside for several weeks, when the operation of embalming, properly so called, began.

As no trace of an opening could be found, Dr Ponnonner was preparing his instruments for dissection, when I observed that it was then past two o'clock. Hereupon it was agreed to postpone the internal examination until the next evening; and we were about to separate for the present, when someone suggested an experiment or two with the Voltaic pile.

The application of electricity to a mummy three or four thousand years old at the least, was an idea, if not very sage, still sufficiently original, and we all caught it at once. About one-tenth in earnest and nine-tenths in jest, we arranged a battery in the doctor's study, and conveyed thither the Egyptian.

It was only after much trouble that we succeeded in laying bare some portions of the temporal muscle which appeared of less stony rigidity than other parts of the frame, but which, as we had anticipated, of course, gave no indication of galvanic susceptibility when brought in contact with the wire. This, the first trial, indeed, seemed decisive, and, with a hearty laugh at our own absurdity, we were bidding each other good-night, when my eyes, happening to fall upon those of the mummy, were there immediately riveted in amazement. My brief glance, in fact, had sufficed to assure me that the orbs which we had all supposed to be glass, and which were originally noticeable for a certain wild stare, were now so far covered by the lids, that only a small portion of the *tunica albuginea* remained visible.

With a shout I called attention to the fact, and it became immediately obvious to all.

I cannot say that I was *alarmed* at the phenomenon, because 'alarmed' is, in my case, not exactly the word. It is possible, however, that, but for the brown stout, I might have been a little nervous. As for the rest of the company, they really made no attempt at concealing the downright fright which possessed them. Dr Ponnonner was a man to be pitied. Mr Gliddon, by some peculiar process, rendered himself invisible. Mr Silk Buckingham, I fancy, will scarcely be so bold as to deny that he made his way, upon all fours, under the table.

After the first shock of astonishment, however, we resolved, as a matter of course, upon further experiment forthwith. Our operations were now directed against the great toe of the right foot. We made an incision over the outside of the exterior *os sesamoideum pollicis pedis*, and thus got at the root of the *abductor* muscle. Readjusting the battery, we now applied the fluid to the bisected nerves, when, with a movement of exceeding lifelikeness, the mummy first drew up its right knee so as to bring it nearly in contact with the abdomen, and then, straightening the limb with inconceivable force, bestowed a kick upon Dr Ponnonner, which had the effect of discharging that gentleman, like an arrow from a catapult, through a window into the street below.

We rushed out *en masse* to bring in the mangled remains of the victim, but had the happiness to meet him upon the staircase, coming up in an unaccountable hurry, brimful of the most ardent philosophy, and more than ever impressed with the necessity of prosecuting our experiments with vigour and with zeal.

It was by his advice, accordingly, that we made, upon the spot, a profound incision into the tip of the subject's nose, while the doctor himself, laying violent hands upon it, pulled it into vehement contact with the wire.

Morally and physically – figuratively and literally – was the effect electric. In the first place, the corpse opened its eyes, and winked very rapidly for several minutes, as does Mr Barnes in the pantomime; in the second place, it sneezed; in the third, it sat up on end; in the fourth, it shook its fist in Dr Ponnonner's face; in the fifth, turning to Messieurs Gliddon and Buckingham, it addressed them, in very capital Egyptian, thus –

'I must say, gentlemen, that I am as much surprised as I am mortified, at your behaviour. Of Dr Ponnonner nothing better was to be expected. He is a poor little fat fool who *knows* no better. I pity and forgive him. But you, Mr Gliddon – and you, Silk – who have travelled and resided in Egypt until one might imagine you to the manner born – you, I say, who have been so much among us that you speak Egyptian fully as well, I think, as you write your mother tongue – you, whom I have always been led to regard as the firm friend of the mummies – I really did anticipate more gentlemanly conduct from *you*. What am I to think of your standing quietly by and seeing me thus unhandsomely used? What am I to suppose by your permitting Tom, Dick, and Harry to strip me of my coffins, and my clothes, in this wretchedly cold climate? In what light (to come to the point) am I to regard your aiding and abetting that miserable little villain, Dr Ponnonner, in pulling me by the nose?'

It will be taken for granted, no doubt, that upon hearing this speech under the circumstances, we all either made for the door, or fell into violent hysterics, or went off in a general swoon. One of these three things, was, I say, to be expected. Indeed each and all of these lines of conduct might have been very plausibly pursued. And, upon my word, I am at a loss to know how or why it was that we pursued neither the one nor the other. But, perhaps, the true reason is to be sought in the spirit of the age, which proceeds by the rule of contraries altogether, and is now usually admitted as the solution of everything in the way of paradox and impossibility. Or perhaps, after all, it was only the mummy's exceedingly natural and matter-of-course air that divested his words of the terrible. However this may be, the facts are clear, and no member of our party betrayed any very particular trepidation, or seemed to consider that anything had gone very especially wrong.

For my part I was convinced it was all right, and merely stepped aside, out of the range of the Egyptian's fist. Dr

Ponnonner thrust his hands into his breeches pockets, looked hard at the mummy, and grew excessively red in the face. Mr Gliddon stroked his whiskers and drew up the collar of his shirt. Mr Buckingham hung down his head, and put his right thumb into the left corner of his mouth.

The Egyptian regarded him with a severe countenance for some minutes, and at length, with a sneer, said – 'Why don't you speak, Mr Buckingham? Did you hear what I asked you, or not? *Do* take your thumb out of your mouth!'

Mr Buckingham, hereupon, gave a slight start, took his right thumb out of the left corner of his mouth, and, by way of indemnification, inserted his left thumb in the right corner of the aperture above mentioned.

Not being able to get an answer from Mr B—, the figure turned peevishly to Mr Gliddon, and, in a peremptory tone, demanded in general terms what we all meant.

Mr Gliddon replied at great length, in phonetics; and but for the deficiency of American printing-offices in hieroglyphical type, it would afford me much pleasure to record here, in the original, the whole of his very excellent speech.

I may as well take this occasion to remark, that all the subsequent conversation in which the mummy took a part, was carried on in primitive Egyptian, through the medium (so far as concerned myself and other untravelled members of the company) – through the medium, I say, of Messieurs Gliddon and Buckingham, as interpreters. These gentlemen spoke the mother-tongue of the mummy with inimitable fluency and grace; but I could not help observing that (owing, no doubt, to the introduction of images entirely modern, and, of course, entirely novel to the stranger) the two travellers were reduced, occasionally, to the employment of sensible forms for the purpose of conveying a particular meaning. Mr Gliddon, at one period, for example, could not make the Egyptian comprehend the term 'politics', until he sketched upon the wall, with a bit of charcoal, a little carbuncle-nosed gentleman, out at elbows, standing upon a stump, with his left leg drawn back, his right arm thrown forward, with his fist shut, the eyes rolled up toward heaven, and the mouth open at an angle of ninety degrees. Just in the same way Mr Buckingham failed to convey the absolutely modern idea, 'Whig', until (at Dr Ponnonner's suggestion) he grew very pale in the face, and consented to take off his own.

It will be readily understood that Mr Gliddon's discourse turned chiefly upon the vast benefits accruing to science from the unrolling and disembowelling of mummies; apologising, upon this score, for any disturbance that might have been occasioned *him*, in particular, the individual mummy called Allamistakeo; and concluding with a mere hint (for it could scarcely be considered more) that, as these little matters were now explained, it might be as well to proceed with the investigation intended. Here Dr Ponnonner made ready his instruments.

In regard to the latter suggestions of the orator, it appears that Allamistakeo had certain scruples of conscience, the nature of which I did not distinctly learn; but he expressed himself satisfied with the apologies tendered, and, getting down from the table, shook hands with the company all round.

When this ceremony was at an end, we immediately busied ourselves in repairing the damages which our subject had sustained from the scalpel. We sewed up the wound in his temple, bandaged his foot, and applied a square inch of black plaster to the tip of his nose.

It was now observed that the count (this was the title, it seems, of Allamistakeo) had a slight fit of shivering – no doubt from the cold. The doctor immediately repaired to his wardrobe, and soon returned with a black dress coat, made in Jennings' best manner, a pair of sky-blue plaid pantaloons, with straps, a pink gingham *chemise*, a flapped vest of brocade, a white sack overcoat, a walking cane with a hook, a hat with no brim, patent-leather boots, straw-coloured kid gloves, an eye-glass, a pair of whiskers, and a waterfall cravat. Owing to the disparity of size between the count and the doctor (the proportion being as two to one), there was some little difficulty in adjusting these habiliments upon the person of the Egyptian; but when all was arranged, he might have been said to be dressed. Mr Gliddon, therefore, gave him his arm, and led him to a comfortable chair by the fire, while the doctor rang the bell upon the spot and ordered a supply of cigars and wine.

The conversation soon grew animated. Much curiosity was, of course, expressed in regard to the somewhat remarkable fact of Allamistakeo's still remaining alive.

'I should have thought,' observed Mr Buckingham, 'that it is high time you were dead.'

'Why,' replied the count, very much astonished, 'I am little more than seven hundred years old! My father lived a thousand, and was by no means in his dotage when he died.'

Here ensued a brisk series of questions and computations, by means of which it became evident that the antiquity of the mummy had been grossly misjudged. It had been five thousand and fifty years, and some months, since he had been consigned to the catacombs at Eleithias.

'But my remark,' resumed Mr Buckingham, 'had no reference to your age at the period of interment (I am willing to grant, in fact, that you are still a young man); and my allusion was to the immensity of time during which, by your own showing, you must have been done up in asphaltum.'

'In what?' said the count.

'In asphaltum,' persisted Mr B.

'Ah, yes; I have some faint notion of what you mean; it might be made to answer, no doubt – but in my time we employed scarcely anything else than the bichloride of mercury.'

'But what we are especially at a loss to understand,' said Dr Ponnonner, 'is, how it happens that, having been dead and buried in Egypt five thousand years ago, you are here today all alive, and looking so delightfully well.'

'Had I been, as you say, *dead*,' replied the count, 'it is more than probable that dead I should still be; for I perceive you are yet in the infancy of galvanism, and cannot accomplish with it what was a common thing among us in the old days. But the fact is, I fell into catalepsy, and it was considered by my best friends that I was either dead or should be; they accordingly embalmed me at once – I presume you are aware of the chief principle of the embalming process?'

'Why, not altogether.'

'Ah, I perceive – a deplorable condition of ignorance! Well, I cannot enter into details just now; but it is necessary to explain that to embalm (properly speaking) in Egypt, was to arrest indefinitely *all* the animal functions subjected to the process. I use the word "animal" in its widest sense, as including the physical not more than the moral and *vital* being. I repeat that the leading principle of embalmment consisted, with us, in the immediately arresting, and holding in perpetual abeyance, *all* the animal functions subjected to the process. To be brief, in whatever condition the individual was, at the period of embalmment, in that condition he remained. Now, as it is my good fortune to be of the blood of the Scarabaeus, I was embalmed *alive*, as you see me at present.'

'The blood of the Scarabaeus!' exclaimed Dr Ponnonner.

'Yes. The Scarabaeus was the *insignium*, or the "arms", of a very distinguished and very rare patrician family. To be "of the blood of the Scarabaeus", is merely to be one of that family of which the Scarabaeus is the *insignium*. I speak figuratively.'

'But what has this to do with your being alive?'

'Why, it is the general custom in Egypt, to deprive a corpse, before embalmment, of its bowels and brains; the race of the Scarabaeus alone did not coincide with the custom. Had I not been a Scarabaeus, therefore, I should have been without bowels and brains; and without either it is inconvenient to live.'

'I perceive that,' said Mr Buckingham; 'and I presume that all the *entire* mummies that come to hand are of the race of Scarabaei.'

'Beyond doubt.'

'I thought,' said Mr Gliddon, very meekly, 'that the Scarabaeus was one of the Egyptian gods.'

'One of the Egyptian *what?*' exclaimed the mummy, starting to its feet.

'Gods!' repeated the traveller.

'Mr Gliddon, I really am astonished to hear you talk in this style,' said the count, resuming his seat. 'No nation upon the face of the earth has ever acknowledged more than *one god*. The Scarabaeus, the Ibis, &c., were with us (as similar creatures have been with others) the symbols, or *media*, through which we offered worship to the Creator too august to be more directly approached.'

There was here a pause. At length the colloquy was renewed by Dr Ponnonner.

'It is not improbable, then, from what you have explained,' said he, 'that among the catacombs near the Nile, there may exist other mummies of the Scarabaeus tribe, in a condition of vitality.'

'There can be no question of it,' replied the count; 'all the Scarabaei embalmed accidentally while alive, are alive. Even some of those *purposely* so embalmed, may have been overlooked by their executors, and still remain in the tombs.'

'Will you be kind enough to explain,' I said, 'what you mean by "purposely so embalmed"?'

'With great pleasure,' answered the mummy, after surveying me leisurely through his eye-glass – for it was the first time I had ventured to address him a direct question.

'With great pleasure,' he said. 'The usual duration of man's life, in my time, was about eight hundred years. Few men died, unless by most extraordinary accident, before the age of six hundred; few lived longer than a decade of centuries; but eight were considered the natural term. After the discovery of the embalming principle, as I have already described it to you, it occurred to our philosophers that a laudable curiosity might be gratified, and, at the same time, the interests of science much advanced, by living this natural term in instalments. In the case of history, indeed, experience demonstrated that something of this kind was indispensable. An historian, for example, having attained the age of five hundred, would write a book with great labour and then get himself carefully embalmed; leaving instructions to his executors *pro tem.*, that they should cause him to be revivified after the lapse of a certain period – say five or six hundred years. Resuming existence at the expiration of this time, he would invariably find his great work converted into a species of haphazard note book – that is to say, into a kind of literary arena for the conflicting guesses, riddles, and personal squabbles of whole herds of exasperated commentators. These guesses, &c., which passed under the name of annotations, or emendations, were found so completely to have enveloped, distorted, and overwhelmed the text, that the author had to go about with a lantern to discover his own book. When discovered, it was never worth the trouble of the search. After rewriting it throughout, it was regarded as the bounden duty of the historian to set himself to work, immediately, in correcting, from his own private knowledge and experience, the traditions of the day concerning the epoch at which he had originally lived. Now this process of rescription and personal rectification, pursued by various individual sages, from time to time, had the effect of preventing our history from degenerating into absolute fable.'

'I beg your pardon,' said Dr Ponnonner at this point, laying his hand gently upon the arm of the Egyptian – 'I beg your pardon, sir, but may I presume to interrupt you for one moment?'

'By all means, *sir*,' replied the count, drawing up.

'I merely wished to ask you a question,' said the doctor. 'You mentioned the historian's personal correction of *traditions* respecting his own epoch. Pray, sir, upon an average, what proportion of these Kabbala were usually found to be right?'

'The Kabbala, as you properly term them, sir, were generally discovered to be precisely on a par with the facts recorded in the un-rewritten histories themselves; that is to say, not one individual iota of either was ever known, under any circumstances, to be not totally and radically wrong.'

'But since it is quite clear,' resumed the doctor, 'that at least five thousand years have elapsed since your entombment, I take it for granted that your histories at that period, if not your traditions, were sufficiently explicit on that one topic of universal interest, the Creation, which took place, as I presume you are aware, only about ten centuries before.'

'Sir!' said the Count Allamistakeo.

The doctor repeated his remarks, but it was only after much additional explanation that the foreigner could be made to comprehend them. The latter at length said, hesitatingly –

'The ideas you have suggested are to me, I confess, utterly novel. During my time I never knew anyone to entertain so singular a fancy as that the universe (or this world, if you will have it so) ever had a beginning at all. I remember once, and once only, hearing something remotely hinted by a man of many speculations concerning the origin *of the human race*; and by this individual the very word *Adam* (or Red Earth), which you make use of, was employed. He employed it, however, in a generical sense, with reference to the spontaneous germination from rank soil (just as a thousand of the lower *genera* of creatures are germinated) – the spontaneous germination, I say, of five vast hordes of men, simultaneously upspringing in five distinct and nearly equal divisions of the globe.'

Here, in general, the company shrugged their shoulders, and one or two of us touched our foreheads with a very significant air. Mr Silk Buckingham, first glancing slightly at the occiput and then at the siniciput of Allamistakeo, spoke as follows –

'The long duration of human life in your time, together with the occasional practice of passing it, as you have explained, in instalments, must have had, indeed, a strong tendency to the general development and conglomeration of knowledge. I presume, therefore, that we are to attribute the marked inferiority of the old Egyptians in all particulars of science, when compared with the moderns, and more especially with the Yankees, altogether to the superior solidity of the Egyptian skull.'

'I confess again,' replied the count, with much suavity, 'that I am somewhat at a loss to comprehend you; pray, to what particulars of science do you allude?'

Here our whole party, joining voices, detailed, at great length, the assumptions of phrenology and the marvels of animal magnetism.

Having heard us to an end, the count proceeded to relate a few anecdotes, which rendered it evident that prototypes of Gall and Spurzheim had flourished and faded in Egypt so long ago as to have been nearly forgotten, and that the manoeuvres of Mesmer were really very contemptible tricks when put in collation with the positive miracles of the Theban *savants*, who created lice, and a great many other similar things.

I here asked the count if his people were able to calculate eclipses. He smiled rather contemptuously, and said they were.

This put me a little out; but I began to make other enquiries in regard to his astronomical knowledge, when a member of the company, who had never as yet opened his mouth, whispered in my ear, that for information on this head I had better consult Ptolemy (whoever Ptolemy is), as well as one Plutarch *de facie lunae*.

I then questioned the mummy about burning-glasses and lenses, and, in general, about the manufacture of glass; but I had not made an end of my queries before the silent member again touched me quietly on the elbow, and begged me, for God's sake, to take a peep at Diodorus Siculus. As for the count, he merely asked me, in the way of reply, if we moderns possessed any such microscopes as would enable us to cut cameos in the style of the Egyptians. While I was thinking how I should answer this question, little Dr Ponnonner committed himself in a very extraordinary way.

'Look at our architecture!' he exclaimed, greatly to the indignation of both the travellers, who pinched him black and blue to no purpose.

'Look!' he cried, with enthusiasm, 'at the Bowling-Green Fountain in New York! or, if this be too vast a contemplation, regard for a moment the Capitol at Washington, DC!' – and the good little medical man went on to detail, very minutely, the proportions of the fabric to which he referred. He explained that the portico alone was adorned with no less than four and twenty columns, five feet in diameter, and ten feet apart.

The count said that he regretted not being able to remember, just at that moment, the precise dimensions of any one of the principal buildings of the City of Aznac, whose foundations were laid in the night of Time, but the ruins of which were still standing, at the epoch of his entombment, in a vast plain of sand to the westward of Thebes. He recollected, however (talking of porticoes), that one affixed to an inferior palace in a kind of suburb called Carnac, consisted of a hundred and forty-four columns, thirty-seven feet each in circumference, and twenty-five feet apart. The approach of this portico, from the Nile, was through an avenue two miles long, composed of sphinxes, statues, and obelisks, twenty, sixty, and a hundred feet in height. The palace itself (as well as he could remember) was, in one direction, two miles long, and might have been, altogether, about seven in circuit. Its walls were richly painted all over, within and without, with hieroglyphics. He would not pretend to *assert* that even fifty or sixty of the doctor's Capitols might have been built within these walls, but he was by no means sure that two or three hundred of them might not have been squeezed in with some trouble. That palace at Carnac was an insignificant little building after all. He (the count), however, could not conscientiously refuse to admit the ingenuity, magnificence, and superiority of the fountain at the Bowling-Green, as described by the doctor. Nothing like it, he was forced to allow, had ever been seen in Egypt or elsewhere.

I here asked the count what he had to say to our railroads.

'Nothing,' he replied, 'in particular.' They were rather slight, rather ill-conceived, and clumsily put together. They could not be compared, of course, with the vast, level, direct, iron-grooved causeways, upon which the Egyptians conveyed entire temples and solid obelisks of a hundred and fifty feet in altitude.

I spoke of our gigantic mechanical forces.

He agreed that we knew something in that way, but enquired how I should have gone to work in getting up the imposts on the lintels of even the little palace at Carnac.

This question I concluded not to hear, and demanded if he had any idea of Artesian wells; but he simply raised his eyebrows; while Mr Gliddon winked at me very hard and said, in a low tone, that one had been recently discovered by the engineers employed to bore for water in the Great Oasis.

I then mentioned our steel; but the foreigner elevated his nose, and asked me if our steel could have executed the sharp carved work seen on the obelisks, and which was wrought altogether by edge-tools of copper.

This disconcerted us so greatly that we thought it advisable to vary the attack to Metaphysics. We sent for a copy of a book called the 'Dial', and read out of it a chapter or two about something which is not very clear, but which the Bostonians call the great movement or progress.

The count merely said that great movements were awfully common things in his day, and as for progress, it was at one time quite a nuisance, but it never progressed.

We then spoke of the great beauty and importance of Democracy, and were at much trouble in impressing the count with a due sense of the advantages we enjoyed in living where there was suffrage *ad libitum* and no king.

He listened with marked interest, and in fact seemed not a little amused. When we had done he said that, a great while ago, there had occurred something of a very similar sort. Thirteen Egyptian provinces determined all at once to be free, and so set a magnificent example to the rest of mankind. They assembled their wise men, and concocted the most ingenious constitution it is possible to conceive. For a while they managed remarkably well; only their habit of bragging was prodigious. The thing ended, however, in the consolidation of the thirteen states, with some fifteen or twenty others, in the most odious and insupportable despotism that ever was heard of upon the face of the Earth.

I asked what was the name of the usurping tyrant.

As well as the count could recollect, it was *Mob*.

Not knowing what to say to this, I raised my voice, and deplored the Egyptian ignorance of steam.

The count looked at me with much astonishment, but made no answer. The silent gentleman, however, gave me a violent nudge in the ribs with his elbows – told me I had sufficiently exposed myself for once – and demanded if I was really such a fool as not to know that the modern steam-engine is derived from the invention of Hero, through Solomon de Caus.

We were now in imminent danger of being discomfited; but, as good luck would have it, Dr Ponnonner, having rallied, returned to our rescue, and enquired if the people of Egypt would seriously pretend to rival the moderns in the all-important particular of dress.

The count, at this, glanced downwards to the straps of his pantaloons, and then taking hold of the end of one of his coat-tails, held it up close to his eyes for some minutes. Letting it fall, at last, his mouth extended itself very gradually from ear to ear; but I do not remember that he said anything in the way of reply.

Hereupon we recovered our spirits, and the doctor, approaching the mummy with great dignity, desired it to say candidly, upon its honour as a gentleman, if the Egyptians had comprehended at *any* period the manufacture of either Ponnonner's lozenges, of Brandreth's pills.

We looked, with profound anxiety, for an answer – but in vain. It was not forthcoming. The Egyptian blushed and hung down his head. Never was triumph more consummate; never was defeat borne with so ill a grace. Indeed, I could not endure the spectacle of the poor mummy's mortification. I reached my hat, bowed to him stiffly, and took leave.

Upon getting home I found it past four o'clock, and went immediately to bed. It is now ten o'clock I have been up since seven, penning these memoranda for the benefit of my family and of mankind. The former I shall behold no more. My wife is a shrew. The truth is, I am heartily sick of this life, and of the nineteenth century in general. I am convinced that everything is going wrong. Besides, I am anxious to know who will be president in 2045. As soon, therefore, as I shave and swallow a cup of coffee, I shall just step over to Ponnonner's and get embalmed for a couple of hundred years.

Tales of the Grotesque and Arabesque

Metzengerstein

Pestis eram vivus – moriens tua mors ero.
MARTIN LUTHER

Horror and fatality have been stalking abroad in all ages. Why then give a date to this story I have to tell? Let it suffice to say, that at the period of which I speak, there existed, in the interior of Hungary, a settled although hidden belief in the doctrines of the Metempsychosis. Of the doctrines themselves – that is, of their falsity, or of their probability – I say nothing. I assert, however, that much of our incredulity – as La Bruyère says of all our unhappiness – *'vient de ne pouvoir être seuls'*.

But there are some points in the Hungarian superstition which were fast verging to absurdity. They – the Hungarians – differed very essentially from their Eastern authorities. For example, 'The soul,' said the former – I give the words of an acute and intelligent Parisian – *'ne demeure qu'une seule fois dans un corps sensible: au reste – un cheval, un chien, un homme même, n'est que la ressemblance peu tangible de ces animaux.'*

The families of Berlifitzing and Metzengerstein had been at variance for centuries. Never before were two houses so illustrious, mutually embittered by hostility so deadly. The origin of this enmity seems to be found in the words of an ancient prophecy – 'A lofty name shall have a fearful fall when, as the rider over his horse, the mortality of Metzengerstein shall triumph over the immortality of Berlifitzing.'

To be sure the words themselves had little or no meaning. But more trivial causes have given rise – and that no long while ago – to consequences equally eventful. Besides, the estates, which were contiguous, had long exercised a rival influence in the affairs of a busy government. Moreover, near neighbours are seldom friends; and the inhabitants of the Castle Berlifitzing might look, from their lofty buttresses, into the very windows of the palace Metzengerstein. Least of all had the more than feudal magnificence, thus discovered, a tendency to allay the irritable feelings of the less ancient and less wealthy Berlifitzings. What wonder then, that the words, however silly, of that prediction, should have succeeded in setting and keeping at variance two families already predisposed to quarrel by every instigation of hereditary jealousy? The prophecy seemed to imply – if it implied anything – a final triumph on the part of the already more powerful house; and was of course remembered with the more bitter animosity by the weaker and less influential.

Wilhelm, Count Berlifitzing, although loftily descended, was, at the epoch of this narrative, an infirm and doting old man, remarkable for nothing but an inordinate and inveterate personal antipathy to the family of his rival, and so passionate a love of horses, and of hunting, that neither bodily infirmity, great age, nor mental incapacity, prevented his daily participation in the dangers of the chase.

Frederick, Baron Metzengerstein, was, on the other hand, not yet of age. His father, the Minister G—, died young. His mother, the Lady Mary, followed him quickly after. Frederick was, at that time, in his fifteenth year. In a city, fifteen years are no long period – a child may be still a child in his third lustrum: but in a wilderness – in so magnificent a wilderness as that old principality, fifteen years have a far deeper meaning.

From some peculiar circumstances attending the administration of his father, the young Baron, at the decease of the former, entered immediately upon his vast possessions. Such estates were seldom held before by a nobleman of Hungary. His castles were without number. The chief in point of splendour and extent was the 'Chateau Metzengerstein'. The boundary line of his dominions was never clearly defined; but his principal park embraced a circuit of fifty miles.

Upon the succession of a proprietor so young, with a character so well known, to a fortune so unparalleled, little speculation was afloat in regard to his probable course of conduct. And, indeed, for the space of three days, the behaviour of the heir out-heroded Herod, and fairly surpassed the expectations of his most enthusiastic admirers. Shameful debaucheries – flagrant treacheries – unheard-of atrocities – gave his trembling vassals quickly to understand that no servile submission on their part – no punctilios of conscience on his own – were thenceforward to prove any security against the remorseless fangs of a petty Caligula. On the night of the fourth day, the stables of the castle Berlifitzing were discovered to be on fire; and the unanimous opinion of the neighbourhood added the crime of the incendiary to the already hideous list of the Baron's misdemeanours and enormities.

But during the tumult occasioned by this occurrence, the young nobleman himself sat apparently buried in meditation, in a vast and desolate upper apartment of the family palace of Metzengerstein. The rich although faded tapestry hangings which swung gloomily upon the walls, represented the shadowy and majestic forms of a thousand illustrious ancestors. *Here*, rich-ermined priests, and pontifical dignitaries, familiarly seated with the autocrat and the sovereign, put a veto on the wishes of a temporal king, or restrained with the fiat of papal supremacy the rebellious sceptre of the Arch-enemy. *There*, the dark, tall statures of the Princes Metzengerstein – their muscular war-coursers plunging over the carcasses of fallen foes – startled the steadiest nerves with their vigorous expression; and *here*, again, the voluptuous and swan-like figures of the dames of days gone by, floated away in the mazes of an unreal dance to the strains of imaginary melody.

But as the Baron listened, or affected to listen, to the gradually increasing uproar in the stables of Berlifitzing – or perhaps pondered upon some more novel, some more decided act of audacity – his eyes became unwittingly riveted to the figure of an enormous, and unnaturally coloured horse, represented in the tapestry as belonging to a Saracen ancestor of the family of his rival. The horse itself, in the foreground of the design, stood motionless and statue-like – while farther back, its discomfited rider perished by the dagger of a Metzengerstein.

On Frederick's lip arose a fiendish expression, as he became aware of the direction which his glance had, without his consciousness, assumed. Yet he did not remove it. On the contrary, he could by no means account for the overwhelming anxiety which appeared falling like a pall upon his senses. It was with difficulty that he reconciled his dreamy and incoherent feelings with the certainty of being awake. The longer he gazed the more absorbing became the spell – the more impossible did it appear that he could ever withdraw his glance from the fascination of that tapestry. But the tumult without becoming suddenly more violent, with a compulsory exertion he diverted his attention to the glare of ruddy light thrown full by the flaming stables upon the windows of the apartment.

The action, however, was but momentary; his gaze returned mechanically to the wall. To his extreme horror and astonishment, the head of the gigantic steed had, in the meantime, altered its position. The neck of the animal, before arched, as if in compassion, over the prostrate body of its lord, was now extended, at full length, in the direction of the Baron. The eyes, before invisible, now wore an energetic and human expression, while they gleamed with a fiery and unusual red; and the distended lips of the apparently enraged horse left in full view his gigantic and disgusting teeth.

Stupefied with terror, the young nobleman tottered to the door. As he threw it open, a flash of red light, streaming far into the chamber, flung his shadow with a clear outline against the quivering tapestry, and he shuddered to perceive that shadow – as he staggered awhile upon the threshold – assuming the exact position, and precisely filling up the contour, of the relentless and triumphant murderer of the Saracen Berlifitzing.

To lighten the depression of his spirits, the Baron hurried into the open air. At the principal gate of the palace he encountered three equerries. With much difficulty, and at the imminent peril of their lives, they were restraining the convulsive plunges of a gigantic and fiery-coloured horse.

'Whose horse? Where did you get him?' demanded the youth, in a querulous and husky tone of voice, as he became instantly aware that the mysterious steed in the tapestried chamber was the very counterpart of the furious animal before his eyes.

'He is your own property, sire,' replied one of the equerries, 'at least he is claimed by no other owner. We caught him flying, all smoking and foaming with rage, from the burning stables of the Castle Berlifitzing. Supposing him to have belonged to the old Count's stud of foreign horses, we led him back as an estray. But the grooms there disclaim any title to the creature; which is strange, since he bears evident marks of having made a narrow escape from the flames.

'The letters WVB are also branded very distinctly on his forehead,' interrupted a second equerry. 'I supposed them, of course, to be the initials of Wilhelm von Berlifitzing – but all at the castle are positive in denying any knowledge of the horse.'

'Extremely singular!' said the young Baron, with a musing air, and apparently unconscious of the meaning of his words. 'He is, as you say, a remarkable horse – a prodigious horse! although, as you very justly observe, of a suspicious and untractable character; let him be mine, however,' he added, after a pause, 'perhaps a rider like Frederick of Metzengerstein may tame even the devil from the stables of Berlifitzing.'

'You are mistaken, my lord; the horse, as I think we mentioned, is *not* from the stables of the Count. If such had been the case, we know our duty better than to bring him into the presence of a noble of your family.'

'True!' observed the Baron, dryly; and at that instant a page of the bedchamber came from the palace with a heightened colour, and a precipitate step. He whispered into his master's ear an account of the sudden disappearance of a small portion of the tapestry, in an apartment which he designated; entering, at the same time, into particulars of a minute and circumstantial character; but from the low tone of voice in which these latter were communicated, nothing escaped to gratify the excited curiosity of the equerries.

The young Frederick, during the conference, seemed agitated by a variety of emotions. He soon, however, recovered his composure, and an expression of determined malignancy settled upon his countenance, as he gave peremptory orders that a certain chamber should be immediately locked up, and the key placed in his own possession.

'Have you heard of the unhappy death of the old hunter Berlifitzing?' said one of his vassals to the Baron, as, after the departure of the page, the huge steed which that nobleman had adopted as his own, plunged and curvetted, with redoubled fury, down the long avenue which extended from the chateau to the stables of Metzengerstein.

'No!' said the Baron, turning abruptly towards the speaker, 'dead! say you?'

'It is indeed true, my lord; and, to a noble of your name, will be, I imagine, no unwelcome intelligence.'

A rapid smile shot over the countenance of the listener. 'How died he?'

'In his rash exertions to rescue a favourite portion of his hunting stud, he has himself perished miserably in the flames.'

'I-n-d-e-e-d!' ejaculated the Baron, as if slowly and deliberately impressed with the truth of some exciting idea.

'Indeed,' repeated the vassal.

'Shocking!' said the youth, calmly, and turned quietly into the chateau.

From this date a marked alteration took place in the outward demeanour of the dissolute young Baron Frederick Von Metzengerstein. Indeed, his behaviour disappointed every expectation, and proved little in accordance with the views of many a manoeuvring mama; while his habits and manner, still less than formerly, offered anything congenial with those of the neighbouring aristocracy. He was never to be seen beyond the limits of his own domain, and, in this wide and social world, was utterly companionless – unless, indeed, that unnatural, impetuous, and fiery-coloured horse, which he henceforward continually bestrode, had any mysterious right to the title of his friend.

Numerous invitations on the part of the neighbourhood for a long time, however, periodically came in. 'Will the Baron honour our festivals with his presence?' 'Will the Baron join us in a hunting of the boar?' – 'Metzengerstein does not hunt,' 'Metzengerstein will not attend,' were the haughty and laconic answers.

These repeated insults were not to be endured by an imperious nobility. Such invitations became less cordial – less frequent – in time they ceased altogether. The widow of the unfortunate Count Berlifitzing was even heard to express a hope 'that the Baron might be at home when he did not wish to be at home, since he disdained the company of his equals; and ride when he did not wish to ride, since he preferred the society of a horse'. This to be sure was a very silly explosion of hereditary pique; and merely proved how singularly unmeaning our sayings are apt to become, when we desire to be unusually energetic.

The charitable, nevertheless, attributed the alteration in the conduct of the young nobleman to the natural sorrow of a son for the untimely loss of his parents – forgetting, however, his atrocious and reckless behaviour during the short period immediately succeeding that bereavement. Some there were, indeed, who suggested a too haughty idea of self-consequence and dignity. Others again (among them may be mentioned the family physician) did not hesitate in speaking of morbid melancholy, and hereditary ill-health; while dark hints, of a more equivocal nature, were current among the multitude.

Indeed, the Baron's perverse attachment to his lately-acquired charger – an attachment which seemed to attain new strength from every fresh example of the animal's ferocious and demon-like propensities – at length became, in the eyes of all reasonable men, a hideous and unnatural fervour. In the glare of noon – at the dead hour of night – in sickness or in health – in calm or in tempest – the young Metzengerstein seemed riveted to the saddle of that colossal horse, whose intractable audacities so well accorded with his own spirit.

There were circumstances, moreover, which, coupled with late events, gave an unearthly and portentous character to the mania of the rider, and to the capabilities of the steed. The space passed over in a single leap had been accurately measured, and was found to exceed, by an astounding difference, the wildest expectations of the most imaginative. The Baron, besides, had no particular *name* for the animal, although all the rest in his collection were distinguished by characteristic appellations. His stable, too, was appointed at a distance from the rest; and with regard to grooming and other necessary offices, none but the owner in person had ventured to officiate, or even to enter the enclosure of that particular stall. It was also to be observed, that although the three grooms, who had caught the steed as he fled from the conflagration at Berlifitzing, had succeeded in arresting his course, by means of a chain-bridle and noose – yet no one of the three could with any certainty affirm that he had, during that dangerous struggle, or at any period thereafter, actually placed his hand upon the body of the beast. Instances of peculiar intelligence in the demeanour of a noble and high-spirited horse are not to be supposed capable of exciting unreasonable attention – especially among men who, daily trained to the labours of the chase, might appear well acquainted with the sagacity of a horse – but there were certain circumstances which intruded themselves perforce upon the most sceptical and phlegmatic; and it is said there were times when the animal caused the gaping crowd who stood around to recoil in horror from the deep and impressive meaning of his terrible stamp – times when the young Metzengerstein turned pale and shrunk away from the rapid and searching expression of his earnest and human-looking eye.

Among all the retinue of the Baron, however, none were found to doubt the ardour of that extraordinary affection which existed on the part of the young nobleman for the fiery qualities of his horse; at least, none but an insignificant and misshapen little page, whose deformities were in everybody's way, and whose opinions were of the least possible importance. He – if his ideas are worth mentioning at all – had the effrontery to assert that his master never vaulted into the saddle without an unaccountable and almost imperceptible shudder, and that, upon his return from every long-continued and habitual ride, an expression of triumphant malignity distorted every muscle in his countenance.

One tempestuous night, Metzengerstein, awaking from a heavy slumber, descended like a maniac from his chamber, and, mounting in hot haste, bounded away into the mazes of the forest. An occurrence so common attracted no particular attention, but his return was looked for with intense anxiety on the part of his domestics, when, after some hours' absence, the stupendous and magnificent battlements of the Chateau Metzengerstein were discovered crackling and rocking to their very foundation, under the influence of a dense and livid mass of ungovernable fire.

As the flames, when first seen, had already made so terrible a progress that all efforts to save any portion of the building were evidently futile, the astonished neighbourhood stood idly around in silent and pathetic wonder. But a new and fearful object soon riveted the attention of the multitude, and proved how much more intense is the excitement wrought in the feelings of a crowd by the contemplation of human agony, than that brought about by the most appalling spectacles of inanimate matter.

Up the long avenue of aged oaks which led from the forest to the main entrance of the Chateau Metzengerstein, a steed, bearing an unbonneted and disordered rider, was seen leaping with an impetuosity which outstripped the very Demon of the Tempest.

The career of the horseman was indisputably, on his own part, uncontrollable. The agony of his countenance, the convulsive struggle of his frame, gave evidence of superhuman exertion: but no sound, save a solitary shriek, escaped from his lacerated lips, which were bitten through and through in the intensity of terror. One instant, and the clattering of hoofs resounded sharply and shrilly above the roaring of the flames and the shrieking of the winds – another, and, clearing at a single plunge the gateway and the moat, the steed bounded far up the tottering staircases of the palace, and, with its rider, disappeared amid the whirlwind of chaotic fire.

The fury of the tempest immediately died away, and a dead calm sullenly succeeded. A white flame still enveloped the building like a shroud, and, streaming far away into the quiet atmosphere, shot forth a glare of preternatural light; while a cloud of smoke settled heavily over the battlements in the distinct colossal figure of – a *horse*.

The Visionary (The Assignation)

Stay for me there! I will not fail
To meet thee in that hollow vale.

Exequy on the death of his wife
by Henry King, Bishop of Chichester

Ill-fated and mysterious man! – bewildered in the brilliancy of thine own imagination, and fallen in the flames of thine own youth! Again in fancy I behold thee! Once more thy form hath risen before me! – not – oh not as thou art – in the cold valley and shadow – but as thou *shouldst be* – squandering away a life of magnificent meditation in that city of dim visions, thine own Venice – which is a star-beloved Elysium of the sea, and the wide windows of whose Palladian palaces look down with a deep and bitter meaning upon the secrets of her silent waters. Yes! I repeat it – as thou *shouldst be*. There are surely other worlds than this – other thoughts than the thoughts of the multitude – other speculations than the speculations of the sophist. Who then shall call thy conduct into question? who blame thee for thy visionary hours, or denounce those occupations as a wasting away of life, which were but the overflowings of thine everlasting energies?

It was at Venice, beneath the covered archway there called the Ponte di Sospiri, that I met for the third or fourth time the person of whom I speak. It is with a confused recollection that I bring to mind the circumstances of that meeting. Yet I remember – ah! how should I forget? – the deep midnight, the Bridge of Sighs, the beauty of woman, and the Genius of Romance that stalked up and down the narrow canal.

It was a night of unusual gloom. The great clock of the Piazza had sounded the fifth hour of the Italian evening. The square of the Campanile lay silent and deserted, and the lights in the old Ducal Palace were dying fast away. I was returning home from the Piazetta, by way of the Grand Canal. But as my gondola arrived opposite the mouth of the canal San Marco, a female voice from its recesses broke suddenly upon the night, in one wild, hysterical, and long-continued shriek. Startled at the sound, I sprang upon my feet; while the gondolier, letting slip his single oar, lost it in the pitchy darkness beyond a chance of recovery, and we were consequently left to the guidance of the current which here sets from the greater into the smaller channel. Like some huge and sable-feathered condor, we were slowly drifting down towards the Bridge of Sighs, when a thousand flambeaus flashing from the windows, and down the staircases of the Ducal Palace, turned all at once that deep gloom into a livid and preternatural day.

A child, slipping from the arms of its own mother, had fallen from an upper window of the lofty structure into the deep and dim canal. The quiet waters had closed placidly over their victim; and, although my own gondola was the only one in sight, many a stout swimmer, already in the stream, was seeking in vain upon the surface, the treasure which was to be found, alas! only within the abyss. Upon the broad black marble flagstones at the entrance of the palace, and a few steps above the water, stood a figure which none who then saw can have ever since forgotten. It was the Marchesa Aphrodite – the adoration of all Venice – the gayest of the gay – the most lovely where all were beautiful – but still the young wife of the old and intriguing Mentoni, and the mother of that fair child, her first and only one, who now, deep beneath the murky water, was thinking in bitterness of heart upon her sweet caresses, and exhausting its little life in struggles to call upon her name.

She stood alone. Her small, bare, and silvery feet gleamed in the black mirror of marble beneath her. Her hair, not as yet more than half loosened for the night from its ballroom array, clustered, amid a shower of diamonds, round and round her classical head, in curls like those of the young hyacinth. A snowy-white and gauze-like drapery seemed to be nearly the sole covering to her delicate form; but the midsummer and midnight air was hot, sullen, and still, and no motion in the statue-like form itself, stirred even the folds of that raiment of very vapour which hung around it as the heavy marble hangs around the Niobe. Yet – strange to say! – her large lustrous eyes were not turned downwards upon that grave wherein her brightest hope lay buried – but riveted in a widely different direction! The prison of the Old

IT WAS THE MARCHESA APHRODITE – THE ADORATION OF ALL VENICE

Republic is, I think, the stateliest building in all Venice – but how could that lady gaze so fixedly upon it, when beneath her lay stifling her only child? Yon dark, gloomy niche, too, yawns right opposite her chamber window – what, then, could there be in its shadows – in its architecture – in its ivy-wreathed and solemn cornices – that the Marchesa di Mentoni had not wondered at a thousand times before? Nonsense! – Who does not remember that, at such a time as this, the eye, like a shattered mirror, multiplies the images of its sorrow, and sees in innumerable far-off places, the woe which is close at hand?

Many steps above the Marchesa, and within the arch of the water-gate, stood, in full dress, the Satyr-like figure of Mentoni himself. He was occasionally occupied in thrumming a guitar, and seemed *ennuyé* to the very death, as at intervals he gave directions for the recovery of his child. Stupefied and aghast, I had myself no power to move from the upright position I had assumed upon first hearing the shriek, and must have presented to the eyes of the agitated group a spectral and ominous appearance, as with pale countenance and rigid limbs, I floated down among them in that funereal gondola.

All efforts proved in vain. Many of the most energetic in the search were relaxing their exertions, and yielding to a gloomy sorrow. There seemed but little hope for the child; (how much less than for the mother!) but now, from the interior of that dark niche which has been already mentioned as forming a part of the Old Republican prison, and as fronting the lattice of the Marchesa, a figure muffled in a cloak, stepped out within reach of the light, and, pausing a moment upon the verge of the giddy descent, plunged headlong into the canal. As, in an instant afterwards, he stood with the still living and breathing child within his grasp, upon the marble flagstones by the side of the Marchesa, his cloak, heavy with the drenching water, became unfastened, and, falling in folds about his feet, discovered to the wonder-stricken spectators the graceful person of a very young man, with the sound of whose name the greater part of Europe was then ringing.

No word spoke the deliverer. But the Marchesa! She will now receive her child – she will press it to her heart – she will cling to its little form, and smother it with her caresses. Alas! *another's* arms have taken it from the stranger – *another's* arms have taken it away, and borne it afar off, unnoticed, into the palace! And the Marchesa! Her lip – her beautiful lip trembles; tears are gathering in her eyes – those eyes which, like Pliny's acanthus, are 'soft and almost liquid'. Yes! tears are gathering in those eyes – and see! the entire woman thrills throughout the soul, and the statue has started into life! The pallor of the marble countenance, the swelling of the marble bosom, the very purity of the marble feet, we behold suddenly flushed over with a tide of ungovernable crimson; and a slight shudder quivers about her delicate frame, as a gentle air at Napoli about the rich silver lilies in the grass.

Why *should* that lady blush! To this demand there is no answer – except that, having left, in the eager haste and terror of a mother's heart, the privacy of her own boudoir, she has neglected to enthral her tiny feet in their slippers, and utterly forgotten to throw over her Venetian shoulders that drapery which is their due. What other possible reason could there have been for her so blushing? – for the glance of those wild appealing eyes? for the unusual tumult of that throbbing bosom? – for the convulsive pressure of that trembling hand? – that hand which fell, as Mentoni turned into the palace, accidentally, upon the hand of the stranger. What reason could there have been for the low – the singularly low tone of those unmeaning words which the lady uttered hurriedly in bidding him adieu? 'Thou hast conquered,' she said, or the murmurs of the water deceived me; 'thou hast conquered – one hour after sunrise – we shall meet – so let it be!'

* * *

The tumult had subsided, the lights had died away within the palace, and the stranger, whom I now recognised, stood alone upon the flags. He shook with inconceivable agitation, and his eye glanced around in search of a gondola. I could not do less than offer him the service of my own; and he accepted the civility. Having obtained an oar at the water-gate, we proceeded together to his residence, while he rapidly recovered his self-possession, and spoke of our former slight acquaintance in terms of great apparent cordiality.

There are some subjects upon which I take pleasure in being minute. The person of the stranger – let me call him by this title, who to all the world was still a stranger – the person of the stranger is one of these subjects. In height he might have been below rather than above the medium size: although there were moments of intense passion when his frame actually *expanded* and belied the assertion. The light, almost slender symmetry of his figure promised more of that ready activity which he evinced at the Bridge of Sighs, than of that Herculean strength which he has been known to wield without an effort, upon occasions of more dangerous emergency. With the mouth and chin of a deity – singular, wild, full, liquid eyes, whose shadows varied from pure hazel to intense and brilliant jet – and a profusion of curling, black hair, from which a forehead of unusual breadth gleamed forth at intervals all light and ivory – his were features than

"I HAD MYSELF NO POWER TO MOVE FROM THE UPRIGHT POSITION I HAD ASSUMED"

which I have seen none more classically regular, except, perhaps, the marble ones of the Emperor Commodus. Yet his countenance was, nevertheless, one of those which all men have seen at some period of their lives, and have never afterwards seen again. It had no peculiar – it had no settled predominant expression to be fastened upon the memory; a countenance seen and instantly forgotten – but forgotten with a vague and never-ceasing desire of recalling it to mind. Not that the spirit of each rapid passion failed, at any time, to throw its own distinct image upon the mirror of that face – but that the mirror, mirror-like, retained no vestige of the passion, when the passion had departed.

Upon leaving him on the night of our adventure, he solicited me, in what I thought an urgent manner, to call upon him very early the next morning. Shortly after sunrise, I found myself accordingly at his Palazzo, one of those huge structures of gloomy, yet fantastic pomp, which tower above the waters of the Grand Canal in the vicinity of the Rialto. I was shown up a broad winding staircase of mosaics, into an apartment whose unparalleled splendour burst through the opening door with an actual glare, making me blind and dizzy with luxuriousness.

I knew my acquaintance to be wealthy. Report had spoken of his possessions in terms which I had even ventured to call terms of ridiculous exaggeration. But as I gazed about me, I could not bring myself to believe that the wealth of any subject in Europe could have supplied the princely magnificence which burned and blazed around.

Although, as I say, the sun had arisen, yet the room was still brilliantly lighted up. I judge from this circumstance, as well as from an air of exhaustion in the countenance of my friend, that he had not retired to bed during the whole of the preceding night. In the architecture and embellishments of the chamber, the evident design had been to dazzle and astound. Little attention had been paid to the *decora* of what is technically called *keeping*, or to the proprieties of nationality. The eye wandered from object to object, and rested upon none – neither the *grotesques* of the Greek painters, nor the sculptures of the best Italian days, nor the huge carvings of untutored Egypt. Rich draperies in every part of the room trembled to the vibration of low, melancholy music, whose origin was not to be discovered. The senses were oppressed by mingled and conflicting perfumes, reeking up from strange convolute censers, together with multitudinous flaring and flickering tongues of emerald and violet fire. The rays of the newly risen sun poured in upon the whole, through windows, formed each of a single pane of crimson-tinted glass. Glancing to and fro, in a thousand reflections, from curtains which rolled from their cornices like cataracts of molten silver, the beams of natural glory mingled at length fitfully with the artificial light, and lay weltering in subdued masses upon a carpet of rich, liquid-looking cloth of Chili gold.

'Ha! ha! ha! – ha! ha! ha!' – laughed the proprietor, motioning me to a seat as I entered the room, and throwing himself back at full-length upon an ottoman. 'I see,' said he, perceiving that I could not immediately reconcile myself to the *bienséance* of so singular a welcome – 'I see you are astonished at my apartment – at my statues – my pictures – my originality of conception in architecture and upholstery! absolutely drunk, eh, with my magnificence? But pardon me, my dear sir (here his tone of voice dropped to the very spirit of cordiality); pardon me for my uncharitable laughter. You appeared so *utterly* astonished. Besides, some things are so completely ludicrous, that a *man* must laugh or die. To die laughing must be the most glorious of all glorious deaths! Sir Thomas More – a very fine man was Sir Thomas More – Sir Thomas More died laughing, you remember. Also in the *Absurdities* of Ravisius Textor, there is a long list of characters who came to the same magnificent end. Do you know, however,' continued he musingly, 'that at Sparta (which is now Palaeochori), at Sparta, I say, to the west of the citadel, among a chaos of scarcely visible ruins, is a kind of *socle*, upon which are still legible the letters ΔΑΞΜ. They are undoubtedly part of ΓΕΔΑΞΜΑ. Now, at Sparta were a thousand temples and shrines to a thousand different divinities. How exceedingly strange that the altar of Laughter should have survived all the others! But in the present instance,' he resumed, with a singular alteration of voice and manner, 'I have no right to be merry at your expense. You might well have been amazed. Europe cannot produce anything so fine as this, my little regal cabinet. My other apartments are by no means of the same order – mere *ultras* of fashionable insipidity. This is better than fashion – is it not? Yet this has but to be seen to become the rage – that is, with those who could afford it at the cost of their entire patrimony. I have guarded, however, against any such profanation. With one exception, you are the only human being besides myself and my *valet*, who has been admitted within the mysteries of these imperial precincts, since they have been bedizened as you see!'

I bowed in acknowledgement – for the overpowering sense of splendour and perfume, and music, together with the unexpected eccentricity of his address and manner, prevented me from expressing, in words, my appreciation of what I might have construed into a compliment.

'Here,' he resumed, arising and leaning on my arm as he sauntered around the apartment, 'here are paintings from the Greeks to Cimabue, and from Cimabue to the present hour. Many are chosen, as you see, with little deference to the opinions of Virtu. They are all, however, fitting tapestry for a chamber such as this. Here, too, are some *chefs d'oeuvre* of the unknown great; and here, unfinished designs by men, celebrated in their day, whose very names the perspicacity of the academies has left to silence and to me. What think you,' said he, turning abruptly as he spoke – 'what think you of this Madonna della Pietà?'

'It is Guido's own!' I said, with all the enthusiasm of my nature, for I had been poring intently over its surpassing loveliness. 'It is Guido's own! – how *could* you have obtained it? – she is undoubtedly in painting what the Venus is in sculpture.'

'Ha!' said he thoughtfully, 'the Venus – the beautiful Venus? – the Venus of the Medici? – she of the diminutive head and the gilded hair? Part of the left arm' (here his voice dropped so as to be heard with difficulty) 'and all the right are restorations; and in the coquetry of that right arm lies, I think, the quintessence of all affectation. Give *me* the Canova! The Apollo, too, is a copy – there can be no doubt of it – blind fool that I am, who cannot behold the boasted inspiration of the Apollo! I cannot help – pity me! – I cannot help preferring the Antinous. Was it not Socrates who said that the statuary found his statue in the block of marble? Then Michael Angelo was by no means original in his couplet:

> Non ha l'ottimo artista alcun concetto
> Che un marmo solo in se non circunscriva.'

It has been, or should be remarked, that, in the manner of the true gentleman, we are always aware of a difference from the bearing of the vulgar, without being at once precisely able to determine in what such difference consists. Allowing the remark to have applied in its full force to the outward demeanour of my acquaintance, I felt it, on that eventful morning, still more fully applicable to his moral temperament and character. Nor can I better define that peculiarity of spirit which seemed to place him so essentially apart from all other human beings, than by calling it a *habit* of intense and continual thought, pervading even his most trivial actions – intruding upon his moments of dalliance – and interweaving itself with his very flashes of merriment – like adders which writhe from out the eyes of the grinning masks in the cornices around the temples of Persepolis.

I could not help, however, repeatedly observing, through the mingled tone of levity and solemnity with which he rapidly descanted upon matters of little importance, a certain air of trepidation – a degree of nervous *unction* in action and in speech – an unquiet excitability of manner which appeared to me at all times unaccountable, and upon some occasions even filled me with alarm. Frequently, too, pausing in the middle of a sentence whose commencement he had apparently forgotten, he seemed to be listening in the deepest attention, as if either in momentary expectation of a visitor, or to sounds which must have had existence in his imagination alone.

It was during one of these reveries or pauses of apparent abstraction, that, in turning over a page of the poet and scholar Politian's beautiful tragedy *The Orfeo* (the first native Italian tragedy), which lay near me upon an ottoman, I discovered a passage underlined in pencil. It was a passage towards the end of the third act – a passage of the most heart-stirring excitement – a passage which, although tainted with impurity, no man shall read without a thrill of novel emotion – no woman without a sigh. The whole page was blotted with fresh tears; and, upon the opposite interleaf, were the following English lines, written in a hand so very different from the peculiar characters of my acquaintance, that I had some difficulty in recognising it as his own:

> Thou wast that all to me, love,
> For which my soul did pine –
> A green isle in the sea, love,
> A fountain and a shrine,
> All wreathed with fairy fruits and flowers;
> And all the flowers were mine.
>
> Ah, dream too bright to last!
> Ah, starry Hope, that didst arise
> But to be overcast!
> A voice from out the Future cries,
> 'Onward!' – but o'er the Past
> (Dim gulf!) my spirit hovering lies,
> Mute – motionless – aghast!
>
> For alas! alas! with me
> The light of life is o'er.
> No more – no more – no more
> (Such language holds the solemn sea
> To the sands upon the shore),
> Shall bloom the thunder-blasted tree,
> Or the stricken eagle soar!
>
> Now all my hours are trances;
> And all my nightly dreams
> Are where the dark eye glances,
> And where thy footstep gleams
> In what ethereal dances,
> By what Italian streams.

Alas! for that accursed time
They bore thee o'er the billow,
From Love to titled age and crime,
And an unholy pillow! –
From me, and from our misty clime,
Where weeps the silver willow!

That these lines were written in English – a language with which I had not believed their author acquainted – afforded me little matter for surprise. I was too well aware of the extent of his acquirements, and of the singular pleasure he took in concealing them from observation, to be astonished at any similar discovery; but the place of date, I must confess, occasioned me no little amazement. It had been originally written London, and afterwards carefully overscored – not, however, so effectually as to conceal the word from a scrutinising eye. I say, this occasioned me no little amazement; for I well remember that, in a former conversation with a friend, I particularly enquired if he had at any time met in *London* the Marchesa di Mentoni (who for some years previous to her marriage had resided in that city), when his answer, if I mistake not, gave me to understand that he had never visited the metropolis of Great Britain. I might as well here mention, that I have more than once heard (without, of course, giving credit to a report involving so many improbabilities), that the person of whom I speak, was not only by birth, but in education, an *Englishman*.

* * *

'There is one painting,' said he, without being aware of my notice of the tragedy – 'there is still one painting which you have not seen.' And throwing aside a drapery, he discovered a full-length portrait of the Marchesa Aphrodite.

Human art could have done no more in the delineation of her superhuman beauty. The same ethereal figure which stood before me the preceding night upon the steps of the Ducal Palace, stood before me once again. But in the expression of the countenance, which was beaming all over with smiles, there still lurked (incomprehensible anomaly!) that fitful stain of melancholy which will ever be found inseparable from the perfection of the beautiful. Her right arm lay folded over her bosom. With her left she pointed downward to a curiously fashioned vase. One small, fairy foot, alone visible, barely touched the earth; and, scarcely discernible in the brilliant atmosphere which seemed to encircle and enshrine her loveliness, floated a pair of the most delicately imagined wings. My glance fell from the painting to the figure of my friend, and the vigorous words of Chapman's *Bussy D'Ambois* quivered instinctively upon my lips:

He is up
There like a Roman statue! He will stand
Till Death hath made him marble!

'Come,' he said at length, turning towards a table of richly enamelled and massive silver, upon which were a few goblets fantastically stained, together with two large Etruscan vases, fashioned in the same extraordinary model as that in the foreground of the portrait, and filled with what I supposed to be Johannisberger. 'Come,' he said, abruptly, 'let us drink! It is early – but let us drink. It is *indeed* early,' he continued, musingly, as a cherub with a heavy golden hammer made the apartment ring with the first hour after sunrise: 'It is *indeed* early – but what matters it? let us drink! Let us pour out an offering to yon solemn sun which these gaudy lamps and censers are so eager to subdue!' And, having made me pledge him in a bumper, he swallowed in rapid succession several goblets of the wine.

'To dream,' he continued, resuming the tone of his desultory conversation, as he held up to the rich light of a censer one of the magnificent vases – 'to dream has been the business of my life. I have therefore framed for myself, as you see, a bower of dreams. In the heart of Venice could I have erected a better? You behold around you, it is true, a medley of architectural embellishments. The chastity of Ionia is offended by antediluvian devices, and the sphinxes of Egypt are outstretched upon carpets of gold. Yet the effect is incongruous to the timid alone. Proprieties of place, and especially of time, are the bugbears which terrify mankind from the contemplation of the magnificent. Once I was myself a decorist; but that sublimation of folly has palled upon my soul. All this is now the fitter for my purpose. Like these arabesque censers, my spirit is writhing in fire, and the delirium of this scene is fashioning me for the wilder visions of that land of real dreams whither I am now rapidly departing.' He here paused abruptly, bent his head to his bosom, and seemed to listen to a sound which I could not hear. At length, erecting his frame, he looked upwards, and ejaculated the lines of the Bishop of Chichester:

'Stay for me there! I will not fail
To meet thee in that hollow vale.'

In the next instant, confessing the power of the wine, he threw himself at full length upon an ottoman.

A quick step was now heard upon the staircase, and a loud knock at the door rapidly succeeded. I was hastening to anticipate a second disturbance, when a page of Mentoni's household burst into the room, and faltered out, in a voice choking with emotion, the incoherent words, 'My mistress! – my mistress! – Poisoned! – poisoned! Oh, beautiful – oh, beautiful Aphrodite!'

Bewildered, I flew to the ottoman, and endeavoured to arouse the sleeper to a sense of the startling intelligence. But his limbs were rigid – his lips were livid – his lately beaming eyes were riveted in *death*. I staggered back towards the table – my hand fell upon a cracked and blackened goblet – and a consciousness of the entire and terrible truth flashed suddenly over my soul.

Morella

Αυτο χαθ' αυτο μεθ' αυτου, μονο ειδες αιει ου.
Itself, by itself, solely, one everlasting, and single.

PLATO, Symposium

With a feeling of deep yet most singular affection I regarded my friend Morella. Thrown by accident into her society many years ago, my soul from our first meeting, burned with fires it had never before known; but the fires were not of Eros, and bitter and tormenting to my spirit was the gradual conviction that I could in no manner define their unusual meaning or regulate their vague intensity. Yet we met; and fate bound us together at the altar, and I never spoke of passion nor thought of love. She, however, shunned society, and, attaching herself to me alone, rendered me happy. It is a happiness to wonder; it is a happiness to dream.

Morella's erudition was profound. As I hope to live, her talents were of no common order – her powers of mind were gigantic. I felt this, and, in many matters, became her pupil. I soon, however, found that, perhaps on account of her Pressburg education, she placed before me a number of those mystical writings which are usually considered the mere dross of the early German literature. These, for what reason I could not imagine, were her favourite and constant study – and that in process of time they became my own, should be attributed to the simple but effectual influence of habit and example.

In all this, if I err not, my reason had little to do. My convictions, or I forget myself, were in no manner acted upon by the ideal, nor was any tincture of the mysticism which I read to be discovered, unless I am greatly mistaken, either in my deeds or in my thoughts. Persuaded of this, I abandoned myself implicitly to the guidance of my wife, and entered with an unflinching heart into the intricacies of her studies. And then – then, when poring over forbidden pages, I felt a forbidden spirit enkindling within me – would Morella place her cold hand upon my own, and rake up from the ashes of a dead philosophy some low, singular words, whose strange meaning burned themselves in upon my memory. And then, hour after hour, would I linger by her side, and dwell upon the music of her voice, until at length its melody was tainted with terror, and there fell a shadow upon my soul, and I grew pale, and shuddered inwardly at those too unearthly tones. And thus, joy suddenly faded into horror, and the most beautiful became the most hideous, as Hinnôm became Gehenna.

It is unnecessary to state the exact character of those disquisitions which, growing out of the volumes I have mentioned, formed, for so long a time, almost the sole conversation of Morella and myself. By the learned in what might be termed theological morality they will be readily conceived, and by the unlearned they would, at all events, be little understood. The wild Pantheism of Fichte; the modified Paliggenedia of the Pythagoreans; and, above all, the doctrines of Identity as urged by Schelling, were generally the points of discussion presenting the most of beauty to the imaginative Morella. That identity which is termed personal, Mr Locke, I think, truly defines to consist in the saneness of rational being. And since by person we understand an intelligent essence having reason, and since there is a consciousness which always accompanies thinking, it is this which makes us all to be that which we call *ourselves*, thereby distinguishing us from other beings that think, and giving us our personal identity. But the *principium individuationis*, the notion of that identity *which at death is or is not lost for ever*, was to me, at all times, a consideration of intense interest; not more from the perplexing and exciting nature of its consequences, than from the marked and agitated manner in which Morella mentioned them.

But, indeed, the time had now arrived when the mystery of my wife's manner oppressed me as a spell. I could no longer bear the touch of her wan fingers, nor the low tone of her musical language, nor the lustre of her melancholy eyes. And she knew all this, but did not upbraid; she seemed conscious of my weakness or my folly, and, smiling, called it fate. She seemed also conscious of a cause, to me unknown, for the gradual alienation of my regard; but she gave me no hint or token of its nature. Yet was she woman, and pined away daily. In time the crimson spot settled steadily upon the cheek, and the blue veins upon the pale forehead became prominent; and one instant my nature melted into pity, but, in the next, I met the glance of her meaning eyes, and then my soul sickened and became giddy with the giddiness of one who gazes downward into some dreary and unfathomable abyss.

Shall I then say that I longed with an earnest and consuming desire for the moment of Morella's decease? I did; but the fragile spirit clung to its tenement of clay for many days, for many weeks and irksome months, until my tortured nerves obtained the mastery over my mind, and I grew furious through delay, and, with the heart of a fiend, cursed the days and the hours and the bitter moments, which seemed to lengthen and lengthen as her gentle life declined, like shadows in the dying of the day.

But one autumnal evening, when the winds lay still in heaven, Morella called me to her bedside. There was a dim mist over all the earth, and a warm glow upon the waters, and amid the rich October leaves of the forest, a rainbow from the firmament had surely fallen.

'It is a day of days,' she said, as I approached; 'a day of all days either to live or die. It is a fair day for the sons of earth and life – ah, more fair for the daughters of heaven and death!'

I kissed her forehead, and she continued: 'I am dying, yet shall I live.'

'Morella!'

'The days have never been when thou couldst love me – but her whom in life thou didst abhor, in death thou shalt adore.'

'Morella!'

'I repeat that I am dying. But within me is a pledge of that affection – ah, how little! – which thou didst feel for me, Morella. And when my spirit departs shall the child live – thy child and mine, Morella's. But thy days shall be days of sorrow – that sorrow which is the most lasting of impressions, as the cypress is the most enduring of trees. For the hours of thy happiness are over and joy is not gathered twice in a life, as the roses of Paestum twice in a year. Thou shalt no longer, then, play the Teian with time, but, being ignorant of the myrtle and the vine, thou shalt bear about with thee thy shroud on the earth, as do the Moslemin at Mecca.'

'Morella!' I cried, 'Morella! how knowest thou this?' but she turned away her face upon the pillow and a slight tremor coming over her limbs, she thus died, and I heard her voice no more.

Yet, as she had foretold, her child, to which in dying she had given birth, which breathed not until the mother breathed no more, her child, a daughter, lived. And she grew strangely in stature and intellect, and was the perfect resemblance of her who had departed, and I loved her with a love more fervent than I had believed it possible to feel for any denizen of earth.

But, ere long, the heaven of this pure affection became darkened, and gloom, and horror, and grief, swept over it in clouds. I said the child grew strangely in stature and intelligence. Strange, indeed, was her rapid increase in bodily size, but terrible, oh! terrible were the tumultuous thoughts which crowded upon me while watching the development of her mental being. Could it be otherwise, when I daily discovered in the conceptions of the child the adult powers and faculties of the woman? when the lessons of experience fell from the lips of infancy? and when the wisdom or the passions of maturity I found hourly gleaming from its full and speculative eye? When, I say, all this became evident to my appalled senses, when I could no longer hide it from my soul, nor throw it off from those perceptions which trembled to receive it, is it to be wondered at that suspicions, of a nature fearful and exciting, crept in upon my spirit, or that my thoughts fell back aghast upon the wild tales and thrilling theories of the entombed Morella? I snatched from the scrutiny of the world a being whom destiny compelled me to adore, and in the rigorous seclusion of my home, watched with an agonising anxiety over all which concerned the beloved.

And as years rolled away, and I gazed day after day upon her holy, and mild, and eloquent face, and pored over her maturing form, day after day did I discover new points of resemblance in the child to her mother, the melancholy and the dead. And hourly grew darker these shadows of similitude, and more full, and more definite, and more perplexing, and more hideously terrible in their aspect. For that her smile was like her mother's I could bear – but then I shuddered at its too perfect identity; that her eyes were like Morella's I could endure – but then they, too, often looked down into the depths of my soul with Morella's own intense and bewildering meaning. And in the contour of the high forehead, and in the ringlets of the silken hair, and in the wan fingers which buried themselves therein, and in the sad musical tones of her speech, and above all – oh, above all, in the phrases and expressions of the dead on the lips of the loved and the

"THE EARTH GREW DARK, AND ITS FIGURES PASSED BY ME, LIKE FLITTING SHADOWS, AND AMONG THEM ALL I BEHELD ONLY – MORELLA"

living, I found food for consuming thought and horror, for a worm that would not die.

Thus passed away two lustra of her life, and as yet my daughter remained nameless upon the earth. 'My child', and 'my love', were the designations usually prompted by a father's affection, and the rigid seclusion of her days precluded all other intercourse. Morella's name died with her at her death. Of the mother I had never spoken to the daughter; it was impossible to speak. Indeed, during the brief period of her existence, the latter had received no impressions from the outward world, save such as might have been afforded by the narrow limits of her privacy. But at length the ceremony of baptism presented to my mind, in its unnerved and agitated condition, a present deliverance from the terrors of my destiny. And at the baptismal font I hesitated for a name. And many titles of the wise and beautiful, of old and modern times, of my own and foreign lands, came thronging to my lips, with many, many fair titles of the gentle, and the happy, and the good. What prompted me then to disturb the memory of the buried dead? What demon urged me to breathe that sound, which in its very recollection was wont to make ebb the purple blood in torrents from the temples to the heart? What fiend spoke from the recesses of my soul, when amid those dim aisles, and in the silence of the night, I whispered within the ears of the holy man the syllables – Morella? What more than fiend convulsed the features of my child, and overspread them with hues of death, as starting at that scarcely audible sound, she turned her glassy eyes from the earth to heaven, and falling prostrate on the black slabs of our ancestral vault, responded – 'I am here!'

Distinct, coldly, calmly distinct, fell those few simple sounds within my ear, and thence like molten lead rolled hissingly into my brain. Years – years may pass away, but the memory of that epoch never. Nor was I indeed ignorant of the flowers and the vine – but the hemlock and the cypress overshadowed me night and day. And I kept no reckoning of time or place, and the stars of my fate faded from heaven, and therefore the earth grew dark, and its figures passed by me like flitting shadows, and among them all I beheld only – Morella. The winds of the firmament breathed but one sound within my ears, and the ripples upon the sea murmured evermore – Morella. But she died; and with my own hands I bore her to the tomb; and I laughed with a long and bitter laugh as I found no traces of the first in the channel where I laid the second Morella.

King Pest

A TALE CONTAINING AN ALLEGORY

The gods do bear and will allow in kings
The things which they abhor in rascal routes.

BUCKHURST, Tragedy of Ferrex and Porrex

About twelve o'clock, one night in the month of October, and during the chivalrous reign of the third Edward, two seamen belonging to the crew of the 'Free and Easy', a trading schooner plying between Sluys and the Thames, and then at anchor in that river, were much astonished to find themselves seated in the taproom of an alehouse in the parish of St Andrews, London – which alehouse bore for sign the portraiture of a 'Jolly Tar'.

The room, although ill-contrived, smoke-blackened, low-pitched, and in every other respect agreeing with the general character of such places at the period – was, nevertheless, in the opinion of the grotesque groups scattered here and there within it, sufficiently well adapted to its purpose.

Of these groups our two seamen formed, I think, the most interesting, if not the most conspicuous.

The one who appeared to be the elder, and whom his companion addressed by the characteristic appellation of 'Legs', was at the same time much the taller of the two. He might have measured six feet and a half, and an habitual stoop in the shoulders seemed to have been the necessary consequence of an altitude so enormous. Superfluities in height were, however, more than accounted for by deficiencies in other respects. He was exceedingly thin; and might, as his associates asserted, have answered, when drunk, for a pennant at the masthead, or, when sober, have served for a jib-boom. But these jests, and others of a similar nature, had evidently produced, at no time, any effect upon the cachinnatory muscles of the tar. With high cheek-bones, a large hawk-nose, retreating chin, fallen under-jaw, and huge protruding white eyes, the expression of his countenance, although tinged with a species of dogged indifference to matters and things in general, was not the less utterly solemn and serious beyond all attempts at imitation or description.

The younger seaman was, in all outward appearance, the converse of his companion. His stature could not have exceeded four feet. A pair of stumpy bow-legs supported his squat, unwieldy figure, while his unusually short and thick arms, with no ordinary fists at their extremities, swung off dangling from his sides like the fins of a sea-turtle. Small eyes, of no particular colour, twinkled far back in his head. His nose remained buried in the mass of flesh which enveloped his round, full, and purple face; and his thick upper-lip rested upon the still thicker one beneath with an air of complacent self-satisfaction, much heightened by the owner's habit of licking them at intervals. He evidently regarded his tall shipmate with a feeling half-wondrous, half-quizzical; and stared up occasionally in his face as the red setting sun stares up at the crags of Ben Nevis.

Various and eventful, however, had been the peregrinations of the worthy couple in and about the different tap-houses of the neighbourhood during the earlier hours of the night. Funds even the most ample, are not always everlasting: and it was with empty pockets our friends had ventured upon the present hostelry.

At the precise period, then, when this history properly commences, Legs, and his fellow Hugh Tarpaulin, sat, each with both elbows resting upon the large oaken table in the middle of the floor, and with a hand upon either cheek. They were eyeing, from behind a huge flagon of unpaid-for 'humming-stuff', the portentous words, 'No Chalk', which to their indignation and astonishment were scored over the doorway by means of that very mineral whose presence they purported to deny. Not that the gift of deciphering written characters – a gift among the commonality of that day considered little less cabbalistical than the art of indicting – could, in strict justice, have been laid to the charge of either disciple of the sea; but there was, to say the truth, a certain twist in the formation of the letters – an indescribable lee-lurch about the whole – which foreboded, in the opinion of both seamen, a long run of dirty weather; and determined them at once, in the allegorical words of Legs himself, to 'pump ship, clew up all sail, and scud before the wind'.

Having accordingly disposed of what remained of the ale, and looped up the points of their short doublets, they finally made a bolt for the street. Although Tarpaulin rolled twice into the fireplace, mistaking it for the door, yet their escape was at length happily effected – and half after twelve o'clock found our heroes ripe for mischief, and running for life down a dark alley in the direction of St Andrew's Stair, hotly pursued by the landlady of the 'Jolly Tar'.

At the epoch of this eventful tale, and periodically, for many years before and after, all England, but more especially the metropolis, resounded with the fearful cry of 'Plague!' The city was in a great measure depopulated – and in those horrible regions, in the vicinity of the Thames, where amid the dark, narrow, and filthy lanes and alleys, the Demon of Disease was supposed to have had his nativity, Awe, Terror, and Superstition were alone to be found stalking abroad.

By authority of the king such districts were placed under ban, and all persons forbidden, under pain of death, to intrude upon their dismal solitude. Yet neither the mandate of the monarch, nor the huge barriers erected at the entrances of the streets, nor the prospect of that loathsome death which, with almost absolute certainty, overwhelmed the wretch whom no peril could deter from the adventure, prevented the unfurnished and untenanted dwellings from being stripped, by the hand of nightly rapine, of every article, such as iron, brass, or lead-work, which could in any manner be turned to a profitable account.

Above all, it was usually found, upon the annual winter opening of the barriers, that locks, bolts, and secret cellars had proved but slender protection to those rich stores of wines and liquors which, in consideration of the risk and trouble of removal, many of the numerous dealers having shops in the neighbourhood had consented to trust, during the period of exile, to so insufficient a security.

But there were very few of the terror-stricken people who attributed these doings to the agency of human hands. Pest-spirits, plague-goblins, and fever-demons were the popular imps of mischief; and tales so blood-chilling were hourly told, that the whole mass of forbidden buildings was, at length, enveloped in terror as in a shroud, and the plunderer himself was often scared away by the horrors his own depredations had created; leaving the entire vast circuit of prohibited district to gloom, silence, pestilence, and death.

It was by one of the terrific barriers already mentioned, and which indicated the region beyond to be under the Pest-ban, that, in scrambling down an alley, Legs and the worthy Hugh Tarpaulin found their progress suddenly impeded. To return was out of the question, and no time was to be lost, as their pursuers were close upon their heels. With thoroughbred seamen to clamber up the roughly fashioned plank-work was a trifle; and, maddened with the twofold excitement of exercise and liquor, they leaped unhesitatingly down within the enclosure, and holding on their drunken course with shouts and yellings, were soon bewildered in its noisome and intricate recesses.

Had they not, indeed, been intoxicated beyond moral sense, their reeling footsteps must have been palsied by the horrors of their situation. The air was cold and misty. The paving-stones, loosened from their beds, lay in wild disorder amid the tall, rank grass, which sprang up around the feet and ankles. Fallen houses choked up the streets. The most fetid and poisonous smells everywhere prevailed – and by the aid of that ghastly light which, even at midnight, never fails to emanate from a vapoury and pestilential atmosphere, might be discerned lying in the by-paths and alleys, or rotting in the windowless habitations, the carcass of many a nocturnal plunderer arrested by the hand of the plague in the very perpetration of his robbery.

But it lay not in the power of images, or sensations, or impediments such as these, to stay the course of men who, naturally brave, and at that time especially, brimful of courage and of 'humming-stuff', would have reeled, as straight as their condition might have permitted, undauntedly into the very jaws of Death. Onward – still onward stalked the grim Legs, making the desolate solemnity echo and re-echo with yells like the terrific war-whoop of the Indian; and onward, still onward rolled the dumpy Tarpaulin, hanging on to the doublet of his more active companion, and far surpassing the latter's most strenuous exertions in the way of vocal music, by bull-roarings in basso, from the profundity of his stentorian lungs.

They had now evidently reached the stronghold of the pestilence. Their way at every step or plunge grew more noisome and more horrible – the paths more narrow and more intricate. Huge stones and beams falling momently from the decaying roofs above them, gave evidence, by their sullen and heavy descent, of the vast height of the surrounding houses; and while actual exertion became necessary to force a passage through frequent heaps of rubbish, it was by no means seldom that the hand fell upon a skeleton or rested upon a more fleshly corpse.

Suddenly, as the seamen stumbled against the entrance of a tall and ghastly-looking building, a yell more than usually shrill from the throat of the excited Legs, was replied to from within, in a rapid succession of wild, laughter-like, and fiendish shrieks. Nothing daunted at sounds which, of such a nature, at such a time, and in such a place, might have curdled the very blood in hearts less irrevocably on fire, the drunken couple rushed headlong against the door, burst it open, and staggered into the midst of things with a volley of curses.

The room within which they found themselves proved to be the shop of an undertaker; but an open trap-door, in a corner of the floor near the entrance, looked down upon a long range of wine-cellars, whose depths the occasional sound of bursting bottles proclaimed to be well stored with their appropriate contents. In the middle of the room stood a table – in the centre of which again arose a huge tub of what appeared to be punch. Bottles of various wines and cordials, together with jugs, pitchers, and flagons of every shape and quality, were scattered profusely upon the board. Around it, upon coffin-trestles, was seated a company of six. This company I will endeavour to delineate one by one.

Fronting the entrance, and elevated a little above his companions, sat a personage who appeared to be the president of the table. His stature was gaunt and tall, and Legs was confounded to behold in him a figure more emaciated than himself. His face was as yellow as saffron – but no feature, excepting one alone, was sufficiently marked to merit a particular description. This one consisted in a forehead so unusually and hideously lofty, as to have the appearance of a bonnet or crown of flesh superadded upon the natural head. His mouth was puckered and dimpled into an expression of ghastly affability, and his eyes, as indeed the eyes of all at table, were glazed over with the fumes of intoxication. This gentleman was clothed from head to foot in a richly embroidered black silk-velvet pall, wrapped negligently around his form after the fashion of a Spanish cloak. His head was stuck full of sable hearse-plumes, which he nodded to and fro with a jaunty and knowing air; and, in his right hand, he held a huge human thigh-bone, with which he appeared to have been just knocking down some member of the company for a song.

Opposite him, and with her back to the door, was a lady of no whit the less extraordinary character. Although quite as tall as the person just described, she had no right to complain of his unnatural emaciation. She was evidently in the last stage of a dropsy; and her figure resembled nearly that of the huge puncheon of October beer which stood, with the head driven in, close by her side, in a corner of the chamber. Her face was exceedingly round, red, and full; and the same peculiarity, or rather want of peculiarity, attached itself to her countenance, which I before mentioned in the case of the president – that is to say, only one feature of her face was sufficiently distinguished to need a separate characterisation: indeed the acute Tarpaulin immediately observed that the same remark might have applied to each individual person of the party; every one of whom seemed to possess a monopoly of some particular portion of physiognomy. With the lady in question this portion proved to be the mouth. Commencing at the right ear, it swept with a terrific chasm to the left – the short pendants which she wore in either auricle continually bobbing into the aperture. She made, however, every exertion to keep her mouth closed and look dignified, in a dress consisting of a newly starched and ironed shroud coming up close under her chin, with a crimpled ruffle of cambric muslin.

At her right hand sat a diminutive young lady whom she appeared to patronise. This delicate little creature, in the trembling of her wasted fingers, in the livid hue of her lips, and in the slight hectic spot which tinged her otherwise leaden complexion, gave evident indications of a galloping consumption. An air of extreme *haut ton*, however, pervaded her whole appearance; she wore in a graceful and *dégagé* manner, a large and beautiful winding-sheet of the finest India lawn; her hair hung in ringlets over her neck; a soft smile played about her mouth; but her nose, extremely long, thin, sinuous, flexible and pimpled, hung down far below her underlip, and in spite of the delicate manner in which she now and then moved it to one side or the other with her tongue, gave to her countenance a somewhat equivocal expression.

Over against her, and upon the left of the dropsical lady, was seated a little puffy, wheezing, and gouty old man, whose cheeks reposed upon the shoulders of their owner, like two huge bladders of Oporto wine. With his arms folded, and with one bandaged leg deposited upon the table, he seemed to think himself entitled to some consideration. He evidently prided himself much upon every inch of his personal appearance, but took more especial delight in calling attention to his gaudy-coloured surtout. This, to say the truth, must have cost him no little money, and was made to fit him exceedingly well – being fashioned from one of the curiously embroidered silken covers appertaining to those glorious escutcheons which, in England and elsewhere, are customarily hung up, in some conspicuous place, upon the dwellings of departed aristocracy.

Next to him, and at the right hand of the president, was a gentleman in long white hose and cotton drawers. His frame shook, in a ridiculous manner, with a fit of what Tarpaulin called 'the horrors'. His jaws, which had been newly shaved, were tightly tied up by a bandage of muslin; and his arms being fastened in a similar way at the wrists, prevented him from helping himself too freely to the liquors upon the table; a precaution rendered necessary, in the opinion of Legs, by the peculiarly sottish and wine-bibbing cast of his visage. A pair of prodigious ears, nevertheless, which it was no doubt found impossible to confine, towered away into the atmosphere of the apartment, and were occasionally pricked up in a spasm, at the sound of the drawing of a cork.

Fronting him, sixthly and lastly, was situated a singularly stiff-looking personage, who, being afflicted with paralysis, must, to speak seriously, have felt very ill at ease in his unaccommodating habiliments. He was habited, somewhat uniquely, in a new and handsome mahogany coffin. Its top or head-piece pressed upon the skull of the wearer, and extended over it in the fashion of a hood, giving to the entire face an air of indescribable interest. Armholes had been cut in the sides, for the sake not more of elegance than of convenience; but the dress, nevertheless, prevented its proprietor from sitting as erect as his associates; and as he lay reclining against his trestle, at an angle of forty-five degrees, a pair of huge goggle eyes rolled up their awful whites towards the ceiling in absolute amazement at their own enormity.

Before each of the party lay a portion of a skull, which was used as a drinking cup. Overhead was suspended a human skeleton, by means of a rope tied round one of the legs and fastened to a ring in the ceiling. The other limb, confined by no such fetter, stuck off from the body at right angles, causing the whole loose and rattling frame to dangle and twirl about at the caprice of every occasional puff of wind which found its way into the apartment. In the cranium of this hideous thing lay a quantity of ignited charcoal, which threw a fitful but vivid light over the entire scene; while coffins, and other wares appertaining to the shop of an undertaker, were piled high up around the room, and against the windows, preventing any ray from escaping into the street.

At sight of this extraordinary assembly, and of their still more extraordinary paraphernalia, our two seamen did not conduct themselves with that degree of decorum which might have been expected. Legs, leaning against the wall near which he happened to be standing, dropped his lower jaw still lower than usual, and spread open his eyes to their fullest extent; while Hugh Tarpaulin, stooping down so as to bring his nose upon a level with the table, and spreading out a palm upon either knee, burst into a long, loud, and obstreperous roar of very ill-timed and immoderate laughter.

Without, however, taking offence at behaviour so excessively rude, the tall president smiled very graciously upon the intruders – nodded to them in a dignified manner with his head of sable plumes – and, arising, took each by an arm, and led him to a seat which some others of the company had placed in the meantime for his accommodation. Legs to all this offered not the slightest resistance, but sat down as he was directed; while the gallant Hugh, removing his coffin trestle from its station near the head of the table, to the vicinity of the little consumptive lady in the winding sheet, plumped down by her side in high glee, and pouring out a skull of red wine, quaffed it to their better acquaintance. But at this presumption the stiff gentleman in the coffin seemed exceedingly nettled; and serious consequences might have

"AVAST THERE A BIT, I SAY, AND TELL US WHO THE DEVIL YE ALL ARE!"

ensued, had not the president, rapping upon the table with his truncheon, diverted the attention of all present to the following speech: 'It becomes our duty upon the present happy occasion – '

'Avast there!' interrupted Legs, looking very serious, 'avast there a bit, I say, and tell us who the devil ye all are, and what business ye have here, rigged off like the foul fiends, and swilling the snug blue ruin stowed away for the winter by my honest shipmate, Will Wimble the undertaker!'

At this unpardonable piece of ill-breeding, all the original company half started to their feet, and uttered the same rapid succession of wild fiendish shrieks which had before caught the attention of the seamen. The president, however, was the first to recover his composure, and at length, turning to Legs with great dignity, recommenced: 'Most willingly will we gratify any reasonable curiosity on the part of guests so illustrious, unbidden though they be. Know then that in these dominions I am monarch, and here rule with undivided empire under the title of "King Pest the First".

'This apartment, which you no doubt profanely suppose to be the shop of Will Wimble the undertaker – a man whom we know not, and whose plebeian appellation has never before this night thwarted our royal ears – this apartment, I say, is the Dais-Chamber of our Palace, devoted to the councils of our kingdom, and to other sacred and lofty purposes.

'The noble lady who sits opposite is Queen Pest, our Serene Consort. The other exalted personages whom you behold are all of our family, and wear the insignia of the blood royal under the respective titles of "His Grace the Arch Duke Pest-Iferous" – "His Grace the Duke Pest-Ilential" – "His Grace the Duke Tem-Pest" – and "Her Serene Highness the Arch Duchess Ana-Pest".

'As regards,' continued he, 'your demand of the business upon which we sit here in council, we might be pardoned for replying that it concerns, and concerns alone, our own private and regal interest, and is in no manner important to any other than ourselves. But in consideration of those rights to which as guests and strangers you may feel yourselves entitled, we will furthermore explain that we are here this night, prepared by deep research and accurate investigation, to examine, analyse, and thoroughly determine the indefinable spirit – the incomprehensible qualities and nature – of those inestimable treasures of the palate, the wines, ales, and liqueurs of this goodly metropolis: by so doing to advance not more our own designs than the true welfare of that unearthly sovereign whose reign is over us all, whose dominions are unlimited, and whose name is "Death".'

'Whose name is Davy Jones!' ejaculated Tarpaulin, helping the lady by his side to a skull of liqueur, and pouring out a second for himself.

'Profane varlet!' said the president, now turning his attention to the worthy Hugh, 'profane and execrable wretch! – we have said, that in consideration of those rights which, even in thy filthy person, we feel no inclination to violate, we have condescended to make reply to thy rude and unseasonable enquiries. We nevertheless, for your unhallowed intrusion upon our councils, believe it our duty to mulct thee and thy companion in each a gallon of Black Strap – having imbibed which to the prosperity of our kingdom – at a single draught – and upon your bended knees – ye shall be forthwith free either to proceed upon your way, or remain and be admitted to the privileges of our table, according to your respective and individual pleasures.'

'It would be a matter of utter impossibility,' replied Legs, whom the assumptions and dignity of King Pest the First had evidently inspired some feelings of respect, and who arose and steadied himself by the table as he spoke – 'it would, please your majesty, be a matter of utter impossibility to stow away in my hold even one-fourth part of the same liquor which your majesty has just mentioned. To say nothing of the stuffs placed on board in the forenoon by way of ballast, and not to mention the various ales and liqueurs shipped this evening at different seaports, I have, at present, a full cargo of "humming stuff" taken in and duly paid for at the sign of the "Jolly Tar". You will, therefore, please your majesty, be so good as to take the will for the deed – for by no manner of means either can I or will I swallow another drop – least of all a drop of that villainous bilge-water that answers to the hail of "Black Strap".'

'Belay that!' interrupted Tarpaulin, astonished not more at the length of his companion's speech than at the nature of his refusal – 'Belay that, you lubber! – and I say, Legs, none of your palaver! My hull is still light, although I confess you yourself seem to be a little top-heavy; and as for the matter of your share of the cargo, why rather than raise a squall I would find stowage room for it myself, but – '

'This proceeding,' interposed the president, 'is by no means in accordance with the terms of the mulct or sentence, which is in its nature Median, and not to be altered or recalled. The conditions we have imposed must be fulfilled to the letter, and that without a moment's hesitation – in failure of which fulfilment we decree that you do here be tied neck and heels together, and duly drowned as rebels in yon hogshead of October beer!'

'A sentence! – a sentence! – a righteous and just sentence! – a glorious decree! – a most worthy and upright, and holy condemnation!' shouted the Pest family altogether. The king elevated his forehead into innumerable wrinkles; the gouty little old man puffed like a pair of bellows; the lady of the winding sheet waved her nose to and fro; the gentleman in the cotton drawers pricked up his ears; she of the shroud gasped like a dying fish; and he of the coffin looked stiff and rolled up his eyes.

'Ugh! ugh! ugh!' chuckled Tarpaulin without heeding the general excitation, 'ugh! ugh! ugh! – ugh! ugh! ugh! – ugh! ugh! ugh! – I was saying,' said he, 'I was saying when Mr King Pest poked in his marlinspike, that as for the matter of two or three gallons more or less of Black Strap, it was a trifle to a tight sea-boat like myself not over-stowed – but when it comes to drinking the health of the Devil (whom God assoilzie) and going down upon my marrow bones to his ill-favoured majesty there, whom I know, as well as I know myself to be a sinner, to be nobody in the whole world, but Tim Hurlygurly the stage-player – why! it's quite another guess sort of a thing, and utterly and altogether past my comprehension.'

He was not allowed to finish this speech in tranquillity. At the name Tim Hurlygurly the whole assembly leaped from their seats.

'Treason!' shouted his Majesty King Pest the First.

'Treason!' said the little man with the gout.

'Treason!' screamed the Arch Duchess Ana-Pest.

'Treason!' muttered the gentleman with his jaws tied up.

'Treason!' growled he of the coffin.

'Treason! treason!' shrieked her majesty of the mouth; and, seizing by the hinder part of his breeches the unfortunate Tarpaulin, who had just commenced pouring out for himself a skull of liqueur, she lifted him high into the air, and let him fall without ceremony into the huge open puncheon of his beloved ale. Bobbing up and down, for a few seconds, like an apple in a bowl of toddy, he, at length, finally disappeared amid the whirlpool of foam which, in the already effervescent liquor, his struggles easily succeeded in creating.

Not tamely, however, did the tall seaman behold the discomfiture of his companion. Jostling King Pest through the open trap, the valiant Legs slammed the door down upon him with an oath, and strode towards the centre of the room. Here tearing down the skeleton which swung over the table, he laid it about him with so much energy and good will, that, as the last glimpses of light died away within the apartment, he succeeded in knocking out the brains of the little gentleman with the gout. Rushing then with all his force against the fatal hogshead full of October ale and Hugh Tarpaulin, he rolled it over and over in an instant. Out burst a deluge of liquor so fierce – so impetuous – so overwhelming – that the room was flooded from wall to wall – the loaded table was overturned – the trestles were thrown upon their backs – the tub of punch into the fireplace – and the ladies into hysterics. Piles of death-furniture floundered about. Jugs, pitchers, and carboys mingled promiscuously in the melee, and wicker flagons encountered desperately with bottles of junk. The man with the horrors was drowned upon the spot – the little stiff gentleman floated off in his coffin – and the victorious Legs, seizing by the waist the fat lady in the shroud, rushed out with her into the street, and made a bee-line for the 'Free and Easy', followed under easy sail by the redoubtable Hugh Tarpaulin, who, having sneezed three or four times, panted and puffed after him with the Arch Duchess Ana-Pest.

The Unparalleled Adventure of One Hans Pfaall

With a heart of furious fancies,
Whereof I am commander,
With a burning spear and a horse of air,
To the wilderness I wander.

Tom o'Bedlam's Song

By late accounts from Rotterdam, that city seems to be in a high state of philosophical excitement. Indeed, phenomena have there occurred of a nature so completely unexpected – so entirely novel – so utterly at variance with preconceived opinions – as to leave no doubt on my mind that long ere this all Europe is in an uproar, all physics in a ferment, all reason and astronomy together by the ears.

It appears that on the — day of — (I am not positive about the date), a vast crowd of people, for purposes not specifically mentioned, were assembled in the great square of the Exchange in the well-conditioned city of Rotterdam. The day was warm – unusually so for the season – there was hardly a breath of air stirring; and the multitude were in no bad humour at being now and then besprinkled with friendly showers of momentary duration, that fell from large white masses of cloud which chequered in a fitful manner the blue vault of the firmament. Nevertheless, about noon, a slight but remarkable agitation became apparent in the assembly: the clattering of ten thousand tongues succeeded; and, in an instant afterwards, ten thousand faces were upturned towards the heavens, ten thousand pipes descended simultaneously from the corners of ten thousand mouths, and a shout, which could be compared to nothing but the roaring of Niagara, resounded long, loudly, and furiously, through all the environs of Rotterdam.

The origin of this hubbub soon became sufficiently evident. From behind the huge bulk of one of those sharply defined masses of cloud already mentioned, was seen slowly to emerge into an open area of blue space, a queer, heterogeneous, but apparently solid substance, so oddly shaped, so whimsically put together, as not to be in any manner comprehended, and never to be sufficiently admired, by the host of sturdy burghers who stood open-mouthed below. What could it be? In the name of all the devils in Rotterdam, what could it possibly portend? No one knew, no one could imagine; no one – not even the burgomaster Mynheer Superbus von Underduk – had the slightest clew by which to unravel the mystery; so, as nothing more reasonable could be done, everyone to a man replaced his pipe carefully in the corner of his mouth, and cocking up his right eye towards the phenomenon, puffed, paused, waddled about, and grunted significantly – then waddled back, grunted, paused, and finally – puffed again.

In the meantime, however, lower and still lower towards the goodly city, came the object of so much curiosity, and the cause of so much smoke. In a very few minutes it arrived near enough to be accurately discerned. It appeared to be – yes! it *was* undoubtedly a species of balloon; but surely no *such* balloon had ever been seen in Rotterdam before. For who, let me ask, ever heard of a balloon manufactured entirely of dirty newspapers? No man in Holland certainly; yet here, under the very noses of the people, or rather at some distance *above* their noses was the identical thing in question, and composed, I have it on the best authority, of the precise material which no one had ever before known to be used for a similar purpose. It was an egregious insult to the good sense of the burghers of Rotterdam. As to the shape of the phenomenon, it was even still more reprehensible, being little or nothing better than a huge foolscap turned upside down. And this similitude was regarded as by no means lessened when, upon nearer inspection, there was perceived a large tassel depending from its apex, and, around the upper rim or base of the cone, a circle of little instruments, resembling sheep-bells, which kept up a continual tinkling to the tune of Betty Martin. But still worse. Suspended by blue ribbons to the end of this fantastic machine, there hung, by way of car, an enormous drab beaver hat, with a brim superlatively broad, and a hemispherical crown with a black band and a silver buckle.

It is, however, somewhat remarkable that many citizens of Rotterdam swore to having seen the same hat repeatedly before; and indeed the whole assembly seemed to regard it with eyes of familiarity; while the frau Grettel Pfaall, upon sight of it, uttered an exclamation of joyful surprise, and declared it to be the identical hat of her good man himself. Now this was a circumstance the more to be observed, as Pfaall, with three companions, had actually disappeared from Rotterdam about five years before, in a very sudden and unaccountable manner, and up to the date of this narrative all attempts had failed of obtaining any intelligence concerning them whatsoever. To be sure, some bones which were thought to be human, mixed up with a quantity of odd-looking rubbish, had been lately discovered in a retired situation to the east of Rotterdam, and some people went so far as to imagine that in this spot a foul murder had been committed, and that the sufferers were in all probability Hans Pfaall and his associates. But to return.

The balloon (for such no doubt it was) had now descended to within a hundred feet of the earth, allowing the crowd below a sufficiently distinct view of the person of its occupant. This was in truth a very droll little somebody. He could not have been more than two feet in height; but this altitude, little as it was, would have been sufficient to destroy his equilibrium, and tilt him over the edge of his tiny car, but for the intervention of a circular rim reaching as high as the breast, and rigged on to the cords of the balloon. The body of the little man was more than proportionately broad, giving to his entire figure a rotundity highly absurd. His feet, of course, could not be seen at all, although a horny substance of suspicious nature was occasionally protruded through a rent in the bottom of the car, or to speak more properly, in the top of the hat. His hands were enormously large. His hair was extremely grey, and collected in a queue behind. His nose was prodigiously long, crooked, and inflammatory; his eyes full, brilliant, and acute; his chin and cheeks, although wrinkled with age, were broad, puffy, and double; but of ears of any kind or character there was not a semblance to be discovered upon any portion of his head. This odd little gentleman was dressed in a loose surtout of sky-blue satin, with tight breeches to match, fastened with silver buckles at the knees. His vest was of some bright yellow material; a white taffety cap was set jauntily on one side of his head; and, to complete his equipment, a blood-red silk handkerchief enveloped his throat, and fell down, in a dainty manner, upon his bosom, in a fantastic bow-knot of super-eminent dimensions.

Having descended, as I said before, to about one hundred feet from the surface of the earth, the little old gentleman was suddenly seized with a fit of trepidation, and appeared disinclined to make any nearer approach to *terra firma*. Throwing out, therefore, a quantity of sand from a canvas bag, which he lifted with great difficulty, he became stationary in an instant. He then proceeded, in a hurried and agitated manner, to extract from a side-pocket in his surtout a large morocco pocketbook. This he poised suspiciously in his hand, then eyed it with an air of extreme surprise, and was evidently astonished at its weight. He at length opened it, and drawing therefrom a huge letter sealed with red sealing-wax and tied carefully with red tape, let it fall precisely at the feet of the burgomaster, Superbus von Underduk. His Excellency stooped to take it up. But the aeronaut, still greatly discomposed, and having apparently no further business to detain him in Rotterdam, began at this moment to make busy preparations for departure; and it being necessary to discharge a portion of ballast to enable him to reascend, the half-dozen bags which he threw out, one after another, without taking the trouble to empty their contents, tumbled, every one of them, most unfortunately upon the back of the burgomaster, and rolled him over and over no less than one-and-twenty times, in the face of every man in Rotterdam. It is not to be supposed, however, that the great Underduk suffered this impertinence on the part of the little old man to pass off with impunity. It is said, on the contrary, that during each and every one of his one-and-twenty circumvolutions he emitted no less than one-and-twenty distinct and furious whiffs from his pipe, to which he held fast the whole time with all his might, and to which he intends holding fast until the day of his death.

In the meantime the balloon arose like a lark, and, soaring far away above the city, at length drifted quietly behind a cloud similar to that from which it had so oddly emerged, and was thus lost for ever to the wondering eyes of the good citizens of Rotterdam. All attention was now directed to the letter, the descent of which, and the consequences attending thereupon, had proved so fatally subversive of both person and personal dignity to his excellency, the illustrious Burgomaster Mynheer Superbus von Underduk. That functionary, however, had not failed, during his circumgyratory movements, to bestow a thought upon the important subject of securing the packet in question, which was seen, upon inspection, to have fallen into the most proper hands, being actually addressed to himself and Professor Rub-a-dub, in their official capacities of president and vice-president of the Rotterdam College of Astronomy.

It was accordingly opened by those dignitaries upon the spot, and found to contain the following extraordinary, and indeed very serious, communication:

'To their Excellencies von Underduk and Rub-a-dub, president and vice-president of the States' College of Astronomers, in the city of Rotterdam.

'Your Excellencies may perhaps be able to remember an humble artisan, by name Hans Pfaall, and by occupation a mender of bellows, who, with three others, disappeared from Rotterdam, about five years ago, in a manner which must have been considered by all parties at once sudden, and extremely unaccountable. If, however, it so please your Excellencies, I, the writer of this communication, am the identical Hans Pfaall himself. It is well known to most of my fellow citizens, that for the period of forty years I continued to occupy the little square brick building, at the head of the alley called Sauerkraut, in which I resided at the time of my disappearance. My ancestors have also resided therein time out of mind – they, as well as myself, steadily following the respectable and indeed lucrative profession of mending of bellows. For, to speak the truth, until of late years, that the heads of all the people have been set agog with politics, no better business than my own could an honest citizen of Rotterdam either desire or deserve. Credit was good, employment was never wanting, and on all hands there was no lack of either money or goodwill. But, as I was saying, we soon began to feel the effects of liberty and long speeches, and radicalism, and all that sort of thing. People who were formerly the very best customers in the world, had now not a moment of time to think of us at all. They had, so they said, as much as they could do to read about the revolutions, and keep up with the march of intellect and the spirit of the age. If a fire wanted fanning, it could readily be fanned with a newspaper, and as the government grew weaker, I have no doubt that leather and iron acquired durability in proportion, for, in a very short time, there was not a pair of bellows in all Rotterdam that ever stood in need of a stitch or required the assistance of a hammer. This was a state of things not to be endured. I soon grew as poor as a rat, and, having a wife and children to provide for, my burdens at length became intolerable, and I spent hour after hour in reflecting upon the most convenient method of putting an end to my life. Duns, in the meantime, left me little leisure for contemplation. My house was literally besieged from morning till night, so that I began to rave, and foam, and fret like a caged tiger against the bars of his enclosure. There were three fellows in particular who worried me beyond endurance, keeping watch continually about my door, and threatening me with the law. Upon these three I internally vowed the bitterest revenge, if ever I should be so happy as to get them within my clutches; and I believe nothing in the world but the pleasure of this anticipation prevented me from putting my plan of suicide into immediate execution, by blowing my brains out with a blunderbuss. I thought it best, however, to dissemble my wrath, and to treat them with promises and fair words, until, by some good turn of fate, an opportunity of vengeance should be afforded me.

'One day, having given my creditors the slip, and feeling more than usually dejected, I continued for a long time to wander about the most obscure streets without object whatever, until at length I chanced to stumble against the corner of a bookseller's stall. Seeing a chair close at hand, for the use of customers, I threw myself doggedly into it, and, hardly knowing why, opened the pages of the first volume which came within my reach. It proved to be a small pamphlet treatise on Speculative Astronomy, written either by Professor Encke of Berlin or by a Frenchman of somewhat similar name. I had some little tincture of information on matters of this nature, and soon became more and more absorbed in the contents of the book, reading it actually through twice before I awoke to a recollection of what was passing around me. By this time it began to grow dark, and I directed my steps towards home. But the treatise had made an indelible impression on my mind, and, as I sauntered along the dusky streets, I revolved carefully over in my memory the wild and sometimes unintelligible reasonings of the writer. There are some particular passages which affected my imagination in a powerful and extraordinary manner. The longer I meditated upon these the more intense grew the interest which had been excited within me. The limited nature of my education in general, and more especially my ignorance on subjects connected with natural philosophy, so far from rendering me diffident of my own ability to comprehend what I had read, or inducing me to mistrust the many vague notions which had arisen in consequence, merely served as a further stimulus to imagination; and I was vain enough, or perhaps reasonable enough, to doubt whether those crude ideas which, arising in ill-regulated minds, have all the appearance, may not often in effect possess all the force, the reality, and other inherent properties, of instinct or intuition; whether, to proceed a step farther, profundity itself might not, in matters of a purely speculative nature, be detected as a legitimate source of falsity and error. In other words, I believed, and still do believe, that truth is frequently of its own essence, superficial, and that, in many cases, the depth lies more in the abysses where we seek her, than in the actual situations wherein she may be found. Nature herself seemed to afford me corroboration of these ideas. In the contemplation of the heavenly bodies it struck me forcibly that I could not distinguish a star with nearly as much precision, when I gazed on it with earnest, direct and undeviating attention, as when I suffered my eye only to glance in its vicinity alone. I was not, of course, at that time aware that this apparent paradox was occasioned by the centre of the visual area being less susceptible of feeble impressions of light than the exterior portions of the retina. This knowledge, and some of another kind, came afterwards in the course of an eventful five years, during which I have dropped the prejudices of my former humble situation in life, and forgotten the bellows-mender in far different occupations. But at the epoch of which I speak, the analogy which a casual observation of a star offered to the conclusions I had already drawn, struck me with the force of positive confirmation, and I then finally made up my mind to the course which I afterwards pursued.

'It was late when I reached home, and I went immediately to bed. My mind, however, was too much occupied to sleep, and I lay the whole night buried in meditation. Arising early in the morning, and contriving again to escape the vigilance of my creditors, I repaired eagerly to the bookseller's stall, and laid out what little ready money I possessed, in the purchase of some volumes of Mechanics and Practical Astronomy. Having arrived at home safely with these, I devoted every spare moment to their perusal, and soon made such proficiency in studies of this nature as I thought sufficient for the execution of my plan. In the intervals of this period, I made every endeavour to conciliate the three creditors who had given me so much annoyance. In this I finally succeeded – partly by selling enough of my household furniture to satisfy a moiety of their claim, and partly by a promise of paying the balance upon completion of a little project which I told them I had in view, and for assistance in which I solicited their services. By these means – for they were ignorant men – I found little difficulty in gaining them over to my purpose.

'Matters being thus arranged, I contrived, by the aid of my wife and with the greatest secrecy and caution, to dispose of what property I had remaining, and to borrow, in small sums, under various pretences, and without paying any attention to my future means of repayment, no inconsiderable quantity of ready money. With the means thus accruing I proceeded to procure at intervals, cambric muslin, very fine, in pieces of twelve yards each; twine; a lot of the varnish of caoutchouc; a large and deep basket of wickerwork, made to order; and several other articles necessary in the construction and equipment of a balloon of extraordinary dimensions. This I directed my wife to make up as soon as possible, and gave her all requisite information as to the particular method of proceeding. In the meantime I worked up the twine into a network of sufficient dimensions; rigged it with a hoop and the necessary cords; bought a quadrant, a compass, a spyglass, a common barometer with some important modifications, and two astronomical instruments not so generally known. I then took opportunities of conveying by night, to a retired situation east of Rotterdam, five iron-bound casks, to contain about fifty gallons each, and one of a larger size; six tin tubes, three inches in diameter, properly shaped, and ten feet in length; a quantity of a particular metallic substance, or semi-metal, which I shall not name, and a dozen demijohns of a very common acid. The gas to be formed from these latter materials is a gas never yet generated by any other person than myself – or at least never applied to any similar purpose. The secret I would make no difficulty in disclosing, but that it of right belongs to a citizen of Nantes, in France, by whom it was conditionally communicated to myself. The same individual submitted to me, without being at all aware of my intentions, a method of constructing balloons from the membrane of a certain animal, through which substance any escape of gas was nearly an impossibility. I found it, however, altogether too expensive, and was not sure, upon the whole, whether cambric muslin with a coating of gum caoutchouc, was not equally as good. I mention this circumstance, because I think it probable that hereafter the individual in question may attempt a balloon ascension with the novel gas and material I have spoken of, and I do not wish to deprive him of the honour of a very singular invention.

'On the spot which I intended each of the smaller casks to occupy respectively during the inflation of the balloon, I privately dug a hole two feet deep; the holes forming in this manner a circle twenty-five feet in diameter. In the centre of this circle, being the station designed for the large cask, I also dug a hole three feet in depth. In each of the five smaller holes, I deposited a canister containing fifty pounds, and in the larger one a keg holding one hundred and fifty pounds, of cannon powder. These – the keg and canisters – I connected in a proper manner with covered trains; and having let into one of the canisters the end of about four feet of slow match, I covered up the hole, and placed the cask over it, leaving the other end of the match protruding about an inch, and barely visible beyond the cask. I then filled up the remaining holes, and placed the barrels over them in their destined situation.

'Besides the articles above enumerated, I conveyed to the depot, and there secreted, one of M. Grimm's improvements upon the apparatus for condensation of the atmospheric air. I found this machine, however, to require considerable alteration before it could be adapted to the purposes to which I intended making it applicable. But, with severe labour and unremitting perseverance, I at length met with entire success in all my preparations. My balloon was soon completed. It would contain more than forty thousand cubic feet of gas; would take me up easily, I calculated, with all my implements, and, if I managed rightly, with one hundred and seventy-five pounds of ballast into the bargain. It had received three coats of varnish, and I found the cambric muslin to answer all the purposes of silk itself, quite as strong and a good deal less expensive.

'Everything being now ready, I exacted from my wife an oath of secrecy in relation to all my actions from the day of my first visit to the bookseller's stall; and promising, on my part, to return as soon as circumstances would permit, I gave her what little money I had left, and bade her farewell. Indeed I had no fear on her account. She was what people call a notable woman, and could manage matters in the world without my assistance. I believe, to tell the truth, she always looked upon me as an idle boy, a mere make-weight, good for nothing but building castles in the air, and was rather glad to get rid of me. It was a dark night when I bade her goodbye, and taking with me, as aides-de-camp, the three creditors who had given me so much trouble, we carried the balloon, with the car and accoutrements, by a roundabout way, to the station where the other articles were deposited. We there found them all unmolested, and I proceeded immediately to business.

'It was the first of April. The night, as I said before, was dark; there was not a star to be seen; and a drizzling rain, falling at intervals, rendered us very uncomfortable. But my chief anxiety was concerning the balloon, which, in spite of the varnish with which it was defended, began to grow rather heavy with the moisture; the powder also was liable to damage. I therefore kept my three duns working with great diligence, pounding down ice around the central cask, and stirring the acid in the others. They did not cease, however, importuning me with questions as to what I intended to do with all this apparatus, and expressed much dissatisfaction at the terrible labour I made them undergo. They could not perceive, so they said, what good was likely to result from their getting wet to the skin, merely to take a part in such horrible incantations. I began to get uneasy, and worked away with all my might, for I verily believe the idiots supposed that I had entered into a compact with the devil, and that, in short, what I was now doing was nothing better than it should be. I was, therefore, in great fear of their leaving me altogether. I contrived, however, to pacify them by promises of payment of all scores in full, as soon as I could bring the present business to a termination. To these speeches they gave, of course, their own interpretation; fancying, no doubt, that at all events I should come into possession of vast quantities of ready money; and provided I paid them all I owed, and a trifle more, in consideration of their services, I dare say they cared very little what became of either my soul or my carcass.

'In about four hours and a half I found the balloon sufficiently inflated. I attached the car, therefore, and put all my implements in it – not forgetting the condensing apparatus, a copious supply of water, and a large quantity of provisions, such as pemmican, in which much nutriment is contained in comparatively little bulk. I also secured in the car a pair of pigeons and a cat. It was now nearly daybreak, and I thought it high time to take my departure. Dropping a lighted cigar on the ground, as if by accident, I took the opportunity, in stooping to pick it up, of igniting privately the piece of slow match, whose end, as I said before, protruded a very little beyond the lower rim of one of the smaller casks. This manoeuvre was totally unperceived on the part of the three duns; and, jumping into the car, I immediately cut the single cord which held me to the earth, and was pleased to find that I shot upward, carrying with all ease one hundred and seventy-five pounds of leaden ballast, and able to have carried up as many more.

'Scarcely, however, had I attained the height of fifty yards, when, roaring and rumbling up after me in the most horrible and tumultuous manner, came so dense a hurricane of fire, and smoke, and sulphur, and legs and arms, and gravel, and burning wood, and blazing metal, that my very heart sunk within me, and I fell down in the bottom of the car, trembling with unmitigated terror. Indeed, I now perceived that I had entirely overdone the business, and that the main consequences of the shock were yet to be experienced. Accordingly, in less than a second, I felt all the blood in my body rushing to my temples, and immediately thereupon, a concussion, which I shall never forget, burst abruptly through the night and seemed to rip the very firmament asunder. When I afterwards had time for reflection, I did not fail to attribute the extreme violence of the explosion, as regarded myself, to its proper cause – my situation directly above it, and in the line of its greatest power. But at the time, I thought only of preserving my life. The balloon at first collapsed, then furiously expanded, then whirled round and round with horrible velocity, and finally, reeling and staggering like a drunken man, hurled me with great force over the rim of the car, and left me dangling, at a terrific height, with my head downwards, and my face outwards, by a piece of slender cord about three feet in length, which hung accidentally through a crevice near the bottom of the wicker-work, and in which, as I fell, my left foot became most providentially entangled. It is impossible – utterly impossible – to form any adequate idea of the horror of my situation. I gasped convulsively for breath – a shudder resembling a fit of the ague agitated every nerve and muscle of my frame – I felt my eyes starting from their sockets – a horrible nausea overwhelmed me – and at length I fainted away.

'How long I remained in this state it is impossible to say. It must, however, have been no inconsiderable time, for when I partially recovered the sense of existence, I found the day breaking, the balloon at a prodigious height over a wilderness of ocean, and not a trace of land to be discovered far and wide within the limits of the vast horizon. My sensations, however, upon thus recovering, were by no means so rife with agony as might have been anticipated. Indeed, there was much of incipient madness in the calm survey which I began to take of my situation. I drew up to my eyes each of my hands, one after the other, and wondered what occurrence could have given rise to the swelling of the veins, and the horrible blackness of the fingernails. I afterwards carefully examined my head, shaking it repeatedly, and feeling it with minute attention, until I succeeded in satisfying myself that it was not, as I had more than half suspected, larger than my balloon. Then, in a knowing manner, I felt in both my breeches pockets, and, missing therefrom a set of tablets and a toothpick case, endeavoured to account for their disappearance, and not being able to do so, felt inexpressibly chagrined. It now occurred to me that I suffered great uneasiness in the joint of my left ankle, and a dim consciousness of my situation began to glimmer through my mind. But, strange to say! I was neither astonished nor horror-stricken. If I felt any emotion at all, it was a kind of chuckling satisfaction at the cleverness I was about to display in extricating myself from this dilemma; and I never, for a moment, looked upon my ultimate safety as a question susceptible of doubt. For a few minutes I remained wrapped in the profoundest meditation. I have a distinct recollection of frequently compressing my lips, putting my forefinger to the side of my nose, and making use of other gesticulations and grimaces common to men who, at ease in their armchairs, meditate upon matters of intricacy or importance. Having, as I thought, sufficiently collected my ideas, I now, with great caution and deliberation, put my hands behind my back, and unfastened the large iron buckle which belonged to the waistband of my inexpressibles. This buckle had three teeth, which, being somewhat rusty, turned with great difficulty on their axis. I brought them, however, after some trouble, at right angles to the body of the buckle, and was glad to find them remain firm in that position. Holding the instrument thus obtained within my teeth, I now proceeded to untie the knot of my cravat. I had to rest several times before I could accomplish this manoeuvre, but it was at length accomplished. To one end of the cravat I then made fast the buckle, and the other end I tied, for greater security, tightly around my wrist. Drawing now my body upwards, with a prodigious exertion of muscular force, I succeeded, at the very first trial, in throwing the buckle over the car, and entangling it, as I had anticipated, in the circular rim of the wickerwork.

'My body was now inclined towards the side of the car, at an angle of about forty-five degrees; but it must not be understood that I was therefore only forty-five degrees below the perpendicular. So far from it, I still lay nearly level with the plane of the horizon; for the change of situation which I had acquired, had forced the bottom of the car considerably outwards from my position, which was accordingly one of the most imminent and deadly peril. It should be remembered, however, that when I fell in the first instance, from the car, if I had fallen with my face turned towards the balloon, instead of turned outwardly from it, as it actually was; or if, in the second place, the cord by which I was suspended had chanced to hang over the upper edge, instead of through a crevice near the bottom of the car – I say it may be readily conceived that, in either of these supposed cases, I should have been unable to accomplish even as much as I had now accomplished, and the wonderful adventures of Hans Pfaall would have been utterly lost to posterity. I had therefore every reason to be grateful; although, in point of fact, I was still too stupid to be anything at all, and hung for, perhaps, a quarter of an hour in that extraordinary manner, without making the slightest farther exertion whatsoever, and in a singularly tranquil state of idiotic enjoyment. But this feeling did not fail to die rapidly away, and thereunto succeeded horror, and dismay, and a chilling sense of utter helplessness and ruin. In fact, the blood so long accumulating in the vessels of my head and throat, and which had hitherto buoyed up my spirits with madness and delirium, had now begun to retire within their proper channels, and the distinctness which was thus added to my perception of the danger, merely served to deprive me of the self-possession and courage to encounter it. But this weakness was, luckily for me, of no very long duration. In good time came to my rescue the spirit of despair, and, with frantic cries and struggles, I jerked my way bodily upwards, till at length, clutching with a vice-like grip the long-desired rim, I writhed my person over it, and fell headlong and shuddering within the car.

'It was not until some time afterwards that I recovered myself sufficiently to attend to the ordinary cares of the balloon. I then, however, examined it with attention, and found it, to my great relief, uninjured. My implements were all safe, and, fortunately, I had lost neither ballast nor provisions. Indeed, I had so well secured them in their places, that such an accident was entirely out of the question. Looking at my watch, I found it six o'clock. I was still rapidly ascending, and my barometer gave a present altitude of three and three-quarter miles. Immediately beneath me in the ocean, lay a small black object, slightly oblong in shape, seemingly about the size, and in every way bearing a great resemblance to one of those childish toys called a domino. Bringing my telescope to bear upon it, I plainly discerned it to be a British ninety-four-gun ship, close-hauled, and pitching heavily in the sea with her head to the west-sou'west. Besides this ship, I saw nothing but the ocean and the sky, and the sun, which had long arisen.

'It is now high time that I should explain to your Excellencies the object of my perilous voyage. Your Excellencies will bear in mind that distressed circumstances in Rotterdam had at length driven me to the resolution of committing suicide. It was not, however, that to life itself I had any positive disgust, but that I was harassed beyond endurance by the adventitious miseries attending my situation. In this state of mind, wishing to live, yet wearied with life, the treatise at the stall of the bookseller opened a resource to my imagination. I then finally made up my mind. I determined to depart, yet live – to leave the world, yet continue to exist – in short, to drop enigmas, I resolved, let what would ensue, to force a passage, if I could, to the moon. Now, lest I should be supposed more of a madman than I actually am, I will detail, as well as I am able, the considerations which led me to believe that an achievement of this nature, although without doubt difficult, and incontestably full of danger, was not absolutely, to a bold spirit, beyond the confines of the possible.

'The moon's actual distance from the earth was the first thing to be attended to. Now, the mean or average interval between the centres of the two planets is 59.9643 of the earth's equatorial radii, or only about 237,000 miles. I say the mean or average interval. But it must be borne in mind that the form of the moon's orbit being an ellipse of eccentricity amounting to no less than 0.05484 of the major semi-axis of the ellipse itself, and the earth's centre being situated in its focus, if I could, in any manner, contrive to meet the moon, as it were, in its perigee, the above-mentioned distance would be materially diminished. But, to say nothing at present of this possibility, it was very certain that, at all events, from the 237,000 miles I would have to deduct the radius of the earth, say 4,000, and the radius of the moon, say 1,080, in all 5,080, leaving an actual interval to be traversed, under average circumstances, of 231,920 miles. Now this, I reflected, was no very extraordinary distance. Travelling on land has been repeatedly accomplished at the rate of thirty miles per hour, and indeed a much greater speed may be anticipated. But even at this velocity, it would take me no more than 322 days to reach the surface of the moon. There were, however, many particulars inducing me to believe that my average rate of travelling might possibly very much exceed that of thirty miles per hour, and, as these considerations did not fail to make a deep impression upon my mind, I will mention them more fully hereafter.

'The next point to be regarded was a matter of far greater importance. From indications afforded by the barometer, we find that, in ascensions from the surface of the earth we have, at the height of 1,000 feet, left below us about one-thirtieth of the entire mass of atmospheric air, that at 10,600 we have ascended through nearly one-third; and that at 18,000, which is not far from the elevation of Cotopaxi, we have surmounted one half of the material, or, at all events, one half of the ponderable, body of air incumbent upon our globe. It is also calculated that at an altitude not exceeding the hundredth part of the earth's diameter – that is, not exceeding eighty miles – the rarefaction would be so excessive that animal life could in no manner be sustained, and, moreover, that the most delicate means we possess of ascertaining the presence of the atmosphere would be inadequate to assure us of its existence. But I did not fail to perceive that these latter calculations are founded altogether on our experimental knowledge of the properties of air, and the mechanical laws regulating its dilation and compression, in what may be called, comparatively speaking, the immediate vicinity of the earth itself; and, at the same time, it is taken for granted that animal life is and must be essentially incapable of modification at any given unattainable distance from the surface. Now, all such reasoning and from such data must, of course, be simply analogical. The greatest height ever reached by man was that of 25,000 feet, attained in the aeronautic expedition of Messieurs Gay-Lussac and Biot. This is a moderate altitude, even when compared with the eighty miles in question; and I could not help thinking that the subject admitted room for doubt and great latitude for speculation.

'But, in point of fact, an ascension being made to any given altitude, the ponderable quantity of air surmounted in any farther ascension is by no means in proportion to the additional height ascended (as may be plainly seen from what has been stated before), but in a ratio constantly decreasing. It is therefore evident that, ascend as high as we may, we cannot, literally speaking, arrive at a limit beyond which no atmosphere is to be found. It must exist, I argued; although it may exist in a state of infinite rarefaction.

'On the other hand, I was aware that arguments have not been wanting to prove the existence of a real and definite limit to the atmosphere, beyond which there is absolutely no air whatsoever. But a circumstance which has been left out of view by those who contend for such a limit seemed to me, although no positive refutation of their creed, still a point worthy very serious investigation. On comparing the intervals between the successive arrivals of Encke's comet at its perihelion, after giving credit, in the most exact manner, for all the disturbances due to the attractions of the planets, it appears that the periods are gradually diminishing; that is to say, the major axis of the comet's ellipse is growing shorter, in a slow but perfectly regular decrease. Now, this is precisely what ought to be the case, if we suppose a resistance experienced from the comet from an extremely rare ethereal medium pervading the regions of its orbit. For it is evident that such a medium must, in retarding the comet's velocity, increase its centripetal, by weakening its centrifugal, force. In other words, the sun's attraction would be constantly attaining greater power, and the comet would be drawn nearer at every revolution. Indeed, there is no other way of accounting for the variation in question. But again: the real diameter of the same comet's nebulosity is observed to contract rapidly as it approaches the sun, and dilate with equal rapidity in its departure towards its aphelion. Was I not justified in supposing with M. Valz, that this apparent condensation of volume has its origin in the compression of the same ethereal medium I have spoken of before, and which is only denser in proportion to its solar vicinity? The lenticular-shaped phenomenon, also called the zodiacal light, was a matter worthy of attention. This radiance, so apparent in the tropics, and which cannot be mistaken for any meteoric lustre, extends from the horizon obliquely upwards, and follows generally the direction of the sun's equator. It appeared to me evidently in the nature of a rare atmosphere extending from the sun outwards, beyond the orbit of Venus at least, and I believed indefinitely farther. Indeed, this medium I could not suppose confined to the path of the comet's ellipse, or to the immediate neighbourhood of the sun. It was easy, on the contrary, to imagine it pervading the entire regions of our planetary system, condensed into what we call atmosphere at the planets themselves, and perhaps at some of them modified by considerations, so to speak, purely geological.

'Having adopted this view of the subject, I had little further hesitation. Granting that on my passage I should meet with atmosphere essentially the same as at the surface of the earth, I conceived that, by means of the very ingenious apparatus of M. Grimm, I should readily be enabled to condense it in sufficient quantity for the purposes of respiration. This would remove the chief obstacle in a journey to the moon. I had indeed spent some money and great labour in adapting the apparatus to the object intended, and confidently looked forward to its successful application, if I could manage to complete the voyage within any reasonable period. This brings me back to the rate at which it might be possible to travel.

'It is true that balloons, in the first stage of their ascensions from the earth, are known to rise with a velocity comparatively moderate. Now, the power of elevation lies altogether in the superior lightness of the gas in the balloon compared with the atmospheric air; and, at first sight, it does not appear probable that, as the balloon acquires altitude, and consequently arrives successively in atmospheric strata of densities rapidly diminishing – I say, it does not appear at all reasonable that, in this its progress upwards, the original velocity should be accelerated. On the other hand, I was not aware that, in any recorded ascension, a diminution was apparent in the absolute rate of ascent; although such should have been the case, if on account of nothing else, on account of the escape of gas through balloons ill-constructed, and varnished with no better material than the ordinary varnish. It seemed, therefore, that the effect of such escape was only sufficient to counterbalance the effect of some accelerating power. I now considered that, provided in my passage I found the medium I had imagined, and provided that it should prove to be actually and essentially what we denominate atmospheric air, it could make comparatively little difference at what extreme state of rarefaction I should discover it – that is to say, in regard to my power of ascending – for the gas in the balloon would not only be itself subject to rarefaction partially similar (in proportion to the occurrence of which, I could suffer an escape of so much as would be requisite to prevent explosion), but, being what it was, would, at all events, continue specifically lighter than any compound whatever of mere nitrogen and oxygen. In the meantime, the force of gravitation would be constantly diminishing, in proportion to the squares of the distances, and thus, with a velocity prodigiously accelerating, I should at length arrive in those distant regions where the force of the earth's attraction would be superseded by that of the moon. In accordance with these ideas, I did not think it worth while to encumber myself with more provisions than would be sufficient for a period of forty days.

'There was still, however, another difficulty, which occasioned me some little disquietude. It has been observed, that, in balloon ascensions to any considerable height, besides the pain attending respiration, great uneasiness is experienced about the head and body, often accompanied with bleeding at the nose, and other symptoms of an alarming kind, and growing more and more inconvenient in proportion to the altitude attained. This was a reflection of a nature somewhat startling. Was it not probable that these symptoms would increase indefinitely, or at least until terminated by death itself? I finally thought not. Their origin was to be looked for in the progressive removal of the customary atmospheric pressure upon the surface of the body, and consequent distention of the superficial blood-vessels – not in any positive disorganisation of the animal system, as in the case of difficulty in breathing, where the atmospheric density is chemically insufficient for the due renovation of blood in a ventricle of the heart. Unless for default of this renovation, I could see no reason, therefore, why life could not be sustained even in a vacuum; for the expansion and compression of chest, commonly called breathing, is action purely muscular, and the cause, not the effect, of respiration. In a word, I conceived that, as the body should become habituated to the want of atmospheric pressure, the sensations of pain would gradually diminish – and to endure them while they continued, I relied with confidence upon the iron hardihood of my constitution.

'Thus, may it please your Excellencies, I have detailed some, though by no means all, the considerations which led me to form the project of a lunar voyage. I shall now proceed to lay before you the result of an attempt so apparently audacious in conception, and, at all events, so utterly unparalleled in the annals of mankind.

'Having attained the altitude before mentioned, that is to say three miles and three-quarters, I threw out from the car a quantity of feathers, and found that I still ascended with sufficient rapidity; there was, therefore, no necessity for discharging any ballast. I was glad of this, for I wished to retain with me as much weight as I could carry, for reasons which will be explained in the sequel. I as yet suffered no bodily inconvenience, breathing with great freedom, and feeling no pain whatever in the head. The cat was lying very demurely upon my coat, which I had taken off, and eyeing the pigeons with an air of nonchalance. These latter being tied by the leg, to prevent their escape, were busily employed in picking up some grains of rice scattered for them in the bottom of the car.

'At twenty minutes past six o'clock, the barometer showed an elevation of 26,400 feet, or five miles to a fraction. The prospect seemed unbounded. Indeed, it is very easily calculated by means of spherical geometry, what a great extent of the earth's area I beheld. The convex surface of any segment of a sphere is, to the entire surface of the sphere itself, as the versed sine of the segment to the diameter of the sphere. Now, in my case, the versed sine – that is to say, the thickness of the segment beneath me – was about equal to my elevation, or the elevation of the point of sight above the surface. "As five miles, then, to eight thousand", would express the proportion of the earth's area seen by me. In other words, I beheld as much as a sixteen-hundredth part of the whole surface of the globe. The sea appeared unruffled as a mirror, although, by means of the spyglass, I could perceive it to be in a state of violent agitation. The ship was no longer visible, having drifted away, apparently to the eastward. I now began to experience, at intervals, severe pain in the head, especially about the ears – still, however, breathing with tolerable freedom. The cat and pigeons seemed to suffer no inconvenience whatsoever.

'At twenty minutes before seven, the balloon entered a long series of dense cloud, which put me to great trouble, by damaging my condensing apparatus and wetting me to the skin. This was, to be sure, a singular *rencontre*, for I had not believed it possible that a cloud of this nature could be sustained at so great an elevation. I thought it best, however, to throw out two five-pound pieces of ballast, reserving still a weight of one hundred and sixty-five pounds. Upon so doing, I soon rose above the difficulty, and perceived immediately, that I had obtained a great increase in my rate of ascent. In a few seconds after my leaving the cloud, a flash of vivid lightning shot from one end of it to the other, and caused it to kindle up, throughout its vast extent, like a mass of ignited and glowing charcoal. This, it must be remembered, was in the broad light of day. No fancy may picture the sublimity which might have been exhibited by a similar phenomenon taking place amid the darkness of the night. Hell itself might have been found a fitting image. Even as it was, my hair stood on end, while I gazed afar down within the yawning abysses, letting imagination descend, as it were, and stalk about in the strange vaulted halls, and ruddy gulfs, and red ghastly chasms of the hideous and unfathomable fire. I had indeed made a narrow escape. Had the balloon remained a very short while longer within the cloud – that is to say, had not the inconvenience of getting wet determined me to discharge the ballast – inevitable ruin would have been the consequence. Such perils, although little considered, are perhaps the greatest which must be encountered in balloons. I had by this time, however, attained too great an elevation to be any longer uneasy on this head.

'I was now rising rapidly, and by seven o'clock the barometer indicated an altitude of no less than nine miles and a half. I began to find great difficulty in drawing my breath. My head, too, was excessively painful; and, having felt for some time a moisture about my cheeks, I at length discovered it to be blood, which was oozing quite fast from the drums of my ears. My eyes, also, gave me great uneasiness. Upon passing the hand over them they seemed to have protruded from their sockets in no inconsiderable degree; and all objects in the car, and even the balloon itself, appeared distorted to my vision. These symptoms were more than I had expected, and occasioned me some alarm. At this juncture, very imprudently, and without consideration, I threw out from the car three five-pound pieces of ballast. The accelerated rate of ascent thus obtained carried me too rapidly, and without sufficient gradation, into a highly rarefied stratum of the atmosphere, and the result had nearly proved fatal to my expedition and to myself. I was suddenly seized with a spasm which lasted for more than five minutes, and even when this, in a measure, ceased, I could catch my breath only at long intervals, and in a gasping manner – bleeding all the while copiously at the nose and ears, and even slightly at the eyes. The pigeons appeared distressed in the extreme, and struggled to escape; while the cat mewed piteously, and, with her tongue hanging out of her mouth, staggered to and fro in the car as if under the influence of poison. I now too late discovered the great rashness of which I had been guilty in discharging the ballast, and my agitation was excessive. I anticipated nothing less than death, and death in a few minutes. The physical suffering I underwent contributed also to render me nearly incapable of making any exertion for the preservation of my life. I had, indeed, little power of reflection left, and the violence of the pain in my head seemed to be greatly on the increase. Thus I found that my senses would shortly give way altogether, and I had already clutched one of the valve ropes with the view of attempting a descent, when the recollection of the trick I had played the three creditors, and the possible consequences to myself, should I return, operated to deter me for the moment. I lay down in the bottom of the car, and endeavoured to collect my faculties. In this I so far succeeded as to determine upon the experiment of losing blood. Having no lancet, however, I was constrained to perform the operation in the best manner I was able, and finally succeeded in opening a vein in my right arm, with the blade of my penknife. The blood had hardly commenced flowing when I experienced a sensible relief, and by the time I had lost about half a moderate basin full, most of the worst symptoms had abandoned me entirely. I nevertheless did not think it expedient to attempt getting on my feet immediately; but, having tied up my arm as well as I could, I lay still for about a quarter of an hour. At the end of this time I arose, and found myself freer from absolute pain of any kind than I had been during the last hour and a quarter of my ascension. The difficulty of breathing, however, was diminished in a very slight degree, and I found that it would soon be positively necessary to make use of my condenser. In the meantime, looking towards the cat, who was again snugly stowed away upon my coat, I discovered, to my infinite surprise, that she had taken the opportunity of my indisposition to bring into light a litter of three little kittens. This was an addition to the number of passengers on my part altogether unexpected; but I was pleased at the occurrence. It would afford me a chance of bringing to a kind of test the truth of a surmise, which, more than anything else, had influenced me in attempting this ascension. I had imagined that the habitual endurance of the atmospheric pressure at the surface of the earth was the cause, or nearly so, of the pain attending animal existence at a distance above the surface. Should the kittens be found to suffer uneasiness in an equal degree with their mother, I must consider my theory in fault, but a failure to do so I should look upon as a strong confirmation of my idea.

'By eight o'clock I had actually attained an elevation of seventeen miles above the surface of the earth. Thus it seemed to me evident that my rate of ascent was not only on the increase, but that the progression would have been apparent in a slight degree even had I not discharged the ballast which I did. The pains in my head and ears returned, at intervals, with violence, and I still continued to bleed occasionally at the nose; but, upon the whole, I suffered much less than might have been expected. I breathed, however, at every moment, with more and more difficulty, and each inhalation was attended with a troublesome spasmodic action of the chest. I now unpacked the condensing apparatus, and got it ready for immediate use.

'The view of the earth, at this period of my ascension, was beautiful indeed. To the westward, the northward, and the southward, as far as I could see, lay a boundless sheet of apparently unruffled ocean, which every moment gained a deeper and a deeper tint of blue and began already to assume a slight appearance of convexity. At a vast distance to the eastward, although perfectly discernible, extended the islands of Great Britain, the entire Atlantic coasts of France and Spain, with a small portion of the northern part of the continent of Africa. Of individual edifices not a trace could be discovered, and the proudest cities of mankind had utterly faded away from the face of the earth. From the rock of Gibraltar, now dwindled into a dim speck, the dark Mediterranean sea, dotted with shining islands as the heaven is dotted with stars, spread itself out to the eastward as far as my vision extended, until its entire mass of waters seemed at length to tumble headlong over the abyss of the horizon, and I found myself listening on tiptoe for the echoes of the mighty cataract. Overhead, the sky was of a jetty black, and the stars were brilliantly visible.

'The pigeons about this time seeming to undergo much suffering, I determined upon giving them their liberty. I first untied one of them, a beautiful grey-mottled pigeon, and placed him upon the rim of the wickerwork. He appeared extremely uneasy, looking anxiously around him, fluttering his wings, and making a loud cooing noise, but could not be persuaded to trust himself from off the car. I took him up at last, and threw him to about half a dozen yards from the balloon. He made, however, no attempt to descend as I had expected, but struggled with great vehemence to get back, uttering at the same time very shrill and piercing cries. He at length succeeded in regaining his former station on the rim, but had hardly done so when his head dropped upon his breast, and he fell dead within the car. The other one did not prove so unfortunate. To prevent his following the example of his companion, and accomplishing a return, I threw him downwards with all my force, and was pleased to find him continue his descent, with great velocity, making use of his wings with ease, and in a perfectly natural manner. In a very short time he was out of sight, and I have no doubt he reached home in safety. Puss, who seemed in a great measure recovered from her illness, now made a hearty meal of the dead bird and then went to sleep with much apparent satisfaction. Her kittens were quite lively, and so far evinced not the slightest sign of any uneasiness whatever.

'At a quarter-past eight, being no longer able to draw breath without the most intolerable pain, I proceeded forthwith to adjust around the car the apparatus belonging to the condenser. This apparatus will require some little explanation, and your Excellencies will please to bear in mind that my object, in the first place, was to surround myself and cat entirely with a barricade against the highly rarefied atmosphere in which I was existing, with the intention of introducing within this barricade, by means of my condenser, a quantity of this same atmosphere sufficiently condensed for the purposes of respiration. With this object in view I had prepared a very strong, perfectly air-tight, but flexible gum-elastic bag. In this bag, which was of sufficient dimensions, the entire car was in a manner placed. That is to say, it (the bag) was drawn over the whole bottom of the car, up its sides, and so on, along the outside of the ropes, to the upper rim or hoop where the network is attached. Having pulled the bag up in this way, and formed a complete enclosure on all sides, and at bottom, it was now necessary to fasten up its top or mouth, by passing its material over the hoop of the network – in other words, between the network and the hoop. But if the network were separated from the hoop to admit this passage, what was to sustain the car in the meantime? Now the network was not permanently fastened to the hoop, but attached by a series of running loops or nooses. I therefore undid only a few of these loops at one time, leaving the car suspended by the remainder. Having thus inserted a portion of the cloth forming the upper part of the bag, I refastened the loops – not to the hoop, for that would have been impossible, since the cloth now intervened – but to a series of large buttons, affixed to the cloth itself, about three feet below the mouth of the bag, the intervals between the buttons having been made to correspond to the intervals between the loops. This done, a few more of the loops were unfastened from the rim, a farther portion of the cloth introduced, and the disengaged loops then connected with their proper buttons. In this way it was possible to insert the whole upper part of the bag between the network and the hoop. It is evident that the hoop would now drop down within the car, while the whole weight of the car itself, with all its contents, would be held up merely by the strength of the buttons. This, at first sight, would seem an inadequate dependence; but it was by no means so, for the buttons were not only very strong in themselves, but so close together that a very slight portion of the whole weight was supported by any one of them. Indeed, had the car and contents been three times heavier than they were, I should not have been at all uneasy. I now raised up the hoop again within the covering of gum-elastic, and propped it at nearly its former height by means of three light poles prepared for the occasion. This was done, of course, to keep the bag distended at the top, and to preserve the lower part of the network in its proper situation. All that now remained was to fasten up the mouth of the enclosure; and this was readily accomplished by gathering the folds of the material together, and twisting them up very tightly on the inside by means of a kind of stationary tourniquet.

'In the sides of the covering thus adjusted round the car, had been inserted three circular panes of thick but clear glass, through which I could see without difficulty around me in every horizontal direction. In that portion of the cloth forming the bottom was likewise a fourth window, of the same kind, and corresponding with a small aperture in the floor of the car itself. This enabled me to see perpendicularly down, but having found it impossible to place any similar contrivance overhead, on account of the peculiar manner of closing up the opening there, and the consequent wrinkles in the cloth, I could expect to see no objects situated directly in my zenith. This, of course, was a matter of little consequence; for had I even been able to place a window at top, the balloon itself would have prevented my making any use of it.

'About a foot below one of the side windows was a circular opening, eight inches in diameter, and fitted with a brass rim adapted in its inner edge to the windings of a screw. In this rim was screwed the large tube of the condenser, the body of the machine being, of course, within the chamber of gum-elastic. Through this tube a quantity of the rare atmosphere circumjacent being drawn by means of a vacuum created in the body of the machine, was thence discharged, in a state of condensation, to mingle with the thin air already in the chamber. This operation being repeated several times, at length filled the chamber with atmosphere proper for all the purposes of respiration. But in so confined a space it would, in a short time, necessarily become foul, and unfit for use from frequent contact with the lungs. It was then ejected by a small valve at the bottom of the car – the dense air readily sinking into the thinner atmosphere below. To avoid the inconvenience of making a total vacuum at any moment within the chamber, this purification was never accomplished all at once, but in a gradual manner – the valve being opened only for a few seconds, then closed again, until one or two strokes from the pump of the condenser had supplied the place of the atmosphere ejected. For the sake of experiment I had put the cat and kittens in a small basket, and suspended it outside the car to a button at the bottom, close by the valve, through which I could feed them at any moment when necessary. I did this at some little risk, and before closing the mouth of the chamber, by reaching under the car with one of the poles before mentioned to which a hook had been attached.

'By the time I had fully completed these arrangements and filled the chamber as explained, it wanted only ten minutes of nine o'clock. During the whole period of my being thus employed, I endured the most terrible distress from difficulty of respiration, and bitterly did I repent the negligence, or rather foolhardiness, of which I had been guilty, of putting off to the last moment a matter of so much importance. But having at length accomplished it, I soon began to reap the benefit of my invention. Once again I breathed with perfect freedom and ease – and indeed why should I not? I was also agreeably surprised to find myself, in a great measure, relieved from the violent pains which had hitherto tormented me. A slight headache, accompanied with a sensation of fullness or distention about the wrists, the ankles, and the throat, was nearly all of which I had now to complain. Thus it seemed evident that a greater part of the uneasiness attending the removal of atmospheric pressure had actually worn off, as I had expected, and that much of the pain endured for the last two hours should have been attributed altogether to the effects of a deficient respiration.

'At twenty minutes before nine o'clock – that is to say, a short time prior to my closing up the mouth of the chamber, the mercury attained its limit, or ran down, in the barometer, which, as I mentioned before, was one of an extended construction. It then indicated an altitude on my part of 132,000 feet, or five-and-twenty miles, and I consequently surveyed at that time an extent of the earth's area amounting to no less than the three-hundred-and-twentieth part of its entire superficies. At nine o'clock I had again lost sight of land to the eastward, but not before I became aware that the balloon was drifting rapidly to the nor'nor-west. The convexity of the ocean beneath me was very evident indeed, although my view was often interrupted by the masses of cloud which floated to and fro. I observed now that even the lightest vapours never rose to more than ten miles above the level of the sea.

'At half-past nine I tried the experiment of throwing out a handful of feathers through the valve. They did not float as I had expected; but dropped down perpendicularly, like a bullet, *en masse*, and with the greatest velocity – being out of sight in a very few seconds. I did not at first know what to make of this extraordinary phenomenon; not being able to believe that my rate of ascent had, of a sudden, met with so prodigious an acceleration. But it soon occurred to me that the atmosphere was now far too rare to sustain even the feathers; that they actually fell, as they appeared to do, with great rapidity; and that I had been surprised by the united velocities of their descent and my own elevation.

'By ten o'clock I found that I had very little to occupy my immediate attention. Affairs went swimmingly, and I believed the balloon to be going upwards with a speed increasing momently although I had no longer any means of ascertaining the progression of the increase. I suffered no pain or uneasiness of any kind, and enjoyed better spirits than I had at any period since my departure from Rotterdam, busying myself now in examining the state of my various apparatus, and now in regenerating the atmosphere within the chamber. This latter point I determined to attend to at regular intervals of forty minutes, more on account of the preservation of my health, than from so frequent a renovation being absolutely necessary. In the meanwhile I could not help making anticipations. Fancy revelled in the wild and dreamy regions of the moon. Imagination, feeling herself for once unshackled, roamed at will among the ever-changing wonders of a shadowy and unstable land. Now there were hoary and time-honoured forests, and craggy precipices, and waterfalls tumbling with a loud noise into abysses without a bottom. Then I came suddenly into still noonday solitudes, where no wind of heaven ever intruded, and where vast meadows of poppies, and slender, lily-looking flowers spread themselves out a weary distance, all silent and motionless for ever. Then again I journeyed far down away into another country where it was all one dim and vague lake, with a boundary line of clouds. And out of this melancholy water arose a forest of tall eastern trees, like a wilderness of dreams. And I have in mind that the shadows of the trees which fell upon the lake remained not on the surface where they fell, but sunk slowly and steadily down, and commingled with the waves, while from the trunks of the trees other shadows were continually coming out, and taking the place of their brothers thus entombed. "This then," I said thoughtfully, "is the very reason why the waters of this lake grow blacker with age, and more melancholy as the hours run on." But fancies such as these were not the sole possessors of my brain. Horrors of a nature most stern and most appalling would too frequently obtrude themselves upon my mind, and shake the innermost depths of my soul with the bare supposition of their possibility. Yet I would not suffer my thoughts for any length of time to dwell upon these latter speculations, rightly judging the real and palpable dangers of the voyage sufficient for my undivided attention.

'At five o'clock p.m., being engaged in regenerating the atmosphere within the chamber, I took that opportunity of observing the cat and kittens through the valve. The cat herself appeared to suffer again very much, and I had no hesitation in attributing her uneasiness chiefly to a difficulty in breathing; but my experiment with the kittens had resulted very strangely. I had expected, of course, to see them betray a sense of pain, although in a less degree than their mother, and this would have been sufficient to confirm my opinion concerning the habitual endurance of atmospheric pressure. But I was not prepared to find them, upon close examination, evidently enjoying a high degree of health, breathing with the greatest ease and perfect regularity, and evincing not the slightest sign of any uneasiness whatever. I could only account for all this by extending my theory, and supposing that the highly rarefied atmosphere around might perhaps not be, as I had taken for granted, chemically insufficient for the purposes of life, and that a person born in such a medium might, possibly, be unaware of any inconvenience attending its inhalation, while, upon removal to the denser strata near the earth, he might endure tortures of a similar nature to those I had so lately experienced. It has since been to me a matter of deep regret that an awkward accident, at this time, occasioned me the loss of my little family of cats, and deprived me of the insight into this matter which a continued experiment might have afforded. In passing my hand through the valve, with a cup of water for the old puss, the sleeves of my shirt became entangled in the loop which sustained the basket, and thus, in a moment, loosened it from the bottom. Had the whole actually vanished into air, it could not have shot from my sight in a more abrupt and instantaneous manner. Positively, there could not have intervened the tenth part of a second between the disengagement of the basket and its absolute and total disappearance with all that it contained. My good wishes followed it to the earth, but of course, I had no hope that either cat or kittens would ever live to tell the tale of their misfortune.

'At six o'clock, I perceived a great portion of the earth's visible area to the eastward involved in thick shadow, which continued to advance with great rapidity, until, at five minutes before seven, the whole surface in view was enveloped in the darkness of night. It was not, however, until long after this time that the rays of the setting sun ceased to illumine the balloon; and this circumstance, although of course fully anticipated, did not fail to give me an infinite deal of pleasure. It was evident that, in the morning, I should behold the rising luminary many hours at least before the citizens of Rotterdam, in spite of their situation so much farther to the eastward, and thus, day after day, in proportion to the height ascended, would I enjoy the light of the sun for a longer and a longer period. I now determined to keep a journal of my passage, reckoning the days from one to twenty-four hours continuously, without taking into consideration the intervals of darkness.

'At ten o'clock, feeling sleepy, I determined to lie down for the rest of the night; but here a difficulty presented itself, which, obvious as it may appear, had escaped my attention up to the very moment of which I am now speaking. If I went to sleep as I proposed, how could the atmosphere in the chamber be regenerated in the interim? To breathe it for more than an hour, at the farthest, would be a matter of impossibility, or, if even this term could be extended to an hour and a quarter, the most ruinous consequences might ensue. The consideration of this dilemma gave me no little disquietude; and it will hardly be believed, that, after the dangers I had undergone, I should look upon this business in so serious a light, as to give up all hope of accomplishing my ultimate design, and finally make up my mind to the necessity of a descent. But this hesitation was only momentary. I reflected that man is the veriest slave of custom, and that many points in the routine of his existence are deemed essentially important, which are only so at all by his having rendered them habitual. It was very certain that I could not do without sleep; but I might easily bring myself to feel no inconvenience from being awakened at intervals of an hour during the whole period of my repose. It would require but five minutes at most to regenerate the atmosphere in the fullest manner, and the only real difficulty was to contrive a method of arousing myself at the proper moment for so doing. But this was a question which, I am willing to confess, occasioned me no little trouble in its solution. To be sure, I had heard of the student who, to prevent his falling asleep over his books, held in one hand a ball of copper, the din of whose descent into a basin of the same metal on the floor beside his chair, served effectually to startle him up, if, at any moment, he should be overcome with drowsiness. My own case, however, was very different indeed, and left me no room for any similar idea; for I did not wish to keep awake, but to be aroused from slumber at regular intervals of time. I at length hit upon the following expedient, which, simple as it may seem, was hailed by me, at the moment of discovery, as an invention fully equal to that of the telescope, the steam-engine, or the art of printing itself.

'It is necessary to premise, that the balloon, at the elevation now attained, continued its course upwards with an even and undeviating ascent, and the car consequently followed with a steadiness so perfect that it would have been impossible to detect in it the slightest vacillation whatever. This circumstance favoured me greatly in the project I now determined to adopt. My supply of water had been put on board in kegs containing five gallons each, and ranged very securely around the interior of the car. I unfastened one of these, and taking two ropes, tied them tightly across the rim of the wickerwork from one side to the other; placing them about a foot apart and parallel so as to form a kind of shelf, upon which I placed the keg, and steadied it in a horizontal position. About eight inches immediately below these ropes, and four feet from the bottom of the car, I fastened another shelf – but made of thin plank, being the only similar piece of wood I had. Upon this latter shelf, and exactly beneath one of the rims of the keg, a small earthern pitcher was deposited. I now bored a hole in the end of the keg over the pitcher, and fitted in a plug of soft wood, cut in a tapering or conical shape. This plug I pushed in or pulled out, as might happen, until, after a few experiments, it arrived at that exact degree of tightness, at which the water, oozing from the hole, and falling into the pitcher below, would fill the latter to the brim in the period of sixty minutes. This, of course, was a matter briefly and easily ascertained, by noticing the proportion of the pitcher filled in any given time. Having arranged all this, the rest of the plan is obvious. My bed was so contrived upon the floor of the car, as to bring my head, in lying down, immediately below the mouth of the pitcher. It was evident that, at the expiration of an hour, the pitcher, getting full, would be forced to run over, and to run over at the mouth, which was somewhat lower than the rim. It was also evident that the water thus falling from a height of more than four feet could not do otherwise than fall upon my face, and that the sure consequence would be to waken me up instantaneously, even from the soundest slumber in the world.

'It was fully eleven by the time I had completed these arrangements, and I immediately betook myself to bed, with full confidence in the efficiency of my invention. Nor in this matter was I disappointed. Punctually every sixty minutes was I aroused by my trusty chronometer, when, having emptied the pitcher into the bung-hole of the keg, and performed the duties of the condenser, I retired again to bed. These regular interruptions to my slumber caused me even less discomfort than I had anticipated; and when I finally arose for the day, it was seven o'clock, and the sun had attained many degrees above the line of my horizon.

'*April 3rd.* I found the balloon at an immense height indeed, and the earth's apparent convexity increased in a material degree. Below me in the ocean lay a cluster of black specks, which undoubtedly were islands. Far away to the northward I perceived a thin, white, and exceedingly brilliant line, or streak, on the edge of the horizon, and I had no hesitation in supposing it to be the southern disc of the ices of the Polar Sea. My curiosity was greatly excited, for I had hopes of passing on much farther to the north, and might possibly, at some period, find myself placed directly above the Pole itself. I now lamented that my great elevation would, in this case, prevent my taking as accurate a survey as I could wish. Much, however, might be ascertained. Nothing else of an extraordinary nature occurred during the day. My apparatus all continued in good order, and the balloon still ascended without any perceptible vacillation. The cold was intense, and obliged me to wrap up closely in an overcoat. When darkness came over the earth, I betook myself to bed, although it was for many hours afterwards broad daylight all around my immediate situation. The water-clock was punctual in its duty, and I slept until next morning soundly, with the exception of the periodical interruption.

'*April 4th.* Arose in good health and spirits, and was astonished at the singular change which had taken place in the appearance of the sea. It had lost, in a great measure, the deep tint of blue it had hitherto worn, being now of a greyish-white, and of a lustre dazzling to the eye. The islands were no longer visible; whether they had passed down the horizon to the south east, or whether my increasing elevation had left them out of sight, it is impossible to say. I was inclined, however, to the latter opinion. The rim of ice to the northward was growing more and more apparent. Cold by no means so intense. Nothing of importance occurred, and I passed the day in reading, having taken care to supply myself with books.

'*April 5th.* Beheld the singular phenomenon of the sun rising while nearly the whole visible surface of the earth continued to be involved in darkness. In time, however, the light spread itself over all, and I again saw the line of ice to the northward. It was now very distinct, and appeared of a much darker hue than the waters of the ocean. I was evidently approaching it, and with great rapidity. Fancied I could again distinguish a strip of land to the eastward, and one also to the westward, but could not be certain. Weather moderate. Nothing of any consequence happened during the day. Went early to bed.

'*April 6th*. Was surprised at finding the rim of ice at a very moderate distance, and an immense field of the same material stretching away off to the horizon in the north. It was evident that if the balloon held its present course, it would soon arrive above the Frozen Ocean, and I had now little doubt of ultimately seeing the Pole. During the whole of the day I continued to near the ice. Towards night the limits of my horizon very suddenly and materially increased, owing undoubtedly to the earth's form being that of an oblate spheroid, and my arriving above the flattened regions in the vicinity of the Arctic circle. When darkness at length overtook me, I went to bed in great anxiety, fearing to pass over the object of so much curiosity when I should have no opportunity of observing it.

'*April 7th*. Arose early, and, to my great joy, at length beheld what there could be no hesitation in supposing the northern Pole itself. It was there, beyond a doubt, and immediately beneath my feet; but, alas! I had now ascended to so vast a distance, that nothing could with accuracy be discerned. Indeed, to judge from the progression of the numbers indicating my various altitudes, respectively, at different periods, between six o'clock on the second of April, and twenty minutes before nine of the same morning (at which time the barometer ran down), it might be fairly inferred that the balloon had now, at four o'clock in the morning of April the seventh, reached a height of not less, certainly, than 7,254 miles above the surface of the sea. This elevation may appear immense, but the estimate upon which it is calculated gave a result in all probability far inferior to the truth. At all events I undoubtedly beheld the whole of the earth's major diameter; the entire northern hemisphere lay beneath me like a chart orthographically projected: and the great circle of the equator itself formed the boundary line of my horizon. Your Excellencies may, however, readily imagine that the confined regions hitherto unexplored within the limits of the Arctic circle, although situated directly beneath me, and therefore seen without any appearance of being foreshortened, were still, in themselves, comparatively too diminutive, and at too great a distance from the point of sight, to admit of any very accurate examination. Nevertheless, what could be seen was of a nature singular and exciting. Northwardly from that huge rim before mentioned, and which, with slight qualification, may be called the limit of human discovery in these regions, one unbroken, or nearly unbroken, sheet of ice continues to extend. In the first few degrees of this its progress, its surface is very sensibly flattened, farther on depressed into a plane, and finally, becoming not a little concave, it terminates, at the Pole itself, in a circular centre, sharply defined, whose apparent diameter subtended at the balloon an angle of about sixty-five seconds, and whose dusky hue, varying in intensity, was, at all times, darker than any other spot upon the visible hemisphere, and occasionally deepened into the most absolute and impenetrable blackness. Farther than this, little could be ascertained. By twelve o'clock the circular centre had materially decreased in circumference, and by seven o'clock I lost sight of it entirely; the balloon passing over the western limb of the ice, and floating away rapidly in the direction of the equator.

'*April 8th*. Found a sensible diminution in the earth's apparent diameter, besides a material alteration in its general colour and appearance. The whole visible area partook in different degrees of a tint of pale yellow, and in some portions had acquired a brilliancy even painful to the eye. My view downwards was also considerably impeded by the dense atmosphere in the vicinity of the surface being loaded with clouds, between whose masses I could only now and then obtain a glimpse of the earth itself. This difficulty of direct vision had troubled me more or less for the last forty-eight hours; but my present enormous elevation brought closer together, as it were, the floating bodies of vapour, and the inconvenience became, of course, more and more palpable in proportion to my ascent. Nevertheless, I could easily perceive that the balloon now hovered above the range of great lakes in the continent of North America, and was holding a course, due south, which would bring me to the tropics. This circumstance did not fail to give me the most heartfelt satisfaction, and I hailed it as a happy omen of ultimate success. Indeed, the direction I had hitherto taken had filled me with uneasiness; for it was evident that, had I continued it much longer, there would have been no possibility of my arriving at the moon at all, whose orbit is inclined to the ecliptic at only the small angle of 5° 8′ 48″.

'*April 9th*. Today the earth's diameter was greatly diminished, and the colour of the surface assumed hourly a deeper tint of yellow. The balloon kept steadily on her course to the southward, and arrived, at nine p.m., over the northern edge of the Mexican Gulf.

'*April 10th*. I was suddenly aroused from slumber, about five o'clock this morning, by a loud, crackling, and terrific sound, for which I could in no manner account. It was of very brief duration, but, while it lasted resembled nothing in the world of which I had any previous experience. It is needless to say that I became excessively alarmed, having, in the first instance, attributed the noise to the bursting of the balloon. I examined all my apparatus, however, with great attention, and could discover nothing out of order. Spent a great part of the day in meditating upon an occurrence so extraordinary, but could find no means whatever of accounting for it. Went to bed dissatisfied, and in a state of great anxiety and agitation.

'*April 11th*. Found a startling diminution in the apparent diameter of the earth, and a considerable increase, now observable for the first time, in that of the moon itself, which wanted only a few days of being full. It now required long and excessive labour to condense within the chamber sufficient atmospheric air for the sustenance of life.

'*April 12th*. A singular alteration took place in regard to the direction of the balloon, and although fully anticipated, afforded me the most unequivocal delight. Having reached, in its former course, about the twentieth parallel of southern latitude, it turned off suddenly, at an acute angle, to the eastward, and thus proceeded throughout the day, keeping nearly, if not altogether, in the exact plane of the lunar ellipse. What was worthy of remark, a very perceptible vacillation in the car was a consequence of this change of route – a vacillation which prevailed, in a more or less degree, for a period of many hours.

'*April 13th*. Was again very much alarmed by a repetition of the loud crackling noise which terrified me on the tenth. Thought long upon the subject, but was unable to form any satisfactory conclusion. Great decrease in the earth's apparent diameter, which now subtended from the balloon an angle of very little more than twenty-five degrees. The moon could not be seen at all, being nearly in my zenith. I still continued in the plane of the ellipse, but made little progress to the eastward.

'*April 14th*. Extremely rapid decrease in the diameter of the earth. Today I became strongly impressed with the idea that the balloon was now actually running up the line of apsides to the point of perigee – in other words, holding the direct course which would bring it immediately to the moon in that part of its orbit the nearest to the earth. The moon itself was directly overhead, and consequently hidden from my view. Great and long-continued labour necessary for the condensation of the atmosphere.

'*April 15th*. Not even the outlines of continents and seas could now be traced upon the earth with anything approaching distinctness. About twelve o'clock I became aware, for the third time, of that appalling sound which had so astonished me before. It now, however, continued for some moments, and gathered intensity as it continued. At length, while, stupefied and terror-stricken, I stood in expectation of I knew not what hideous destruction, the car vibrated with excessive violence, and a gigantic and flaming mass of some material which I could not distinguish, came with a voice of a thousand thunders, roaring and booming by the balloon. When my fears and astonishment had in some degree subsided, I had little difficulty in supposing it to be some mighty volcanic fragment ejected from that world to which I was so rapidly approaching, and, in all probability, one of that singular class of substances occasionally picked up on the earth, and termed meteoric stones for want of a better appellation.

'*April 16th*. Today, looking upwards as well as I could, through each of the side windows alternately, I beheld, to my great delight, a very small portion of the moon's disc protruding, as it were, on all sides beyond the huge circumference of the balloon. My agitation was extreme; for I had now little doubt of soon reaching the end of my perilous voyage. Indeed, the labour now required by the condenser had increased to a most oppressive degree, and allowed me scarcely any respite from exertion. Sleep was a matter nearly out of the question. I became quite ill, and my frame trembled with exhaustion. It was impossible that human nature could endure this state of intense suffering much longer. During the now brief interval of darkness a meteoric stone again passed in my vicinity, and the frequency of these phenomena began to occasion me much apprehension.

'*April 17th*. This morning proved an epoch in my voyage. It will be remembered that, on the thirteenth, the earth subtended an angular breadth of twenty-five degrees. On the fourteenth this had greatly diminished; on the fifteenth a still more remarkable decrease was observable; and, on retiring on the night of the sixteenth, I had noticed an angle of no more than about seven degrees and fifteen minutes. What, therefore, must have been my amazement, on awakening from a brief and disturbed slumber, on the morning of this day, the seventeenth, at finding the surface beneath me so suddenly and wonderfully augmented in volume, as to subtend no less than thirty-nine degrees in apparent angular diameter! I was thunderstruck! No words can give any adequate idea of the extreme, the absolute horror and astonishment, with which I was seized, possessed, and altogether overwhelmed. My knees tottered beneath me – my teeth chattered – my hair started up on end. "The balloon, then, had actually burst!" These were the first tumultuous ideas that hurried through my mind: "The balloon had positively burst! – I was falling – falling with the most impetuous, the most unparalleled velocity! To judge by the immense distance already so quickly passed over, it could not be more than ten minutes, at the farthest, before I should meet the surface of the earth, and be hurled into annihilation!" But at length reflection came to my relief. I paused; I considered; and I began to doubt. The matter was impossible. I could not in any reason have so rapidly come down. Besides, although I was evidently approaching the surface below me, it was with a speed by no means commensurate with the velocity I had at first so horribly conceived. This consideration served to calm the perturbation of my mind, and I finally succeeded in regarding the phenomenon in its proper point of view. In fact, amazement must have fairly deprived me of my senses, when I could not see the vast difference, in appearance, between the surface below me, and the surface of my mother earth. The latter was indeed over my head, and completely hidden by the balloon, while the moon – the moon itself in all its glory – lay beneath me, and at my feet.

'The stupor and surprise produced in my mind by this extraordinary change in the posture of affairs was perhaps, after all, that part of the adventure least susceptible of explanation. For the *bouleversement* in itself was not only natural and inevitable, but had been long actually anticipated as a circumstance to be expected whenever I should arrive at that exact point of my voyage where the attraction of the planet should be superseded by the attraction of the satellite – or, more precisely, where the gravitation of the balloon towards the earth should be less powerful than its gravitation towards the moon. To be sure I arose from a sound slumber, with all my senses in confusion, to the contemplation of a very startling phenomenon, and one which, although expected, was not expected at the moment. The revolution itself must, of course, have taken place in an easy and gradual manner, and it is by no means clear that, had I even been awake at the time of the occurrence, I should have been made aware of it by any internal evidence of an inversion – that is to say, by any inconvenience or disarrangement, either about my person or about my apparatus.

'It is almost needless to say that, upon coming to a due sense of my situation, and emerging from the terror which had absorbed every faculty of my soul, my attention was, in the first place, wholly directed to the contemplation of the general physical appearance of the moon. It lay beneath me like a chart – and although I judged it to be still at no inconsiderable distance, the indentures of its surface were defined to my vision with a most striking and altogether unaccountable distinctness. The entire absence of ocean or sea, and indeed of any lake or river, or body of water whatsoever, struck me, at first glance, as the most extraordinary feature in its geological condition. Yet, strange to say, I beheld vast level regions of a character decidedly alluvial, although by far the greater portion of the hemisphere in sight was covered with innumerable volcanic mountains, conical in shape, and having more the appearance of artificial than of natural protuberance. The highest among them does not exceed three and three-quarter miles in perpendicular elevation; but a map of the volcanic districts of the Campi Phlegraei would afford to your Excellencies a better idea of their general surface than any unworthy description I might think proper to attempt. The greater part of them were in a state of evident eruption, and gave me fearfully to understand their fury and their power, by the repeated thunders of the miscalled meteoric stones, which now rushed upwards by the balloon with a frequency more and more appalling.

'*April 18th.* Today I found an enormous increase in the moon's apparent bulk – and the evidently accelerated velocity of my descent began to fill me with alarm. It will be remembered that, in the earliest stage of my speculations upon the possibility of a passage to the moon, the existence, in its vicinity, of an atmosphere, dense in proportion to the bulk of the planet, had entered largely into my calculations; this too in spite of many theories to the contrary, and, it may be added, in spite of a general disbelief in the existence of any lunar atmosphere at all. But, in addition to what I have already urged in regard to Encke's comet and the zodiacal light, I had been strengthened in my opinion by certain observations of Mr Schroeter, of Lilienthal. He observed the moon when two days and a half old, in the evening soon after sunset, before the dark part was visible, and continued to watch it until it became visible. The two cusps appeared tapering in a very sharp faint prolongation, each exhibiting its farthest extremity faintly illuminated by the solar rays, before any part of the dark hemisphere was visible. Soon afterwards, the whole dark limb became illuminated. This prolongation of the cusps beyond the semicircle, I thought, must have arisen from the refraction of the sun's rays by the moon's atmosphere. I computed, also, the height of the atmosphere (which could refract light enough into its dark hemisphere to produce a twilight more luminous than the light reflected from the earth when the moon is about 32° from the new) to be 1,356 Paris feet; in this view, I supposed the greatest height capable of refracting the solar ray to be 5,376 feet. My ideas on this topic had also received confirmation by a passage in the eighty-second volume of the Philosophical Transactions, in which it is stated that at an occultation of Jupiter's satellites, the third disappeared after having been about 1" or 2" of time indistinct, and the fourth became indiscernible near the limb.

'Upon the resistance or, more properly, upon the support of an atmosphere, existing in the state of density imagined, I had, of course, entirely depended for the safety of my ultimate descent. Should I then, after all, prove to have been mistaken, I had in consequence nothing better to expect, as a finale to my adventure, than being dashed into atoms against the rugged surface of the satellite. And, indeed, I had now every reason to be terrified. My distance from the moon was comparatively trifling, while the labour required by the condenser was diminished not at all, and I could discover no indication whatever of a decreasing rarity in the air.

'*April 19th.* This morning, to my great joy, about nine o'clock, the surface of the moon being frightfully near, and my apprehensions excited to the utmost, the pump of my condenser at length gave evident tokens of an alteration in the atmosphere. By ten, I had reason to believe its density considerably increased. By eleven, very little labour was necessary at the apparatus; and at twelve o'clock, with some hesitation, I ventured to unscrew the tourniquet, when, finding no inconvenience from having done so, I finally threw open the gum-elastic chamber, and unrigged it from around the car. As might have been expected, spasms and violent headache were the immediate consequences of an experiment so precipitate and full of danger. But these and other difficulties attending respiration, as they were by no means so great as to put me in peril of my life, I determined to endure as I best could, in consideration of my leaving them behind me momently in my approach to the denser strata near the moon. This approach, however, was still impetuous in the extreme; and it soon became alarmingly certain that, although I had probably not been deceived in the expectation of an atmosphere dense in proportion to the mass of the satellite, still I had been wrong in supposing this density, even at the surface, at all adequate to the support of the great weight contained in the car of my balloon. Yet this should have been the case, and in an equal degree as at the surface of the earth, the actual gravity of bodies at either planet supposed in the ratio of the atmospheric condensation. That it was not the case, however, my precipitous downfall gave testimony enough; why it was not so, can only be explained by a reference to those possible geological disturbances to which I have formerly alluded. At all events I was now close upon the planet, and coming down with the most terrible impetuosity. I lost not a moment, accordingly, in throwing overboard first my ballast, then my water-kegs, then my condensing apparatus and gum-elastic chamber, and finally every article within the car. But it was all to no purpose. I still fell with horrible rapidity, and was now not more than half a mile from the surface. As a last resource, therefore, having got rid of my coat, hat, and boots, I cut loose from the balloon the car itself, which was of no inconsiderable weight, and thus, clinging with both hands to the network, I had barely time to observe that the whole country, as far as the eye could reach, was thickly interspersed with diminutive habitations, ere I tumbled headlong into the very heart of a fantastical-looking city, and into the middle of a vast crowd of ugly little people, who none of them uttered a single syllable, or gave themselves the least trouble to render me assistance, but stood, like a parcel of idiots, grinning in a ludicrous manner, and eyeing me and my balloon askant, with their arms set akimbo. I turned from them in contempt, and, gazing upward at the earth so lately left, and left perhaps for ever, beheld it like a huge, dull, copper shield, about two degrees in diameter, fixed immovably in the heavens overhead, and tipped on one of its edges with a crescent border of the most brilliant gold. No traces of land or water could be discovered, and the whole was clouded with variable spots, and belted with tropical and equatorial zones.

'Thus, may it please your Excellencies, after a series of great anxieties, unheard-of dangers, and unparalleled escapes, I had, at length, on the nineteenth day of my departure from Rotterdam, arrived in safety at the conclusion of a voyage undoubtedly the most extraordinary, and the most momentous, ever accomplished, undertaken, or conceived by any denizen of earth. But my adventures yet remain to be related. And indeed your Excellencies may well imagine that, after a residence of five years upon a planet not only deeply interesting in its own peculiar character, but rendered doubly so by its intimate connection, in capacity of satellite, with the world inhabited by man, I may have intelligence for the private ear of the States' College of Astronomers of far more importance than the details, however wonderful, of the mere voyage which so happily concluded. This is, in fact, the case. I have much – very much which it would give me the greatest pleasure to communicate. I have much to say of the climate of the planet; of its wonderful alternations of heat and cold, of unmitigated and burning sunshine for one fortnight, and more than polar frigidity for the next; of a constant transfer of moisture, by distillation like that *in vacuo*, from the point beneath the sun to the point the farthest from it; of a variable zone of running water, of the people themselves; of their manners, customs, and political institutions; of their peculiar physical construction; of their ugliness; of their want of ears, those useless appendages in an atmosphere so peculiarly modified; of their consequent ignorance of the use and properties of speech; of their substitute for speech in a singular method of intercommunication; of the incomprehensible connection between each particular individual in the moon with some particular individual on the earth – a connection analogous with, and depending upon, that of the orbs of the planet and the satellites, and by means of which the lives and destinies of the inhabitants of the one are interwoven with the lives and destinies of the inhabitants of the other; and above all, if it so please your Excellencies – above all, of those dark and hideous mysteries which lie in the outer regions of the moon – regions which, owing to the almost miraculous accordance of the satellite's rotation on its own axis with its sidereal revolution about the earth, have never yet been turned, and, by God's mercy, never shall be turned, to the scrutiny of the telescopes of man. All this, and more – much more – would I most willingly detail. But, to be brief, I must have my reward. I am pining for a return to my family and to my home, and as the price of any further communication on my part – in consideration of the light which I have it in my power to throw upon many very important branches of physical and metaphysical science – I must solicit, through the influence of your honourable body, a pardon for the crime of which I have been guilty in the death of the creditors upon my departure from Rotterdam. This, then, is the object of the present paper. Its bearer, an inhabitant of the moon, whom I have prevailed upon, and properly instructed, to be my messenger to the earth, will await your Excellencies' pleasure, and return to me with the pardon in question, if it can, in any manner, be obtained.

'I have the honour to be, etc., your Excellencies' very humble servant,

HANS PFAALL.'

Upon finishing the perusal of this very extraordinary document, Professor Rub-a-dub, it is said, dropped his pipe upon the ground in the extremity of his surprise, and Mynheer Superbus von Underduk having taken off his spectacles, wiped them, and deposited them in his pocket, so far forgot both himself and his dignity, as to turn round three times upon his heel in the quintessence of astonishment and admiration. There was no doubt about the matter – the pardon should be obtained. So at least swore, with a round oath, Professor Rub-a-dub, and so finally thought the illustrious von Underduk, as he took the arm of his brother in science, and without saying a word, began to make the best of his way home to deliberate upon the measures to be adopted. Having reached the door, however, of the burgomaster's dwelling, the professor ventured to suggest that as the messenger had thought proper to disappear – no doubt frightened to death by the savage appearance of the burghers of Rotterdam – the pardon would be of little use, as no one but a man of the moon would undertake a voyage to so vast a distance. To the truth of this observation the burgomaster assented, and the matter was therefore at an end. Not so, however, rumours and speculations. The letter, having been published, gave rise to a variety of gossip and opinion. Some of the over-wise even made themselves ridiculous by decrying the whole business as nothing better than a hoax. But hoax, with these sort of people, is, I believe, a general term for all matters above their comprehension. For my part, I cannot conceive upon what data they have founded such an accusation. Let us see what they say:

Imprimis. That certain wags in Rotterdam have certain especial antipathies to certain burgomasters and astronomers.

Don't understand at all.

Secondly. That an odd little dwarf and bottle conjurer, both of whose ears, for some misdemeanour, have been cut off close to his head, has been missing for several days from the neighbouring city of Bruges.

Well – what of that?

Thirdly. That the newspapers which were stuck all over the little balloon were newspapers of Holland, and therefore could not have been made in the moon. They were dirty papers – very dirty – and Gluck, the printer, would take his Bible oath to their having been printed in Rotterdam.

He was mistaken – undoubtedly – mistaken.

Fourthly. That Hans Pfaall himself, the drunken villain, and the three very idle gentlemen styled his creditors, were all seen, no longer than two or three days ago, in a tippling house in the suburbs, having just returned, with money in their pockets, from a trip beyond the sea.

Don't believe it – don't believe a word of it.

Lastly. That it is an opinion very generally received, or which ought to be generally received, that the College of Astronomers in the city of Rotterdam, as well as other colleges in all other parts of the world – not to mention colleges and astronomers in general – are, to say the least of the matter, not a whit better, nor greater, nor wiser than they ought to be.

NOTE – Strictly speaking, there is but little similarity between the above sketchy trifle and the celebrated 'Moon-Story' of Mr Locke; but as both have the character of *hoaxes* (although the one is in a tone of banter, the other of downright earnest), and as both hoaxes are on the same subject, the moon – moreover, as both attempt to give plausibility by scientific detail – the author of 'Hans Pfaall' thinks it necessary to say, in *self-defence*, that his own *jeu d'esprit* was published in the *Southern Literary Messenger* about three weeks before the commencement of Mr L—'s in the *New York Sun*. Fancying a likeness which, perhaps, does not exist, some of the New York papers copied 'Hans Pfaall', and collated it with the 'Moon-Hoax', by way of detecting the writer of the one in the writer of the other.

As many more persons were actually gulled by the 'Moon-Hoax' than would be willing to acknowledge the fact, it may here afford some little amusement to show why no one should have been deceived – to point out those particulars of the story which should have been sufficient to establish its real character. Indeed, however rich the imagination displayed in this ingenious fiction, it wanted much of the force which might have been given it by a more scrupulous attention to facts and to general analogy. That the public were misled, even for an instant, merely proves the gross ignorance which is so generally prevalent upon subjects of an astronomical nature.

The moon's distance from the earth is, in round numbers, 240,000 miles. If we desire to ascertain how near, apparently, a lens would bring the satellite (or any distant object), we, of course, have but to divide the distance by the magnifying or, more strictly, by the space-penetrating power of the glass. Mr L— makes his lens have a power of 42,000 times. By this divide 240,000 (the moon's real distance), and we have five miles and five-sevenths, as the apparent distance. No animal at all could be seen so far; much less the minute points particularised in the story. Mr L— speaks about Sir John Herschel's perceiving flowers (the *Papaver rheas*, etc.), and even detecting the colour and the shape of the eyes of small birds. Shortly before, too, he has himself observed that the lens would not render perceptible objects of less than eighteen inches in diameter; but even this, as I have said, is giving the glass by far too great power. It may be observed, in passing, that this prodigious glass is said to have been moulded at the glasshouse of Messrs Hartley and Grant, in Dumbarton; but Messrs H and G's establishment had ceased operations for many years previous to the publication of the hoax.

On page 13, pamphlet edition, speaking of 'a hairy veil' over the eyes of a species of bison, the author says: 'It immediately occurred to the acute mind of Dr Herschel that this was a providential contrivance to protect the eyes of the animal from the great extremes of light and darkness to which all the inhabitants of our side of the moon are periodically subjected.' But this cannot be thought a very 'acute' observation of the doctor's. The inhabitants of our side of the moon have, evidently, no darkness at all, so there can be nothing of the 'extremes' mentioned. In the absence of the sun they have a light from the earth equal to that of thirteen full unclouded moons.

The topography throughout, even when professing to accord with Blunt's Lunar Chart, is entirely at variance with that or any other lunar chart, and even grossly at variance with itself. The points of the compass, too, are in inextricable confusion; the writer appearing to be ignorant that, on a lunar map, these are not in accordance with terrestrial points; the east being to the left, etc.

Deceived, perhaps, by the vague titles, *Mare Nubium, Mare Tranquillitatis, Mare Faecunditatis*, etc., given to the dark spots by former astronomers, Mr L— has entered into details regarding oceans and other large bodies of water in the moon; whereas there is no astronomical point more positively ascertained than that no such bodies exist there. In examining the boundary between light and darkness (in the crescent or gibbous moon) where this boundary crosses any of the dark places, the line of division is found to be rough and jagged; but, were these dark places liquid, it would evidently be even.

The description of the wings of the man-bat, on page 21, is but a literal copy of Peter Wilkins' account of the wings of his flying islanders. This simple fact should have induced suspicion, at least, it might be thought.

On page 23, we have the following: 'What a prodigious influence must our thirteen times larger globe have exercised upon this satellite when an embryo in the womb of time, the passive subject of chemical affinity!' This is very fine; but it should be observed that no astronomer would have made such remark, especially to any journal of Science; for the earth, in the sense intended, is not only thirteen, but forty-nine times larger than the moon. A similar objection applies to the whole of the concluding pages, where, by way of introduction to some discoveries in Saturn, the philosophical correspondent enters into a minute schoolboy account of that planet – this to the *Edinburgh Journal of Science*!

But there is one point, in particular, which should have betrayed the fiction. Let us imagine the power actually possessed of seeing animals upon the moon's surface – what would first arrest the attention of an observer from the earth? Certainly neither their shape, size, nor any other such peculiarity, so soon as their remarkable *situation*. They would appear to be walking, with heels up and head down, in the manner of flies on a ceiling. The *real* observer would have uttered an instant ejaculation of surprise (however prepared by previous knowledge) at the singularity of their position; the *fictitious* observer has not even mentioned the subject, but speaks of seeing the entire bodies of such creatures, when it is demonstrable that he could have seen only the diameter of their heads!

It might as well be remarked, in conclusion, that the size, and particularly the powers of the man-bats (for example, their ability to fly in so rare an atmosphere – if, indeed, the moon have any), with most of the other fancies in regard to animal and vegetable existence, are at variance, generally, with all analogical reasoning on these themes; and that analogy here will often amount to conclusive demonstration. It is, perhaps, scarcely necessary to add, that all the suggestions attributed to Brewster and Herschel, in the beginning of the article, about 'a transfusion of artificial light through the focal object of vision', etc., etc., belong to that species of figurative writing which comes, most properly, under the denomination of rigmarole.

There is a real and very definite limit to optical discovery among the stars – a limit whose nature need only be stated to be understood. If, indeed, the casting of large lenses were all that is required, man's ingenuity would ultimately prove equal to the task, and we might have them of any size demanded. But, unhappily, in proportion to the increase of size in the lens, and consequently of space-penetrating power, is the diminution of light from the object, by diffusion of its rays. And for this evil there is no remedy within human ability; for an objéct is seen by means of that light alone which proceeds from itself, whether direct or reflected. Thus the only 'artificial' light which could avail Mr Locke, would be some artificial light which he should be able to throw – not upon the 'focal object of vision', but upon the real object to be viewed – to wit: upon the moon. It has been easily calculated that, when the light proceeding from a star becomes so diffused as to be as weak as the natural light proceeding from the whole of the stars, in a clear and moonless night, then the star is no longer visible for any practical purpose.

The Earl of Ross's telescope, lately constructed in England, has a *speculum* with a reflecting surface of .4071 square inches; the Herschel telescope having one of only .1811. The metal of the Earl of Ross's is 6 feet in diameter; it is 51Ú2 inches thick at the edges, and 5 at the centre. The weight is 3 tons. The focal length is 50 feet.

I have lately read a singular and somewhat ingenious little book, whose title-page runs thus: '*L'Homme dans la Lune où le Voyage Chimerique fait au Monde de la Lune, nouvellement decouvert par Dominique Gonzales, Advanturier Espagnol, autrement dit le Courier volant. Mis en notre langue par J.B.D.A., Paris, chez François Piot, près la Fontaine de Saint Benoist. Et chez J. Goignard, au premier pilier de la grand'salle du Palais, proché les Consultations,* MDCXLVII.'

The writer professes to have translated his work from the English of one Mr D'Avisson (Davidson?) although there is a terrible ambiguity in the statement. '*J'en ai eu,*' says he, '*l'original de M. D'Avisson, medecin des mieux versez qui soient aujourd'huy dans la conaissance des belles lettres, et sur tout de la philosophie naturelle. Je lui ai cette obligation entre les autres, de m'avoir non seulement mis en main ce livre en anglais, mais encore le manuscrit du Sieur Thomas D'Anan, gentilhomme Eccossais, récommandable pour sa vertu, sur la version duquel j'advoue que j'ay tiré le plan de la mienne.*'

After some irrelevant adventures, much in the manner of Gil Blas, and which occupy the first thirty pages, the author relates that, being ill during a sea voyage, the crew abandoned him, together with a negro servant, on the island of St Helena. To increase the chances of obtaining food, the two separate, and live as far apart as possible. This brings about a training of birds, to serve the purpose of carrier-pigeons between them. By and by these are taught to carry parcels of some weight – and this weight is gradually increased. At length the idea is entertained of uniting the force of a great number of the birds, with a view to raising the author himself. A machine is contrived for the purpose, and we have a minute description of it, which is materially helped out by a steel engraving. Here we perceive the Signor Gonzales, with point ruffles and a huge periwig, seated astride something which resembles very closely a broomstick, and borne aloft by a multitude of wild swans (*ganzas*) who had strings reaching from their tails to the machine.

The main event detailed in the Signor's narrative depends upon a very important fact, of which the reader is kept in ignorance until near the end of the book. The *ganzas*, with whom he had become so familiar, were not really denizens of St Helena, but of the moon. Thence it had been their custom, time out of mind, to migrate annually to some portion of the earth. In proper season, of course, they would return home; and the author, happening, one day, to require their services for a short voyage, is unexpectedly carried straight up, and in a very brief period arrives at the satellite. Here he finds, among other odd things, that the people enjoy extreme happiness; that they have no law; that they die without pain; that they are from ten to thirty feet in height; that they live five thousand years; that they have an emperor called Irdonozur; and that they can jump sixty feet high, when, being out of the gravitating influence, they fly about with fans.

I cannot forbear giving a specimen of the general *philosophy* of the volume.

'I must now declare to you,' says the Signor Gonzales, 'the nature of the place in which I found myself. All the clouds were beneath my feet, or, if you please, spread between me and the earth. As to the stars, *since there was no night where I was, they always had the same appearance; not brilliant, as usual, but pale, and very nearly like the moon of a morning.* But few of them were visible, and these ten times larger (as well as I could judge) than they seem to the inhabitants of the earth. The moon, which wanted two days of being full, was of a terrible bigness.

'I must not forget here, that the stars appeared only on that side of the globe turned towards the moon, and that the closer they were to it the larger they seemed. I have also to inform you that, whether it was calm weather or stormy, I found myself *always immediately between the moon and the earth*. I was convinced of this for two reasons – because my birds always flew in a straight line; and because whenever we attempted to rest, *we were carried insensibly around the globe of the earth*. For I admit the opinion of Copernicus, who maintains that it never ceases to revolve *from the east to the west*, not upon the poles of the Equinoctial, commonly called the poles of the world, but upon those of the Zodiac, a question of which I propose to speak more at length hereafter, when I shall have leisure to refresh my memory in regard to the astrology which I learned at Salamanca when young, and have since forgotten.'

Notwithstanding the blunders italicised, the book is not without some claim to attention, as affording a naive specimen of the current astronomical notions of the time. One of these assumed, that the 'gravitating power' extended but a short distance from the earth's surface, and, accordingly, we find our voyager 'carried insensibly around the globe', etc.

There have been other 'voyages to the moon', but none of higher merit than the one just mentioned. That of Bergerac is utterly meaningless. In the third volume of the *American Quarterly Review* will be found quite an elaborate criticism upon a certain 'journey' of the kind in question – a criticism in which it is difficult to say whether the critic most exposes the stupidity of the book, or his own absurd ignorance of astronomy. I forget the title of the work; but the *means* of the voyage are more deplorably ill conceived than are even the *ganzas* of our friend the Signor Gonzales. The adventurer, in digging the earth, happens to discover a peculiar metal for which the moon has a strong attraction, and straightway constructs of it a box, which, when cast loose from its terrestrial fastenings, flies with him, forthwith, to the satellite. The *Flight of Thomas O'Rourke* is a *jeu d'esprit* not altogether contemptible, and has been translated into German. Thomas, the hero, was, in fact, the gamekeeper of an Irish peer, whose eccentricities gave rise to the tale. The 'flight' is made on an eagle's back, from Hungry Hill, a lofty mountain at the end of Bantry Bay.

In these various *brochures* the aim is always satirical; the theme being a description of Lunarian customs as compared with ours. In none is there any effort at *plausibility* in the details of the voyage itself. The writers seem, in each instance, to be utterly uninformed in respect to astronomy. In 'Hans Pfaall' the design is original, inasmuch as regards an attempt at *verisimilitude*, in the application of scientific principles (so far as the whimsical nature of the subject would permit), to the actual passage between the earth and the moon.

Berenice

Dicebant mihi sodales, si sepulchrum amicae
visitarem, curas meas aliquantulum fore levatas.

Ebn Zaiat

Misery is manifold. The wretchedness of earth is multiform. Overreaching the wide horizon as the rainbow, its hues are as various as the hues of that arch – as distinct too, yet as intimately blended. Overreaching the wide horizon as the rainbow! How is it that from beauty I have derived a type of unloveliness? – from the covenant of peace, a simile of sorrow? But as, in ethics, evil is a consequence of good, so, in fact, out of joy is sorrow born. Either the memory of past bliss is the anguish of today, or the agonies which are, have their origin in the ecstasies which *might have been*.

My baptismal name is Egaeus; that of my family I will not mention. Yet there are no towers in the land more time-honoured than my gloomy, grey, hereditary halls. Our line has been called a race of visionaries; and in many striking particulars – in the character of the family mansion – in the frescos of the chief saloon – in the tapestries of the dormitories – in the chiselling of some buttresses in the armoury – but more especially in the gallery of antique paintings – in the fashion of the library chamber – and, lastly, in the very peculiar nature of the library's contents – there is more than sufficient evidence to warrant the belief.

The recollections of my earliest years are connected with that chamber, and with its volumes – of which latter I will say no more. Here died my mother. Herein was I born. But it is mere idleness to say that I had not lived before – that the soul has no previous existence. You deny it? – let us not argue the matter. Convinced myself, I seek not to convince. There is, however, a remembrance of aerial forms – of spiritual and meaning eyes – of sounds, musical yet sad – a remembrance which will not be excluded; a memory like a shadow – vague, variable, indefinite, unsteady; and like a shadow, too, in the impossibility of my getting rid of it while the sunlight of my reason shall exist.

In that chamber was I born. Thus awaking from the long night of what seemed, but was not, nonentity, at once into the very regions of fairy land – into a palace of imagination – into the wild dominions of monastic thought and erudition – it is not singular that I gazed around me with a startled and ardent eye – that I loitered away my boyhood in books, and dissipated my youth in reverie; but it is singular that as years rolled away, and the noon of manhood found me still in the mansion of my fathers – it is wonderful what stagnation there fell upon the springs of my life – wonderful how total an inversion took place in the character of my commonest thought. The realities of the world affected me as visions, and as visions only, while the wild ideas of the land of dreams became, in turn, not the material of my everyday existence, but in very deed that existence utterly and solely in itself.

* * *

Berenice and I were cousins, and we grew up together in my paternal halls. Yet differently we grew – I, ill of health, and buried in gloom – she, agile, graceful, and overflowing with energy; hers, the ramble on the hillside – mine, the studies of the cloister; I, living within my own heart, and addicted, body and soul, to the most intense and painful meditation – she, roaming carelessly through life, with no thought of the shadows in her path, or the silent flight of the raven-winged hours. Berenice! – I call upon her name – Berenice! – and from the grey ruins of memory a thousand tumultuous recollections are startled at the sound! Ah, vividly is her image before me now, as in the early days of her light-heartedness and joy! Oh, gorgeous yet fantastic beauty! Oh, sylph amid the shrubberies of Arnheim! Oh, Naiad among its fountains! And then – then all is mystery and terror, and a tale which should not be told. Disease – a fatal disease, fell like the simoon upon her frame; and, even while I gazed upon her, the spirit of change swept over her, pervading her mind, her habits, and her character, and, in a manner the most subtle and terrible, disturbing even the identity of her person! Alas! the destroyer came and went! – and the victim –where is she? I knew her not – or knew her no longer as Berenice.

Among the numerous train of maladies superinduced by that fatal and primary one which effected a revolution of so horrible a kind in the moral and physical being of my cousin, may be mentioned as the most distressing and obstinate in its nature, a species of epilepsy not unfrequently terminating in *trance* itself – trance very nearly resembling positive dissolution, and from which her manner of recovery was, in most instances, startlingly abrupt. In the meantime my own disease – for I have been told that I should call it by no other appellation – my own disease, then, grew rapidly upon me, and assumed finally a monomaniac character of a novel and extraordinary form – hourly and momently gaining vigour – and at length obtaining over me the most incomprehensible ascendancy. This monomania, if I must so term it, consisted in a morbid irritability of those properties of the mind in metaphysical science termed the *attentive*. It is more than probable that I am not understood; but I fear, indeed, that it is in no manner possible to convey to the mind of the merely general reader, an adequate idea of that nervous *intensity of interest* with which, in my case, the powers of meditation (not to speak technically) busied and buried themselves, in the contemplation of even the most ordinary objects of the universe.

To muse for long unwearied hours, with my attention riveted to some frivolous device on the margin, or in the typography of a book; to become absorbed, for the better part of a summer's day, in a quaint shadow falling aslant upon the tapestry or upon the floor; to lose myself, for an entire night, in watching the steady flame of a lamp, or the embers of a fire; to dream away whole days over the perfume of a flower; to repeat, monotonously, some common word, until the sound, by dint of frequent repetition, ceased to convey any idea whatever to the mind; to lose all sense of motion or physical existence, by means of absolute bodily quiescence long and obstinately persevered in: such were a few of the most common and least pernicious vagaries induced by a condition of the mental faculties, not, indeed, altogether unparalleled, but certainly bidding defiance to anything like analysis or explanation.

Yet let me not be misapprehended. The undue, earnest, and morbid attention thus excited by objects in their own nature frivolous, must not be confounded in character with that ruminating propensity common to all mankind, and more especially indulged in by persons of ardent imagination. It was not even, as might be at first supposed, an extreme condition, or exaggeration of such propensity, but primarily and essentially distinct and different. In the one instance, the dreamer, or enthusiast, being interested by an object usually *not* frivolous, imperceptibly loses sight of this object in a wilderness of deductions and suggestions issuing therefrom, until, at the conclusion of a daydream *often replete with luxury*, he finds the incitamentum, or first cause of his musings, entirely vanished and forgotten. In my case, the primary object was *invariably frivolous*, although assuming, through the medium of my distempered vision, a refracted and unreal importance. Few deductions, if any, were made; and those few pertinaciously returning in upon the original object as a centre. The meditations were *never* pleasurable; and, at the termination of the reverie, the first cause, so far from being out of sight, had attained that supernaturally exaggerated interest which was the prevailing feature of the disease. In a word, the powers of mind more particularly exercised were, with me, as I have said before, the *attentive*, and are, with the daydreamer, the *speculative*.

My books, at this epoch, if they did not actually serve to

irritate the disorder, partook, it will be perceived, largely, in their imaginative and inconsequential nature, of the characteristic qualities of the disorder itself. I well remember, among others, the treatise of the noble Italian, Coelius Secundus Curio, *De Amplitudine Beati Regni Dei*; St Austin's great work, the *City of God*; and Tertullian's *De Carne Christi*, in which the paradoxical sentence '*Mortuus est Dei filius; credible est quia ineptum est; et sepultus resurrexit; certum est quia impossibile est*', occupied my undivided time, for many weeks of laborious and fruitless investigation.

Thus it will appear that, shaken from its balance only by trivial things, my reason bore resemblance to that ocean-crag spoken of by Ptolemy Hephestion, which steadily resisting the attacks of human violence, and the fiercer fury of the waters and the winds, trembled only to the touch of the flower called Asphodel. And although, to a careless thinker, it might appear a matter beyond doubt, that the alteration produced by her unhappy malady, in the moral condition of Berenice, would afford me many objects for the exercise of that intense and abnormal meditation whose nature I have been at some trouble in explaining, yet such was not in any degree the case. In the lucid intervals of my infirmity, her calamity, indeed, gave me pain, and, taking deeply to heart that total wreck of her fair and gentle life, I did not fail to ponder, frequently and bitterly, upon the wonder-working means by which so strange a revolution had been so suddenly brought to pass. But these reflections partook not of the idiosyncrasy of my disease, and were such as would have occurred, under similar circumstances, to the ordinary mass of mankind. True to its own character, my disorder revelled in the less important but more startling changes wrought in the *physical* frame of Berenice – in the singular and most appalling distortion of her personal identity.

During the brightest days of her unparalleled beauty, most surely I had never loved her. In the strange anomaly of my existence, feelings with me, *had never been* of the heart, and my passions *always* were of the mind. Through the grey of the early morning – among the trellised shadows of the forest at noonday – and in the silence of my library at night – she had flitted by my eyes, and I had seen her – not as the living and breathing Berenice, but as the Berenice of a dream; not as a being of the earth, earthy, but as the abstraction of such a being; not as a thing to admire, but to analyse; not as an object of love, but as the theme of the most abstruse although desultory speculation. And *now* – now I shuddered in her presence, and grew pale at her approach; yet, bitterly lamenting her fallen and desolate condition, I called to mind that she had loved me long, and, in an evil moment, I spoke to her of marriage.

And at length the period of our nuptials was approaching, when, upon an afternoon in the winter of the year – one of those unseasonably warm, calm, and misty days which are the nurse of the beautiful Halcyon – I sat (and sat, as I thought, alone) in the inner apartment of the library. But, uplifting my eyes, I saw that Berenice stood before me.

Was it my own excited imagination – or the misty influence of the atmosphere – or the uncertain twilight of the chamber – or the grey draperies which fell around her figure – that caused in it so vacillating and indistinct an outline? I could not tell. She spoke no word; and I – not for worlds could I have uttered a syllable. An icy chill ran through my frame; a sense of insufferable anxiety oppressed me; a consuming curiosity pervaded my soul; and sinking back upon the chair, I remained for some time breathless and motionless, with my eyes riveted upon her person. Alas! its emaciation was excessive, and not one vestige of the former being lurked in any single line of the contour. My burning glances at length fell upon the face.

The forehead was high, and very pale, and singularly placid; and the once jetty hair fell partially over it, and overshadowed the hollow temples with innumerable ringlets, now of a vivid yellow, and jarring discordantly, in their fantastic character, with the reigning melancholy of the countenance. The eyes were lifeless, and lustreless, and seemingly pupilless, and I shrank involuntarily from their glassy stare to the contemplation of the thin and shrunken lips. They parted; and in a smile of peculiar meaning, *the teeth* of the changed Berenice disclosed themselves slowly to my view. Would to God that I had never beheld them, or that, having done so, I had died!

* * *

The shutting of a door disturbed me, and, looking up, I found that my cousin had departed from the chamber. But from the disordered chamber of my brain, had not, alas! departed, and would not be driven away, the white and ghastly *spectrum* of the teeth. Not a speck on their surface – not a shade on their enamel – not an indenture in their edges – but what that period of her smile had sufficed to brand in upon my memory. I saw them *now* even more unequivocally than I beheld them *then*. The teeth! – the teeth! – they were here, and there, and everywhere, and visibly and palpably before me; long, narrow, and excessively white, with the pale lips writhing about them, as in the very moment of their first terrible development. Then came the full fury of my *monomania*, and I struggled in vain against its strange and irresistible influence. In the multiplied objects of the external world I had no thoughts but for the teeth. For these I longed with a frenzied desire. All other matters and all different interests became absorbed in their single

"IT WAS A FEARFUL PAGE IN THE RECORD OF MY EXISTENCE"

contemplation. They – they alone were present to the mental eye, and they, in their sole individuality, became the essence of my mental life. I held them in every light. I turned them in every attitude. I surveyed their characteristics. I dwelt upon their peculiarities. I pondered upon their conformation. I mused upon the alteration in their nature. I shuddered as I assigned to them in imagination a sensitive and sentient power, and even when unassisted by the lips, a capability of moral expression. Of Mlle Salle it has been well said, '*Que tous ses pas étaient des sentiments,*' and of Berenice I more seriously believed *que toutes ses dents étaient des idées. Des idées!* – ah here was the idiotic thought that destroyed me! *Des idées!* – ah *therefore* it was that I coveted them so madly! I felt that their possession could alone ever restore me to peace, in giving me back to reason.

And the evening closed in upon me thus – and then the darkness came, and tarried, and went – and the day again dawned – and the mists of a second night were now gathering around – and still I sat motionless in that solitary room – and still I sat buried in meditation – and still the phantasma of the teeth maintained its terrible ascendancy, as, with the most vivid hideous distinctness, it floated about amid the changing lights and shadows of the chamber. At length there broke in upon my dreams a cry as of horror and dismay; and thereunto, after a pause, succeeded the sound of troubled voices, intermingled with many low moanings of sorrow or of pain. I arose from my seat, and throwing open one of the doors of the library, saw standing out in the antechamber a servant maiden, all in tears, who told me that Berenice was – no more! She had been seized with epilepsy in the early morning, and now, at the closing in of the night, the grave was ready for its tenant, and all the preparations for the burial were completed.

* * *

I found myself sitting in the library, and again sitting there alone. It seemed that I had newly awakened from a confused and exciting dream. I knew that it was now midnight, and I was well aware, that since the setting of the sun, Berenice had been interred. But of that dreary period which intervened I had no positive, at least no definite, comprehension. Yet its memory was replete with horror – horror more horrible from being vague, and terror more terrible from ambiguity. It was a fearful page in the record of my existence, written all over with dim, and hideous, and unintelligible recollections. I strived to decipher them, but in vain; while ever and anon, like the spirit of a departed sound, the shrill and piercing shriek of a female voice seemed to be ringing in my ears. I had done a deed – what was it? I asked myself the question aloud, and the whispering echoes of the chamber answered me, '*What was it?*'

On the table beside me burned a lamp, and near it lay a little box. It was of no remarkable character, and I had seen it frequently before, for it was the property of the family physician; but how came it *there*, upon my table, and why did I shudder in regarding it? These things were in no manner to be accounted for, and my eyes at length dropped to the open pages of a book, and to a sentence underscored therein. The words were the singular but simple ones of the poet Ebn Zaiat – '*Dicebant mihi sodales si sepulchrum amicae visitarem, curas meas aliquantulum fore levatas.*' Why then, as I perused them, did the hairs of my head erect themselves on end, and the blood of my body become congealed within my veins?

There came a light tap at the library door – and, pale as the tenant of a tomb, a menial entered upon tiptoe. His looks were wild with terror, and he spoke to me in a voice tremulous, husky, and very low. What said he? – some broken sentences I heard. He told of a wild cry disturbing the silence of the night – of the gathering together of the household – of a search in the direction of the sound; and then his tones grew thrillingly distinct as he whispered me of a violated grave – of a disfigured body enshrouded, yet still breathing – still palpitating – *still alive*!

He pointed to garments – they were muddy and clotted with gore. I spoke not, and he took me gently by the hand: it was indented with the impress of human nails. He directed my attention to some object against the wall. I looked at it for some minutes: it was a spade. With a shriek I bounded to the table, and grasped the box that lay upon it. But I could not force it open; and in my tremor, it slipped from my hands, and fell heavily, and burst into pieces; and from it, with a rattling sound, there rolled out some instruments of dental surgery, intermingled with thirty-two small, white and ivory-looking substances that were scattered to and fro about the floor.

Mystification

Slid, if these be your 'passados' and
'montantes', I'll have none o' them.

NED KNOWLES

The Baron Ritzner von Jung was of a noble Hungarian family, every member of which (at least as far back into antiquity as any certain records extend) was more or less remarkable for talent of some description – the majority for that species of *grotesquerie* in conception of which Tieck, a scion of the house, has given a vivid, although by no means the most vivid exemplifications. My acquaintance with Ritzner commenced at the magnificent Chateau Jung, into which a train of droll adventures, not to be made public, threw me during the summer months of the year 18—. Here it was that I obtained a place in his regard, and here, with somewhat more difficulty, a partial insight into his mental conformation. In later days this insight grew more clear, as the intimacy which had at first permitted it became more close; and when, after three years' separation, we met at G—n, I knew all that it was necessary to know of the character of the Baron Ritzner von Jung.

I remember the buzz of curiosity which his advent excited within the college precincts on the night of the twenty-fifth of June. I remember still more distinctly, that while he was pronounced by all parties at first sight 'the most remarkable man in the world', no person made any attempt at accounting for his opinion. That he was unique appeared so undeniable that it was deemed impertinent to enquire wherein the uniquity consisted. But, letting this matter pass for the present, I will merely observe that, from the first moment of his setting foot within the limits of the university, he began to exercise over the habits, manners, persons, purses, and propensities of the whole community which surrounded him, an influence the most extensive and despotic, yet at the same time the most indefinite and altogether unaccountable. Thus the brief period of his residence at the university forms an era in its annals, and is characterised by all classes of people appertaining to it or its dependencies as 'that very extraordinary epoch forming the domination of the Baron Ritzner von Jung'.

Upon his advent to G—n, he sought me out in my apartments. He was then of no particular age, by which I mean that it *was* impossible to form a guess respecting his age by any data personally afforded. He might have been fifteen or fifty, and *was* twenty-one years and seven months. He was by no means a handsome man – perhaps the reverse. The contour of his face was somewhat angular and harsh. His forehead was lofty and very fair; his nose a snub; his eyes large, heavy, glassy, and meaningless. About the mouth there was more to be observed. The lips were gently protruded, and rested the one upon the other, after such a fashion that it is impossible to conceive any, even the most complex, combination of human features, conveying so entirely, and so singly, the idea of unmitigated gravity, solemnity and repose.

It will be perceived, no doubt, from what I have already said, that the Baron was one of those human anomalies now and then to be found, who make the science of mystification the study and the business of their lives. For this science a peculiar turn of mind gave him instinctively the cue, while his physical appearance afforded him unusual facilities for carrying his projects into effect. I firmly believe that no student at G—n, during that renowned epoch so quaintly termed the domination of the Baron Ritzner von Jung, ever rightly entered into the mystery which overshadowed his character. I truly think that no person at the university, with the exception of myself, ever suspected him to be capable of a joke, verbal or practical – the old bulldog at the garden-gate would sooner have been accused – the ghost of Heraclitus – or the wig of the Emeritus Professor of Theology. This, too, when it was evident that the most egregious and unpardonable of all conceivable tricks, whimsicalities and buffooneries were brought about, if not directly by him, at least plainly through his intermediate agency or connivance. The beauty, if I may so call it, of his art *mystifique*, lay in that consummate ability (resulting from an almost intuitive knowledge of human nature, and a most wonderful self-possession), by means of which he never failed to make it appear that the drolleries he was occupied in bringing to a point, arose partly in spite, and partly in consequence of the laudable efforts he was making for their prevention, and for the preservation of the good order and dignity of Alma Mater. The deep, the poignant, the overwhelming mortification, which upon each such failure of his praiseworthy endeavours would suffuse every lineament of his countenance, left not the slightest room for doubt of his sincerity in the bosoms of even his most sceptical companions. The adroitness, too, was no less worthy of observation by which he contrived to shift the sense of the grotesque from the creator to the created – from his own person to the absurdities to which he had given rise. In no instance before that of which I speak, have I known the habitual mystific escape the natural consequence of his manoeuvres – an attachment of the ludicrous to his own character and person. Continually enveloped in an atmosphere of whim, my friend appeared to live only for the severities of society; and not even his own household have for a moment associated other ideas than those of the rigid and august with the memory of the Baron Ritzner von Jung.

During the epoch of his residence at G—n it really appeared that the demon of the *dolce far niente* lay like an incubus upon the university. Nothing, at least, was done beyond eating and drinking and making merry. The apartments of the students were converted into so many pot-houses, and there was no pot-house of them all more famous or more frequented than that of the Baron. Our carousals here were many, and boisterous, and long, and never unfruitful of events.

Upon one occasion we had protracted our sitting until nearly daybreak, and an unusual quantity of wine had been drunk. The company consisted of seven or eight individuals besides the Baron and myself. Most of these were young men of wealth, of high connection, of great family pride, and all alive with an exaggerated sense of honour. They abounded in the most ultra German opinions respecting the *duello*. To these Quixotic notions some recent Parisian publications, backed by three or four desperate and fatal rencounters at G—n, had given new vigour and impulse; and thus the conversation, during the greater part of the night, had run wild upon the all-engrossing topic of the times. The Baron, who had been unusually silent and abstracted in the earlier portion of the evening, at length seemed to be aroused from his apathy, took a leading part in the discourse, and dwelt upon the benefits, and more especially upon the beauties, of the received code of etiquette in passages of arms with an ardour, an eloquence, an impressiveness, and an affectionateness of manner, which elicited the warmest enthusiasm from his hearers in general, and absolutely staggered even myself, who well knew him to be at heart a ridiculer of those very points for which he contended, and especially to hold the entire *fanfaronade* of duelling etiquette in the sovereign contempt which it deserves.

Looking around me during a pause in the Baron's discourse (of which my readers may gather some faint idea when I say that it bore resemblance to the fervid, chanting, monotonous, yet musical sermonic manner of Coleridge), I perceived symptoms of even more than the general interest in the countenance of one of the party. This gentleman, whom I shall call Hermann, was an original in every respect – except, perhaps, in the single particular that he was a very great fool. He contrived to bear, however, among a particular set at the university, a reputation for deep metaphysical thinking, and, I believe, for some logical talent. As a duellist he had acquired great renown, even at G—n. I forget the precise number of victims who had fallen at his hands; but they were many. He was a man of courage undoubtedly. But it was upon his minute acquaintance with the etiquette of the *duello*, and the nicety of his sense of honour, that he most especially prided himself. These things were a hobby which he rode to the death. To Ritzner, ever upon the lookout for the grotesque, his peculiarities had for a long time past afforded food for mystification. Of this, however, I was not aware; although, in the present instance, I saw clearly that something of a whimsical nature was upon the *tapis* with my friend, and that Hermann was its especial object.

As the former proceeded in his discourse, or rather monologue, I perceived the excitement of the latter momently increasing. At length he spoke; offering some objection to a point insisted upon by R—, and giving his reasons in detail. To these the Baron replied at length (still maintaining his exaggerated tone of sentiment) and concluding, in what I thought very bad taste, with a sarcasm and a sneer. The hobby of Hermann now took the bit in his teeth. This I could discern by the studied hair-splitting *farrago* of his rejoinder. His last words I distinctly remember. 'Your opinions, allow me to say, Baron von Jung, although in the main correct, are, in many nice points, discreditable to yourself and to the university of which you are a member. In a few respects they are even unworthy of serious refutation. I would say more than this, sir, were it not for the fear of giving you offence (here the speaker smiled blandly), I would say, sir, that your opinions are not the opinions to be expected from a gentleman.'

As Hermann completed this equivocal sentence, all eyes were turned upon the Baron. He became pale, then excessively red; then, dropping his pocket-handkerchief, stooped to recover it, when I caught a glimpse of his countenance, while it could be seen by no one else at the table. It was radiant with the quizzical expression which was its natural character, but which I had never seen it assume except when we were alone together, and when he unbent himself freely. In an instant afterwards he stood erect, confronting

Hermann; and so total an alteration of countenance in so short a period I certainly never saw before. For a moment I even fancied that I had misconceived him, and that he was in sober earnest. He appeared to be stifling with passion, and his face was cadaverously white. For a short time he remained silent, apparently striving to master his emotion. Having at length seemingly succeeded, he reached a decanter which stood near him, saying as he held it firmly clenched – 'The language you have thought proper to employ, Mynheer Hermann, in addressing yourself to me, is objectionable in so many particulars, that I have neither temper nor time for specification. That my opinions, however, are not the opinions to be expected from a gentleman, is an observation so directly offensive as to allow me but one line of conduct. Some courtesy, nevertheless, is due to the presence of this company, and to yourself, at this moment, as my guest. You will pardon me, therefore, if, upon this consideration, I deviate slightly from the general usage among gentlemen in similar cases of personal affront. You will forgive me for the moderate tax I shall make upon your imagination, and endeavour to consider, for an instant, the reflection of your person in yonder mirror as the living Mynheer Hermann himself. This being done, there will be no difficulty whatever. I shall discharge this decanter of wine at your image in yonder mirror, and thus fulfil all the spirit, if not the exact letter, of resentment for your insult, while the necessity of physical violence to your real person will be obviated.'

With these words he hurled the decanter, full of wine, against the mirror which hung directly opposite Hermann; striking the reflection of his person with great precision, and of course shattering the glass into fragments. The whole company at once started to their feet, and, with the exception of myself and Ritzner, took their departure. As Hermann went out, the Baron whispered me that I should follow him and make an offer of my services. To this I agreed; not knowing precisely what to make of so ridiculous a piece of business.

The duellist accepted my aid with his stiff and *ultra recherché* air, and, taking my arm, led me to his apartment. I could hardly forbear laughing in his face while he proceeded to discuss, with the profoundest gravity, what he termed 'the refinedly peculiar character' of the insult he had received. After a tiresome harangue in his ordinary style, he took down from his book shelves a number of musty volumes on the subject of the *duello*, and entertained me for a long time with their contents; reading aloud, and commenting earnestly as he read. I can just remember the titles of some of the works. There were the *Ordonnance of Philip le Bel on Single Combat*; the *Theatre of Honour*, by Favyn, and a treatise *On the Permission of Duels*, by Andiguier. He displayed, also, with much pomposity, Brantome's *Memoirs of Duels*, published at Cologne, 1666, in the types of Elzevir – a precious and unique vellum-paper volume, with a fine margin, and bound by Derôme. But he requested my attention particularly, and with an air of mysterious sagacity, to a thick octavo, written in barbarous Latin by one Hedelin, a Frenchman, and having the quaint title, *Duelli Lex Scripta, et non; aliterque*. From this he read me one of the drollest chapters in the world concerning '*Injuriae per applicationem, per constructionem, et per se*', about half of which, he averred, was strictly applicable to his own 'refinedly peculiar' case, although not one syllable of the whole matter could I understand for the life of me. Having finished the chapter, he closed the book, and demanded what I thought necessary to be done. I replied that I had entire confidence in his superior delicacy of feeling, and would abide by what he proposed. With this answer he seemed flattered, and sat down to write a note to the Baron. It ran thus:

> SIR – My friend, Mr P—, will hand you this note. I find it incumbent upon me to request, at your earliest convenience, an explanation of this evening's occurrences at your chambers. In the event of your declining this request, Mr P— will be happy to arrange, with any friend whom you may appoint, the steps preliminary to a meeting.
>
> With sentiments of perfect respect,
> Your most humble servant,
>
> JOHANN HERMANN
> *To the Baron Ritzner von Jung*
> *August 18th 18—*

Not knowing what better to do, I called upon Ritzner with this epistle. He bowed as I presented it; then, with a grave countenance, motioned me to a seat. Having perused the cartel, he wrote the following reply, which I carried to Hermann.

> SIR – Through our common friend, Mr P—, I have received your note of this evening. Upon due reflection I frankly admit the propriety of the explanation you suggest. This being admitted, I still find great difficulty (owing to the refinedly peculiar nature of our disagreement, and of the personal affront offered on my part) in so wording what I have to say by way of apology, as to meet all the minute exigencies, and all the variable shadows, of the case. I have great reliance, however, on that extreme delicacy of discrimination, in matters appertaining to the rules

of etiquette, for which you have been so long and so pre-eminently distinguished. With perfect certainty, therefore, of being comprehended, I beg leave, in lieu of offering any sentiments of my own, to refer you to the opinions of Sieur Hedelin, as set forth in the ninth paragraph of the chapter of '*Injuriae per applicationem, per constructionem, et per se*', in his *Duelli Lex Scripta, et non; aliterque*. The nicety of your discernment in all the matters here treated, will be sufficient, I am assured, to convince you that the mere circumstance of me referring you to this admirable passage, ought to satisfy your request, as a man of honour, for explanation.

With sentiments of profound respect,
Your most obedient servant,

VON JUNG
The Herr Johann Hermann
August 18th 18—

Hermann commenced the perusal of this epistle with a scowl, which, however, was converted into a smile of the most ludicrous self-complacency as he came to the rigmarole about *Injuriae per applicationem, per constructionem, et per se*. Having finished reading, he begged me, with the blandest of all possible smiles, to be seated, while he made reference to the treatise in question. Turning to the passage specified, he read it with great care to himself, then closed the book, and desired me, in my character of confidential acquaintance, to express to the Baron von Jung his exalted sense of his chivalrous behaviour, and, in that of second, to assure him that the explanation offered was of the fullest, the most honourable, and the most unequivocally satisfactory nature.

Somewhat amazed at all this, I made my retreat to the Baron. He seemed to receive Hermann's amicable letter as a matter of course, and after a few words of general conversation, went to an inner room and brought out the everlasting treatise *Duelli Lex Scripta, et non; aliterque*. He handed me the volume and asked me to look over some portion of it. I did so, but to little purpose, not being able to gather the least particle of meaning. He then took the book himself, and read me a chapter aloud. To my surprise, what he read proved to be a most horribly absurd account of a duel between two baboons. He now explained the mystery; showing that the volume, as it appeared *prima facie*, was written upon the plan of the nonsense verses of Du Bartas; that is to say, the language was ingeniously framed so as to present to the ear all the outward signs of intelligibility, and even of profundity, while in fact not a shadow of meaning existed. The key to the whole was found in leaving out every second and third word alternately, when there appeared a series of ludicrous quizzes upon a single combat as practised in modern times.

The Baron afterwards informed me that he had purposely thrown the treatise in Hermann's way two or three weeks before the adventure, and that he was satisfied, from the general tenor of his conversation, that he had studied it with the deepest attention, and firmly believed it to be a work of unusual merit. Upon this hint he proceeded. Hermann would have died a thousand deaths rather than acknowledge his inability to understand anything and everything in the universe that had ever been written about the *duello*.

How to Write a *Blackwood* Article

'In the name of the Prophet – figs!!'
Cry of the Turkish fig-pedlar

I presume everybody has heard of me. My name is the Signora Psyche Zenobia. This I know to be a fact. Nobody but my enemies ever calls me Suky Snobbs. I have been assured that Suky is but a vulgar corruption of Psyche, which is good Greek, and means 'the soul' (that's me, I'm all soul) and sometimes 'a butterfly', which latter meaning undoubtedly alludes to my appearance in my new crimson satin dress, with the sky-blue Arabian *mantelet*, and the trimmings of green *agraffas*, and the seven flounces of orange-coloured *auriculas*. As for Snobbs – any person who should look at me would be instantly aware that my name wasn't Snobbs. Miss Tabitha Turnip propagated that report through sheer envy. Tabitha Turnip indeed! Oh the little wretch! But what can we expect from a turnip? Wonder if she remembers the old adage about 'blood out of a turnip', &c.? [Mem. put her in mind of it the first opportunity.] [Mem. again – pull her nose.] Where was I? Ah! I have been assured that Snobbs is a mere corruption of Zenobia, and that Zenobia was a queen – (So am I. Dr Moneypenny always calls me the Queen of Hearts) – and that Zenobia, as well as Psyche, is good Greek, and that my father was 'a Greek', and that consequently I have a right to our patronymic, which is Zenobia and not by any means Snobbs. Nobody but Tabitha Turnip calls me Suky Snobbs. I am the Signora Psyche Zenobia.

As I said before, everybody has heard of me. I am that very Signora Psyche Zenobia, so justly celebrated as corresponding secretary to the 'Philadelphia, Regular, Exchange, Tea, Total, Young, Belles, Lettres, Universal, Experimental, Bibliographical, Association, To, Civilise, Humanity'. Dr Moneypenny made the title for us, and says he chose it because it sounded big like an empty rum-puncheon. (A vulgar man that sometimes – but he's deep.) We all sign the initials of the society after our names, in the fashion of the RSA, Royal Society of Arts – the SDUK, Society for the Diffusion of Useful Knowledge, &c., &c. Dr Moneypenny says that S stands for stale, and that DUK spells duck (but it don't), that SDUK stands for Stale Duck and not for Lord Brougham's society – but then Dr Moneypenny is such a queer man that I am never sure when he is telling me the truth. At any rate we always add the initials PRETTYBLUEBATCH to our names – that is to say, Philadelphia, Regular, Exchange, Tea, Total, Young, Belles, Lettres, Universal, Experimental, Bibliographical, Association, To, Civilise, Humanity – one letter for each word, which is a decided improvement upon Lord Brougham. Dr Moneypenny will have it that our initials give our true character – but for my life I can't see what he means.

Notwithstanding the good offices of the doctor, and the strenuous exertions of the association to get itself into notice, it met with no very great success until I joined it. The truth is, the members indulged in too flippant a tone of discussion. The papers read every Saturday evening were characterised less by depth than buffoonery. They were all whipped syllabub. There was no investigation of first causes, first principles. There was no investigation of anything at all. There was no attention paid to that great point, the 'fitness of things'. In short there was no fine writing like this. It was all low – very! No profundity, no reading, no metaphysics – nothing which the learned call spirituality, and which the unlearned choose to stigmatise as cant. [Dr M— says I ought to spell 'cant' with a capital K – but I know better.]

When I joined the society it was my endeavour to introduce a better style of thinking and writing, and all the world knows how well I have succeeded. We get up as good papers now in the PRETTYBLUEBATCH as any to be found even in *Blackwood*. I say, *Blackwood*, because I have been assured that the finest writing, upon every subject, is to be discovered in the pages of that justly celebrated magazine. We now take it for our model upon all themes, and are getting into rapid notice accordingly. And, after all, it's not so very difficult a matter to compose an article of the genuine *Blackwood* stamp, if one only goes properly about it. Of course I don't speak of the political articles. Everybody knows how they are managed, since Dr Moneypenny explained it. Mr Blackwood has a pair of tailor's-shears, and three apprentices who stand by him for orders. One hands him *The Times*, another the Examiner and a third a Gulley's *New Compendium of Slang-Whang*. Mr B— merely cuts out and intersperses. It is soon done – nothing but *Examiner*, *Slang-Whang*, and *Times* – then *Times*, *Slang-Whang*, and *Examiner* – and then *Times*, *Examiner*, and *Slang-Whang*.

But the chief merit of the magazine lies in its miscellaneous articles; and the best of these come under the head of what Dr Moneypenny calls the *bizarreries* (whatever that may mean) and what everybody else calls the intensities. This is a species of writing which I have long known how to appreciate, although it is only since my late visit to Mr Blackwood (deputed by the society) that I have been made aware of the exact method of composition. This method is very simple, but not so much so as the politics. Upon my calling at Mr B—'s, and making known to him the wishes of the society, he received me with great civility, took me into his study, and gave me a clear explanation of the whole process.

'My dear madam,' said he, evidently struck with my majestic appearance, for I had on the crimson satin, with the green *agraffas*, and orange-coloured *auriculas*. 'My dear madam,' said he, 'sit down. The matter stands thus: in the first place your writer of intensities must have very black ink, and a very big pen, with a very blunt nib. And, mark me, Miss Psyche Zenobia!' he continued, after a pause, with the most expressive energy and solemnity of manner, 'mark me! – that pen – must – never be mended! Herein, madam, lies the secret, the soul, of intensity. I assume upon myself to say, that no individual, of however great genius ever wrote with a good pen – understand me – a good article. You may take it for granted, that when manuscript can be read it is never worth reading. This is a leading principle in our faith, to which if you cannot readily assent, our conference is at an end.'

He paused. But, of course, as I had no wish to put an end to the conference, I assented to a proposition so very obvious, and one, too, of whose truth I had all along been sufficiently aware. He seemed pleased, and went on with his instructions.

'It may appear invidious in me, Miss Psyche Zenobia, to

refer you to any article, or set of articles, in the way of model or study, yet perhaps I may as well call your attention to a few cases. Let me see. There was "The Dead Alive", a capital thing! – the record of a gentleman's sensations when entombed before the breath was out of his body – full of taste, terror, sentiment, metaphysics, and erudition. You would have sworn that the writer had been born and brought up in a coffin. Then we had the "Confessions of an Opium-eater" – fine, very fine! – glorious imagination – deep philosophy – acute speculation – plenty of fire and fury, and a good spicing of the decidedly unintelligible. That was a nice bit of flummery, and went down the throats of the people delightfully. They would have it that Coleridge wrote the paper – but not so. It was composed by my pet baboon, Juniper, over a rummer of Hollands and water, "hot, without sugar".' [This I could scarcely have believed had it been anybody but Mr Blackwood, who assured me of it.] 'Then there was "The Involuntary Experimentalist", all about a gentleman who got baked in an oven, and came out alive and well, although certainly done to a turn. And then there was "The Diary of a Late Physician", where the merit lay in good rant, and indifferent Greek – both of them taking things with the public. And then there was "The Man in the Bell", a paper by the by, Miss Zenobia, which I cannot sufficiently recommend to your attention. It is the history of a young person who goes to sleep under the clapper of a church bell, and is awakened by its tolling for a funeral. The sound drives him mad, and, accordingly, pulling out his tablets, he gives a record of his sensations. Sensations are the great things after all. Should you ever be drowned or hung, be sure and make a note of your sensations – they will be worth to you ten guineas a sheet. If you wish to write forcibly, Miss Zenobia, pay minute attention to the sensations.'

'That I certainly will, Mr Blackwood,' said I.

'Good!' he replied. 'I see you are a pupil after my own heart. But I must put you *au fait* to the details necessary in composing what may be denominated a genuine *Blackwood* article of the sensation stamp – the kind which you will understand me to say I consider the best for all purposes.

'The first thing requisite is to get yourself into such a scrape as no one ever got into before. The oven, for instance, that was a good hit. But if you have no oven, or big bell, at hand, and if you cannot conveniently tumble out of a balloon, or be swallowed up in an earthquake, or get stuck fast in a chimney, you will have to be contented with simply imagining some similar misadventure. I should prefer, however, that you have the actual fact to bear you out. Nothing so well assists the fancy, as an experimental knowledge of the matter in hand. "Truth is strange", you know, "stranger than fiction" – besides being more to the purpose.'

Here I assured him I had an excellent pair of garters, and would go and hang myself forthwith.

'Good!' he replied, 'do so; although hanging is somewhat hackneyed. Perhaps you might do better. Take a dose of Brandreth's pills, and then give us your sensations. However, my instructions will apply equally well to any variety of misadventure, and in your way home you may easily get knocked in the head, or run over by an omnibus, or bitten by a mad dog, or drowned in a gutter. But to proceed.

'Having determined upon your subject, you must next consider the tone, or manner, of your narration. There is the tone didactic, the tone enthusiastic, the tone natural – all commonplace enough. But then there is the tone laconic, or curt, which has lately come much into use. It consists in short sentences. Somehow thus: Can't be too brief. Can't be too snappish. Always a full stop. And never a paragraph.

'Then there is the tone elevated, diffusive, and interjectional. Some of our best novelists patronise this tone. The words must be all in a whirl, like a humming-top, and make a noise very similar, which answers remarkably well instead of meaning. This is the best of all possible styles where the writer is in too great a hurry to think.

'The tone metaphysical is also a good one. If you know any big words this is your chance for them. Talk of the Ionic and Eleatic schools – of Archytas, Gorgias, and Alcmaeon. Say something about objectivity and subjectivity. Be sure and abuse a man named Locke. Turn up your nose at things in general, and when you let slip anything a little too absurd, you need not be at the trouble of scratching it out, but just add a footnote and say that you are indebted for the above profound observation to the *Kritik der reinem Vernunft*, or to the *Metaphysische Anfangsgründe der Naturwissenschaft*. This would look erudite and – and – and frank.

'There are various other tones of equal celebrity, but I shall mention only two more – the tone transcendental and the tone heterogeneous. In the former the merit consists in seeing into the nature of affairs a very great deal farther than anybody else. This second sight is very efficient when properly managed. A little reading of the *Dial* will carry you a great way. Eschew, in this case, big words; get them as small as possible, and write them upside down. Look over Channing's poems and quote what he says about a "fat little man with a delusive show of Can". Put in something about the supernal oneness. Don't say a syllable about the infernal twoness. Above all, study innuendo. Hint everything – assert nothing. If you feel inclined to say "bread and butter", do not by any means say it outright. You may say anything and everything approaching to "bread and butter". You may hint at buckwheat cake, or you may even go so far as to insinuate oatmeal porridge, but if bread and butter be your real meaning, be cautious, my dear Miss Psyche, not on any account to say "bread and butter"!'

I assured him that I should never say it again as long as I lived. He kissed me and continued: 'As for the tone heterogeneous, it is merely a judicious mixture, in equal proportions, of all the other tones in the world, and is consequently made up of everything deep, great, odd, piquant, pertinent, and pretty.

'Let us suppose now you have determined upon your incidents and tone. The most important portion – in fact, the soul of the whole business, is yet to be attended to – I allude to the filling up. It is not to be supposed that a lady, or gentleman either, has been leading the life of a bookworm. And yet above all things it is necessary that your article have an air of erudition, or at least afford evidence of extensive general reading. Now I'll put you in the way of accomplishing this point. See here!' (pulling down some three or four ordinary-looking volumes, and opening them at random). 'By casting your eye down almost any page of any book in the world, you will be able to perceive at once a host of little scraps of either learning or bel-espritism, which are the very thing for the spicing of a *Blackwood* article. You might as well note down a few while I read them to you. I shall make two divisions: first, "Piquant facts for the manufacture of similes"; and, second, "Piquant expressions to be introduced as occasion may require". Write now!' – and I wrote as he dictated.

'Piquant facts for similes. "There were originally but three muses – Melete, Mneme, Aoede – meditation, memory, and singing." You may make a good deal of that little fact if properly worked. You see it is not generally known, and looks *recherché*. You must be careful and give the thing with a downright *improviso* air.

'Again. "The river Alpheus passed beneath the sea, and emerged without injury to the purity of its waters." Rather stale that, to be sure, but, if properly dressed and dished up, will look quite as fresh as ever.

'Here is something better. "The Persian iris appears to some persons to possess a sweet and very powerful perfume, while to others it is perfectly scentless." Fine that, and very delicate! Turn it about a little, and it will do wonders. We'll have something else in the botanical line. There's nothing goes down so well, especially with the help of a little Latin. Write!

' "*The Epidendrum Flos Aeris*, of Java, bears a very beautiful flower, and will live when pulled up by the roots. The natives suspend it by a cord from the ceiling, and enjoy its fragrance for years." That's capital! That will do for the similes. Now for the "Piquant expressions".

'Piquant expressions. "The venerable Chinese novel *Ju-Kiao-Li*." Good! By introducing these few words with dexterity you will evince your intimate acquaintance with the language and literature of the Chinese. With the aid of this you may either get along without either Arabic, or Sanscrit, or Chickasaw. There is no passing muster, however, without Spanish, Italian, German, Latin, and Greek. I must look you out a little specimen of each. Any scrap will answer, because you must depend upon your own ingenuity to make it fit into your article. Now write!

' "*Aussi tendre que Zaire*" – as tender as Zaire – French. Alludes to the frequent repetition of the phrase, *la tendre Zaire*, in the French tragedy of that name. Properly introduced, will show not only your knowledge of the language, but your general reading and wit. You can say, for instance, that the chicken you were eating (write an article about being choked to death by a chicken-bone) was not altogether *aussi tendre que Zaire*. Write!

Van muerte tan escondida,
Que no te sienta venir,
Porque el plazer del morir,
No mestorne a dar la vida.

That's Spanish – from Miguel de Cervantes. "Come quickly, O death! but be sure and don't let me see you coming, lest thes pleasure I shall feel at your appearance should unfortunately bring me back again to life." This you may slip in quite apropos when you are struggling in the last agonies with the chicken-bone. Write!

Il pover' huomo che non se'n era accorto,
Andava combattendo, e era morto.

That's Italian, you perceive – from Ariosto. It means that a great hero, in the heat of combat, not perceiving that he had been fairly killed, continued to fight valiantly, dead as he was. The application of this to your own case is obvious – for I trust, Miss Psyche, that you will not neglect to kick for at least an hour and a half after you have been choked to death by that chicken-bone. Please to write!

Und sterb' ich doch, so sterb' ich denn
Durch sie – durch sie!

That's German – from Schiller. "And if I die, at least I die – for thee – for thee!" Here it is clear that you are apostrophising the cause of your disaster, the chicken. Indeed what gentleman (or lady either) of sense, *wouldn't* die, I should like to know, for a well fattened capon of the right Molucca breed, stuffed with capers and mushrooms, and served up in a salad-bowl, with orange-jellies *en mosaïques*. Write! (You can get them that way at Tortoni's.) – Write, if you please!

'Here is a nice little Latin phrase, and rare too, (one can't be too *recherché* or brief in one's Latin, it's getting so common – *ignoratio elenchi*. He has committed an *ignoratio elenchi* – that is to say, he has understood the words of your proposition, but not the idea. The man was a fool, you see. Some poor fellow whom you address while choking with that chicken-bone, and who therefore didn't precisely understand what you were talking about. Throw the *ignoratio elenchi* in his teeth, and, at once, you have him annihilated. If he dares to reply, you can tell him from Lucan (here it is) that speeches are mere *anemonae verborum*, anemone words. The anemone, with great brilliancy, has no smell. Or, if he begins to bluster, you may be down upon him with *insomnia Jovis*, reveries of Jupiter – a phrase which Silius Italicus (see here!) applies to thoughts pompous and inflated. This will be sure and cut him to the heart. He can do nothing but roll over and die. Will you be kind enough to write?

'In Greek we must have something pretty – from Demosthenes, for example. Ανερο φευγων και παλιν. [Anero pheugoen kai palin makesetai.] There is a tolerably good translation of it in *Hudibras*:

> For he that flies may fight again,
> Which he can never do that's slain.

In a *Blackwood* article nothing makes so fine a show as your Greek. The very letters have an air of profundity about them. Only observe, madam, the astute look of that epsilon! That phi ought certainly to be a bishop! Was ever there a smarter fellow than that omicron? Just twig that tau! In short, there is nothing like Greek for a genuine sensation-paper. In the present case your application is the most obvious thing in the world. Rap out the sentence, with a huge oath, and by way of *ultimatum* at the good-for-nothing dunderheaded villain who couldn't understand your plain English in relation to the chicken-bone. He'll take the hint and be off, you may depend upon it.'

These were all the instructions Mr B— could afford me upon the topic in question, but I felt they would be entirely sufficient. I was, at length, able to write a genuine *Blackwood* article, and determined to do it forthwith. In taking leave of me, Mr B— made a proposition for the purchase of the paper when written; but as he could offer me only fifty guineas a sheet, I thought it better to let our society have it, than sacrifice it for so paltry a sum. Notwithstanding this niggardly spirit, however, the gentleman showed his consideration for me in all other respects, and indeed treated me with the greatest civility. His parting words made a deep impression upon my heart, and I hope I shall always remember them with gratitude.

'My dear Miss Zenobia,' he said, while the tears stood in his eyes, 'is there *anything* else I can do to promote the success of your laudable undertaking? Let me reflect! It is just possible that you may not be able, so soon as convenient, to – to – get yourself drowned, or – choked with a chicken-bone, or – or hung – or – bitten by a – but stay! Now I think me of it, there are a couple of very excellent bulldogs in the yard – fine fellows, I assure you – savage, and all that – indeed just the thing for your money – they'll have you eaten up, *auriculas* and all, in less than five minutes (here's my watch!) – and then only think of the sensations! Here! I say – Tom! – Peter! – Dick, you villain! – let out those – ' but as I was really in a great hurry, and had not another moment to spare, I was reluctantly forced to expedite my departure, and accordingly took leave *at once* – somewhat more abruptly, I admit, than strict courtesy would have otherwise allowed.

It was my primary object upon quitting Mr Blackwood, to get into some immediate difficulty, pursuant to his advice, and with this view I spent the greater part of the day in wandering about Edinburgh, seeking for desperate adventures – adventures adequate to the intensity of my feelings, and adapted to the vast character of the article I intended to write. In this excursion I was attended by one negro servant, Pompey, and my little lap-dog Diana, whom I had brought with me from Philadelphia. It was not, however, until late in the afternoon that I fully succeeded in my arduous undertaking. An important event then happened of which the following *Blackwood* article, in the tone heterogeneous, is the substance and result.

A Predicament

What chance, good lady, hath bereft you thus?
COMUS

It was a quiet and still afternoon when I strolled forth in the goodly city of Edina. The confusion and bustle in the streets were terrible. Men were talking. Women were screaming. Children were choking. Pigs were whistling. Carts they rattled. Bulls they bellowed. Cows they lowed. Horses they neighed. Cats they caterwauled. Dogs they danced. *Danced*! Could it then be possible? *Danced*! Alas, thought I, my dancing days are over! Thus it is ever. What a host of gloomy recollections will ever and anon be awakened in the mind of genius and imaginative contemplation, especially of a genius doomed to the everlasting and eternal, and continual, and, as one might say, the – *continued* – yes, the *continued and continuous*, bitter, harassing, disturbing, and, if I may be allowed the expression, the very disturbing influence of the serene, and godlike, and heavenly, and exalted, and elevated, and purifying effect of what may be rightly termed the most enviable, the most *truly* enviable – nay! the most benignly beautiful, the most deliciously ethereal, and, as it were, the most *pretty* (if I may use so bold an expression) thing (pardon me, gentle reader!) in the world – but I am always led away by my feelings. In *such* a mind, I repeat, what a host of recollections are stirred up by a trifle! The dogs danced! I – I *could* not! They frisked – I wept. They capered – I sobbed aloud. Touching circumstances! which cannot fail to bring to the recollection of the classical reader that exquisite passage in relation to the fitness of things, which is to be found in the commencement of the third volume of that admirable and venerable Chinese novel the *Jo-Go-Slow*.

In my solitary walk through the city I had two humble but faithful companions. Diana, my poodle! sweetest of creatures! She had a quantity of hair over her one eye, and a blue ribband tied fashionably around her neck. Diana was not more than five inches in height, but her head was somewhat bigger than her body, and her tail being cut off exceedingly close, gave an air of injured innocence to the interesting animal which rendered her a favourite with all.

And Pompey, my negro! – sweet Pompey! how shall I ever forget thee? I had taken Pompey's arm. He was three feet in height (I like to be particular) and about seventy, or perhaps eighty, years of age. He had bow-legs and was corpulent. His mouth should not be called small, nor his ears short. His teeth, however, were like pearl, and his large full eyes were deliciously white. Nature had endowed him with no neck, and had placed his ankles (as usual with that race) in the middle of the upper portion of the feet. He was clad with a striking simplicity. His sole garments were a stock of nine inches in height, and a nearly-new drab overcoat which had formerly been in the service of the tall, stately, and illustrious Dr Moneypenny. It was a good overcoat. It was well cut. It was well made. The coat was nearly new. Pompey held it up out of the dirt with both hands.

There were three persons in our party, and two of them have already been the subject of remark. There was a third – that person was myself. I am the Signora Psyche Zenobia. I am not Suky Snobbs. My appearance is commanding. On the memorable occasion of which I speak I was habited in a crimson satin dress, with a sky-blue Arabian *mantelet*. And the dress had trimmings of green *agraffas*, and seven graceful flounces of the orange-coloured *auricula*. I thus formed the third of the party. There was the poodle. There was Pompey. There was myself. We were *three*. Thus it is said there were originally but three Furies – Melty, Nimmy, and Hetty – Meditation, Memory, and Fiddling.

Leaning upon the arm of the gallant Pompey, and attended at a respectable distance by Diana, I proceeded down one of the populous and very pleasant streets of the now deserted Edina. On a sudden, there presented itself to view a church – a Gothic cathedral – vast, venerable, and with a tall steeple, which towered into the sky. What madness now possessed me? Why did I rush upon my fate? I was seized with an uncontrollable desire to ascend the giddy pinnacle, and then survey the immense extent of the city. The door of the cathedral stood invitingly open. My destiny prevailed. I entered the ominous archway. Where then was my guardian angel? – if indeed such angels there be. If! Distressing monosyllable! what world of mystery, and meaning, and doubt, and uncertainty is there involved in thy two letters! I entered the ominous archway! I entered; and, without injury to my orange-coloured *auriculas*, I passed beneath the portal, and emerged within the vestibule. Thus it is said the immense river Alfred passed, unscathed, and unwetted, beneath the sea.

I thought the staircase would never have an end. *Round!* Yes, they went round and up, and round and up and round and up, until I could not help surmising, with the sagacious Pompey, upon whose supporting arm I leaned in all the confidence of early affection – I *could* not help surmising that the upper end of the continuous spiral ladder had been accidentally, or perhaps designedly, removed. I paused for breath; and, in the meantime, an accident occurred of too momentous a nature in a moral, and also in a metaphysical point of view, to be passed over without notice. It appeared to me – indeed I was quite confident of the fact – I could not be mistaken – no! I had, for some moments, carefully and anxiously observed the motions of my Diana – I say that *I could not be* mistaken – Diana *smelt a rat*! At once I called Pompey's attention to the subject, and he – he agreed with me. There was then no longer any reasonable room for doubt. The rat had been smelled – and by Diana. Heavens! shall I ever forget the intense excitement of the moment? Alas! what is the boasted intellect of man? The rat! – it was there – that is to say, it was somewhere. Diana smelled the rat. I – I *could* not! Thus it is said the Prussian Isis has, for some persons, a sweet and very powerful perfume, while to others it is perfectly scentless.

The staircase had been surmounted, and there were now only three or four more upward steps intervening between us and the summit. We still ascended, and now only one step remained. One step! One little, little step! Upon one such little step in the great staircase of human life how vast a sum of human happiness or misery depends! I thought of myself, then of Pompey, and then of the mysterious and inexplicable destiny which surrounded us. I thought of Pompey! – alas, I thought of love! I thought of my many false *steps* which have been taken, and may be taken again. I resolved to be more cautious, more reserved. I abandoned the arm of Pompey, and, without his assistance, surmounted the one remaining step, and gained the chamber of the belfry. I was followed immediately afterwards by my poodle. Pompey alone remained behind. I stood at the head of the staircase, and encouraged him to ascend. He stretched forth to me his hand, and unfortunately in so doing was forced to abandon his firm hold upon the overcoat. Will the gods never cease their persecution? The overcoat is dropped, and, with one of his feet, Pompey stepped upon the long and trailing skirt of the overcoat. He stumbled and fell – this consequence was inevitable. He fell forward, and, with his accursed head, striking me full in the – in the breast, precipitated me headlong, together with himself, upon the hard, filthy, and detestable floor of the belfry. But my revenge was sure, sudden, and complete. Seizing him furiously by the wool with both hands, I tore out a vast quantity of black, and crisp, and curling material, and tossed it from me with every manifestation of disdain. It fell among the ropes of the belfry and remained. Pompey arose, and said no word. But he regarded me piteously with his large eyes and – sighed. Ye Gods – that sigh! It sunk into my heart. And the hair – the wool! Could I have reached that wool I would have bathed it with my tears, in testimony of regret. But alas! it was now far beyond my grasp. As it dangled among the cordage of the bell, I fancied it alive. I fancied that it stood on end with indignation. Thus the *happy-dandy Flos Aeris* of Java bears, it is said, a beautiful flower, which will live when pulled up by the roots. The natives suspend it by a cord from the ceiling and enjoy its fragrance for years.

Our quarrel was now made up, and we looked about the room for an aperture through which to survey the city of Edina. Windows there were none. The sole light admitted into the gloomy chamber proceeded from a square opening, about a foot in diameter, at a height of about seven feet from the floor. Yet what will the energy of true genius not effect? I resolved to clamber up to this hole. A vast quantity of wheels, pinions, and other cabbalistic-looking machinery stood opposite the hole, close to it; and through the hole there passed an iron rod from the machinery. Between the wheels and the wall where the hole lay there was barely room for my body – yet I was desperate, and determined to persevere. I called Pompey to my side.

'You perceive that aperture, Pompey. I wish to look through it. You will stand here just beneath the hole – so. Now, hold out one of your hands, Pompey, and let me step upon it – thus. Now, the other hand, Pompey, and with its aid I will get upon your shoulders.'

He did everything I wished, and I found, upon getting up, that I could easily pass my head and neck through the aperture. The prospect was sublime. Nothing could be more magnificent. I merely paused a moment to bid Diana behave herself, and assure Pompey that I would be considerate and bear as lightly as possible upon his shoulders. I told him I would be tender of his feelings – *ossi tender que beefsteak*. Having done this justice to my faithful friend, I gave myself up with great zest and enthusiasm to the enjoyment of the scene which so obligingly spread itself out before my eyes.

Upon this subject, however, I shall forbear to dilate. I will not describe the city of Edinburgh. Everyone has been to the city of Edinburgh. Everyone has been to Edinburgh – the classic Edina. I will confine myself to the momentous details of my own lamentable adventure. Having, in some measure, satisfied my curiosity in regard to the extent, situation, and general appearance of the city, I had leisure to survey the church in which I was, and the delicate architecture of the steeple. I observed that the aperture through which I had thrust my head was an opening in the dial-plate of a gigantic clock, and must have appeared, from the street, as a large keyhole, such as we see in the face of the French watches. No doubt the true object was to admit the arm of an attendant, to adjust, when necessary, the hands of the clock from within. I observed also, with surprise, the immense size of these hands, the longest of which could not have been less than ten feet in length, and, where broadest, eight or nine inches in breadth. They were of solid steel apparently, and their edges appeared to be sharp. Having noticed these particulars, and some others, I again turned my eyes upon the glorious prospect below, and soon became absorbed in contemplation.

From this, after some minutes, I was aroused by the voice of Pompey, who declared that he could stand it no longer, and requested that I would be so kind as to come down. This was unreasonable, and I told him so in a speech of some length. He replied, but with an evident misunderstanding of my ideas upon the subject. I accordingly grew angry, and told him in plain words, that he was a fool, that he had committed an *ignoramus e-clench-eye*, that his notions were mere *insommary Bovis*, and his words little better than an *ennemywerrybor'em*. With this he appeared satisfied, and I resumed my contemplations.

It might have been half an hour after this altercation when, as I was deeply absorbed in the heavenly scenery beneath me, I was startled by something very cold which pressed with a gentle pressure on the back of my neck. It is needless to say that I felt inexpressibly alarmed. I knew that Pompey was beneath my feet, and that Diana was sitting, according to my explicit directions, upon her hind legs, in the farthest corner of the room. What could it be? Alas! I but too soon discovered. Turning my head gently to one side, I perceived, to my extreme horror, that the huge, glittering, scimitar-like minute-hand of the clock had, in the course of its hourly revolution, *descended upon my neck*. There was, I knew, not a second to be lost. I pulled back at once – but it was too late. There was no chance of forcing my head through the mouth of that terrible trap in which it was so fairly caught, and which grew narrower and narrower with a rapidity too horrible to be conceived. The agony of that moment is not to be imagined. I threw up my hands and endeavoured, with all my strength, to force upward the ponderous iron bar. I might as well have tried to lift the cathedral itself. Down, down, down it came, closer and yet closer. I screamed to Pompey for aid; but he said that I had hurt his feelings by calling him 'an ignorant old squint-eye': I yelled to Diana; but she only said 'bow-wow-wow', and that I had told her 'on no account to stir from the corner'. Thus I had no relief to expect from my associates.

Meantime the ponderous and terrific *Scythe of Time* (for I now discovered the literal import of that classical phrase) had not stopped, nor was it likely to stop, in its career. Down and still down, it came. It had already buried its sharp edge a full inch in my flesh, and my sensations grew indistinct and confused. At one time I fancied myself in Philadelphia with the stately Dr Moneypenny, at another in the back parlour of Mr Blackwood receiving his invaluable instructions. And then again the sweet recollection of better and earlier times came over me, and I thought of that happy period when the world was not all a desert, and Pompey not altogether cruel.

The ticking of the machinery amused me. *Amused me*, I say, for my sensations now bordered upon perfect happiness, and the most trifling circumstances afforded me pleasure. The eternal *click-clack, click-clack, click-clack* of the clock was the most melodious of music in my ears, and occasionally even put me in mind of the graceful sermonic harangues of Dr Ollapod. Then there were the great figures upon the dial-plate – how intelligent, how intellectual, they all looked! And presently they took to dancing the Mazurka, and I think it was the figure V who performed the most to my satisfaction. She was evidently a lady of breeding. None of your swaggerers, and nothing at all indelicate in her motions. She did the pirouette to admiration – whirling round upon her apex. I made an endeavour to hand her a chair, for I saw that she appeared fatigued with her exertions – and it was not until then that I fully perceived my lamentable situation. Lamentable indeed! The bar had buried itself two inches in my neck. I was aroused to a sense of exquisite pain. I prayed for death, and, in the agony of the moment, could not help repeating those exquisite verses of the poet Miguel de Cervantes:

> *Vanny Buren, tan escondida*
> *Query no te senty venny*
> *Pork and pleasure, delly morry*
> *Nommy, torny, darry, widdy!*

But now a new horror presented itself, and one indeed sufficient to startle the strongest nerves. My eyes, from the cruel pressure of the machine, were absolutely starting from their sockets. While I was thinking how I should possibly manage without them, one actually tumbled out of my head, and, rolling down the steep side of the steeple, lodged in the rain gutter which ran along the eaves of the main building. The loss of the eye was not so much as the insolent air of independence and contempt with which it regarded me after it was out. There it lay in the gutter just under my nose, and the airs it gave itself would have been ridiculous had they not been disgusting. Such a winking and blinking were never before seen. This behaviour on the part of my eye in the gutter was not only irritating on account of its manifest insolence and shameful ingratitude, but was also exceedingly inconvenient on account of the sympathy which always exists between two eyes of the same head, however far apart. I was forced, in a manner, to wink and to blink, whether I would or not, in exact concert with the scoundrelly thing that lay just under my nose. I was presently relieved, however, by the dropping out of the other eye. In falling it took the same direction (possibly a concerted plot) as its fellow. Both rolled out of the gutter together, and in truth I was very glad to get rid of them.

The bar was now four inches and a half deep in my neck, and there was only a little bit of skin to cut through. My sensations were those of entire happiness, for I felt that in a few minutes, at farthest, I should be relieved from my disagreeable situation. And in this expectation I was not at all deceived. At twenty-five minutes past five in the afternoon, precisely, the huge minute-hand had proceeded sufficiently far on its terrible revolution to sever the small remainder of my neck. I was not sorry to see the head which had occasioned me so much embarrassment at length make a final separation from my body. It first rolled down the side of the steeple, then lodged, for a few seconds, in the gutter, and then made its way, with a plunge, into the middle of the street.

I will candidly confess that my feelings were now of the most singular – nay, of the most mysterious, the most perplexing and incomprehensible character. My senses were here and there at one and the same moment. With my head I imagined, at one time, that I, the head, was the real Signora Psyche Zenobia – at another I felt convinced that myself, the body, was the proper identity. To clear my ideas on this topic I felt in my pocket for my snuff-box, but, upon getting it, and endeavouring to apply a pinch of its grateful contents in the ordinary manner, I became immediately aware of my peculiar deficiency, and threw the box at once down to my head. It took a pinch with great satisfaction, and smiled me an acknowledgement in return. Shortly afterwards it made me a speech, which I could hear but indistinctly without ears. I gathered enough, however, to know that it was astonished at my wishing to remain alive under such circumstances. In the concluding sentences it quoted the noble words of Ariosto:

Il pover hommy che non sera corty
And have a combat tenty erry morty;

thus comparing me to the hero who, in the heat of the combat, not perceiving that he was dead, continued to contest the battle with inextinguishable valour. There was nothing now to prevent my getting down from my elevation, and I did so. What it was that Pompey saw so very peculiar in my appearance I have never yet been able to find out. The fellow opened his mouth from ear to ear, and shut his two eyes as if he were endeavouring to crack nuts between the lids. Finally, throwing off his overcoat, he made one spring for the staircase and disappeared. I hurled after the scoundrel these vehement words of Demosthenes:

Andrew O'Phlegethon, you really make haste to fly –

and then turned to the darling of my heart, to the one-eyed! the shaggy-haired Diana. Alas! what a horrible vision affronted my eyes? Was that a rat I saw skulking into his hole? Are these the picked bones of the little angel who has been cruelly devoured by the monster? Ye gods! and what do I behold – is that the departed spirit, the shade, the ghost, of my beloved puppy, which I perceive sitting with a grace so melancholy, in the corner? Hearken! for she speaks, and, heavens! it is in the German of Schiller:

'Unt stubby duk, so stubby dun
Duk she! duk she!'

Alas! and are not her words too true?

And if I died, at least I died
For thee – for thee.

Sweet creature! she *too* has sacrificed herself in my behalf. Dogless, niggerless, headless, what *now* remains for the unhappy Signora Psyche Zenobia? Alas – *nothing*! I have done.

The Man that was Used Up

A TALE OF THE LATE BUGABOO AND KICKAPOO CAMPAIGN

Pleurez, pleurez, mes yeux, et fondez vous en eau!
La moitié de ma vie a mis l'autre au tombeau.

CORNEILLE

I cannot just now remember when or where I first made the acquaintance of that truly fine-looking fellow, Brevet Brigadier General John A. B. C. Smith. Someone *did* introduce me to the gentleman, I am sure – at some public meeting, I know very well – held about something of great importance, no doubt – at some place or other, I feel convinced – whose name I have unaccountably forgotten. The truth is – that the introduction was attended, upon my part, with a degree of anxious embarrassment which operated to prevent any definite impressions of either time or place. I am constitutionally nervous – this, with me, is a family failing, and I can't help it. In especial, the slightest appearance of mystery – of any point I cannot exactly comprehend – puts me at once into a pitiable state of agitation.

There was something, as it were, remarkable – yes, *remarkable*, although this is but a feeble term to express my full meaning – about the entire individuality of the personage in question. He was, perhaps, six feet in height, and of a presence singularly commanding. There was an *air distingué* pervading the whole man, which spoke of high breeding, and hinted at high birth. Upon this topic – the topic of Smith's personal appearance – I have a kind of melancholy satisfaction in being minute. His head of hair would have done honour to a Brutus – nothing could be more richly flowing, or possess a brighter gloss. It was of a jetty black; which was also the colour, or more properly the no colour of his unimaginable whiskers. You perceive I cannot speak of these latter without enthusiasm; it is not too much to say that they were the handsomest pair of whiskers under the sun. At all events, they encircled, and at times partially overshadowed, a mouth utterly unequalled. Here were the most entirely even, and the most brilliantly white of all conceivable teeth. From between them, upon every proper occasion, issued a voice of surpassing clearness, melody, and strength. In the matter of eyes, also, my acquaintance was pre-eminently endowed. Either one of such a pair was worth a couple of the ordinary ocular organs. They were of a deep hazel, exceedingly large and lustrous; and there was perceptible about them, ever and anon, just that amount of interesting obliquity which gives pregnancy to expression.

The bust of the General was unquestionably the finest bust I ever saw. For your life you could not have found a fault with its wonderful proportion. This rare peculiarity set off to great advantage a pair of shoulders which would have called up a blush of conscious inferiority into the countenance of the marble Apollo. I have a passion for fine shoulders, and may say that I never beheld them in perfection before. The arms altogether were admirably modelled. Nor were the lower limbs less superb. These were, indeed, the *ne plus ultra* of good legs. Every connoisseur in such matters admitted the legs to be good. There was neither too much flesh, nor too little, neither rudeness nor fragility. I could not imagine a more graceful curve than that of the *os femoris*, and there was just that due gentle prominence in the rear of the *fibula* which goes to the conformation of a properly proportioned calf. I wish to God my young and talented friend Chiponchipino, the sculptor, had but seen the legs of Brevet Brigadier General John A. B. C. Smith.

But although men so absolutely fine-looking are neither as plenty as reasons or blackberries, still I could not bring myself to believe that *the remarkable* something to which I alluded just now – that the odd air of *je ne sais quoi* which hung about my new acquaintance – lay altogether, or indeed at all, in the supreme excellence of his bodily endowments. Perhaps it might be traced to the *manner* – yet here again I could not pretend to be positive. There *was* a primness, not to say stiffness, in his carriage – a degree of measured, and, if I may so express it, of rectangular precision, attending his every movement, which, observed in a more diminutive figure, would have had the least little savour in the world, of affectation, pomposity or constraint, but which noticed in a gentleman of his undoubted dimensions, was readily placed to the account of reserve, *hauteur* – of a commendable sense, in short, of what is due to the dignity of colossal proportion.

The kind friend who presented me to General Smith whispered in my ear some few words of comment upon the man. He was a *remarkable* man – a *very* remarkable man – indeed one of the *most* remarkable men of the age. He was an especial favourite, too, with the ladies – chiefly on account of his high reputation for courage.

'In *that* point he is unrivalled – indeed he is a perfect desperado – a downright fire-eater, and no mistake,' said my friend, here dropping his voice excessively low, and thrilling me with the mystery of his tone.

'A downright fire-eater, and *no* mistake. Showed *that*, I should say, to some purpose, in the late tremendous swamp-fight away down South, with the Bugaboo and Kickapoo Indians.' [Here my friend opened his eyes to some extent.] 'Bless my soul! – blood and thunder, and all that! – *prodigies* of valour! – heard of him of course? – you know he's the man – '

'Man alive, how *do* you do? why, how *are ye? very* glad to see ye, indeed!' here interrupted the General himself, seizing my companion by the hand as he drew near, and bowing stiffly, but profoundly, as I was presented. I then thought (and I think so still), that I never heard a clearer nor a stronger voice, nor beheld a finer set of teeth: but I *must* say that I was sorry for the interruption just at that moment, as, owing to the whispers and insinuations aforesaid, my interest had been greatly excited in the hero of the Bugaboo and Kickapoo campaign.

However, the delightfully luminous conversation of Brevet Brigadier General John A. B. C. Smith soon completely dissipated this chagrin. My friend leaving us immediately, we had quite a long *tête-à-tête*, and I was not only pleased but *really* – instructed. I never heard a more fluent talker, or a man of greater general information. With becoming modesty, he forbore, nevertheless, to touch upon the theme I had just then most at heart – I mean the mysterious circumstances attending the Bugaboo war – and, on my own part, what I conceive to be a proper sense of delicacy forbade me to broach the subject; although, in truth, I was exceedingly tempted to do so. I perceived, too, that the gallant soldier preferred topics of philosophical interest, and that he delighted, especially, in commenting upon the rapid march of mechanical invention. Indeed, lead him where I would, this was a point to which he invariably came back.

'There is nothing at all like it,' he would say; 'we are a wonderful people, and live in a wonderful age. Parachutes and railroads – mantraps and spring-guns! Our steamboats are upon every sea, and the Nassau balloon packet is about to run regular trips (fare either way only twenty pounds sterling) between London and Timbuktu. And who shall calculate the immense influence upon social life – upon arts – upon commerce – upon literature – which will be the immediate result of the great principles of electro-magnetics! Nor is this all, let me assure you! There is really no end to the march of invention. The most wonderful – the most ingenious – and let me add, Mr – Mr – Thompson, I believe, is your name – let me add, I say, the most *useful* – the most truly *useful* mechanical contrivances, are daily springing up like mushrooms, if I may so express myself, or, more figuratively, like – ah – grasshoppers – like grasshoppers, Mr Thompson – about us and ah – ah – ah – around us!'

Thompson, to be sure, is not my name; but it is needless to say that I left General Smith with a heightened interest in the man, with an exalted opinion of his conversational powers, and a deep sense of the valuable privileges we enjoy in living in this age of mechanical invention. My curiosity, however, had not been altogether satisfied, and I resolved to prosecute immediate enquiry among my acquaintances touching the Brevet Brigadier General himself, and particularly respecting the tremendous events *quorum pars magna fuit*, during the Bugaboo and Kickapoo campaign.

The first opportunity which presented itself, and which (*horresco referens*) I did not in the least scruple to seize, occurred at the Church of the Revd Dr Drummummupp, where I found myself established, one Sunday, just at sermon time, not only in the pew, but by the side, of that worthy and communicative little friend of mine, Miss Tabitha T. Thus seated, I congratulated myself, and with much reason, upon the very flattering state of affairs. If any person knew anything about Brevet Brigadier General John A. B. C. Smith, that person, it was clear to me, was Miss Tabitha T. We telegraphed a few signals, and then commenced, *sotto voce*, a brisk *tête-à-tête*.

'Smith!' said she, in reply to my very earnest enquiry; 'Smith! – why, not General John A. B. C.? Bless me, I thought you *knew* all about *him*! This is a wonderfully inventive age! Horrid affair that! A bloody set of wretches, those Kickapoos! Fought like a hero – prodigies of valour – immortal renown. Smith! – Brevet Brigadier General John A. B. C.! why, you know he's the man – '

'Man,' here broke in Doctor Drummummupp, at the top of his voice, and with a thump that came near knocking the pulpit about our ears; 'man that is born of a woman hath but a short time to live; he cometh up and is cut down like a flower!' I started to the extremity of the pew, and perceived by the animated looks of the divine, that the wrath which had nearly proved fatal to the pulpit had been excited by the whispers of the lady and myself. There was no help for it; so I submitted with a good grace, and listened, in all the martyrdom of dignified silence, to the balance of that very capital discourse.

Next evening found me a somewhat late visitor at the Rantipole Theatre, where I felt sure of satisfying my curiosity at once, by merely stepping into the box of those exquisite specimens of affability and omniscience, the Misses Arabella and Miranda Cognoscenti. That fine tragedian, Climax, was doing Iago to a very crowded house, and I experienced some little difficulty in making my wishes understood; especially as our box was next the slips, and completely overlooked the stage.

'Smith?' said Miss Arabella, as she at length comprehended the purport of my query; 'Smith? – why, not General John A. B. C.?'

'Smith?' enquired Miranda, musingly. 'God bless me, did you ever behold a finer figure?'

'Never, madam, but *do* tell me – '

'Or so inimitable grace?'

'Never, upon my word! – But pray inform me – '

'Or so just an appreciation of stage effect?'

'Madam!'

'Or a more delicate sense of the true beauties of Shakespeare? Be so good as to look at that leg!'

'The devil!' and I turned again to her sister.

'Smith?' said she, 'why, not General John A. B. C.? Horrid affair that, wasn't it? – great wretches, those Bugaboos – savage and so on – but we live in a wonderfully inventive age! – Smith! – O yes! great man! – perfect desperado – immortal renown – prodigies of valour! *Never heard!*' [This was given in a scream.] 'Bless my soul! why, he's the man – '

> '... mandragora
> Nor all the drowsy syrups of the world
> Shall ever medicine thee to that sweet sleep
> Which thou ow'dst yesterday!'

here roared out Climax just in my ear, and shaking his fist in my face all the time, in a way that I *couldn't* stand, and I *wouldn't*. I left the Misses Cognoscenti immediately, went behind the scenes forthwith, and gave the beggarly scoundrel such a thrashing as I trust he will remember to the day of his death.

At the *soirée* of the lovely widow, Mrs Kathleen O'Trump, I was confident that I should meet with no similar disappointment. Accordingly, I was no sooner seated at the card-table, with my pretty hostess for a *vis-à-vis*, than I propounded those questions the solution of which had become a matter so essential to my peace.

'Smith?' said my partner, 'why, not General John A. B. C.? Horrid affair that, wasn't it? – diamonds, did you say? – terrible wretches those Kickapoos! – we are playing *whist*, if you please, Mr Tattle – however, this is the age of invention, most certainly *the* age, one may say – *the* age *par excellence* – speak French? – oh, quite a hero – perfect desperado! – *no hearts*, Mr Tattle? I don't believe it! – immortal renown and all that! – prodigies of valour! *Never heard*!! – why, bless me, he's the man – '

'Mann? – *Captain* Mann?' here screamed some little feminine interloper from the farthest corner of the room. 'Are you talking about Captain Mann and the duel? – oh, I *must* hear – do tell – go on, Mrs O'Trump! – do now go on!' And go on Mrs O'Trump did – all about a certain Captain Mann, who was either shot or hung, or should have been both shot and hung. Yes! Mrs O'Trump, she went on, and I – I went off. There was no chance of hearing anything farther that evening in regard to Brevet Brigadier General John A. B. C. Smith.

Still I consoled myself with the reflection that the tide of ill luck would not run against me for ever, and so determined to make a bold push for information at the rout of that bewitching little angel, the graceful Mrs Pirouette.

'Smith?' said Mrs P, as we twirled about together in a *pas de zephyr*, 'Smith? – why, not General John A. B. C.? Dreadful business that of the Bugaboos, wasn't it? – dreadful creatures, those Indians! – do turn out your toes! I really am ashamed of you – man of great courage, poor fellow! – but this is a wonderful age for invention – O dear me, I'm out of breath – quite a desperado – prodigies of valour – *never heard*!! – can't believe it – I shall have to sit down and enlighten you – Smith! why, he's the man – '

'Man-*Fred*, I tell you!' here bawled out Miss Bas-Bleu, as I led Mrs Pirouette to a seat. 'Did ever anybody hear the like? It's Man-*Fred*, I say, and not at all by any means Man-*Friday*.' Here Miss Bas-Bleu beckoned to me in a very peremptory manner; and I was obliged, willy-nilly, to leave Mrs P for the purpose of deciding a dispute touching the title of a certain poetical drama of Lord Byron's. Although I pronounced, with great promptness, that the true title was Man-*Friday*, and not by any means Man-*Fred*, yet when I returned to seek Mrs Pirouette she was not to be discovered, and I made my retreat from the house in a very bitter spirit of animosity against the whole race of the Bas-Bleus.

Matters had now assumed a really serious aspect, and I resolved to call at once upon my particular friend, Mr Theodore Sinivate; for I knew that here at least I should get something like definite information.

'Smith?' said he, in his well-known peculiar way of drawling out his syllables; 'Smith? – why, not General John A. B. C.? Savage affair that with the Kickapo–o–o–os, wasn't it? Say! don't you think so? – perfect despera–a–ado – great pity, 'pon my honour! – wonderfully inventive age! – pro–o–odigies of valour! By the by, did you ever hear about Captain Ma–a–a–a–n?'

'Captain Mann be d—d!' said I; 'please to go on with your story.'

'Hem! – oh well! – quite *la même cho–o–ose*, as we say in France. Smith, eh? Brigadier-General John A. B. C.? I say' – [here Mr S thought proper to put his finger to the side of his nose] – 'I say, you don't mean to insinuate now, really and truly, and conscientiously, that you don't know all about that affair of Smith's, as well as I do, eh? Smith? John A–B–C.? Why, bless me, he's the ma–a–an – '

'*Mr* Sinivate,' said I, imploringly, 'is he the man in the mask?'

'No–o–o!' said he, looking wise, 'nor the man in the mo–o–on.'

This reply I considered a pointed and positive insult, and so left the house at once in high dudgeon, with a firm resolve to call my friend, Mr Sinivate, to a speedy account for his ungentlemanly conduct and ill-breeding.

In the meantime, however, I had no notion of being thwarted touching the information I desired. There was one resource left me yet. I would go to the fountain-head. I would call forthwith upon the General himself, and demand, in explicit terms, a solution of this abominable piece of mystery. Here, at least, there should be no chance for equivocation. I would be plain, positive, peremptory – as short as pie-crust – as concise as Tacitus or Montesquieu.

It was early when I called, and the General was dressing; but I pleaded urgent business, and was shown at once into his bedroom by an old negro valet, who remained in attendance during my visit. As I entered the chamber, I looked about, of course, for the occupant, but did not immediately perceive him. There was a large and exceedingly odd-looking bundle of something which lay close by my feet on the floor, and, as I was not in the best humour in the world, I gave it a kick out of the way.

'Hem! ahem! rather civil that, I should say!' said the bundle, in one of the smallest, and altogether the funniest little voices, between a squeak and a whistle, that I ever heard in all the days of my existence.

'Ahem! rather civil that, I should observe.'

I fairly shouted with terror, and made off, at a tangent, into the farthest extremity of the room.

'God bless me! my dear fellow,' here again whistled the bundle, 'what – what – what – why, what *is* the matter? I really believe you don't know me at all.'

What *could* I say to all this – what *could* I? I staggered into an armchair, and, with staring eyes and open mouth, awaited the solution of the wonder.

'Strange you shouldn't know me though, isn't it?' presently resqueaked the nondescript, which I now perceived was performing, upon the floor, some inexplicable evolution, very analogous to the drawing on of a stocking. There was only a single leg, however, apparent.

'Strange you shouldn't know me, though, isn't it? Pompey, bring me that leg!' Here Pompey handed the bundle a very capital cork leg, already dressed, which it screwed on in a trice; and then it stood up before my eyes.

'And a bloody action it *was*,' continued the thing, as if in a soliloquy; 'but then one mustn't fight with the Bugaboos and Kickapoos, and think of coming off with a mere scratch. Pompey, I'll thank you now for that arm. Thomas' [turning to me] 'is decidedly the best hand at a cork leg; but if you should ever want an arm, my dear fellow, you must really let me recommend you to Bishop.' Here Pompey screwed on an arm.

'We had rather hot work of it, that you may say. Now, you dog, slip on my shoulders and bosom! Pettit makes the best shoulders, but for a bosom you will have to go to Ducrow.'

'Bosom!' said I.

'Pompey, will you *never* be ready with that wig? Scalping is a rough process after all; but then you can procure such a capital scratch at De L'Orme's.'

'Scratch!'

'Now, you nigger, my teeth! For a good set of these you had better go to Parmly's at once; high prices, but excellent work. I swallowed some very capital articles, though, when the big Bugaboo rammed me down with the butt end of his rifle.'

'Butt end! ram down!! my eye!!'

'O yes, by the by, my eye – here, Pompey, you scamp, screw it in! Those Kickapoos are not so very slow at a gouge; but he's a belied man, that Dr Williams, after all; you can't imagine how well I see with the eyes of his make.'

I now began very clearly to perceive that the object before me was nothing more nor less than my new acquaintance, Brevet Brigadier General John A. B. C. Smith. The manipulations of Pompey had made, I must confess, a very striking difference in the appearance of the personal man. The voice, however, still puzzled me no little; but even this apparent mystery was speedily cleared up.

'Pompey, you black rascal,' squeaked the General, 'I really do believe you would let me go out without my palate.'

Hereupon, the negro, grumbling out an apology, went up

to his master, opened his mouth with the knowing air of a horse-jockey, and adjusted therein a somewhat singular-looking machine, in a very dexterous manner, that I could not altogether comprehend. The alteration, however, in the entire expression of the General's countenance was instantaneous and surprising. When he again spoke, his voice had resumed all that rich melody and strength which I had noticed upon our original introduction.

'D—n the vagabonds!' said he, in so clear a tone that I positively started at the change, 'D—n the vagabonds! they not only knocked in the roof of my mouth, but took the trouble to cut off at least seven-eighths of my tongue. There isn't Bonfanti's equal, however, in America, for really good articles of this description. I can recommend you to him with confidence' [here the General bowed], 'and assure you that I have the greatest pleasure in so doing.'

I acknowledged his kindness in my best manner, and took leave of him at once, with a perfect understanding of the true state of affairs – with a full comprehension of the mystery which had troubled me so long. It was evident. It was a clear case. Brevet Brigadier General John A. B. C. Smith was the man – was *the man that was used up*.

William Wilson

What say of it? what say of CONSCIENCE grim,
That spectre in my path?

CHAMBERLAYNE'S PHARRONIDA

Let me call myself, for the present, William Wilson. The fair page now lying before me need not be sullied with my real appellation. This has been already too much an object for the scorn – for the horror – for the detestation of my race. To the uttermost regions of the globe have not the indignant winds bruited its unparalleled infamy? Oh, outcast of all outcasts most abandoned! – to the earth art thou not forever dead? to its honours, to its flowers, to its golden aspirations? – and a cloud, dense, dismal, and limitless, does it not hang eternally between thy hopes and heaven?

I would not, if I could, here or today, embody a record of my later years of unspeakable misery, and unpardonable crime. This epoch – these later years – took unto themselves a sudden elevation in turpitude, whose origin alone it is my present purpose to assign. Men usually grow base by degrees. From me, in an instant, all virtue dropped bodily as a mantle. From comparatively trivial wickedness I passed, with the stride of a giant, into more than the enormities of an Elagabalus. What chance – what one event brought this evil thing to pass, bear with me while I relate. Death approaches; and the shadow which foreruns him has thrown a softening influence over my spirit. I long, in passing through the dim valley, for the sympathy – I had nearly said for the pity – of my fellow men. I would fain have them believe that I have been, in some measure, the slave of circumstances beyond human control. I would wish them to seek out for me, in the details I am about to give, some little oasis of fatality amid a wilderness of error. I would have them allow – what they cannot refrain from allowing – that, although temptation may have erewhile existed as great, man was never thus, at least, tempted before – certainly, never thus fell. And is it therefore that he has never thus suffered? Have I not indeed been living in a dream? And am I not now dying a victim to the horror and the mystery of the wildest of all sublunary visions?

I am the descendant of a race whose imaginative and easily excitable temperament has at all times rendered them remarkable; and, in my earliest infancy, I gave evidence of having fully inherited the family character. As I advanced in years it was more strongly developed; becoming, for many reasons, a cause of serious disquietude to my friends, and of positive injury to myself. I grew self-willed, addicted to the wildest caprices, and a prey to the most ungovernable passions. Weak-minded, and beset with constitutional infirmities akin to my own, my parents could do but little to check the evil propensities which distinguished me. Some feeble and ill-directed efforts resulted in complete failure on their part, and, of course, in total triumph on mine. Thenceforward my voice was a household law; and at an age when few children have abandoned their leading-strings, I was left to the guidance of my own will, and became, in all but name, the master of my own actions.

My earliest recollections of a school-life, are connected with a large, rambling, Elizabethan house, in a misty-looking village of England, where were a vast number of gigantic and gnarled trees, and where all the houses were excessively ancient. In truth, it was a dream-like and spirit-soothing place, that venerable old town. At this moment, in fancy, I feel the refreshing chilliness of its deeply-shadowed avenues, inhale the fragrance of its thousand shrubberies, and thrill anew with undefinable delight, at the deep hollow note of the church-bell, breaking, each hour, with sullen and sudden roar, upon the stillness of the dusky atmosphere in which the fretted Gothic steeple lay embedded and asleep.

It gives me, perhaps, as much of pleasure as I can now in any manner experience, to dwell upon minute recollections of the school and its concerns. Steeped in misery as I am – misery, alas! only too real – I shall be pardoned for seeking relief, however slight and temporary, in the weakness of a few rambling details. These, moreover, utterly trivial, and even ridiculous in themselves, assume, to my fancy, adventitious importance, as connected with a period and a locality when and where I recognise the first ambiguous monitions of the destiny which afterwards so fully overshadowed me. Let me then remember.

The house, I have said, was old and irregular. The grounds were extensive, and a high and solid brick wall, topped with a bed of mortar and broken glass, encompassed the whole. This prison-like rampart formed the limit of our domain; beyond it we saw but thrice a week – once every Saturday afternoon, when, attended by two ushers, we were permitted to take brief walks in a body through some of the neighbouring fields – and twice during Sunday, when we were paraded in the same formal manner to the morning and evening service in the one church of the village. Of this church the principal of our school was pastor. With how deep a spirit of wonder and perplexity was I wont to regard him from our remote pew in the gallery, as, with step solemn and slow, he ascended the pulpit! This reverend man, with countenance so demurely benign, with robes so glossy and so clerically flowing, with wig so minutely powdered, so rigid and so vast – could this be he who, of late, with sour visage, and in snuffy habiliments, administered, ferule in hand, the Draconian laws of the academy? Oh, gigantic paradox, too utterly monstrous for solution!

At an angle of the ponderous wall frowned a more ponderous gate. It was riveted and studded with iron bolts, and surmounted with jagged iron spikes. What impressions of deep awe did it inspire! It was never opened save for the three periodical egressions and ingressions already mentioned; then, in every creak of its mighty hinges, we found a plenitude of mystery – a world of matter for solemn remark, or for more solemn meditation.

The extensive enclosure was irregular in form, having many capacious recesses. Of these, three or four of the largest constituted the playground. It was level, and covered with fine hard gravel. I well remember it had no trees, nor benches, nor anything similar within it. Of course it was in the rear of the house. In front lay a small parterre, planted with box and other shrubs; but through this sacred division we passed only upon rare occasions indeed – such as a first advent to school or final departure thence, or perhaps, when a parent or friend having called for us, we joyfully took our way home for the Christmas or Midsummer holy-days.

But the house! – how quaint an old building was this! – to me how veritably a palace of enchantment! There was really no end to its windings – to its incomprehensible subdivisions. It was difficult, at any given time, to say with certainty upon which of its two storeys one happened to be. From each room to every other there were sure to be found three or four steps either in ascent or descent. Then the lateral branches were innumerable – inconceivable – and so returning in upon themselves, that our most exact ideas in regard to the whole mansion were not very far different from those with which we pondered upon infinity. During the five years of my residence here, I was never able to ascertain with precision, in what remote locality lay the little sleeping apartment assigned to myself and some eighteen or twenty other scholars.

The schoolroom was the largest in the house – I could not help thinking, in the world. It was very long, narrow, and dismally low, with pointed Gothic windows and a ceiling of oak. In a remote and terror-inspiring angle was a square enclosure of eight or ten feet, comprising the sanctum, 'during hours', of our principal, the Revd Dr Bransby. It was a solid structure, with massy door, sooner than open which in the absence of the 'Dominie', we would all have willingly perished by the *peine forte et dure*. In other angles were two other similar boxes, far less reverenced, indeed, but still greatly matters of awe. One of these was the pulpit of the 'classical' usher, one of the 'English and mathematical'. Interspersed about the room, crossing and recrossing in endless irregularity, were innumerable benches and desks, black, ancient, and time-worn, piled desperately with much-bethumbed books, and so beseamed with initial letters, names at full length, grotesque figures, and other multiplied efforts of the knife, as to have entirely lost what little of original form might have been their portion in days long departed. A huge bucket with water stood at one extremity of the room, and a clock of stupendous dimensions at the other.

Encompassed by the massy walls of this venerable academy, I passed, yet not in tedium or disgust, the years of the third lustrum of my life. The teeming brain of childhood requires no external world of incident to occupy or amuse it; and the apparently dismal monotony of a school was replete with more intense excitement than my riper youth has derived from luxury, or my full manhood from crime. Yet I must believe that my first mental development had in it much of the uncommon – even much of the *outré*. Upon mankind at large the events of very early existence rarely leave in mature age any definite impression. All is grey shadow – a weak and irregular remembrance – an indistinct regathering of feeble pleasures and phantasmagoric pains. With me this is not so. In childhood I must have felt with the energy of a man what I now find stamped upon memory in lines as vivid, as deep, and as durable as the *exergues* of the Carthaginian medals.

Yet in fact – in the fact of the world's view – how little was there to remember! The morning's awakening, the nightly summons to bed; the connings, the recitations; the periodical half-holidays, and perambulations; the playground, with its broils, its pastimes, its intrigues; these, by a mental sorcery long forgotten, were made to involve a wilderness of sensation, a world of rich incident, an universe of varied emotion, of excitement the most passionate and spirit-stirring. '*Oh, le bon temps, que ce siècle de fer!*'

In truth, the ardour, the enthusiasm, and the imperiousness of my disposition, soon rendered me a marked character among my schoolmates, and by slow, but natural gradations, gave me an ascendancy over all not greatly older than myself – over all with a single exception. This exception was found in the person of a scholar, who, although no relation, bore the same Christian and surname as myself – a circumstance, in fact, little remarkable for, notwithstanding a noble descent, mine was one of those everyday appellations which seem, by prescriptive right, to have been, time out of mind, the common property of the mob. In this narrative I have therefore designated myself as William Wilson – a fictitious title not very dissimilar to the real. My namesake alone, of those who in school phraseology constituted 'our set', presumed to compete with me in the studies of the class – in the sports and broils of the playground – to refuse implicit belief in my assertions, and submission to my will – indeed, to interfere with my arbitrary dictation in any respect whatsoever. If there is on earth a supreme and unqualified despotism, it is the despotism of a mastermind in boyhood over the less energetic spirits of its companions.

Wilson's rebellion was to me a source of the greatest embarrassment – the more so as, in spite of the bravado with which in public I made a point of treating him and his pretensions, I secretly felt that I feared him, and could not help thinking the equality which he maintained so easily with myself, a proof of his true superiority; since not to be overcome cost me a perpetual struggle. Yet this superiority – even this equality – was in truth acknowledged by no one but myself; our associates, by some unaccountable blindness, seemed not even to suspect it. Indeed, his competition, his resistance, and especially his impertinent and dogged interference with my purposes, were not more pointed than private. He appeared to be destitute alike of the ambition which urged, and of the passionate energy of mind which enabled me to excel. In his rivalry he might have been supposed actuated solely by a whimsical desire to thwart, astonish, or mortify myself; although there were times when I could not help observing, with a feeling made up of wonder, abasement, and pique, that he mingled with his injuries, his insults, or his contradictions, a certain most inappropriate, and assuredly most unwelcome affectionateness of manner. I could only conceive this singular behaviour to arise from a consummate self-conceit assuming the vulgar airs of patronage and protection.

Perhaps it was this latter trait in Wilson's conduct, conjoined with our identity of name, and the mere accident of our having entered the school upon the same day, which set afloat the notion that we were brothers, among the senior classes in the academy. These do not usually enquire with much strictness into the affairs of their juniors. I have before said, or should have said, that Wilson was not, in the most remote degree, connected with my family. But assuredly if we had been brothers we must have been twins; for, after leaving Dr Bransby's, I casually learned that my namesake was born on the nineteenth of January, 1813 – and this is a somewhat remarkable coincidence; for the day is precisely that of my own nativity.

It may seem strange that in spite of the continual anxiety occasioned me by the rivalry of Wilson, and his intolerable spirit of contradiction, I could not bring myself to hate him altogether. We had, to be sure, nearly every day a quarrel in which, yielding me publicly the palm of victory, he, in some manner, contrived to make me feel that it was he who had deserved it; yet a sense of pride on my part, and a veritable dignity on his own, kept us always upon what are called 'speaking terms', while there were many points of strong congeniality in our tempers, operating to awake in me a sentiment which our position alone, perhaps, prevented from ripening into friendship. It is difficult, indeed, to define, or even to describe, my real feelings towards him. They formed a motley and heterogeneous admixture – some petulant animosity, which was not yet hatred, some esteem, more respect, much fear, with a world of uneasy curiosity. To the moralist it will be unnecessary to say, in addition, that Wilson and myself were the most inseparable of companions.

It was no doubt the anomalous state of affairs existing between us, which turned all my attacks upon him (and they were many, either open or covert) into the channel of banter or practical joke (giving pain while assuming the aspect of mere fun) rather than into a more serious and determined hostility. But my endeavours on this head were by no means uniformly successful, even when my plans were the most wittily concocted; for my namesake had much about him, in character, of that unassuming and quiet austerity which, while enjoying the poignancy of its own jokes, has no heel of Achilles in itself, and absolutely refuses to be laughed at. I could find, indeed, but one vulnerable point, and that, lying in a personal peculiarity, arising, perhaps, from constitutional disease, would have been spared by any antagonist less at his wit's end than myself – my rival had a weakness in the faucial or guttural organs, which precluded him from raising his voice at any time above a very low whisper. Of this defect I did not fail to take what poor advantage lay in my power.

Wilson's retaliations in kind were many; and there was one form of his practical wit that disturbed me beyond measure. How his sagacity first discovered at all that so petty a thing would vex me, is a question I never could solve; but, having discovered, he habitually practised the annoyance. I had always felt aversion to my uncourtly patronymic, and its very common, if not plebeian praenomen. The words were venom in my ears; and when, upon the day of my arrival, a second William Wilson came also to the academy, I felt angry with him for bearing the name, and doubly disgusted with the name because a stranger bore it, who would be the cause of its twofold repetition, who would be constantly in my presence, and whose concerns, in the ordinary routine of the school business, must inevitably, on account of the detestable coincidence, be often confounded with my own.

The feeling of vexation thus engendered grew stronger with every circumstance tending to show resemblance, moral or physical, between my rival and myself. I had not then discovered the remarkable fact that we were of the same age; but I saw that we were of the same height, and I perceived that we were even singularly alike in general contour of person and outline of feature. I was galled, too, by the rumour touching a relationship, which had grown current in the upper forms. In a word, nothing could more seriously disturb me (although I scrupulously concealed such disturbance) than any allusion to a similarity of mind, person, or condition existing between us. But, in truth, I had no reason to believe that (with the exception of the matter of relationship, and in the case of Wilson himself) this similarity had ever been made a subject of comment, or even observed at all by our schoolfellows. That he observed it in all its bearings, and as fixedly as I, was apparent; but that he could discover in such circumstances so fruitful a field of annoyance, can only be attributed, as I said before, to his more than ordinary penetration.

His cue, which was to perfect an imitation of myself, lay both in words and in actions; and most admirably did he play his part. My dress it was an easy matter to copy; my gait and general manner were, without difficulty, appropriated; in spite of his constitutional defect, even my voice did not escape him. My louder tones were, of course, unattempted, but then the key, it was identical; and his singular whisper, it grew the very echo of my own.

How greatly this most exquisite portraiture harassed me (for it could not justly be termed a caricature) I will not now venture to describe. I had but one consolation – in the fact that the imitation, apparently, was noticed by myself alone, and that I had to endure only the knowing and strangely sarcastic smiles of my namesake himself. Satisfied with having produced in my bosom the intended effect, he seemed to chuckle in secret over the sting he had inflicted, and was characteristically disregardful of the public applause which the success of his witty endeavours might have so easily elicited. That the school, indeed, did not feel his design, perceive its accomplishment, and participate in his sneer, was, for many anxious months, a riddle I could not resolve. Perhaps the gradation of his copy rendered it not so readily perceptible; or, more possibly, I owed my security to the master air of the copyist, who, disdaining the letter (which in a painting is all the obtuse can see), gave but the full spirit of his original for my individual contemplation and chagrin.

I have already more than once spoken of the disgusting air of patronage which he assumed towards me, and of his frequent officious interference with my will. This interference often took the ungracious character of advice; advice not openly given, but hinted or insinuated. I received it with a repugnance which gained strength as I grew in years. Yet, at this distant day, let me do him the simple justice to acknowledge that I can recall no occasion when the suggestions of my rival were on the side of those errors or follies so usual to his immature age and seeming inexperience; that his moral sense, at least, if not his general talents and worldly wisdom, was far keener than my own; and that I might, today, have been a better, and thus a happier man, had I less frequently rejected the counsels embodied in those meaning whispers which I then but too cordially hated and too bitterly despised.

As it was, I at length grew restive in the extreme under his distasteful supervision, and daily resented more and more openly what I considered his intolerable arrogance. I have said that, in the first years of our connection as schoolmates, my feelings in regard to him might have been easily ripened into friendship: but, in the latter months of my residence at the academy, although the intrusion of his ordinary manner had, beyond doubt, in some measure, abated, my sentiments, in nearly similar proportion, partook very much of positive hatred. Upon one occasion he saw this, I think, and afterwards avoided, or made a show of avoiding me.

It was about the same period, if I remember aright, that, in an altercation of violence with him, in which he was more than usually thrown off his guard, and spoke and acted with an openness of demeanour rather foreign to his nature, I discovered, or fancied I discovered, in his accent, his air, and general appearance, a something which first startled, and then deeply interested me, by bringing to mind dim visions of my earliest infancy – wild, confused and thronging memories of a time when memory herself was yet unborn. I cannot better describe the sensation which oppressed me than by saying that I could with difficulty shake off the belief of my having been acquainted with the being who stood before me, at some epoch very long ago – some point of the past even infinitely remote. The delusion, however, faded rapidly as it came; and I mention it at all but to define the day of the last conversation I there held with my singular namesake.

The huge old house, with its countless subdivisions, had several large chambers communicating with each other, where slept the greater number of the students. There were, however (as must necessarily happen in a building so awkwardly planned), many little nooks or recesses, the odds and ends of the structure; and these the economic ingenuity of Dr Bransby had also fitted up as dormitories; although, being the merest closets, they were capable of accommodating but a single individual. One of these small apartments was occupied by Wilson.

One night, about the close of my fifth year at the school, and immediately after the altercation just mentioned, finding everyone wrapped in sleep, I arose from bed, and, lamp in hand, stole through a wilderness of narrow passages from my own bedroom to that of my rival. I had long been plotting one of those ill-natured pieces of practical wit at his expense in which I had hitherto been so uniformly unsuccessful. It was my intention, now, to put my scheme in operation, and I resolved to make him feel the whole extent of the malice with which I was imbued. Having reached his closet, I noiselessly entered, leaving the lamp, with a shade over it, on the outside. I advanced a step, and listened to the sound of his tranquil breathing. Assured of his being asleep, I returned, took the light, and with it again approached the bed. Close curtains were around it, which, in the prosecution of my plan, I slowly and quietly withdrew, when the bright rays fell vividly upon the sleeper, and my eyes, at the same moment, upon his countenance. I looked – and a numbness, an iciness of feeling instantly pervaded my frame. My breast heaved, my knees tottered, my whole spirit became possessed with an objectless yet intolerable horror. Gasping for breath, I lowered the lamp in still nearer proximity to the face. Were these – *these* the lineaments of William Wilson? I saw, indeed, that they were his, but I shook as if with a fit of the ague in fancying they were not. What was there about them to confound me in this manner? I gazed – while my brain reeled with a multitude of incoherent thoughts. Not thus he appeared – assuredly not thus – in the vivacity of his waking hours. The same name! the same contour of person! the same day of arrival at the academy! And then his dogged and meaningless imitation of my gait, my voice, my habits, and my manner! Was it, in truth, within the bounds of human possibility, that what I now saw was the result, merely, of the habitual practice of this sarcastic imitation? Awestricken, and with a creeping shudder, I extinguished the lamp, passed silently from the chamber, and left, at once, the halls of that old academy, never to enter them again.

After a lapse of some months, spent at home in mere idleness, I found myself a student at Eton. The brief interval had been sufficient to enfeeble my remembrance of the events at Dr Bransby's, or at least to effect a material change in the nature of the feelings with which I remembered them. The truth – the tragedy – of the drama was no more. I could now find room to doubt the evidence of my senses; and seldom called up the subject at all but with wonder at the extent of human credulity, and a smile at the vivid force of the imagination which I hereditarily possessed. Neither was this species of scepticism likely to be diminished by the character of the life I led at Eton. The vortex of thoughtless folly into which I there so immediately and so recklessly plunged, washed away all but the froth of my past hours, engulfed at once every solid or serious impression, and left to memory only the veriest levities of a former existence.

I do not wish, however, to trace the course of my miserable profligacy here – a profligacy which set at defiance the laws, while it eluded the vigilance of the institution. Three years of folly, passed without profit, had but given me rooted habits of vice, and added, in a somewhat unusual degree, to my bodily stature, when, after a week of soulless dissipation, I invited a small party of the most dissolute students to a secret carousal in my chambers. We met at a late hour of the night; for our debaucheries were to be faithfully protracted until morning. The wine flowed freely, and there were not wanting other and perhaps more dangerous seductions; so that the grey dawn had already faintly appeared in the east, while our delirious extravagance was at its height. Madly flushed with cards and intoxication, I was in the act of insisting upon a toast of more than wonted profanity, when my attention was suddenly diverted by the violent, although partial unclosing of the door of the apartment, and by the eager voice of a servant from without. He said that some person, apparently in great haste, demanded to speak with me in the hall.

Wildly excited with wine, the unexpected interruption rather delighted than surprised me. I staggered forward at once, and a few steps brought me to the vestibule of the building. In this low and small room there hung no lamp; and now no light at all was admitted, save that of the exceedingly feeble dawn which made its way through the semicircular window. As I put my foot over the threshold, I became aware of the figure of a youth about my own height, and habited in a white kerseymere morning frock, cut in the novel fashion of the one I myself wore at the moment. This the faint light enabled me to perceive; but the features of his face I could not distinguish. Upon my entering he strode hurriedly up to me, and, seizing me by the arm with a gesture of petulant impatience, whispered the words 'William Wilson!' in my ear.

I grew perfectly sober in an instant. There was that in the manner of the stranger, and in the tremulous shake of his uplifted finger, as he held it between my eyes and the light, which filled me with unqualified amazement; but it was not this which had so violently moved me. It was the pregnancy of solemn admonition in the singular, low, hissing utterance; and, above all, it was the character, the tone, the key, of those few, simple, and familiar, yet whispered syllables, which came with a thousand thronging memories of bygone days, and struck upon my soul with the shock of a galvanic battery. Ere I could recover the use of my senses he was gone.

Although this event failed not of a vivid effect upon my disordered imagination, yet was it evanescent as vivid. For some weeks, indeed, I busied myself in earnest enquiry, or was wrapped in a cloud of morbid speculation. I did not pretend to disguise from my perception the identity of the singular individual who thus perseveringly interfered with my affairs, and harassed me with his insinuated counsel. But who and what was this Wilson? – and whence came he? – and what were his purposes? Upon neither of these points could I be satisfied; merely ascertaining, in regard to him, that a sudden accident in his family had caused his removal from Dr Bransby's academy on the afternoon of the day in which I myself had eloped. But in a brief period I ceased to think upon the subject; my attention being all absorbed in a contemplated departure for Oxford. Thither I soon went; the uncalculating vanity of my parents furnishing me with an outfit and annual establishment, which would enable me to indulge at will in the luxury already so dear to my heart – to vie in profuseness of expenditure with the haughtiest heirs of the wealthiest earldoms in Great Britain.

Excited by such appliances to vice, my constitutional temperament broke forth with redoubled ardour, and I spurned even the common restraints of decency in the mad infatuation of my revels. But it were absurd to pause in the detail of my extravagance. Let it suffice, that among spendthrifts I out-Heroded Herod, and that, giving name to a multitude of novel follies, I added no brief appendix to the long catalogue of vices then usual in the most dissolute university of Europe.

It could hardly be credited, however, that I had, even here, so utterly fallen from the gentlemanly estate, as to seek acquaintance with the vilest arts of the gambler by profession, and, having become an adept in his despicable science, to practise it habitually as a means of increasing my already enormous income at the expense of the weak-minded among my fellow-collegians. Such, nevertheless, was the fact. And the very enormity of this offence against all manly and honourable sentiment proved, beyond doubt, the main if not the sole reason of the impunity with which it was committed. Who, indeed, among my most abandoned associates, would not rather have disputed the clearest evidence of his senses, than have suspected of such courses, the gay, the frank, the generous William Wilson – the noblest and most liberal commoner at Oxford – him whose follies (said his parasites) were but the follies of youth and unbridled fancy – whose errors but inimitable whim – whose darkest vice but a careless and dashing extravagance?

I had been now two years successfully busied in this way, when there came to the university a young *parvenu* nobleman, Glendinning – rich, said report, as Herodes Atticus – his riches, too, as easily acquired. I soon found him of weak intellect, and, of course, marked him as a fitting subject for my skill. I frequently engaged him in play, and contrived, with the gambler's usual art, to let him win considerable sums, the more effectually to entangle him in my snares. At length, my schemes being ripe, I met him (with the full intention that this meeting should be final and decisive) at the chambers of a fellow-commoner (Mr Preston), equally intimate with both, but who, to do him justice, entertained not even a remote suspicion of my design. To give to this a better colouring, I had contrived to have assembled a party of some eight or ten, and was solicitously careful that the introduction of cards should appear accidental, and originate in the proposal of my contemplated dupe himself. To be brief upon a vile topic, none of the low finesse was omitted, so customary upon similar occasions that it is a just matter for wonder how any are still found so besotted as to fall its victim.

We had protracted our sitting far into the night, and I had at length effected the manoeuvre of getting Glendinning as my sole antagonist. The game, too, was my favourite *écarté*. The rest of the company, interested in the extent of our play, had abandoned their own cards, and were standing around us as spectators. The *parvenu*, who had been induced by my artifices in the early part of the evening, to drink deeply, now shuffled, dealt, or played, with a wild nervousness of manner for which his intoxication, I thought, might partially, but could not altogether account. In a very short period he had become my debtor to a large amount, when, having taken a long draught of port, he did precisely what I had been coolly anticipating – he proposed to double our already extravagant stakes. With a well-feigned show of reluctance, and not until after my repeated refusal had seduced him into some angry words which gave a colour of pique to my compliance, did I finally comply. The result, of course, did but prove how entirely the prey was in my toils; in less than an hour he had quadrupled his debt. For some time his countenance had been losing the florid tinge lent it by the wine; but now, to my astonishment, I perceived that it had grown to a pallor truly fearful. I say to my astonishment. Glendinning had been represented to my eager enquiries as immeasurably wealthy; and the sums which he had as yet lost, although in themselves vast, could not, I supposed, very seriously annoy, much less so violently affect him. That he was overcome by the wine just swallowed, was the idea which most readily presented itself; and, rather with a view to the preservation of my own character in the eyes of my associates, than from any less interested motive, I was about to insist, peremptorily, upon a discontinuance of the play, when some expressions at my elbow from among the company, and an ejaculation evincing utter despair on the part of Glendinning, gave me to understand that I had effected his total ruin under circumstances which, rendering him an object for the pity of all, should have protected him from the ill offices even of a fiend.

What now might have been my conduct it is difficult to say. The pitiable condition of my dupe had thrown an air of embarrassed gloom over all; and, for some moments, a profound silence was maintained, during which I could not help feeling my cheeks tingle with the many burning glances of scorn or reproach cast upon me by the less abandoned of the party. I will even own that an intolerable weight of anxiety was for a brief instant lifted from my bosom by the sudden and extraordinary interruption which ensued. The wide, heavy folding doors of the apartment were all at once thrown open, to their full extent, with a vigorous and rushing impetuosity that extinguished, as if by magic, every candle in the room. Their light, in dying, enabled us just to perceive that a stranger had entered, about my own height, and closely muffled in a cloak. The darkness, however, was now total; and we could only feel that he was standing in our midst. Before any one of us could recover from the extreme astonishment into which this rudeness had thrown all, we heard the voice of the intruder.

'Gentlemen,' he said, in a low, distinct, and never-to-be-forgotten whisper which thrilled to the very marrow of my bones, 'Gentlemen, I make no apology for this behaviour, because in thus behaving, I am but fulfilling a duty. You are, beyond doubt, uninformed of the true character of the person who has tonight won at *écarté* a large sum of money from Lord Glendinning. I will therefore put you upon an expeditious and decisive plan of obtaining this very necessary information. Please to examine, at your leisure, the inner linings of the cuff of his left sleeve, and the several little packages which may be found in the somewhat capacious pockets of his embroidered morning wrapper.'

While he spoke, so profound was the stillness that one might have heard a pin drop upon the floor. In ceasing, he departed at once, and as abruptly as he had entered. Can I – shall I describe my sensations? – must I say that I felt all the horrors of the damned? Most assuredly I had little time given for reflection. Many hands roughly seized me upon the spot, and lights were immediately reprocured. A search ensued. In the lining of my sleeve were found all the court cards essential in *écarté*, and, in the pockets of my wrapper, a number of packs, facsimiles of those used at our sittings, with the single exception that mine were of the species called, technically, *arrondées* – the honours being slightly convex at the ends, the lower cards slightly convex at the sides. In this disposition, the dupe who cuts, as customary, at the length of the pack, will invariably find that he cuts his antagonist an honour; while the gambler, cutting at the breadth, will, as certainly, cut nothing for his victim which may count in the records of the game.

Any burst of indignation upon this discovery would have affected me less than the silent contempt, or the sarcastic composure, with which it was received.

'Mr Wilson,' said our host, stooping to remove from beneath his feet an exceedingly luxurious cloak of rare furs, 'Mr Wilson, this is your property.' (The weather was cold; and, upon quitting my own room, I had thrown a cloak over my dressing wrapper, putting it off upon reaching the scene of play.) 'I presume it is supererogatory to seek here (eyeing the folds of the garment with a bitter smile) for any farther evidence of your skill. Indeed, we have had enough. You will see the necessity, I hope, of quitting Oxford – at all events, of quitting instantly my chambers.'

Abased, humbled to the dust as I then was, it is probable that I should have resented this galling language by immediate personal violence, had not my whole attention been at the moment arrested by a fact of the most startling character. The cloak which I had worn was of a rare description of fur; how rare, how extravagantly costly, I shall not venture to say. Its fashion, too, was of my own fantastic invention; for I was fastidious to an absurd degree of coxcombry, in matters of this frivolous nature. When, therefore, Mr Preston reached me that which he had picked up upon the floor, and near the folding doors of the apartment, it was with an astonishment nearly bordering upon terror that I perceived my own already hanging on my arm (where I had no doubt unwittingly placed it), and that the one presented me was but its exact counterpart in every, in even the minutest possible particular. The singular being who had so disastrously exposed me, had been muffled, I remembered, in a cloak; and none had been worn at all by any of the members of our party with the exception of myself. Retaining some presence of mind, I took the one offered me by Preston; placed it, unnoticed, over my own; left the apartment with a resolute scowl of defiance; and, next morning ere dawn of day, commenced a hurried journey from Oxford to the continent, in a perfect agony of horror and of shame.

I fled in vain. My evil destiny pursued me as if in exultation, and proved, indeed, that the exercise of its mysterious dominion had as yet only begun. Scarcely had I set foot in Paris ere I had fresh evidence of the detestable interest taken by this Wilson in my concerns. Years flew, while I experienced no relief. Villain! – at Rome, with how untimely, yet with how spectral an officiousness, stepped he in between me and my ambition! At Vienna, too – at Berlin – and at Moscow! Where, in truth, had I not bitter cause to curse him within my heart? From his inscrutable tyranny did I at length flee, panic-stricken, as from a pestilence; and to the very ends of the earth I fled in vain.

And again, and again, in secret communion with my own spirit, would I demand the questions 'Who is he? – whence came he? – and what are his objects?' But no answer was there found. And then I scrutinised, with a minute scrutiny, the forms, and the methods, and the leading traits of his impertinent supervision. But even here there was very little upon which to base a conjecture. It was noticeable, indeed, that, in no one of the multiplied instances in which he had of late crossed my path, had he so crossed it except to frustrate those schemes, or to disturb those actions, which, if fully carried out, might have resulted in bitter mischief. Poor justification this, in truth, for an authority so imperiously assumed! Poor indemnity for natural rights of self-agency so pertinaciously, so insultingly denied!

I had also been forced to notice that my tormentor, for a very long period of time (while scrupulously and with miraculous dexterity maintaining his whim of an identity of apparel with myself), had so contrived it, in the execution of his varied interference with my will, that I saw not, at any moment, the features of his face. Be Wilson what he might, *this*, at least, was but the veriest of affectation, or of folly. Could he, for an instant, have supposed that, in my admonisher at Eton – in the destroyer of my honour at Oxford – in him who thwarted my ambition at Rome, my revenge at Paris, my passionate love at Naples, or what he falsely termed my avarice in Egypt – that in this, my archenemy and evil genius, could fail to recognise the William Wilson of my schoolboy days – the namesake, the companion, the rival – the hated and dreaded rival at Dr Bransby's? Impossible! – But let me hasten to the last eventful scene of the drama.

Thus far I had succumbed supinely to this imperious domination. The sentiment of deep awe with which I habitually regarded the elevated character, the majestic wisdom, the apparent omnipresence and omnipotence of Wilson, added to a feeling of even terror, with which certain other traits in his nature and assumptions inspired me, had operated, hitherto, to impress me with an idea of my own utter weakness and helplessness, and to suggest an implicit, although bitterly reluctant submission to his arbitrary will. But, of late days, I had given myself up entirely to wine; and its maddening influence upon my hereditary temper rendered me more and more impatient of control. I began to murmur – to hesitate – to resist. And was it only fancy which induced me to believe that, with the increase of my own firmness, that of my tormentor underwent a proportional diminution? Be this as it may, I now began to feel the inspiration of a burning hope, and at length nurtured in my secret thoughts a stern and desperate resolution that I would submit no longer to be enslaved.

It was at Rome, during the Carnival of 18—, that I attended a masquerade in the palazzo of the Neapolitan Duke di Broglio. I had indulged more freely than usual in the excesses of the wine-table; and now the suffocating atmosphere of the crowded rooms irritated me beyond endurance. The difficulty, too, of forcing my way through the mazes of the company contributed not a little to the ruffling of my temper; for I was anxiously seeking (let me not say with what unworthy motive) the young, the gay, the beautiful wife of the aged and doting di Broglio. With a too unscrupulous confidence she had previously communicated to me the secret of the costume in which she would be

"IN MY DEATH, SEE BY THIS IMAGE, WHICH IS THINE OWN, HOW UTTERLY THOU HAST MURDERED THYSELF"

habited, and now, having caught a glimpse of her person, I was hurrying to make my way into her presence. At this moment I felt a light hand placed upon my shoulder, and that ever-remembered, low, damnable whisper within my ear.

In an absolute frenzy of wrath, I turned at once upon him who had thus interrupted me, and seized him violently by the collar. He was attired, as I had expected, in a costume altogether similar to my own; wearing a Spanish cloak of blue velvet, begirt about the waist with a crimson belt sustaining a rapier. A mask of black silk entirely covered his face.

'Scoundrel!' I said, in a voice husky with rage, while every syllable I uttered seemed as new fuel to my fury, 'scoundrel! impostor! accursed villain! you shall not – you shall not dog me unto death! Follow me, or I stab you where you stand!' – and I broke my way from the ballroom into a small antechamber adjoining – dragging him unresistingly with me as I went.

Upon entering, I thrust him furiously from me. He staggered against the wall, while I closed the door with an oath, and commanded him to draw. He hesitated but for an instant; then, with a slight sigh, drew in silence, and put himself upon his defence.

The contest was brief indeed. I was frantic with every species of wild excitement, and felt within my single arm the energy and power of a multitude. In a few seconds I forced him by sheer strength against the wainscoting, and thus, getting him at my mercy, plunged my sword, with brute ferocity, repeatedly through and through his bosom.

At that instant some person tried the latch of the door. I hastened to prevent an intrusion, and then immediately returned to my dying antagonist. But what human language can adequately portray that astonishment, that horror which possessed me at the spectacle then presented to view? The brief moment in which I averted my eyes had been sufficient to produce, apparently, a material change in the arrangements at the upper or farther end of the room. A large mirror – so at first it seemed to me in my confusion – now stood where none had been perceptible before; and, as I stepped up to it in extremity of terror, mine own image, but with features all pale and dabbled in blood, advanced to meet me with a feeble and tottering gait.

Thus it appeared, I say, but was not. It was my antagonist – it was Wilson, who then stood before me in the agonies of his dissolution. His mask and cloak lay, where he had thrown them, upon the floor. Not a thread in all his raiment – not a line in all the marked and singular lineaments of his face which was not, even in the most absolute identity, *mine own*!

It was Wilson; but he spoke no longer in a whisper, and I could have fancied that I myself was speaking while he said: 'You have conquered, and I yield. Yet, henceforward art thou also dead – dead to the World, to Heaven and to Hope! In me didst thou exist – and, in my death, see by this image, which is thine own, how utterly thou hast murdered thyself.'

Eleonora

Sub conservatione formae specificae salva anima.

RAYMOND LULLY

I am come of a race noted for vigour of fancy and ardour of passion. Men have called me mad; but the question is not yet settled, whether madness is or is not the loftiest intelligence – whether much that is glorious – whether all that is profound – does not spring from disease of thought – from moods of mind exalted at the expense of the general intellect. They who dream by day are cognisant of many things which escape those who dream only by night. In their grey visions they obtain glimpses of eternity, and thrill, in awakening, to find that they have been upon the verge of the great secret. In snatches, they learn something of the wisdom which is of good, and more of the mere knowledge which is of evil. They penetrate, however, rudderless or compassless into the vast ocean of the 'light ineffable', and again, like the adventures of the Nubian geographer, '*agressi sunt mare tenebrarum, quid in eo esset exploraturi*'.

We will say, then, that I am mad. I grant, at least, that there are two distinct conditions of my mental existence: the condition of a lucid reason – not to be disputed, and belonging to the memory of events forming the first epoch of my life – and a condition of shadow and doubt, appertaining to the present, and to the recollection of what constitutes the second great era of my being. Therefore, what I shall tell of the earlier period, believe; and to what I may relate of the later time, give only such credit as may seem due, or doubt it altogether; or, if doubt it ye cannot, then play unto its riddle the Oedipus.

She whom I loved in youth, and of whom I now pen calmly and distinctly these remembrances, was the sole daughter of the only sister of my mother long departed. Eleonora was the name of my cousin. We had always dwelled together, beneath a tropical sun, in the Valley of the Many-Coloured Grass. No unguided footstep ever came upon that vale; for it lay away up among a range of giant hills that hung beetling around about it, shutting out the sunlight from its sweetest recesses. No path was trodden in its vicinity; and, to reach our happy home, there was need of putting back, with force, the foliage of many thousands of forest trees, and of crushing to death the glories of many millions of fragrant flowers. Thus it was that we lived all alone, knowing nothing of the world without the valley – I, and my cousin, and her mother.

From the dim regions beyond the mountains at the upper end of our encircled domain, there crept out a narrow and deep river, brighter than all save the eyes of Eleonora; and, winding stealthily about in mazy courses, it passed away, at length, through a shadowy gorge, among hills still dimmer than those whence it had issued. We called it the 'River of Silence'; for there seemed to be a hushing influence in its flow. No murmur arose from its bed, and so gently it wandered along, that the pearly pebbles upon which we loved to gaze, far down within its bosom, stirred not at all, but lay in a motionless content, each in its own old station, shining on gloriously for ever.

The margin of the river, and of the many dazzling rivulets that glided through devious ways into its channel, as well as the spaces that extended from the margins away down into the depths of the streams until they reached the bed of pebbles at the bottom – these spots, not less than the whole surface of the valley, from the river to the mountains that girdled it in, were carpeted all by a soft green grass, thick, short, perfectly even, and vanilla-perfumed, but so besprinkled throughout with the yellow buttercup, the white daisy, the purple violet, and the ruby-red asphodel, that its exceeding beauty spoke to our hearts in loud tones, of the love and of the glory of God.

And, here and there, in groves about this grass, like wildernesses of dreams, sprang up fantastic trees, whose tall slender stems stood not upright, but slanted gracefully towards the light that peered at noonday into the centre of the valley. Their bark was speckled with the vivid alternate splendour of ebony and silver, and was smoother than all save the cheeks of Eleonora; so that, but for the brilliant green of the huge leaves that spread from their summits in long, tremulous lines, dallying with the Zephyrs, one might have fancied them giant serpents of Syria doing homage to their sovereign the Sun.

Hand in hand about this valley, for fifteen years, roamed I with Eleonora before Love entered within our hearts. It was one evening at the close of the third lustrum of her life, and of the fourth of my own, that we sat, locked in each other's embrace, beneath the serpent-like trees, and looked down within the water of the River of Silence at our images therein. We spoke no words during the rest of that sweet day, and our words even upon the morrow were tremulous and few. We had drawn the God Eros from that wave, and now we felt that he had enkindled within us the fiery souls of our forefathers. The passions which had for centuries distinguished our race, came thronging with the fancies for which they had been equally noted, and together breathed a delirious bliss over the Valley of the Many-Coloured Grass. A change fell upon all things. Strange, brilliant flowers, star-shaped, burst out upon the trees where no flowers had been known before. The tints of the green carpet deepened; and when, one by one, the white daisies shrank away, there sprang up in place of them, ten by ten of the ruby-red asphodel. And life arose in our paths; for the tall flamingo, hitherto unseen, with all gay glowing birds, flaunted his scarlet plumage before us. The golden and silver fish haunted the river, out of the bosom of which issued, little by little, a murmur that swelled, at length, into a lulling melody more divine than that of the harp of Aeolus – sweeter than all save the voice of Eleonora. And now, too, a voluminous cloud, which we had long watched in the regions of Hesper, floated out thence, all gorgeous in crimson and gold, and settling in peace above us, sank, day by day, lower and lower, until its edges rested upon the tops of the mountains, turning all their dimness into magnificence, and shutting us up, as if for ever, within a magic prison-house of grandeur and of glory.

The loveliness of Eleonora was that of the Seraphim; but she was a maiden artless and innocent as the brief life she had led among the flowers. No guile disguised the fervour of love which animated her heart, and she examined with me its inmost recesses as we walked together in the Valley of the Many-Coloured Grass, and discoursed of the mighty changes which had lately taken place therein.

At length, having spoken one day, in tears, of the last sad change which must befall Humanity, she thenceforward dwelt only upon this one sorrowful theme, interweaving it into all our converse, as, in the songs of the bard of Schiraz, the same images are found occurring, again and again, in every impressive variation of phrase.

She had seen that the finger of Death was upon her bosom – that, like the ephemeron, she had been made perfect in loveliness only to die; but the terrors of the grave to her lay solely in a consideration which she revealed to me, one evening at twilight, by the banks of the River of Silence. She grieved to think that, having entombed her in the Valley of the Many-Coloured Grass, I would quit for ever its happy recesses, transferring the love which now was so passionately her own to some maiden of the outer and everyday world. And, then and there, I threw myself hurriedly at the feet of Eleonora, and offered up a vow, to herself and to Heaven, that I would never bind myself in marriage to any daughter of Earth – that I would in no manner prove recreant to her dear memory, or to the memory of the devout affection with which she had blessed me. And I called the Mighty Ruler of the Universe to witness the pious solemnity of my vow. And the curse which I invoked of Him and of her, a saint in Helusion should I prove traitorous to that promise, involved a penalty the exceeding great horror of which will not permit me to make record of it here. And the bright eyes of Eleonora grew brighter at my words; and she sighed as if a deadly burden had been taken from her breast; and she trembled and very bitterly wept; but she made acceptance of the vow (for what was she but a child?) and it made easy to her the bed of her death. And she said to me, not many days afterwards, tranquilly dying, that, because of what I had done for the comfort of her spirit she would watch over me in that spirit when departed, and, if so it were permitted her, return to me visibly in the watches of the night; but, if this thing were, indeed, beyond the power of the souls in Paradise, that she would, at least, give me frequent indications of her presence, sighing upon me in the evening winds, or filling the air which I breathed with perfume from the censers of the angels. And, with these words upon her lips, she yielded up her innocent life, putting an end to the first epoch of my own.

Thus far I have faithfully said. But as I pass the barrier in Time's path, formed by the death of my beloved, and proceed with the second era of my existence, I feel that a shadow gathers over my brain, and I mistrust the perfect sanity of the record. But let me on. – Years dragged themselves along heavily, and still I dwelled within the Valley of the Many-Coloured Grass; but a second change had come upon all things. The star-shaped flowers shrank into the stems of the trees, and appeared no more. The tints of the green carpet faded; and, one by one, the ruby-red asphodels withered away; and there sprang up, in place of them, ten by ten, dark, eye-like violets, that writhed uneasily and were ever encumbered with dew. And Life departed from our paths; for the tall flamingo flaunted no longer his scarlet plumage before us, but flew sadly from the vale into the hills, with all the gay glowing birds that had arrived in his company. And the golden and silver fish swam down through the gorge at the lower end of our domain and bedecked the sweet river never again. And the lulling melody that had been softer than the wind-harp of Aeolus, and more divine than all save the voice of Eleonora, it died little by little away, in murmurs growing lower and lower, until the stream returned, at length, utterly, into the solemnity of its original silence. And then, lastly, the voluminous cloud uprose, and, abandoning the tops of the mountains to the dimness of old, fell back into the regions of Hesper, and took away all its manifold golden and gorgeous glories from the Valley of the Many-Coloured Grass.

Yet the promises of Eleonora were not forgotten; for I heard the sounds of the swinging of the censers of the angels; and streams of a holy perfume floated ever and ever about the valley; and at lone hours, when my heart beat heavily, the winds that bathed my brow came unto me laden with soft sighs; and indistinct murmurs filled often the night air, and once – oh, but once only! I was awakened from a slumber, like the slumber of death, by the pressing of spiritual lips upon my own.

But the void within my heart refused, even thus, to be filled. I longed for the love which had before filled it to overflowing. At length the valley pained me through its memories of Eleonora, and I left it for ever for the vanities and the turbulent triumphs of the world.

* * *

I found myself within a strange city, where all things might have served to blot from recollection the sweet dreams I had dreamed so long in the Valley of the Many-Coloured Grass. The pomps and pageantries of a stately court, and the mad clangour of arms, and the radiant loveliness of women, bewildered and intoxicated my brain. But as yet my soul had proved true to its vows, and the indications of the presence of Eleonora were still given me in the silent hours of the night. Suddenly these manifestations they ceased, and the world grew dark before mine eyes, and I stood aghast at the burning thoughts which possessed, at the terrible temptations which beset me; for there came from some far, far distant and unknown land, into the gay court of the king I served, a maiden to whose beauty my whole recreant heart yielded at once – at whose footstool I bowed down without a struggle, in the most ardent, in the most abject worship of love. What, indeed, was my passion for the young girl of the valley in comparison with the fervour, and the delirium, and the spirit-lifting ecstasy of adoration with which I poured out my whole soul in tears at the feet of the ethereal

Ermengarde? – Oh, bright was the seraph Ermengarde! and in that knowledge I had room for none other. – Oh, divine was the angel Ermengarde! and as I looked down into the depths of her memorial eyes, I thought only of them – and *of her*.

I wedded – nor dreaded the curse I had invoked; and its bitterness was not visited upon me. And once – but once again in the silence of the night – there came through my lattice the soft sighs which had forsaken me; and they modelled themselves into familiar and sweet voice, saying: 'Sleep in peace! – for the spirit of love reigneth and ruleth, and, in taking to thy passionate heart her who is Ermengarde, thou art absolved, for reasons which shall be made known to thee in Heaven, of thy vows unto Eleonora.'

The Island of the Fay

Nullus enim locus sine genio est.
SERVIUS

'*La musique*,' says Marmontel, in those '*contes moraux*' which, in all our translations, we have insisted upon calling 'moral tales', as if in mockery of their spirit – '*la musique est le seul des talents qui jouissent de lui-même; tous les autres veulent des temoins.*' He here confounds the pleasure derivable from sweet sounds with the capacity for creating them. No more than any other talent, is that for music susceptible of complete enjoyment, where there is no second party to appreciate its exercise. And it is only in common with other talents that it produces effects which may be fully enjoyed in solitude. The idea which the *raconteur* has either failed to entertain clearly, or has sacrificed in its expression to his national love of *point*, is, doubtless, the very tenable one that the higher order of music is the most thoroughly estimated when we are exclusively alone. The proposition, in this form, will be admitted at once by those who love the lyre for its own sake, and for its spiritual uses. But there is one pleasure still within the reach of fallen mortality – and perhaps only one – which owes even more than does music to the accessory sentiment of seclusion. I mean the happiness experienced in the contemplation of natural scenery. In truth, the man who would behold aright the glory of God upon earth must in solitude behold that glory. To me, at least, the presence – not of human life only, but of life in any other form than that of the green things which grow upon the soil and are voiceless – is a stain upon the landscape – is at war with the genius of the scene. I love, indeed, to regard the dark valleys, and the grey rocks, and the waters that silently smile, and the forests that sigh in uneasy slumbers, and the proud watchful mountains that look down upon all – I love to regard these as themselves but the colossal members of one vast animate and sentient whole – a whole whose form (that of the sphere) is the most perfect and most inclusive of all; whose path is among associate planets; whose meek handmaiden is the moon, whose mediate sovereign is the sun; whose life is eternity, whose thought is that of a God; whose enjoyment is knowledge; whose destinies are lost in immensity, whose cognisance of ourselves is akin with our own cognisance of the *animalculae* which infest the brain – a being which we, in consequence, regard as purely inanimate and material, much in the same manner as these *animalculae* must thus regard us.

Our telescopes and our mathematical investigations assure us on every hand – notwithstanding the cant of the more ignorant of the priesthood – that space, and therefore that bulk, is an important consideration in the eyes of the Almighty. The cycles in which the stars move are those best adapted for the evolution, without collision, of the greatest possible number of bodies. The forms of those bodies are accurately such as, within a given surface, to include the greatest possible amount of matter – while the surfaces themselves are so disposed as to accommodate a denser population than could be accommodated on the same surfaces otherwise arranged. Nor is it any argument against bulk being an object with God, that space itself is infinite; for there may be an infinity of matter to fill it. And since we see clearly that the endowment of matter with vitality is a principle – indeed, as far as our judgements extend, the leading principle in the operations of Deity – it is scarcely logical to imagine it confined to the regions of the minute, where we daily trace it, and not extending to those of the august. As we find cycle within cycle without end – yet all revolving around one far-distant centre which is the Godhead, may we not analogically suppose in the same manner, life within life, the less within the greater, and all within the Spirit Divine? In short, we are madly erring, through self-esteem, in believing man, in either his temporal or future destinies, to be of more moment in the universe than that vast 'clod of the valley' which he tills and contemns, and to which he denies a soul for no more profound reason than that he does not behold it in operation.

These fancies, and such as these, have always given to my meditations among the mountains and the forests, by the rivers and the ocean, a tinge of what the everyday world would not fail to term fantastic. My wanderings amid such scenes have been many, and far-searching, and often solitary; and the interest with which I have strayed through many a dim, deep valley, or gazed into the reflected Heaven of many a bright lake, has been an interest greatly deepened by the thought that I have strayed and gazed alone. What flippant Frenchman was it who said in allusion to the well-known work of Zimmerman, that, *'la solitude est une belle chose; mais il faut quelqu'un pour vous dire que la solitude est une belle chose'*? The epigram cannot be gainsaid; but the necessity is a thing that does not exist.

It was during one of my lonely journeyings, amid a far distant region of mountain locked within mountain, and sad rivers and melancholy tarn writhing or sleeping within all – that I chanced upon a certain rivulet and island. I came upon them suddenly in the leafy June, and threw myself upon the turf, beneath the branches of an unknown odorous shrub, that I might doze as I contemplated the scene. I felt that thus only should I look upon it – such was the character of phantasm which it wore.

On all sides – save to the west, where the sun was about sinking – arose the verdant walls of the forest. The little river which turned sharply in its course, and was thus immediately lost to sight, seemed to have no exit from its prison, but to be absorbed by the deep green foliage of the trees to the east – while in the opposite quarter (so it appeared to me as I lay at length and glanced upwards) there poured down noiselessly and continuously into the valley, a rich golden and crimson waterfall from the sunset fountains of the sky.

About midway in the short vista which my dreamy vision took in, one small circular island, profusely verdured, reposed upon the bosom of the stream.

> So blended bank and shadow there
> That each seemed pendulous in air –

so mirror-like was the glassy water, that it was scarcely possible to say at what point upon the slope of the emerald turf its crystal dominion began.

My position enabled me to include in a single view both the eastern and western extremities of the islet; and I observed a singularly marked difference in their aspects. The latter was all one radiant harem of garden beauties. It glowed and blushed beneath the eyes of the slant sunlight, and fairly laughed with flowers. The grass was short, springy, sweet-scented, and asphodel-interspersed. The trees were lithe, mirthful, erect – bright, slender, and graceful – of eastern figure and foliage, with bark smooth, glossy, and parti-coloured. There seemed a deep sense of life and joy about all; and although no airs blew from out the heavens, yet everything had motion through the gentle sweepings to and fro of innumerable butterflies, that might have been mistaken for tulips with wings.

The other or eastern end of the isle was whelmed in the blackest shade. A sombre, yet beautiful and peaceful gloom here pervaded all things. The trees were dark in colour, and mournful in form and attitude, wreathing themselves into sad, solemn, and spectral shapes that conveyed ideas of mortal sorrow and untimely death. The grass wore the deep tint of the cypress, and the heads of its blades hung droopingly, and hither and thither among it were many small unsightly hillocks, low and narrow, and not very long, that had the aspect of graves, but were not; although over and all about them the rue and the rosemary clambered. The shade of the trees fell heavily upon the water, and seemed to bury itself therein, impregnating the depths of the element with darkness. I fancied that each shadow, as the sun descended lower and lower, separated itself sullenly from the trunk that gave it birth, and thus became absorbed by the stream; while other shadows issued momently from the trees, taking the place of their predecessors thus entombed.

This idea, having once seized upon my fancy, greatly excited it, and I lost myself forthwith in reverie. 'If ever island were enchanted,' said I to myself, 'this is it. This is the haunt of the few gentle Fays who remain from the wreck of the race. Are these green tombs theirs? – or do they yield up their sweet lives as mankind yield up their own? In dying, do they not rather waste away mournfully, rendering unto God, little by little, their existence, as these trees render up shadow after shadow, exhausting their substance unto dissolution? What the wasting tree is to the water that imbibes its shade, growing thus blacker by what it preys upon, may not the life of the Fay be to the death which engulfs it?'

As I thus mused, with half-shut eyes, while the sun sank rapidly to rest, and eddying currents careered round and round the island, bearing upon their bosom large, dazzling, white flakes of the bark of the sycamore – flakes which, in their multiform positions upon the water, a quick imagination might have converted into anything it pleased, while I thus mused, it appeared to me that the form of one of those very Fays about whom I had been pondering made its way slowly into the darkness from out the light at the western end of the island. She stood erect in a singularly fragile canoe, and urged it with the mere phantom of an oar. While within the influence of the lingering sunbeams, her attitude seemed indicative of joy – but sorrow deformed it as she passed within the shade. Slowly she glided along, and at length rounded the islet and re-entered the region of light. 'The revolution which has just been made by the Fay,' continued I, musingly, 'is the cycle of the brief year of her life. She has floated through her winter and through her summer. She is a year nearer unto Death; for I did not fail to see that, as she came into the shade, her shadow fell from her, and was swallowed up in the dark water, making its blackness more black.'

And again the boat appeared, and the Fay, but about the attitude of the latter there was more of care and uncertainty and less of elastic joy. She floated again from out the light and into the gloom (which deepened momently) and again her shadow fell from her into the ebony water, and became absorbed into its blackness. And again and again she made the circuit of the island (while the sun rushed down to his slumbers), and at each issuing into the light there was more sorrow about her person, while it grew feebler and far fainter and more indistinct, and at each passage into the gloom there fell from her a darker shade, which became whelmed in a shadow more black. But at length when the sun had utterly departed, the Fay, now the mere ghost of her former self, went disconsolately with her boat into the region of the ebony flood, and that she issued thence at all I cannot say, for darkness fell over all things and I beheld her magical figure no more.

The Balloon Hoax

Astounding news by express, via Norfolk! – The Atlantic crossed in three days! Signal triumph of Mr Monck Mason's flying machine! – Arrival at Sullivan's Island, near Charlestown, SC, of Mr Mason, Mr Robert Holland, Mr Henson, Mr Harrison Ainsworth, and four others, in the steering balloon *Victoria*, after a passage of seventy-five hours from land to land! Full particulars of the voyage!

The subjoined *jeu d'esprit* with the preceding heading in magnificent capitals, well interspersed with notes of admiration, was originally published, as matter of fact, in the *New York Sun*, a daily newspaper, and therein fully subserved the purpose of creating indigestible aliment for the *quidnuncs* during the few hours intervening between a couple of the Charleston mails. The rush for the 'sole paper which had the news', was something beyond even the prodigious; and, in fact, if (as some assert) the *Victoria did* not absolutely accomplish the voyage recorded, it will be difficult to assign a reason why she *should* not have accomplished it.

The great problem is at length solved! The air, as well as the earth and the ocean, has been subdued by science, and will become a common and convenient highway for mankind. *The Atlantic has been actually crossed in a Balloon!* and this too without difficulty – without any great apparent danger – with thorough control of the machine – and in the inconceivably brief period of seventy-five hours from shore to shore! By the energy of an agent at Charleston, SC, we are enabled to be the first to furnish the public with a detailed account of this most extraordinary voyage, which was performed between Saturday, the 6th instant, at 11 a.m., and 2 p.m. on Tuesday, the 9th instant, by Sir Everard Bringhurst; Mr Osborne, a nephew of Lord Bentinck's; Mr Monck Mason and Mr Robert Holland, the well-known aeronauts; Mr Harrison Ainsworth, author of *Jack Sheppard*, etc.; and Mr Henson, the projector of the late unsuccessful flying machine – with two seamen from Woolwich – in all, eight persons. The particulars furnished below may be relied on as authentic and accurate in every respect, as, with a slight exception, they are copied verbatim from the joint diaries of Mr Monck Mason and Mr Harrison Ainsworth, to whose politeness our agent is also indebted for much verbal information respecting the balloon itself, its construction, and other matters of interest. The only alteration in the manuscript received, has been made for the purpose of throwing the hurried account of our agent, Mr Forsyth, into a connected and intelligible form.

THE BALLOON

Two very decided failures, of late – those of Mr Henson and Sir George Cayley – had much weakened the public interest in the subject of aerial navigation. Mr Henson's scheme (which at first was considered very feasible even by men of science) was founded upon the principle of an inclined plane, started from an eminence by an extrinsic force, applied and continued by the revolution of impinging vanes, in form and number resembling the vanes of a windmill. But, in all the experiments made with models at the Adelaide Gallery, it was found that the operation of these fans not only did not propel the machine, but actually impeded its flight. The only propelling force it ever exhibited was the mere *impetus* acquired from the descent of the inclined plane; and this *impetus* carried the machine farther when the vanes were at rest, than when they were in motion – a fact which sufficiently demonstrates their inutility; and in the absence of the propelling, which was also the *sustaining* power, the whole fabric would necessarily descend. This consideration led Sir George Cayley to think only of adapting a propeller to some machine having of itself an independent power of support – in a word, to a balloon; the idea, however, being novel, or original, with Sir George, only so far as regards the mode of its application to practice. He exhibited a model of his invention at the Polytechnic Institution. The propelling principle, or power, was here, also, applied to interrupted surfaces, or vanes, put in revolution. These vanes were four in number, but were found entirely ineffectual in moving the balloon, or in aiding its ascending power. The whole project was thus a complete failure.

It was at this juncture that Mr Monck Mason (whose voyage from Dover to Weilburg in the balloon, *Nassau*, occasioned so much excitement in 1837) conceived the idea of employing the principle of the Archimedean screw for the purpose of propulsion through the air – rightly attributing the failure of Mr Henson's scheme, and of Sir George Cayley's, to the interruption of surface in the independent vanes. He made the first public experiment at Willis's Rooms, but afterwards removed his model to the Adelaide Gallery.

Like Sir George Cayley's balloon, his own was an ellipsoid. Its length was thirteen feet six inches – height, six feet eight inches. It contained about three hundred and twenty cubic feet of gas, which, if pure hydrogen, would support twenty-one pounds upon its first inflation, before the gas has time to deteriorate or escape. The weight of the whole machine and apparatus was seventeen pounds – leaving about four pounds to spare. Beneath the centre of the balloon was a frame of light wood, about nine feet long, and rigged on to the balloon itself with a network in the customary manner. From this framework was suspended a wicker basket or car.

The screw consists of an axis of hollow brass tube, eighteen inches in length, through which, upon a semi-spiral inclined at fifteen degrees, pass a series of steel wire radii, two feet long, and thus projecting a foot on either side. These radii are connected at the outer extremities by two bands of flattened wire – the whole in this manner forming the framework of the screw, which is completed by a covering of oiled silk cut into gores, and tightened so as to present a tolerably uniform surface. At each end of its axis this screw is supported by pillars of hollow brass tube descending from the hoop. In the lower ends of these tubes are holes in which the pivots of the axis revolve. From the end of the axis which is next the car, proceeds a shaft of steel, connecting the screw with the pinion of a piece of spring machinery fixed in the car. By the operation of this spring, the screw is made to revolve with great rapidity, communicating a progressive motion to the whole. By means of the rudder, the machine was readily turned in any direction. The spring was of great power, compared with its dimensions, being capable of raising forty-five pounds upon a barrel of four inches diameter, after the first turn, and gradually increasing as it was wound up. It weighed, altogether, eight pounds six ounces. The rudder was a light frame of cane covered with silk, shaped somewhat like a battledore, and was about three feet long, and at the widest, one foot. Its weight was about two ounces. It could be turned *flat*, and directed upwards or downwards, as well as to the right or left; and thus enabled the aeronaut to transfer the resistance of the air which in an inclined position it must generate in its passage, to any side upon which he might desire to act; thus determining the balloon in the opposite direction.

This model (which, through want of time, we have necessarily described in an imperfect manner) was put in action at the Adelaide Gallery, where it accomplished a velocity of five miles per hour; although, strange to say, it excited very little interest in comparison with the previous complex machine of Mr Henson – so resolute is the world to despise anything which carries with it an air of simplicity. To accomplish the great desideratum of aerial navigation, it was very generally supposed that some exceedingly complicated application must be made of some unusually profound principle in dynamics.

So well satisfied, however, was Mr Mason of the ultimate success of his invention, that he determined to construct immediately, if possible, a balloon of sufficient capacity to test the question by a voyage of some extent – the original design being to cross the British Channel, as before, in the *Nassau* balloon. To carry out his views, he solicited and obtained the patronage of Sir Everard Bringhurst and Mr Osborne, two gentlemen well known for scientific acquirement, and especially for the interest they have exhibited in the progress of aerostation. The project, at the desire of Mr Osborne, was kept a profound secret from the public – the only persons entrusted with the design being those actually engaged in the construction of the machine, which was built (under the superintendence of Mr Mason, Mr Holland, Sir Everard Bringhurst, and Mr Osborne) at the seat of the latter gentleman near Penstruthal, in Wales. Mr Henson, accompanied by his friend Mr Ainsworth, was admitted to a private view of the balloon, on Saturday last – when the two gentlemen made final arrangements to be included in the adventure. We are not informed for what reason the two seamen were also included in the party – but, in the course of a day or two, we shall put our readers in possession of the minutest particulars respecting this extraordinary voyage.

The balloon is composed of silk, varnished with the liquid gum caoutchouc. It is of vast dimensions, containing more than 40,000 cubic feet of gas; but as coal gas was employed in place of the more expensive and inconvenient hydrogen, the supporting power of the machine, when fully inflated, and immediately after inflation, is not more than about 2,500 pounds. The coal gas is not only much less costly, but is easily procured and managed.

For its introduction into common use for purposes of aerostation, we are indebted to Mr Charles Green. Up to his discovery, the process of inflation was not only exceedingly expensive, but uncertain. Two, and even three days, have frequently been wasted in futile attempts to procure a sufficiency of hydrogen to fill a balloon, from which it had great tendency to escape, owing to its extreme subtlety, and its affinity for the surrounding atmosphere. In a balloon sufficiently perfect to retain its contents of coal gas unaltered, in quantity or amount, for six months, an equal quantity of hydrogen could not be maintained in equal purity for six weeks.

The supporting power being estimated at 2,500 pounds, and the united weights of the party amounting only to about 1,200, there was left a surplus of 1,300, of which again 1,200 was exhausted by ballast, arranged in bags of different sizes, with their respective weights marked upon them – by cordage, barometers, telescopes, barrels containing provision for a fortnight, water-casks, cloaks, carpet-bags, and various other indispensable matters, including a coffee-warmer, contrived for warming coffee by means of slack-lime, so as to dispense altogether with fire, if it should be judged prudent to do so. All these articles, with the exception of the ballast, and a few trifles, were suspended from the hoop overhead. The car is much smaller and lighter, in proportion, than the one appended to the model. It is formed of a light wicker, and is wonderfully strong, for so frail-looking a machine. Its rim is about four feet deep. The rudder is also very much larger, in proportion, than that of the model; and the screw is considerably smaller. The balloon is furnished besides with a grapnel, and a guide-rope; which latter is of the most indispensable importance. A few words, in explanation, will here be necessary for such of our readers as are not conversant with the details of aerostation.

As soon as the balloon quits the earth, it is subjected to the influence of many circumstances tending to create a difference in its weight; augmenting or diminishing its ascending power. For example, there may be a deposition of dew upon the silk, to the extent, even, of several hundred pounds; ballast has then to be thrown out, or the machine may descend. This ballast being discarded, and a clear sunshine evaporating the dew, and at the same time expanding the gas in the silk, the whole will again rapidly ascend. To check this ascent, the only recourse is (or rather was, until Mr Green's invention of the guide-rope) the permission of the escape of gas from the valve; but, in the loss of gas, is a proportionate general loss of ascending power; so that, in a comparatively brief period, the best-constructed balloon must necessarily exhaust all its resources, and come to the earth. This was the great obstacle to voyages of length.

The guide-rope remedies the difficulty in the simplest manner conceivable. It is merely a very long rope which is suffered to trail from the car, and the effect of which is to prevent the balloon from changing its level in any material degree. If, for example, there should be a deposition of moisture upon the silk, and the machine begins to descend in consequence, there will be no necessity for discharging ballast to remedy the increase of weight, for it is remedied, or counteracted, in an exactly just proportion, by the deposit on the ground of just so much of the end of the rope as is necessary. If, on the other hand, any circumstances should cause undue levity, and consequent ascent, this levity is immediately counteracted by the additional weight of rope upraised from the earth. Thus, the balloon can neither ascend or descend, except within very narrow limits, and its resources, either in gas or ballast, remain comparatively unimpaired. When passing over an expanse of water, it becomes necessary to employ small kegs of copper or wood, filled with liquid ballast of a lighter nature than water. These float, and serve all the purposes of a mere rope on land. Another most important office of the guide-rope is to point out the *direction* of the balloon. The rope *drags*, either on land or sea, while the balloon is free; the latter, consequently, is always in advance, when any progress whatever is made: a comparison, therefore, by means of the compass, of the relative positions of the two objects, will always indicate the *course*. In the same way, the angle formed by the rope with the vertical axis of the machine, indicates the *velocity*. When there is *no* angle – in other words, when the rope hangs perpendicularly, the whole apparatus is stationary; but the larger the angle, that is to say, the farther the balloon precedes the end of the rope, the greater the velocity; and the converse.

As the original design was to cross the British Channel, and alight as near Paris as possible, the voyagers had taken the precaution to prepare themselves with passports directed to all parts of the Continent, specifying the nature of the expedition, as in the case of the *Nassau* voyage, and entitling the adventurers to exemption from the usual formalities of office: unexpected events, however, rendered these passports superfluous.

The inflation was commenced very quietly at daybreak, on Saturday morning, the 6th instant, in the courtyard of Weal-Vor House, Mr Osborne's seat, about a mile from Penstruthal, in North Wales; and at seven minutes past eleven, everything being ready for departure, the balloon was set free, rising gently but steadily, in a direction nearly south; no use being made, for the first half-hour, of either the screw or the rudder. We proceed now with the journal, as transcribed by Mr Forsyth from the joint manuscripts of Mr Monck Mason, and Mr Ainsworth. The body of the journal, as given, is in the handwriting of Mr Mason, and a PS is appended, each day, by Mr Ainsworth, who has in preparation, and will shortly give the public a more minute, and no doubt, a thrillingly interesting account of the voyage.

THE JOURNAL

Saturday, April the 6th – Every preparation likely to embarrass us having been made overnight, we commenced the inflation this morning at daybreak; but owing to a thick fog, which encumbered the folds of the silk and rendered it unmanageable, we did not get through before nearly eleven o'clock. Cut loose, then, in high spirits, and rose gently but steadily, with a light breeze at north, which bore us in the direction of the British Channel. Found the ascending force greater than we had expected; and as we arose higher and so got clear of the cliffs, and more in the sun's rays, our ascent became very rapid. I did not wish, however, to lose gas at so early a period of the adventure, and so concluded to ascend for the present. We soon ran out our guide-rope; but even when we had raised it clear of the earth, we still went up very rapidly. The balloon was unusually steady, and looked beautiful. In about ten minutes after starting, the barometer indicated an altitude of 15,000 feet. The weather was remarkably fine, and the view of the subjacent country – a most romantic one when seen from any point – was now especially sublime. The numerous deep gorges presented the appearance of lakes, on account of the dense vapours with which they were filled, and the pinnacles and crags to the south east, piled in inextricable confusion, resembling nothing so much as the giant cities of Eastern fable. We were rapidly approaching the mountains in the south; but our elevation was more than sufficient to enable us to pass them in safety. In a few minutes we soared over them in fine style; and Mr Ainsworth, with the seamen, was surprised at their apparent want of altitude when viewed from the car, the tendency of great elevation in a balloon being to reduce inequalities of the surface below, to nearly a dead level. At half-past eleven still proceeding nearly south, we obtained our first view of the Bristol Channel; and, in fifteen minutes afterwards, the line of breakers on the coast appeared immediately beneath us, and we were fairly out at sea. We now resolved to let off enough gas to bring our guide-rope, with the buoys affixed, into the water. This was immediately done, and we commenced a gradual descent. In about twenty minutes our first buoy dipped, and at the touch of the second soon afterwards, we remained stationary as to elevation. We were all now anxious to test the efficiency of the rudder and screw, and we put them both into requisition forthwith, for the purpose of altering our direction more to the eastward, and in a line for Paris. By means of the rudder we instantly effected the necessary change of direction, and our course was brought nearly at right angles to that of the wind; when we set in motion the spring of the screw, and were rejoiced to find it propel us readily as desired. Upon this we gave nine hearty cheers, and dropped in the sea a bottle, enclosing a slip of parchment with a brief account of the principle of the invention. Hardly, however, had we done with our rejoicings, when an unforeseen accident occurred which discouraged us in no little degree. The steel rod connecting the spring with the propeller was suddenly jerked out of place at the car end (by a swaying of the car through some movement of one of the two seamen we had taken up) and in an instant hung dangling out of reach, from the pivot of the axis of the screw. While we were endeavouring to regain it, our attention being completely absorbed, we became involved in a strong current of wind from the east, which bore us, with rapidly increasing force, towards the Atlantic. We soon found ourselves driving out to sea at the rate of not less, certainly, than fifty or sixty miles an hour, so that we came up with Cape Clear, at some forty miles to our north, before we had secured the rod, and had time to think what we were about. It was now that Mr Ainsworth made an extraordinary, but to my fancy, a by no means unreasonable or chimerical proposition, in which he was instantly seconded by Mr Holland – viz.: that we should take advantage of the strong gale which bore us on, and in place of beating back to Paris, make an attempt to reach the coast of North America. After slight reflection I gave a willing assent to this bold proposition, which (strange to say) met with objection from the two seamen only. As the stronger party, however, we overruled their fears, and kept resolutely upon our course. We steered due west; but as the trailing of the buoys materially impeded our progress, and we had the balloon abundantly at command, either for ascent or descent, we first threw out fifty pounds of ballast, and then wound up (by means of a windlass) so much of the rope as brought it quite clear of the sea. We perceived the effect of this manoeuvre immediately, in a vastly increased rate of progress; and, as the gale freshened, we flew with a velocity nearly inconceivable; the guide-rope flying out behind the car, like a streamer from a vessel. It is needless to say that a very short time sufficed us to lose sight of the coast. We passed over innumerable vessels of all kinds, a few of which were endeavouring to beat up, but the most of them lying to. We occasioned the greatest excitement on board all – an excitement greatly relished by ourselves, and especially by our two men, who, now under the influence of a dram of Geneva, seemed resolved to give all scruple, or fear, to the wind. Many of the vessels fired signal guns; and in all we were saluted with loud cheers (which we heard with surprising distinctness) and the waving of caps and handkerchiefs. We kept on in this manner throughout the day, with no material incident, and, as the shades of night closed around us, we made a rough estimate of the distance traversed. It could not have been less than five hundred miles, and was probably much more. The propeller was kept in constant operation, and, no doubt, aided our progress materially. As the sun went down, the gale freshened into an absolute hurricane, and the ocean beneath was clearly visible on account of its phosphorescence. The wind was from the east all night, and gave us the brightest omen of success. We suffered no little from cold, and the dampness of the atmosphere was most unpleasant; but the ample space in the car enabled us to lie down, and by means of cloaks and a few blankets, we did sufficiently well.

PS (by Mr Ainsworth). The last nine hours have been unquestionably the most exciting of my life. I can conceive nothing more sublimating than the strange peril and novelty of an adventure such as this. May God grant that we succeed! I ask not success for mere safety to my insignificant person, but for the sake of human knowledge and – for the vastness of the triumph. And yet the feat is only so evidently feasible that the sole wonder is why men have scrupled to attempt it before. One single gale such as now befriends us – let such a tempest whirl forward a balloon for four or five days (these gales often last longer) and the voyager will be easily borne, in that period, from coast to coast. In view of such a gale the broad Atlantic becomes a mere lake. I am more struck, just now, with the supreme silence which reigns in the sea beneath us, notwithstanding its agitation, than with any other phenomenon presenting itself. The waters give up no voice to the heavens. The immense flaming ocean writhes and is tortured uncomplainingly. The mountainous surges suggest the idea of innumerable dumb gigantic fiends struggling in impotent agony. In a night such as is this to me, a man *lives* – lives a whole century of ordinary life – nor would I forgo this rapturous delight for that of a whole century of ordinary existence.

Sunday, the seventh (Mr Mason's manuscript). This morning the gale, by ten, had subsided to an eight- or nine-knot breeze (for a vessel at sea) and bears us, perhaps, thirty miles per hour, or more. It has veered, however, very considerably to the north; and now, at sundown, we are holding our course due west, principally by the screw and rudder, which answer their purposes to admiration. I regard the project as thoroughly successful, and the easy navigation of the air in any direction (not exactly in the teeth of a gale) as no longer problematical. We could not have made head against the strong wind of yesterday; but, by ascending, we might have got out of its influence, if requisite. Against a pretty stiff breeze, I feel convinced, we can make our way with the propeller. At noon, today, ascended to an elevation of nearly 25,000 feet, by discharging ballast. Did this to search for a more direct current, but found none so favourable as the one we are now in. We have an abundance of gas to take us across this small pond, even should the voyage last three weeks. I have not the slightest fear for the result. The difficulty has been strangely exaggerated and misapprehended. I can choose my current, and should I find *all* currents against me, I can make very tolerable headway with the propeller. We have had no incidents worth recording. The night promises fair.

PS (by Mr Ainsworth). I have little to record, except the fact (to me quite a surprising one) that, at an elevation equal to that of Cotopaxi, I experienced neither very intense cold, nor headache, nor difficulty of breathing; neither, I find, did Mr Mason, nor Mr Holland, nor Sir Everard. Mr Osborne complained of constriction of the chest – but this soon wore off. We have flown at a great rate during the day, and we must be more than halfway across the Atlantic. We have passed over some twenty or thirty vessels of various kinds, and all seem to be delightfully astonished. Crossing the ocean in a balloon is not so difficult a feat after all. *Omne ignotum pro magnifico. Mem.*: at 25,000 feet elevation the sky appears nearly black, and the stars are distinctly visible; while the sea does not seem convex (as one might suppose) but absolutely and most unequivocally *concave*.

Monday, the 8th (Mr Mason's manuscript). This morning we had again some little trouble with the rod of the propeller, which must be entirely remodelled, for fear of serious accident – I mean the steel rod – not the vanes. The latter could not be improved. The wind has been blowing steadily and strongly from the north east all day and so far fortune seems bent upon favouring us. Just before day, we were all somewhat alarmed at some odd noises and concussions in the balloon, accompanied with the apparent rapid subsidence of the whole machine. These phenomena were occasioned by the expansion of the gas, through increase of heat in the atmosphere, and the consequent disruption of the minute particles of ice with which the network had become encrusted during the night. Threw down several bottles to the vessels below. Saw one of them picked up by a large ship – seemingly one of the New York line packets. Endeavoured to make out her name, but could not be sure of it. Mr Osborne's telescope made it out something like *Atalanta*. It is now 12 at night and we are still going nearly west, at a rapid pace. The sea is peculiarly phosphorescent.

PS (by Mr Ainsworth). It is now 2 a.m., and nearly calm, as well as I can judge – but it is very difficult to determine this point, since we move *with* the air so completely. I have not slept since quitting Wheal-Vor, but can stand it no longer, and must take a nap. We cannot be far from the American coast.

Tuesday, the 9th (Mr Ainsworth's manuscript). 1 p.m. *We are in full view of the low coast of South Carolina*. The great problem is accomplished. We have crossed the Atlantic – fairly and *easily* crossed it in a balloon! God be praised! Who shall say that anything is impossible hereafter?

The journal here ceases. Some particulars of the descent were communicated, however, by Mr Ainsworth to Mr Forsyth. It was nearly dead calm when the voyagers first came in view of the coast, which was immediately recognised by both the seamen, and by Mr Osborne. The latter gentleman having acquaintances at Fort Moultrie, it was immediately resolved to descend in its vicinity. The balloon was brought over the beach (the tide being out and the sand hard, smooth, and admirably adapted for a descent) and the grapnel let go, which took firm hold at once. The inhabitants of the island, and of the fort, thronged out, of course, to see the balloon; but it was with the greatest difficulty that anyone could be made to credit the actual voyage – *the crossing of the Atlantic*. The grapnel caught at 2 p.m., precisely; and thus the whole voyage was completed in seventy-five hours; or rather less, counting from shore to shore. No serious accident occurred. No real danger was at any time apprehended. The balloon was exhausted and secured without trouble; and when the manuscript from which this narrative is compiled was despatched from Charleston, the party were still at Fort Moultrie. Their farther intentions were not ascertained; but we can safely promise our readers some additional information either on Monday or in the course of the next day, at farthest.

This is unquestionably the most stupendous, the most interesting, and the most important undertaking ever accomplished or even attempted by man. What magnificent events may ensue, it would be useless now to think of determining.

The System of Dr Tarr and Professor Fether

During the autumn of 18—, while on a tour through the extreme southern provinces of France, my route led me within a few miles of a certain *maison de santé* or private madhouse, about which I had heard much in Paris from my medical friends. As I had never visited a place of the kind, I thought the opportunity too good to be lost; and so proposed to my travelling companion (a gentleman with whom I had made casual acquaintance a few days before) that we should turn aside, for an hour or so, and look through the establishment. To this he objected – pleading haste in the first place, and, in the second, a very usual horror at the sight of a lunatic. He begged me, however, not to let any mere courtesy towards himself interfere with the gratification of my curiosity, and said that he would ride on leisurely, so that I might overtake him during the day, or, at all events, during the next. As he bade me goodbye, I bethought me that there might be some difficulty in obtaining access to the premises, and mentioned my fears on this point. He replied that, in fact, unless I had personal knowledge of the superintendent, M. Maillard, or some credential in the way of a letter, a difficulty might be found to exist, as the regulations of these private madhouses were more rigid than the public hospital laws. For himself, he added, he had, some years since, made the acquaintance of Maillard, and would so far assist me as to ride up to the door and introduce me; although his feelings on the subject of lunacy would not permit of his entering the house.

I thanked him, and, turning from the main road, we entered a grass-grown by-path, which, in half an hour, nearly lost itself in a dense forest, clothing the base of a mountain. Through this dank and gloomy wood we rode some two miles, when the *maison de santé* came in view. It was a fantastic chateau, much dilapidated, and indeed scarcely tenantable through age and neglect. Its aspect inspired me with absolute dread, and, checking my horse, I half resolved to turn back. I soon, however, grew ashamed of my weakness, and proceeded.

As we rode up to the gateway, I perceived it slightly open, and the visage of a man peering through. In an instant afterwards, this man came forth, accosted my companion by name, shook him cordially by the hand, and begged him to alight. It was M. Maillard himself. He was a portly, fine-looking gentleman of the old school, with a polished manner, and a certain air of gravity, dignity, and authority which was very impressive.

My friend, having presented me, mentioned my desire to inspect the establishment, and received M. Maillard's assurance that he would show me all attention, now took leave, and I saw him no more.

When he had gone, the superintendent ushered me into a small and exceedingly neat parlour, containing, among other indications of refined taste, many books, drawings, pots of flowers, and musical instruments. A cheerful fire blazed upon the hearth. At a piano, singing an aria from Bellini, sat a young and very beautiful woman, who, at my entrance, paused in her song, and received me with graceful courtesy. Her voice was low, and her whole manner subdued. I thought, too, that I perceived the traces of sorrow in her countenance, which was excessively, although to my taste, not unpleasingly, pale. She was attired in deep mourning, and excited in my bosom a feeling of mingled respect, interest, and admiration.

I had heard, at Paris, that the institution of M. Maillard was managed upon what is vulgarly termed the 'system of soothing' – that all punishments were avoided – that even confinement was seldom resorted to – that the patients, while secretly watched, were left much apparent liberty, and that most of them were permitted to roam about the house and grounds in the ordinary apparel of persons in right mind.

Keeping these impressions in view, I was cautious in what I said before the young lady; for I could not be sure that she was sane; and, in fact, there was a certain restless brilliancy about her eyes which half led me to imagine she was not. I confined my remarks, therefore, to general topics, and to such as I thought would not be displeasing or exciting even to a lunatic. She replied in a perfectly rational manner to all that I said; and even her original observations were marked with the soundest good sense, but a long acquaintance with the metaphysics of mania had taught me to put no faith in such evidence of sanity, and I continued to practise, throughout the interview, the caution with which I commenced it.

Presently a smart footman in livery brought in a tray with fruit, wine, and other refreshments, of which I partook, the lady soon afterwards leaving the room. As she departed I turned my eyes in an enquiring manner towards my host.

'No,' he said, 'oh, no – a member of my family – my niece, and a most accomplished woman.'

'I beg a thousand pardons for the suspicion,' I replied, 'but of course you will know how to excuse me. The excellent administration of your affairs here is well understood in Paris, and I thought it just possible, you know – '

'Yes, yes – say no more – or rather it is myself who should thank you for the commendable prudence you have displayed. We seldom find so much of forethought in young men; and, more than once, some unhappy contretemps has occurred in consequence of thoughtlessness on the part of our visitors. While my former system was in operation, and my patients were permitted the privilege of roaming to and fro at will, they were often aroused to a dangerous frenzy by injudicious persons who called to inspect the house. Hence I was obliged to enforce a rigid system of exclusion; and none obtained access to the premises upon whose discretion I could not rely.'

'While your former system was in operation!' I said, repeating his words – 'do I understand you, then, to say that the "soothing system" of which I have heard so much is no longer in force?'

'It is now,' he replied, 'several weeks since we have concluded to renounce it for ever.'

'Indeed! you astonish me!'

'We found it, sir,' he said, with a sigh, 'absolutely necessary to return to the old usages. The danger of the soothing system was, at all times, appalling; and its advantages have been much overrated. I believe, sir, that in this house it has been given a fair trial, if ever in any. We did everything that rational humanity could suggest. I am sorry that you could not have paid us a visit at an earlier period, that you might have judged for yourself. But I presume you are conversant with the soothing practice – with its details.'

'Not altogether. What I have heard has been at third or fourth hand.'

'I may state the system, then, in general terms, as one in which the patients were *ménagés* – humoured. We contradicted no fancies which entered the brains of the mad. On the contrary, we not only indulged but encouraged them; and many of our most permanent cures have been thus effected. There is no argument which so touches the feeble reason of the madman as the *reductio ad absurdum*. We have had men, for example, who fancied themselves chickens. The cure was, to insist upon the thing as a fact – to accuse the patient of stupidity in not sufficiently perceiving it to be a fact – and thus to refuse him any other diet for a week than that which properly appertains to a chicken. In this manner a little corn and gravel were made to perform wonders.'

'But was this species of acquiescence all?'

'By no means. We put much faith in amusements of a simple kind, such as music, dancing, gymnastic exercises generally, cards, certain classes of books, and so forth. We affected to treat each individual as if for some ordinary physical disorder, and the word "lunacy" was never employed. A great point was to set each lunatic to guard the actions of all the others. To repose confidence in the understanding or discretion of a madman, is to gain him body and soul. In this way we were enabled to dispense with an expensive body of keepers.'

'And you had no punishments of any kind?'

'None.'

'And you never confined your patients?'

'Very rarely. Now and then, the malady of some individual growing to a crisis, or taking a sudden turn of fury, we conveyed him to a secret cell, lest his disorder should infect the rest, and there kept him until we could dismiss him to his friends – for with the raging maniac we have nothing to do. He is usually removed to the public hospitals.'

'And you have now changed all this – and you think for the better?'

'Decidedly. The system had its disadvantages, and even its dangers. It is now, happily, exploded throughout all the *maisons de santé* of France.'

'I am very much surprised,' I said, 'at what you tell me; for I made sure that, at this moment, no other method of treatment for mania existed in any portion of the country.'

'You are young yet, my friend,' replied my host, 'but the time will arrive when you will learn to judge for yourself of what is going on in the world, without trusting to the gossip of others. Believe nothing you hear, and only one half that you see. Now about our *maisons de santé*, it is clear that some ignoramus has misled you. After dinner, however, when you have sufficiently recovered from the fatigue of your ride, I will be happy to take you over the house, and introduce to you a system which, in my opinion, and in that of everyone who has witnessed its operation, is incomparably the most effectual as yet devised.'

'Your own?' I enquired – 'one of your own invention?'

'I am proud,' he replied, 'to acknowledge that it is – at least in some measure.'

In this manner I conversed with M. Maillard for an hour or two, during which he showed me the gardens and conservatories of the place.

'I cannot let you see my patients,' he said, 'just at present. To a sensitive mind there is always more or less of the shocking in such exhibitions; and I do not wish to spoil your appetite for dinner. We will dine. I can give you some veal *à la St Menehoult*, with cauliflowers in *velouté* sauce – after that a glass of Clos de Vougeôt – then your nerves will be sufficiently steadied.'

At six, dinner was announced; and my host conducted me into a large *salle à manger*, where a very numerous company were assembled – twenty-five or thirty in all. They were, apparently, people of rank – certainly of high breeding – although their habiliments, I thought, were extravagantly rich, partaking somewhat too much of the ostentatious finery of the *ville cour*. I noticed that at least two-thirds of these guests were ladies; and some of the latter were by no means accoutred in what a Parisian would consider good taste at the present day. Many females, for example, whose age could not have been less than seventy, were bedecked with a profusion of jewellery, such as rings, bracelets, and earrings, and wore their bosoms and arms shamefully bare. I observed, too, that very few of the dresses were well made – or, at least, that very few of them fitted the wearers. In looking about, I discovered the interesting girl to whom M. Maillard had presented me in the little parlour; but my surprise was great to see her wearing a hoop and farthingale, with high-heeled shoes, and a dirty cap of Brussels lace, so much too large for her that it gave her face a ridiculously diminutive expression. When I had first seen her, she was attired, most becomingly, in deep mourning. There was an air of oddity, in short, about the dress of the whole party, which, at first, caused me to recur to my original idea of the 'soothing system', and to fancy that M. Maillard had been willing to deceive me until after dinner, that I might experience no uncomfortable feelings during the repast, at finding myself dining with lunatics; but I remembered having been informed, in Paris, that the southern provincialists were a peculiarly eccentric people, with a vast number of antiquated notions; and then, too, upon conversing with several members of the company, my apprehensions were immediately and fully dispelled.

The dining room itself, although perhaps sufficiently comfortable and of good dimensions, had nothing too much of elegance about it. For example, the floor was uncarpeted; in France, however, a carpet is frequently dispensed with. The windows, too, were without curtains; the shutters, being shut, were securely fastened with iron bars, applied diagonally, after the fashion of our ordinary shop-shutters. The apartment, I observed, formed, in itself, a wing of the chateau, and thus the windows were on three sides of the parallelogram, the door being at the other. There were no less than ten windows in all.

The table was superbly set out. It was loaded with plate, and more than loaded with delicacies. The profusion was absolutely barbaric. There were meats enough to have feasted the Anakim. Never, in all my life, had I witnessed so lavish, so wasteful an expenditure of the good things of life. There seemed very little taste, however, in the arrangements; and my eyes, accustomed to quiet lights, were sadly offended by the prodigious glare of a multitude of wax candles, which, in silver candelabra, were deposited upon the table, and all about the room, wherever it was possible to find a place. There were several active servants in attendance; and, upon a large table, at the farther end of the apartment, were seated seven or eight people with fiddles, fifes, trombones, and a drum. These fellows annoyed me very much, at intervals, during the repast, by an infinite variety of noises, which were intended for music, and which appeared to afford much entertainment to all present, with the exception of myself.

Upon the whole, I could not help thinking that there was much of the bizarre about everything I saw – but then the world is made up of all kinds of persons, with all modes of thought, and all sorts of conventional customs. I had travelled, too, so much, as to be quite an adept at the *nil admirari*; so I took my seat very coolly at the right hand of my host, and, having an excellent appetite, did justice to the good cheer set before me.

The conversation, in the meantime, was spirited and general. The ladies, as usual, talked a great deal. I soon found that nearly all the company were well educated; and my host was a world of good-humoured anecdote in himself. He seemed quite willing to speak of his position as superintendent of a *maison de santé*; and, indeed, the topic of lunacy was, much to my surprise, a favourite one with all present. A great many amusing stories were told, having reference to the whims of the patients.

'We had a fellow here once,' said a fat little gentleman, who sat at my right – 'a fellow that fancied himself a teapot; and by the way, is it not especially singular how often this particular crotchet has entered the brain of the lunatic? There is scarcely an insane asylum in France which cannot supply a human teapot. *Our* gentleman was a Britannia-ware teapot, and was careful to polish himself every morning with buckskin and whiting.'

'And then,' said a tall man just opposite, 'we had here, not long ago, a person who had taken it into his head that he was a donkey – which allegorically speaking, you will say, was quite true. He was a troublesome patient; and we had much ado to keep him within bounds. For a long time he would eat nothing but thistles; but of this idea we soon cured him by insisting upon his eating nothing else. Then he was perpetually kicking out his heels – so – so – '

'M. de Kock! I will thank you to behave yourself!' here interrupted an old lady, who sat next to the speaker. 'Please keep your feet to yourself! You have spoiled my brocade! Is it necessary, pray, to illustrate a remark in so practical a style? Our friend here can surely comprehend you without all this. Upon my word, you are nearly as great a donkey as the poor unfortunate imagined himself. Your acting is very natural, as I live.'

'*Mille pardons, mademoiselle*!' replied M. de Kock, thus addressed – 'a thousand pardons! I had no intention of offending. Mlle Laplace – M. de Kock will do himself the honour of taking wine with you.'

Here M. de Kock bowed low, kissed his hand with much ceremony, and took wine with Mlle Laplace.

'Allow me, *mon ami*,' now said M. Maillard, addressing myself, 'allow me to send you a morsel of this veal *à la St Menehoult* – you will find it particularly fine.'

At this instant three sturdy waiters had just succeeded in depositing safely upon the table an enormous dish, or trencher, containing what I supposed to be the '*monstrum, horrendum, informe, ingens, cui lumen ademptum*'. A closer scrutiny assured me, however, that it was only a small calf roasted whole, and set upon its knees, with an apple in its mouth, as is the English fashion of dressing a hare.

'Thank you, no,' I replied; 'to say the truth, I am not particularly partial to veal *à la St* – what is it? – for I do not find that it altogether agrees with me. I will change my plate, however, and try some of the rabbit.'

There were several side-dishes on the table, containing what appeared to be the ordinary French rabbit – a very delicious *morceau*, which I can recommend.

'Pierre,' cried the host, 'change this gentleman's plate, and give him a side-piece of this rabbit *au-chat*.'

'This what?' said I.

'This rabbit *au-chat*.'

'Why, thank you – upon second thoughts, no. I will just help myself to some of the ham.'

There is no knowing what one eats, thought I to myself, at the tables of these people of the province. I will have none of their rabbit *au-chat* – and, for the matter of that, none of their cat *au*-rabbit either.

'And then,' said a cadaverous-looking personage, near the foot of the table, taking up the thread of the conversation where it had been broken off, 'and then, among other oddities, we had a patient, once upon a time, who very pertinaciously maintained himself to be a Cordova cheese, and went about, with a knife in his hand, soliciting his friends to try a small slice from the middle of his leg.'

'He was a great fool, beyond doubt,' interposed someone, 'but not to be compared with a certain individual whom we all know, with the exception of this strange gentleman. I mean the man who took himself for a bottle of champagne, and always went off with a pop and a fizz, in this fashion.'

Here the speaker, very rudely, as I thought, put his right thumb in his left cheek, withdrew it with a sound resembling the popping of a cork, and then, by a dexterous movement of the tongue upon the teeth, created a sharp hissing and fizzing, which lasted for several minutes, in imitation of the frothing of champagne. This behaviour, I saw plainly, was not very pleasing to M. Maillard; but that gentleman said nothing, and the conversation was resumed by a very lean little man in a big wig.

'And then there was an ignoramus,' said he, 'who mistook himself for a frog, which, by the way, he resembled in no little degree. I wish you could have seen him, sir,' – here the speaker addressed myself – 'it would have done your heart good to see the natural airs that he put on. Sir, if that man was not a frog, I can only observe that it is a pity he was not. His croak thus – o-o-o-o-gh – o-o-o-o-gh! was the finest note in the world – B flat; and when he put his elbows upon the table thus – after taking a glass or two of wine – and distended his mouth, thus, and rolled up his eyes, thus, and winked them with excessive rapidity, thus, why then, sir, I take it upon myself to say, positively, that you would have been lost in admiration of the genius of the man.'

'I have no doubt of it,' I said.

'And then,' said somebody else, 'then there was Petit Gaillard, who thought himself a pinch of snuff, and was truly distressed because he could not take himself between his own finger and thumb.'

'And then there was Jules Desoulières, who was a very singular genius, indeed, and went mad with the idea that he was a pumpkin. He persecuted the cook to make him up into pies – a thing which the cook indignantly refused to do. For my part, I am by no means sure that a pumpkin pie *à la Desoulières* would not have been very capital eating indeed!'

'You astonish me!' said I; and I looked inquisitively at M. Maillard.

'Ha! ha! ha!' said that gentleman – 'he! he! he! – hi! hi! hi! – ho! ho! ho! – hu! hu! hu! hu! – very good indeed! You must not be astonished, *mon ami*; our friend here is a wit – a *drôle* – you must not understand him to the letter.'

'And then,' said some other one of the party, 'then there was Bouffon Le Grand – another extraordinary personage in his way. He grew deranged through love, and fancied himself possessed of two heads. One of these he maintained to be the head of Cicero; the other he imagined a composite one, being Demosthenes' from the top of the forehead to the mouth, and Lord Brougham's from the mouth to the chin. It is not impossible that he was wrong; but he would have convinced you of his being in the right; for he was a man of great eloquence. He had an absolute passion for oratory, and could not refrain from display. For example, he used to leap upon the dinner-table thus, and – and – '

Here a friend, at the side of the speaker, put a hand upon his shoulder and whispered a few words in his ear, upon which he ceased talking with great suddenness, and sank back within his chair.

'And then,' said the friend who had whispered, 'there was Boullard, the tee-totum. I call him the tee-totum because, in fact, he was seized with the droll but not altogether irrational crotchet, that he had been converted into a tee-totum. You would have roared with laughter to see him spin. He would turn round upon one heel by the hour, in this manner – so – '

Here the friend whom he had just interrupted by a whisper, performed an exactly similar office for himself.

'But then,' cried the old lady, at the top of her voice, 'your M. Boullard was a madman, and a very silly madman at best; for who, allow me to ask you, ever heard of a human tee-totum? The thing is absurd. Mme Joyeuse was a more sensible person, as you know. She had a crotchet, but it was instinct with common sense, and gave pleasure to all who had the honour of her acquaintance. She found, upon mature deliberation, that, by some accident, she had been turned into a chicken-cock; but, as such, she behaved with propriety. She flapped her wings with prodigious effect – so – so – and, as for her crow, it was delicious! Cock-a-doodle-doo! – cock-a-doodle-doo! – cock-a-doodle-de-doo-dooo-do-o-o-o-o-o-o!'

'Mme Joyeuse, I will thank you to behave yourself!' here interrupted our host, very angrily. 'You can either conduct yourself as a lady should do, or you can quit the table forthwith – take your choice.'

The lady (whom I was much astonished to hear addressed as Mme Joyeuse, after the description of Mme Joyeuse she had just given) blushed up to the eyebrows, and seemed exceedingly abashed at the reproof. She hung down her head, and said not a syllable in reply. But another and younger lady resumed the theme. It was my beautiful girl of the little parlour.

'Oh, Mme Joyeuse *was* a fool!' she exclaimed, 'but there was really much sound sense, after all, in the opinion of Eugénie Salsafette. She was a very beautiful and painfully modest young lady, who thought the ordinary mode of habiliment indecent, and wished to dress herself, always, by getting outside instead of inside of her clothes. It is a thing very easily done, after all. You have only to do so – and then so – so – so – and then so – so – so – and then so – so – and then –'

'*Mon dieu*! Mlle Salsafette!' here cried a dozen voices at once. 'What are you about? – forbear! – that is sufficient! – we see, very plainly, how it is done! – hold! hold!' and several persons were already leaping from their seats to withhold Mlle Salsafette from putting herself upon a par with the Medicean Venus, when the point was very effectually and suddenly accomplished by a series of loud screams, or yells, from some portion of the main body of the chateau.

My nerves were very much affected, indeed, by these yells; but the rest of the company I really pitied. I never saw any set of reasonable people so thoroughly frightened in my life. They all grew as pale as so many corpses, and, shrinking within their seats, sat quivering and gibbering with terror, and listening for a repetition of the sound. It came again – louder and seemingly nearer – and then a third time very loud, and then a fourth time with a vigour evidently diminished. At this apparent dying away of the noise, the spirits of the company were immediately regained, and all was life and anecdote as before. I now ventured to enquire the cause of the disturbance.

'A mere bagatelle,' said M. Maillard. 'We are used to these things, and care really very little about them. The lunatics, every now and then, get up a howl in concert; one starting another, as is sometimes the case with a bevy of dogs at night. It occasionally happens, however, that the concerto yells are succeeded by a simultaneous effort at breaking loose, when, of course, some little danger is to be apprehended.'

'And how many have you in charge?'

'At present we have not more than ten, altogether.'

'Principally females, I presume?'

'Oh, no – every one of them men, and stout fellows, too, I can tell you.'

'Indeed! I have always understood that the majority of lunatics were of the gentler sex.'

'It is generally so, but not always. Some time ago, there were about twenty-seven patients here; and, of that number, no less than eighteen were women; but, lately, matters have changed very much, as you see.'

'Yes – have changed very much, as you see,' here interrupted the gentleman who had broken the shins of Mlle Laplace.

'Yes – have changed very much, as you see!' chimed in the whole company at once.

'Hold your tongues, every one of you!' said my host, in a great rage. Whereupon the whole company maintained a dead silence for nearly a minute. As for one lady, she obeyed M. Maillard to the letter, and thrusting out her tongue, which was an excessively long one, held it very resignedly, with both hands, until the end of the entertainment.

'And this gentlewoman,' said I, to M. Maillard, bending over and addressing him in a whisper – 'this good lady who has just spoken, and who gives us the cock-a-doodle-de-doo – she, I presume, is harmless – quite harmless, eh?'

'Harmless!' ejaculated he, in unfeigned surprise, 'why – why, what can you mean?'

'Only slightly touched?' said I, touching my head. 'I take it for granted that she is not particularly – not dangerously affected, eh?'

'*Mon dieu!* what is it you imagine? This lady, my particular old friend Mme Joyeuse, is as absolutely sane as myself. She has her little eccentricities, to be sure – but then, you know, all old women – all very old women – are more or less eccentric!'

'To be sure,' said I, 'to be sure – and then the rest of these ladies and gentlemen –'

'Are my friends and keepers,' interrupted M. Maillard, drawing himself up with hauteur, 'my very good friends and assistants.'

'What! all of them?' I asked, 'the women and all?'

'Assuredly,' he said, 'we could not do at all without the women; they are the best lunatic nurses in the world; they have a way of their own, you know; their bright eyes have a marvellous effect – something like the fascination of the snake, you know.'

'To be sure,' said I, 'to be sure! They behave a little odd, eh? – they are a little queer, eh? – don't you think so?'

'Odd! – queer! – why, do you really think so? We are not very prudish, to be sure, here in the South – do pretty much as we please – enjoy life, and all that sort of thing, you know –'

'To be sure,' said I, 'to be sure.'

'And then, perhaps, this Clos de Vougeôt is a little heady, you know – a little strong – you understand, eh?'

'To be sure,' said I, 'to be sure. By the by, *monsieur*, did I understand you to say that the system you have adopted, in place of the celebrated soothing system, was one of very rigorous severity?'

'By no means. Our confinement is necessarily close; but the treatment – the medical treatment, I mean – is rather agreeable to the patients than otherwise.'

'And the new system is one of your own invention?'

'Not altogether. Some portions of it are referable to Professor Tarr, of whom you have, necessarily, heard; and, again, there are modifications in my plan which I am happy to acknowledge as belonging of right to the celebrated Fether, with whom, if I mistake not, you have the honour of an intimate acquaintance.'

'I am quite ashamed to confess,' I replied, 'that I have never even heard the names of either gentleman before.'

'Good heavens!' ejaculated my host, drawing back his chair abruptly, and uplifting his hands. 'I surely do not hear you aright! You did not intend to say, eh? that you had never heard either of the learned Doctor Tarr, or of the celebrated Professor Fether?'

'I am forced to acknowledge my ignorance,' I replied; 'but the truth should be held inviolate above all things. Nevertheless, I feel humbled to the dust, not to be acquainted with the works of these, no doubt, extraordinary men. I will seek out their writings forthwith, and peruse them with deliberate care. M. Maillard, you have really – I must confess it – you have really – made me ashamed of myself!'

And this was the fact.

'Say no more, my good young friend,' he said kindly, pressing my hand, 'join me now in a glass of Sauterne.'

We drank. The company followed our example without stint. They chatted – they jested – they laughed – they perpetrated a thousand absurdities – the fiddles shrieked – the drum row-de-dowed – the trombones bellowed like so many brazen bulls of Phalaris – and the whole scene, growing gradually worse and worse, as the wines gained the ascendancy, became at length a sort of pandemonium *in petto*. In the meantime, M. Maillard and myself, with some bottles of Sauterne and Vougeôt between us, continued our conversation at the top of the voice. A word spoken in an ordinary key stood no more chance of being heard than the voice of a fish from the bottom of Niagara Falls.

'And, sir,' said I, screaming in his ear, 'you mentioned something before dinner about the danger incurred in the old system of soothing. How is that?'

'Yes,' he replied, 'there was, occasionally, very great danger indeed. There is no accounting for the caprices of madmen; and, in my opinion as well as in that of Dr Tarr and Professor Fether, it is never safe to permit them to run at large unattended. A lunatic may be "soothed", as it is called, for a time, but, in the end, he is very apt to become obstreperous. His cunning, too, is proverbial and great. If he has a project in view, he conceals his design with a marvellous wisdom; and the dexterity with which he counterfeits sanity, presents, to the metaphysician, one of the most singular problems in the study of mind. When a madman appears thoroughly sane, indeed, it is high time to put him in a straitjacket.'

'But the danger, my dear sir, of which you were speaking, in your own experience – during your control of this house – have you had practical reason to think liberty hazardous in the case of a lunatic?'

'Here? – in my own experience? – why, I may say, yes. For example – no very long while ago, a singular circumstance occurred in this very house. The "soothing system", you know, was then in operation, and the patients were at large. They behaved remarkably well – especially so – anyone of sense might have known that some devilish scheme was brewing from that particular fact, that the fellows behaved so remarkably well. And, sure enough, one fine morning the keepers found themselves pinioned hand and foot, and thrown into the cells, where they were attended, as if they were the lunatics, by the lunatics themselves, who had usurped the offices of the keepers.'

'You don't tell me so! I never heard of anything so absurd in my life!'

'Fact – it all came to pass by means of a stupid fellow – a lunatic – who, by some means, had taken it into his head that he had invented a better system of government than any ever heard of before – of lunatic government, I mean. He wished to give his invention a trial, I suppose, and so he persuaded the rest of the patients to join him in a conspiracy for the overthrow of the reigning powers.'

'And he really succeeded?'

'No doubt of it. The keepers and kept were soon made to exchange places. Not that exactly either – for the madmen had been free, but the keepers were shut up in cells forthwith, and treated, I am sorry to say, in a very cavalier manner.'

'But I presume a counter-revolution was soon effected. This condition of things could not have long existed. The country people in the neighbourhood – visitors coming to see the establishment – would have given the alarm.'

'There you are out. The head rebel was too cunning for that. He admitted no visitors at all – with the exception, one day, of a very stupid-looking young gentleman of whom he had no reason to be afraid. He let him in to see the place – just by way of variety – to have a little fun with him. As soon as he had gammoned him sufficiently, he let him out, and sent him about his business.'

'And how long, then, did the madmen reign?'

'Oh, a very long time, indeed – a month certainly – how much longer I can't precisely say. In the meantime, the lunatics had a jolly season of it – that you may swear. They doffed their own shabby clothes, and made free with the family wardrobe and jewels. The cellars of the chateau were well stocked with wine; and these madmen are just the devils that know how to drink it. They lived well, I can tell you.'

'And the treatment – what was the particular species of treatment which the leader of the rebels put into operation?'

'Why, as for that, a madman is not necessarily a fool, as I have already observed; and it is my honest opinion that his treatment was a much better treatment than that which it superseded. It was a very capital system indeed – simple – neat – no trouble at all – in fact it was delicious – it was – '

Here my host's observations were cut short by another series of yells, of the same character as those which had previously disconcerted us. This time, however, they seemed to proceed from persons rapidly approaching.

'Gracious heavens!' I ejaculated – 'the lunatics have most undoubtedly broken loose.'

'I very much fear it is so,' replied M. Maillard, now becoming excessively pale. He had scarcely finished the sentence, before loud shouts and imprecations were heard beneath the windows; and, immediately afterwards, it became evident that some persons outside were endeavouring to gain entrance into the room. The door was beaten with what appeared to be a sledgehammer, and the shutters were wrenched and shaken with prodigious violence.

A scene of the most terrible confusion ensued. M. Maillard, to my excessive astonishment, threw himself under the sideboard. I had expected more resolution at his hands. The members of the orchestra, who, for the last fifteen minutes, had been seemingly too much intoxicated to do duty, now sprang all at once to their feet and to their instruments, and, scrambling upon their table, broke out, with one accord, into 'Yankee Doodle', which they performed, if not exactly in tune, at least with an energy superhuman, during the whole of the uproar.

Meantime, upon the main dining-table, among the bottles and glasses, leaped the gentleman who, with such difficulty, had been restrained from leaping there before. As soon as he fairly settled himself, he commenced an oration, which, no doubt, was a very capital one, if it could only have been heard. At the same moment, the man with the tee-totum predilection set himself to spinning around the apartment, with immense energy, and with arms outstretched at right angles with his body; so that he had all the air of a tee-totum in fact, and knocked everybody down that happened to get in his way. And now, too, hearing an incredible popping and fizzing of champagne, I discovered at length, that it proceeded from the person who performed the bottle of that delicate drink during dinner. And then, again, the frog-man croaked away as if the salvation of his soul depended upon every note that he uttered. And, in the midst of all this, the continuous braying of a donkey arose over all. As for my old friend, Mme Joyeuse, I really could have wept for the poor lady, she appeared so terribly perplexed. All she did, however, was to stand up in a corner, by the fireplace, and sing out incessantly at the top of her voice, 'Cock-a-doodle-de-dooooooh!'

And now came the climax – the catastrophe of the drama. As no resistance, beyond whooping and yelling and cock-a-doodling, was offered to the encroachments of the party without, the ten windows were very speedily, and almost simultaneously, broken in. But I shall never forget the emotions of wonder and horror with which I gazed, when, leaping through these windows, and down among us pell-mell, fighting, stamping, scratching, and howling, there rushed a perfect army of what I took to be chimpanzees, orang-utans, or big black baboons of the Cape of Good Hope.

I received a terrible beating – after which I rolled under a sofa and lay still. After lying there some fifteen minutes, during which time I listened with all my ears to what was going on in the room, I came to same satisfactory denouement of this tragedy. M. Maillard, it appeared, in giving me the account of the lunatic who had excited his fellows to rebellion, had been merely relating his own exploits. This gentleman had, indeed, some two or three years before, been the superintendent of the establishment, but grew crazy himself, and so became a patient. This fact was unknown to the travelling companion who introduced me. The keepers, ten in number, having been suddenly overpowered, were first well tarred, then carefully feathered, and then shut up in underground cells. They had been so imprisoned for more than a month, during which period M. Maillard had generously allowed them not only the tar and feathers (which constituted his 'system'), but some bread and abundance of water. The latter was pumped on them daily. At length, one escaping through a sewer, gave freedom to all the rest.

The 'soothing system', with important modifications, has been resumed at the chateau; yet I cannot help agreeing with M. Maillard, that his own 'treatment' was a very capital one of its kind. As he justly observed, it was 'simple – neat – and gave no trouble at all – not the least'.

I have only to add that, although I have searched every library in Europe for the works of Dr Tarr and Professor Fether, I have, up to the present day, utterly failed in my endeavours at procuring an edition.

Mesmeric Revelation

Whatever doubt may still envelop the *rationale* of mesmerism, its startling *facts* are now almost universally admitted. Of these latter, those who doubt, are your mere doubters by profession – an unprofitable and disreputable tribe. There can be no more absolute waste of time than the attempt to *prove*, at the present day, that man, by mere exercise of will, can so impress his fellow, as to cast him into an abnormal condition, of which the phenomena resemble very closely those of *death*, or at least resemble them more nearly than they do the phenomena of any other normal condition within our cognisance; that, while in this state, the person so impressed employs only with effort, and then feebly, the external organs of sense, yet perceives, with keenly refined perception, and through channels supposed unknown, matters beyond the scope of the physical organs; that, moreover, his intellectual faculties are wonderfully exalted and invigorated; that his sympathies with the person so impressing him are profound; and, finally, that his susceptibility to the impression increases with its frequency, while, in the same proportion, the peculiar phenomena elicited are more extended and more *pronounced*.

I say that these – which are the laws of mesmerism in its general features – it would be supererogation to demonstrate; nor shall I inflict upon my readers so needless a demonstration today. My purpose at present is a very different one indeed. I am impelled, even in the teeth of a world of prejudice, to detail without comment the very remarkable substance of a colloquy, occurring between a sleep-waker and myself.

I had been long in the habit of mesmerising the person in question (Mr Vankirk), and the usual acute susceptibility and exaltation of the mesmeric perception had supervened. For many months he had been labouring under confirmed phthisis, the more distressing effects of which had been relieved by my manipulations; and on the night of Wednesday, the fifteenth instant, I was summoned to his bedside.

The invalid was suffering with acute pain in the region of the heart, and breathed with great difficulty, having all the ordinary symptoms of asthma. In spasms such as these he had usually found relief from the application of mustard to the nervous centres, but tonight this had been attempted in vain.

As I entered his room he greeted me with a cheerful smile, and although evidently in much bodily pain, appeared to be, mentally, quite at ease.

'I sent for you tonight,' he said, 'not so much to administer to my bodily ailment, as to satisfy me concerning certain psychic impressions which, of late, have occasioned me much anxiety and surprise. I need not tell you how sceptical I have hitherto been on the topic of the soul's immortality. I cannot deny that there has always existed, as if in that very soul which I have been denying, a vague half-sentiment of its own existence. But this half-sentiment at no time amounted to conviction. With it my reason had nothing to do. All attempts at logical enquiry resulted, indeed, in leaving me more sceptical than before. I had been advised to study Cousin. I studied him in his own works as well as in those of his European and American echoes. The "Charles Elwood" of Mr Brownson, for example, was placed in my hands. I read it with profound attention. Throughout I found it logical, but the portions which were not *merely* logical were unhappily the initial arguments of the disbelieving hero of the book. In his summing up it seemed evident to me that the reasoner had not even succeeded in convincing himself. His end had plainly forgotten his beginning, like the government of Trinculo. In short, I was not long in perceiving that if man is to be intellectually convinced of his own immortality, he will never be so convinced by the mere abstractions which have been so long the fashion of the moralists of England, of France, and of Germany. Abstractions may amuse and exercise, but take no hold on the mind. Here upon earth, at least, philosophy, I am persuaded, will always in vain call upon us to look upon qualities as things. The will may assent – the soul – the intellect, never.

'I repeat, then, that I only half felt, and never intellectually believed. But latterly there has been a certain deepening of the feeling, until it has come so nearly to resemble the acquiescence of reason, that I find it difficult to distinguish between the two. I am enabled, too, plainly to trace this effect to the mesmeric influence. I cannot better explain my meaning than by the hypothesis that the mesmeric exaltation enables me to perceive a train of ratiocination which, in my abnormal existence, convinces, but which, in full accordance with the mesmeric phenomena, does not extend, except through its *effect*, into my normal condition. In sleep-waking, the reasoning and its conclusion – the cause and its effect – are present together. In my natural state, the cause vanishing, the effect only, and perhaps only partially, remains.

'These considerations have led me to think that some good results might ensue from a series of well-directed questions propounded to me while mesmerised. You have often observed the profound self-cognisance evinced by the sleep-waker – the extensive knowledge he displays upon all points relating to the mesmeric condition itself; and from this self-cognisance may be deduced hints for the proper conduct of a catechism.'

I consented of course to make this experiment. A few passes threw Mr Vankirk into the mesmeric sleep. His breathing became immediately more easy, and he seemed to suffer no physical uneasiness. The following conversation then ensued – V in the dialogue representing the patient, and P myself.

P: Are you asleep?

V: Yes – no; I would rather sleep more soundly.

P: [*After a few more passes*] Do you sleep now?

V: Yes.

P: How do you think your present illness will result?

V: [*After a long hesitation and speaking as if with effort*] I must die.

P: Does the idea of death afflict you?

V: [*Very quickly*] No – no!

P: Are you pleased with the prospect?

V: If I were awake I should like to die, but now it is no matter. The mesmeric condition is so near death as to content me.

P: I wish you would explain yourself, Mr Vankirk.

V: I am willing to do so, but it requires more effort than I feel able to make. You do not question me properly.

P: What then shall I ask?

V: You must begin at the beginning.

P: The beginning! but where is the beginning?

V: You know that the beginning is GOD. [*This was said in a low, fluctuating tone, and with every sign of the most profound veneration*]

P: What then is God?

V: [*Hesitating for many minutes*] I cannot tell.

P: Is not God spirit?

V: While I was awake I knew what you meant by 'spirit', but now it seems only a word – such for instance as truth, beauty – a quality, I mean.

P: Is not God immaterial?

V: There is no immateriality – it is a mere word. That which is not matter, is not at all – unless qualities are things.

P: Is God, then, material?

V: No. [*This reply startled me very much*]

P: What then is he?

V: [*After a long pause, and mutteringly*] I see – but it is a thing difficult to tell. [*Another long pause*] He is not spirit, for he exists. Nor is he matter, *as you understand it*. But there are *gradations* of matter of which man knows nothing; the grosser impelling the finer, the finer pervading the grosser. The atmosphere, for example, impels the electric principle, while the electric principle permeates the atmosphere. These gradations of matter increase in rarity or fineness, until we arrive at a matter *unparticled* – without particles – indivisible – *one*; and here the law of impulsion and permeation is modified. The ultimate, or unparticled matter, not only permeates all things but impels all things – and thus is all things within itself. This matter is God. What men attempt to embody in the word 'thought', is this matter in motion.

P: The metaphysicians maintain that all action is reducible to motion and thinking, and that the latter is the origin of the former.

V: Yes; and I now see the confusion of idea. Motion is the action of *mind* – not of *thinking*. The unparticled matter, or God, in quiescence, is (as nearly as we can conceive it) what men call mind. And the power of self-movement (equivalent in effect to human volition) is, in the unparticled matter, the result of its unity and omniprevalence; *how*, I know not, and now clearly see that I shall never know. But the unparticled matter, set in motion by a law, or quality, existing within itself, is thinking.

P: Can you give me no more precise idea of what you term the unparticled matter?

V: The matters of which man is cognisant, escape the senses in gradation. We have, for example, a metal, a piece of wood, a drop of water, the atmosphere, a gas, caloric, electricity, the luminiferous ether. Now we call all these things matter, and embrace all matter in one general definition; but in spite of this, there can be no two ideas more essentially distinct than that which we attach to a metal, and that which we attach to the luminiferous ether. When we reach the latter, we feel an almost irresistible inclination to class it with spirit, or with nihility. The only consideration which restrains us is our conception of its atomic constitution; and here, even, we have to seek aid from our notion of an atom, as something possessing in infinite minuteness, solidity, palpability, weight. Destroy the idea of the atomic constitution and we should no longer be able to regard the ether as an entity, or at least as matter. For want of a better word we might term it spirit. Take, now, a step beyond the luminiferous ether – conceive a matter as much more rare than the ether, as this ether is more rare than the metal, and we arrive at once (in spite of all the school dogmas) at a unique mass – an unparticled matter. For although we may admit infinite littleness in the atoms themselves, the infinitude of littleness in the spaces between them is an absurdity. There will be a point – there will be a degree of rarity, at which, if the atoms are sufficiently numerous, the interspaces must vanish, and the mass absolutely coalesce. But the consideration of the atomic constitution being now taken away, the nature of the mass inevitably glides into what we conceive of spirit. It is clear, however, that it is as fully matter as before. The truth is, it is impossible to conceive spirit, since it is impossible to imagine what is not. When we flatter ourselves that we have formed its conception, we have merely deceived our understanding by the consideration of infinitely rarefied matter.

P: There seems to me an insurmountable objection to the idea of absolute coalescence – and that is the very slight resistance experienced by the heavenly bodies in their revolutions through space – a resistance now ascertained, it is true, to exist in some degree, but which is, nevertheless, so slight as to have been quite overlooked by the sagacity even of Newton. We know that the resistance of bodies is, chiefly, in proportion to their density. Absolute coalescence is absolute density. Where there are no interspaces, there can be no yielding. An ether, absolutely dense, would put an infinitely more effectual stop to the progress of a star than would an ether of adamant or of iron.

V: Your objection is answered with an ease which is nearly in the ratio of its apparent unanswerability. As regards the progress of the star, it can make no difference whether the star passes through the ether *or the ether through it*. There is no astronomical error more unaccountable than that which reconciles the known retardation of the comets with the idea of their passage through an ether: for, however rare this ether be supposed, it would put a stop to all sidereal revolution in a very far briefer period than has been admitted by those astronomers who have endeavoured to slur over a point which they found it impossible to comprehend. The retardation actually experienced is, on the other hand, about that which might be expected from the *friction* of the ether in the instantaneous passage through the orb. In the one case, the retarding force is momentary and complete within itself – in the other it is endlessly accumulative.

P: But in all this – in this identification of mere matter with God – is there nothing of irreverence? [*I was forced to repeat this question before the sleep-waker fully comprehended my meaning*]

V: Can you say *why* matter should be less reverenced than mind? But you forget that the matter of which I speak is, in all respects, the very 'mind' or 'spirit' of the schools, so far as regards its high capacities, and is, moreover, the 'matter' of these schools at the same time. God, with all the powers attributed to spirit, is but the perfection of matter.

P: You assert, then, that the unparticled matter, in motion, is thought?

V: In general, this motion is the universal thought of the universal mind. This thought creates. All created things are but the thoughts of God.

P: You say, 'in general'.

V: Yes. The universal mind is God. For new individualities, *matter* is necessary.

P: But you now speak of 'mind' and 'matter' as do the metaphysicians.

V: Yes – to avoid confusion. When I say 'mind', I mean the unparticled or ultimate matter; by 'matter', I intend all else.

P: You were saying that 'for new individualities matter is necessary'.

V: Yes; for mind, existing unincorporate, is merely God. To create individual, thinking beings, it was necessary to incarnate portions of the divine mind. Thus man is individualised. Divested of corporate investiture, he were God. Now, the particular motion of the incarnated portions of the unparticled matter is the thought of man; as the motion of the whole is that of God.

P: You say that divested of the body man will be God?

V: [*After much hesitation*] I could not have said this; it is an absurdity.

P: [*Referring to my notes*] You did say that 'divested of corporate investiture man were God'.

V: And this is true. Man thus divested *would be* God – would be unindividualised. But he can never be thus divested – at least never *will be* – else we must imagine an action of God returning upon itself – a purposeless and futile action. Man is a creature. Creatures are thoughts of God. It is the nature of thought to be irrevocable.

P: I do not comprehend. You say that man will never put off the body?

V: I say that he will never be bodiless.

P: Explain.

V: There are two bodies – the rudimental and the complete; corresponding with the two conditions of the worm and the butterfly. What we call 'death', is but the painful metamorphosis. Our present incarnation is progressive, preparatory, temporary. Our future is perfected, ultimate, immortal. The ultimate life is the full design.

P: But of the worm's metamorphosis we are palpably cognisant.

V: *We*, certainly – but not the worm. The matter of which our rudimental body is composed, is within the ken of the organs of that body; or, more distinctly, our rudimental organs are adapted to the matter of which is formed the rudimental body; but not to that of which the ultimate is composed. The ultimate body thus escapes our rudimental senses, and we perceive only the shell which falls, in decaying, from the inner form; not that inner form itself; but this inner form, as well as the shell, is appreciable by those who have already acquired the ultimate life.

P: You have often said that the mesmeric state very nearly resembles death. How is this?

V: When I say that it resembles death, I mean that it resembles the ultimate life; for when I am entranced the senses of my rudimental life are in abeyance, and I perceive external things directly, without organs, through a medium which I shall employ in the ultimate, unorganised life.

P: Unorganised?

V: Yes; organs are contrivances by which the individual is brought into sensible relation with particular classes and forms of matter, to the exclusion of other classes and forms. The organs of man are adapted to his rudimental condition, and to that only; his ultimate condition, being unorganised, is of unlimited comprehension in all points but one – the nature of the volition of God – that is to say, the motion of the unparticled matter. You will have a distinct idea of the ultimate body by conceiving it to be entire brain. This it is *not*; but a conception of this nature will bring you near a comprehension of what it *is*. A luminous body imparts vibration to the luminiferous ether. The vibrations generate similar ones within the retina; these again communicate similar ones to the optic nerve. The nerve conveys similar ones to the brain; the brain, also, similar ones to the unparticled matter which permeates it. The motion of this latter is thought, of which perception is the first undulation. This is the mode by which the mind of the rudimental life communicates with the external world; and this external world is, to the rudimental life, limited, through the idiosyncrasy of its organs. But in the ultimate, unorganised life, the external world reaches the whole body (which is of a substance having affinity to brain, as I have said), with no other intervention than that of an infinitely rarer ether than even the luminiferous; and to this ether – in unison with it – the whole body vibrates, setting in motion the unparticled matter which permeates it. It is to the absence of idiosyncratic organs, therefore, that we must attribute the nearly unlimited perception of the ultimate life. To rudimental beings, organs are the cages necessary to confine them until fledged.

P: You speak of rudimental 'beings'. Are there other rudimental thinking beings than man?

V: The multitudinous conglomeration of rare matter into nebulae, planets, suns, and other bodies which are neither nebulae, suns, nor planets, is for the sole purpose of supplying *pabulum* for the idiosyncrasy of the organs of an infinity of rudimental beings. But for the necessity of the rudimental, prior to the ultimate life, there would have been no bodies such as these. Each of these is tenanted by a distinct variety of organic, rudimental, thinking creatures. In all, the organs vary with the features of the place tenanted. At death, or metamorphosis, these creatures, enjoying the ultimate life – immortality – and cognisant of all secrets but *the one*, act all things and pass everywhere by mere volition – indwelling, not the stars, which to us seem the sole palpabilities, and for the accommodation of which we blindly deem space created – but that SPACE itself – that infinity of which the truly substantive vastness swallows up the star-shadows – blotting them out as nonentities from the perception of the angels.

P: You say that 'but for the *necessity* of the rudimental life' there would have been no stars. But why this necessity?

V: In the inorganic life, as well as in the inorganic matter generally, there is nothing to impede the action of one simple *unique* law – the Divine Volition. With the view of producing impediment, the organic life and matter (complex, substantial, and law-encumbered) were contrived.

P: But again – why need this impediment have been produced?

V: The result of law inviolate is perfection – right – negative happiness. The result of law violate is imperfection, wrong, positive pain. Through the impediments afforded by the number, complexity, and substantiality of the laws of organic life and matter, the violation of law is rendered, to a certain extent, practicable. Thus pain, which in the inorganic life is impossible, is possible in the organic.

P: But to what good end is pain thus rendered possible?

V: All things are either good or bad by comparison. A sufficient analysis will show that pleasure, in all cases, is but the contrast of pain. *Positive* pleasure is a mere idea. To be happy at any one point we must have suffered at the same. Never to suffer would have been never to have been blessed. But it has been shown that, in the inorganic life, pain cannot be thus the necessity for the organic. The pain of the primitive life of Earth is the sole basis of the bliss of the ultimate life in Heaven.

P: Still, there is one of your expressions which I find it impossible to comprehend – 'the truly *substantive* vastness of infinity'.

V: This, probably, is because you have no sufficiently generic conception of the term '*substance*' itself. We must not regard it as a quality, but as a sentiment – it is the perception, in thinking beings, of the adaptation of matter to their organisation. There are many things on the Earth, which would be nihility to the inhabitants of Venus – many things visible and tangible in Venus, which we could not be brought to appreciate as existing at all. But to the inorganic beings – to the angels – the whole of the unparticled matter is substance; that is to say, the whole of what we term 'space' is to them the truest substantiality – the stars, meantime, through what we consider their materiality, escaping the angelic sense, just in proportion as the unparticled matter, through what we consider its immateriality, eludes the organic.

As the sleep-waker pronounced these latter words, in a feeble tone, I observed on his countenance a singular expression, which somewhat alarmed me, and induced me to awake him at once. No sooner had I done this, than, with a bright smile irradiating all his features, he fell back upon his pillow and expired. I noticed that in less than a minute afterwards his corpse had all the stern rigidity of stone. His brow was of the coldness of ice. Thus, ordinarily, should it have appeared, only after long pressure from Azrael's hand. Had the sleep-waker, indeed, during the latter portion of his discourse, been addressing me from out the region of the shadows?

A Tale of the Ragged Mountains

During the fall of the year 1827, while residing near Charlottesville, Virginia, I casually made the acquaintance of Mr Augustus Bedloe. This young gentleman was remarkable in every respect, and excited in me a profound interest and curiosity. I found it impossible to comprehend him either in his moral or his physical relations. Of his family I could obtain no satisfactory account. Whence he came, I never ascertained. Even about his age – although I call him a young gentleman – there was something which perplexed me in no little degree. He certainly seemed young – and he made a point of speaking about his youth – yet there were moments when I should have had little trouble in imagining him a hundred years of age. But in no regard was he more peculiar than in his personal appearance. He was singularly tall and thin. He stooped much. His limbs were exceedingly long and emaciated. His forehead was broad and low. His complexion was absolutely bloodless. His mouth was large and flexible, and his teeth were more wildly uneven, although sound, than I had ever before seen teeth in a human head. The expression of his smile, however, was by no means unpleasing, as might be supposed; but it had no variation whatever. It was one of profound melancholy – of a phaseless and unceasing gloom. His eyes were abnormally large, and round like those of a cat. The pupils, too, upon any accession or diminution of light, underwent contraction or dilation, just such as is observed in the feline tribe. In moments of excitement the orbs grew bright to a degree almost inconceivable; seeming to emit luminous rays, not of a reflected but of an intrinsic lustre, as does a candle or the sun; yet their ordinary condition was so totally vapid, filmy, and dull as to convey the idea of the eyes of a long-interred corpse.

These peculiarities of person appeared to cause him much annoyance, and he was continually alluding to them in a sort of half-explanatory, half-apologetic strain, which, when I first heard it, impressed me very painfully. I soon, however, grew accustomed to it, and my uneasiness wore off. It seemed to be his design rather to insinuate than directly to assert that, physically, he had not always been what he was – that a long series of neuralgic attacks had reduced him from a condition of more than usual personal beauty, to that which I saw. For many years past he had been attended by a physician, named Templeton – an old gentleman, perhaps seventy years of age – whom he had first encountered at Saratoga, and from whose attention, while there, he either received, or fancied that he received, great benefit. The result was that Bedloe, who was wealthy, had made an arrangement with Dr Templeton, by which the latter, in consideration of a liberal annual allowance, had consented to devote his time and medical experience exclusively to the care of the invalid.

Doctor Templeton had been a traveller in his younger days, and at Paris had become a convert, in great measure, to the doctrines of Mesmer. It was altogether by means of magnetic remedies that he had succeeded in alleviating the acute pains of his patient; and this success had very naturally inspired the latter with a certain degree of confidence in the opinions from which the remedies had been educed. The Doctor, however, like all enthusiasts, had struggled hard to make a thorough convert of his pupil, and finally so far gained his point as to induce the sufferer to submit to numerous experiments. By a frequent repetition of these, a result had arisen, which of late days has become so common as to attract little or no attention, but which, at the period of which I write, had very rarely been known in America. I mean to say, that between Doctor Templeton and Bedloe there had grown up, little by little, a very distinct and strongly marked rapport, or magnetic relation. I am not prepared to assert, however, that this rapport extended beyond the limits of the simple sleep-producing power, but this power itself had attained great intensity. At the first attempt to induce the magnetic somnolency, the mesmerist entirely failed. In the fifth or sixth he succeeded very partially, and after long continued effort. Only at the twelfth was the triumph complete. After this the will of the patient succumbed rapidly to that of the physician, so that, when I first became acquainted with the two, sleep was brought about almost instantaneously by the mere volition of the operator, even when the invalid was unaware of his presence. It is only now, in the year 1845, when similar miracles are witnessed daily by thousands, that I dare venture to record this apparent impossibility as a matter of serious fact.

The temperature of Bedloe was in the highest degree sensitive, excitable, enthusiastic. His imagination was singularly vigorous and creative; and no doubt it derived additional force from the habitual use of morphine, which he swallowed in great quantity, and without which he would have found it impossible to exist. It was his practice to take a very large dose of it immediately after breakfast each morning – or, rather, immediately after a cup of strong coffee, for he ate nothing in the forenoon – and then set forth alone, or attended only by a dog, upon a long ramble among the chain of wild and dreary hills that lie westward and southward of Charlottesville, and are there dignified by the title of the Ragged Mountains.

Upon a dim, warm, misty day, towards the close of November, and during the strange interregnum of the seasons which in America is termed the Indian summer, Mr Bedloe departed as usual for the hills. The day passed, and still he did not return.

About eight o'clock at night, having become seriously alarmed at his protracted absence, we were about setting out in search of him, when he unexpectedly made his appearance, in health no worse than usual, and in rather more than ordinary spirits. The account which he gave of his expedition, and of the events which had detained him, was a singular one indeed.

'You will remember,' said he, 'that it was about nine in the morning when I left Charlottesville. I bent my steps immediately to the mountains, and, about ten, entered a gorge which was entirely new to me. I followed the windings of this pass with much interest. The scenery which presented itself on all sides, although scarcely entitled to be called grand, had about it an indescribable and to me a delicious aspect of dreary desolation. The solitude seemed absolutely virgin. I could not help believing that the green sods and the grey rocks upon which I trod had been trodden never before by the foot of a human being. So entirely secluded, and in fact inaccessible, except through a series of accidents, is the entrance of the ravine, that it is by no means impossible that I was indeed the first adventurer – the very first and sole adventurer who had ever penetrated its recesses.

'The thick and peculiar mist, or smoke, which distinguishes the Indian summer, and which now hung heavily over all objects, served, no doubt, to deepen the vague impressions which these objects created. So dense was this pleasant fog that I could at no time see more than a dozen yards of the path before me. This path was excessively sinuous, and as the sun could not be seen, I soon lost all idea of the direction in which I journeyed. In the meantime the morphine had its customary effect – that of enduing all the external world with an intensity of interest. In the quivering of a leaf – in the hue of a blade of grass – in the shape of a trefoil – in the humming of a bee – in the gleaming of a dew drop – in the breathing of the wind – in the faint odours that came from the forest – there came a whole universe of suggestion – a gay and motley train of rhapsodical and immethodical thought.

'Busied in this, I walked on for several hours, during which the mist deepened around me to so great an extent that at length I was reduced to an absolute groping of the way. And now an indescribable uneasiness possessed me – a species of nervous hesitation and tremor. I feared to tread, lest I should be precipitated into some abyss. I remembered, too, strange stories told about these Ragged Hills, and of the uncouth and fierce races of men who tenanted their groves and caverns. A thousand vague fancies oppressed and disconcerted me – fancies the more distressing because vague. Very suddenly my attention was arrested by the loud beating of a drum.

'My amazement was, of course, extreme. A drum in these hills was a thing unknown. I could not have been more surprised at the sound of the trump of the Archangel. But a new and still more astounding source of interest and perplexity arose. There came a wild rattling or jingling sound, as if of a bunch of large keys, and upon the instant a dusky-visaged and half-naked man rushed past me with a shriek. He came so close to my person that I felt his hot breath upon my face. He bore in one hand an instrument composed of an assemblage of steel rings, and shook them vigorously as he ran. Scarcely had he disappeared in the mist before, panting after him, with open mouth and glaring eyes, there darted a huge beast. I could not be mistaken in its character. It was a hyena.

'The sight of this monster rather relieved than heightened my terrors – for I now made sure that I dreamed, and endeavoured to arouse myself to waking consciousness. I stepped boldly and briskly forward. I rubbed my eyes. I called aloud. I pinched my limbs. A small spring of water presented itself to my view, and here, stooping, I bathed my hands and my head and neck. This seemed to dissipate the equivocal sensations which had hitherto annoyed me. I arose, as I thought, a new man, and proceeded steadily and complacently on my unknown way.

'At length, quite overcome by exertion, and by a certain oppressive closeness of the atmosphere, I seated myself beneath a tree. Presently there came a feeble gleam of sunshine, and the shadow of the leaves of the tree fell faintly but definitely upon the grass. At this shadow I gazed wonderingly for many minutes. Its character stupefied me with astonishment. I looked upwards. The tree was a palm.

'I now arose hurriedly, and in a state of fearful agitation – for the fancy that I dreamed would serve me no longer. I saw – I felt that I had perfect command of my senses – and these senses now brought to my soul a world of novel and singular sensation. The heat became all at once intolerable. A strange odour loaded the breeze. A low, continuous murmur, like that arising from a full, but gently flowing river, came to my ears, intermingled with the peculiar hum of multitudinous human voices.

'While I listened in an extremity of astonishment which I need not attempt to describe, a strong and brief gust of wind bore off the incumbent fog as if by the wand of an enchanter.

'I found myself at the foot of a high mountain, and looking down into a vast plain, through which wound a majestic river. On the margin of this river stood an Eastern-looking city, such as we read of in the Arabian Tales, but of a character even more singular than any there described. From my position, which was far above the level of the town, I could perceive its every nook and corner, as if delineated on a map. The streets seemed innumerable, and crossed each other irregularly in all directions, but were rather long winding alleys than streets, and absolutely swarmed with inhabitants. The houses were wildly picturesque. On every hand was a wilderness of balconies, of verandas, of minarets, of shrines, and fantastically carved oriels. Bazaars abounded; and in these were displayed rich wares in infinite variety and profusion – silks, muslins, the most dazzling cutlery, the most magnificent jewels and gems. Besides these things, were seen, on all sides, banners and palanquins, litters with stately dames close veiled, elephants gorgeously caparisoned, idols grotesquely hewn, drums, banners, and gongs, spears, silver and gilded maces. And amid the crowd, and the clamour, and the general intricacy and confusion – amid the million of black and yellow men, turbaned and robed, and of flowing beard, there roamed a countless multitude of holy filleted bulls, while vast legions of the filthy but sacred ape clambered, chattering and shrieking, about the cornices of the mosques, or clung to the minarets and oriels. From the swarming streets to the banks of the river, there descended innumerable flights of steps leading to bathing places, while the river itself seemed to force a passage with difficulty through the vast fleets of deeply burdened ships that far and wide encountered its surface. Beyond the limits of the city arose, in frequent majestic groups, the palm and the cocoa, with other gigantic and weird trees of vast age, and here and there might be seen a field of rice, the thatched hut of a peasant, a tank, a stray temple, a gypsy camp, or a solitary graceful maiden taking her way, with a pitcher upon her head, to the banks of the magnificent river.

'You will say now, of course, that I dreamed; but not so. What I saw – what I heard – what I felt – what I thought – had about it nothing of the unmistakable idiosyncrasy of the dream. All was rigorously self-consistent. At first, doubting that I was really awake, I entered into a series of tests, which soon convinced me that I really was. Now, when one dreams, and, in the dream, suspects that he dreams, the suspicion never fails to confirm itself, and the sleeper is almost immediately aroused. Thus Novalis errs not in saying that "we are near waking when we dream that we dream". Had the vision occurred to me as I describe it, without my suspecting it as a dream, then a dream it might absolutely have been, but, occurring as it did, and suspected and tested as it was, I am forced to class it among other phenomena.'

'In this I am not sure that you are wrong,' observed Dr Templeton, 'but proceed. You arose and descended into the city.'

'I arose,' continued Bedloe, regarding the Doctor with an air of profound astonishment, 'I arose, as you say, and descended into the city. On my way I fell in with an immense populace, crowding through every avenue, all in the same direction, and exhibiting in every action the wildest excitement. Very suddenly, and by some inconceivable impulse, I became intensely imbued with personal interest in what was going on. I seemed to feel that I had an important part to play, without exactly understanding what it was. Against the crowd which environed me, however, I experienced a deep sentiment of animosity. I shrank from amid them, and, swiftly, by a circuitous path, reached and entered the city. Here all was the wildest tumult and contention. A small party of men, clad in garments half-Indian, half-European, and officered by gentlemen in a uniform partly British, were engaged, at great odds, with the swarming rabble of the alleys. I joined the weaker party, arming myself with the weapons of a fallen officer, and fighting I knew not whom with the nervous ferocity of despair. We were soon overpowered by numbers, and driven to seek refuge in a species of kiosk. Here we barricaded ourselves, and, for the present, were secure. From a loophole near the summit of the kiosk, I perceived a vast crowd, in furious agitation, surrounding and assaulting a gay palace that overhung the river. Presently, from an upper window of this place, there descended an effeminate-looking person, by means of a string made of the turbans of his attendants. A boat was at hand, in which he escaped to the opposite bank of the river.

'And now a new object took possession of my soul. I spoke a few hurried but energetic words to my companions, and, having succeeded in gaining over a few of them to my purpose made a frantic sally from the kiosk. We rushed amid the crowd that surrounded it. They retreated, at first, before us. They rallied, fought madly, and retreated again. In the meantime we were borne far from the kiosk, and became bewildered and entangled among the narrow streets of tall, overhanging houses, into the recesses of which the sun had never been able to shine. The rabble pressed impetuously upon us, harassing us with their spears, and overwhelming us with flights of arrows. These latter were very remarkable, and resembled in some respects the writhing *kris* of the Malay. They were made to imitate the body of a creeping serpent, and were long and black, with a poisoned barb. One of them struck me upon the right temple. I reeled and fell. An instantaneous and dreadful sickness seized me. I struggled – I gasped – I died.'

'You will hardly persist now,' said I, smiling, 'that the whole of your adventure was not a dream. You are not prepared to maintain that you are dead?'

When I said these words, I of course expected some lively sally from Bedloe in reply, but, to my astonishment, he hesitated, trembled, became fearfully pallid, and remained silent. I looked towards Templeton. He sat erect and rigid in his chair – his teeth chattered, and his eyes were starting from their sockets. 'Proceed!' he at length said hoarsely to Bedloe.

'For many minutes,' continued the latter, 'my sole sentiment – my sole feeling – was that of darkness and nonentity, with the consciousness of death. At length there seemed to pass a violent and sudden shock through my soul, as if of electricity. With it came the sense of elasticity and of light. This latter I felt – not saw. In an instant I seemed to rise from the ground. But I had no bodily, no visible, audible, or palpable presence. The crowd had departed. The tumult had ceased. The city was in comparative repose. Beneath me lay my corpse, with the arrow in my temple, the whole head greatly swollen and disfigured. But all these things I felt – not saw. I took interest in nothing. Even the corpse seemed a matter in which I had no concern. Volition I had none, but appeared to be impelled into motion, and flitted buoyantly out of the city, retracing the circuitous path by which I had entered it. When I had attained that point of the ravine in the mountains at which I had encountered the hyena, I again experienced a shock as of a galvanic battery, the sense of weight, of volition, of substance, returned. I became my original self, and bent my steps eagerly homewards – but the past had not lost the vividness of the real – and not now, even for an instant, can I compel my understanding to regard it as a dream.'

'Nor was it,' said Templeton, with an air of deep solemnity, 'yet it would be difficult to say how otherwise it should be termed. Let us suppose only, that the soul of the man of today is upon the verge of some stupendous psychic discoveries. Let us content ourselves with this supposition. For the rest I have some explanation to make. Here is a watercolour drawing, which I should have shown you before, but which an unaccountable sentiment of horror has hitherto prevented me from showing.'

We looked at the picture which he presented. I saw nothing in it of an extraordinary character, but its effect upon Bedloe was prodigious. He nearly fainted as he gazed. And yet it was but a miniature portrait – a miraculously accurate one, to be sure – of his own very remarkable features. At least this was my thought as I regarded it.

'You will perceive,' said Templeton, 'the date of this picture – it is here, scarcely visible, in this corner – 1780. In this year was the portrait taken. It is the likeness of a dead friend – a Mr Oldeb – to whom I became much attached at Calcutta, during the administration of Warren Hastings. I was then only twenty years old. When I first saw you, Mr Bedloe, at Saratoga, it was the miraculous similarity which existed between yourself and the painting which induced me to accost you, to seek your friendship, and to bring about those arrangements which resulted in my becoming your constant companion. In accomplishing this point, I was urged partly, and perhaps principally, by a regretful memory of the deceased, but also, in part, by an uneasy, and not altogether horrorless curiosity respecting yourself.

'In your detail of the vision which presented itself to you amid the hills, you have described, with the minutest accuracy, the Indian city of Benares, upon the Holy River. The riots, the combat, the massacre, were the actual events of the insurrection of Cheyte Sing, which took place in 1780, when Hastings was put in imminent peril of his life. The man escaping by the string of turbans was Cheyte Sing himself. The party in the kiosk were sepoys and British officers, headed by Hastings. Of this party I was one, and did all I could to prevent the rash and fatal sally of the officer who fell, in the crowded alleys, by the poisoned arrow of a Bengalee. That officer was my dearest friend. It was Oldeb. You will perceive by these manuscripts' (here the speaker produced a notebook in which several pages appeared to have been freshly written) 'that at the very period in which you fancied these things amid the hills, I was engaged in detailing them upon paper here at home.'

In about a week after this conversation, the following paragraphs appeared in a Charlottesville paper:

> We have the painful duty of announcing the death of Mr Augustus Bedlo, a gentleman whose amiable manners and many virtues have long endeared him to the citizens of Charlottesville.
>
> Mr B—, for some years past, has been subject to neuralgia, which has often threatened to terminate fatally; but this can be regarded only as the mediate cause of his decease. The proximate cause was one of especial singularity. In an excursion to the Ragged Mountains, a few days since, a slight cold and fever were contracted, attended with great determination of blood to the head. To relieve this, Dr Templeton resorted to

topical bleeding. Leeches were applied to the temples. In a fearfully brief period the patient died, when it appeared that in the jar containing the leeches, had been introduced, by accident, one of the venomous vermicular *sangsues* which are now and then found in the neighbouring ponds. This creature fastened itself upon a small artery in the right temple. Its close resemblance to the medicinal leech caused the mistake to be overlooked until too late.

NB – The poisonous *sangsue* of Charlottesville may always be distinguished from the medicinal leech by its blackness, and especially by its writhing or vermicular motions, which very nearly resemble those of a snake.

I was speaking with the editor of the paper in question, upon the topic of this remarkable accident, when it occurred to me to ask how it happened that the name of the deceased had been given as Bedlo.

'I presume,' I said, 'you have authority for this spelling, but I have always supposed the name to be written with an e at the end.'

'Authority? – no,' he replied. 'It is a mere typographical error. The name is Bedlo with an e, all the world over, and I never knew it to be spelt otherwise in my life.'

'Then,' said I mutteringly, as I turned upon my heel, 'then indeed has it come to pass that one truth is stranger than any fiction – for Bedloe, without the e, what is it but Oldeb conversed! And this man tells me that it is a typographical error.'

The Spectacles

Many years ago, it was the fashion to ridicule the idea of 'love at first sight'; but those who think, not less than those who feel deeply, have always advocated its existence. Modern discoveries, indeed, in what may be termed ethical magnetism or magneto-aesthetics, render it probable that the most natural, and, consequently, the truest and most intense of the human affections are those which arise in the heart as if by electric sympathy – in a word, that the brightest and most enduring of the psychic fetters are those which are riveted by a glance. The confession I am about to make will add another to the already almost innumerable instances of the truth of the position.

My story requires that I should be somewhat minute. I am still a very young man – not yet twenty-two years of age. My name, at present, is a very usual and rather plebeian one – Simpson. I say 'at present'; for it is only lately that I have been so called – having legislatively adopted this surname within the last year in order to receive a large inheritance left me by a distant male relative, Adolphus Simpson, Esq. The bequest was conditioned upon my taking the name of the testator – the family, not the Christian name; my Christian name is Napoleon Bonaparte – or, more properly, these are my first and middle appellations.

I assumed the name, Simpson, with some reluctance, as in my true patronym, Froissart, I felt a very pardonable pride – believing that I could trace a descent from the immortal author of the *Chronicles*. While on the subject of names, by the by, I may mention a singular coincidence of sound attending the names of some of my immediate predecessors. My father was a M. Froissart, of Paris. His wife – my mother, whom he married at fifteen – was a Mlle Croissart, eldest daughter of Croissart the banker, whose wife, again, being only sixteen when married, was the eldest daughter of one Victor Voissart. M. Voissart, very singularly, had married a lady of similar name – a Mlle Moissart. She, too, was quite a child when married; and her mother, also, Mme Moissart, was only fourteen when led to the altar. These early marriages are usual in France. Here, however, are Moissart, Voissart, Croissart, and Froissart, all in the direct line of descent. My own name, though, as I say, became Simpson, by act of Legislature, and with so much repugnance on my part, that, at one period, I actually hesitated about accepting the legacy with the useless and annoying proviso attached.

As to personal endowments, I am by no means deficient. On the contrary, I believe that I am well made, and possess what nine-tenths of the world would call a handsome face. In height I am five feet eleven. My hair is black and curling. My nose is sufficiently good. My eyes are large and grey; and although, in fact, they are weak to a very inconvenient degree, still no defect in this regard would be suspected from their appearance. The weakness itself, however, has always much annoyed me, and I have resorted to every remedy –

short of wearing glasses. Being youthful and good-looking, I naturally dislike these, and have resolutely refused to employ them. I know nothing, indeed, which so disfigures the countenance of a young person, or so impresses every feature with an air of demureness, if not altogether of sanctimoniousness and of age. An eyeglass, on the other hand, has a savour of downright foppery and affectation. I have hitherto managed as well as I could without either. But something too much of these merely personal details, which, after all, are of little importance. I will content myself with saying, in addition, that my temperament is sanguine, rash, ardent, enthusiastic – and that all my life I have been a devoted admirer of the women.

One night last winter I entered a box at the P— Theatre, in company with a friend, Mr Talbot. It was an opera night, and the bills presented a very rare attraction, so that the house was excessively crowded. We were in time, however, to obtain the front seats which had been reserved for us, and into which, with some little difficulty, we elbowed our way.

For two hours my companion, who was a musical *fanatico*, gave his undivided attention to the stage; and, in the meantime, I amused myself by observing the audience, which consisted, in chief part, of the very elite of the city. Having satisfied myself upon this point, I was about turning my eyes to the prima donna, when they were arrested and riveted by a figure in one of the private boxes which had escaped my observation.

If I live a thousand years, I can never forget the intense emotion with which I regarded this figure. It was that of a female, the most exquisite I had ever beheld. The face was so far turned towards the stage that, for some minutes, I could not obtain a view of it – but the form was divine; no other word can sufficiently express its magnificent proportion – and even the term 'divine' seems ridiculously feeble as I write it.

The magic of a lovely form in woman – the necromancy of female gracefulness – was always a power which I had found it impossible to resist, but here was grace personified, incarnate, the beau ideal of my wildest and most enthusiastic visions. The figure, almost all of which the construction of the box permitted to be seen, was somewhat above the medium height, and nearly approached, without positively reaching, the majestic. Its perfect fullness and *tournure* were delicious. The head, of which only the back was visible, rivalled in outline that of the Greek Psyche, and was rather displayed than concealed by an elegant cap of *gaze aérienne*, which put me in mind of the *ventum textilem* of Apuleius. The right arm hung over the balustrade of the box, and thrilled every nerve of my frame with its exquisite symmetry. Its upper portion was draperied by one of the loose open sleeves now in fashion. This extended but little below the elbow. Beneath it was worn an under one of some frail material, close-fitting, and terminated by a cuff of rich lace, which fell gracefully over the top of the hand, revealing only the delicate fingers, upon one of which sparkled a diamond ring, which I at once saw was of extraordinary value. The admirable roundness of the wrist was well set off by a bracelet which encircled it, and which also was ornamented and clasped by a magnificent *aigrette* of jewels – telling, in words that could not be mistaken, at once of the wealth and fastidious taste of the wearer.

I gazed at this queenly apparition for at least half an hour, as if I had been suddenly converted to stone; and, during this period, I felt the full force and truth of all that has been said or sung concerning 'love at first sight'. My feelings were totally different from any which I had hitherto experienced, in the presence of even the most celebrated specimens of female loveliness. An unaccountable, and what I am compelled to consider a magnetic, sympathy of soul for soul, seemed to rivet, not only my vision, but my whole powers of thought and feeling, upon the admirable object before me. I saw – I felt – I knew that I was deeply, madly, irrevocably in love – and this even before seeing the face of the person beloved. So intense, indeed, was the passion that consumed me, that I really believe it would have received little if any abatement had the features, yet unseen, proved of merely ordinary character, so anomalous is the nature of the only true love – of the love at first sight – and so little really dependent is it upon the external conditions which only seem to create and control it.

While I was thus wrapped in admiration of this lovely vision, a sudden disturbance among the audience caused her to turn her head partially towards me, so that I beheld the entire profile of the face. Its beauty even exceeded my anticipations – and yet there was something about it which disappointed me without my being able to tell exactly what it was. I said 'disappointed', but this is not altogether the word. My sentiments were at once quieted and exalted. They partook less of transport and more of calm enthusiasm – of enthusiastic repose. This state of feeling arose, perhaps, from the Madonna-like and matronly air of the face; and yet I at once understood that it could not have arisen entirely from this. There was something else – some mystery which I could not develop – some expression about the countenance which slightly disturbed me while it greatly heightened my interest. In fact, I was just in that condition of mind which prepares a young and susceptible man for any act of extravagance. Had the lady been alone, I should undoubtedly have entered her box and accosted her at all hazards; but, fortunately, she was attended by two companions – a gentleman, and a strikingly beautiful woman, to all appearance a few years younger than herself.

I revolved in my mind a thousand schemes by which I might obtain, hereafter, an introduction to the elder lady, or, for the present, at all events, a more distinct view of her beauty. I would have removed my position to one nearer her own, but the crowded state of the theatre rendered this impossible; and the stern decrees of Fashion had, of late, imperatively prohibited the use of the opera-glass in a case such as this, even had I been so fortunate as to have one with me – but I had not – and was thus in despair.

At length I bethought me of applying to my companion.

'Talbot,' I said, 'you have an opera-glass. Let me have it.'

'An opera-glass! – no! – what do you suppose I would be doing with an opera-glass?' Here he turned impatiently towards the stage.

'But, Talbot,' I continued, pulling him by the shoulder, 'listen to me, will you? Do you see the stage-box? – there! – no, the next. – Did you ever behold as lovely a woman?'

'She is very beautiful, no doubt,' he said.

'I wonder who she can be?'

'Why, in the name of all that is angelic, don't you know who she is? "Not to *know* her argues yourself unknown." She is the celebrated Mme Lalande – the beauty of the day *par excellence*, and the talk of the whole town. Immensely wealthy too – a widow, and a great match. She has just arrived from Paris.'

'Do you know her?'

'Yes; I have the honour.'

'Will you introduce me?'

'Assuredly, with the greatest pleasure; when shall it be?'

'Tomorrow, at one, I will call upon you at B—'s.'

'Very good; and now *do* hold your tongue, *if* you can.'

In this latter respect I was forced to take Talbot's advice; for he remained obstinately deaf to every further question or suggestion, and occupied himself exclusively for the rest of the evening with what was transacting upon the stage.

In the meantime I kept my eyes riveted on Mme Lalande, and at length had the good fortune to obtain a full front view of her face. It was exquisitely lovely – this, of course, my heart had told me before, even had not Talbot fully satisfied me upon the point – but still the unintelligible something disturbed me. I finally concluded that my senses were impressed by a certain air of gravity, sadness, or, still more properly, of weariness, which took something from the youth and freshness of the countenance, only to endow it with a seraphic tenderness and majesty, and thus, of course, to my enthusiastic and romantic temperament, with an interest tenfold.

While I thus feasted my eyes, I perceived, at last, to my great trepidation, by an almost imperceptible start on the part of the lady, that she had become suddenly aware of the intensity of my gaze. Still, I was absolutely fascinated, and could not withdraw it, even for an instant. She turned aside her face, and again I saw only the chiselled contour of the back portion of the head. After some minutes, as if urged by curiosity to see if I was still looking, she gradually brought her face again around and again encountered my burning gaze. Her large dark eyes fell instantly, and a deep blush mantled her cheek. But what was my astonishment at perceiving that she not only did not a second time avert her head, but that she actually took from her girdle a double eyeglass – elevated it – adjusted it – and then regarded me through it, intently and deliberately, for the space of several minutes.

Had a thunderbolt fallen at my feet I could not have been more thoroughly astounded – astounded only – not offended or disgusted in the slightest degree; although an action so bold in any other woman would have been likely to offend or disgust. But the whole thing was done with so much quietude – so much nonchalance – so much repose – with so evident an air of the highest breeding, in short – that nothing of mere effrontery was perceptible, and my sole sentiments were those of admiration and surprise.

I observed that, upon her first elevation of the glass, she had seemed satisfied with a momentary inspection of my person, and was withdrawing the instrument, when, as if struck by a second thought, she resumed it, and so continued to regard me with fixed attention for the space of several minutes – for five minutes, at the very least, I am sure.

This action, so remarkable in an American theatre, attracted very general observation, and gave rise to an indefinite movement, or buzz, among the audience, which for a moment filled me with confusion, but produced no visible effect upon the countenance of Mme Lalande.

Having satisfied her curiosity – if such it was – she dropped the glass, and quietly gave her attention again to the stage; her profile now being turned towards myself, as before. I continued to watch her unremittingly, although I was fully conscious of my rudeness in so doing. Presently I saw the head slowly and slightly change its position; and soon I became convinced that the lady, while pretending to look at the stage was, in fact, attentively regarding myself. It is needless to say what effect this conduct, on the part of so fascinating a woman, had upon my excitable mind.

Having thus scrutinised me for perhaps a quarter of an hour, the fair object of my passion addressed the gentleman who attended her, and while she spoke, I saw distinctly, by the glances of both, that the conversation had reference to myself.

Upon its conclusion, Mme Lalande again turned towards the stage, and, for a few minutes, seemed absorbed in the performance. At the expiration of this period, however, I was thrown into an extremity of agitation by seeing her unfold, for the second time, the eyeglass which hung at her side, fully confront me as before, and, disregarding the renewed buzz of the audience, survey me, from head to foot, with the same miraculous composure which had previously so delighted and confounded my soul.

This extraordinary behaviour, by throwing me into a perfect fever of excitement – into an absolute delirium of love – served rather to embolden than to disconcert me. In the mad intensity of my devotion, I forgot everything but the presence and the majestic loveliness of the vision which confronted my gaze. Watching my opportunity, when I thought the audience were fully engaged with the opera, I at length caught the eyes of Mme Lalande, and, upon the instant, made a slight but unmistakable bow.

She blushed very deeply – then averted her eyes – then slowly and cautiously looked around, apparently to see if my rash action had been noticed – then leaned over towards the gentleman who sat by her side.

I now felt a burning sense of the impropriety I had committed, and expected nothing less than instant exposure; while a vision of pistols upon the morrow floated rapidly and uncomfortably through my brain. I was greatly and immediately relieved, however, when I saw the lady merely hand the gentleman a playbill, without speaking; but the reader may form some feeble conception of my astonishment – of my profound amazement – my delirious bewilderment of heart and soul – when, instantly afterwards, having again glanced furtively around, she allowed her bright eyes to set fully and steadily upon my own, and then, with a faint smile, disclosing a bright line of her pearly teeth, made two distinct, pointed, and unequivocal affirmative inclinations of the head.

It is useless, of course, to dwell upon my joy – upon my transport – upon my illimitable ecstasy of heart. If ever man was mad with excess of happiness, it was myself at that moment. I loved. This was my first love – so I felt it to be. It was love supreme – indescribable. It was 'love at first sight'; and at first sight, too, it had been appreciated and returned.

Yes, returned. How and why should I doubt it for an instant. What other construction could I possibly put upon such conduct, on the part of a lady so beautiful – so wealthy – evidently so accomplished – of so high breeding – of so lofty a position in society – in every regard so entirely respectable as I felt assured was Mme Lalande? Yes, she loved me – she returned the enthusiasm of my love, with an enthusiasm as blind – as uncompromising – as uncalculating – as abandoned – and as utterly unbounded as my own! These delicious fancies and reflections, however, were now interrupted by the falling of the drop-curtain. The audience arose; and the usual tumult immediately supervened. Quitting Talbot abruptly, I made every effort to force my way into closer proximity with Mme Lalande. Having failed in this, on account of the crowd, I at length gave up the chase, and bent my steps homewards; consoling myself for my disappointment in not having been able to touch even the hem of her robe by the reflection that I should be introduced by Talbot, in due form, upon the morrow.

This morrow at last came; that is to say, a day finally dawned upon a long and weary night of impatience; and then the hours until 'one' were snail-paced, dreary, and innumerable. But even Stamboul, it is said, shall have an end, and there came an end to this long delay. The clock struck. As the last echo ceased, I stepped into B—'s and enquired for Talbot.

'Out,' said the footman – Talbot's own.

'Out!' I replied, staggering back half a dozen paces – 'let me tell you, my fine fellow, that this thing is thoroughly impossible and impracticable; Mr Talbot is not out. What do you mean?'

'Nothing, sir; only Mr Talbot is not in, that's all. He rode over to S—, immediately after breakfast, and left word that he would not be in town again for a week.'

I stood petrified with horror and rage. I endeavoured to reply, but my tongue refused its office. At length I turned on my heel, livid with wrath, and inwardly consigning the whole tribe of the Talbots to the innermost regions of Erebus. It was evident that my considerate friend, *il fanatico*, had quite forgotten his appointment with myself – had forgotten it as soon as it was made. At no time was he a very scrupulous man of his word. There was no help for it; so smothering my vexation as well as I could, I strolled moodily up the street, propounding futile enquiries about Mme Lalande to every male acquaintance I met. By report she was known, I found, to all – to many by sight – but she had been in town only a few weeks, and there were very few, therefore, who claimed her personal acquaintance. These few, being still comparatively strangers, could not, or would not, take the liberty of introducing me through the formality of a morning call. While I stood thus in despair, conversing with a trio of friends upon the all-absorbing subject of my heart, it so happened that the subject itself passed by.

'As I live, there she is!' cried one.

'Surprisingly beautiful!' exclaimed a second.

'An angel upon earth!' ejaculated a third.

I looked; and in an open carriage which approached us,

passing slowly down the street, sat the enchanting vision of the opera, accompanied by the younger lady who had occupied a portion of her box.

'Her companion also wears remarkably well,' said the one of my trio who had spoken first.

'Astonishingly,' said the second; 'still quite a brilliant air, but art will do wonders. Upon my word, she looks better than she did at Paris five years ago. A beautiful woman still – don't you think so, Froissart? – Simpson, I mean.'

'Still!' said I, 'and why shouldn't she be? But compared with her friend she is as a rush-light to the evening star – a glow-worm to Antares.'

'Ha! ha! ha! – why, Simpson, you have an astonishing tact at making discoveries – original ones, I mean.' And here we separated, while one of the trio began humming a gay vaudeville, of which I caught only the lines:

> Ninon, Ninon, Ninon à bas –
> Ë bas Ninon de L'Enclos!

During this little scene, however, one thing had served greatly to console me, although it fed the passion by which I was consumed. As the carriage of Mme Lalande rolled by our group, I had observed that she recognised me; and more than this, she had blessed me, by the most seraphic of all imaginable smiles, with no equivocal mark of the recognition.

As for an introduction, I was obliged to abandon all hope of it until such time as Talbot should think proper to return from the country. In the meantime I perseveringly frequented every reputable place of public amusement; and, at length, at the theatre, where I first saw her, I had the supreme bliss of meeting her, and of exchanging glances with her once again. This did not occur, however, until the lapse of a fortnight. Every day, in the interim, I had enquired for Talbot at his hotel, and every day had been thrown into a spasm of wrath by the everlasting 'Not come home yet' of his footman.

Upon the evening in question, therefore, I was in a condition little short of madness. Mme Lalande, I had been told, was a Parisian – had lately arrived from Paris – might she not suddenly return? – return before Talbot came back – and might she not be thus lost to me for ever? The thought was too terrible to bear. Since my future happiness was at issue, I resolved to act with a manly decision. In a word, upon the breaking up of the play, I traced the lady to her residence, noted the address, and the next morning sent her a full and elaborate letter, in which I poured out my whole heart.

I spoke boldly, freely – in a word, I spoke with passion. I concealed nothing – nothing even of my weakness. I alluded to the romantic circumstances of our first meeting – even to the glances which had passed between us. I went so far as to say that I felt assured of her love; while I offered this assurance, and my own intensity of devotion, as two excuses for my otherwise unpardonable conduct. As a third, I spoke of my fear that she might quit the city before I could have the opportunity of a formal introduction. I concluded the most wildly enthusiastic epistle ever penned, with a frank declaration of my worldly circumstances – of my affluence – and with an offer of my heart and of my hand.

In an agony of expectation I awaited the reply. After what seemed the lapse of a century it came.

Yes, actually came. Romantic as all this may appear, I really received a letter from Mme Lalande – the beautiful, the wealthy, the idolised Mme Lalande. Her eyes – her magnificent eyes, had not belied her noble heart. Like a true Frenchwoman as she was she had obeyed the frank dictates of her reason – the generous impulses of her nature – despising the conventional pruderies of the world. She had not scorned my proposals. She had not sheltered herself in silence. She had not returned my letter unopened. She had even sent me, in reply, one penned by her own exquisite fingers. It ran thus:

> M. Simpson vill pardonne me for not compose de butefulle tong of his contrée so vell as might. It is only de late dat I am arrive, and not yet ave do opportunité for to – l'étudier.
>
> Vid dis apologie for the manière, I vill now say dat, hélas! – M. Simpson ave guess but de too true. Need I say de more? Hélas! am I not ready speak de too moshe?
>
> EUGÉNIE LALANDE

This noble-spirited note I kissed a million times, and committed, no doubt, on its account, a thousand other extravagances that have now escaped my memory. Still Talbot would not return. Alas! could he have formed even the vaguest idea of the suffering his absence had occasioned his friend, would not his sympathising nature have flown immediately to my relief? Still, however, he came not. I wrote. He replied. He was detained by urgent business – but would shortly return. He begged me not to be impatient – to moderate my transports – to read soothing books – to drink nothing stronger than Hock – and to bring the consolations of philosophy to my aid. The fool! if he could not come himself, why, in the name of everything rational, could he not have enclosed me a letter of presentation? I wrote him again, entreating him to forward one forthwith. My letter was returned by that footman, with the following endorsement in pencil. The scoundrel had joined his master in the country:

> Left S— yesterday, for parts unknown – did not say where – or when be back – so thought best to return letter, knowing your handwriting, and as how you is always, more or less, in a hurry.
>
> Yours sincerely,
>
> STUBBS

After this, it is needless to say that I devoted to the infernal deities both master and valet – but there was little use in anger, and no consolation at all in complaint.

But I had yet a resource left, in my constitutional audacity. Hitherto it had served me well, and I now resolved to make it avail me to the end. Besides, after the correspondence which had passed between us, what act of mere informality could I commit, within bounds, that ought to be regarded as indecorous by Mme Lalande? Since the affair of the letter, I had been in the habit of watching her house, and thus discovered that, about twilight, it was her custom to promenade, attended only by a negro in livery, in a public square overlooked by her windows. Here, amid the luxuriant and shadowing groves, in the grey gloom of a sweet midsummer evening, I observed my opportunity and accosted her.

The better to deceive the servant in attendance, I did this with the assured air of an old and familiar acquaintance. With a presence of mind truly Parisian, she took the cue at once, and, to greet me, held out the most bewitchingly little of hands. The valet at once fell into the rear, and now, with hearts full to overflowing, we discoursed long and unreservedly of our love.

As Mme Lalande spoke English even less fluently than she wrote it, our conversation was necessarily in French. In this sweet tongue, so adapted to passion, I gave loose to the impetuous enthusiasm of my nature, and, with all the eloquence I could command, besought her to consent to an immediate marriage.

At this impatience she smiled. She urged the old story of decorum – that bugbear which deters so many from bliss until the opportunity for bliss has forever gone by. I had most imprudently made it known among my friends, she observed, that I desired her acquaintance – thus that I did not possess it – thus, again, there was no possibility of concealing the date of our first knowledge of each other. And then she adverted, with a blush, to the extreme recency of this date. To wed immediately would be improper – would be indecorous – would be *outré*. All this she said with a charming air of *naïveté* which enraptured while it grieved and convinced me. She went even so far as to accuse me, laughingly, of rashness – of imprudence. She bade me remember that I really even knew not who she was – what were her prospects, her connections, her standing in society. She begged me, but with a sigh, to reconsider my proposal, and termed my love an infatuation – a will o' the wisp – a fancy or fantasy of the moment – a baseless and unstable creation rather of the imagination than of the heart. These things she uttered as the shadows of the sweet twilight gathered darkly and more darkly around us – and then, with a gentle pressure of her fairy-like hand, overthrew, in a single sweet instant, all the argumentative fabric she had reared.

I replied as best I could – as only a true lover can. I spoke at length, and perseveringly of my devotion, of my passion – of her exceeding beauty, and of my own enthusiastic admiration. In conclusion, I dwelt, with a convincing energy, upon the perils that encompass the course of love – that course of true love that never did run smooth – and thus deduced the manifest danger of rendering that course unnecessarily long.

This latter argument seemed finally to soften the rigour of her determination. She relented; but there was yet an obstacle, she said, which she felt assured I had not properly considered. This was a delicate point – for a woman to urge, especially so; in mentioning it, she saw that she must make a sacrifice of her feelings; still, for me, every sacrifice should be made. She alluded to the topic of age. Was I aware – was I fully aware of the discrepancy between us? That the age of the husband should surpass by a few years – even by fifteen or twenty – the age of the wife, was regarded by the world as admissible, and, indeed, as even proper, but she had always entertained the belief that the years of the wife should never exceed in number those of the husband. A discrepancy of this unnatural kind gave rise, too frequently, alas! to a life of unhappiness. Now she was aware that my own age did not exceed two and twenty; and I, on the contrary, perhaps, was not aware that the years of my Eugénie extended very considerably beyond that sum.

About all this there was a nobility of soul – a dignity of candour – which delighted – which enchanted me – which eternally riveted my chains. I could scarcely restrain the excessive transport which possessed me.

'My sweetest Eugénie,' I cried, 'what is all this about which you are discoursing? Your years surpass in some measure my own. But what then? The customs of the world are so many conventional follies. To those who love as ourselves, in what respect differs a year from an hour? I am twenty-two, you say; granted: indeed, you may as well call me, at once, twenty-three. Now you yourself, my dearest Eugénie, can have numbered no more than – can have numbered no more than – no more than – than – than – than – '

Here I paused for an instant, in the expectation that Mme Lalande would interrupt me by supplying her true age. But a Frenchwoman is seldom direct, and has always, by way of answer to an embarrassing query, some little practical reply of her own. In the present instance, Eugénie, who for a few moments past had seemed to be searching for something in her bosom, at length let fall upon the grass a miniature, which I immediately picked up and presented to her.

'Keep it!' she said, with one of her most ravishing smiles. 'Keep it for my sake – for the sake of her whom it too flatteringly represents. Besides, upon the back of the trinket you may discover, perhaps, the very information you seem to desire. It is now, to be sure, growing rather dark – but you can examine it at your leisure in the morning. In the meantime, you shall be my escort home tonight. My friends are about holding a little musical *levée*. I can promise you, too, some good singing. We French are not nearly so punctilious as you Americans, and I shall have no difficulty in smuggling you in, in the character of an old acquaintance.'

With this, she took my arm, and I attended her home. The mansion was quite a fine one, and, I believe, furnished in good taste. Of this latter point, however, I am scarcely qualified to judge; for it was just dark as we arrived; and in American mansions of the better sort lights seldom, during the heat of summer, make their appearance at this, the most pleasant period of the day. In about an hour after my arrival, to be sure, a single shaded solar lamp was lit in the principal drawing room; and this apartment, I could thus see, was arranged with unusual good taste and even splendour; but two other rooms of the suite, and in which the company chiefly assembled, remained, during the whole evening, in a very agreeable shadow. This is a well-conceived custom, giving the party at least a choice of light or shade, and one which our friends over the water could not do better than immediately adopt.

The evening thus spent was unquestionably the most delicious of my life. Mme Lalande had not overrated the musical abilities of her friends; and the singing I here heard I had never heard excelled in any private circle out of Vienna. The instrumental performers were many and of superior talents. The vocalists were chiefly ladies, and no individual sang less than well. At length, upon a peremptory call for 'Mme Lalande', she arose at once, without affectation or demur, from the *chaise longue* upon which she had sat by my side, and, accompanied by one or two gentlemen and her female friend of the opera, repaired to the piano in the main drawing room. I would have escorted her myself, but felt that, under the circumstances of my introduction to the house, I had better remain unobserved where I was. I was thus deprived of the pleasure of seeing, although not of hearing, her sing.

The impression she produced upon the company seemed electrical – but the effect upon myself was something even more. I know not how adequately to describe it. It arose in part, no doubt, from the sentiment of love with which I was imbued; but chiefly from my conviction of the extreme sensibility of the singer. It is beyond the reach of art to endow either air or recitative with more impassioned expression than was hers. Her utterance of the romance in *Otello* – the tone with which she gave the words '*Sul mio sasso*', in the Capuletti – is ringing in my memory yet. Her lower tones were absolutely miraculous. Her voice embraced three complete octaves, extending from the contralto D to the D upper soprano, and, though sufficiently powerful to have filled the San Carlos, executed, with the minutest precision, every difficulty of vocal composition – ascending and descending scales, cadences, or *fioriturі*. In the final of the *somnambula*, she brought about a most remarkable effect at the words:

Ah! non guinge uman pensiero
Al contento ond 'io son piena.

Here, in imitation of Malibran, she modified the original phrase of Bellini, so as to let her voice descend to the tenor G, when, by a rapid transition, she struck the G above the treble stave, springing over an interval of two octaves.

Upon rising from the piano after these miracles of vocal execution, she resumed her seat by my side; when I expressed to her, in terms of the deepest enthusiasm, my delight at her performance. Of my surprise I said nothing, and yet was I most unfeignedly surprised; for a certain feebleness, or rather a certain tremulous indecision of voice in ordinary conversation, had prepared me to anticipate that, in singing, she would not acquit herself with any remarkable ability.

Our conversation was now long, earnest, uninterrupted, and totally unreserved. She made me relate many of the earlier passages of my life, and listened with breathless attention to every word of the narrative. I concealed nothing – felt that I had a right to conceal nothing – from her confiding affection. Encouraged by her candour upon the delicate point of her age, I entered, with perfect frankness, not only into a detail of my many minor vices, but made full confession of those moral and even of those physical infirmities, the disclosure of which, in demanding so much higher a degree of courage, is so much surer an evidence of love. I touched upon my college indiscretions – upon my extravagances – upon my carousals – upon my debts – upon my flirtations. I even went so far as to speak of a slightly hectic cough with which, at one time, I had been troubled – of a chronic rheumatism – of a twinge of hereditary gout – and, in conclusion, of the disagreeable and inconvenient, but hitherto carefully concealed, weakness of my eyes.

'Upon this latter point,' said Mme Lalande, laughingly, 'you have been surely injudicious in coming to confession; for, without the confession, I take it for granted that no one would have accused you of the crime. By the by,' she continued, 'have you any recollection – ' and here I fancied that a blush, even through the gloom of the apartment, became distinctly visible upon her cheek – 'have you any recollection, *mon cher ami*, of this little ocular assistant, which now depends from my neck?'

As she spoke she twirled in her fingers the identical double eyeglass which had so overwhelmed me with confusion at the opera.

'Full well – alas! do I remember it,' I exclaimed, pressing passionately the delicate hand which offered the glasses for my inspection. They formed a complex and magnificent toy, richly chased and filigreed, and gleaming with jewels, which, even in the deficient light, I could not help perceiving were of high value.

'Eh bien! mon ami,' she resumed with a certain *empressment* of manner that rather surprised me – *'Eh bien! mon ami*, you have earnestly besought of me a favour which you have been pleased to denominate priceless. You have demanded of me my hand upon the morrow. Should I yield to your entreaties – and, I may add, to the pleadings of my own bosom – would I not be entitled to demand of you a very – a very little boon in return?'

'Name it!' I exclaimed with an energy that had nearly drawn upon us the observation of the company, and restrained by their presence alone from throwing myself impetuously at her feet. 'Name it, my beloved, my Eugénie, my own! – name it! – but, alas! it is already yielded ere named.'

'You shall conquer, then, *mon ami*,' said she, 'for the sake of the Eugénie whom you love, this little weakness which you have at last confessed – this weakness more moral than physical – and which, let me assure you, is so unbecoming the nobility of your real nature – so inconsistent with the candour of your usual character – and which, if permitted further control, will assuredly involve you, sooner or later, in some very disagreeable scrape. You shall conquer, for my sake, this affectation which leads you, as you yourself acknowledge, to the tacit or implied denial of your infirmity of vision. For, this infirmity you virtually deny, in refusing to employ the customary means for its relief. You will understand me to say, then, that I wish you to wear spectacles – ah, hush! – you have already consented to wear them, for my sake. You shall accept the little toy which I now hold in my hand, and which, though admirable as an aid to vision, is really of no very immense value as a gem. You perceive that, by a trifling modification thus – or thus – it can be adapted to the eyes in the form of spectacles, or worn in the waistcoat pocket as an eyeglass. It is in the former mode, however, and habitually, that you have already consented to wear it for my sake.'

This request – must I confess it? – confused me in no little degree. But the condition with which it was coupled rendered hesitation, of course, a matter altogether out of the question.

'It is done!' I cried, with all the enthusiasm that I could muster at the moment. 'It is done – it is most cheerfully agreed. I sacrifice every feeling for your sake. Tonight I wear this dear eyeglass, as an eyeglass, and upon my heart; but with the earliest dawn of that morning which gives me the pleasure of calling you wife, I will place it upon my – upon my nose – and there wear it ever afterwards, in the less romantic, and less fashionable, but certainly in the more serviceable, form which you desire.'

Our conversation now turned upon the details of our arrangements for the morrow. Talbot, I learned from my betrothed, had just arrived in town. I was to see him at once, and procure a carriage. The *soirée* would scarcely break up before two; and by this hour the vehicle was to be at the door, when, in the confusion occasioned by the departure of the company, Mme L— could easily enter it unobserved. We were then to call at the house of a clergyman who would be in waiting; there be married, drop Talbot, and proceed on a short tour to the East, leaving the fashionable world at home to make whatever comments upon the matter it thought best.

Having planned all this, I immediately took leave, and went in search of Talbot, but, on the way, I could not refrain from stepping into a hotel, for the purpose of inspecting the miniature; and this I did by the powerful aid of the glasses. The countenance was a surpassingly beautiful one! Those large luminous eyes! – that proud Grecian nose! – those dark luxuriant curls! – 'Ah!' said I, exultingly to myself, 'this is indeed the speaking image of my beloved!' I turned the reverse, and discovered the words – 'Eugénie Lalande – aged twenty-seven years and seven months.'

I found Talbot at home, and proceeded at once to acquaint him with my good fortune. He professed excessive astonishment, of course, but congratulated me most cordially, and proffered every assistance in his power. In a word, we carried out our arrangement to the letter, and, at two in the morning, just ten minutes after the ceremony, I found myself in a close carriage with Mme Lalande – with

Mrs Simpson, I should say – and driving at a great rate out of town, in a direction nor'east by north, half-north.

It had been determined for us by Talbot, that, as we were to be up all night, we should make our first stop at C—, a village about twenty miles from the city, and there get an early breakfast and some repose, before proceeding upon our route. At four precisely, therefore, the carriage drew up at the door of the principal inn. I handed my adored wife out, and ordered breakfast forthwith. In the meantime we were shown into a small parlour, and sat down.

It was now nearly if not altogether daylight; and, as I gazed, enraptured, at the angel by my side, the singular idea came, all at once, into my head, that this was really the very first moment since my acquaintance with the celebrated loveliness of Mme Lalande that I had enjoyed a near inspection of that loveliness by daylight at all.

'And now, *mon ami*,' said she, taking my hand, and so interrupting this train of reflection, 'and now, *mon cher ami*, since we are indissolubly one – since I have yielded to your passionate entreaties, and performed my portion of our agreement – I presume you have not forgotten that you also have a little favour to bestow – a little promise which it is your intention to keep. Ah! let me see! Let me remember! Yes; full easily do I call to mind the precise words of the dear promise you made to Eugénie last night. Listen! You spoke thus: "It is done! – it is most cheerfully agreed! I sacrifice every feeling for your sake. Tonight I wear this dear eyeglass as an eyeglass, and upon my heart; but with the earliest dawn of that morning which gives me the privilege of calling you wife, I will place it upon my – upon my nose – and there wear it ever afterwards, in the less romantic, and less fashionable, but certainly in the more serviceable, form which you desire." These were the exact words, my beloved husband, were they not?'

'They were,' I said; 'you have an excellent memory; and assuredly, my beautiful Eugénie, there is no disposition on my part to evade the performance of the trivial promise they imply. See! Behold! they are becoming – rather – are they not?' And here, having arranged the glasses in the ordinary form of spectacles, I applied them gingerly in their proper position; while Mme Simpson, adjusting her cap, and folding her arms, sat bolt upright in her chair, in a somewhat stiff and prim, and indeed, in a somewhat undignified position.

'Goodness gracious me!' I exclaimed, almost at the very instant that the rim of the spectacles had settled upon my nose – 'My goodness gracious me! – why, what can be the matter with these glasses?' and taking them quickly off, I wiped them carefully with a silk handkerchief, and adjusted them again.

But if, in the first instance, there had occurred something which occasioned me surprise, in the second, this surprise became elevated into astonishment; and this astonishment was profound – was extreme –indeed I may say it was horrific. What, in the name of everything hideous, did this mean? Could I believe my eyes? – could I? – that was the question. Was that – was that – was that rouge? And were those – and were those – were those wrinkles, upon the visage of Eugénie Lalande? And oh! Jupiter, and every one of the gods and goddesses, little and big! what – what – what – what had become of her teeth? I dashed the spectacles violently to the ground, and, leaping to my feet, stood erect in the middle of the floor, confronting Mrs Simpson, with my arms set akimbo, and grinning and foaming, but, at the same time, utterly speechless with terror and with rage.

Now I have already said that Mme Eugénie Lalande – that is to say, Simpson – spoke the English language but very little better than she wrote it, and for this reason she very properly never attempted to speak it upon ordinary occasions. But rage will carry a lady to any extreme; and in the present case it carried Mrs Simpson to the very extraordinary extreme of attempting to hold a conversation in a tongue that she did not altogether understand.

'Vell, *monsieur*,' said she, after surveying me, in great apparent astonishment, for some moments – 'Vell, *monsieur*? – and vat den? – vat de matter now? Is it de dance of de St Vitusse dat you ave? If not like me, vat for vy buy de pig in the poke?'

'You wretch!' said I, catching my breath – 'you – you – you villainous old hag!'

'Ag? – ole? – me not so ver ole, after all! Me not one single day more dan de eighty-doo.'

'Eighty-two!' I ejaculated, staggering to the wall – 'eighty-two hundred thousand baboons! The miniature said twenty-seven years and seven months!'

'To be sure! – dat is so! – ver true! but den de portraite has been take for dese fifty-five year. Ven I go marry my segonde usbande, M. Lalande, at dat time I had de portraite take for my daughter by my first usbande, M. Moissart!'

'Moissart!' said I.

'Yes, Moissart,' said she, mimicking my pronunciation, which, to speak the truth, was none of the best, 'and vat den? Vat you know about de Moissart?'

'Nothing, you old fright! – I know nothing about him at all; only I had an ancestor of that name, once upon a time.'

'Dat name! and vat you ave for say to dat name? 'Tis ver goot name; and so is Voissart – dat is *ver* goot name too. My daughter, Mlle Moissart, she marry von M. Voissart – and de name is both ver respectaable name.'

'Moissart?' I exclaimed, 'and Voissart! Why, what is it you mean?'

'Vat I mean? – I mean Moissart and Voissart; and for de matter of dat, I mean Croissart and Froissart, too, if I only tink proper to mean it. My daughter's daughter, Mlle Voissart, she marry von M. Croissart, and den again, my daughter's granddaughter, Mlle Croissart, she marry von M. Froissart; and I suppose you say dat *dat* is not von *ver* respectaable name.'

'Froissart!' said I, beginning to faint, 'why, surely you don't say Moissart, and Voissart, and Croissart, and Froissart?'

'Yes,' she replied, leaning fully back in her chair, and stretching out her lower limbs at great length; 'yes, Moissart, and Voissart, and Croissart, and Froissart. But M. Froissart, he vas von ver big vat you call fool – he vas von ver great big donce like yourself – for he lef *la belle France* for come to dis stupide Amérique – and ven he get here he went and ave von *ver* stupide, von *ver, ver* stupide sonn, so I hear, dough I not yet av ad de plaisir to meet vid him – neither me nor my companion, de Mme Stephanie Lalande. He is name de Napoleon Bonaparte Froissart, and I suppose you say dat *dat*, too, is not von *ver* respectable name.'

Either the length or the nature of this speech had the effect of working up Mrs Simpson into a very extraordinary passion indeed; and as she made an end of it, with great labour, she jumped up from her chair like somebody bewitched, dropping upon the floor an entire universe of bustle as she jumped. Once upon her feet, she gnashed her gums, brandished her arms, rolled up her sleeves, shook her fist in my face, and concluded the performance by tearing the cap from her head, and with it an immense wig of the most valuable and beautiful black hair, the whole of which she dashed upon the ground with a yell, and there trampled and danced a fandango upon it, in an absolute ecstasy and agony of rage.

Meantime I sank aghast into the chair which she had vacated. 'Moissart and Voissart!' I repeated, thoughtfully, as she cut one of her pigeon-wings, and, 'Croissart and Froissart!' as she completed another – 'Moissart and Voissart and Croissart and Napoleon Bonaparte Froissart! – why, you ineffable old serpent, that's me – that's me – d'ye hear? that's me' – here I screamed at the top of my voice – 'that's me–e–e! I am Napoleon Bonaparte Froissart! and if I haven't married my great-great-grandmother, I wish I may be everlastingly confounded!'

Mme Eugénie Lalande, quasi Simpson – formerly Moissart – was, in sober fact, my great-great-grandmother. In her youth she had been beautiful, and even at eighty-two, retained the majestic height, the sculptural contour of head, the fine eyes and the Grecian nose of her girlhood. By the aid of these, of pearl-powder, of rouge, of false hair, false teeth, and false *tournure*, as well as of the most skilful modistes of Paris, she contrived to hold a respectable footing among the beauties *en peu passées* of the French metropolis. In this respect, indeed, she might have been regarded as little less than the equal of the celebrated Ninon de L'Enclos.

She was immensely wealthy, and being left, for the second time, a widow without children, she bethought herself of my existence in America, and for the purpose of making me her heir, paid a visit to the United States, in company with a distant and exceedingly lovely relative of her second husband's – a Mme Stephanie Lalande.

At the opera, my great-great-grandmother's attention was arrested by my notice; and, upon surveying me through her eyeglass, she was struck with a certain family resemblance to herself. Thus interested, and knowing that the heir she sought was actually in the city, she made enquiries of her party respecting me. The gentleman who attended her knew my person, and told her who I was. The information thus obtained induced her to renew her scrutiny; and this scrutiny it was which so emboldened me that I behaved in the absurd manner already detailed. She returned my bow, however, under the impression that, by some odd accident, I had discovered her identity. When, deceived by my weakness of vision, and the arts of the toilet, in respect to the age and charms of the strange lady, I demanded so enthusiastically of Talbot who she was, he concluded that I meant the younger beauty, as a matter of course, and so informed me, with perfect truth, that she was 'the celebrated widow, Mme Lalande'.

In the street, next morning, my great-great-grandmother encountered Talbot, an old Parisian acquaintance; and the conversation, very naturally, turned upon myself. My deficiencies of vision were then explained; for these were notorious, although I was entirely ignorant of their notoriety, and my good old relative discovered, much to her chagrin, that she had been deceived in supposing me aware of her identity, and that I had been merely making a fool of myself in making open love, in a theatre, to an old woman unknown. By way of punishing me for this imprudence, she concocted with Talbot a plot. He purposely kept out of my way to avoid giving me the introduction. My street enquiries about 'the lovely widow, Mme Lalande', were supposed to refer to the younger lady, of course, and thus the conversation with the three gentlemen whom I encountered shortly after leaving Talbot's hotel will be easily explained, as also their allusion to Ninon de L'Enclos. I had no opportunity of seeing Mme Lalande closely during daylight; and, at her musical *soirée*, my silly weakness in refusing the aid of glasses effectually prevented me from making a discovery of her age. When 'Mme Lalande' was called upon to sing, the younger lady was intended; and it was she who arose to obey the call; my great-great-grandmother, to further the deception, arising at the same moment and accompanying her to the piano in the main drawing room. Had I decided upon escorting her thither, it had been her design to suggest the propriety of my remaining where I was; but my own prudential views rendered this unnecessary. The songs which I so much admired, and which so confirmed my impression of the youth of my mistress, were executed by Mme Stephanie Lalande. The eyeglass was presented by way of adding a reproof to the hoax – a sting to the epigram of the deception. Its presentation afforded an opportunity for the lecture upon affectation with which I was so especially edified. It is almost superfluous to add that the glasses of the instrument, as worn by the old lady, had been exchanged by her for a pair better adapted to my years. They suited me, in fact, to a T.

The clergyman, who merely pretended to tie the fatal knot, was a boon companion of Talbot's, and no priest. He was an excellent 'whip', however; and having doffed his cassock to put on a greatcoat, he drove the hack which conveyed the 'happy couple' out of town. Talbot took a seat at his side. The two scoundrels were thus 'in at the death', and through a half-open window of the back parlour of the inn, amused themselves in grinning at the denouement of the drama. I believe I shall be forced to call them both out.

Nevertheless, I am not the husband of my great-great-grandmother; and this is a reflection which affords me infinite relief – but I am the husband of Mme Lalande – of Mme Stephanie Lalande – with whom my good old relative, besides making me her sole heir when she dies – if she ever does – has been at the trouble of concocting me a match. In conclusion: I am done for ever with *billets doux* and am never to be met without SPECTACLES.

The Imp of the Perverse

In the consideration of the faculties and impulses – of the *prima mobilia* of the human soul, the phrenologists have failed to make room for a propensity which, although obviously existing as a radical, primitive, irreducible sentiment, has been equally overlooked by all the moralists who have preceded them. In the pure arrogance of the reason, we have all overlooked it. We have suffered its existence to escape our senses, solely through want of belief – of faith – whether it be faith in Revelation, or faith in the Kabbala. The idea of it has never occurred to us, simply because of its supererogation. We saw no need of the impulse – for the propensity. We could not perceive its necessity. We could not understand, that is to say, we could not have understood, had the notion of this *primum mobile* ever obtruded itself – we could not have understood in what manner it might be made to further the objects of humanity, either temporal or eternal. It cannot be denied that phrenology and, in great measure, all metaphysicianism have been concocted *a priori*. The intellectual or logical man, rather than the understanding or observant man, set himself to imagine designs – to dictate purposes to God. Having thus fathomed, to his satisfaction, the intentions of Jehovah, out of these intentions he built his innumerable systems of mind. In the matter of phrenology, for example, we first determined, naturally enough, that it was the design of the deity that man should eat. We then assigned to man an organ of alimentiveness, and this organ is the scourge with which the deity compels man, willy-nilly, into eating. Secondly, having settled it to be God's will that man should continue his species, we discovered an organ of amativeness, forthwith. And so with combativeness, with ideality, with causality, with constructiveness – so, in short, with every organ, whether representing a propensity, a moral sentiment, or a faculty of the pure intellect. And in these arrangements of the *principia* of human action, the Spurzheimites, whether right or wrong, in part, or upon the whole, have but followed, in principle, the footsteps of their predecessors: deducing and establishing everything from the preconceived destiny of man, and upon the ground of the objects of his creator.

It would have been wiser, it would have been safer, to classify (if classify we must) upon the basis of what man usually or occasionally did, and was always occasionally doing, rather than upon the basis of what we took it for granted the deity intended him to do. If we cannot comprehend God in his visible works, how then in his inconceivable thoughts, that call the works into being? If we cannot understand him in his objective creatures, how then in his substantive moods and phases of creation?

Induction, *a posteriori*, would have brought phrenology to admit, as an innate and primitive principle of human action, a paradoxical something, which we may call perverseness, for want of a more characteristic term. In the sense I intend, it is, in fact, a *mobile* without motive, a motive not *motiviert*. Through its promptings we act without comprehensible object; or, if this shall be understood as a contradiction in terms, we may so far modify the proposition as to say, that through its promptings we act, for the reason that we should *not*. In theory, no reason can be more unreasonable, but, in fact, there is none more strong. With certain minds, under certain conditions, it becomes absolutely irresistible. I am not more certain that I breathe, than that the assurance of the wrong or error of any action is often the one unconquerable force which impels us, and alone impels us to its prosecution. Nor will this overwhelming tendency to do wrong for the wrong's sake, admit of analysis, or resolution into ulterior elements. It is a radical, a primitive impulse – elementary. It will be said, I am aware, that when we persist in acts because we feel we should not persist in them, our conduct is but a modification of that which ordinarily springs from the combativeness of phrenology. But a glance will show the fallacy of this idea. The phrenological combativeness has for its essence, the necessity of self-defence. It is our safeguard against injury. Its principle regards our well-being; and thus the desire to be well is excited simultaneously with its development. It follows, that the desire to be well must be excited simultaneously with any principle which shall be merely a modification of combativeness, but in the case of that something which I term perverseness, the desire to be well is not only not aroused, but a strongly antagonistical sentiment exists.

An appeal to one's own heart is, after all, the best reply to the sophistry just noticed. No one who trustingly consults and thoroughly questions his own soul, will be disposed to deny the entire radicalness of the propensity in question. It is not more incomprehensible than distinctive. There lives no man who at some period has not been tormented, for example, by an earnest desire to tantalise a listener by circumlocution. The speaker is aware that he displeases; he has every intention to please, he is usually curt, precise, and clear, the most laconic and luminous language is struggling for utterance upon his tongue, it is only with difficulty that he restrains himself from giving it flow; he dreads and deprecates the anger of him whom he addresses; yet, the thought strikes him, that by certain involutions and parentheses this anger may be engendered. That single thought is enough. The impulse increases to a wish, the wish to a desire, the desire to an uncontrollable longing, and the longing (to the deep regret and mortification of the speaker, and in defiance of all consequences) is indulged.

We have a task before us which must be speedily performed. We know that it will be ruinous to make delay. The most important crisis of our life calls, trumpet-tongued, for immediate energy and action. We glow, we are consumed with eagerness to commence the work, with the anticipation of whose glorious result our whole souls are on fire. It must, it shall be undertaken today, and yet we put it off until tomorrow, and why? There is no answer, except that we feel perverse, using the word with no comprehension of the principle. Tomorrow arrives, and with it a more impatient anxiety to do our duty, but with this very increase of anxiety arrives, also, a nameless, a positively fearful, because unfathomable, craving for delay. This craving gathers strength as the moments fly. The last hour for action is at hand. We tremble with the violence of the conflict within us – of the definite with the indefinite – of the substance with the shadow. But, if the contest have proceeded thus far, it is the shadow which prevails – we struggle in vain. The clock strikes, and is the knell of our welfare. At the same time, it is the chanticleer-note to the ghost that has so long overawed us. It flies – it disappears – we are free. The old energy returns. We will labour now. Alas, it is too late!

We stand upon the brink of a precipice. We peer into the abyss – we grow sick and dizzy. Our first impulse is to shrink from the danger. Unaccountably we remain. By slow degrees our sickness and dizziness and horror become merged in a cloud of nameable feeling. By gradations, still more imperceptible, this cloud assumes shape, as did the vapour from the bottle out of which arose the genius in the Arabian Nights. But out of this our cloud upon the precipice's edge, there grows into palpability, a shape, far more terrible than any genius or any demon of a tale, and yet it is but a thought, although a fearful one, and one which chills the very marrow of our bones with the fierceness of the delight of its horror. It is merely the idea of what would be our sensations during the sweeping precipitancy of a fall from such a height. And this fall – this rushing annihilation – for the very reason that it involves that one most ghastly and loathsome of all the most ghastly and loathsome images of death and suffering which have ever presented themselves to our imagination – for this very cause do we now the most vividly desire it. And because our reason violently deters us from the brink, therefore do we the most impetuously approach it. There is no passion in nature so demoniacally impatient, as that of him who, shuddering upon the edge of a precipice, thus meditates a plunge. To indulge, for a moment, in any attempt at thought, is to be inevitably lost; for reflection but urges us to forbear, and therefore it is, I say, that we cannot. If there be no friendly arm to check us, or if we fail in a sudden effort to prostrate ourselves backwards from the abyss, we plunge, and are destroyed.

Examine these similar actions as we will, we shall find them resulting solely from the spirit of the perverse. We perpetrate them because we feel that we should not. Beyond or behind this there is no intelligible principle; and we might, indeed, deem this perverseness a direct instigation of the arch-fiend, were it not occasionally known to operate in furtherance of good.

I have said thus much, that in some measure I may answer your question, that I may explain to you why I am here, that I may assign to you something that shall have at least the faint aspect of a cause for my wearing these fetters, and for my tenanting this cell of the condemned. Had I not been thus prolix, you might either have misunderstood me altogether, or, with the rabble, have fancied me mad. As it is, you will easily perceive that I am one of the many uncounted victims of the Imp of the Perverse.

It is impossible that any deed could have been wrought with a more thorough deliberation. For weeks, for months, I pondered upon the means of the murder. I rejected a thousand schemes, because their accomplishment involved a chance of detection. At length, in reading some French memoirs, I found an account of a nearly fatal illness that occurred to Mme Pilau, through the agency of a candle accidentally poisoned. The idea struck my fancy at once. I knew my victim's habit of reading in bed. I knew, too, that his apartment was narrow and ill-ventilated. But I need not vex you with impertinent details. I need not describe the easy artifices by which I substituted, in his bedroom candlestand, a wax-light of my own making for the one which I there found. The next morning he was discovered dead in his bed, and the coroner's verdict was – 'Death by the visitation of God'.

Having inherited his estate, all went well with me for years. The idea of detection never once entered my brain. Of the remains of the fatal taper I had myself carefully disposed. I had left no shadow of a clue by which it would be possible to convict, or even to suspect me of the crime. It is inconceivable how rich a sentiment of satisfaction arose in my bosom as I reflected upon my absolute security. For a very long period of time I was accustomed to revel in this sentiment. It afforded me more real delight than all the mere worldly advantages accruing from my sin. But there arrived at length an epoch, from which the pleasurable feeling grew, by scarcely perceptible gradations, into a haunting and harassing thought. It harassed because it haunted. I could scarcely get rid of it for an instant. It is quite a common thing to be thus annoyed with the ringing in our ears, or rather in our memories, of the burthen of some ordinary song, or some unimpressive snatches from an opera. Nor will we be the less tormented if the song in itself be good, or the opera air meritorious. In this manner, at last, I would perpetually catch myself pondering upon my security, and repeating, in a low undertone, the phrase, 'I am safe.'

One day, whilst sauntering along the streets, I arrested myself in the act of murmuring, half aloud, these customary syllables. In a fit of petulance, I remodelled them thus: 'I am safe – I am safe – yes – if I be not fool enough to make open confession!'

No sooner had I spoken these words, than I felt an icy chill creep to my heart. I had had some experience in these fits of perversity (whose nature I have been at some trouble to explain), and I remembered well that in no instance had I successfully resisted their attacks. And now my own casual self-suggestion that I might possibly be fool enough to confess the murder of which I had been guilty, confronted me, as if the very ghost of him whom I had murdered – and beckoned me on to death.

At first, I made an effort to shake off this nightmare of the soul. I walked vigorously – faster – still faster – at length I ran. I felt a maddening desire to shriek aloud. Every succeeding wave of thought overwhelmed me with new terror, for, alas! I well, too well, understood that to think, in my situation, was to be lost. I still quickened my pace. I bounded like a madman through the crowded thoroughfares. At length, the populace took the alarm, and pursued me. I felt then the consummation of my fate. Could I have torn out my tongue, I would have done it, but a rough voice resounded in my ears – a rougher grasp seized me by the shoulder. I turned – I gasped for breath. For a moment I experienced all the pangs of suffocation; I became blind, and deaf, and giddy; and then some invisible fiend, I thought, struck me with his broad palm upon the back. The long imprisoned secret burst forth from my soul.

They say that I spoke with a distinct enunciation, but with marked emphasis and passionate hurry, as if in dread of interruption before concluding the brief but pregnant sentences that consigned me to the hangman and to hell.

Having related all that was necessary for the fullest judicial conviction, I fell prostrate in a swoon.

But why shall I say more? Today I wear these chains, and am here! Tomorrow I shall be fetterless! – *but where?*

The Sphinx

During the dread reign of cholera in New York, I had accepted the invitation of a relative to spend a fortnight with him in the retirement of his *cottage ornée* on the banks of the Hudson. We had here around us all the ordinary means of summer amusement; and what with rambling in the woods, sketching, boating, fishing, bathing, music, and books, we should have passed the time pleasantly enough, but for the fearful intelligence which reached us every morning from the populous city. Not a day elapsed which did not bring us news of the decease of some acquaintance. Then as the fatality increased, we learned to expect daily the loss of some friend. At length we trembled at the approach of every messenger. The very air from the South seemed to us redolent with death. That palsying thought, indeed, took entire possession of my soul. I could neither speak, think, nor dream of anything else. My host was of a less excitable temperament, and, although greatly depressed in spirits, exerted himself to sustain my own. His richly philosophical intellect was not at any time affected by unrealities. To the substances of terror he was sufficiently alive, but of its shadows he had no apprehension.

His endeavours to arouse me from the condition of abnormal gloom into which I had fallen, were frustrated, in great measure, by certain volumes which I had found in his library. These were of a character to force into germination whatever seeds of hereditary superstition lay latent in my bosom. I had been reading these books without his knowledge, and thus he was often at a loss to account for the forcible impressions which had been made upon my fancy.

A favourite topic with me was the popular belief in omens – a belief which, at this one epoch of my life, I was almost seriously disposed to defend. On this subject we had long and animated discussions – he maintaining the utter groundlessness of faith in such matters – I contending that a popular sentiment arising with absolute spontaneity – that is to say, without apparent traces of suggestion – had in itself the unmistakable elements of truth, and was entitled to as much respect as that intuition which is the idiosyncrasy of the individual man of genius.

The fact is, that soon after my arrival at the cottage there had occurred to myself an incident so entirely inexplicable, and which had in it so much of the portentous character, that I might well have been excused for regarding it as an omen. It appalled, and at the same time so confounded and bewildered me, that many days elapsed before I could make up my mind to communicate the circumstances to my friend.

Near the close of exceedingly warm day, I was sitting, book in hand, at an open window, commanding, through a long vista of the river banks, a view of a distant hill, the face of which nearest my position had been denuded by what is termed a landslide, of the principal portion of its trees. My thoughts had been long wandering from the volume before me to the gloom and desolation of the neighbouring city. Uplifting my eyes from the page, they fell upon the naked face of the hill, and upon an object – upon some living monster of hideous conformation, which very rapidly made its way from the summit to the bottom, disappearing finally in the dense forest below. As this creature first came in sight, I doubted my own sanity – or at least the evidence of my own eyes; and many minutes passed before I succeeded in convincing myself that I was neither mad nor in a dream. Yet when I described the monster (which I distinctly saw, and calmly surveyed through the whole period of its progress), my readers, I fear, will feel more difficulty in being convinced of these points than even I did myself.

Estimating the size of the creature by comparison with the diameter of the large trees near which it passed – the few giants of the forest which had escaped the fury of the landslide – I concluded it to be far larger than any ship of the line in existence. I say ship of the line, because the shape of the monster suggested the idea – the hull of one of our seventy-fours might convey a very tolerable conception of the general outline. The mouth of the animal was situated at the extremity of a proboscis some sixty or seventy feet in length, and about as thick as the body of an ordinary elephant. Near the root of this trunk was an immense quantity of black shaggy hair – more than could have been supplied by the coats of a score of buffaloes; and projecting from this hair downwardly and laterally, sprang two gleaming tusks not unlike those of the wild boar, but of infinitely greater dimensions. Extending forward, parallel with the proboscis, and on each side of it, was a gigantic staff, thirty or forty feet in length, formed seemingly of pure crystal and in shape a perfect prism – it reflected in the most gorgeous manner the rays of the declining sun. The trunk was fashioned like a wedge with the apex to the earth. From it there were outspread two pairs of wings – each wing nearly one hundred yards in length – one pair being placed above the other, and all thickly covered with metal scales; each scale apparently some ten or twelve feet in diameter. I observed that the upper and lower tiers of wings were connected by a strong chain. But the chief peculiarity of this horrible thing was the representation of a Death's Head, which covered nearly the whole surface of its breast, and which was as accurately traced in glaring white, upon the dark ground of the body, as if it had been there carefully designed by an artist. While I regarded the terrific animal, and more especially the appearance on its breast, with a feeling or horror and awe – with a sentiment of forthcoming evil, which I found it impossible to quell by any effort of the reason, I perceived the huge jaws at the extremity of the proboscis suddenly expand themselves, and from them there proceeded a sound so loud and so expressive of woe, that it struck upon my nerves like a knell, and as the monster disappeared at the foot of the hill, I fell at once, fainting, to the floor.

Upon recovering, my first impulse, of course, was to inform my friend of what I had seen and heard – and I can scarcely explain what feeling of repugnance it was which, in the end, operated to prevent me.

At length, one evening, some three or four days after the occurrence, we were sitting together in the room in which I had seen the apparition – I occupying the same seat at the same window, and he lounging on a sofa near at hand. The association of the place and time impelled me to give him an account of the phenomenon. He heard me to the end – at first laughed heartily – and then lapsed into an excessively grave demeanour, as if my insanity was a thing beyond suspicion. At this instant I again had a distinct view of the monster – to which, with a shout of absolute terror, I now directed his attention. He looked eagerly – but maintained that he saw nothing – although I designated minutely the course of the creature, as it made its way down the naked face of the hill.

I was now immeasurably alarmed, for I considered the vision either as an omen of my death, or, worse, as the forerunner of an attack of mania. I threw myself passionately back in my chair, and for some moments buried my face in my hands. When I uncovered my eyes, the apparition was no longer visible.

My host, however, had in some degree resumed the calmness of his demeanour, and questioned me very rigorously in respect to the conformation of the visionary creature. When I had fully satisfied him on this head, he sighed deeply, as if relieved of some intolerable burden, and went on to talk, with what I thought a cruel calmness, of various points of speculative philosophy, which had heretofore formed subject of discussion between us. I remember his insisting very especially (among other things) upon the idea that the principal source of error in all human investigations lay in the liability of the understanding to underrate or to overvalue the importance of an object, through mere mis-admeasurement of its propinquity. 'To estimate properly, for example,' he said, 'the influence to be exercised on mankind at large by the thorough diffusion of Democracy, the distance of the epoch at which such diffusion may possibly be accomplished should not fail to form an item in the estimate. Yet can you tell me one writer on the subject of government who has ever thought this particular branch of the subject worthy of discussion at all?'

He here paused for a moment, stepped to a bookcase, and brought forth one of the ordinary synopses of Natural History. Requesting me then to exchange seats with him, that he might the better distinguish the fine print of the volume, he took my armchair at the window, and, opening the book, resumed his discourse very much in the same tone as before.

'But for your exceeding minuteness,' he said, 'in describing the monster, I might never have had it in my power to demonstrate to you what it was. In the first place, let me read to you a schoolboy account of the genus Sphinx, of the family *Crepuscularia*, of the order *Lepidoptera*, of the class of *Insecta* – or insects. The account runs thus:

> 'Four membranous wings covered with little coloured scales of metallic appearance; mouth forming a rolled proboscis, produced by an elongation of the jaws, upon the sides of which are found the rudiments of mandibles and downy palpi; the inferior wings retained to the superior by a stiff hair; antennae in the form of an elongated club, prismatic; abdomen pointed. The Death's-headed Sphinx has occasioned much terror among the vulgar, at times, by the melancholy kind of cry which it utters, and the insignia of death which it wears upon its corslet.'

He here closed the book and leaned forward in the chair, placing himself accurately in the position which I had occupied at the moment of beholding 'the monster'.

'Ah, here it is,' he presently exclaimed – 'it is reascending the face of the hill, and a very remarkable-looking creature I admit it to be. Still, it is by no means so large or so distant as you imagined it, for the fact is that, as it wriggles its way up this thread, which some spider has wrought along the window-sash, I find it to be about the sixteenth of an inch in its extreme length, and also about the sixteenth of an inch distant from the pupil of my eye.'

The Domain of Arnheim or The Landscape Garden

The garden like a lady fair was cut,
That lay as if she slumbered in delight,
And to the open skies her eyes did shut.
The azure fields of Heaven were 'sembled right
In a large round, set with the flowers of light.
The flowers *de luce*, and the round sparks of dew
That hung upon their azure leaves did shew
Like twinkling stars that sparkle in the evening
blue.

GILES FLETCHER

From his cradle to his grave a gale of prosperity bore my friend Ellison along. Nor do I use the word prosperity in its mere worldly sense. I mean it as synonymous with happiness. The person of whom I speak seemed born for the purpose of foreshadowing the doctrines of Turgot, Price, Priestley, and Condorcet – of exemplifying by individual instance what has been deemed the chimera of the perfectionists. In the brief existence of Ellison I fancy that I have seen refuted the dogma, that in man's very nature lies some hidden principle, the antagonist of bliss. An anxious examination of his career has given me to understand that, in general, from the violation of a few simple laws of humanity arises the wretchedness of mankind – that as a species we have in our possession the as yet unwrought elements of content – and that, even now, in the present darkness and madness of all thought on the great question of the social condition, it is not impossible that man, the individual, under certain unusual and highly fortuitous conditions, may be happy.

With opinions such as these my young friend, too, was fully imbued, and thus it is worthy of observation that the uninterrupted enjoyment which distinguished his life was, in great measure, the result of preconcert. It is indeed evident that with less of the instinctive philosophy which, now and then, stands so well in the stead of experience, Mr Ellison would have found himself precipitated, by the very extraordinary success of his life, into the common vortex of unhappiness which yawns for those of pre-eminent endowments. But it is by no means my object to pen an essay on happiness. The ideas of my friend may be summed up in a few words. He admitted but four elementary principles, or more strictly, conditions of bliss. That which he considered chief was (strange to say!) the simple and purely physical one of free exercise in the open air. 'The health,' he said, 'attainable by other means is scarcely worth the name.' He instanced the ecstasies of the fox-hunter, and pointed to the tillers of the earth, the only people who, as a class, can be fairly considered happier than others. His second condition was the love of woman. His third, and most difficult of realisation, was the contempt of ambition. His fourth was an object of unceasing pursuit; and he held that, other things being equal, the extent of attainable happiness was in proportion to the spirituality of this object.

Ellison was remarkable in the continuous profusion of good gifts lavished upon him by fortune. In personal grace and beauty he exceeded all men. His intellect was of that order to which the acquisition of knowledge is less a labour than an intuition and a necessity. His family was one of the most illustrious of the empire. His bride was the loveliest and most devoted of women. His possessions had been always ample; but on the attainment of his majority, it was discovered that one of those extraordinary freaks of fate had been played in his behalf which startle the whole social world amid which they occur, and seldom fail radically to alter the moral constitution of those who are their objects.

It appears that about a hundred years before Mr Ellison's coming of age, there had died, in a remote province, one Mr Seabright Ellison. This gentleman had amassed a princely fortune, and, having no immediate connections, conceived the whim of suffering his wealth to accumulate for a century after his decease. Minutely and sagaciously directing the various modes of investment, he bequeathed the aggregate amount to the nearest of blood, bearing the name of Ellison, who should be alive at the end of the hundred years. Many attempts had been made to set aside this singular bequest; their *ex post facto* character rendered them abortive; but the attention of a jealous government was aroused, and a legislative act finally obtained, forbidding all similar accumulations. This act, however, did not prevent young Ellison from entering into possession, on his twenty-first birthday, as the heir of his ancestor Seabright, of a fortune of $450,000,000.

When it had become known that such was the enormous wealth inherited, there were, of course, many speculations as to the mode of its disposal. The magnitude and the immediate availability of the sum bewildered all who thought on the topic. The possessor of any appreciable amount of money might have been imagined to perform any one of a thousand things. With riches merely surpassing those of any citizen, it would have been easy to suppose him engaging to supreme excess in the fashionable extravagances of his time – or busying himself with political intrigue – or aiming at ministerial power – or purchasing increase of nobility – or collecting large museums of virtu – or playing the munificent patron of letters, of science, of art – or endowing, and bestowing his name upon extensive institutions of charity. But for the inconceivable wealth in the actual possession of the heir, these objects and all ordinary objects were felt to afford too limited a field. Recourse was had to figures, and these but sufficed to confound. It was seen that, even at three per cent, the annual income of the inheritance amounted to no less than $13,500,000; which was $1,125,000 per month; or $36,986 per day; or $1,541 per hour; or $26 every minute that flew. Thus the usual track of supposition was thoroughly broken up. Men knew not what to imagine. There were some who even conceived that Mr Ellison would divest himself of at least one-half of his fortune, as of utterly superfluous opulence – enriching whole troops of his relatives by division of his superabundance. To the nearest of these he did, in fact, abandon the very unusual wealth which was his own before the inheritance.

I was not surprised, however, to perceive that he had long made up his mind on a point which had occasioned so much discussion to his friends. Nor was I greatly astonished at the nature of his decision. In regard to individual charities he had satisfied his conscience. In the possibility of any improvement, properly so called, being effected by man himself in the general condition of man, he had (I am sorry to confess it) little faith. Upon the whole, whether happily or unhappily, he was thrown back, in very great measure, upon self.

In the widest and noblest sense he was a poet. He comprehended, moreover, the true character, the august aims, the supreme majesty and dignity of the poetic sentiment. The fullest, if not the sole proper satisfaction of this sentiment he instinctively felt to lie in the creation of novel forms of beauty. Some peculiarities, either in his early education, or in the nature of his intellect, had tinged with what is termed materialism all his ethical speculations; and it was this bias, perhaps, which led him to believe that the most advantageous at least, if not the sole legitimate field for the poetic exercise, lies in the creation of novel moods of purely physical loveliness. Thus it happened he became neither musician nor poet – if we use this latter term in its everyday acceptation. Or it might have been that he neglected to become either, merely in pursuance of his idea that in contempt of ambition is to be found one of the essential principles of happiness on earth. Is it not, indeed, possible that, while a high order of genius is necessarily ambitious, the highest is above that which is termed ambition? And may it not thus happen that many far greater than Milton have contentedly remained 'mute and inglorious'? I believe that the world has never seen – and that, unless through some series of accidents goading the noblest order of mind into distasteful exertion, the world will never see – that full extent of triumphant execution, in the richer domains of art, of which the human nature is absolutely capable.

Ellison became neither musician nor poet; although no man lived more profoundly enamoured of music and poetry. Under other circumstances than those which invested him, it is not impossible that he would have become a painter. Sculpture, although in its nature rigorously poetical, was too limited in its extent and consequences to have occupied, at any time, much of his attention. And I have now mentioned all the provinces in which the common understanding of the poetic sentiment has declared it capable of expatiating. But Ellison maintained that the richest, the truest, and most natural, if not altogether the most extensive province, had been unaccountably neglected. No definition had spoken of the landscape-gardener as of the poet; yet it seemed to my friend that the creation of the landscape-garden offered to the proper Muse the most magnificent of opportunities. Here, indeed, was the fairest field for the display of imagination in the endless combining of forms of novel beauty; the elements to enter into combination being, by a vast superiority, the most glorious which the earth could afford. In the multiform and multicolour of the flowers and the trees, he recognised the most direct and energetic efforts of Nature at physical loveliness. And in the direction or concentration of this effort – or, more properly, in its adaptation to the eyes which were to behold it on earth – he perceived that he should be employing the best means – labouring to the greatest advantage – in the fulfilment, not only of his own destiny as poet, but of the august purposes for which the deity had implanted the poetic sentiment in man.

'Its adaptation to the eyes which were to behold it on earth.' In his explanation of this phraseology, Mr Ellison did much towards solving what has always seemed to me an enigma – I mean the fact (which none but the ignorant dispute) that no such combination of scenery exists in nature as the painter of genius may produce. No such paradises are to be found in reality as have glowed on the canvas of Claude. In the most enchanting of natural landscapes, there will always be found a defect or an excess – many excesses and defects. While the component parts may defy, individually, the highest skill of the artist, the arrangement of these parts will always be susceptible of improvement. In short, no position can be attained on the wide surface of the natural earth, from which an artistical eye, looking steadily, will not find matter of offence in what is termed the 'composition' of the landscape. And yet how unintelligible is this! In all other matters we are justly instructed to regard nature as supreme. With her details we shrink from competition. Who shall presume to imitate the colours of the tulip, or to improve the proportions of the lily of the valley? The criticism which says, of sculpture or portraiture, that here nature is to be exalted or idealised rather than imitated, is in error. No pictorial or sculptural combinations of points of human liveliness do more than approach the living and breathing beauty. In landscape alone is the principle of the critic true; and, having felt its truth here, it is but the headlong spirit of generalisation which has led him to pronounce it true throughout all the domains of art. Having, I say, felt its truth here; for the feeling is no affectation or chimera. The mathematics afford no more absolute demonstrations than the sentiments of his art yields the artist. He not only believes, but positively knows, that such and such apparently arbitrary arrangements of matter constitute and alone constitute the true beauty. His reasons, however, have not yet been matured into expression. It remains for a more profound analysis than the world has yet seen, fully to investigate and express them. Nevertheless he is confirmed in his instinctive opinions by the voice of all his brethren. Let a 'composition' be defective; let an emendation be wrought in its mere arrangement of form; let this emendation be submitted to every artist in the world; by each will its necessity be admitted. And even far more than this – in remedy of the defective composition, each insulated member of the fraternity would have suggested the identical emendation.

I repeat that in landscape arrangements alone is the physical nature susceptible of exaltation, and that, therefore, her susceptibility of improvement at this one point, was a mystery I had been unable to solve. My own thoughts on the subject had rested in the idea that the primitive intention of nature would have so arranged the earth's surface as to have fulfilled at all points man's sense of perfection in the beautiful, the sublime, or the picturesque; but that this primitive intention had been frustrated by the known geological disturbances – disturbances of form and colour-grouping, in the correction or allaying of which lies the soul of art. The force of this idea was much weakened, however, by the necessity which it involved of considering the disturbances abnormal and unadapted to any purpose. It was Ellison who suggested that they were prognostic of death. He thus explained: Admit the earthly immortality of man to have been the first intention. We have then the primitive arrangement of the earth's surface adapted to his blissful estate, as not existent but designed. The disturbances were the preparations for his subsequently conceived deathful condition.

'Now,' said my friend, 'what we regard as exaltation of the landscape may be really such as respects only the moral or human point of view. Each alteration of the natural scenery may possibly effect a blemish in the picture, if we can suppose this picture viewed at large – in mass – from some point distant from the earth's surface, although not beyond the limits of its atmosphere. It is easily understood that what might improve a closely scrutinised detail, may at the same time injure a general or more distantly observed effect. There may be a class of beings, human once, but now invisible to humanity, to whom, from afar, our disorder may seem order – our unpicturesqueness picturesque; in a word, the earth-angels, for whose scrutiny more especially than our own, and for whose death-refined appreciation of the beautiful, may have been set in array by God the wide landscape-gardens of the hemispheres.'

In the course of discussion, my friend quoted some passages from a writer on landscape-gardening who has been supposed to have well treated his theme:

> There are properly but two styles of landscape-gardening, the natural and the artificial. One seeks to recall the original beauty of the country, by adapting its means to the surrounding scenery, cultivating trees in harmony with the hills or plains of the neighbouring land; detecting and bringing into practice those nice relations of size, proportion, and colour which, hid from the common observer, are revealed everywhere to the experienced student of nature. The result of the natural style of gardening, is seen rather in the absence of all defects and incongruities – in the prevalence of a healthy harmony and order – than in the creation of any special wonders or miracles. The artificial style has as many varieties as there are different tastes to gratify.

> It has a certain general relation to the various styles of building. There are the stately avenues and retirements of Versailles; Italian terraces; and a various mixed old English style, which bears some relation to the domestic Gothic or English Elizabethan architecture. Whatever may be said against the abuses of the artificial landscape-gardening, a mixture of pure art in a garden scene adds to it a great beauty. This is partly pleasing to the eye, by the show of order and design, and partly moral. A terrace, with an old moss-covered balustrade, calls up at once to the eye the fair forms that have passed there in other days. The slightest exhibition of art is an evidence of care and human interest.

'From what I have already observed,' said Ellison, 'you will understand that I reject the idea, here expressed, of recalling the original beauty of the country. The original beauty is never so great as that which may be introduced. Of course, everything depends on the selection of a spot with capabilities. What is said about detecting and bringing into practice nice relations of size, proportion, and colour, is one of those mere vaguenesses of speech which serve to veil inaccuracy of thought. The phrase quoted may mean anything, or nothing, and guides in no degree. That the true result of the natural style of gardening is seen rather in the absence of all defects and incongruities than in the creation of any special wonders or miracles, is a proposition better suited to the grovelling apprehension of the herd than to the fervid dreams of the man of genius. The negative merit suggested appertains to that hobbling criticism which, in letters, would elevate Addison into apotheosis. In truth, while that virtue which consists in the mere avoidance of vice appeals directly to the understanding, and can thus be circumscribed in rule, the loftier virtue, which flames in creation, can be apprehended in its results alone. Rule applies but to the merits of denial – to the excellencies which refrain. Beyond these, the critical art can but suggest. We may be instructed to build a "Cato", but we are in vain told how to conceive a Parthenon or an "Inferno". The thing done, however; the wonder accomplished; and the capacity for apprehension becomes universal. The sophists of the negative school who, through inability to create, have scoffed at creation, are now found the loudest in applause. What, in its chrysalis condition of principle, affronted their demure reason, never fails, in its maturity of accomplishment, to extort admiration from their instinct of beauty.

'The author's observations on the artificial style,' continued Ellison, 'are less objectionable. A mixture of pure art in a garden scene adds to it a great beauty. This is just; as also is the reference to the sense of human interest. The principle expressed is incontrovertible – but there may be something beyond it. There may be an object in keeping with the principle – an object unattainable by the means ordinarily possessed by individuals, yet which, if attained, would lend a charm to the landscape-garden far surpassing that which a sense of merely human interest could bestow. A poet, having very unusual pecuniary resources, might, while retaining the necessary idea of art or culture, or, as our author expresses it, of interest, so imbue his designs at once with extent and novelty of beauty, as to convey the sentiment of spiritual interference. It will be seen that, in bringing about such result, he secures all the advantages of interest or design, while relieving his work of the harshness or technicality of the worldly art. In the most rugged of wildernesses – in the most savage of the scenes of pure nature – there is apparent the art of a creator; yet this art is apparent to reflection only; in no respect has it the obvious force of a feeling. Now let us suppose this sense of the Almighty design to be one step depressed – to be brought into something like harmony or consistency with the sense of human art – to form an intermedium between the two – let us imagine, for example, a landscape whose combined vastness and definitiveness – whose united beauty, magnificence, and strangeness, shall convey the idea of care, or culture, or superintendence, on the part of beings superior, yet akin to humanity – then the sentiment of interest is preserved, while the art intervolved is made to assume the air of an intermediate or secondary nature – a nature which is not God, nor an emanation from God, but which still is nature in the sense of the handiwork of the angels that hover between man and God.'

It was in devoting his enormous wealth to the embodiment of a vision such as this – in the free exercise in the open air ensured by the personal superintendence of his plans – in the unceasing object which these plans afforded – in the high spirituality of the object – in the contempt of ambition which it enabled him truly to feel – in the perennial springs with which it gratified, without possibility of satiating, that one master passion of his soul, the thirst for beauty; above all, it was in the sympathy of a woman, not unwomanly, whose loveliness and love enveloped his existence in the purple atmosphere of Paradise, that Ellison thought to find, and found, exemption from the ordinary cares of humanity, with a far greater amount of positive happiness than ever glowed in the rapt daydreams of De Staël.

I despair of conveying to the reader any distinct conception of the marvels which my friend did actually accomplish. I wish to describe, but am disheartened by the difficulty of description, and hesitate between detail and generality.

Perhaps the better course will be to unite the two in their extremes.

Mr Ellison's first step regarded, of course, the choice of a locality, and scarcely had he commenced thinking on this point, when the luxuriant nature of the Pacific Islands arrested his attention. In fact, he had made up his mind for a voyage to the South Seas, when a night's reflection induced him to abandon the idea. 'Were I misanthropic,' he said, 'such a locale would suit me. The thoroughness of its insulation and seclusion, and the difficulty of ingress and egress, would in such case be the charm of charms; but as yet I am not Timon. I wish the composure but not the depression of solitude. There must remain with me a certain control over the extent and duration of my repose. There will be frequent hours in which I shall need, too, the sympathy of the poetic in what I have done. Let me seek, then, a spot not far from a populous city – whose vicinity, also, will best enable me to execute my plans.'

In search of a suitable place so situated, Ellison travelled for several years, and I was permitted to accompany him. A thousand spots with which I was enraptured he rejected without hesitation, for reasons which satisfied me, in the end, that he was right. We came at length to an elevated tableland of wonderful fertility and beauty, affording a panoramic prospect very little less in extent than that of Etna, and, in Ellison's opinion as well as my own, surpassing the far-famed view from that mountain in all the true elements of the picturesque.

'I am aware,' said the traveller, as he drew a sigh of deep delight after gazing on this scene, entranced, for nearly an hour, 'I know that here, in my circumstances, nine-tenths of the most fastidious of men would rest content. This panorama is indeed glorious, and I should rejoice in it but for the excess of its glory. The taste of all the architects I have ever known leads them, for the sake of "prospect", to put up buildings on hilltops. The error is obvious. Grandeur in any of its moods, but especially in that of extent, startles, excites – and then fatigues, depresses. For the occasional scene nothing can be better – for the constant view nothing worse. And, in the constant view, the most objectionable phase of grandeur is that of extent; the worst phase of extent, that of distance. It is at war with the sentiment and with the sense of seclusion – the sentiment and sense which we seek to humour in "retiring to the country". In looking from the summit of a mountain we cannot help feeling abroad in the world. The heartsick avoid distant prospects as a pestilence.'

It was not until towards the close of the fourth year of our search that we found a locality with which Ellison professed himself satisfied. It is, of course, needless to say where was the locality. The late death of my friend, in causing his domain to be thrown open to certain classes of visitors, has given to Arnheim a species of secret and subdued if not solemn celebrity, similar in kind, although infinitely superior in degree, to that which so long distinguished Fonthill.

The usual approach to Arnheim was by the river. The visitor left the city in the early morning. During the forenoon he passed between shores of a tranquil and domestic beauty, on which grazed innumerable sheep, their white fleeces spotting the vivid green of rolling meadows. By degrees the idea of cultivation subsided into that of merely pastoral care. This slowly became merged in a sense of retirement – this again in a consciousness of solitude. As the evening approached, the channel grew more narrow, the banks more and more precipitous; and these latter were clothed in rich, more profuse, and more sombre foliage. The water increased in transparency. The stream took a thousand turns, so that at no moment could its gleaming surface be seen for a greater distance than a furlong. At every instant the vessel seemed imprisoned within an enchanted circle, having insuperable and impenetrable walls of foliage, a roof of ultramarine satin, and no floor – the keel balancing itself with admirable nicety on that of a phantom bark which, by some accident having been turned upside down, floated in constant company with the substantial one, for the purpose of sustaining it. The channel now became a gorge – although the term is somewhat inapplicable, and I employ it merely because the language has no word which better represents the most striking – not the most distinctive – feature of the scene. The character of gorge was maintained only in the height and parallelism of the shores; it was lost altogether in their other traits. The walls of the ravine (through which the clear water still tranquilly flowed) arose to an elevation of a hundred and occasionally of a hundred and fifty feet, and inclined so much towards each other as, in a great measure, to shut out the light of day; while the long plume-like moss which depended densely from the intertwining shrubberies overhead, gave the whole chasm an air of funereal gloom. The windings became more frequent and intricate, and seemed often as if returning in upon themselves, so that the voyager had long lost all idea of direction. He was, moreover, enwrapt in an exquisite sense of the strange. The thought of nature still remained, but her character seemed to have undergone modification, there was a weird symmetry, a thrilling uniformity, a wizard propriety in these her works. Not a dead branch – not a withered leaf – not a stray pebble – not a patch of the brown earth was anywhere visible. The crystal water welled up against the clean granite, or the unblemished moss, with a sharpness of outline that delighted while it bewildered the eye.

Having threaded the mazes of this channel for some hours, the gloom deepening every moment, a sharp and unexpected turn of the vessel brought it suddenly, as if dropped from heaven, into a circular basin of very considerable extent when compared with the width of the gorge. It was about two hundred yards in diameter, and girt in at all points but one – that immediately fronting the vessel as it entered – by hills equal in general height to the walls of the chasm, although of a thoroughly different character. Their sides sloped from the water's edge at an angle of some forty-five degrees, and they were clothed from base to summit – not a perceptible point escaping – in a drapery of the most gorgeous flower-blossoms; scarcely a green leaf being visible among the sea of odorous and fluctuating colour. This basin was of great depth, but so transparent was the water that the bottom, which seemed to consist of a thick mass of small round alabaster pebbles, was distinctly visible by glimpses – that is to say, whenever the eye could permit itself not to see, far down in the inverted heaven, the duplicate blooming of the hills. On these latter there were no trees, nor even shrubs of any size. The impressions wrought on the observer were those of richness, warmth, colour, quietude, uniformity, softness, delicacy, daintiness, voluptuousness, and a miraculous extremeness of culture that suggested dreams of a new race of fairies, laborious, tasteful, magnificent, and fastidious; but as the eye traced upwards the myriad-tinted slope, from its sharp junction with the water to its vague termination amid the folds of overhanging cloud, it became, indeed, difficult not to fancy a panoramic cataract of rubies, sapphires, opals, and golden onyxes, rolling silently out of the sky.

The visitor, shooting suddenly into this bay from out the gloom of the ravine, is delighted but astounded by the full orb of the declining sun, which he had supposed to be already far below the horizon, but which now confronts him, and forms the sole termination of an otherwise limitless vista seen through another chasm-like rift in the hills.

But here the voyager quits the vessel which has borne him so far, and descends into a light canoe of ivory, stained with arabesque devices in vivid scarlet, both within and without. The poop and beak of this boat arise high above the water, with sharp points, so that the general form is that of an irregular crescent. It lies on the surface of the bay with the proud grace of a swan. On its ermined floor reposes a single feathery paddle of satinwood; but no oarsmen or attendant is to be seen. The guest is bidden to be of good cheer – that the fates will take care of him. The larger vessel disappears, and he is left alone in the canoe, which lies apparently motionless in the middle of the lake. While he considers what course to pursue, however, he becomes aware of a gentle movement in the fairy bark. It slowly swings itself around until its prow points towards the sun. It advances with a gentle but gradually accelerated velocity, while the slight ripples it creates seem to break about the ivory side in divinest melody – seem to offer the only possible explanation of the soothing yet melancholy music for whose unseen origin the bewildered voyager looks around him in vain.

The canoe steadily proceeds, and the rocky gate of the vista is approached, so that its depths can be more distinctly seen. To the right arise a chain of lofty hills rudely and luxuriantly wooded. It is observed, however, that the trait of exquisite cleanness where the bank dips into the water, still prevails. There is not one token of the usual river dèbris. To the left the character of the scene is softer and more obviously artificial. Here the bank slopes upwards from the stream in a very gentle ascent, forming a broad sward of grass of a texture resembling nothing so much as velvet, and of a brilliancy of green which would bear comparison with the tint of the purest emerald. This plateau varies in width from ten to three hundred yards; reaching from the river-bank to a wall, fifty feet high, which extends, in an infinity of curves, but following the general direction of the river, until lost in the distance to the westward. This wall is of one continuous rock, and has been formed by cutting perpendicularly the once rugged precipice of the stream's southern bank, but no trace of the labour has been suffered to remain. The chiselled stone has the hue of ages, and is profusely overhung and overspread with the ivy, the coral honeysuckle, the eglantine, and the clematis. The uniformity of the top and bottom lines of the wall is fully relieved by occasional trees of gigantic height, growing singly or in small groups, both along the plateau and in the domain behind the wall, but in close proximity to it; so that frequent limbs (of the black walnut especially) reach over and dip their pendent extremities into the water. Farther back within the domain, the vision is impeded by an impenetrable screen of foliage.

These things are observed during the canoe's gradual approach to what I have called the gate of the vista. On drawing nearer to this, however, its chasm-like appearance vanishes; a new outlet from the bay is discovered to the left – in which direction the wall is also seen to sweep, still following the general course of the stream. Down this new opening the eye cannot penetrate very far; for the stream, accompanied by the wall, still bends to the left, until both are swallowed up by the leaves.

The boat, nevertheless, glides magically into the winding channel; and here the shore opposite the wall is found to resemble that opposite the wall in the straight vista. Lofty hills, rising occasionally into mountains, and covered with vegetation in wild luxuriance, still shut in the scene.

Floating gently onwards, but with a velocity slightly augmented, the voyager, after many short turns, finds his progress apparently barred by a gigantic gate or rather door of burnished gold, elaborately carved and fretted, and reflecting the direct rays of the now fast-sinking sun with an effulgence that seems to wreathe the whole surrounding forest in flames. This gate is inserted in the lofty wall; which here appears to cross the river at right angles. In a few moments, however, it is seen that the main body of the water still sweeps in a gentle and extensive curve to the left, the wall following it as before, while a stream of considerable volume, diverging from the principal one, makes its way, with a slight ripple, under the door, and is thus hidden from sight. The canoe falls into the lesser channel and approaches the gate. Its ponderous wings are slowly and musically expanded. The boat glides between them, and commences a rapid descent into a vast amphitheatre entirely begirt with purple mountains, whose bases are laved by a gleaming river throughout the full extent of their circuit. Meantime the whole Paradise of Arnheim bursts upon the view. There is a gush of entrancing melody; there is an oppressive sense of strange sweet odour – there is a dream-like intermingling to the eye of tall slender Eastern trees – bosky shrubberies – flocks of golden and crimson birds – lily-fringed lakes – meadows of violets, tulips, poppies, hyacinths, and tuberoses – long intertangled lines of silver streamlets – and, upspringing confusedly from amid all, a mass of semi-Gothic, semi-Saracenic architecture sustaining itself by miracle in mid-air, glittering in the red sunlight with a hundred oriels, minarets, and pinnacles; and seeming the phantom handiwork, conjointly, of the sylphs, of the fairies, of the genii and of the gnomes.

Von Kempelen and His Discovery

After the very minute and elaborate paper by Arago, to say nothing of the summary in *Silliman's Journal*, with the detailed statement just published by Lieutenant Maury, it will not be supposed, of course, that in offering a few hurried remarks in reference to Von Kempelen's discovery, I have any design to look at the subject in a scientific point of view. My object is simply, in the first place, to say a few words of Von Kempelen himself (with whom, some years ago, I had the honour of a slight personal acquaintance), since everything which concerns him must necessarily, at this moment, be of interest; and, in the second place, to look in a general way, and speculatively, at the results of the discovery.

It may be as well, however, to premise the cursory observations which I have to offer, by denying, very decidedly, what seems to be a general impression (gleaned, as usual in a case of this kind, from the newspapers), viz.: that this discovery, astounding as it unquestionably is, is unanticipated.

By reference to the *Diary of Sir Humphrey Davy* (Cottle and Munroe, London, pp. 150), it will be seen at pp. 53 and 82, that this illustrious chemist had not only conceived the idea now in question, but had actually made no inconsiderable progress, experimentally, in the very identical analysis now so triumphantly brought to an issue by Von Kempelen, who although he makes not the slightest allusion to it, is, without doubt (I say it unhesitatingly, and can prove it, if required), indebted to the *Diary* for at least the first hint of his own undertaking.

The paragraph from the *Courier and Enquirer*, which is now going the rounds of the press, and which purports to claim the invention for a Mr Kissam, of Brunswick, Maine, appears to me, I confess, a little apocryphal, for several reasons; although there is nothing either impossible or very improbable in the statement made. I need not go into details. My opinion of the paragraph is founded principally upon its manner. It does not look true. Persons who are narrating facts are seldom so particular as Mr Kissam seems to be, about day and date and precise location. Besides, if Mr Kissam actually did come upon the discovery he says he did, at the period designated – nearly eight years ago – how happens it that he took no steps, on the instant, to reap the immense benefits which the merest bumpkin must have known would have resulted to him individually, if not to the world at large, from the discovery? It seems to me quite incredible that any man of common understanding could have discovered what Mr Kissam says he did, and yet have subsequently acted so like a baby – so like an owl – as Mr Kissam admits that he did. By the way, who *is* Mr Kissam? and is not the whole paragraph in the *Courier and Enquirer* a fabrication got up to 'make a talk'? It must be confessed that it has an amazingly moon-hoaxy-air. Very little dependence is to be placed upon it, in my humble opinion; and if I were not well aware, from experience, how very easily men of science are mystified, on points out of their usual range of enquiry, I should be profoundly astonished at finding so eminent a chemist as Professor Draper, discussing Mr Kissam's (or is it Mr Quizzem's?) pretensions to the discovery, in so serious a tone.

But to return to the *Diary* of Sir Humphrey Davy. This pamphlet was not designed for the public eye, even upon the decease of the writer, as any person at all conversant with authorship may satisfy himself at once by the slightest inspection of the style. At page 13, for example, near the middle, we read, in reference to his researches about the protoxide of azote: 'In less than half a minute the respiration being continued, diminished gradually and were succeeded by analogous to gentle pressure on all the muscles.' That the respiration was not 'diminished', is not only clear by the subsequent context, but by the use of the plural, 'were'. The sentence, no doubt, was thus intended: 'In less than half a minute, the respiration being continued, [these feelings] diminished gradually, and were succeeded by [a sensation] analogous to gentle pressure on all the muscles.' A hundred similar instances go to show that the manuscript so inconsiderately published, was merely a rough notebook, meant only for the writer's own eye, but an inspection of the pamphlet will convince almost any thinking person of the truth of my suggestion. The fact is, Sir Humphrey Davy was about the last man in the world to commit himself on scientific topics. Not only had he a more than ordinary dislike to quackery, but he was morbidly afraid of appearing empirical; so that, however fully he might have been convinced that he was on the right track in the matter now in question, he would never have spoken out, until he had everything ready for the most practical demonstration. I verily believe that his last moments would have been rendered wretched, could he have suspected that his wishes in regard to burning this *Diary* (full of crude speculations) would have been unattended to; as, it seems, they were. I say 'his wishes', for that he meant to include this notebook among the miscellaneous papers directed 'to be burnt', I think there can be no manner of doubt. Whether it escaped the flames by good fortune or by bad, yet remains to be seen. That the passages quoted above, with the other similar ones referred to, gave Von Kempelen the hint, I do not in the slightest degree question; but I repeat, it yet remains to be seen whether this momentous discovery itself (momentous under any circumstances) will be of service or disservice to mankind at large. That Von Kempelen and his immediate friends will reap a rich harvest, it would be folly to doubt for a moment. They will scarcely be so weak as not to 'realise', in time, by large purchases of houses and land, with other property of intrinsic value.

In the brief account of Von Kempelen which appeared in the *Home Journal*, and has since been extensively copied, several misapprehensions of the German original seem to have been made by the translator, who professes to have taken the passage from a late number of the Presburg *Schnellpost*. '*Viele*' has evidently been misconceived (as it often is), and what the translator renders by 'sorrows', is probably '*lieden*', which, in its true version, 'sufferings', would give a totally different complexion to the whole account; but, of course, much of this is merely guess, on my part.

Von Kempelen, however, is by no means a 'misanthrope', in appearance at least, whatever he may be in fact. My acquaintance with him was casual altogether; and I am scarcely warranted in saying that I know him at all; but to have seen and conversed with a man of so prodigious a notoriety as he has attained, or will attain in a few days, is not a small matter, as times go.

The *Literary World* speaks of him, confidently, as a native of Presburg (misled, perhaps, by the account in the *Home Journal*), but I am pleased in being able to state positively, since I have it from his own lips, that he was born in Utica, in the State of New York, although both his parents, I believe, are of Presburg descent. The family is connected, in some way, with Maelzel, of automaton-chess-player memory. In person, he is short and stout, with large, fat, blue eyes, sandy hair and whiskers, a wide but pleasing mouth, fine teeth, and I think a Roman nose. There is some defect in one of his feet. His address is frank, and his whole manner noticeable for *bonhomie*. Altogether, he looks, speaks, and acts as little like 'a misanthrope' as any man I ever saw. We were fellow-sojourners for a week about six years ago, at Earl's Hotel, in Providence, Rhode Island; and I presume that I conversed with him, at various times, for some three or four hours altogether. His principal topics were those of the day, and nothing that fell from him led me to suspect his scientific attainments. He left the hotel before me, intending to go to New York, and thence to Bremen; it was in the latter city that his great discovery was first made public; or, rather, it was there that he was first suspected of having made it. This is about all that I personally know of the now immortal Von Kempelen; but I have thought that even these few details would have interest for the public.

There can be little question that most of the marvellous rumours afloat about this affair are pure inventions, entitled to about as much credit as the story of Aladdin's lamp; and yet, in a case of this kind, as in the case of the discoveries in

California, it is clear that the truth may be stranger than fiction. The following anecdote, at least, is so well authenticated, that we may receive it implicitly.

Von Kempelen had never been even tolerably well off during his residence at Bremen; and often, it was well known, he had been put to extreme shifts in order to raise trifling sums. When the great excitement occurred about the forgery on the house of Gutsmuth & Co., suspicion was directed towards Von Kempelen, on account of his having purchased a considerable property in Gasperitch Lane, and his refusing, when questioned, to explain how he became possessed of the purchase money. He was at length arrested, but nothing decisive appearing against him, was in the end set at liberty. The police, however, kept a strict watch upon his movements, and thus discovered that he left home frequently, taking always the same road, and invariably giving his watchers the slip in the neighbourhood of that labyrinth of narrow and crooked passages known by the flash name of the 'Dondergat'. Finally, by dint of great perseverance, they traced him to a garret in an old house of seven storeys, in an alley called Flatzplatz – and, coming upon him suddenly, found him, as they imagined, in the midst of his counterfeiting operations. His agitation is represented as so excessive that the officers had not the slightest doubt of his guilt. After handcuffing him, they searched his room, or rather rooms, for it appears he occupied all the mansard.

Opening into the garret where they caught him, was a closet, ten feet by eight, fitted up with some chemical apparatus, of which the object has not yet been ascertained. In one corner of the closet was a very small furnace, with a glowing fire in it, and on the fire a kind of duplicate crucible – two crucibles connected by a tube. One of these crucibles was nearly full of lead in a state of fusion, but not reaching up to the aperture of the tube, which was close to the brim. The other crucible had some liquid in it, which, as the officers entered, seemed to be furiously dissipating in vapour. They relate that, on finding himself taken, Kempelen seized the crucibles with both hands (which were encased in gloves that afterwards turned out to be asbestic), and threw the contents on the tiled floor. It was now that they handcuffed him; and before proceeding to ransack the premises they searched his person, but nothing unusual was found about him, excepting a paper parcel, in his coat-pocket, containing what was afterwards ascertained to be a mixture of antimony and some unknown substance, in nearly, but not quite, equal proportions. All attempts at analysing the unknown substance have, so far, failed, but that it will ultimately be analysed, is not to be doubted.

Passing out of the closet with their prisoner, the officers went through a sort of antechamber, in which nothing material was found, to the chemist's sleeping room. They here rummaged some drawers and boxes, but discovered only a few papers, of no importance, and some good coin, silver and gold. At length, looking under the bed, they saw a large, common hair trunk, without hinges, hasp, or lock, and with the top lying carelessly across the bottom portion. Upon attempting to draw this trunk out from under the bed, they found that, with their united strength (there were three of them, all powerful men), they 'could not stir it one inch'. Much astonished at this, one of them crawled under the bed, and looking into the trunk, said: 'No wonder we couldn't move it – why it's full to the brim of old bits of brass!'

Putting his feet, now, against the wall, so as to get a good purchase, and pushing with all his force, while his companions pulled with all theirs, the trunk, with much difficulty, was slid out from under the bed, and its contents examined. The supposed brass with which it was filled was all in small, smooth pieces, varying from the size of a pea to that of a dollar; but the pieces were irregular in shape, although more or less flat-looking, upon the whole, 'very much as lead looks when thrown upon the ground in a molten state, and there suffered to grow cool'. Now, not one of these officers for a moment suspected this metal to be anything but brass. The idea of its being gold never entered their brains, of course; how could such a wild fancy have entered it? And their astonishment may be well conceived, when the next day it became known, all over Bremen, that the 'lot of brass' which they had carted so contemptuously to the police office, without putting themselves to the trouble of pocketing the smallest scrap, was not only gold – real gold – but gold far finer than any employed in coinage – gold, in fact, absolutely pure, virgin, without the slightest appreciable alloy!

I need not go over the details of Von Kempelen's confession (as far as it went) and release, for these are familiar to the public. That he has actually realised, in spirit and in effect, if not to the letter, the old chimaera of the philosopher's stone, no sane person is at liberty to doubt. The opinions of Arago are, of course, entitled to the greatest consideration; but he is by no means infallible; and what he says of bismuth, in his report to the Academy, must be taken *cum grano salis*. The simple truth is, that up to this period all analysis has failed; and until Von Kempelen chooses to let us have the key to his own published enigma, it is more than probable that the matter will remain, for years, *in statu quo*. All that as yet can fairly be said to be known is, that 'pure gold can be made at will, and very readily from lead in connection with certain other substances, in kind and in proportions, unknown'.

Speculation, of course, is busy as to the immediate and ultimate results of this discovery – a discovery which few thinking persons will hesitate in referring to an increased interest in the matter of gold generally, by the late developments in California; and this reflection brings us inevitably to another – the exceeding inopportuneness of Von Kempelen's analysis. If many were prevented from adventuring to California, by the mere apprehension that gold would so materially diminish in value, on account of its plentifulness in the mines there, as to render the speculation of going so far in search of it a doubtful one – what impression will be wrought now, upon the minds of those about to emigrate, and especially upon the minds of those actually in the mineral region, by the announcement of this astounding discovery of Von Kempelen? a discovery which declares, in so many words, that beyond its intrinsic worth for manufacturing purposes (whatever that worth may be), gold now is, or at least soon will be (for it cannot be supposed that Von Kempelen can long retain his secret), of no greater value than lead, and of far inferior value to silver. It is, indeed, exceedingly difficult to speculate prospectively upon the consequences of the discovery, but one thing may be positively maintained – that the announcement of the discovery six months ago would have had material influence in regard to the settlement of California.

In Europe, as yet, the most noticeable results have been a rise of two hundred per cent in the price of lead, and nearly twenty-five per cent in that of silver.

X-ing a Paragrab

As it is well known that the 'wise men' came 'from the East', and as Mr Touch-and-go Bullet-head came from the East, it follows that Mr Bullet-head was a wise man; and if collateral proof of the matter be needed, here we have it – Mr B— was an editor. Irascibility was his sole foible, for in fact the obstinacy of which men accused him was anything but his foible, since he justly considered it his forte. It was his strong point – his virtue; and it would have required all the logic of a Brownson to convince him that it was 'anything else'.

I have shown that Touch-and-go Bullet-head was a wise man; and the only occasion on which he did not prove infallible, was when, abandoning that legitimate home for all wise men, the East, he migrated to the city of Alexander-the-Great-o-nopolis, or some place of a similar title, out West.

I must do him the justice to say, however, that when he made up his mind finally to settle in that town, it was under the impression that no newspaper, and consequently no editor, existed in that particular section of the country. In establishing *The Teapot* he expected to have the field all to himself. I feel confident he never would have dreamed of taking up his residence in Alexander-the-Great-o-nopolis had he been aware that, in Alexander-the-Great-o-nopolis, there lived a gentleman named John Smith (if I rightly remember), who for many years had there quietly grown fat in editing and publishing The *Alexander-the-Great-o-nopolis Gazette*. It was solely, therefore, on account of having been misinformed, that Mr Bullet-head found himself in Alex— suppose we call it Nopolis, 'for short' – but, as he *did* find himself there, he determined to keep up his character for obst— for firmness, and remain. So remain he did; and he did more; he unpacked his press, type, etc., etc., rented an office exactly opposite to that of *The Gazette*, and, on the third morning after his arrival, issued the first number of *The Alexan*— that is to say, of *The Nopolis Teapot* – as nearly as I can recollect, this was the name of the new paper.

The leading article, I must admit, was brilliant – not to say severe. It was especially bitter about things in general – and as for the editor of *The Gazette*, he was torn all to pieces in particular. Some of Bullet-head's remarks were really so fiery that I have always, since that time, been forced to look upon John Smith, who is still alive, in the light of a salamander. I cannot pretend to give all *The Teapot's* paragraphs verbatim, but one of them runs thus: 'Oh, yes! – Oh, we perceive! Oh, no doubt! The editor over the way is a genius – Oh, my! Oh, goodness, gracious! – what is this world coming to? Oh, *tempora*! Oh, Moses!'

A philippic at once so caustic and so classical, alighted like a bombshell among the hitherto peaceful citizens of Nopolis. Groups of excited individuals gathered at the corners of the streets. Everyone awaited, with heartfelt anxiety, the reply of the dignified Smith. Next morning it appeared as follows:

> We quote from *The Teapot* of yesterday the subjoined paragraph: 'Oh, yes! Oh, we perceive! Oh, no doubt! Oh, my! Oh, goodness! Oh, *tempora*! Oh, Moses!' Why, the fellow is all O! That accounts for his reasoning in a circle, and explains why there is neither beginning nor end to him, nor to anything he says. We

really do not believe the vagabond can write a word that hasn't an O in it. Wonder if this O-ing is a habit of his? By the by, he came away from down-east in a great hurry. Wonder if he O's as much there as he does here? 'O! it is pitiful.'

The indignation of Mr Bullet-head at these scandalous insinuations, I shall not attempt to describe. On the eel-skinning principle, however, he did not seem to be so much incensed at the attack upon his integrity as one might have imagined. It was the sneer at his style that drove him to desperation. What! – *he*, Touch-and-go Bullet-head! – not able to write a word without an O in it! He would soon let the jackanapes see that he was mistaken. Yes! he would let him see how much he was mistaken, the puppy! He, Touch-and-go Bullet-head, of Frogpondium, would let Mr John Smith perceive that he, Bullet-head, could indict, if it so pleased him, a whole paragraph – aye! a whole article – in which that contemptible vowel should not once – not even once – make its appearance. But no – that would be yielding a point to the said John Smith. He, Bullet-head, would make no alteration in his style, to suit the caprices of any Mr Smith in Christendom. Perish so vile a thought! The O for ever! He would persist in the O. He would be as O-wy as O-wy could be.

Burning with the chivalry of this determination, the great Touch-and-go, in the next *Teapot*, came out merely with this simple but resolute paragraph, in reference to this unhappy affair:

> The editor of *The Teapot* has the honour of advising the editor of *The Gazette* that he (*The Teapot*) will take an opportunity in tomorrow morning's paper, of convincing him *(The Gazette)* that he *(The Teapot)* both can and will be his own master, as regards style; he *(The Teapot)* intending to show him (the *Gazette*) the supreme, and indeed the withering contempt with which the criticism of him (*The Gazette*) inspires the independent bosom of him (*The Teapot*) by composing for the especial gratification (?) of him (*The Gazette*) a leading article, of some extent, in which the beautiful vowel – the emblem of eternity – yet so offensive to the hyper-exquisite delicacy of him (*The Gazette*) shall most certainly not be avoided by his (*The Gazette's*) most obedient, humble servant, *The Teapot*. 'So much for Buckingham!'

In fulfilment of the awful threat thus darkly intimated rather than decidedly enunciated, the great Bullet-head, turning a deaf ear to all entreaties for 'copy', and simply requesting his foreman to 'go to the d—l', when he (the foreman) assured him (*The Teapot!*) that it was high time to 'go to press': turning a deaf ear to everything, I say, the great Bullet-head sat up until daybreak, consuming the midnight oil, and absorbed in the composition of the really unparalleled paragraph, which follows:

> So ho, John! how now? Told you so, you know. Don't crow, another time, before you're out of the woods! Does your mother know you're out? Oh, no, no! – so go home at once, now, John, to your odious old woods of Concord! Go home to your woods, old owl – go! You won't? Oh, poh, poh, John don't do so! You've *got* to go, you know! So go at once, and don't go slow, for nobody owns you here, you know! Oh! John, John, if you *don't* go you're no *homo* – no! You're only a fowl, an owl, a cow, a sow – a doll, a poll; a poor, old, good-for-nothing-to-nobody, log, dog, hog, or frog, come out of a Concord bog. Cool, now – cool! *Do* be cool, you fool! None of your crowing, old cock! Don't frown so – don't! Don't hollo, nor howl nor growl, nor bow-wow-wow! Good Lord, John, how you do look! Told you so, you know – but stop rolling your goose of an old poll about so, and go and drown your sorrows in a bowl!

Exhausted, very naturally, by so stupendous an effort, the great Touch-and-go could attend to nothing farther that night. Firmly, composedly, yet with an air of conscious power, he handed his manuscript to the devil in waiting, and then, walking leisurely home, retired, with ineffable dignity, to bed.

Meantime the devil, to whom the copy was entrusted, ran upstairs to his case, in an unutterable hurry, and forthwith made a commencement at setting the manuscript up.

In the first place, of course – as the opening word was 'So', he made a plunge into the capital S hole and came out in triumph with a capital S. Elated by this success, he immediately threw himself upon the little-o box with a blindfold impetuosity – but who shall describe his horror when his fingers came up without the anticipated letter in their clutch? who shall paint his astonishment and rage at perceiving, as he rubbed his knuckles, that he had been only thumping them to no purpose, against the bottom of an empty box. Not a single little-o was in the little-o hole; and, glancing fearfully at the capital-O partition, he found *that*, to his extreme terror, in a precisely similar predicament. Awe-stricken, his first impulse was to rush to the foreman.

'Sir!' said he, gasping for breath, 'I can't never set up nothing without no o's.'

'What do you mean by that?' growled the foreman, who was in a very ill humour at being kept so late.

'Why, sir, there beant an o in the office, neither a big un nor a little un!'

'What – what the d—l has become of all that were in the case?'

'I don't know, sir,' said the boy, 'but one of them ere *G'zette* devils is bin prowling 'bout here all night, and I spect he's gone and cabbaged 'em every one.'

'Dod rot him! I haven't a doubt of it,' replied the foreman, getting purple with rage – 'but I tell you what you do, Bob, that's a good boy – you go over the first chance you get and hook every one of their i's and (d—n them!) their izzards.'

'Jist so,' replied Bob, with a wink and a frown – 'I'll be into 'em, I'll let 'em know a thing or two; but in de meantime, that ere paragrab? Mus go in tonight, you know – else there'll be the d—l to pay, and – '

'And not a *bit* of pitch hot,' interrupted the foreman, with a deep sigh, and an emphasis on the 'bit'. 'Is it a very *long* paragraph, Bob?'

'Shouldn't call it a wery long paragrab,' said Bob.

'Ah, well, then! do the best you can with it! We must get to press,' said the foreman, who was over head and ears in work; 'just stick in some other letter for o; nobody's going to read the fellow's trash anyhow.'

'Wery well,' replied Bob, 'here goes it!' and off he hurried to his case, muttering as he went: 'Considdeble vell, them ere expressions, perticcler for a man as doesn't swar. So I's to gouge out all their eyes, eh? and d—n all their gizzards! Vell! this here's the chap as is just able for to do it.' The fact is that although Bob was but twelve years old and four feet high, he was equal to any amount of fight, in a small way.

The exigency here described is by no means of rare occurrence in printing offices; and I cannot tell how to account for it, but the fact is indisputable, that when the exigency does occur, it almost always happens that x is adopted as a substitute for the letter deficient. The true reason, perhaps, is that x is rather the most superabundant letter in the cases, or at least was so in the old times – long enough to render the substitution in question an habitual thing with printers. As for Bob, he would have considered it heretical to employ any other character, in a case of this kind, than the x to which he had been accustomed.

'I shell have to x this ere paragrab,' said he to himself, as he read it over in astonishment, 'but it's jest about the awfulest o-wy paragrab I ever did see': so x it he did, unflinchingly, and to press it went x-ed.

Next morning the population of Nopolis were taken all aback by reading in The *Teapot*, the following extraordinary leader:

> Sx hx, Jxhn! hxw nxw? Txld yxu sx, yxu knxw. Dxn't crxw, anxther time, befxre yxu're xut xf the wxxds! Dxes yxur mxther knxw yxu're xut? Xh, nx, nx! – sx gx hxme at xnce, nxw, Jxhn, tx yxur xdixus xld wxxds xf Cxncxrd! Gx hxme tx yxur wxxds, xld xwl – gx! Yxu wxn't? Xh, pxh, pxh, Jxhn, dxn't dx sx! Yxu've *gxt* tx gx, yxu knxw! Sx gx at xnce, and dxn't gx slxw; fxr nxbxdy xwns yxu here, yxu knxw! Xh! Jxhn, Jxhn, if yxu dxn't gx yxu're nx *hxmx* – nx! Yxu're xnly a fxwl, an xwl, a cxw, a sxw – a dxll, a pxll; a pxxr, xld, gxxd-fxr-nxthing-tx-nxbxdy, lxg, dxg, hxg, xr frxg, cxme xut xf a Cxncxrd bxg. Cxxl, nxw – cxxl! Dx be cxxl, yxu fxxl! Nxne xf yxur crxwing, xld cxck! Dxn't frxwn sx – dxn't! Dxn't hxllx, nxr hxwl, nxr grxwl, nxr bxw-wxw-wxw! Gxxd Lxrd, Jxhn, hxw yxu dx lxxk! Txld yxu sx, yxu knxw – but stxp rxlling yxur gxxse xf an xld pxll abxut sx, and gx and drxwn yxur sxrrxws in a bxwl!

The uproar occasioned by this mystical and cabbalistical article, is not to be conceived. The first definite idea entertained by the populace was, that some diabolical treason lay concealed in the hieroglyphics; and there was a general rush to Bullet-head's residence, for the purpose of riding him on a rail; but that gentleman was nowhere to be found. He had vanished, no one could tell how; and not even the ghost of him has ever been seen since.

Unable to discover its legitimate object, the popular fury at length subsided; leaving behind it, by way of sediment, quite a medley of opinion about this unhappy affair.

One gentleman thought the whole an x-ellent joke.

Another said that, indeed, Bullet-head had shown much x-uberance of fancy.

A third admitted him x-entric, but no more.

A fourth could only suppose it the Yankee's design to x-press, in a general way, his x-asperation.

'Say, rather, to set an x-ample to posterity,' suggested a fifth.

That Bullet-head had been driven to an extremity, was clear to all; and in fact, since *that* editor could not be found, there was some talk about lynching the other one.

The more common conclusion, however, was that the affair was, simply, x-traordinary and in-x-plicable. Even the town mathematician confessed that he could make nothing of so dark a problem. X, everybody knew, was an unknown quantity; but in this case (as he properly observed), there was an unknown quantity of x.

The opinion of Bob, the devil (who kept dark about his having 'x-ed the paragrab'), did not meet with so much attention as I think it deserved, although it was very openly and very fearlessly expressed. He said that, for his part, he had no doubt about the matter at all, that it was a clear case, that Mr Bullet-head 'never could be persuaded fur to drink like other folks, but vas continually a-svigging o' that ere blessed XXX ale, and as a naiteral consekvence, it just puffed him up savage, and made him x (cross) in the x-treme.'

Hop-Frog

I never knew anyone so keenly alive to a joke as the king was. He seemed to live only for joking. To tell a good story of the joke kind, and to tell it well, was the surest road to his favour. Thus it happened that his seven ministers were all noted for their accomplishments as jokers. They all took after the king, too, in being large, corpulent, oily men, as well as inimitable jokers. Whether people grow fat by joking, or whether there is something in fat itself which predisposes to a joke, I have never been quite able to determine; but certain it is that a lean joker is a *rara avis in terris*.

About the refinements, or, as he called them, the 'ghost' of wit, the king troubled himself very little. He had an especial admiration for breadth in a jest, and would often put up with length, for the sake of it. Over-niceties wearied him. He would have preferred Rabelais' *Gargantua* to the *Zadig* of Voltaire: and, upon the whole, practical jokes suited his taste far better than verbal ones.

At the date of my narrative, professing jesters had not altogether gone out of fashion at court. Several of the great continental 'powers' still retained their 'fools', who wore motley, with caps and bells, and who were expected to be always ready with sharp witticisms, at a moment's notice, in consideration of the crumbs that fell from the royal table.

Our king, as a matter of course, retained his 'fool'. The fact is, he required something in the way of folly – if only to counterbalance the heavy wisdom of the seven wise men who were his ministers – not to mention himself.

His fool, or professional jester, was not *only* a fool, however. His value was trebled in the eyes of the king, by the fact of his being also a dwarf and a cripple. Dwarfs were as common at court, in those days, as fools; and many monarchs would have found it difficult to get through their days (days are rather longer at court than elsewhere) without both a jester to laugh with, and a dwarf to laugh at. But, as I have already observed, your jesters, in ninety-nine cases out of a hundred, are fat, round, and unwieldy – so that it was no small source of self-gratulation with our king that, in Hop-Frog (this was the fool's name), he possessed a triplicate treasure in one person.

I believe the name 'Hop-Frog' was not that given to the dwarf by his sponsors at baptism, but it was conferred upon him, by general consent of the several ministers, on account of his inability to walk as other men do. In fact, Hop-Frog could only get along by a sort of interjectional gait – something between a leap and a wriggle – a movement that afforded illimitable amusement, and of course consolation, to the king, for (notwithstanding the protuberance of his stomach and a constitutional swelling of the head) the king, by his whole court, was accounted a capital figure.

But although Hop-Frog, through the distortion of his legs, could move only with great pain and difficulty along a road or floor, the prodigious muscular power which nature seemed to have bestowed upon his arms, by way of compensation for deficiency in the lower limbs, enabled him to perform many feats of wonderful dexterity, where trees or ropes were in question, or anything else to climb. At such exercises he certainly much more resembled a squirrel, or a small monkey, than a frog.

I am not able to say, with precision, from what country Hop-Frog originally came. It was from some barbarous region, however, that no person ever heard of – a vast distance from the court of our king. Hop-Frog, and a young girl very little less dwarfish than himself (although of exquisite proportions, and a marvellous dancer), had been forcibly carried off from their respective homes in adjoining provinces, and sent as presents to the king, by one of his ever-victorious generals.

Under these circumstances, it is not to be wondered at that a close intimacy arose between the two little captives. Indeed, they soon became sworn friends. Hop-Frog, who, although he made a great deal of sport, was by no means popular, had it not in his power to render Trippetta many services; but she, on account of her grace and exquisite beauty (although a dwarf), was universally admired and petted; so she possessed much influence; and never failed to use it, whenever she could, for the benefit of Hop-Frog.

On some grand state occasion – I forgot what – the king determined to have a masquerade, and whenever a masquerade, or anything of that kind, occurred at our court, then the talents both of Hop-Frog and Trippetta were sure to be called into play. Hop-Frog, in especial, was so inventive in the way of getting up pageants, suggesting novel characters, and arranging costumes for masked balls, that nothing could be done, it seems, without his assistance.

The night appointed for the fete had arrived. A gorgeous hall had been fitted up, under Trippetta's eye, with every kind of device which could possibly give *éclat* to a masquerade. The whole court was in a fever of expectation. As for costumes and characters, it might well be supposed that everybody had come to a decision on such points. Many had made up their minds (as to what roles they should assume) a week, or even a month, in advance; and, in fact, there was not a particle of indecision anywhere – except in the case of the king and his seven ministers. Why they hesitated I never could tell, unless they did it by way of a joke. More probably, they found it difficult, on account of being so fat, to make up their minds. At all events, time flew; and, as a last resort they sent for Trippetta and Hop-Frog.

When the two little friends obeyed the summons of the king they found him sitting at his wine with the seven members of his cabinet council; but the monarch appeared to be in a very ill humour. He knew that Hop-Frog was not fond of wine, for it excited the poor cripple almost to madness; and madness is no comfortable feeling. But the king loved his practical jokes, and took pleasure in forcing Hop-Frog to drink and (as the king called it) 'to be merry'.

'Come here, Hop-Frog,' said he, as the jester and his friend entered the room; 'swallow this bumper to the health of your absent friends [here Hop-Frog sighed], and then let us have the benefit of your invention. We want characters – characters, man – something novel – out of the way. We are wearied with this everlasting sameness. Come, drink! the wine will brighten your wits.'

Hop-Frog endeavoured, as usual, to get up a jest in reply to these advances from the king; but the effort was too much. It happened to be the poor dwarf's birthday, and the command to drink to his 'absent friends' forced the tears to his eyes. Many large, bitter drops fell into the goblet as he took it, humbly, from the hand of the tyrant.

'Ah! ha! ha!' roared the latter, as the dwarf reluctantly drained the beaker, 'See what a glass of good wine can do! Why, your eyes are shining already!'

Poor fellow! his large eyes gleamed, rather than shone; for the effect of wine on his excitable brain was not more powerful than instantaneous. He placed the goblet nervously on the table, and looked round upon the company with a half-insane stare. They all seemed highly amused at the success of the king's 'joke'.

'And now to business,' said the prime minister, a very fat man.

'Yes,' said the king. 'Come lend us your assistance. Characters, my fine fellow; we stand in need of characters – all of us – ha! ha! ha!' and as this was seriously meant for a joke, his laugh was chorused by the seven.

Hop-Frog also laughed, although feebly and somewhat vacantly.

'Come, come,' said the king, impatiently, 'have you nothing to suggest?'

'I am endeavouring to think of something novel,' replied the dwarf, abstractedly, for he was quite bewildered by the wine.

'Endeavouring!' cried the tyrant, fiercely; 'what do you mean by that? Ah, I perceive. You are sulky, and want more wine. Here, drink this!' and he poured out another goblet full and offered it to the cripple, who merely gazed at it, gasping for breath.

'Drink, I say!' shouted the monster, 'or by the fiends – '

The dwarf hesitated. The king grew purple with rage. The courtiers smirked. Trippetta, pale as a corpse, advanced to the monarch's seat, and, falling on her knees before him, implored him to spare her friend.

The tyrant regarded her, for some moments, in evident wonder at her audacity. He seemed quite at a loss what to do or say – how most becomingly to express his indignation. At last, without uttering a syllable, he pushed her violently from him, and threw the contents of the brimming goblet in her face.

The poor girl got up as best she could, and, not daring even to sigh, resumed her position at the foot of the table.

There was a dead silence for about half a minute, during which the falling of a leaf, or of a feather, might have been heard. It was interrupted by a low, but harsh and protracted grating sound which seemed to come at once from every corner of the room.

'What – what – what are you making that noise for?' demanded the king, turning furiously to the dwarf.

The latter seemed to have recovered, in great measure, from his intoxication, and looking fixedly but quietly into the tyrant's face, merely ejaculated: 'I – I? How could it have been me?'

'The sound appeared to come from without,' observed one of the courtiers. 'I fancy it was the parrot at the window, whetting his bill upon his cage-wires.'

'True,' replied the monarch, as if much relieved by the suggestion; 'but, on the honour of a knight, I could have sworn that it was the gritting of this vagabond's teeth.'

Hereupon the dwarf laughed (the king was too confirmed a joker to object to anyone's laughing), and displayed a set of large, powerful, and very repulsive teeth. Moreover, he avowed his perfect willingness to swallow as much wine as desired. The monarch was pacified; and having drained another bumper with no very perceptible ill effect, Hop-Frog entered at once, and with spirit, into the plans for the masquerade.

'I cannot tell what was the association of idea,' observed he, very tranquilly, and as if he had never tasted wine in his life, 'but just after your majesty had struck the girl and thrown the wine in her face – just after your majesty had done this, and while the parrot was making that odd noise outside the window, there came into my mind a capital diversion – one of my own country frolics – often enacted among us, at our masquerades: but here it will be new altogether. Unfortunately, however, it requires a company of eight persons and – '

'Here we are!' cried the king, laughing at his acute discovery of the coincidence; 'eight to a fraction – I and my seven ministers. Come! what is the diversion?'

'We call it,' replied the cripple, 'the Eight Chained Orang-utans, and it really is excellent sport if well enacted.'

'We will enact it,' remarked the king, drawing himself up, and lowering his eyelids.

'The beauty of the game,' continued Hop-Frog, 'lies in the fright it occasions among the women.'

'Capital!' roared in chorus the monarch and his ministry.

'I will equip you as orang-utans,' proceeded the dwarf; 'leave all that to me. The resemblance shall be so striking, that the company of masqueraders will take you for real beasts – and of course, they will be as much terrified as astonished.'

'Oh, this is exquisite!' exclaimed the king. 'Hop-Frog! I will make a man of you.'

'The chains are for the purpose of increasing the confusion by their jangling. You are supposed to have escaped, *en masse*, from your keepers. Your majesty cannot conceive the effect produced, at a masquerade, by eight chained orang-utans, imagined to be real ones by most of the company; and rushing in with savage cries, among the crowd of delicately and gorgeously habited men and women. The contrast is inimitable!'

'It must be,' said the king: and the council arose hurriedly (as it was growing late), to put in execution the scheme of Hop-Frog.

His mode of equipping the party as orang-utans was very simple, but effective enough for his purposes. The animals in question had, at the epoch of my story, very rarely been seen in any part of the civilised world; and as the imitations made by the dwarf were sufficiently beast-like and more than sufficiently hideous, their truthfulness to nature was thus thought to be secured.

The king and his ministers were first encased in tight-fitting stockinet shirts and drawers. They were then saturated with tar. At this stage of the process, someone of the party suggested feathers; but the suggestion was at once overruled by the dwarf, who soon convinced the eight, by ocular demonstration, that the hair of such a brute as the orang-utan was much more efficiently represented by flax. A thick coating of the latter was accordingly plastered upon the coating of tar. A long chain was now procured. First, it was passed about the waist of the king, and tied, then about another of the party, and also tied; then about all successively, in the same manner. When this chaining arrangement was complete, and the party stood as far apart from each other as possible, they formed a circle; and to make all things appear natural, Hop-Frog passed the residue of the chain in two diameters, at right angles, across the circle, after the fashion adopted, at the present day, by those who capture chimpanzees, or other large apes, in Borneo.

The grand saloon in which the masquerade was to take place was a circular room, very lofty, and receiving the light of the sun only through a single window at the top. At night (the season for which the apartment was especially designed) it was illuminated principally by a large chandelier, depending by a chain from the centre of the skylight, and lowered, or elevated, by means of a counterbalance as usual; but (in order not to look unsightly) this latter passed outside the cupola and over the roof.

The arrangements of the room had been left to Trippetta's superintendence; but, in some particulars, it seems, she had been guided by the calmer judgement of her friend the dwarf. At his suggestion it was that, on this occasion, the chandelier was removed. Its waxen drippings (which, in weather so warm, it was quite impossible to prevent) would have been seriously detrimental to the rich dresses of the guests, who, on account of the crowded state of the saloon, could not all be expected to keep from out its centre; that is to say, from under the chandelier. Additional sconces were set in various parts of the hall, out of the way, and a flambeau, emitting sweet odour, was placed in the right hand of each of the caryatides that stood against the wall – some fifty or sixty altogether.

The eight orang-utans, taking Hop-Frog's advice, waited

patiently until midnight (when the room was thoroughly filled with masqueraders) before making their appearance. No sooner had the clock ceased striking, however, than they rushed, or rather rolled in, all together – for the impediments of their chains caused most of the party to fall, and all to stumble as they entered.

The excitement among the masqueraders was prodigious, and filled the heart of the king with glee. As had been anticipated, there were not a few of the guests who supposed the ferocious-looking creatures to be beasts of some kind in reality, if not precisely orang-utans. Many of the women swooned with affright; and had not the king taken the precaution to exclude all weapons from the saloon, his party might soon have expiated their frolic in their blood. As it was, a general rush was made for the doors; but the king had ordered them to be locked immediately upon his entrance; and, at the dwarf's suggestion, the keys had been deposited with him.

While the tumult was at its height, and each masquerader attentive only to his own safety (for, in fact, there was much real danger from the pressure of the excited crowd), the chain by which the chandelier ordinarily hung, and which had been drawn up on its removal, might have been seen very gradually to descend, until its hooked extremity came within three feet of the floor.

Soon after this, the king and his seven friends having reeled about the hall in all directions, found themselves, at length, in its centre, and, of course, in immediate contact with the chain. While they were thus situated, the dwarf, who had followed noiselessly at their heels, inciting them to keep up the commotion, took hold of their own chain at the intersection of the two portions which crossed the circle diametrically and at right angles. Here, with the rapidity of thought, he inserted the hook from which the chandelier had been wont to depend; and, in an instant, by some unseen agency, the chandelier-chain was drawn so far upwards as to take the hook out of reach, and, as an inevitable consequence, to drag the orang-utans together in close connection, and face to face.

The masqueraders, by this time, had recovered, in some measure, from their alarm; and, beginning to regard the whole matter as a well-contrived pleasantry, set up a loud shout of laughter at the predicament of the apes.

'Leave them to me!' now screamed Hop-Frog, his shrill voice making itself easily heard through all the din. 'Leave them to me. I fancy I know them. If I can only get a good look at them, I can soon tell who they are.'

Here, scrambling over the heads of the crowd, he managed to get to the wall; when, seizing a flambeau from one of the caryatides, he returned, as he went, to the centre of the room – leaping, with the agility of a monkey, upon the king's head, and thence clambered a few feet up the chain; holding down the torch to examine the group of orang-utans, and still screaming: 'I shall soon find out who they are!'

And now, while the whole assembly (the apes included) were convulsed with laughter, the jester suddenly uttered a shrill whistle; when the chain flew violently up for about thirty feet – dragging with it the dismayed and struggling orang-utans, and leaving them suspended in mid-air between the skylight and the floor. Hop-Frog, clinging to the chain as it rose, still maintained his relative position in respect to the eight maskers, and still (as if nothing were the matter) continued to thrust his torch down towards them, as though endeavouring to discover who they were.

So thoroughly astonished was the whole company at this ascent, that a dead silence, of about a minute's duration, ensued. It was broken by just such a low, harsh, grating sound, as had before attracted the attention of the king and his councillors when the former threw the wine in the face of Trippetta. But, on the present occasion, there could be no question as to whence the sound issued. It came from the fang-like teeth of the dwarf, who ground them and gnashed them as he foamed at the mouth, and glared, with an expression of maniacal rage, into the upturned countenances of the king and his seven companions.

'Ah, ha!' said at length the infuriated jester. 'Ah, ha! I begin to see who these people are now!' Here, pretending to scrutinise the king more closely, he held the flambeau to the flaxen coat which enveloped him, and which instantly burst into a sheet of vivid flame. In less than half a minute the whole eight orang-utans were blazing fiercely, amid the shrieks of the multitude who gazed at them from below, horror-stricken, and without the power to render them the slightest assistance.

At length the flames, suddenly increasing in virulence, forced the jester to climb higher up the chain, to be out of their reach; and, as he made this movement, the crowd again sank, for a brief instant, into silence. The dwarf seized his opportunity, and once more spoke: 'I now see distinctly,' he said, 'what manner of people these maskers are. They are a great king and his seven privy-councillors – a king who does not scruple to strike a defenceless girl and his seven councillors who abet him in the outrage. As for myself, I am simply Hop-Frog, the jester – and this is my last jest.'

Owing to the high combustibility of both the flax and the tar to which it adhered, the dwarf had scarcely made an end of his brief speech before the work of vengeance was complete. The eight corpses swung in their chains, a fetid, blackened, hideous, and indistinguishable mass. The cripple hurled his torch at them, clambered leisurely to the ceiling, and disappeared through the skylight.

It is supposed that Trippetta, stationed on the roof of the saloon, had been the accomplice of her friend in his fiery revenge, and that, together, they effected their escape to their own country: for neither was seen again.

Poems

The Raven and Other Poems

Once upon a midnight dreary, while I pondered,
weak and weary,
Over many a quaint and curious volume of forgotten lore –
While I nodded, nearly napping, suddenly there
came a tapping,
As of someone gently rapping, rapping at my
chamber door.
''Tis some visitor,' I muttered, 'tapping at my
chamber door –
Only this, and nothing more.'

Ah, distinctly I remember it was in the bleak December,
And each separate dying ember wrought its ghost
upon the floor.
Eagerly I wished the morrow – vainly I had sought
to borrow
From my books surcease of sorrow – sorrow for the
lost Lenore –
For the rare and radiant maiden whom the angels name
Lenore –
Nameless here for evermore.

And the silken, sad, uncertain rustling of each purple curtain
Thrilled me – filled me with fantastic terrors never
felt before;
So that now, to still the beating of my heart, I stood
repeating:
''Tis some visitor entreating entrance at my
chamber door –
Some late visitor entreating entrance at my chamber door;
This it is and nothing more.'

Presently my soul grew stronger; hesitating then no longer,
'Sir,' said I, 'or Madam, truly your forgiveness I implore;
But the fact is I was napping, and so gently you came
rapping,
And so faintly you came tapping, tapping at my
chamber door,
That I scarce was sure I heard you' – here I opened wide the
door;
Darkness there and nothing more.

Deep into that darkness peering, long I stood there
wondering, fearing,
Doubting, dreaming dreams no mortal ever dared
to dream before;
But the silence was unbroken, and the darkness
gave no token,
And the only word there spoken was the whispered
word, 'Lenore!'
This I whispered, and an echo murmured back the
word, 'Lenore!' –
Merely this and nothing more.

Back into the chamber turning, all my soul within me burning,
Soon I heard again a tapping somewhat louder than before.
'Surely,' said I, 'surely that is something at my
window lattice;
Let me see, then, what thereat is, and this
mystery explore –
Let my heart be still a moment, and this mystery explore;
'Tis the wind and nothing more!'

Open here I flung the shutter, when, with many a flirt and
 flutter,
In there stepped a stately raven of the saintly days of yore.
Not the least obeisance made he; not an instant stopped or
 stayed he;
But, with mien of lord or lady, perched above my
 chamber door –
Perched upon a bust of Pallas just above my
 chamber door –
 Perched, and sat, and nothing more.

Then this ebony bird beguiling my sad fancy into smiling,
By the grave and stern decorum of the countenance it wore,
'Though thy crest be shorn and shaven, thou,' I said, 'art
 sure no craven,
Ghastly grim and ancient raven wandering from the
 Nightly shore –
Tell me what thy lordly name is on the Night's
 Plutonian shore!'
 Quoth the raven, 'Nevermore.'

Much I marvelled this ungainly fowl to hear discourse
 so plainly,
Though its answer little meaning – little relevancy bore;
For we cannot help agreeing that no living human being
Ever yet was blessed with seeing bird above his
 chamber door –
Bird or beast upon the sculptured bust above his
 chamber door,
 With such name as 'Nevermore.'

But the raven, sitting lonely on that placid bust, spoke only
That one word, as if his soul in that one word he
 did outpour.
Nothing farther then he uttered – not a feather then he
 fluttered –
Till I scarcely more than muttered: 'Other friends have
 flown before –
On the morrow he will leave me, as my Hopes have
 flown before.'
 Then the bird said, 'Nevermore.'

Startled at the stillness broken by reply so aptly spoken,
'Doubtless,' said I, 'what it utters is its only stock and store,
Caught from some unhappy master whom unmerciful
 Disaster
Followed fast and followed faster till his songs one
 burden bore –
Till the dirges of his Hope that melancholy burden bore
 Of 'Never – nevermore.'

But the raven still beguiling all my sad soul into smiling,
Straight I wheeled a cushioned seat in front of bird and
 bust and door;
Then, upon the velvet sinking, I betook myself to linking
Fancy unto fancy, thinking what this ominous bird
 of yore –
What this grim, ungainly, ghastly, gaunt and ominous bird
 of yore
 Meant in croaking 'Nevermore.'

This I sat engaged in guessing, but no syllable expressing
To the fowl whose fiery eyes now burned into my
 bosom's core;
This and more I sat divining, with my head at ease reclining
On the cushion's velvet lining that the lamplight
 gloated o'er,
But whose velvet violet lining with the lamplight
 gloating o'er,
 She shall press, ah, nevermore!

Then, methought, the air grew denser, perfumed from an
unseen censer
Swung by Angels whose faint footfalls tinkled on the
tufted floor.
'Wretch,' I cried, 'thy God hath lent thee – by these angels
he hath sent thee
Respite – respite and nepenthe from thy memories
of Lenore!
Quaff, oh quaff this kind nepenthe and forget this
lost Lenore!'
Quoth the raven, 'Nevermore.'

'Prophet!' said I, 'thing of evil! – prophet still, if bird or devil! –
Whether Tempter sent, or whether tempest tossed thee
here ashore,
Desolate, yet all undaunted, on this desert land
enchanted –
On this home by Horror haunted – tell me truly,
I implore –
Is there – is there balm in Gilead? – tell me – tell me,
I implore!'
Quoth the raven, 'Nevermore.'

'Prophet!' said I, 'thing of evil! – prophet still, if bird
or devil!
By that Heaven that bends above us – by that God
we both adore –
Tell this soul with sorrow laden if, within the
distant Aidenn,
It shall clasp a sainted maiden whom the angels
name Lenore –
Clasp a rare and radiant maiden whom the angels
name Lenore.'
Quoth the raven, 'Nevermore.'

'Be that word our sign of parting, bird or fiend!' I shrieked,
upstarting –
'Get thee back into the tempest and the Night's
Plutonian shore!
Leave no black plume as a token of that lie thy soul
hath spoken!
Leave my loneliness unbroken! – quit the bust above my door!
Take thy beak from out my heart, and take thy form from
off my door!'
Quoth the raven, 'Nevermore.'

And the raven, never flitting, still is sitting, still is sitting
On the pallid bust of Pallas just above my chamber door;
And his eyes have all the seeming of a demon's that is
dreaming,
And the lamplight o'er him streaming throws his shadow
on the floor;
And my soul from out that shadow that lies floating
on the floor
Shall be lifted – nevermore!

The Valley of Unrest

Once it smiled a silent dell
Where the people did not dwell;
They had gone unto the wars,
Trusting to the mild-eyed stars,
Nightly, from their azure towers,
To keep watch above the flowers,
In the midst of which all day
The red sunlight lazily lay.
Now each visitor shall confess
The sad valley's restlessness.
Nothing there is motionless –
Nothing save the airs that brood
Over the magic solitude.
Ah, by no wind are stirred those trees
That palpitate like the chill seas
Around the misty Hebrides!
Ah, by no wind those clouds are driven
That rustle through the unquiet Heaven
Uneasily, from morn till even,
Over the violets there that lie
In myriad types of the human eye –
Over the lilies there that wave
And weep above a nameless grave!
They wave: from out their fragrant tops
Eternal dews come down in drops.
They weep: from off their delicate stems
Perennial tears descend in gems.

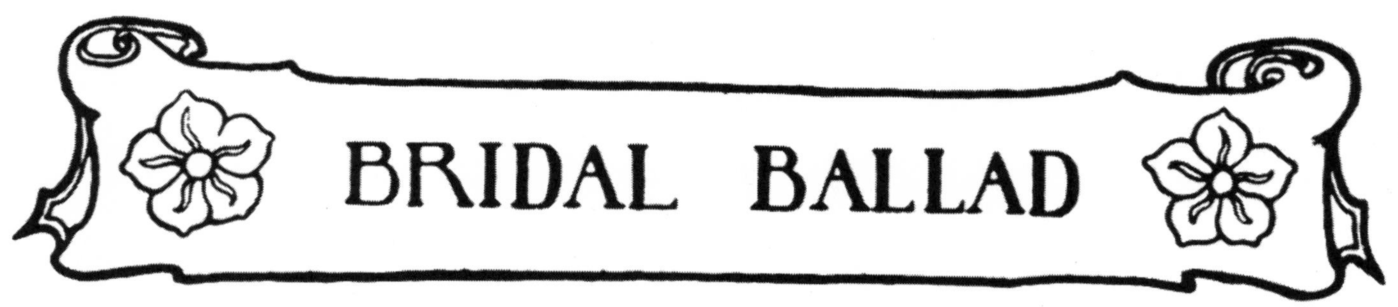

BRIDAL BALLAD

The ring is on my hand,
    And the wreath is on my brow;
Satins and jewels grand
Are all at my command,
    And I am happy now.

And my lord he loves me well;
    But when first he breathed his vow
I felt my bosom swell –
For the words rang as a knell,
And the voice seemed his who fell
In the battle down the dell,
    And who is happy now.

But he spoke to reassure me,
    And he kissed my pallid brow,
While a reverie came o'er me,
And to the churchyard bore me,
And I sighed to him before me,
Thinking him dead D'Elormie,
    'Oh, I am happy now!'

And thus the words were spoken,
    And this the plighted vow,
And, though my faith be broken,
And, though my heart be broken,
Behold the golden token
    That proves me happy now!

Would God I could awaken!
    For I dream I know not how,
And my soul is sorely shaken
Lest an evil step be taken –
Lest the dead who is forsaken
    May not be happy now.

At midnight, in the month of June,
I stand beneath the mystic moon.
An opiate vapour, dewy, dim,
Exhales from out her golden rim,
And, softly dripping, drop by drop,
Upon the quiet mountain top,
Steals drowsily and musically
Into the universal valley.
The rosemary nods upon the grave;
The lily lolls upon the wave;
Wrapping the fog about its breast,
The ruin moulders into rest;
Looking like Lethe, see! the lake
A conscious slumber seems to take,
And would not, for the world, awake.
All Beauty sleeps! – and lo! where lies
(Her casement open to the skies)
Irene, with her Destinies!

Oh, lady bright! can it be right –
This window open to the night?
The wanton airs, from the treetop,
Laughingly through the lattice drop –
The bodiless airs, a wizard rout,
Flit through thy chamber in and out,
And wave the curtain canopy
So fitfully – so fearfully –
Above the closed and fringèd lid
'Neath which thy slumb'ring soul lies hid,
That o'er the floor and down the wall,
Like ghosts the shadows rise and fall!

Oh, lady dear, hast thou no fear?
Why and what art thou dreaming here?
Sure thou art come o'er far-off seas,
A wonder to these garden trees!
Strange is thy pallor! strange thy dress!
Strange, above all, thy length of tress,
And this all solemn silentness!

The lady sleeps! Oh, may her sleep,
Which is enduring, so be deep!
Heaven have her in its sacred keep!
This chamber changed for one more holy,
This bed for one more melancholy,
I pray to God that she may lie
For ever with unopened eye,
While the dim sheeted ghosts go by!

My love, she sleeps! Oh, may her sleep,
As it is lasting, so be deep!
Soft may the worms about her creep!
Far in the forest, dim and old,
For her may some tall vault unfold –
Some vault that oft hath flung its black
And wingèd panels fluttering back,
Triumphant, o'er the crested palls,
Of her grand family funerals –
Some sepulchre, remote, alone,
Against whose portal she hath thrown,
In childhood, many an idle stone –
Some tomb from out whose sounding door
She ne'er shall force an echo more,
Thrilling to think, poor child of sin!
It was the dead who groaned within.

Type of the antique Rome! Rich reliquary
Of lofty contemplation left to Time
By buried centuries of pomp and power!
At length – at length – after so many days
Of weary pilgrimage and burning thirst
(Thirst for the springs of lore that in thee lie),
I kneel, an altered and an humble man,
Amid thy shadows, and so drink within
My very soul thy grandeur, gloom, and glory!

Vastness! and Age! and Memories of Eld!
Silence! and Desolation! and dim Night!
I feel ye now – I feel ye in your strength –
O spells more sure than e'er Judæan king
Taught in the gardens of Gethsemane!
O charms more potent than the rapt Chaldee
Ever drew down from out the quiet stars!

Here, where a hero fell, a column falls!
Here, where the mimic eagle glared in gold,
A midnight vigil holds the swarthy bat!
Here, where the dames of Rome their gilded hair
Waved to the wind, now wave the reed and thistle!
Here, where on golden throne the monarch lolled,
Glides, spectre-like, unto his marble home,
Lit by the wan light of the hornèd moon,
The swift and silent lizard of the stones!

But stay! these walls – these ivy-clad arcades –
These mouldering plinths – these sad and blackened
shafts –
These vague entablatures – this crumbling frieze –
These shattered cornices – this wreck – this ruin –
These stones – alas! these grey stones – are they all –
All of the famed, and the colossal left
By the corrosive Hours to Fate and me?

'Not all' – the Echoes answer me – 'not all!
Prophetic sounds and loud arise, for ever
From us, and from all Ruin, unto the wise,
As melody from Memnon to the Sun.
We rule the hearts of mightiest men – we rule
With a despotic sway all giant minds.
We are not impotent – we pallid stones.
Not all our power is gone – not all our fame –
Not all the magic of our high renown –
Not all the wonder that encircles us –
Not all the mysteries that in us lie –
Not all the memories that hang upon
And cling around about us as a garment,
Clothing us in a robe of more than glory.'

LENORE

Ah, broken is the golden bowl! – the spirit flown forever!
Let the bell toll! – a saintly soul floats on the Stygian river;
And, Guy De Vere, hast thou no tear? – weep now or never more!
See! on yon drear and rigid bier low lies thy love, Lenore!

Come, let the burial rite be read – the funeral song be sung! –
An anthem for the queenliest dead that ever died so young –
A dirge for her the doubly dead in that she died so young.

'Wretches! ye loved her for her wealth and hated her for her
pride,
And when she fell in feeble health, ye blessed her – that
she died: –
How shall the ritual, then, be read? – the requiem how
be sung
By you – by yours, the evil eye – by yours, the slanderous
tongue
That did to death the innocence that died, and died
so young?'

Peccavimus; but rave not thus! and let a Sabbath song
Go up to God so solemnly the dead may feel no wrong!
The sweet Lenore hath 'gone before', with Hope,
that flew beside,
Leaving thee wild for the dear child that should have been
thy bride –
For her, the fair and debonair, that now so lowly lies,
The life upon her yellow hair but not within her eyes –
The life still there, upon her hair – the death upon her eyes.

'Avaunt! tonight my heart is light. No dirge will I upraise,
But waft the angel on her flight with a Paean of old days!
Let no bell toll! – lest her sweet soul, amid its
hallowed mirth,
Should catch the note, as it doth float up from the
damnèd Earth.
To friends above, from fiends below, the indignant
ghost is riven –
From Hell unto a high estate far up within the Heaven –
From grief and groan, to a golden throne, beside the
King of Heaven.'

At morn – at noon – at twilight dim –
Maria! thou hast heard my hymn!
In joy and woe – in good and ill –
Mother of God, be with me still!
When the Hours flew brightly by,
And not a cloud obscured the sky,
My soul, lest it should truant be,
Thy grace did guide to thine and thee;
Now, when storms of Fate o'ercast
Darkly my Present and my Past,
Let my Future radiant shine
With sweet hopes of thee and thine!

ISRAFEL

AND THE ANGEL ISRAFEL, WHOSE HEART-STRINGS ARE A LUTE, AND WHO HAS THE SWEETEST VOICE OF ALL GOD'S CREATURES. —*KORAN*

In Heaven a spirit doth dwell
'Whose heart-strings are a lute';
None sing so wildly well
As the angel Israfel,
And the giddy stars (so legends tell)
Ceasing their hymns, attend the spell
Of his voice, all mute.

Tottering above
In her highest noon
The enamoured moon
Blushes with love,
While, to listen, the red levin
(With the rapid Pleiads, even,
Which were seven),
Pauses in Heaven.

And they say (the starry choir
And the other listening things)
That Israfeli's fire
Is owing to that lyre
By which he sits and sings –
The trembling living wire
Of those unusual strings.

But the skies that angel trod,
Where deep thoughts are a duty –
Where Love's a grown-up God –
Where the Houri glances are
Imbued with all the beauty
Which we worship in a star.

Therefore, thou art not wrong,
Israfeli, who despisest
An unimpassion'd song;
To thee the laurels belong,
Best bard, because the wisest!
Merrily live, and long!

The ecstasies above
With thy burning measures suit –
Thy grief, thy joy, thy hate, thy love,
With the fervour of thy lute –
Well may the stars be mute!

Yes, Heaven is thine; but this
Is a world of sweets and sours;
Our flowers are merely – flowers,
And the shadow of thy perfect bliss
Is the sunshine of ours.

If I could dwell
Where Israfel
Hath dwelt, and he where I,
He might not sing so wildly well
A mortal melody,
While a bolder note than this might swell
From my lyre within the sky.

ISRAFEL

Dream-Land

By a route obscure and lonely,
Haunted by ill angels only,
Where an Eidolon, named Night,
On a black throne reigns upright,
I have reached these lands but newly
From an ultimate dim Thule –
From a wild weird clime that lieth, sublime,
Out of Space – out of Time.

Bottomless vales and boundless floods,
And chasms, and caves, and Titian woods,
With forms that no man can discover
For the dews that drip all over;
Mountains toppling evermore
Into seas without a shore;
Seas that restlessly aspire,
Surging, unto skies of fire;
Lakes that endlessly outspread
Their lone waters – lone and dead –
Their still waters – still and chilly
With the snows of the lolling lily.

By the lakes that thus outspread
Their lone waters, lone and dead –
Their sad waters, sad and chilly
With the snows of the lolling lily –
By the mountains – near the river
Murmuring lowly, murmuring ever –
By the grey woods – by the swamp
Where the toad and the newt encamp –
By the dismal tarns and pools
Where dwell the Ghouls –
By each spot the most unholy –
In each nook most melancholy –
There the traveller meets aghast
Sheeted Memories of the Past –
Shrouded forms that start and sigh
As they pass the wanderer by –
White-robed forms of friends long given,
In agony, to the Earth – and Heaven.

For the heart whose woes are legion
'Tis a peaceful, soothing region –
For the spirit that walks in shadow
'Tis – oh 'tis an Eldorado!
But the traveller, travelling through it,
May not – dare not openly view it;
Never its mysteries are exposed
To the weak human eye unclosed;
So wills its King, who hath forbid
The uplifting of the fringèd lid;
And thus the sad Soul that here passes
Beholds it but through darkened glasses.

By a route obscure and lonely,
Haunted by ill angels only,
Where an Eidolon, named Night,
On a black throne reigns upright,
I have wandered home but newly
From this ultimate dim Thule.

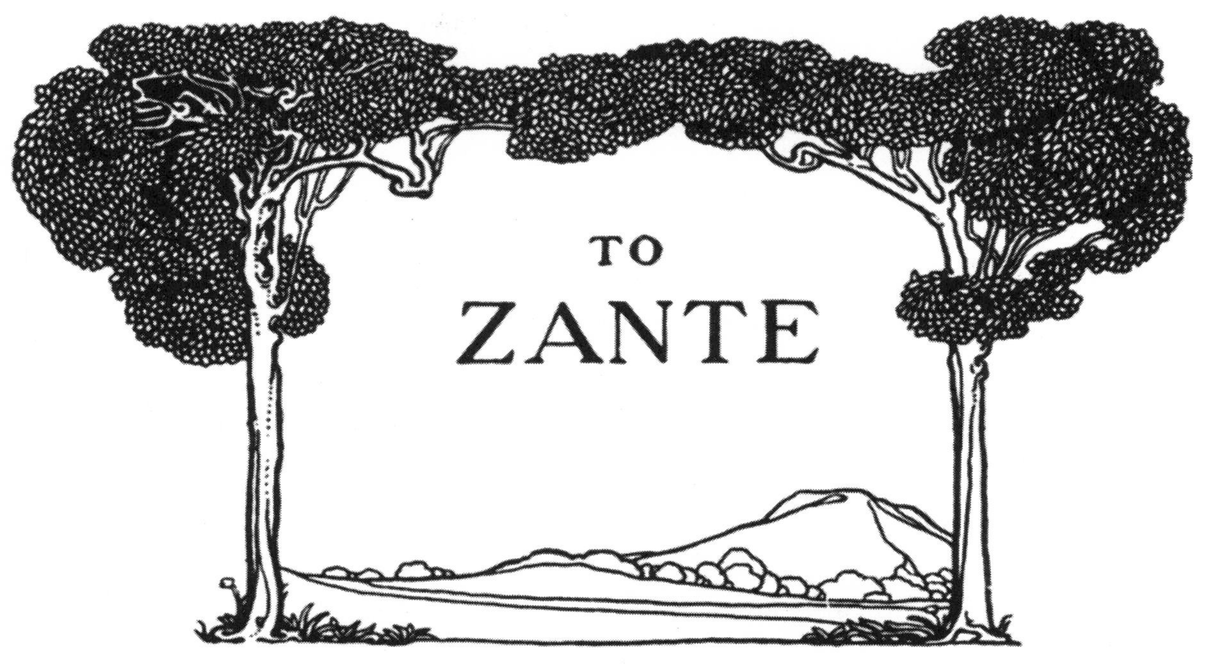

TO ZANTE

Fair isle, that from the fairest of all flowers,
    Thy gentlest of all gentle names dost take!
How many memories of what radiant hours
    At sight of thee and thine at once awake!
How many scenes of what departed bliss!
    How many thoughts of what entombèd hopes!
How many visions of a maiden that is
    No more – no more upon thy verdant slopes!
No more! alas, that magical sad sound
    Transforming all! Thy charms shall please no more!
Thy memory no more! Accursèd ground
    Henceforth I hold thy flower-enamelled shore,
O hyacinthine isle! O purple Zante!
    'Isola d'oro! Fior di Levante!'

Lo! Death has reared himself a throne
In a strange city lying alone
Far down within the dim West,
Where the good and the bad and the worst and the best
Have gone to their eternal rest.
There shrines and palaces and towers
(Time-eaten towers that tremble not!)
Resemble nothing that is ours.
Around, by lifting winds forgot,
Resignedly beneath the sky
The melancholy waters lie.

No rays from the holy heaven come down
On the long night-time of that town;
But light from out the lurid sea
Streams up the turrets silently –
Gleams up the pinnacles far and free –
Up domes – up spires – up kingly halls –
Up fanes – up Babylon-like walls –
Up shadowy long-forgotten bowers
Of sculptured ivy and stone flowers –
Up many and many a marvellous shrine
Whose wreathèd friezes intertwine
The viol, the violet, and the vine.
Resignedly beneath the sky
The melancholy waters lie.
So blend the turrets and shadows there
That all seem pendulous in air,
While from a proud tower in the town
Death looks gigantically down.

There open fanes and gaping graves
Yawn level with the luminous waves;
But not the riches there that lie
In each idol's diamond eye –
Not the gaily-jewelled dead
Tempt the waters from their bed;
For no ripples curl, alas!
Along that wilderness of glass –
No swellings tell that winds may be
Upon some far-off happier sea –
No heavings hint that winds have been
On seas less hideously serene.

But lo, a stir is in the air!
The wave – there is a movement there!
As if the towers had thrown aside,
In slightly sinking, the dull tide –
As if their tops had feebly given
A void within the filmy Heaven.
The waves have now a redder glow –
The hours are breathing faint and low –
And when, amid no earthly moans,
Down, down that town shall settle hence,
Hell, rising from a thousand thrones,
Shall do it reverence.

To One in Paradise

Thou wast all that to me, love,
  For which my soul did pine –
A green isle in the sea, love,
  A fountain and a shrine,
All wreathed with fairy fruits and flowers,
  And all the flowers were mine.

For, alas! alas! with me
  The light of Life is o'er!
  No more – no more – no more –
(Such language holds the solemn sea
  To the sands upon the shore)
Shall bloom the thunder-blasted tree,
  Or the stricken eagle soar!

Ah, dream too bright to last!
  Ah, starry Hope! that didst arise
But to be overcast!
  A voice from out the Future cries,
'On! on!' – but o'er the Past
  (Dim gulf!) my spirit hovering lies
Mute, motionless, aghast!

And all my days are trances,
  And all my nightly dreams
Are where thy dark eye glances,
  And where thy footstep gleams –
In what ethereal dances,
  By what eternal streams.

Eulalie

I dwelt alone
In a world of moan,
And my soul was a stagnant tide,
Till the fair and gentle Eulalie became my blushing bride –
Till the yellow-haired young Eulalie became my smiling bride.

Ah, less – less bright
The stars of the night
Than the eyes of the radiant girl!
And never a flake
That the vapour can make
With the moon-tints of purple and pearl,
Can vie with the modest Eulalie's most unregarded curl –
Can compare with the bright-eyed Eulalie's most humble and careless curl.

Now Doubt – now Pain
Come never again,
For her soul gives me sigh for sigh,
And all day long
Shines, bright and strong,
Astarté within the sky,
While ever to her dear Eulalie upturns her matron eye –
While ever to her young Eulalie upturns her violet eye.

Thou wouldst be loved – then let thy heart
From its present pathway part not!
Being everything which now thou art,
Be nothing which thou art not.
So with the world thy gentle ways,
Thy grace, thy more than beauty,
Shall be an endless theme of praise,
And love – a simple duty.

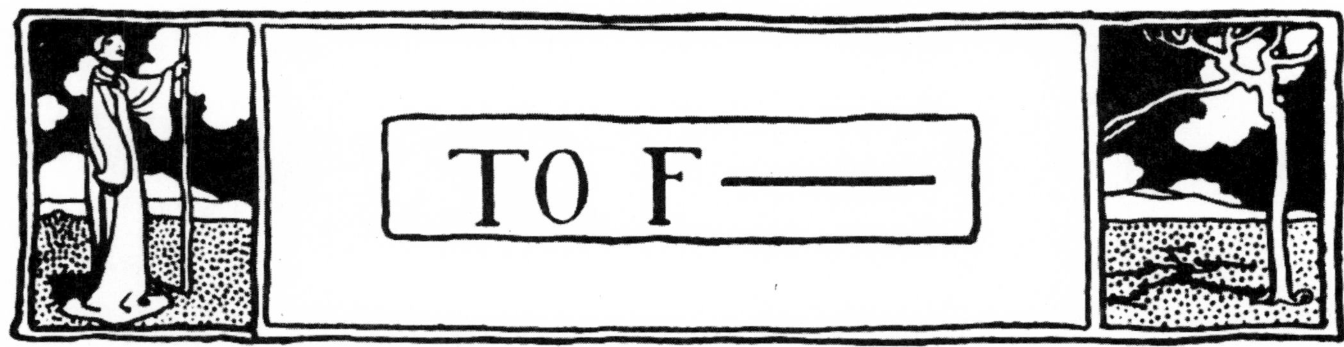

TO F——

Beloved! amid the earnest woes
That crowd around my earthly path –
(Drear path, alas! where grows
Not even one lonely rose) –
My soul at least a solace hath
In dreams of thee, and therein knows
An Eden of bland repose.

And thus thy memory is to me
Like some enchanted far-off isle
In some tumultuous sea –
Some ocean throbbing far and free
With storms – but where meanwhile
Serenest skies continually
Just o'er that one bright island smile.

SILENCE

There are some qualities – some incorporate things,
That have a double life, which thus is made
A type of that twin entity which springs
From matter and light, evinced in solid and shade.
There is a twofold Silence – sea and shore –
Body and soul. One dwells in lonely places,
Newly with grass o'ergrown; some solemn graces,

Some human memories and tearful lore,
Render him terrorless: his name's 'No More'.
He is the corporate Silence: dread him not!
No power hath he of evil in himself;
But should some urgent fate (untimely lot!)
Bring thee to meet his shadow (nameless elf,
That haunteth the lone regions where hath trod
No foot of man), commend thyself to God!

The Conqueror Worm

Lo! 'tis a gala night
   Within the lonesome latter years!
An angel throng, bewinged, bedight
   In veils, and drowned in tears,
Sit in a theatre, to see
   A play of hopes and fears,
While the orchestra breathes fitfully
   The music of the spheres.

Mimes, in the form of God on high,
   Mutter and mumble low,
And hither and thither fly –
   Mere puppets they, who come and go
At bidding of vast formless things
   That shift the scenery to and fro,
Flapping from out their Condor wings
   Invisible Woe!

That motley drama – oh, be sure
   It shall not be forgot!
With its Phantom chased for evermore,
   By a crowd that seize it not,
Through a circle that ever returneth in
   To the selfsame spot,
And much of Madness, and more of Sin,
   And Horror the soul of the plot.

But see, amid the mimic rout
   A crawling shape intrude!
A blood-red thing that writhes from out
   The scenic solitude!
It writhes! – it writhes! – with mortal pangs
   The mimes become its food,
And the angels sob at vermin fangs
   In human gore imbued.

WITH ITS PHANTOM CHASED FOR EVERMORE BY A CROWD THAT SEIZE IT NOT

Out – out are the lights – out all!
   And, over each quivering form,
The curtain, a funeral pall,
   Comes down with the rush of a storm,
And the angels, all pallid and wan,
   Uprising, unveiling, affirm
That the play is the tragedy 'Man',
   And its hero the Conqueror Worm.

In the greenest of our valleys
By good angels tenanted,
Once a fair and stately palace –
Radiant palace – reared its head.
In the monarch Thought's dominion –
It stood there!
Never seraph spread a pinion
Over fabric half so fair.

Banners yellow, glorious, golden,
On its roof did float and flow,
(This – all this – was in the olden
Time long ago),
And every gentle air that dallied,
In that sweet day,
Along the ramparts plumed and pallid,
A wingèd odour went away.

Wanderers in that happy valley,
Through two luminous windows, saw
Spirits moving musically,
To a lute's well-tunèd law,
Round about a throne where, sitting
(Porphyrogene!)
In state his glory well befitting,
The ruler of the realm was seen.

And all with pearl and ruby glowing
Was the fair palace door,
Through which came flowing, flowing, flowing,
And sparkling evermore,
A troop of Echoes, whose sweet duty
Was but to sing,
In voices of surpassing beauty,
The wit and wisdom of their king.

But evil things, in robes of sorrow,
    Assailed the monarch's high estate.
(Ah, let us mourn! – for never morrow
    Shall dawn upon him desolate!)
And round about his home, the glory
    That blushed and bloomed
Is but a dim-remembered story
    Of the old time entombed.

And travellers, now, within that valley,
    Through the red-litten windows see
Vast forms, that move fantastically
    To a discordant melody,
While, lie a ghastly rapid river,
    Through the pale door
A hideous throng rush out for ever
    And laugh – but smile no more.

An Unpublished Drama

I

Rome – A Hall in a Palace. ALESSANDRA *and* CASTIGLIONE.

ALESSANDRA
Thou art sad, Castiglione.

CASTIGLIONE
Sad! – not I.
Oh, I'm the happiest, happiest man in Rome!
A few days more, thou knowest, my Alessandra,
Will make thee mine. Oh, I am very happy!

ALESSANDRA
Methinks thou hast a singular way of showing
Thy happiness! – what ails thee, cousin of mine?
Why didst thou sigh so deeply?

CASTIGLIONE
Did I sigh?
I was not conscious of it. It is a fashion,
A silly – a most silly fashion I have
When I am *very* happy. Did I sigh? (*sighing*)

ALESSANDRA
Thou didst. Thou art not well. Thou hast indulged
Too much of late, and I am vexed to see it.
Late hours and wine, Castiglione, – these
Will ruin thee! thou art already altered –
Thy looks are haggard – nothing so wears away
The constitution as late hours and wine.

CASTIGLIONE
(*musing*) Nothing, fair cousin, nothing – not even deep sorrow –
Wears it away like evil hours and wine.
I will amend.

ALESSANDRA
Do it! I would have thee drop
Thy riotous company, too – fellows low born –
Ill suit the like with old Di Broglio's heir
And Alessandra's husband.

CASTIGLIONE
I will drop them.

ALESSANDRA
Thou wilt – thou must. Attend thou also more
To thy dress and equipage – they are over plain
For thy lofty rank and fashion – much depends
Upon appearances.

CASTIGLIONE
I'll see to it.

ALESSANDRA

Then see to it! – pay more attention, sir,
To a becoming carriage – much thou wantest
In dignity.

CASTIGLIONE

Much, much, oh much I want
In proper dignity.

ALESSANDRA

(*haughtily*) Thou mockest me, sir!

CASTIGLIONE

(*abstractedly*) Sweet, gentle Lalage!

ALESSANDRA

Heard I aright?
I speak to him – he speaks of Lalage!
Sir Count! (*places her hand on his shoulder*) what art thou dreaming? he's not well!
What ails thee, sir?

CASTIGLIONE

(*starting*) Cousin! fair cousin! – madam!
I crave thy pardon – indeed I am not well –
Your hand from off my shoulder, if you please.
This air is most oppressive! – Madam – the Duke!

Enter DI BROGLIO.

DI BROGLIO

My son, I've news for thee! – hey? – what 's the matter? (*observing* ALESSANDRA)
I' the pouts? Kiss her, Castiglione! kiss her,
You dog! and make it up, I say, this minute!
I've news for you both. Politian is expected
Hourly in Rome – Politian, Earl of Leicester!
We'll have him at the wedding. 'T is his first visit
To the imperial city.

ALESSANDRA

What! Politian
Of Britain, Earl of Leicester?

DI BROGLIO

The same, my love.
We'll have him at the wedding. A man quite young
In years, but grey in fame. I have not seen him,
But Rumour speaks of him as of a prodigy
Pre-eminent in arts and arms, and wealth,
And high descent. We'll have him at the wedding.

ALESSANDRA

I have heard much of this Politian.
Gay, volatile and giddy – is he not?
And little given to thinking.

DI BROGLIO

Far from it, love.
No branch, they say, of all philosophy
So deep abstruse he has not mastered it.
Learned as few are learned.

ALESSANDRA

'T is very strange!
I have known men have seen Politian
And sought his company. They speak of him
As of one who entered madly into life,
Drinking the cup of pleasure to the dregs.

CASTIGLIONE

Ridiculous! Now *I* have seen Politian
And know him well – nor learned nor mirthful he.
He is a dreamer and a man shut out
From common passions.

DI BROGLIO

Children, we disagree.
Let us go forth and taste the fragrant air
Of the garden. Did I dream, or did I hear
Politian was *a melancholy* man?

(*exeunt*)

II

A Lady's apartment, with a window open and looking into a garden. Lalage, in deep mourning, reading at a table on which lie some books and a hand mirror. In the back ground JACINTA *(a servant maid) leans carelessly upon a chair.*

LALAGE

Jacinta! is it thou?

JACINTA

(*pertly*) Yes, Ma'am, I'm here.

LALAGE

I did not know, Jacinta, you were in waiting.
Sit down! – let not my presence trouble you –
Sit down! – for I am humble, most humble.

JACINTA

(*aside*) 'T is time.

(JACINTA *seats herself in a side-long manner upon the chair, resting her elbows upon the back, and regarding her mistress with a contemptuous look.* LALAGE *continues to read*)

LALAGE

'It in another climate, so he said,
'Bore a bright golden flower, but not i' this soil!'
(*pauses – turns over some leaves, and resumes*)
'No lingering winters there, nor snow, nor shower –
'But Ocean ever to refresh mankind
'Breathes the shrill spirit of the western wind.'
Oh, beautiful! – most beautiful! – how like
To what my fevered soul doth dream of Heaven!
O happy land! (*pauses*) She died! – the maiden died!
O still more happy maiden who couldst die!
Jacinta!
(JACINTA *returns no answer, and Lalage presently resumes*)
Again! – a similar tale
Told of a beauteous dame beyond the sea!
Thus speaketh one Ferdinand in the words of the play –
'She died full young' – one Bossola answers him –
'I think not so – her infelicity
'Seemed to have years too many' – Ah luckless lady!
Jacinta! (*still no answer*)
Here's a far sterner story
But like – oh, very like in its despair –
Of that Egyptian queen, winning so easily
A thousand hearts – losing at length her own.
She died. Thus endeth the history – and her maids
Lean over her and weep – two gentle maids
With gentle names – Eiros and Charmion!
Rainbow and Dove! – Jacinta!

JACINTA

(*pettishly*) Madam, what is it?

LALAGE

Wilt thou, my good Jacinta, be so kind
As go down in the library and bring me
The Holy Evangelists.

JACINTA

Pshaw! (*exit*)

LALAGE

If there be balm
For the wounded spirit in Gilead it is there!
Dew in the night time of my bitter trouble
Will there be found – 'dew sweeter far than that
Which hangs like chains of pearl on Hermon Hill.'
(*re-enter* JACINTA, *and throws a volume on the table*)
There, ma'am, 's the book. Indeed she is very troublesome. (*aside*)

LALAGE

(*astonished*) What didst thou say, Jacinta?
Have I done aught
To grieve thee or to vex thee? – I am sorry.
For thou hast served me long and ever been
Trust-worthy and respectful. (*resumes her reading*)

JACINTA

I can't believe
She has any more jewels – no – no – she gave me all. (*aside*)

LALAGE

What didst thou say, Jacinta? Now I bethink me
Thou hast not spoken lately of thy wedding.
How fares good Ugo? – and when is it to be?
Can I do aught? – is there no farther aid
Thou needest, Jacinta?

JACINTA

Is there no *farther* aid!
That's meant for me. (*aside*) I'm sure, Madam, you need not
Be always throwing those jewels in my teeth.

LALAGE

Jewels! Jacinta, – now indeed, Jacinta,
I thought not of the jewels.

JACINTA

Oh! perhaps not!
But then I might have sworn it. After all,
There's Ugo says the ring is only paste,
For he's sure the Count Castiglione never
Would have given a real diamond to such as you;
And at the best I 'm certain, Madam, you cannot
Have use for jewels *now*. But I might have sworn it.
(*exit*)

(LALAGE *bursts into tears and leans her head upon the table – after a short pause raises it*)

LALAGE

Poor Lalage! – and is it come to this?
Thy servant maid! – but courage! – 't is but a viper
Whom thou hast cherished to sting thee to the soul!
(*taking up the mirror*)
Ha! here at least 's a friend – too much a friend
In earlier days – a friend will not deceive thee.
Fair mirror and true! now tell me (for thou canst)
A tale – a pretty tale – and heed thou not
Though it be rife with woe. It answers me.
It speaks of sunken eyes, and wasted cheeks,
And Beauty long deceased – remembers me
Of joy departed – Hope, the Seraph Hope,
Inurned and entombed! – now, in a tone
Low, sad, and solemn, but most audible,
Whispers of early grave untimely yawning
For ruined maid. Fair mirror and true! – thou liest not!
Thou hast no end to gain – no heart to break –

Castiglione lied who said he loved –
Thou true – he false! – false! – false!

(*while she speaks, a monk enters her apartment, and approaches unobserved*)

MONK

Refuge thou hast,
Sweet daughter! in Heaven. Think of eternal things!
Give up thy soul to penitence, and pray!

LALAGE

(*arising hurriedly*) I *cannot* pray! – My soul is at war with God!
The frightful sounds of merriment below
Disturb my senses – go! I cannot pray –
The sweet airs from the garden worry me!
Thy presence grieves me – go! – thy priestly raiment
Fills me with dread – thy ebony crucifix
With horror and awe!

MONK

Think of thy precious soul!

LALAGE

Think of my early days! – think of my father
And mother in Heaven! think of our quiet home,
And the rivulet that ran before the door!
Think of my little sisters! – think of them!
And think of me! – think of my trusting love
And confidence – his vows – my ruin – think – think
Of my unspeakable misery! – begone!
Yet stay! yet stay! – what was it thou saidst of prayer
And penitence? Didst thou not speak of faith
And vows before the throne?

MONK

I did.

LALAGE

'T is well.
There is a vow were fitting should be made –
A sacred vow, imperative, and urgent,
A solemn vow!

MONK

Daughter, this zeal is well!

LALAGE

Father, this zeal is anything but well!
Hast thou a crucifix fit for this thing?
A crucifix whereon to register
This sacred vow? (*he hands her his own*)
Not that – Oh! no! – no! – no! (*shuddering*)
Not that! Not that! – I tell thee, holy man.
Thy raiments and thy ebony cross affright me!

Stand back! I have a crucifix myself, –
I have a crucifix! Methinks 't were fitting
The deed – the vow – the symbol of the deed –
And the deed's register should tally, father!
(*draws a cross-handled dagger and raises it on high*)
Behold the cross wherewith a vow like mine
Is written in Heaven!

MONK

Thy words are madness, daughter,
And speak a purpose unholy – thy lips are livid –
Thine eyes are wild – tempt not the wrath divine!
Pause ere too late! – oh be not – be not rash!
Swear not the oath – oh swear it not!

LALAGE

'T is sworn!

III

An apartment in a palace. POLITIAN *and* BALDAZZAR.

BALDAZZAR

– Arouse thee now, Politian!
Thou must not – nay indeed, indeed, thou shalt not
Give way unto these humours. Be thyself!
Shake off the idle fancies that beset thee,
And live, for now thou diest!

POLITIAN

Not so, Baldazzar!
Surely I live.

BALDAZZAR

Politian, it doth grieve me
To see thee thus.

POLITIAN

Baldazzar, it doth grieve me
To give thee cause for grief, my honoured friend.
Command me, sir! what wouldst thou have me do?
At thy behest I will shake off that nature
Which from my forefathers I did inherit,
Which with my mother's milk I did imbibe,
And be no more Politian, but some other.
Command me, sir!

BALDAZZAR

To the field then – to the field –
To the senate or the field.

POLITIAN

Alas! alas!
There is an imp would follow me even there!
There is an imp *hath* followed me even there!
There is – what voice was that?

BALDAZZAR

I heard it not.
I heard not any voice except thine own,
And the echo of thine own.

POLITIAN

Then I but dreamed.

BALDAZZAR

Give not thy soul to dreams: the camp – the court
Befit thee – Fame awaits thee – Glory calls –
And her the trumpet-tongued thou wilt not hear
In hearkening to imaginary sounds
And phantom voices.

POLITIAN

It is a phantom voice!
Didst thou not hear it *then?*

BALDAZZAR

I heard it not.

POLITIAN

Thou heardst it not! – Baldazzar, speak no more
To me, Politian, of thy camps and courts.
Oh! I am sick, sick, sick, even unto death,
Of the hollow and high-sounding vanities
Of the populous Earth! Bear with me yet awhile!
We have been boys together – school-fellows –
And now are friends – yet shall not be so long –
For in the eternal city thou shalt do me
A kind and gentle office, and a Power –
A Power August, benignant and supreme –
Shall then absolve thee of all farther duties
Unto thy friend.

BALDAZZAR

Thou speakest a fearful riddle
I *will* not understand.

POLITIAN

Yet now as Fate
Approaches, and the Hours are breathing low,
The sands of Time are changed to golden grains,
And dazzle me, Baldazzar. Alas! alas!
I *cannot* die, having within my heart
So keen a relish for the beautiful
As hath been kindled within it. Methinks the air
Is balmier now than it was wont to be –
Rich melodies are floating in the winds –
A rarer loveliness bedecks the earth –

And with a holier lustre the quiet moon
Sitteth in Heaven. – Hist! hist! thou canst not say
Thou hearest not *now*, Baldazzar?

BALDAZZAR

Indeed I hear not.

POLITIAN

Not hear it! – listen now – listen! – the faintest sound
And yet the sweetest that ear ever heard!
A lady's voice! – and sorrow in the tone!
Baldazzar, it oppresses me like a spell!
Again! – again! – how solemnly it falls
Into my heart of hearts! that eloquent voice
Surely I never heard – yet it were well
Had I *but* heard it with its thrilling tones
In earlier days!

BALDAZZAR

I myself hear it now.
Be still! – the voice, if I mistake not greatly,
Proceeds from yonder lattice – which you may see
Very plainly through the window – it belongs,
Does it not? unto this palace of the Duke.
The singer is undoubtedly beneath
The roof of his Excellency – and perhaps
Is even that Alessandra of whom he spoke
As the betrothed of Castiglione,
His son and heir.

POLITIAN

Be still! – it comes again!

VOICE

(*very faintly*) 'And is thy heart so strong
As for to leave me thus
Who hath loved thee so long
In wealth and wo among?
And is thy heart so strong
As for to leave me thus?
Say nay – say nay!'

BALDAZZAR

The song is English, and I oft have heard it
In merry England – never so plaintively –
Hist! hist! it comes again!

VOICE

(*more loudly*) 'Is it so strong
As for to leave me thus
Who hath loved thee so long
In wealth and wo among?
And is thy heart so strong
As for to leave me thus?
Say nay – say nay!'

BALDAZZAR

'T is hushed and all is still!

POLITIAN

All *is not* still.

BALDAZZAR

Let us go down.

POLITIAN

Go down, Baldazzar, go!

BALDAZZAR

The hour is growing late – the Duke awaits us, –
Thy presence is expected in the hall
Below. What ails thee, Earl Politian?

VOICE

(*distinctly*) 'Who hath loved thee so long,
In wealth and wo among,
And is thy heart so strong?
Say nay – say nay!'

BALDAZZAR

Let us descend! – 't is time. Politian, give
These fancies to the wind. Remember, pray,
Your bearing lately savoured much of rudeness
Unto the Duke. Arouse thee! and remember!

POLITIAN

Remember? I do. Lead on! I *do* remember.
(*going*)
Let us descend. Believe me I would give,
Freely would give the broad lands of my earldom
To look upon the face hidden by yon lattice –
'To gaze upon that veiled face, and hear
Once more that silent tongue.'

BALDAZZAR

Let me beg you, sir,
Descend with me – the Duke may be offended.
Let us go down, I pray you.
(*Voice loudly*) *Say nay! – say nay!*

POLITIAN

(*aside*) 'T is strange! – 't is very strange – methought the voice
Chimed in with my desires and bade me stay!
(*approaching the window*)
Sweet voice! I heed thee, and will surely stay.
Now be this Fancy, by Heaven, or be it Fate,
Still will I not descend. Baldazzar, make
Apology unto the Duke for me;
I go not down to-night.

BALDAZZAR

Your lordship's pleasure
Shall be attended to. Good night, Politian.

POLITIAN

Good night, my friend, good night.

IV

The gardens of a palace – Moonlight. LALAGE *and* POLITAN

LALAGE

And dost thou speak of love
To *me*, Politian? – dost thou speak of love
To Lalage? – ah wo – ah wo is me!
This mockery is most cruel – most cruel indeed!

POLITIAN

Weep not! oh, sob not thus! – thy bitter tears
Will madden me. Oh mourn not, Lalage –
Be comforted! I know – I know it all,
And *still I* speak of love. Look at me, brightest,
And beautiful Lalage! – turn here thine eyes!
Thou askest me if I could speak of love,
Knowing what I know, and seeing what I have seen.
Thou askest me that – and thus I answer thee –
Thus on my bended knee I answer thee. (*kneeling*)
Sweet Lalage, *I love thee – love thee – love thee;*
Thro' good and ill – thro' weal and wo I *love thee.*
Not mother, with her first born on her knee,
Thrills with intenser love than I for thee.
Not on God's altar, in any time or clime,
Burned there a holier fire than burneth now
Within my spirit for *thee*. And do I love? (*arising*)
Even for thy woes I love thee – even for thy woes –
Thy beauty and thy woes.

LALAGE

Alas, proud Earl,
Thou dost forget thyself, remembering me!
How, in thy father's halls, among the maidens
Pure and reproachless of thy princely line,
Could the dishonoured Lalage abide?
Thy wife, and with a tainted memory –
My seared and blighted name, how would it tally
With the ancestral honours of thy house,
And with thy glory?

POLITIAN

Speak not to me of glory!
I hate – I loathe the name; I do abhor
The unsatisfactory and ideal thing.
Art thou not Lalage and I Politian?
Do I not love – art thou not beautiful –
What need we more? Ha! glory! – now speak not of it!
By all I hold most sacred and most solemn –
By all my wishes now – my fears hereafter –
By all I scorn on earth and hope in heaven –
There is no deed I would more glory in,
Than in thy cause to scoff at this same glory
And trample it under foot. What matters it –
What matters it, my fairest, and my best,
That we go down unhonoured and forgotten
Into the dust – so we descend together.
Descend together – and then – and then perchance –

LALAGE

Why dost thou pause, Politian?

POLITIAN

And then perchance
Arise together, Lalage, and roam
The starry and quiet dwellings of the blest,
And still –

LALAGE

Why dost thou pause, Politian?

POLITIAN

And still *together – together.*

LALAGE

Now Earl of Leicester!
Thou *lovest* me, and in my heart of hearts
I feel thou lovest me truly.

POLITIAN

Oh, Lalage! (*throwing himself upon his knee*)
And lovest thou *me?*

LALAGE

Hist! hush! within the gloom
Of yonder trees methought a figure past –
A spectral figure, solemn, and slow, and noiseless –
Like the grim shadow Conscience, solemn and noiseless. (*walks across and returns*)
I was mistaken – 't was but a giant bough
Stirred by the autumn wind. Politian!

POLITIAN

My Lalage – my love! why art thou moved?
Why dost thou turn so pale? Not Conscience' self,
Far less a shadow which thou likenest to it,

Should shake the firm spirit thus. But the night wind
Is chilly – and these melancholy boughs
Throw over all things a gloom.

LALAGE

Politian!
Thou speakest to me of love. Knowest thou the land
With which all tongues are busy – a land new found –
Miraculously found by one of Genoa –
A thousand leagues within the golden west?
A fairy land of flowers, and fruit, and sunshine,
And crystal lakes, and over-arching forests,
And mountains, around whose towering summits the winds
Of Heaven untrammelled flow – which air to breathe
Is Happiness now, and will be Freedom hereafter
In days that are to come?

POLITIAN

O, wilt thou – wilt thou
Fly to that Paradise – my Lalage, wilt thou
Fly thither with me? There Care shall be forgotten,
And Sorrow shall be no more, and Eros be all.
And life shall then be mine, for I will live
For thee, and in thine eyes – and thou shalt be
No more a mourner – but the radiant Joys
Shall wait upon thee, and the angel Hope
Attend thee ever; and I will kneel to thee
And worship thee, and call thee my beloved,
My own, my beautiful, my love, my wife,
My all; – oh, wilt thou – wilt thou, Lalage,
Fly thither with me?

LALAGE

A deed is to be done –
Castiglione lives!

POLITIAN

And he shall die! (*exit*)

LALAGE

(*after a pause*) And – he – shall – die! alas!
Castiglione die? Who spoke the words?
Where am I? – what was it he said? – Politian!
Thou *art* not gone – thou art not *gone*, Politian!
I *feel* thou art not gone – yet dare not look,
Lest I behold thee not; thou *couldst* not go
With those words upon thy lips – O, speak to me!
And let me hear thy voice – one word – one word,
To say thou art not gone, – one little sentence,
To say how thou dost scorn – how thou dost hate
My womanly weakness. Ha! ha! thou *art* not gone –
O speak to me! I *knew* thou wouldst not go!
I knew thou wouldst not, couldst not, *durst* not go.
Villain, thou *art* not gone – thou mockest me!
And thus I clutch thee – thus! – He is gone, he is gone –
Gone – gone. Where am I? – 't is well – 't is very well!
So that the blade be keen – the blow be sure,
'T is well, 't is *very* well – alas! alas! (*exit*)

V

The suburbs. Politian alone.

POLITIAN

This weakness grows upon me. I am faint,
And much I fear me ill – it will not do
To die ere I have lived! Stay – stay thy hand,
O Azrael, yet awhile! – Prince of the Powers
Of Darkness and the Tomb, O pity me!
O pity me! let me not perish now,
In the budding of my Paradisal Hope!
Give me to live yet – yet a little while:
'T is I who pray for life – I who so late
Demanded but to die! – what sayeth the Count?

Enter BALDAZZAR.

BALDAZZAR

That knowing no cause of quarrel or of feud
Between the Earl Politian and himself,
He doth decline your cartel.

POLITIAN

What didst thou say?
What answer was it you brought me, good Baldazzar?
With what excessive fragrance the zephyr comes
Laden from yonder bowers! – a fairer day,
Or one more worthy Italy, methinks
No mortal eyes have seen! – *what* said the Count?

BALDAZZAR

That he, Castiglione, not being aware
Of any feud existing, or any cause
Of quarrel between your lordship and himself
Cannot accept the challenge.

POLITIAN

It is most true –
All this is very true. When saw you, sir,
When saw you now, Baldazzar, in the frigid
Ungenial Britain which we left so lately,
A heaven so calm as this – so utterly free
From the evil taint of clouds? – and he did *say*?

BALDAZZAR

No more, my lord, than I have told you, sir:
The Count Castiglione will not fight,
Having no cause for quarrel.

POLITIAN

Now this is true –
All very true. Thou art my friend, Baldazzar,
And I have not forgotten it – thou 'lt do me
A piece of service; wilt thou go back and say
Unto this man, that I, the Earl of Leicester,
Hold him a villain? – thus much, I prythee, say
Unto the Count – it is exceeding just
He should have cause for quarrel.

BALDAZZAR

My lord! – my friend! –

POLITIAN

(*aside*) 'T is he – he comes himself! (*aloud*) thou reasonest well.
I know what thou wouldst say – not send the message –
Well! – I will think of it – I will not send it.
Now prythee, leave me – hither doth come a person
With whom affairs of a most private nature
I would adjust.

BALDAZZAR

I go – to-morrow we meet,
Do we not? – at the Vatican.

POLITIAN

At the Vatican.

(*exit* BAL)

Enter CASTIGLIONE.

CASTIGLIONE

The Earl of Leicester here!

POLITIAN

I *am* the Earl of Leicester, and thou seest,
Dost thou not? that I am here.

CASTIGLIONE

My lord, some strange,
Some singular mistake – misunderstanding –
Hath without doubt arisen: thou hast been urged
Thereby, in heat of anger, to address
Some words most unaccountable, in writing,
To me, Castiglione; the bearer being
Baldazzar, Duke of Surrey. I am aware
Of nothing which might warrant thee in this thing,
Having given thee no offence. Ha! – am I right?
'T was a mistake? – undoubtedly – we all
Do err at times.

POLITIAN

Draw, villain, and prate no more!

CASTIGLIONE

Ha! – draw? – and villain? have at thee then at once,
Proud Earl!
(*draws*)

POLITIAN

(*drawing*) Thus to the expiatory tomb,
Untimely sepulchre, I do devote thee
In the name of Lalage!

CASTIGLIONE

(*letting fall his sword and recoiling to the extremity of the stage*)
Of Lalage!
Hold off – thy sacred hand! – avaunt I say!
Avaunt – I will not fight thee – indeed I dare not.

POLITIAN

Thou wilt not fight with me didst say, Sir Count?
Shall I be baffled thus? – now this is well;
Didst say thou *darest* not? Ha!

CASTIGLIONE

I dare not – dare not –
Hold off thy hand – with that beloved name
So fresh upon thy lips I will not fight thee –
I cannot – dare not.

POLITIAN

Now by my halidom
I do believe thee! – coward, I do believe thee!

CASTIGLIONE

Ha! – coward! – this may not be!

(*clutches his sword and staggers towards* POLITIAN, *but his purpose is changed before reaching him, and he falls upon his knee at the feet of the Earl*)

Alas! my lord,
It is – it is – most true. In such a cause
I am the veriest coward. O pity me!

POLITIAN

(*greatly softened*) Alas! – I do – indeed I pity thee.

CASTIGLIONE

And Lalage

POLITIAN

Scoundrel! – arise and die!

CASTIGLIONE

It needeth not be – thus – thus – O let me die
Thus on my bended knee. It were most fitting
That in this deep humiliation I perish.
For in the fight I will not raise a hand

Against thee, Earl of Leicester. Strike thou home – (*baring his bosom*)
Here is no let or hindrance to thy weapon –
Strike home. I *will not* fight thee.

POLITIAN

Now's Death and Hell!
Am I not – am I not sorely – grievously tempted
To take thee at thy word? But mark me, sir!
Think not to fly me thus. Do thou prepare
For public insult in the streets – before
The eyes of the citizens. I'll follow thee –
Like an avenging spirit I'll follow thee
Even unto death. Before those whom thou lovest –
Before all Rome I'll taunt thee, villain, – I'll taunt thee,
Dost hear? with *cowardice* – thou *will not* fight me?
Thou liest! thou *shalt!*
(*exit*)

CASTIGLIONE

Now this indeed is just!
Most righteous, and most just, avenging Heaven!

THE BELLS
W.H. ROBINSON

Later Poems

The Bells

1

Hear the sledges with the bells –
Silver bells!
What a world of merriment their melody foretells!
How they tinkle, tinkle, tinkle,
In the icy air of night!
While the stars that oversprinkle
All the heavens seem to twinkle
With a crystalline delight;
Keeping time, time, time,
In a sort of Runic rhyme,
To the tintinnabulation that so musically wells
From the bells, bells, bells, bells,
Bells, bells, bells –
From the jingling and the tinkling of the bells.

2

Hear the mellow wedding bells
Golden bells!
What a world of happiness their harmony foretells!
Through the balmy air of night
How they ring out their delight!
From the molten-golden notes,
And all in tune,
What a liquid ditty floats
To the turtledove that listens, while she gloats
On the moon!
Oh, from out the sounding cells,
What a gush of euphony voluminously wells!
How it swells!
How it dwells
On the Future! – how it tells
Of the rapture that impels
To the swinging and the ringing
Of the bells, bells, bells,
Of the bells, bells, bells, bells,
Bells, bells, bells –
To the rhyming and the chiming of the bells!

3

Hear the loud alarum bells –
Brazen bells!
What tale of terror, now, their turbulency tells!
In the startled ear of night
How they scream out their affright!
Too much horrified to speak,
They can only shriek, shriek,
Out of tune,
In a clamorous appealing to the mercy of the fire,
In a mad expostulation with the deaf and frantic fire,
Leaping higher, higher, higher,
With a desperate desire,
And a resolute endeavour
Now – now to sit, or never,
By the side of the pale-faced moon.
Oh, the bells, bells, bells!
What a tale their terror tells
Of Despair!
How they clang, and clash, and roar!
What a horror they outpour
On the bosom of the palpitating air!
Yet the ear it fully knows,

By the twanging,
And the clanging,
How the danger ebbs and flows;
Yet the ear distinctly tells,
In the jangling
And the wrangling,
How the danger sinks and swells,
By the sinking or the swelling in the anger of the bells –
Of the bells –
Of the bells, bells, bells, bells,
Bells, bells, bells –
In the clamour and the clangour of the bells!

4

Hear the tolling of the bells –
Iron bells!
What a world of solemn thought their melody compels!
In the silence of the night,
How we shiver with affright
At the melancholy meaning of their tone!
For every sound that floats
From the rust within their throats
Is a groan.
And the people – ah, the people –
They that dwell up in the steeple,
All alone,

And who, tolling, tolling, tolling,
In that muffled monotone,
Feel a glory in so rolling
On the human heart a stone –
They are neither man nor woman –
They are neither brute nor human –
They are Ghouls:
And their king it is who tolls;
And he rolls, rolls, rolls,
Rolls
A paean from the bells!
And his merry bosom swells
With the paean of the bells!
And he dances, and he yells;
Keeping time, time, time,
In a sort of Runic rhyme,
To the paean of the bells –
Of the bells:
Keeping time, time, time,
In a sort of Runic rhyme,
To the throbbing of the bells –
Of the bells, bells, bells –
To the sobbing of the bells;
Keeping time, time, time,
As he knells, knells, knells,
In a happy Runic rhyme,
To the rolling of the bells –
Of the bells, bells, bells –
To the tolling of the bells,
Of the bells, bells, bells, bells –
Bells, bells, bells –
To the moaning and the groaning of the bells.

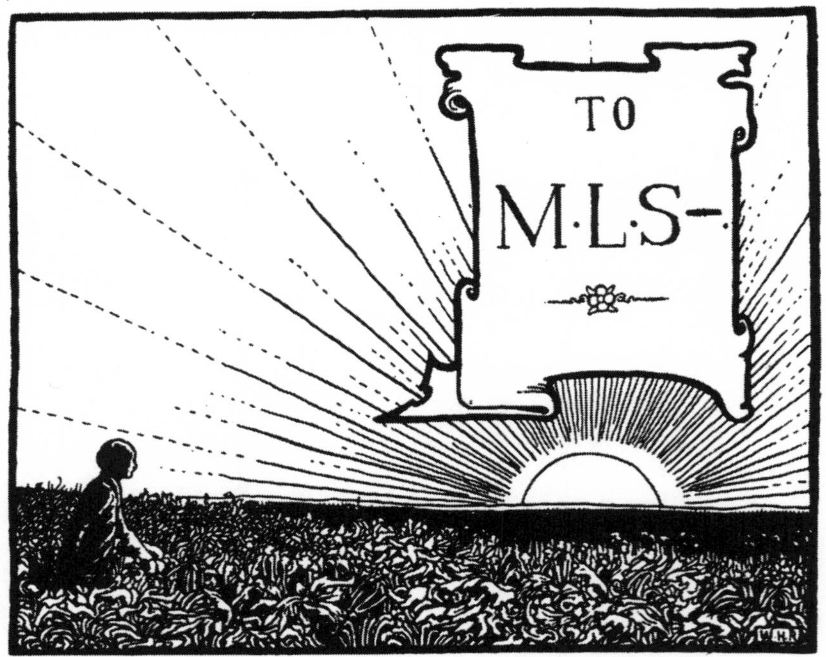

Of all who hail thy presence as the morning –
Of all to whom thine absence is the night –
The blotting utterly from out high heaven
The sacred sun – of all who, weeping, bless thee
Hourly for hope – for life – ah, above all,
For the resurrection of deep-buried faith
In truth, in virtue, in humanity –
Of all who, on despair's unhallowed bed
Lying down to die, have suddenly arisen
At thy soft-murmured words, 'Let there be light!'
At the soft-murmured words that were fulfilled
In the seraphic glancing of thine eyes –
Of all who owe thee most, whose gratitude
Nearest resembles worship, – oh, remember
The truest, the most fervently devoted,
And think that these weak lines are written by him –
By him, who, as he pens them, thrills to think
His spirit is communing with an angel's.

To——

Not long ago, the writer of these lines,
In the mad pride of intellectuality,
Maintained 'the power of words' – denied that ever
A thought arose within the human brain
Beyond the utterance of the human tongue:
And now, as if in mockery of that boast,
Two words – two foreign soft dissyllables –
Italian tones, made only to be murmured
By angels dreaming in the moonlit 'dew
That hangs like chains of pearl on Hermon hill' –
Have stirred from out the abysses of his heart,
Unthought-like thoughts that are the souls of thought,
Richer, far wilder, far diviner visions
Than even the seraph harper, Israfel
(Who has 'the sweetest voice of all God's creatures'),
Could hope to utter. And I! my spells are broken.
The pen falls powerless from my shivering hand.
With thy dear name as text, though bidden by thee,
I cannot write – I cannot speak or think –
Alas, I cannot feel; for 'tis not feeling,
This standing motionless upon the golden
Threshold of the wide-open gate of dreams,
Gazing, entranced, adown the gorgeous vista,
And thrilling as I see, upon the right,
Upon the left, and all the way along,
Amid unpurpled vapours, far away
To where the prospect terminates – thee only.

'Seldom we find,' says Solomon Don Dunce,
'Half an idea in the profoundest sonnet.
Through all the flimsy things we see at once
As easily as through a Naples bonnet –
Trash of all trash! – how can a lady don it?
Yet heavier far than your Petrarchan stuff–
Owl-downy nonsense that the faintest puff
Twirls into trunk-paper the while you con it.'
And, veritably, Sol is right enough.
The general tuckermanities are arrant
Bubbles – ephemeral and so transparent –
But this is, now – you may depend upon it –
Stable, opaque, immortal – all by dint
Of the dear names that lie concealed within 't.

I saw thee once – once only – years ago;
I must not say how many – but not many.
It was a July midnight; and from out
A full-orbed moon, that, like thine own soul, soaring,
Sought a precipitate pathway up through heaven,
There fell a silvery-silken veil of light,
With quietude, and sultriness, and slumber,
Upon the upturn'd faces of a thousand
Roses that grew in an enchanted garden,
Where no wind dared to stir, unless on tiptoe –
Fell on the upturn'd faces of these roses
That gave out, in return for the love-light,
Their odorous souls in an ecstatic death –
Fell on the upturn'd faces of these roses
That smiled and died in this parterre, enchanted
By thee, and by the poetry of thy presence.

Clad all in white, upon a violet bank
I saw thee half reclining; while the moon
Fell on the upturn'd faces of the roses,
And on thine own, upturn'd – alas, in sorrow!

Was it not Fate that, on this July midnight –
Was it not Fate (whose name is also Sorrow),
That bade me pause before that garden-gate,
To breathe the incense of those slumbering roses?
No footsteps stirred; the hated world all slept,
Save only thee and me. (Oh, Heaven! – oh, God!
How my heart beats in coupling those two words!)
Save only thee and me. I paused – I looked –
And in an instant all things disappeared.
(Ah, bear in mind this garden was enchanted!)
The pearly lustre of the moon went out;
The mossy banks and the meandering paths,
The happy flowers and the repining trees,
Were seen no more: the very roses' odours
Died in the arms of the adoring airs.
All – all expired save thee – save less than thou:
Save only the divine light in thine eyes –
Save but the soul in thine uplifted eyes.
I saw but them – they were the world to me.
I saw but them – saw only them for hours –
Saw only them until the moon went down.
What wild heart-histories seemed to lie enwritten
Upon those crystalline, celestial spheres!
How dark a woe, yet how sublime a hope!
How silently serene a sea of pride!
How daring an ambition; yet how deep –
How fathomless a capacity for love!

But now, at length, dear Dian sank from sight,
Into a western couch of thunder-cloud;
And thou, a ghost, amid the entombing trees
Didst glide away. Only thine eyes remained.

They would not go – they never yet have gone.
Lighting my lonely pathway home that night,
They have not left me (as my hopes have) since;
They follow me – they lead me through the years.
They are my ministers – yet I their slave.
Their office is to illumine and enkindle –
My duty, to be saved by their bright light,
And purified in their electric fire,
And sanctified in their Elysian fire.
They fill my soul with Beauty (which is Hope),
And are far up in Heaven – the stars I kneel to
In the sad, silent watches of my night;
While even in the meridian glare of day
I see them still – two sweetly scintillant
Venuses, unextinguished by the sun!

A Valentine

For her this rhyme is penned, whose luminous eyes,
Brightly expressive as the twins of Lœda,
Shall find her own sweet name, that, nestling lies
Upon the page, enwrapped from every reader.
Search narrowly the lines! – they hold a treasure
Divine – a talisman – an amulet
That must be worn at heart. Search well the measure –
The words – the syllables! Do not forget
The trivialest point, or you may lose your labour!
And yet there is in this no Gordian knot
Which one might not undo without a sabre,
If one could merely comprehend the plot.
Enwritten upon the leaf where now are peering
Eyes' scintillating soul, there lie perdus
Three eloquent words oft uttered in the hearing
Of poets, by poets – as the name is a poet's too.
Its letters, although naturally lying
Like the knight Pinto – Mendez Ferdinando –
Still form a synonym for Truth. Cease trying!
You will not read the riddle, though you do the best you can do.

Thank Heaven! the crisis –
The danger is past,
And the lingering illness
Is over at last –
And the fever called 'Living'
Is conquered at last.

Sadly, I know
I am shorn of my strength,
And no muscle I move
As I lie at full length –
But no matter! – I feel
I am better at length.

And I rest so composed,
Now, in my bed,
That any beholder
Might fancy me dead –
Might start at beholding me,
Thinking me dead.

The moaning and groaning,
The sighing and sobbing,
Are quieted now,
With that horrible throbbing
At heart: ah, that horrible,
Horrible throbbing!
The sickness – the nausea –
The pitiless pain –
Have ceased, with the fever
That maddened my brain –
With the fever called 'Living'
That burned in my brain.

And oh! of all tortures
That torture the worst
Has abated – the terrible
Torture of thirst
For the naphthaline river
Of Passion accurst:
I have drank of a water
That quenches all thirst:

Of a water that flows,
With a lullaby sound,
From a spring but a very few
Feet under ground –
From a cavern not very far
Down under ground.

And ah! let it never
Be foolishly said
That my room it is gloomy
And narrow my bed;
For man never slept
In a different bed –
And, to sleep, you must slumber
In just such a bed.

My tantalised spirit
Here blandly reposes,
Forgetting, or never
Regretting, its roses –
Its old agitations
Of myrtles and roses:

For now, while so quietly
Lying, it fancies
A holier odour
About it, of pansies –
A rosemary odour,
Commingled with pansies –
With rue and the beautiful
Puritan pansies.

And so it lies happily,
Bathing in many
A dream of the truth
And the beauty of Annie –
Drowned in a bath
Of the tresses of Annie.

She tenderly kissed me,
  She fondly caressed,
And then I fell gently
  To sleep on her breast –
Deeply to sleep
  From the heaven of her breast.

When the light was extinguished,
  She covered me warm,
And she prayed to the angels
  To keep me from harm –
To the queen of the angels
  To shield me from harm.

And I lie so composedly,
  Now in my bed,
(Knowing her love),
  That you fancy me dead –
And I rest so contentedly,
  Now in my bed,
(With her love at my breast),
  That you fancy me dead –
That you shudder to look at me,
  Thinking me dead:

But my heart it is brighter
  Than all of the many
Stars in the sky,
  For it sparkles with Annie –
It glows with the light
  Of the love of my Annie –
With the thought of the light
  Of the eyes of my Annie.

Because I feel that, in the Heavens above,
  The angels, whispering to one another,
Can find, among their burning terms of love,
  None so devotional as that of 'Mother',
Therefore by that dear name I long have called you –
  You who are more than mother unto me,
And fill my heart of hearts, where Death installed you,
  In setting my Virginia's spirit free.
My mother – my own mother, who died early,
  Was but the mother of myself; but you
Are mother to the one I loved so dearly,
  And thus are dearer than the mother I knew
By that infinity with which my wife
  Was dearer to my soul than its soul-life.

Eldorado

Gaily bedight,
A gallant knight,
In sunshine and in shadow,
Had journeyed long,
Singing a song,
In search of Eldorado.

But he grew old –
This knight so bold –
And o'er his heart a shadow
Fell, as he found
No spot of ground
That looked like Eldorado.

And, as his strength
Failed him at length,
He met a pilgrim shadow –
'Shadow,' said he,
'Where can it be –
This land of Eldorado?'

'Over the Mountains
Of the Moon,
Down the Valley of the Shadow,
Ride, boldly ride,'
The shade replied –
'If you seek for Eldorado!'

It was many and many a year ago,
In a kingdom by the sea,
That a maiden lived whom you may know
By the name of Annabel Lee;
And this maiden she lived with no other thought
Than to love and be loved by me.

I was a child and she was a child,
In this kingdom by the sea,
But we loved with a love that was more than love –
I and my Annabel Lee;
With a love that the wingèd seraphs of Heaven
Coveted her and me.

And this was the reason that, long ago,
In this kingdom by the sea,
A wind blew out of a cloud, chilling
My beautiful Annabel Lee;
So that her high-born kinsmen came
And bore her away from me,
To shut her up in a sepulchre
In this kingdom by the sea.

The angels, not half so happy in Heaven,
Went envying her and me;
Yes! that was the reason (as all men know,
In this kingdom by the sea)
That the wind came out of the cloud by night,
Chilling and killing my Annabel Lee.

But our love it was stronger by far than the love
Of those who were older than we –
Of many far wiser than we –
And neither the angels in Heaven above,
Nor the demons down under the sea,
Can ever dissever my soul from the soul
Of the beautiful Annabel Lee:

For the moon never beams without bringing me dreams
Of the beautiful Annabel Lee;
And the stars never rise but I see the bright eyes
Of the beautiful Annabel Lee;
And so, all the night-tide, I lie down by the side
Of my darling, my darling, my life and my bride,
In her sepulchre there by the sea –
In her tomb by the sounding sea.

ULALUME

Ulalume

The skies they were ashen and sober;
The leaves they were crisped and sere –
The leaves they were withering and sere;
It was night in the lonesome October
Of my most immemorial year;
It was hard by the dim lake of Auber,
In the misty mid region of Weir –
It was down by the dank tarn of Auber,
In the ghoul-haunted woodland of Weir.

Here once, through an alley Titanic,
Of cypress, I roamed with my Soul –
Of cypress, with Psyche, my Soul.
There were days when my heart was volcanic
As the scoriac rivers that roll –
As the lavas that restlessly roll
Their sulphurous currents down Yaanek,
In the ultimate climes of the Pole –
That groan as they roll down Mount Yaanek
In the realms of the Boreal Pole.

Our talk had been serious and sober,
But our thoughts they were palsied and sere –
Our memories were treacherous and sere;
For we knew not the month was October,
And we marked not the night of the year
(Ah, night of all nights in the year!)
We noted not the dim lake of Auber
(Though once we had journeyed down here) –
Remembered not the dank tarn of Auber,
Nor the ghoul-haunted woodland of Weir.

And now, as the night was senescent,
And star-dials pointed to morn –
As the star-dials hinted of morn –
At the end of our path a liquescent
And nebulous lustre was born,
Out of which a miraculous crescent
Arose with a duplicate horn –
Astarte's be-diamonded crescent,
Distinct with its duplicate horn.

And I said: 'She is warmer than Dian:
She rolls through an ether of sighs –
She revels in a region of sighs.
She has seen that the tears are not dry on
These cheeks, where the worm never dies,

And has come past the stars of the Lion,
   To point us the path to the skies –
   To the Lethean peace of the skies –
Come up, in despite of the Lion,
   To shine on us with her bright eyes –
Come up, through the lair of the Lion,
   With love in her luminous eyes.'

But Psyche, uplifting her finger,
   Said: 'Sadly this star I mistrust –
   Her pallor I strangely mistrust –
Oh, hasten! – oh, let us not linger!
   Oh, fly! – let us fly! – for we must.'
In terror she spoke, letting sink her
   Wings till they trailed in the dust –
In agony sobbed, letting sink her
   Plumes till they trailed in the dust –
   Till they sorrowfully trailed in the dust.

I replied: 'This is nothing but dreaming.
   Let us on, by this tremulous light!
   Let us bathe in this crystalline light!
Its Sybillic splendour is beaming
   With Hope and in Beauty tonight –
   See! – it flickers up the sky through the night!
Ah, we safely may trust to its gleaming,
   And be sure it will lead us aright –
We safely may trust to a gleaming
   That cannot but guide us aright,
   Since it flickers up to Heaven through the night.'

Thus I pacified Psyche and kissed her,
   And tempted her out of her gloom –
   And conquered her scruples and gloom;
And we passed to the end of the vista,
   But were stopped by the door of a tomb –
   By the door of a legended tomb;
And I said: 'What is written, sweet sister,
   On the door of this legended tomb?'
   She replied: 'Ulalume – Ulalume –
   'Tis the vault of thy lost Ulalume!'

Then my heart it grew ashen and sober
   As the leaves that were crisped and sere –
   As the leaves that were withering and sere –
And I cried: 'It was surely October
   On this very night of last year,
   That I journeyed – I journeyed down here! –
   That I brought a dread burden down here –
   On this night of all nights in the year,
   Ah, what demon has tempted me here?
Well I know, now, this dim lake of Auber –
   This misty mid region of Weir –
Well I know, now, this dank tarn of Auber,
   This ghoul-haunted woodland of Weir.'
Kind solace in a dying hour!

ULALUME.

POEMS
WRITTEN IN YOUTH
W.H.R.

Tamerlane

Such, father, is not (now) my theme –
I will not madly deem that power
Of Earth may shrive me of the sin
Unearthly pride hath revell'd in –
I have no time to dote or dream:
You call it hope – that fire of fire!
It is but agony of desire:
If I *can* hope – Oh God! I can –
Its fount is holier – more divine –
I would not call thee fool, old man,
But such is not a gift of thine.

Know thou the secret of a spirit
Bow'd from its wild pride into shame.
O yearning heart! I did inherit
Thy withering portion with the fame,
The searing glory which hath shone
Amid the Jewels of my throne,
Halo of Hell! and with a pain
Not hell shall make me fear again –

O craving heart, for the lost flowers
And sunshine of my summer hours!
The undying voice of that dead time,
With its interminable chime,
Rings, in the spirit of a spell,
Upon thy emptiness – a knell.

I have not always been as now:
The fever'd diadem on my brow
I claim'd and won usurpingly –
Hath not the same fierce heirdom given
Rome to the Cæsar – this to me?
The heritage of a kingly mind,
And a proud spirit which hath striven
Triumphantly with human kind.

On mountain soil I first drew life:
The mists of the Taglay have shed
Nightly their dews upon my head,
And, I believe, the winged strife
And tumult of the headlong air
Have nestled in my very hair.

So late from Heaven – that dew – it fell
('Mid dreams of an unholy night)
Upon me with the touch of Hell,
While the red flashing of the light
From clouds that hung, like banners, o'er,
Appeared to my half-closing eye
The pageantry of monarchy,
And the deep trumpet-thunder's roar
Came hurriedly upon me, telling
Of human battle, where my voice,
My own voice, silly child! – was swelling
(O! how my spirit would rejoice,
And leap within me at the cry)
The battle-cry of Victory!

The rain came down upon my head
Unshelter'd – and the heavy wind
Rendered me mad and deaf and blind.
It was but man, I thought, who shed
Laurels upon me: and the rush –

The torrent of the chilly air
Gurgled within my ear the crush
Of empires – with the captive's prayer –
The hum of suitors – and the tone
Of flattery 'round a sovereign's throne.

My passions, from that hapless hour,
Usurp'd a tyranny which men
Have deem'd, since I have reach'd to power,
My innate nature – be it so:
But, father, there liv'd one who, then,
Then – in my boyhood – when their fire
Burn'd with a still intenser glow
(For passion must, with youth, expire)
E'en *then* who knew this iron heart
In woman's weakness had a part.

I have no words – alas! – to tell
The loveliness of loving well!
Nor would I now attempt to trace
The more than beauty of a face
Whose lineaments, upon my mind,
Are – shadows on th' unstable wind:
Thus I remember having dwelt
Some page of early lore upon,
With loitering eye, till I have felt
The letters – with their meaning – melt
To fantasies – with none.

O, she was worthy of all love!
Love – as in infancy was mine –
'T was such as angel minds above
Might envy; her young heart the shrine
On which my every hope and thought
Were incense – then a goodly gift,
For they were childish and upright –
Pure – as her young example taught:
Why did I leave it, and, adrift,
Trust to the fire within, for light?

We grew in age – and love – together –
Roaming the forest, and the wild;
My breast her shield in wintry weather –
And, when the friendly sunshine smil'd,
And she would mark the opening skies,
I saw no Heaven – but in her eyes.

Young Love's first lesson is – the heart:
For 'mid that sunshine, and those smiles,
When, from our little cares apart,

And laughing at her girlish wiles,
I'd throw me on her throbbing breast,
And pour my spirit out in tears –
There was no need to speak the rest –
No need to quiet any fears
Of her – who ask'd no reason why,
But turn'd on me her quiet eye!

Yet *more* than worthy of the love
My spirit struggled with, and strove,
When, on the mountain peak, alone,
Ambition lent it a new tone –
I had no being – but in thee:
The world, and all it did contain
In the earth – the air – the sea –
Its joy – its little lot of pain
That was new pleasure – the ideal,
Dim, vanities of dreams by night –
And dimmer nothings which were real –
(Shadows – and a more shadowy light!)
Parted upon their misty wings,
And, so, confusedly, became
Thine image and – a name – a name!
Two separate – yet most intimate things.

I was ambitious – have you known
The passion, father? You have not:
A cottager, I mark'd a throne
Of half the world as all my own,
And murmur'd at such lowly lot –
But, just like any other dream,
Upon the vapour of the dew
My own had past, did not the beam
Of beauty which did while it thro'
The minute – the hour – the day – oppress
My mind with double loveliness.

We walk'd together on the crown
Of a high mountain which look'd down
Afar from its proud natural towers
Of rock and forest, on the hills –
The dwindled hills! begirt with bowers
And shouting with a thousand rills.

I spoke to her of power and pride,
But mystically – in such guise
That she might deem it nought beside
The moment's converse; in her eyes
I read, perhaps too carelessly –
A mingled feeling with my own –
The flush on her bright cheek, to me
Seem'd to become a queenly throne
Too well that I should let it be
Light in the wilderness alone.

I wrapp'd myself in grandeur then
And donn'd a visionary crown –
Yet it was not that Fantasy
Had thrown her mantle over me –
But that, among the rabble – men,

Lion ambition is chain'd down –
And crouches to a keeper's hand –
Not so in deserts where the grand –
The wild – the terrible conspire
With their own breath to fan his fire.
Look 'round thee now on Samarcand! –
Is she not queen of Earth? her pride
Above all cities? in her hand
Their destinies? in all beside
Of glory which the world hath known
Stands she not nobly and alone?
Falling – her veriest stepping-stone
Shall form the pedestal of a throne –
And who her sovereign? Timour – he
Whom the astonished people saw
Striding o'er empires haughtily
A diadem'd outlaw!

O, human love! thou spirit given,
On Earth, of all we hope in Heaven!
Which fall'st into the soul like rain
Upon the Siroc-wither'd plain,
And, failing in thy power to bless,
But leav'st the heart a wilderness!
Idea! which bindest life around
With music of so strange a sound
And beauty of so wild a birth –
Farewell! for I have won the Earth.

When Hope, the eagle that tower'd, could see
No cliff beyond him in the sky,
His pinions were bent droopingly –
And homeward turn'd his soften'd eye.
'T was sunset: when the sun will part
There comes a sullenness of heart
To him who still would look upon
The glory of the summer sun.
That soul will hate the ev'ning mist
So often lovely, and will list
To the sound of the coming darkness (known
To those whose spirits harken) as one
Who, in a dream of night, *would* fly
But *cannot* from a danger nigh.

What tho' the moon – the white moon
Shed all the splendour of her noon,
Her smile is chilly – and *her* beam,
In that time of dreariness, will seem
(So like you gather in your breath)
A portrait taken after death.

And boyhood is a summer sun
Whose waning is the dreariest one –
For all we live to know is known
And all we seek to keep hath flown –
Let life, then, as the day-flower, fall
With the noon-day beauty – which is all.

I reach'd my home – my home no more –
  For all had flown who made it so.
I pass'd from out its mossy door,
  And, tho' my tread was soft and low,
A voice came from the threshold stone
Of one whom I had earlier known –
  O, I defy thee, Hell, to show
  On beds of fire that burn below,
  An humbler heart – a deeper wo.

Father, I firmly do believe –
  I *know* – for Death who comes for me
    From regions of the blest afar,
Where there is nothing to deceive,
    Hath left his iron gate ajar,
  And rays of truth you cannot see
  Are flashing thro' Eternity –
I do believe that Eblis hath
A snare in every human path –
Else how, when in the holy grove
I wandered of the idol, Love,
Who daily scents his snowy wings
With incense of burnt offerings
From the most unpolluted things,
Whose pleasant bowers are yet so riven
Above with trellis'd rays from Heaven
No mote may shun – no tiniest fly –
The light'ning of his eagle eye –
How was it that Ambition crept,
  Unseen, amid the revels there,
Till growing bold, he laughed and leapt
In the tangles of Love's very hair?

Science! true daughter of Old Time thou art!
Who alterest all things with thy peering eyes.
Why preyest thou thus upon the poet's heart,
Vulture, whose wings are dull realities?
How should he love thee? or how deem thee wise,
Who wouldst not leave him in his wandering
To seek for treasure in the jewelled skies,
Albeit he soared with an undaunted wing?
Hast thou not dragged Diana from her car?
And driven the Hamadryad from the wood
To seek a shelter in some happier star?
Hast thou not torn the Naiad from her flood,
The Elfin from the green grass, and from me
The summer dream beneath the tamarind tree?

AL AARAAF

W.H. ROBINSON

O! nothing earthly save the ray
(Thrown back from flowers) of Beauty's eye,
As in those gardens where the day
Springs from the gems of Circassy –
O! nothing earthly save the thrill
Of melody in woodland rill –
Or (music of the passion-hearted)
Joy's voice so peacefully departed
That like the murmur in the shell,
Its echo dwelleth and will dwell –
Oh, nothing of the dross of ours –
Yet all the beauty – all the flowers
That list our Love, and deck our bowers –
Adorn yon world afar, afar –
The wandering star.

'T was a sweet time for Nesace – for there
Her world lay lolling on the golden air,
Near four bright suns – a temporary rest –
An oasis in desert of the blest.
Away – away – 'mid seas of rays that roll
Empyrean splendour o'er th' unchained soul –
The soul that scarce (the billows are so dense)
Can struggle to its destin'd eminence –
To distant spheres, from time to time, she rode,
And late to ours, the favour'd one of God –
But, now, the ruler of an anchor'd realm,
She throws aside the sceptre – leaves the helm,
And, amid incense and high spiritual hymns,
Laves in quadruple light her angel limbs.

Now happiest, loveliest in yon lovely Earth,
Whence sprang the 'Idea of Beauty' into birth,
(Falling in wreaths thro' many a startled star,
Like woman's hair 'mid pearls, until, afar,
It lit on hills Achaian, and there dwelt)
She look'd into Infinity – and knelt.
Rich clouds, for canopies, about her curled –
Fit emblems of the model of her world –
Seen but in beauty – not impeding sight
Of other beauty glittering thro' the light –
A wreath that twined each starry form around,
And all the opal'd air in colour bound.

All hurriedly she knelt upon a bed
Of flowers: of lilies such as rear'd the head
On the fair Capo Deucato, and sprang
So eagerly around about to hang
Upon the flying footsteps of – deep pride –
Of her who lov'd a mortal – and so died.
The Sephalica, budding with young bees,
Uprear'd its purple stem around her knees:
And gemmy flower, of Trebizond misnam'd –
Inmate of highest stars, where erst it sham'd
All other loveliness: its honied dew
(The fabled nectar that the heathen knew)
Deliriously sweet, was dropp'd from Heaven,
And fell on gardens of the unforgiven
In Trebizond – and on a sunny flower
So like its own above that, to this hour,
It still remaineth, torturing the bee
With madness, and unwonted reverie:
In Heaven, and all its environs, the leaf
And blossom of the fairy plant, in grief
Disconsolate linger – grief that hangs her head,
Repenting follies that full long have fled,
Heaving her white breast to the balmy air,
Like guilty beauty, chasten'd, and more fair:

Nyctanthes too, as sacred as the light
She fears to perfume, perfuming the night:
And Clytia pondering between many a sun,
While pettish tears adown her petals run:
And that aspiring flower that sprang on earth –
And died, ere scarce exalted into birth,
Bursting its odorous heart in spirit to wing
Its way to Heaven, from garden of a king:
And Valisnerian lotus thither flown
From struggling with the waters of the Rhone:
And thy most lovely purple perfume, Zante!
Isola d'oro! – Fior di Levante!
And the Nelumbo bud that floats for ever
With Indian Cupid down the holy river –
Fair flowers, and fairy! to whose care is given
To bear the Goddess' song, in odours, up to Heaven:

'Spirit! that dwellest where,
In the deep sky,
The terrible and fair,
In beauty vie!
Beyond the line of blue –
The boundary of the star
Which turneth at the view
Of thy barrier and thy bar –
Of the barrier overgone
By the cornets who were cast
From their pride, and from their throne
To be drudges till the last –
To be carriers of fire
(The red fire of their heart)
With speed that may not tire
And with pain that shall not part –
Who livest – *that* we know –
In Eternity – we feel –
But the shadow of whose brow
What spirit shall reveal?
Tho' the beings whom thy Nesace,
Thy messenger hath known
Have dream'd for thy Infinity
A model of their own –
Thy will is done, Oh, God!
The star hath ridden high
Thro' many a tempest, but she rode
Beneath thy burning eye;
And here, in thought, to thee –
In thought that can alone
Ascend thy empire and so be
A partner of thy throne –
By winged Fantasy,
My embassy is given,
Till secrecy shall knowledge be
In the environs of Heaven.'

She ceas'd – and buried then her burning cheek
Abash'd, amid the lilies there, to seek
A shelter from the fervour of His eye;
For the stars trembled at the Deity.
She stir'd not – breath'd not – for a voice was there
How solemnly pervading the calm air!
A sound of silence on the startled ear
Which dreamy poets name 'the music of the sphere.'
Ours is a world of words: Quiet we call
'Silence' – which is the merest word of all.
All Nature speaks, and ev'n ideal things
Flap shadowy sounds from visionary wings –
But ah! not so when, thus, in realms on high
The eternal voice of God is passing by,
And the red winds are withering in the sky!

'What tho' in worlds which sightless cycles run,
Link'd to a little system, and one sun –
Where all my love is folly and the crowd

Still think my terrors but the thunder cloud,
The storm, the earthquake, and the ocean-wrath –
(Ah! will they cross me in my angrier path?)
What tho' in worlds which own a single sun
The sands of Time grow dimmer as they run,
Yet thine is my resplendency, so given
To bear my secrets thro' the upper Heaven.
Leave tenantless thy crystal home, and fly,
With all thy train, athwart the moony sky –
Apart – like fire-flies in Sicilian night,
And wing to other worlds another light!
Divulge the secrets of thy embassy
To the proud orbs that twinkle – and so be
To ev'ry heart a barrier and a ban
Lest the stars totter in the guilt of man!'

Up rose the maiden in the yellow night,
The single-moonèd eve! – on Earth we plight
Our faith to one love – and one moon adore –
The birth-place of young Beauty had no more.
As sprang that yellow star from downy hours
Up rose the maiden from her shrine of flowers,
And bent o'er sheeny mountain and dim plain
Her way – but left not yet her Therasæan reign.

High on a mountain of enamell'd head –
Such as the drowsy shepherd on his bed
Of giant pasturage lying at his ease,
Raising his heavy eyelid, starts and sees
With many a mutter'd 'hope to be forgiven'
What time the moon is quadrated in Heaven –
Of rosy head, that towering far away
Into the sunlit ether, caught the ray
Of sunken suns at eve – at noon of night,
While the moon danc'd with the fair stranger light –
Uprear'd upon such height arose a pile
Of gorgeous columns on th' unburthen'd air,
Flashing from Parian marble that twin smile
Far down upon the wave that sparkled there,
And nursed the young mountain in its lair.
Of molten stars their pavement, such as fall
Thro' the ebon air, besilvering the pall
Of their own dissolution, while they die –
Adorning then the dwellings of the sky.
A dome, by linkèd light from Heaven let down,
Sat gently on these columns as a crown –
A window of one circular diamond, there,
Look'd out above into the purple air,
And rays from God shot down that meteor chain
And hallow'd all the beauty twice again,
Save when, between th' Empyrean and that ring,
Some eager spirit flapp'd his dusky wing.
But on the pillars Seraph eyes have seen
The dimness of this world: that greyish green
That Nature loves the best for Beauty's grave
Lurk'd in each cornice, round each architrave –
And every sculptur'd cherub thereabout
That from his marble dwelling peerèd out,
Seem'd earthly in the shadow of his niche –
Achaian statues in a world so rich.
Friezes from Tadmor and Persepolis –
From Balbec, and the stilly, clear abyss
Of beautiful Gomorrah! O, the wave
Is now upon thee – but too late to save!

Sound loves to revel in a summer night:
Witness the murmur of the grey twilight
That stole upon the ear, in Eyraco,
Of many a wild star-gazer long ago –
That stealeth ever on the ear of him
Who, musing, gazeth on the distance dim,

And sees the darkness coming as a cloud –
Is not its form – its voice – most palpable and loud?

 But what is this? – it cometh – and it brings
A music with it – 't is the rush of wings –
A pause – and then a sweeping, falling strain
And Nesace is in her halls again.
From the wild energy of wanton haste
 Her cheeks were flushing, and her lips apart;
And zone that clung around her gentle waist
 Had burst beneath the heaving of her heart
Within the centre of that hall to breathe
She paus'd and panted, Zanthe! all beneath,
The fairy light that kiss'd her golden hair
And long'd to rest, yet could but sparkle there!

Young flowers were whispering in melody
To happy flowers that night – and tree to tree;
Fountains were gushing music as they fell
In many a star-lit grove, or moon-lit dell;
Yet silence came upon material things –
Fair flowers, bright waterfalls and angel wings –
And sound alone that from the spirit sprang
Bore burthen to the charm the maiden sang:

 "Neath blue-bell or streamer –
  Or tufted wild spray
 That keeps, from the dreamer,
  The moonbeam away –
 Bright beings! that ponder,
  With half closing eyes,
 On the stars which your wonder
  Hath drawn from the skies,
 'Till they glance thro' the shade, and
  Come down to your brow
 Like – eyes of the maiden
  Who calls on you now –
 Arise! from your dreaming
  In violet bowers,
 To duty beseeming
  These star-litten hours –
 And shake from your tresses
  Encumber'd with dew
 The breath of those kisses
  That cumber them too –
 (O! how, without you, Love!
  Could angels be blest?)
 Those kisses of true love
  That lull'd ye to rest!
 Up! – shake from your wing
  Each hindering thing:
 The dew of the night –
  It would weigh down your flight;
 And true love caresses –
  O! leave them apart!
 They are light on the tresses,
  But lead on the heart.

 Ligeia! Ligeia!
  My beautiful one!
 Whose harshest idea
  Will to melody run,
 O! is it thy will
  On the breezes to toss?
 Or, capriciously still,
  Like the lone Albatross,
 Incumbent on night
  (As she on the air)
 To keep watch with delight
  On the harmony there?
 Ligeia! wherever
  Thy image may be,
 No magic shall sever
  Thy music from thee.
 Thou hast bound many eyes
  In a dreamy sleep–
 But the strains still arise
  Which *thy* vigilance keep –
 The sound of the rain
  Which leaps down to the flower,
 And dances again
  In the rhythm of the shower –
 The murmur that springs
  From the growing of grass
 Are the music of things –
  But are modell'd, alas! –
 Away, then my dearest,
  O! hie thee away
 To springs that lie clearest
  Beneath the moon-ray –
 To lone lake that smiles,
  In its dream of deep rest,
 At the many star-isles
  That enjewel its breast –
 Where wild flowers, creeping,
  Have mingled their shade,
 On its margin is sleeping
  Full many a maid –
 Some have left the cool glade, and
  Have slept with the bee –

Arouse then my maiden,
  On moorland and lea –
Go! breathe on their slumber,
  All softly in ear,
The musical number
  They slumber'd to hear –
For what can awaken
  An angel so soon
Whose sleep hath been taken
  Beneath the cold moon,
As the spell which no slumber
  Of witchery may test,
The rhythmical number
  Which lull'd him to rest?'

Spirits in wing, and angels to the view,
A thousand seraphs burst th' Empyrean thro',
Young dreams still hovering on their drowsy flight –
Seraphs in all but 'Knowledge,' the keen light
That fell, refracted, thro' thy bounds, afar
O Death! from eye of God upon that star:
Sweet was that error – sweeter still that death –
Sweet was that error – ev'n with *us* the breath
Of Science dims the mirror of our joy –
To them 't were the Simoom, and would destroy –
For what (to them) availeth it to know
That Truth is Falsehood – or that Bliss is Woe?
Sweet was their death – with them to die was rife
With the last ecstasy of satiate life –
Beyond that death no immortality –
But sleep that pondereth and is not 'to be' –
And there – oh! may my weary spirit dwell –
Apart from Heaven's Eternity – and yet how far from Hell!
What guilty spirit, in what shrubbery dim,
Heard not the stirring summons of that hymn?
But two: they fell: for Heaven no grace imparts
To those who hear not for their beating hearts.
A maiden-angel and her seraph-lover –
O! where (and ye may seek the wide skies over)
Was Love, the blind, near sober Duty known?
Unguided Love hath fallen – 'mid 'tears of perfect moan'.
He was a goodly spirit – he who fell:
A wanderer by moss-y-mantled well –
A gazer on the lights that shine above –
A dreamer in the moonbeam by his love:
What wonder? for each star is eye-like there,
And looks so sweetly down on Beauty's hair –
And they, and ev'ry mossy spring were holy
To his love-haunted heart and melancholy.
The night had found (to him a night of wo)
Upon a mountain crag, young Angelo –
Beetling it bends athwart the solemn sky,
And scowls on starry worlds that down beneath it lie.
Here sate he with his love – his dark eye bent
With eagle gaze along the firmament:
Now turn'd it upon her – but ever then
It trembled to the orb of Earth again.

'Ianthe, dearest, see! how dim that ray!
How lovely 't is to look so far away!
She seem'd not thus upon that autumn eve
I left her gorgeous halls – nor mourn'd to leave.
That eve – that eve – I should remember well –
The sun-ray dropp'd, in Lemnos, with a spell
On th' Arabesque carving of a gilded hall
Wherein I sate, and on the draperied wall –
And on my eye-lids – O the heavy light!
How drowsily it weigh'd them into night!
On flowers, before, and mist, and love they ran
With Persian Saadi in his Gulistan:
But O that light! – I slumber'd – Death, the while,
Stole o'er my senses in that lovely isle
So softly that no single silken hair
Awoke that slept – or knew that he was there.
The last spot of Earth's orb I trod upon
Was a proud temple call'd the Parthenon –
More beauty clung around her column'd wall
Than ev'n thy glowing bosom beats withal,
And when old Time my wing did disenthrall
Thence sprang I – as the eagle from his tower,
And years I left behind me in an hour.
What time upon her airy bounds I hung
One half the garden of her globe was flung
Unrolling as a chart unto my view –
Tenantless cities of the desert too!
Ianthe, beauty crowded on me then,
And half I wish'd to be again of men."
'My Angelo! and why of them to be?
A brighter dwelling-place is there for thee –
And greener fields than in yon world above,
And woman's loveliness – and passionate love.'

'But, list, Ianthe! when the air so soft
Fail'd, as my pennon'd spirit leapt aloft,
Perhaps my brain grew dizzy – but the world
I left so late was into chaos hurl'd –
Sprang from her station, on the winds apart,
And roll'd, a flame, the fiery Heaven athwart.
Methought, my sweet one, then I ceased to soar
And fell – not swiftly as I rose before,

But with a downward, tremulous motion thro'
Light, brazen rays, this golden star unto!
Nor long the measure of my falling hours,
For nearest of all stars was thine to ours –
Dread star! that came, amid a night of mirth,
A red Dædalion on the timid Earth.

'We came – and to thy Earth – but not to us
Be given our lady's bidding to discuss:
We came, my love; around, above, below,
Gay fire-fly of the night we come and go,
Nor ask a reason save the angel-nod
She grants to us, as granted by her God –
But, Angelo, than thine grey Time unfurl'd
Never his fairy wing o'er fairier world!
Dim was its little disk, and angel eyes
Alone could see the phantom in the skies,
When first Al Aaraaf knew her course to be
Headlong thitherward o'er the starry sea –
But when its glory swell'd upon the sky,
As glowing Beauty's bust beneath man's eye,
We paus'd before the heritage of men,
And thy star trembled – as doth Beauty then!'

Thus, in discourse, the lovers whiled away
The night that waned and waned and brought no day.
They fell: for Heaven to them no hope imparts
Who hear not for the beating of their hearts.

ROMANCE

Romance, who loves to nod and sing,
With drowsy head and folded wing,
Among the green leaves as they shake
Far down within some shadowy lake,
To me a painted paroquet
Hath been – a most familiar bird –
Taught me my alphabet to say –
To lisp my very earliest word
While in the wild wood I did lie,
A child – with a most knowing eye.
Of late, eternal Condor years
So shake the very Heaven on high
With tumult as they thunder by,
I have no time for idle cares
Through gazing on the unquiet sky.
And when an hour with calmer wings
Its down upon my spirit flings –
That little time with lyre and rhyme
To while away – forbidden things!
My heart would feel to be a crime
Unless it trembled with the strings.

I saw thee on thy bridal day –
    When a burning blush came o'er thee,
Though happiness around thee lay,
    The world all love before thee:

And in thine eye a kindling light
    (Whatever it might be)
Was all on Earth my aching sight
    Of Loveliness could see.

That blush, perhaps, was maiden shame –
    As such it well may pass –
Though its glow hath raised a fiercer flame
    In the breast of him, alas!

Who saw thee on that bridal day,
    When that deep blush *would* come o'er thee,
Though happiness around thee lay,
    The world all love before thee.

Oh! that my young life were a lasting dream!
My spirit not awakening, till the beam
Of an Eternity should bring the morrow.
Yes! tho' that long dream were of hopeless sorrow,
'T were better than the cold reality
Of waking life, to him whose heart must be,
And hath been still, upon the lovely earth,
A chaos of deep passion, from his birth.
But should it be – that dream eternally
Continuing – as dreams have been to me
In my young boyhood – should it thus be given,
'T were folly still to hope for higher Heaven.
For I have revell'd when the sun was bright
I' the summer sky, in dreams of living light,
And loveliness, – have left my very heart
Inclines of my imagining, apart
From mine own home, with beings that have been
Of mine own thought – what more could I have seen?
'T was once – and only once – and the wild hour
From my remembrance shall not pass – some power
Or spell had bound me – 't was the chilly wind
Came o'er me in the night, and left behind
Its image on my spirit – or the moon
Shone on my slumbers in her lofty noon
Too coldly – or the stars – howe'er it was
That dream was as that night-wind – let it pass.

I *have been* happy, tho' in a dream.
I have been happy – and I love the theme:
Dreams! in their vivid colouring of life
As in that fleeting, shadowy, misty strife
Of semblance with reality which brings
To the delirious eye, more lovely things
Of Paradise and Love – and all our own!
Than young Hope in his sunniest hour hath known.

I

Thy soul shall find itself alone
'Mid dark thoughts of the gray tomb-stone –
Not one, of all the crowd, to pry
Into thine hour of secrecy:

II

Be silent in that solitude,
Which is not loneliness – for then
The spirits of the dead who stood
In life before thee are again
In death around thee – and their will
Shall overshadow thee: be still.

III

The night – tho' clear – shall frown –
And the stars shall look not down,
From their high thrones in the heaven,
With light like Hope to mortals given –
But their red orbs, without beam,
To thy weariness shall seem
As a burning and a fever
Which would cling to thee for ever.

IV

Now are thoughts thou shalt not banish –
Now are visions ne'er to vanish –
From thy spirit shall they pass
No more – like dew-drops from the grass.

V

The breeze – the breath of God – is still –
And the mist upon the hill
Shadowy – shadowy – yet unbroken,
Is a symbol and a token –
How it hangs upon the trees,
A mystery of mysteries! –

'T was noontide of summer,
And mid-time of night;
And stars, in their orbits,
Shone pale, thro' the light
Of the brighter, cold moon,
'Mid planets her slaves,
Herself in the Heavens,
Her beam on the waves.
I gazed awhile
On her cold smile;
Too cold – too cold for me –
There pass'd, as a shroud,
A fleecy cloud,
And I turn'd away to thee,
Proud Evening Star,
In thy glory afar,
And dearer thy beam shall be;
For joy to my heart
Is the proud part
Thou bearest in Heaven at night,
And more I admire
Thy distant fire,
Than that colder, lowly light.

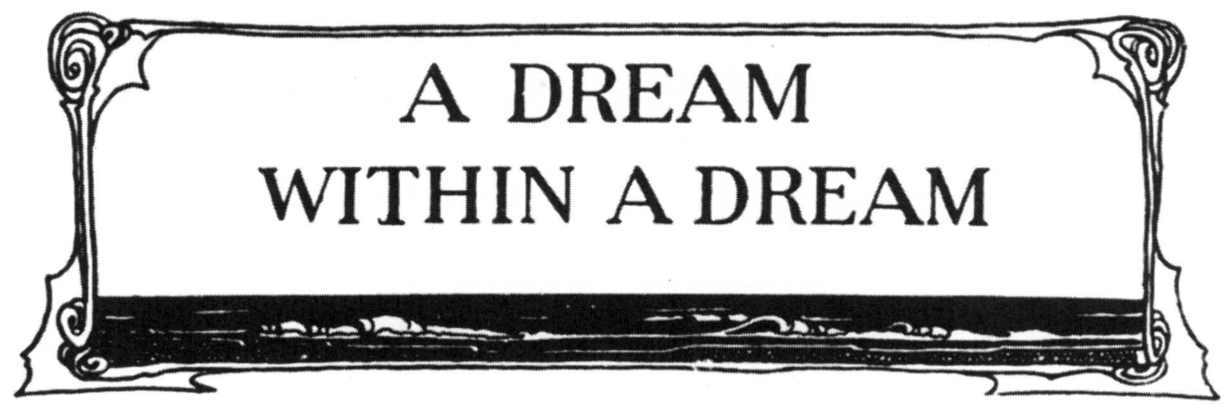

A DREAM WITHIN A DREAM

Take this kiss upon the brow!
And, in parting from you now,
Thus much let me avow –
You are not wrong, who deem
That my days have been a dream;
Yet if hope has flown away
In a night, or in a day,
In a vision, or in none,
Is it therefore the less gone?
All that we see or seem
Is but a dream within a dream.

I stand amid the roar
Of a surf-tormented shore,
And I hold within my hand
Grains of the golden sand –
How few! yet how they creep
Through my fingers to the deep,
While I weep – while I weep!
O God! can I not grasp
Them with a tighter clasp?
O God! can I not save
One from the pitiless wave?
Is all that we see or seem
But a dream within a dream?

> How often we forget all time, when lone
> Admiring Nature's universal throne;
> Her woods – her wilds – her mountains – the
> intense
> Reply of hers to our intelligence!
>
> BYRON

1

In youth have I known one with whom the Earth
In secret communing held – as he with it,
In daylight, and in beauty from his birth:
Whose fervid, flickering torch of life was lit
From the sun and stars, whence he had drawn forth
A passionate light – such for his spirit was fit –
And yet that spirit knew not, in the hour
Of its own fervour, what had o'er it power.

2

Perhaps it may be that my mind is wrought
To a fervour by the moonbeam that hangs o'er,
But I will half believe that wild light fraught
With more of sovereignty than ancient lore
Hath ever told – or is it of a thought
The unembodied essence, and no more,
That with a quickening spell doth o'er us pass
As dew of the night-time o'er the summer grass?

3

Doth o'er us pass, when, as th' expanding eye
To the loved object – so the tear to the lid
Will start, which lately slept in apathy?
And yet it need not be – (that object) hid
From us in life – but common – which doth lie
Each hour before us – but *then* only, bid
With a strange sound, as of a harp-string broken,
To awake us – 'T is a symbol and a token

4

Of what in other worlds shall be – and given
In beauty by our God, to those alone
Who otherwise would fall from life and Heaven
Drawn by their heart's passion, and that tone,
That high tone of the spirit which hath striven,
Tho' not with Faith – with godliness – whose throne
With desperate energy 't hath beaten down;
Wearing its own deep feeling as a crown.

In visions of the dark night
    I have dreamed of joy departed –
But a waking dream of life and light
    Hath left me broken-hearted.

Ah! what is not a dream by day
    To him whose eyes are cast
On things around him with a ray
    Turned back upon the past?

That holy dream – that holy dream,
    While all the world were chiding,
Hath cheered me as a lovely beam
    A lonely spirit guiding.

What though that light, thro' storm and
        night,
    So trembled from afar –
What could there be more purely bright
    In Truth's day-star?

The happiest day – the happiest hour
    My sear'd and blighted heart hath
        known,
The highest hope of pride and power,
    I feel hath flown.

Of power! said I? yes! such I ween;
    But they have vanish'd long, alas!
The visions of my youth have been –
    But let them pass.

And, pride, what have I now with thee?
    Another brow may even inherit
The venom thou hast pour'd on me –
    Be still, my spirit!

The happiest day – the happiest hour
    Mine eyes shall see – have ever seen,
The brightest glance of pride and power,
    I feel – have been:

But were that hope of pride and power
    Now offer'd, with the pain
Even *then* I felt – that brightest hour
    I would not live again:

For on its wing was dark alloy,
    And, as it flutter'd – fell
An essence – powerful to destroy
    A soul that knew it well.

In youth's spring it was my lot
To haunt of the wide world a spot
The which I could not love the less,
So lovely was the loneliness
Of a wild lake with black rock bound,
And the tall pines that tower'd around –

But when the night had thrown her pall
Upon that spot, as upon all,
And the ghastly wind went by
In a dirge-like melody,
Then – ah then I would awake
To the terror of that lone lake.

Yet that terror was not fright,
But a tremulous delight –
A feeling not the jewell'd mine
Could teach or bribe me to define,
Nor love – although the love were thine.

Death was in that poison'd wave,
And in its depth a fitting grave
For him who thence could solace bring
To his lone imagining –
Whose solitary soul could make
An Eden of that dim lake.

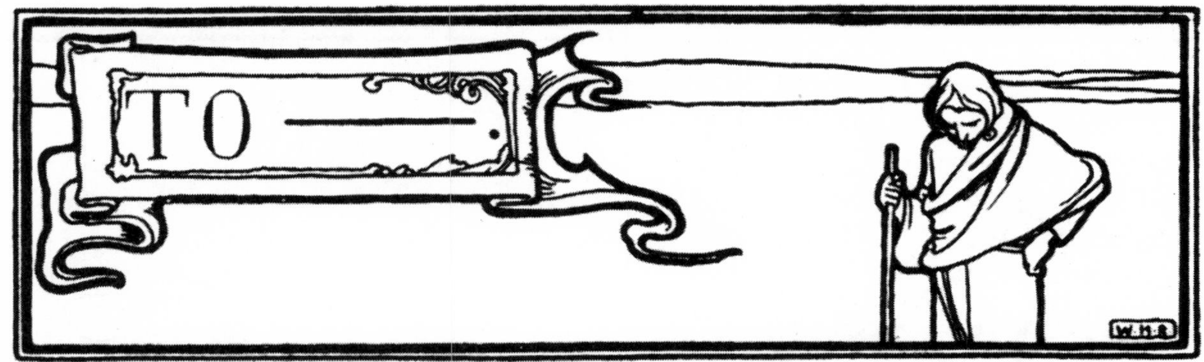

The bowers whereat, in dreams, I see
  The wantonest singing birds,
Are lips – and all thy melody
  Of lip-begotten words –

Thine eyes, in Heaven of heart enshrined
  Then desolately fall,
O God! on my funereal mind
  Like starlight on a pall –

Thy heart – *thy* heart! – I wake and sigh,
  And sleep to dream till day
Of the truth that gold can never buy –
  Of the baubles that it may.

Fair river! in thy bright, clear flow
  Of crystal, wandering water,
Thou art an emblem of the glow
    Of beauty – the unhidden heart –
    The playful maziness of art
  In old Alberto's daughter;

But when within thy wave she looks –
  Which glistens then, and trembles –
Why, then, the prettiest of brooks
  Her worshipper resembles;

For in his heart, as in thy stream,
  Her image deeply lies –
His heart which trembles at the beam
  Of her soul-searching eyes.

To——

I heed not that my earthly lot
Hath little of Earth in it –
That years of love have been forgot
In the hatred of a minute:
I mourn not that the desolate
Are happier, sweet, than I,
But that you sorrow for my fate
Who am a passer-by.

Dim vales – and shadowy floods –
And cloudy-looking woods,
Whose forms we can't discover
For the tears that drip all over.
Huge moons there wax and wane –
Again – again – again –
Every moment of the night –
Forever changing places –
And they put out the star-light
With the breath from their pale faces.
About twelve by the moon-dial
One more filmy than the rest
(A kind which, upon trial,
They have found to be the best)
Comes down – still down – and down
With its centre on the crown
Of a mountain's eminence,
While its wide circumference
In easy drapery falls
Over hamlets, over halls,
Wherever they may be –
O'er the strange woods – o'er the sea –
Over spirits on the wing –
Over every drowsy thing –
And buries them up quite
In a labyrinth of light –
And then, how deep! – O, deep!
Is the passion of their sleep.
In the morning they arise,
And their moony covering
Is soaring in the skies,
With the tempests as they toss,
Like – almost any thing –
Or a yellow Albatross.
They use that moon no more
For the same end as before –
Videlicet a tent –
Which I think extravagant:
Its atomies, however,
Into a shower dissever,
Of which those butterflies,
Of Earth, who seek the skies,
And so come down again
(Never-contented things!)
Have brought a specimen
Upon their quivering wings.

Helen, thy beauty is to me
Like those Nicéan barks of yore,
That gently, o'er a perfumed sea,
The weary, way-worn wanderer bore
To his own native shore.

On desperate seas long wont to roam,
Thy hyacinth hair, thy classic face,
Thy Naiad airs have brought me home
To the glory that was Greece,
And the grandeur that was Rome.

Lo! in yon brilliant window-niche
How statue-like I see thee stand,
The agate lamp within thy hand!
Ah, Psyche, from the regions which
Are Holy-Land!

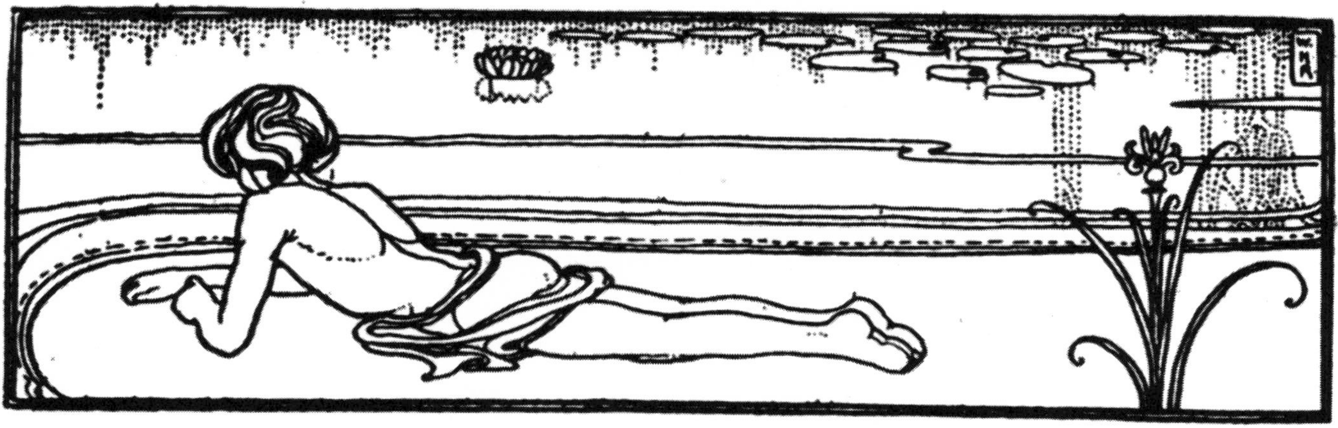

Alone

From childhood's hour I have not been
As others were – I have not seen
As others saw – I could not bring
My passions from a common spring –
From the same source I have not taken
My sorrow – I could not awaken
My heart to joy at the same tone –
And all I lov'd – I lov'd alone –
Then – in my childhood – in the dawn
Of a most stormy life – was drawn
From ev'ry depth of good and ill
The mystery which binds me still –
From the torrent, or the fountain –
From the red cliff of the mountain –
From the sun that 'round me roll'd
In its autumn tint of gold –
From the lightning in the sky
As it pass'd me flying by –
From the thunder, and the storm –
And the cloud that took the form
(When the rest of Heaven was blue)
Of a demon in my view –

Poems Now First Collected

Spiritual Song

Hark, echo! – Hark; echo!
    'T is the sound
  Of archangels, in happiness wrapt

Elizabeth

Elizabeth – it surely is most fit
[Logic and common usage so commanding]
In thy own book that *first* thy name be writ,
Zeno and other sages notwithstanding;
And I have other reasons for so doing
Besides my innate love of contradiction;
Each poet – *if* a poet – in pursuing
The muses thro' their bowers of Truth or Fiction,
Has studied very little of his part,
Read nothing, written less – in short's a fool
Endued with neither soul, nor sense, nor art,
Being ignorant of one important rule,
Employed in even the theses of the school –
Called – I forget the heathenish Greek name –
[Called anything, its meaning is the same]
'Always write *first* things uppermost in the heart.'

From an Album

Elizabeth it is in vain you say
'Love not' – thou sayest it in so sweet a way:
In vain those words from thee or L. E. L.
Zantippe's talents had enforced so well:
Ah! if that language from thy heart arise,
Breathe it less gently forth – and veil thine eyes.
Endymion, recollect, when Luna tried
To cure his love – was cured of all beside –
His folly – pride – and passion – for he died.

To Sarah

When melancholy and alone,
I sit on some moss-covered stone
Beside a murm'ring stream;
I think I hear thy voice's sound
In every tuneful thing around,
Oh! what a pleasant dream.

The silvery streamlet gurgling on,
The mock-bird chirping on the thorn,
Remind me, love, of thee.
They seem to whisper thoughts of love,
As thou didst when the stars above
Witnessed thy vows to me; –

The gentle zephyr floating by,
In chorus to my pensive sigh,
Recalls the hour of bliss,
When from thy balmy lips I drew
Fragrance as sweet as Hermia's dew,
And left the first fond kiss.

In such an hour, when are forgot,
The world, its cares, and my own lot,
Thou seemest then to be,
A gentle guarding spirit given
To guide my wandering thoughts to heaven,
If they should stray from thee.

The Great Man

The great man lives forever shrived in the hearts of men,
Albeit form and feature may fade from human ken;
Recorded are his actions on history's living page –
They shine with purer lustre with each successive age.
Immortal aye immortal, undying as a God
The sands of time are printed wherever his feet have trod.
Above his dust no monument may proudly rear its head
To mark the spot where resteth, the mighty and the dead.
He needeth no mausoleum, nor shaft need pierce the sky
To point to coming ages, where his sacred ashes lie.
No! that may be forgotten, but around his glorious name
Will shine the dazzling halo of a never dying fame.
His requiem will be chanted in the wild bird's sweetest song,
The summer breeze and wintry gale the sad notes will prolong,
The flowers of spring time and the leaves of autumn be his pall,
Long as the one shall blossom, long as the other fall.
Here is a noble lesson. Oh! let it graven be
In characters unfading on the page of memory.
Like the needle to the mariner amidst the tempest wrath
Let it fire your hopes and guide you as you tread life's thorny path.

Gratitude To ——

As turns the eye to bless the hand that led its infant years,
A list'ning still for that sweet voice which every tone endears,
So I to thee, through mental power, would each remembrance trace,
And bless the hand that led me on to fonts of lasting grace.
As sailor on the billowy deep hath seen some light afar,
And shunned the rock that lies between his pathway and the star,
So hast thou been o'er stormy wave to me, 'mid sorrow's night,
A beacon true whose glory spreads afar its rays of light.
As flow sweet sounds of melody from strings drawn out by skill,
As roll its wavelets o'er the soul and all its chambers fill,
So came the words of holy truth endued with wisdom's zeal,
So fell their impress on my heart and stamped it with their seal.

As runs the rivulet its course and swifter as it flows,
Still murmuring of the hidden depths where first its waters rose,
So evermore as life glides on expanding far and wide,
Will turn the heart to where at first was ope'd its holiest tide.
As pours the captive bird its song to him who sets it free,
So flows my breath in song of praise in gratitude to thee.
As o'er the earth the sun reflects its rays of living light,
So thou by thy pure rays of thought art power to mental sight.

An Enigma

First, find out a word that doth silence proclaim,
And that backwards and forwards is always the same;
Then next you must find out a feminine name
That backwards and forwards is always the same;
An act, or a writing on parchment whose name
Both backwards and forwards is always the same;
A fruit that is rare, whose botanical name
Read backwards and forwards is always the same;
A note used in music, which time doth proclaim,
And backwards and forwards is always the same;
Their initials connected, a title will frame,
That is justly the due of the fair married dame,
Which backwards and forwards is always the same.

Impromptu

To Kate Carol

When from your gems of thought I turn
To those pure orbs, your heart to learn,
I scarce know what to prize most high –
The bright *i-dea,* or bright *dear-eye.*

Additional Poems Attributed to Poe

Song of Triumph

From the tale 'Four Beasts In One'; *Southern Literary Messenger*

Who is king but Epiphanes?
Say – do you know?
Who is king but Epiphanes?
Bravo – bravo!
There is none but Epiphanes,
No – there is none:
So tear down the temples,
And put out the sun!
Who is king but Epiphanes?
Say – do you know?
Who is king but Epiphanes?
Bravo – bravo!

Latin Hymn

From the tale 'Four Beasts In One'; *Southern Literary Messenger*

A thousand, a thousand, a thousand,
A thousand, a thousand, a thousand,
We, with one warrior, have slain!
A thousand, a thousand, a thousand, a thousand,
Sing a thousand over again!
Soho! – let us sing
Long life to our king,
Who knocked over a thousand so fine!
Soho! – let us roar,
He has given us more
Red gallons of gore
Than all Syria can furnish of wine!

The Skeleton-Hand

Attributed to Poe; from *The Yankee*, August, 1829

Lo! one is on the mountain side,
While the clouds are passing by –
With their black wings flapping heavily,
Like eagles in the sky;
Or lying up in the forest trees,
And waiting there for the mountain-breeze.

And now he passes through the clouds –
And up to the mountain-top,
Nor yet to look for the joyous sun
Does the hasty traveller stop.

But he leapeth down in the broken path
With a step as light and free –
As ever in his days of mirth,
In the dance and revelry.

Why endeth he his hasty speed?
Why stoppeth on his way?
In truth it is a fearful thing,
For human tongue to say.

He fears that toward him pointeth there,
A fleshless human hand;
Where the mountain rains have swept away,
Its covering of sand;
That hand his very soul doth stir,
For it proveth him a murderer.

Ay long ago on the mountain side,
The fearful deed was done;
And the murderer thought him safe, that none
Could see, save the broad bright sun,
As he rolled in the heavens the dead above,
And flooded the earth with his rays of love.

Now lifted he his clouded eye,
To the mountain crests behind;
And o'er them came the broad black clouds,
Upheaving with the wind;
And on them their thick darkness spread –
A crown upon the mountain's head.
And then shone out the flaming sun,
From the waters of the sea;
And God's own bow came in the clouds,
And looked out gloriously;
But its colours were of wo and wrath,
That threw their light o'er the murderer's path.

And now God's chariots – the clouds,
Came rolling down with might;
Their wheels like many horsemen were,
In battle or in flight.
And yet no power to move hath *he*,
His soul is in an agony.

Over the murderer and dead
They rolled their mighty host;
Old ocean's waves come not so thick,
By northern tempests tost.

Forth from their mighty bosom came,
A flash of heaven's wrath,
And away the heavy clouds – and sun,
Rolled from the murder-path.
And the sun shone out where the murderer lay,
Before the dead in the narrow way –
With his hand all seared, and his breast torn bare –
God's vengeance had been working there.

The Magician

Attributed to Poe; from *The Yankee*, December, 1829

MAGICIAN

Thou dark, sea-stirring storm,
Whence comest thou in thy might –
Nay – wait, thou dim and dreamy form –
Storm spirit, I call thee – 't is mine of right –
Arrest thee in thy troubled flight.

STORM SPIRIT

Thou askest me whence I came –
I came o'er the sleeping sea,
It roused at my torrent of storm and flame,
And it howled aloud in its agony,
And swelled to the sky – that sleeping sea.

Thou askest me what I met –
A ship from the Indian shore,
A tall proud ship with her sails all set –
Far down in the sea that ship I bore,
My storms wild rushing wings before.

And her men will forever lie,
Below the unquiet sea;
And tears will dim full many an eye,
Of those who shall widows and orphans be,
And their days be years – for their misery.

A boat with a starving crew –
For hunger they howled and swore;
While the blood from a fellow's veins they drew
I came upon them with rush and roar –
Far under the waves that boat I bore.

Two ships in a fearful fight –
When a hundred guns did flash
I came upon them – no time for flight –
But under the sea their timbers crash
And over their guns the wild waters dash

A wretch on a single plank –
And I tossed him on the shore –
A night and a day of the sea he drank,
But the wearied wretch to the land I bore –
And now he walketh the earth once more –

MAGICIAN

Storm spirit – go on thy path –

The spirit has spread his wings –
And comes on the sea with a rush of wrath,
As a war horse when he springs –
And over the earth his winds he flings –
And over the earth – nor stop nor stay –
The winds of the storm king go out on their way.

Translation: Hymn to Aristogeiton and Harmodius

Attributed to Poe; from the *Southern Literary Messenger*, December, 1835

I

Wreathed in myrtle, my sword I'll conceal,
   Like those champions devoted and brave,
When they plunged in the tyrant their steel,
   And to Athens deliverance gave.

II

Beloved heroes! your deathless souls roam
   In the joy breathing isles of the blest;
Where the mighty of old have their home –
   Where Achilles and Diomed rest.

III

In fresh myrtle my blade I'll entwine,
   Like Harmodius, the gallant and good,
When he made at the tutelar shrine
   A libation of Tyranny's blood.

IV

Ye deliverers of Athens from shame!
   Ye avengers of Liberty's wrongs!
Endless ages shall cherish your fame,
   Embalmed in their echoing songs!

The Mammoth Squash

W. M. Griswold's Correspondence of R. W. Griswold

Green and specked with spots of golden,
Never since the ages olden –
Since the time of Cain and Abel,
Never such a vegetable,
So with odours sweetest laden
Thus our halls appearance made in.
Who – oh! who in kindness sent thee
To afford my soul nepenthe?

Rude men seeing thee, say 'Gosh!
'T is a most enormous squash!'
But the one who peers within,
Knowledge of himself to win,
    Says, while total silence reigns,
Silence, from the Stygian shore –
(Grim silence, darkling o'er)
'This may perchance be but the skull
Of Arthur Cleveland Coxe so dull –
    Its streaked, yellow flesh – his brains.'

Oh, Tempora! Oh, Mores!

Attributed to Poe; from *No Name Magazine*, Baltimore, October, 1889

Oh Times! Oh Manners! It is my opinion
That you are changing sadly your dominion –
I mean the reign of manners hath long ceased,
For men have none at all, or bad at least;
And as for times, although 't is said by many
The 'good old times' were far the worst of any,
Of which sound doctrine I believe each tittle,
Yet still I think these worse than them a little.

I've been a thinking, isn't that the phrase?
– I like your Yankee words and Yankee ways –
I've been a thinking, whether it were best
To take things seriously or all in jest;
Whether with Heraclitus of yore
To weep, as he did, till his eyes were sore,
Or rather laugh with him, that queer Philosopher,
Democritus of Thrace, who used to toss over
The page of life and grin at the dog-ears,
As though he'd say, 'Why who the devil cares?'

This is a question which, Oh Heaven, withdraw
The luckless query from a Member's claw!
Instead of two sides, Job has nearly eight,
Each fit to furnish forth four hours debate.
What shall be done? I'll lay it on the table,
And take the matter up when I'm more able,
And in the meantime, to prevent all bother,
I'll neither laugh with one or cry with t'other,
Nor deal in flattery or aspersions foul,
But, taking one by each hand, merely growl.

Ah growl, say you, my friend, and pray at what?
Why really, sir, I almost had forgot –
But damn it, sir, I deem it a disgrace
That things should stare us boldly in the face,
And daily strut the street with bows and scrapes,
Who would be men by imitating apes.
I beg your pardon, reader, for the oath,
The monkey made me swear, though something loath;
I'm apt to be discursive in my style,
But pray be patient: yet a little while
Will change me, and as politicians do
I'll mend my manners and my measures too.

Of all the cities, and I've seen no few, –
For I have travelled, friend, as well as you, –
I don't remember one, upon my soul,
But take it generally upon the whole,
(As Members say they like their logic taken
Because divided it may chance be shaken)
So pat, agreeable, and vastly proper
As this for a neat, frisky counter-hopper;
Here he may revel to his heart's content,
Flounce like a fish in his own element,
Toss back his fine curls from their forehead fair
And hop o'er counters with a Vestris air,
Complete at night what he began A. M.,
And having cheated ladies, dance with them;

For at a ball what fair one can escape
The pretty little hand that sold her tape,
Or who so cold, so callous to refuse
The youth who cut the ribbon for her shoes!

One of these fish, par excellence the beau,
God help me, it has been my lot to know,
At least by sight, for I'm a timid man
And always keep from laughing when I can;
But speak to him, he'll make you such grimace.
Lord! to be grave exceeds the power of face.
The hearts of all the ladies are with him,
Their bright eyes on his Tom and Jerry brim
And dove-tailed coat, obtained at cost; while then
Those won't turn on anything like men.

His very voice is musical delight,
His form once seen becomes a part of sight,
In short his shirt-collar, his look, his tone is
The 'beau ideal' fancied for Adonis.
Philosophers have often held dispute
As to the seat of thought in man and brute,
For that the power of thought attend the latter
My friend, the beau, hath made a settled matter,
And spite all dogmas current in all ages,
One settled fact is better than ten sages.

For he does think, although I'm oft in doubt
If I can tell exactly what about.
Ah yes! his little foot and ankle trim,
'T is there the seat of reason lies in him;
A wise philosopher would shake his head,
He then, of course, must shake his foot instead.
At me in vengeance shall that foot be shaken –
Another proof of thought, I'm not mistaken –
Because to his cat's eyes I hold a glass
And let him see himself a proper ass?
I think he'll take this likeness to himself,
But if he won't *he shall*, the stupid elf,
And, lest the guessing throw the fool in fits,
I close the portrait with the name of Pitts.